Dan Simmons, a former teacher and director of pro-
grammes for gifted children, now writes full time. He
lives with his wife and daughter in Colorado, USA.
He has always been interested in writing, composing
his first short stories at the age of nine. Since then he
has been co-winner of the first *Twilight Zone Magazine* short story contest, winner of the Rod Serling
Memorial Award and the winner of the World Fantasy
Award for Best Novel with *Song of Kali*.

Dan Simmons is also the author of the internationally
acclaimed *Hyperion*, winner of the 1990 Hugo Award
and Locus Award for Best Science Fiction Novel,
Phases of Gravity, and *Carrion Comfort*, winner of
the 1990 Bram Stoker Award, British Fantasy Society
Award and Locus Award for Best Horror Novel.

The Fall of Hyperion

Dan Simmons

First published in Great Britain in 1991
by HEADLINE BOOK PUBLISHING

First published in paperback in 1991
by HEADLINE BOOK PUBLISHING

A HEADLINE FEATURE paperback

10 9

ISBN 0 7472 3604 6

Typeset in 10/12 pt Plantin
by Colset Private Limited, Singapore

Printed and bound in Great Britain by
Mackays of Chatham PLC, Chatham, Kent

HEADLINE BOOK PUBLISHING
A division of Hodder Headline PLC
338 Euston Road
London NW1 3BH

**To John Keats
Whose Name Was Writ
in Eternity**

'Can God play a significant game with his own creature? Can any creator, even a limited one, play a significant game with his own creature?'

     – NORBERT WIENER, *God and Golem, Inc.*

'. . . May there not be superior beings amused with any graceful, though instinctive attitude my mind may fall into, as I am entertained with the alertness of a Stoat or the anxiety of a Deer? Though a quarrel in the streets is a thing to be hated, the energies displayed in it are fine . . . By a superior being our reasonings may take the same tone – though erroneous they may be fine – This is the very thing in which consists poetry . . .'

     – JOHN KEATS, in a letter to his brother

'The Imagination may be compared to Adam's dream – he awoke and found it truth.'

     – JOHN KEATS, in a letter to a friend

PART ONE

ONE

On the day the armada went off to war, on the last day of life as we knew it, I was invited to a party. There were parties everywhere that evening, on more than a hundred and fifty worlds in the Web, but *this* was the only party that mattered.

I signified acceptance via the datasphere, checked to make sure that my finest formal jacket was clean, took my time bathing and shaving, dressed with meticulous care, and used the one-time diskey in the invitation chip to farcast from Esperance to Tau Ceti Center at the appointed time.

It was evening in this hemisphere of TC^2, and a low, rich light illuminated the hills and vales of Deer Park, the gray towers of the Administration complex far to the south, the weeping willows and radiant fernfire which lined the banks of River Tethys, and the white colonnades of Government House itself. Thousands of guests were arriving, but security personnel greeted each of us, checked our invitation codes against DNA patterns, and showed the way to bar and buffet with a graceful gesture of arm and hand.

'M Joseph Severn?' the guide confirmed politely.

'Yes,' I lied. It was now my name but never my identity.

'CEO Gladstone still wishes to see you later in the evening. You will be notified when she is free for the appointment.'

'Very good.'

'If you desire anything in the way of refreshment or entertainment that is not set out, merely speak your wish aloud and the grounds monitors will seek to provide it.'

3

I nodded, smiled, and left the guide behind. Before I had strolled a dozen steps, he had turned to the next guests alighting from the terminex platform.

From my vantage point on a low knoll, I could see several thousand guests milling across several hundred acres of manicured lawn, many of them wandering among forests of topiary. Above the stretch of grass where I stood, its broad sweep already shaded by the line of trees along the river, lay the formal gardens, and beyond them rose the imposing bulk of Government House. A band was playing on the distant patio, and hidden speakers carried the sound to the farthest reaches of Deer Park. A constant line of EMVs spiraled down from a farcaster portal far above. For a few seconds I watched their brightly clad passengers disembark at the platform near the pedestrian terminex. I was fascinated by the variety of aircraft; evening light glinted not only on the shells of the standard Vikkens and Altz and Sumatsos, but also on the rococo decks of levitation barges and the metal hulls of antique skimmers which had been quaint when Old Earth still existed.

I wandered down the long, gradual slope to the River Tethys, past the dock where an incredible assortment of river craft disgorged their passengers. The Tethys was the only webwide river, flowing past its permanent farcaster portals through sections of more than two hundred worlds and moons, and the folk who lived along its banks were some of the wealthiest in the Hegemony. The vehicles on the river showed this: great, crenelated cruisers, canvas-laden barks, and five-tiered barges, many showing signs of being equipped with levitation gear; elaborate houseboats, obviously fitted with their own farcasters; small, motile isles imported from the oceans of Maui-Covenant; sporty pre-Hegira speedboats and submersibles; an assortment of hand-carved nautical EMVs from Renaissance Vector; and a few contemporary go-everywhere yachts, their outlines hidden by the seamless reflective ovoid surfaces of containment fields.

The guests who alighted from these craft were no less flamboyant and impressive than their vehicles: personal styles ranged from pre-Hegira conservative evening wear on bodies obviously never touched by Poulsen treatments to this week's highest fashion from TC² draped on figures molded by the Web's most famous ARNists. Then I moved on, pausing at a long table just long enough to fill my plate with roast beef, salad, sky squid filet, Parvati curry, and fresh-baked bread.

The low evening light had faded to twilight by the time I found a place to sit near the gardens, and the stars were coming out. The lights of the nearby city and Administration Complex had been dimmed for tonight's viewing of the armada, and Tau Ceti Center's night sky was more clear than it had been for centuries.

A woman near me glanced over and smiled. 'I'm sure that we've met before.'

I smiled back, sure that we had not. She was very attractive, perhaps twice my age, in her late fifties, standard, but looking younger than my own twenty-six years, thanks to money and Poulsen. Her skin was so fair that it looked almost translucent. Her hair was done in a rising braid. Her breasts, more revealed than hidden by the wispwear gown, were flawless. Her eyes were cruel.

'Perhaps we have,' I said, 'although it seems unlikely. My name is Joseph Severn.'

'Of course,' she said. 'You're an artist!'

I was not an artist. I was . . . had been . . . a poet. But the Severn identity, which I had inhabited since my real persona's death and birth a year before, stated that I was an artist. It was in my All Thing file.

'I remembered,' laughed the lady. She lied. She had used her expensive comlog implants to access the datasphere.

I did not need to access . . . a clumsy, redundant word which I despised despite its antiquity. I mentally closed my eyes and was *in* the datasphere, sliding past the superficial

5

All Thing barriers, slipping beneath the waves of surface data, and following the glowing strand of her access umbilical far into the darkened depths of 'secure' information flow.

'My name is Diana Philomel,' she said. 'My husband is sector transport administrator for Sol Draconi Septem.'

I nodded and took the hand she offered. She had said nothing about the fact that her husband had been head goon for the mold-scrubbers union on Heaven's Gate before political patronage had promoted him to Sol Draconi . . . or that her name once had been Dinee Teats, former crib doxie and hopstop hostess to lungpipe proxies in the Midsump Barrens . . . or that she had been arrested twice for Flashback abuse, the second time seriously injuring a halfway house medic . . . or that she had poisoned her half-brother when she was nine, after he had threatened to tell her stepfather that she was seeing a Mudflat miner named . . .

'Pleased to meet you, M Philomel,' I said. Her hand was warm. She held the handshake an instant too long.

'Isn't it exciting?' she breathed.

'What's that?'

She made an expansive gesture that included the night, the glow-globes just coming on, the gardens, and the crowds. 'Oh, the party, the war, *everything*,' she said.

I smiled, nodded, and tasted the roast beef. It was rare and quite good, but gave the salty hint of the Lusus clone vats. The squid seemed authentic. Stewards had come by offering champagne, and I tried mine. It was inferior. Quality wine, Scotch, and coffee had been the three irreplaceable commodities after the death of Old Earth. 'Do you think the war is necessary?' I asked.

'Goddamn right it's necessary.' Diana Philomel had opened her mouth, but it was her husband who answered. He had come up from behind and now took a seat on the faux log where we dined. He was a big man, at least a foot and a half taller than I. But then, I am short. My memory tells me that I once wrote a verse ridiculing myself as '. . . Mr John

6

Keats, five feet high,' although I am five feet one, slightly short when Napoleon and Wellington were alive and the average height for men was five feet six, ridiculously short now that men from average-g worlds range from six feet tall to almost seven. I obviously did not have the musculature or frame to claim I had come from a high-g world, so to all eyes I was merely short. (I report my thoughts above in the units in which I think . . . of all the mental changes since my rebirth into the Web, thinking in metric is by far the hardest. Sometimes I refuse to try.)

'Why is the war necessary?' I asked Hermund Philomel, Diana's husband.

'Because they goddamn *asked for it*,' growled the big man. He was a molar grinder and a cheek-muscle flexer. He had almost no neck and a subcutaneous beard that obviously defied depilatory, blade, and shaver. His hands were half again as large as mine and many times more powerful.

'I see,' I said.

'The goddamn Ousters goddamn *asked for it*,' he repeated, reviewing the high points of his argument for me. 'They fucked with us on Bressia and now they're fucking with us on . . . in . . . whatsis . . .'

'Hyperion system,' said his wife, her eyes never leaving mine.

'Yeah,' said her lord and husband, 'Hyperion system. They fucked with us, and now we've got to go out there and show them that the Hegemony isn't going to stand for it. Understand?'

Memory told me that as a boy I had been sent off to John Clarke's academy at Enfield and that there had been more than a few small-brained, ham-fisted bullies like this there. When I first arrived, I avoided them or placated them. After my mother died, after the world changed, I went after them with rocks in my small fists and rose from the ground to swing again, even after they had bloodied my nose and loosened my teeth with their blows.

7

'I understand,' I said softly. My plate was empty. I raised the last of my bad champagne to toast Diana Philomel.

'Draw me,' she said.

'I beg your pardon?'

'Draw me, M Severn. You're an artist.'

'A painter,' I said, making a helpless gesture with an empty hand. 'I'm afraid I have no stylus.'

Diana Philomel reached into her husband's tunic pocket and handed me a light pen. 'Draw me. Please.'

I drew her. The portrait took shape in the air between us, lines rising and falling and turning back on themselves like neon filaments in a wire sculpture. A small crowd gathered to watch. Mild applause rippled when I finished. The drawing was not bad. It caught the lady's long, voluptuous curve of neck, high braid bridge of hair, prominent cheekbones . . . even the slight, ambiguous glint of eye. It was as good as I could do after the RNA medication and lessons had prepared me for the persona. The real Joseph Severn could do better . . . had done better. I remember him sketching me as I lay dying.

M Diana Philomel beamed approval. M Hermund Philomel glowered.

A shout went up. 'There they are!'

The crowd murmured, gasped, and hushed. Glow-globes and garden lights dimmed and went off. Thousands of guests raised their eyes to the heavens. I erased the drawing and tucked the light pen back in Hermund's tunic.

'It's the armada,' said a distinguished-looking older man in FORCE dress black. He lifted his drink to point something out to his young female companion. 'They've just opened the portal. The scouts will come through first, then the torchship escorts.'

The FORCE military farcaster portal was not visible from our vantage point; even in space, I imagine it would look like nothing more than a rectangular aberration in the starfield. But the fusion tails of the scoutships were certainly visible – first as a score of fireflies or radiant gossamers, then as blazing comets as they ignited their main drives and swept out through Tau Ceti System's cislunar traffic region. Another cumulative gasp went up as the torchships farcast into existence, their firetails a hundred times longer than the scouts'. TC²'s night sky was scarred from zenith to horizon with gold-red streaks.

Somewhere the applause began, and within seconds the fields and lawns and formal gardens of Government House's Deer Park were filled with riotous applause and raucous cheering as the well-dressed crowd of billionaires and government officials and members of noble houses from a hundred worlds forgot everything except a jingoism and war lust awakened now after more than a century and a half of dormancy.

I did not applaud. Ignored by those around me, I finished my toast – not to Lady Philomel now, but to the enduring stupidity of my race – and downed the last of the champagne. It was flat.

Above, the more important ships of the flotilla had translated in-system. I knew from the briefest touch of the datasphere – its surface now agitated with surges of information until it resembled a storm-tossed sea – that the main line of the FORCE:space armada consisted of more than a hundred capital spinships: matte-black attack carriers, looking like thrown spears, with their launch-arms lashed down; Three-C command ships, as beautiful and awkward as meteors made of black crystal; bulbous destroyers resembling the overgrown torchships they were; perimeter defense pickets, more energy than matter, their massive containment shields now set to total reflection – brilliant mirrors reflecting Tau Ceti and the hundreds of flame trails around them; fast cruisers, moving like sharks among the slower schools of ships; lumbering troop transports carrying thousands of FORCE:Marines in their zero-g holds; and scores of support ships – frigates; fast attack fighters; torpedo ALRs;

fatline relay pickets; and the farcaster JumpShips themselves, massive dodecahedrons with their fairyland arrays of antennae and probes.

All around the fleet, kept at a safe distance by traffic control, flitted the yachts and sunjammers and private in-system ships, their sails catching sunlight and reflecting the glory of the armada.

The guests on the Government House grounds cheered and applauded. The gentleman in FORCE black was weeping silently. Nearby, concealed cameras and wideband imagers carried the moment to every world in the Web and – via fatline – to scores of worlds which were not.

I shook my head and remained seated.

'M Severn?' A security guard stood over me.

'Yes?'

She nodded toward the executive mansion. 'CEO Gladstone will see you now.'

TWO

Every age fraught with discord and danger seems to spawn a leader meant only for that age, a political giant whose absence, in retrospect, seems inconceivable when the history of that age is written. Meina Gladstone was just such a leader for our Final Age, although none then could have dreamed that there would be no one but me to write the true history of her and her time.

Gladstone had been compared to the classical figure of Abraham Lincoln so many times that when I was finally ushered into her presence that night of the armada party, I was half surprised not to find her in a black frock coat and stovepipe hat. The CEO of the Senate and leader of a government serving a hundred and thirty billion people was wearing a gray suit of soft wool, trousers and tunic top ornamented only by the slightest hint of red cord piping at seams and cuffs. I did not think she looked like Abraham Lincoln . . . nor like Alvarez-Temp, the second most common hero of antiquity cited as her Doppelganger by the press. I thought that she looked like an old lady.

Meina Gladstone was tall and thin, but her countenance was more aquiline than Lincolnesque, with her blunt beak of a nose; sharp cheekbones; the wide, expressive mouth with thin lips; and gray hair rising in a roughly cropped wave, which did indeed resemble feathers. But to my mind, the most memorable aspect of Meina Gladstone's appearance was her eyes: large, brown, and infinitely sad.

11

We were not alone. I had been led into a long, softly lighted room lined with wooden shelves holding many hundreds of printed books. A long holoframe simulating a window gave a view of the gardens. A meeting was in the process of breaking up, and a dozen men and women stood or sat in a rough half-circle that held Gladstone's desk at its cusp. The CEO leaned back casually on her desk, resting her weight on the front of it, her arms folded. She looked up as I entered.

'M Severn?'

'Yes.'

'Thank you for coming.' Her voice was familiar from a thousand All Thing debates, its timbre rough with age and its tone as smooth as an expensive liqueur. Her accent was famous – blending precise syntax with an almost forgotten lilt of pre-Hegira English, evidently now found only in the river-delta regions of her home world of Patawpha. 'Gentlemen and ladies, let me introduce M Joseph Severn,' she said.

Several of the group nodded, obviously at a loss as to why I was there. Gladstone made no further introductions, but I touched the datasphere to identify everyone: three cabinet members, including the Minister of Defense; two FORCE chiefs of staff; two aides to Gladstone; four senators, including the influential Senator Kolchev; and a projection of a TechnoCore Councilor known as Albedo.

'M Severn has been invited here to bring an artist's perspective to the proceedings,' said CEO Gladstone.

FORCE:ground General Morpurgo snorted a laugh. 'An *artist*'s perspective? With all due respect, CEO, what the hell does that mean?'

Gladstone smiled. Instead of answering the General, she turned back to me. 'What do you think of the passing of the armada, M Severn?'

'It's pretty,' I said.

General Morpurgo made a noise again. '*Pretty?* He looks at the greatest concentration of space-force firepower in the history of the galaxy and calls it *pretty*?' He turned toward another military man and shook his head.

Gladstone's smile had not wavered. 'And what of the war?' she asked me. 'Do you have an opinion on our attempt to rescue Hyperion from the Ouster barbarians?'

'It's stupid,' I said.

The room became very silent. Current real-time polling in the All Thing showed 98 percent approval of CEO Gladstone's decision to fight rather than cede the colonial world of Hyperion to the Ousters. Gladstone's political future rested on a positive outcome of the conflict. The men and women in that room had been instrumental in formulating the policy, making the decision to invade, and carrying out the logistics. The silence stretched.

'Why is it stupid?' Gladstone asked softly.

I made a gesture with my right hand. 'The Hegemony's not been at war since its founding seven centuries ago,' I said. 'It is foolish to test its basic stability this way.'

'Not at war!' shouted General Morpurgo. He gripped his knees with massive hands. 'What the hell do you call the Glennon-Height Rebellion?'

'A rebellion,' I said. 'A mutiny. A police action.'

Senator Kolchev showed his teeth in a smile that held no amusement. He was from Lusus and seemed more muscle than man. 'Fleet actions,' he said, 'half a million dead, two FORCE divisions locked in combat for more than a year. Some police action, son.'

I said nothing.

Leigh Hunt, an older, consumptive-looking man reported to be Gladstone's closest aide, cleared his throat. 'But what M Severn says is interesting. Where do you see the difference between this . . . ah . . . conflict and the Glennon-Height wars, sir?'

'Glennon-Height was a former FORCE officer,' I said, aware that I was stating the obvious. 'The Ousters have been an unknown quantity for centuries. The rebels' forces were known, their potential easily gauged; the Ouster Swarms have been outside the Web since the Hegira. Glennon-Height stayed within the Protectorate, raiding worlds no farther than two months' time-debt from the Web; Hyperion is *three years* from Parvati, the closest Web staging area.'

'You think we haven't thought of all this?' asked General Morpurgo. 'What about the Battle of Bressia? We've already fought the Ousters there. That was no . . . rebellion.'

'Quiet, please,' said Leigh Hunt. 'Go on, M Severn.'

I shrugged again. 'The primary difference is that in this case we are dealing with Hyperion,' I said.

Senator Richeau, one of the women present, nodded as if I had explained myself in full. 'You're afraid of the Shrike,' she said. 'Do you belong to the Church of the Final Atonement?'

'No,' I said, 'I'm not a member of the Shrike Cult.'

'What *are* you?' demanded Morpurgo.

'An artist,' I lied.

Leigh Hunt smiled and turned to Gladstone. 'I agree that we needed this perspective to sober us, CEO,' he said, gesturing toward the window and the holo images showing the still-applauding crowds, 'but while our artist friend has brought up necessary points, they have all been reviewed and weighed in full.'

Senator Kolchev cleared his throat. 'I hate to mention the obvious when it seems we are all intent on ignoring it, but does this . . . *gentleman* . . . have the proper security clearance to be present at such a discussion?'

Gladstone nodded and showed the slight smile so many caricaturists had tried to capture. 'M Severn has been commissioned by the Arts Ministry to do a series of drawings of me during the next few days or weeks. The theory is, I believe, that these will have some historical significance and may lead to a formal portrait. At any rate, M Severn has been granted a T-level gold security clearance, and we may speak

14

freely in front of him. Also, I appreciate his candor. Perhaps his arrival serves to suggest that our meeting has reached its conclusion. I will join you all in the War Room at 0800 hours tomorrow morning, just before the fleet translates to Hyperion space.'

The group broke up at once. General Morpurgo glowered at me as he left. Senator Kolchev stared with some curiosity as he passed. Councilor Albedo merely faded into nothingness. Leigh Hunt was the only one besides Gladstone and me to remain behind. He made himself more comfortable by draping one leg over the arm of the priceless pre-Hegira chair in which he sat. 'Sit down,' said Hunt.

I glanced at the CEO. She had taken her seat behind the massive desk, and now she nodded. I sat in the straight-backed chair General Morpurgo had occupied. CEO Gladstone said, 'Do you really think that defending Hyperion is stupid?'

'Yes.'

Gladstone steepled her fingers and tapped at her lower lip. Behind her, the window showed the armada party continuing in silent agitation. 'If you have any hope of being reunited with your . . . ah . . . counterpart,' she said, 'it would seem to be in your interest for us to carry out the Hyperion campaign.'

I said nothing. The window view shifted to show the night sky still ablaze with fusion trails.

'Did you bring drawing materials?' asked Gladstone.

I brought out the pencil and small sketchpad I had told Diana Philomel I did not have.

'Draw while we talk,' said Meina Gladstone.

I began sketching, roughing in the relaxed, almost slumped posture, and then working on the details of the face. The eyes intrigued me.

I was vaguely aware that Leigh Hunt was staring intently at me. 'Joseph Severn,' he said. 'An interesting choice of names.'

I used quick, bold lines to give the sense of Gladstone's high brow and strong nose.

'Do you know why people are leery of cybrids?' Hunt asked.

'Yes,' I said. 'The Frankenstein monster syndrome. Fear of anything in human form that is not completely human. It's the real reason androids were outlawed, I suppose.'

'Uh-huh,' agreed Hunt. 'But cybrids *are* completely human, aren't they?'

'Genetically they are,' I said. I found myself thinking of my mother, remembering the times I had read to her during her illness. I thought of my brother Tom. 'But they are also part of the Core,' I said, 'and thus fit the description of "not completely human." '

'Are you part of the Core?' asked Meina Gladstone, turning full face toward me. I started a new sketch.

'Not really,' I said. 'I can travel freely through the regions they allow me in, but it is more like someone accessing the datasphere than a true Core personality's ability.' Her face had been more interesting in three-quarters profile, but the eyes were more powerful when viewed straight on. I worked on the latticework of lines radiating from the corners of those eyes. Meina Gladstone obviously had never indulged in Poulsen treatments.

'If it were possible to keep secrets from the Core,' said Gladstone, 'it would be folly to allow you free access to the councils of government. As it is . . .' She dropped her hands and sat up. I flipped to a new page.

'As it is,' said Gladstone, 'you have information I need. Is it true that you can read the mind of your counterpart, the first retrieval persona?'

'No,' I said. It was difficult to capture the complicated interplay of line and muscle at the corners of her mouth. I sketched in my attempt to do so, moved on to the strong chin and shaded the area beneath the underlip.

Hunt frowned and glanced at the CEO. M Gladstone

brought her fingertips together again. 'Explain,' she said.

I looked up from the drawing. 'I dream,' I said. 'The contents of the dream appear to correspond to the events occurring around the person carrying the implant of the previous Keats persona.'

'A woman named Brawne Lamia,' said Leigh Hunt.

'Yes.'

Gladstone nodded. 'So the original Keats persona, the one thought killed on Lusus, is still alive?'

I paused. 'It . . . he . . . is still aware,' I said. 'You know that the primary personality substrate was extracted from the Core, probably by the cybrid himself, and implanted in a Schrön-loop bio-shunt carried by M Lamia.'

'Yes, yes,' said Leigh Hunt. 'But the fact is, you are *in contact* with the Keats persona, and through him, with the Shrike pilgrims.'

Quick, dark strokes provided a dark background to give the sketch of Gladstone more depth. 'I am not actually in contact,' I said. 'I dream dreams about Hyperion that your fatline broadcasts have confirmed as conforming to real-time events. I cannot communicate to the passive Keats persona, nor to its host or the other pilgrims.'

CEO Gladstone blinked. 'How did you know about the fatline broadcasts?'

'The Consul told the other pilgrims about his comlog's ability to relay through the fatline transmitter in his ship. He told them just before they descended into the valley.'

Gladstone's tone hinted of her years as a lawyer before entering politics. 'And how did the others respond to the Consul's revelation?'

I put the pencil back in my pocket. 'They knew that a spy was in their midst,' I said. 'You told each of them.'

Gladstone glanced at her aide. Hunt's expression was blank. 'If you're in touch with them,' she said, 'you must know that we've received no message since before they left Keep Chronos to descend to the Time Tombs.'

I shook my head. 'Last night's dream ended just as they approached the valley.'

Meina Gladstone rose, paced to the window, raised a hand, and the image went black. 'So you don't know if any of them are still alive?'

'No.'

'What was their status the last time you . . . dreamt?'

Hunt was watching me as intensely as ever. Meina Gladstone was staring at the dark screen, her back to both of us. 'All of the pilgrims were alive,' I said, 'with the possible exception of Het Masteen, the True Voice of the Tree.'

'He was dead?' asked Hunt.

'He disappeared from the windwagon on the Sea of Grass two nights before, only hours after the Ouster scouts had destroyed the treeship *Yggdrasill*. But shortly before the pilgrims descended from Keep Chronos, they saw a robed figure crossing the sands toward the Tombs.'

'Het Masteen?' asked Gladstone.

I lifted a hand. 'They assumed so. They were not sure.'

'Tell me about the others,' said the CEO.

I took a breath. I knew from the dreams that Gladstone had known at least two of the people on the last Shrike Pilgrimage; Brawne Lamia's father had been a fellow senator, and the Hegemony Consul had been Gladstone's personal representative in secret negotiations with the Ousters. 'Father Hoyt is in great pain,' I said. 'He told the story of the cruciform. The Consul learned that Hoyt also wears one . . . two actually, Father Duré's and his own.'

Gladstone nodded. 'So he still carries the resurrection parasite?'

'Yes.'

'Does it bother him more as he approaches the Shrike's lair?'

'I believe so,' I said.

'Go on.'

'The poet, Silenus, has been drunk much of the time. He

is convinced that his unfinished poem predicted and determines the course of events.'

'On Hyperion?' asked Gladstone, her back still turned.

'Everywhere,' I said.

Hunt glanced at the chief executive and then looked back at me. 'Is Silenus insane?'

I returned his gaze but said nothing. In truth, I did not know.

'Go on,' Gladstone said again.

'Colonel Kassad continues with his twin obsessions of finding the woman named Moneta and of killing the Shrike. He is aware that they may be one and the same.'

'Is he armed?' Gladstone's voice was very soft.

'Yes.'

'Go on.'

'Sol Weintraub, the scholar from Barnard's World, hopes to enter the tomb called the Sphinx as soon as—'

'Excuse me,' said Gladstone, 'but is his daughter still with him?'

'Yes.'

'And how old is Rachel now?'

'Five days, I believe.' I closed my eyes to remember the previous night's dream in greater detail. 'Yes,' I said, 'five days.'

'And still aging backward in time?'

'Yes.'

'Go on, M Severn. Please tell me about Brawne Lamia and the Consul.'

'M Lamia is carrying out the wishes of her former client . . . and lover,' I said. 'The Keats persona felt it was necessary for him to confront the Shrike. M Lamia is doing it in his stead.'

'M Severn,' began Leigh Hunt, 'you speak of "the Keats persona" as if it had no relevance or connection to your own . . .'

'Later, please, Leigh,' said Meina Gladstone. She turned

19

to look at me. 'I'm curious about the Consul. Did he take his turn at telling his reason for joining the pilgrimage?'

'Yes,' I said.

Gladstone and Hunt waited.

'The Consul told them about his grandmother,' I said. 'The woman called Siri who started the Maui-Covenant rebellion more than half a century ago. He told them about the death of his own family during the battle for Bressia, and he revealed his secret meetings with the Ousters.'

'Is that all?' asked Gladstone. Her brown eyes were very intense.

'No,' I said. 'The Consul told them that he had been the one to trigger an Ouster device which hastened the opening of the Time Tombs.'

Hunt sat straight up, his leg dropping off the arm of the chair. Gladstone visibly took a breath. 'Is that all?'

'Yes.'

'How did the others respond to his revelation of . . . betrayal?' she asked.

I paused, tried to reconstruct the dream images in a more linear fashion than memory provided. 'Some were outraged,' I said. 'But none feels overwhelming loyalty to the Hegemony at this point. They decided to go on. I believe that each of the pilgrims feels that punishment will be dealt out by the Shrike, not by human agency.'

Hunt slammed his fist down on the arm of the chair. 'If the Consul were here,' he snapped, 'he'd fast discover otherwise.'

'Quiet, Leigh.' Gladstone paced back to her desk, touched some papers there. All of the comm lights were glowing impatiently. I found myself amazed that she could spend so much time talking to me at such an hour. 'Thank you, M Severn,' she said. 'I want you to be with us for the next few days. Someone will show you to your suite in the residential wing of Government House.'

I rose. 'I'll return to Esperance for my things,' I said.

'No need,' said Gladstone. 'They were brought here before you had stepped off the terminex platform. Leigh will show you out.'

I nodded and followed the taller man toward the door.

'Oh, M Severn . . .' called Meina Gladstone.

'Yes?'

The CEO smiled. 'I did appreciate your candor earlier,' she said. 'But from this point on, let us assume you are a court artist and a court artist alone, *sans* opinions, *sans* visibility, *sans* mouth. Understood?'

'Understood, M Executive,' I said.

Gladstone nodded, already turning her attention to the blinking phone lights. 'Very good. Please bring your sketch-book to the meeting in the War Room at 0800 hours.'

A security guard met us in the anteroom and started to lead me toward the maze of corridors and checkpoints. Hunt called out for him to stop and strode across the wide hall, his steps echoing on the tile. He touched my arm. 'Make no mistake,' he said. 'We know . . . *she* knows . . . who you are and what you are and whom you represent.'

I met his gaze and calmly extracted my arm. 'That's good,' I said, 'because at this point, I am quite sure that I do *not* know.'

THREE

Six adults and an infant in a hostile landscape. Their fire seems a small thing against the darkness falling. Above them and beyond them, the hills of the valley rise like walls while closer in, wrapped in the darkness of the valley itself, the huge shapes of the Tombs seem to creep closer like saurian apparitions from some antediluvian age.

Brawne Lamia is tired and aching and very irritable. The sound of Sol Weintraub's baby crying sets her teeth on edge. She knows the others are also tired; none has slept more than a few hours in the past three nights, and the day just ending has been filled with tension and unresolved terrors. She sets the last piece of wood on the fire.

'There's no more where that came from,' snaps Martin Silenus. The fire lights the poet's satyrish features from below.

'I know it,' says Brawne Lamia, too tired to put anger or any other energy into her voice. The firewood is from a cache carried in by the pilgrim groups of years gone by. Their three small tents are set in the area traditionally used by the pilgrims on their last night before confronting the Shrike. They are camped close to the Time Tomb called the Sphinx, and the black sweep of what may be a wing blots out some of the sky.

'We'll use the lantern when this is gone,' says the Consul. The diplomat looks even more exhausted than the others. The flickering light casts a red tint over his sad features. He had dressed in diplomatic finery for the day, but now the cape and tricorne cap look as soiled and wilted as the Consul himself.

Colonel Kassad returns to the fire and slides the night visor up on to the top of his helmet. Kassad is wearing full combat gear, and the activated chameleon polymer shows only his face, floating two meters above the ground. 'Nothing,' he says. 'No movement. No heat traces. No sound besides the wind.' Kassad leans the FORCE multipurpose assault rifle against a rock and sits near the others, the fibers of his impact armor deactivating into a matte black not much more visible than before.

'Do you think the Shrike will come tonight?' asks Father Hoyt. The priest has his black cloak wrapped around him and seems as much a part of the night as Colonel Kassad. The thin man's voice is strained.

Kassad leans forward and pokes the fire with his baton. 'There is no way to tell. I'll stand watch just in case.'

Suddenly all six look up as the star-filled sky spasms with color, orange and red blossoms unfolding silently, obliterating the starfield.

'There hasn't been much of that in the past few hours,' says Sol Weintraub, rocking his infant. Rachel has quit crying and now tries to grasp her father's short beard. Weintraub kisses her tiny hand.

'They're testing Hegemony defenses again,' says Kassad. Sparks rise from the prodded fire, embers floating into the sky as if seeking to join the brighter flames there.

'Who won?' asks Lamia, referring to the silent space battle which had filled the sky with violence all the night before and much of that day.

'Who fucking cares?' says Martin Silenus. He searches through the pockets of his fur coat as if he might find a full bottle there. He does not. 'Who fucking cares,' he mutters again.

'I care,' the Consul says tiredly. 'If the Ousters break through, they may destroy Hyperion before we find the Shrike.'

Silenus laughs derisively. 'Oh, that would be terrible, wouldn't it? To die before we discover death? To be killed before we are scheduled to be killed? To go out swiftly and without pain, rather than to writhe forever on the Shrike's thorns? Oh, terrible thought, that.'

'Shut up,' says Brawne Lamia, and her voice again is without emotion but this time is not devoid of threat. She looks at the Consul. 'So where is the Shrike? Why didn't we find it?'

The diplomat stares at the fire. 'I don't know. Why should I know?'

'Perhaps the Shrike is gone,' says Father Hoyt. 'Perhaps by collapsing the anti-entropic fields you've freed it forever. Perhaps it's carried its scourge elsewhere.'

The Consul shakes his head and says nothing.

'No,' says Sol Weintraub. The baby is sleeping against his shoulder. 'It will be here. I feel it.'

Brawne Lamia nods. 'So do I. It's waiting.' She had retrieved several ration units from her pack, and now she pulls heating tabs and passes the units around.

'I know that anticlimax is the warp and woof of the world,' says Silenus. 'But this is fucking ridiculous. All dressed up with nowhere to die.'

Brawne Lamia glowers but says nothing, and for a while they eat in silence. The flames fade from the sky, and the densely packed stars return, but embers continue to rise as if seeking escape.

Wrapped in the dream-hazy tumble of Brawne Lamia's thoughts twice-removed, I try to reassemble the events since last I dreamt their lives.

The pilgrims had descended into the valley before dawn, singing, their shadows thrown before them by the light from the battle a billion kilometers above. All day they had explored the Time Tombs. Each minute they expected to die. After some hours, as the sun rose and the high desert

24

cold gave way to heat, their fear and exultation faded.

The long day was silent except for the rasp of sand, occasional shouts, and the constant, almost subliminal moan of the wind around rocks and tombs. Kassad and the Consul each had brought an instrument that measured the intensity of the anti-entropic fields, but Lamia had been the first to notice that these were not needed, that the ebb and flow of the time tides could be felt as a slight nausea overladen with a sense of *déjà vu* which did not fade.

Nearest to the entrance of the valley had been the Sphinx; then came the Jade Tomb, its walls translucent only in morning and evening twilight; then, less than a hundred meters farther in, rose the tomb called the Obelisk; the pilgrim path then led up the widening arroyo to the largest tomb of them all, centrally placed, the Crystal Monolith, its surface devoid of design or opening, its flat-topped roof flush with the tops of the valley walls; then came the three Cave Tombs, their entrances visible only because of the well-worn paths that led to them; and finally – almost a kilometer farther down the valley – sat the so-called Shrike Palace, its sharp flanges and outflung spires reminiscent of the spikes of the creature said to haunt this valley.

All day they had moved from tomb to tomb, none venturing off alone, the group pausing before entering those artifacts which might be entered. Sol Weintraub had been all but overcome with emotion upon seeing and entering the Sphinx, the same tomb where his daughter had contracted the Merlin sickness twenty-six years earlier. The instruments set out by her university team still sat on tripods outside the tomb, although none in the group could tell if they still functioned, carrying out their monitoring duties. The passageways in the Sphinx were as narrow and labyrinthine as Rachel's comlog entries had suggested, the strings of glow-globes and electric lights left behind by various research groups now dark and depleted. They used hand torches and Kassad's night visor to explore the place. There was no sign of the room Rachel had been in when the walls closed in on her and the sickness began. There were only vestigial remnants of the once-powerful time tides. There was no sign of the Shrike.

Each tomb had offered its moment of terror, of hopeful and dreadful anticipation, only to be replaced by an hour or more of anticlimax as dusty, empty rooms appeared just as they had to the tourists and Shrike Pilgrims of centuries past.

Eventually the day had ended in disappointment and fatigue, the shadows from the eastern valley wall drawing across the Tombs and valley like a curtain closing an unsuccessful play. The day's heat had vanished, and the high desert cold returned quickly, borne on a wind that smelled of snow and the high reaches of the Bridle Range, twenty kilometers to the southwest. Kassad suggested that they make camp. The Consul had shown the way to the traditional grounds where Shrike Pilgrims had waited their last night before meeting the creature they sought. The flat area near the Sphinx, showing traces of litter from research groups as well as pilgrims, pleased Sol Weintraub, who imagined his daughter had camped there. No one else objected.

Now, in full darkness with the last piece of wood burning, I sensed the six of them drawing closer . . . not merely to the fire's warmth, but to each other . . . drawn by the fragile but tangible cords of shared experience forged during their voyage upriver on the levitation barge *Benares* and in their crossing to Keep Chronos. More than that, I sensed a unity more palpable than emotional bonds; it took a moment, but I soon realized that the group was connected in a microsphere of shared data and senseweb. On a world whose primitive, regional data relays had been shredded by the first hint of combat, this group had linked comlogs and biomonitors to share information and to watch over one another as best they could.

While the entry barriers were obvious and solid, I had no trouble sliding past, through, and under them, picking up the finite but numerous clues – pulse, skin temperature, cortical wave activity, access request, data inventory – which allowed me some insight into what each pilgrim was thinking, feeling, and doing. Kassad, Hoyt, and Lamia had implants, the flow of their thoughts were easiest to sense. At that second, Brawne Lamia was wondering if it had not been a mistake to seek out the Shrike; something was nagging at her, just under the surface but unrelenting in its demand to be heard. She felt as if she were ignoring some terribly important clue which held the solution to . . . what?

Brawne Lamia had always despised mysteries; it was one of the reasons she had left a life of some comfort and leisure to become a private investigator. But what mystery? She had all but solved the murder of her cybrid client . . . and lover . . . and had come to Hyperion to fulfill his final wish. Yet she sensed that this nagging doubt had little to do with the Shrike. What?

Lamia shook her head and poked the dying fire. Her body was strong, raised to resist Lusus's 1.3 standard gravity, and trained to even greater strength, but she had not slept in several days and she was very, very tired. She became vaguely aware that someone was speaking.

'. . . just to take a shower and get some food,' says Martin Silenus. 'Perhaps use your comm unit and fatline link to see who's winning the war.'

The Consul shakes his head. 'Not yet. The ship is for an emergency.'

Silenus gestures toward the night, the Sphinx, and the rising wind. 'You think that this isn't an emergency?'

Brawne Lamia realizes that they are talking about the Consul bringing his spacecraft here from the city of Keats. 'Are you sure that the absence of alcohol isn't the emergency you're referring to?' she asks.

27

Silenus glares at her. 'Would it hurt to have a drink?'

'No,' says the Consul. He rubs his eyes, and Lamia remembers that he too is addicted to alcohol. But his answer to bringing the ship here had been no. 'We'll wait until we have to.'

'What about the fatline transmitter?' says Kassad.

The Consul nods and removes the antique comlog from his small pack. The instrument had belonged to his grandmother Siri and to her grandparents before her. The Consul touches the diskey. 'I can broadcast with this, but not receive.'

Sol Weintraub has set his sleeping child in the opening of the closest tent. Now he turns toward the fire. 'And the last time you transmitted a message was when we arrived in the Keep?'

'Yes.'

Martin Silenus's tone is sarcastic. 'And we're supposed to believe that . . . from a confessed traitor?'

'Yes.' The Consul's voice is a distillation of pure weariness.

Kassad's thin face floats in the darkness. His body, legs, and arms are discernible only as a blackness against the already dark background. 'But it will serve to call the ship if we need it?'

'Yes.'

Father Hoyt hugs his cloak tighter around him to keep it from flapping in the rising wind. Sand scrapes against wool and tent fabric. 'Aren't you afraid that the port authorities or FORCE will move the ship or tamper with it?' he asks the Consul.

'No.' The Consul's head moves only slightly, as if he is too tired to shake it completely. 'Our clearance pip was from Gladstone herself. Also, the Governor-General is a friend of mine . . . was a friend.'

The others had met the recently promoted Hegemony governor shortly after landing; to Brawne Lamia, Theo Lane

28

had seemed a man catapulted into events too large for his talents.

'The wind's coming up,' says Sol Weintraub. He turns his body to protect the baby from flying sand. Still squinting into the gale, the scholar says, 'I wonder if Het Masteen is out there?'

'We searched everywhere,' says Father Hoyt. His voice is muffled because he has lowered his head into the folds of his cloak.

Martin Silenus laughs. 'Pardon me, priest,' he says, 'but you're full of shit.' The poet stands and walks to the edge of the firelight. The wind ruffles the fur of his coat and rips his words away into the night. 'The cliff walls hold a thousand hiding places. The Crystal Monolith hides its entrance to us . . . but to a Templar? And besides, you saw the stairway to the labyrinth in the deepest room of the Jade Tomb.'

Hoyt looks up, squinting against the pinpricks of blowing sand. 'You think he's there? In the labyrinth?'

Silenus laughs and raises his arms. The silk of his loose blouse ripples and billows. 'How the fuck should I know, Padre? All I know is that Het Masteen could be out there now, watching us, waiting to come back to claim his luggage.' The poet gestures toward the Möbius cube in the center of their small pile of gear. 'Or he could be dead already. Or worse.'

'Worse?' says Hoyt. The priest's face has aged in the past few hours. His eyes are sunken mirrors of pain, his smile a rictus.

Martin Silenus strides back to the dying fire. 'Worse,' he says. 'He could be twisting on the Shrike's steel tree. Where we'll be in a few—'

Brawne Lamia rises suddenly and grasps the poet by his shirtfront. She lifts him off the ground, shakes him, lowers him until his face is on a level with hers. 'Once more,' she says softly, 'and I'll do very painful things to you. I won't kill you, but you will wish I had.'

The poet shows his satyr's smile. Lamia drops him and turns her back. Kassad says, 'We're tired. Everyone turn in. I'll stand watch.'

My dreams of Lamia are mixed with Lamia's dreams. It is not unpleasant to share a woman's dreams, a woman's thoughts, even those of a woman separated from me by a gulf of time and culture far greater than any imagined gap of gender. In a strange and oddly mirrorlike way, she dreamed of her dead lover, Johnny, of his too-small nose and his too-stubborn jaw, his too-long hair curling over his collar, and his eyes – those too-expressive, too-revealing, eyes that too-freely animated a face which might, except for those eyes, belong to any one of a thousand peasants born within a day's ride of London.

The face she dreamed was mine. The voice she heard in that dream was mine. But the lovemaking she dreamed of – remembering now – was nothing that I had shared. I sought to escape her dream, if only to find my own. If I were to be a voyeur, it might as well be in the tumble of manufactured memories which passed for my own dreams.

But I was not allowed to dream my own dreams. Not yet. I suspect that I was born – and born again from my death-bed – simply to dream those dreams of my dead and distant twin.

I resigned myself, ceased my struggles to awaken, and dreamed.

Brawne Lamia comes awake swiftly, jarringly, shaken from a pleasant dream by some sound or movement. For a long second she is disoriented; it is dark, there is a noise – not mechanical – which is louder than most sounds in the Lusus Hive where she lives; she is drunk with fatigue but knows that she has awakened after very little sleep; she is alone in a small, confined space, in something resembling an oversized body bag.

Raised on a world where enclosed places mean security from vicious air, winds, and animals, where many people suffer from agoraphobia when confronting the rare open space but few know the meaning of claustrophobia, Brawne Lamia nonetheless reacts as a claustrophobe: clawing for air, pushing aside bedroll and tent flaps in a panicked rush to escape the small cocoon of fiberplastic, crawling, pulling herself along by her hands and forearms and elbows until there is sand under her palms and sky above.

Not really sky, she realizes, suddenly seeing and remembering where she is. Sand. A blowing, raging, whirling sandstorm of particles, stinging her face like pinpricks. The campfire is out and covered with sand. Sand has banked on the windward side of all three of the tents, their sides flapping, cracking like rifle shots in the wind, and dunes of new-blown sand have grown up around the camp, leaving streaks and furrows and ridges in the lee of tents and gear. No one stirs from the other tents. The tent she was sharing with Father Hoyt is half-collapsed, all but buried by the rising dunes.

Hoyt.

It had been his absence which awakened her. Even in her dreams, some part of her consciousness had been aware of the soft breathing and almost indistinguishable moans from the sleeping priest as he wrestled with his pain. Sometime in the past half hour, he had left. Probably not more than a few minutes before; Brawne Lamia knew that even as she had dreamed of Johnny she had been half aware of a rustling, sliding sound above the rasp of sand and roar of the wind.

Lamia gets to her feet and shields her eyes from the sandstorm. It is very dark, the stars are occluded by high cloud and the surface storm, but a faint, almost electrical radiance fills the air and reflects from rock and dune surface. Lamia realizes that it *is* electrical, that the air is filled with a static which makes the curls of her hair leap and writhe in Medusalike gyrations. Static charges creep along her tunic sleeves and float over the tent surfaces like St Elmo's fire. As her eyes adapt, Lamia realizes that the shifting dunes are aglow with pale fire. Forty meters to the east, the tomb called the Sphinx is a crackling, pulsing outline in the night. Waves of current move along the outflung appendages often called the wings.

Brawne Lamia looks around, sees no sign of Father Hoyt, and considers calling for help. She realizes that her voice will not be heard above the wind roar. She wonders for a second whether the priest has merely gone to one of the other tents or to the crude latrine twenty meters west, but something tells her that this is not the case. She looks at the Sphinx and – for the briefest second – seems to see the shape of a man, black cloak flapping like a falling pennant, shoulders hunched against the wind, outlined against the static glow of the tomb.

A hand falls on her shoulder.

Brawne Lamia twists away, falls into a fighting crouch, left fist extended, right hand rigid. She recognizes Kassad standing there. The Colonel is half again as tall as Lamia – and half as broad – and miniature lightning plays across his thin form as he leans closer to shout in her ear. 'He went that way!' The long, black, scarecrow arm extends toward the Sphinx.

Lamia nods and shouts back, her voice almost inaudible to herself above the roar. 'Shall we wake the others?' She had forgotten that Kassad was standing watch. Did the man never sleep?

Fedmahn Kassad shakes his head. His visors are up and the helmet destructured to form a hood on the back of his combat-armored coverall. Kassad's face looks very pale in the glow from his suit. He gestures toward the Sphinx. His multipurpose FORCE rifle is nestled in the crook of his left arm. Grenades, binocular case, and more-mysterious items are draped from hooks and web belts on his impact armor. He points again toward the Sphinx.

Lamia leans forward and shouts. 'Did the Shrike take him?'

Kassad shakes his head.

'Can you see him?' She gestures toward his night visor and binoculars.

'No,' says Kassad. 'The storm. Fouls up heat signatures.'

Brawne Lamia turns her back to the wind, feeling the particles striking her neck like needles from a fléchette gun. She queries her comlog but it tells her only that Hoyt is alive and moving; nothing else is being transmitted on the common band. She moves until she is next to Kassad, their backs forming a wall against the gale. 'Are we going to follow him?' she shouts.

Kassad shakes his head. 'We can't leave the perimeter unguarded. I left telltales, but . . .' He gestures toward the storm.

Brawne Lamia ducks back in the tent, tugs on her boots, and emerges with her all-weather cape and her father's automatic pistol. A more conventional weapon, a Gier stunner, is in the breast pocket of the cape. 'I'll go then,' she says.

At first she thinks that the Colonel has not heard her, but then she sees something in his pale eyes and knows that he has. He taps the military comlog on his wrist.

Lamia nods and makes sure that her own implant and comlog are set to the widest bandwidth. 'I'll be back,' she says and wades up the growing dune. Her pant legs glow with static discharge, and the sand seems alive with silver-white pulses of current fleeting across its variegated surface.

Twenty meters from the camp, and she can see nothing of it. Ten meters farther, and the Sphinx rises above her. There is no sign of Father Hoyt; footprints do not survive ten seconds in the storm.

The wide entrance to the Sphinx is open, has been open as long as mankind has known of this place. Now it is a black rectangle in a faintly glowing wall. Logic suggested that Hoyt would have gone there, if only to get out of the storm, but something quite beyond logic tells her that this is not the priest's destination.

Brawne Lamia trudges past the Sphinx, rests in its lee for several moments to wipe the sand from her face and to breathe freely again, and then she moves on, following a faint, hard-packed trail between the dunes. Ahead of her, the Jade Tomb glows a milky green in the night, its smooth curves and crests oily with an ominous glow.

Squinting, Lamia looks again and sees someone or something outlined against that glow for the most fleeting of instants. Then the figure is gone, either inside the tomb or invisible against the black semicircle of its entrance.

Lamia puts her head down and moves forward, the wind pushing and shoving at her as if hurrying her toward something important.

FOUR

The military briefing droned on toward midmorning. I suspect that such meetings had shared the same qualities – brisk monotone continuing like a background buzz, the stale taste of too much coffee, the pall of smoke in the air, stacks of hard copy and the cortical overlay vertigo of implant access – for many centuries. I suspect it was simpler when I was a boy; Wellington rounded up his men, those he dispassionately and accurately called 'the scum of the earth,' told them nothing, and sent them off to die.

I brought my attention back to the group. We were in a large room, gray walls relieved by white rectangles of light, gray carpet, gunmetal gray horseshoe table with black diskeys and the occasional carafe of water. CEO Meina Gladstone sat at the center of the arc of table, ranking senators and cabinet ministers near her, military officers and other second-rank decision makers farther along the curve. Behind them all, not at the table, sat the inevitable clusters of aides, none of the FORCE people below the rank of colonel, and behind them – on less comfortable looking chairs – the aides to the aides.

I had no chair. With a cluster of other invited but obviously purposeless personnel, I sat on a stool near a rear corner of the room, twenty meters from the CEO and even farther from the briefing officer, a young colonel with a pointer in his hand and no hesitation whatsoever in his voice. Behind the colonel was the gold and gray slab of a callup template, before him the slightly raised omnisphere of the kind found in any holopit. From time to time, the callup clouded and leaped to life; at other times the air misted with complex holos. Miniatures of these diagrams glowed on every diskey plate and hovered above some comlogs.

I sat on my stool, watched Gladstone, and drew an occasional sketch.

Awakening that morning in the Government House guest room, bright Tau Ceti sunlight streaming between peach-colored drapes which had opened automatically at my 0630 wake-up time, there was a second when I was lost, displaced, still in pursuit of Lenar Hoyt and in fear of the Shrike and Het Masteen. Then, as if some power had granted my wish to leave me to dream my own dreams, there was a minute where confusion compounded, and I sat up gasping, looking around in alarm, expecting the lemon carpet and peach-colored light to fade like the fever dream it was, leaving only the pain and phlegm and terrible hemorrhages, blood on linen, the light-filled room dissolving into the shadows of the dark apartment on the Piazza di Spagna, and looming over all, the sensitive face of Joseph Severn leaning forward, leaning forward, watching and waiting for me to die.

I showered twice, first with water and then with sonic, dressed in a new gray suit that lay set out for me on the just-made bed when I emerged from the bathroom, and set off to find the east courtyard where – a courtesy pip left near my new clothing had told me – breakfast was being served for Government House guests.

The orange juice was fresh squeezed. The bacon was crisp and authentic. The newspaper said that CEO Gladstone would be addressing the Web via All Thing and media at 1030 hours Web standard. The pages were full of war news. Flat photos of the armada glowed in full color. General Morpurgo stared out grimly from page three; the paper called him 'the hero of the Second Height Rebellion.' Diana Philomel glanced over toward me from a nearby table where she dined with her Neanderthal husband. Her gown was more formal this morning, dark blue and far less revealing, but a slit up the side allowed a hint of last night's show. She kept her eyes on me as she lifted a strip of bacon with lacquered nails and took a careful bite. Hermund Philomel grunted as he read something agreeable on the folded financial pages.

'The Ouster migration cluster . . . commonly known as a Swarm . . . was detected by Hawking distortion-sensing equipment in the Camn System a little more than three standard years ago,' the young briefing officer was saying. 'Immediately upon detection, FORCE Task Force 42, preconfigured for evacuation of Hyperion System, spun up to C-plus status from Parvati with sealed orders to create a farcaster capability within portal range of Hyperion. At the same time, Task Force 87.2 was dispatched from Solkov-Tikata Staging Area around Camn III with orders to rendezvous with the evacuation force in Hyperion System, to find the Ouster migration cluster, and to engage and destroy their military components . . .' Images of the armada appeared on the callup temp and in front of the young colonel. He gestured with his pointer and a line of ruby light cut through the larger holo to illuminate one of the Three-C ships in the formation. 'Task Force 87.2 is under the command of Admiral Nashita aboard the HS *Hebrides* . . .'

'Yes, yes,' grumbled General Morpurgo, 'we know all this, Yani. Cut to the quick.'

The young colonel simulated a smile, nodded imperceptibly toward the General and CEO Gladstone, and resumed in a voice a trifle less confident. 'Coded fatline transmissions from TF 42 during the past seventy-two hours, standard, report pitched battles between scouting elements of the evacuation task force and forward elements of the Ouster migration cluster—'

'The Swarm,' interrupted Leigh Hunt.

'Yes,' said Yani. He turned toward the callup, and five

37

meters of frosted glass burned to life. To me the display was an incomprehensible maze of arcane symbols, colored vector lines, substrate codes, and FORCE acronyms which added up to total gibberish. Perhaps it made no sense to the big brass and senior politicians in the room either, but no one let on that this was the case. I began a new drawing of Gladstone, with the bulldog profile of Morpurgo in the background.

'Although first reports suggested Hawking wakes in the neighborhood of four thousand drives, this is a misleading figure,' continued the colonel named Yani. I wondered whether that was his first or last name. 'As you know, Ouster . . . ah . . . Swarms can be constituted of up to ten thousand separate drive units, but the vast majority of these are small and either unarmed or of negligible military significance. Microwave, fatline, and other emission signature evaluation suggests—'

'Excuse me,' said Meina Gladstone, her weathered voice in sharp contrast to the briefing officer's syrupy flow, 'but could you tell us how many of the Ouster ships *are* of military significance?'

'Ah . . .' said the colonel, and glanced toward his superiors.

General Morpurgo cleared his throat. 'We think about six . . . seven hundred, tops,' he said. 'Nothing to worry about.'

CEO Gladstone raised an eyebrow. 'And the size of our battle groups?'

Morpurgo nodded toward the young colonel to stand at ease. Morpurgo answered. 'Task Force 42 has about sixty ships, CEO. Task Force—'

'Task Force 42 is the evacuation group?' said Gladstone.

General Morpurgo nodded, and I thought I saw a hint of condescension in his smile. 'Yes, ma'am. Task Force 87.2, the battle group, which translated in-system about an hour ago, will—'

'Were sixty ships adequate to face six or seven hundred?' asked Gladstone.

Morpurgo glanced toward one of his fellow officers as if asking for patience. 'Yes,' he said, 'more than adequate. You have to understand, CEO, that six hundred Hawking drives may sound like a lot, but they're nothing to worry about when they're pushing singleships, or scouts, or one of those little five-person attack craft they call lancers. Task Force 42 consisted of almost *two dozen* main line spinships, including the carriers *Olympus Shadow* and *Neptune Station*. Each of these can launch more than a hundred fighters or ALRs.' Morpurgo fumbled in his pocket, pulled out a recom smokestick the size of a cigar, appeared to remember that Gladstone disapproved of them, and stuck it back in his coat. He frowned. 'When Task Force 87.2 completes its deployment, we'll have more than enough firepower to deal with a dozen Swarms.' Still frowning, he nodded toward Yani to continue.

The colonel cleared his throat and gestured with his pointer toward the callup display. 'As you can see, Task Force 42 had no trouble clearing the necessary volume of space to initiate farcaster construction. This construction was begun six weeks ago, WST, and completed yesterday at 1624 hours, standard. Initial Ouster harassing attacks were beaten off with no casualties for TF 42, and during the past forty-eight hours, a major battle has been waged between advance units of the task force and main Ouster forces. The focus of this skirmish has been here'—Yani gestured again, and a section of the callup pulsed with blue light beyond the tip of his pointer—'twenty-nine degrees above the plane of the ecliptic, thirty AU from Hyperion's sun, approximately 0.35 AU from the hypothetical rim of the system's Oört cloud.'

'Casualties?' said Leigh Hunt.

'Quite within acceptable limits for a firefight of this duration,' said the young colonel, who looked like he had never been within a light-year of hostile fire. His blond hair was carefully combed to the side and gleamed under the intense glow of the spots. 'Twenty-six Hegemony fast attack fighters destroyed or missing, twelve torpedo-carrying ALRs, three torchships, the fuel transport *Asquith's Pride*, and the cruiser *Draconi III*.'

'How many *people* lost?' asked CEO Gladstone. Her voice was very quiet.

Yani glanced quickly at Morpurgo but answered the question himself. 'Around twenty-three hundred,' he said. 'But rescue operations are currently being carried out, and there is some hope of finding survivors of the *Draconi*.' He smoothed his tunic and went on quickly. 'This should be weighed against confirmed kills of at least a hundred and fifty Ouster warships. Our own raids into the migration clust— the Swarm have resulted in an additional thirty to sixty destroyed craft, including comet farms, ore-processing ships, and at least one command cluster.'

Meina Gladstone rubbed her gnarled fingers together. 'Did the casualty estimate – *our* casualties – include the passengers and crew of the destroyed treeship *Yggdrasill*, which we had chartered for the evacuation?'

'No, ma'am,' Yani responded briskly. 'Although there was an Ouster raid in progress at the time, our analysis shows that the *Yggdrasill* was not destroyed by enemy action.'

Gladstone again raised an eyebrow. 'What then?'

'Sabotage, as far as we can tell at this time,' said the Colonel. He prompted another Hyperion System diagram on to the callup.

General Morpurgo glanced at his comlog and said, 'Uh-uh, skip to the ground defenses, Yani. The CEO has to deliver her speech in thirty minutes.'

I completed the sketch of Gladstone and Morpurgo, stretched, and looked around for another subject. Leigh Hunt seemed a challenge, with his nondescript, almost pinched features. When I glanced back up, a holoed globe of Hyperion ceased spinning and unwound itself into a series of flattened projections: oblique equirectangular, Bonne, orthographic, rosette, Van der Grinten, Gores, interrupted Goode homolosine, gnomonic, sinusoidal, azimuthal equidistant, polyconic, hypercorrected Kuwatsi, computer-eschered, Briesemeister, Buckminster, Miller cylindrical, multicoligraphed, and satplot standard, before resolving into a standard Robinson-Baird map of Hyperion.

I smiled. That had been the most enjoyable thing I'd seen since the briefing began. Several of Gladstone's people were shifting with impatience. They wanted at least ten minutes with the CEO before the broadcast began.

'As you know,' began the colonel, 'Hyperion is Old Earth standard to nine point eight nine on the Thuron-Laumier Scale of—'

'Oh, for Chrissakes,' growled Morpurgo, 'get to the troop dispositions and get it over with.'

'Yessir.' Yani swallowed and lifted his pointer. His voice was no longer confident. 'As you know . . . I mean . . .' He pointed to the northernmost continent, floating like a poorly done sketch of a horse's head and neck, terminating jaggedly where the beast's chest and back muscles would begin. 'This is Equus. It has a different official name, but everyone's called it that since . . . this is Equus. The chain of islands running southeast . . . here and here . . . is called the Cat and Nine Tails. Actually, it's an archipelago with more than a hundred . . . anyway, the second major continent is called Aquila, and perhaps you can see it's shaped something like an Old Earth eagle, with the beak here . . . on the northwest coast . . . and the talons extended here, to the southwest . . . and at least one wing raised here, running to the northeast coast. This section is the so-called Pinion Plateau and is almost inaccessible due to the flame forests, but here . . . and here . . . to the southwest, are the main fiberplastic plantations . . .'

'The *disposition* of troops,' growled Morpurgo.

I sketched Yani. I discovered that it is impossible to convey the sheen of sweat with graphite.

'Yessir. The third continent is Ursus . . . looks a bit like a bear . . . but no FORCE troops landed there because it's south polar, almost uninhabitable, although the Hyperion Self-defense Force keeps a listening post there . . .' Yani seemed to sense he was babbling. He drew himself up, wiped his upper lip with the back of his hand, and continued in a more composed tone. 'Primary FORCE:ground installations here . . . here . . . and here.' His pointer illuminated areas near the capital of Keats, high on the neck of Equus. 'FORCE:space units have secured the primary spaceport at the capital as well as secondary fields here . . . and here.' He touched the cities of Endymion and Port Romance, both on the continent of Aquila. 'FORCE:ground units have prepared defensive installations here . . .' Two dozen red lights winked on; most on the neck and mane areas of Equus, but several in Aquila's Beak and Port Romance regions. 'These include elements of the Marines, as well as ground defenses, ground-to-air and ground-to-space components. High Command expects that, unlike Bressia, there will be no battles on the planet itself, but should they attempt an invasion, we will be ready for them.'

Meina Gladstone checked her comlog. Seventeen minutes remained until her live broadcast. 'What about evacuation plans?'

Yani's regained composure crumbled. He looked in some desperation toward his superior officers.

'No evacuation,' said Admiral Singh. 'It was a feint, a lure for the Ousters.'

Gladstone tapped her fingers together. 'There are several million people on Hyperion, Admiral.'

'Yes,' said Singh, 'and we'll protect them, but an evacuation of even the sixty thousand or so Hegemony citizens is quite out of the question. It would be chaos if we allowed all three million into the Web. Besides, for security reasons, it is not possible.'

'The Shrike?' queried Leigh Hunt.

'Security reasons,' repeated General Morpurgo. He stood up, took the pointer from Yani. The young man stood there for a second, irresolute, seeing no place to sit or stand, and then he moved to the rear of the room near me, stood at parade rest, and stared at something near the ceiling – possibly the end of his military career.

'Task Force 87.2 is in-system,' said Morpurgo. 'The Ousters have pulled back to their Swarm center, about sixty AU from Hyperion. To all intents and purposes, the system is secure. Hyperion is secure. We're waiting for a counterattack, but we know that we can contain it. Again, to all intents and purposes, Hyperion is now part of the Web. Questions?'

There were none. Gladstone left with Leigh Hunt, a pack of senators, and her aides. The military brass gravitated to huddles, apparently as dictated by rank. Aides scattered. The few reporters allowed in the room ran to their imager crews waiting outside. The young colonel, Yani, remained at parade rest, his eyes unfocused, his face very pale.

I sat for a moment, staring at the callup map of Hyperion. The continent Equus's resemblance to a horse was greater at this distance. From where I sat, I could just make out the mountains of the Bridle Range and the orange-yellow coloring of the high desert below the horse's 'eye.' There were no FORCE defensive positions marked northeast of the mountains, no symbols at all besides a tiny red glow which might have been the dead City of Poets. The Time Tombs were not marked at all. It was as if the Tombs had no military significance, no part to play in the day's proceedings. But somehow I knew better. Somehow I suspected that the entire war, the movement of thousands, the fate of millions – perhaps billions – depended upon the actions of six people in that unmarked stretch of orange and yellow.

I folded my sketchbook, stuffed my pencils in pockets, looked for an exit, found and used it.

*　　*　　*

43

Leigh Hunt met me in one of the long hallways that led to the main entrance. 'You are leaving?'

I took a breath. 'Aren't I allowed to?'

Hunt smiled, if one could call that upward folding of thin lips a smile. 'Of course, M Severn. But CEO Gladstone has asked me to tell you that she would like to speak to you again this afternoon.'

'When?'

Hunt shrugged. 'Any time after her speech. At your convenience.'

I nodded. Literally millions of lobbyists, job seekers, would-be biographers, business people, fans of the CEO, and potential assassins would give almost anything to have a minute with the Hegemony's most visible leader, a few seconds with CEO Gladstone, and I could see her 'at my convenience.' No one ever said the universe was sane.

I brushed past Leigh Hunt and made for the front door.

By long tradition, Government House had no public farcaster portals within its walls. It was a short walk past the main-entrance security baffles, across the garden, to the low, white building that served as press headquarters and terminex. The newsteeps were clustered around a central viewing pit, where the familiar face and voice of Lewellyn Drake, 'the voice of the All Thing,' gave background to CEO Gladstone's speech 'of vital importance to the Hegemony.' I nodded in his direction, found an unused portal, presented my universal card, and went in search of a bar.

The Grand Concourse was, once you got there, the one place in the Web where you could farcast for free. Every world in the Web had offered at least one of its finest urban blocks – TC^2 provided twenty-three blocks – for shopping, entertainment, fine restaurants, and bars. Especially bars.

Like River Tethys, the Grand Concourse flowed between

military-sized farcaster portals two hundred meters high. With wraparound, the effect was of an infinite main street, a hundred-kilometer torus of material delights. One could stand, as I did that morning, under the brilliant sun of Tau Ceti and look down the Concourse to the night-time midway of Deneb Drei, alive with neon and holos, and catch a glimpse of the hundred-tiered Main Mall of Lusus, while knowing that beyond it lay the shadow-dappled boutiques of God's Grove with its brick concourse and elevators to Treetops, the most expensive eatery in the Web.

I didn't give a damn about all that. I just wanted to find a quiet bar.

TC^2 bars were too filled with bureaucrats, teeps, and business types, so I caught one of the Concourse shuttles and stepped off on Sol Draconi Septem's main drag. The gravity discouraged many – it discouraged *me* – but it meant that the bars were less full, and those there had come to drink.

The place I chose was a ground-level bar, almost hidden under the support pillars and service chutes to the main shopping trellis, and it was dark inside: dark walls, dark wood, dark patrons – their skin as black as mine was pale. It was a good place to drink, and I did so, starting with a double Scotch and getting more serious as I went along.

Even there I couldn't be free of Gladstone. Far across the room, a flatscreen TV showed the CEO's face with the blue-and-gold background she used for state broadcasts. Several of the other drinkers had gathered to watch. I heard snatches of the speech: '. . . to insure the safety of Hegemony citizens and . . . cannot be allowed to endanger the safety of the Web or our allies in . . . thus, I have authorized a full military response to . . .'

'Turn that goddamned thing down!' I was amazed to realize that it was me shouting. The patrons glowered over their shoulders, but they turned it down. I watched Gladstone's mouth move a moment, and then I waved to the bartender for another double.

Sometime later, it might have been hours, I looked up from my drink to realize that there was someone sitting across from me in the dark booth. It took me a second, blinking, to recognize who it was in the dim light. For an instant my heart raced as I thought, *Fanny*, but then I blinked again and said, 'Lady Philomel.'

She still wore the dark blue dress I'd seen her in at breakfast. Somehow it seemed cut lower now. Her face and shoulders seemed to glow in the near-darkness. 'M Severn,' she said, her voice almost a whisper. 'I've come to redeem your promise.'

'Promise?' I waved the bartender over, but he did not respond. I frowned and looked at Diana Philomel. 'What promise?'

'To draw me, of course. Did you forget your promise at the party?'

I snapped my fingers, but the insolent barkeep still did not deign to look my way. 'I did draw you,' I said.

'Yes,' said Lady Philomel, 'but not *all* of me.'

I sighed and drained the last of my Scotch. 'Drinking,' I said.

Lady Philomel smiled. 'So I see.'

I started to stand to go after the bartender, thought better of it, and sat back slowly on to the weathered wood of the bench. 'Armageddon,' I said. 'They're playing with Armageddon.' I looked at the woman carefully, squinting slightly to bring her into focus. 'Do you know that word, m'lady?'

'I don't believe he will serve you any more alcohol,' she said. 'I have drinks at my place. You could have one while you draw.'

I squinted again, craftily now. I might have had a few too many Scotches, but they hadn't impaired my awareness. 'Husband,' I said.

Diana Philomel smiled again, and that too was radiant. 'Spending several days at Government House,' she said,

46

truly whispering now. 'He can't be far from the source of power at such an important time. Come, my vehicle is just outside.'

I don't remember paying, but I assume I did. Or Lady Philomel did. I don't remember her helping me outside, but I assume that someone did. Perhaps a chauffeur. I remember a man in gray tunic and trousers, remember leaning against him.

The EMV had a bubble top, polarized from the outside but quite transparent from where we sat in deep cushions and looked out. I counted one, two portals, and then we were out and away from the Concourse and gaining altitude above blue fields under a yellow sky. Elaborate homes, made from some ebony wood, sat on hilltops surrounded by poppy fields and bronze lakes. Renaissance Vector? It was too difficult a puzzle to work on right then, so I laid my head against the bubble and decided to rest for a moment or two. Had to be rested for Lady Philomel's portrait . . . heh, heh.

The countryside passed below.

47

FIVE

Colonel Fedmahn Kassad follows Brawne Lamia and
Father Hoyt through the dust storm toward the Jade Tomb.
He had lied to Lamia; his night visor and sensors worked well
despite the electrical discharge flickering around them. Following the two seemed the best chance for finding the
Shrike. Kassad remembered the rock-lion hunts on Hebron
– one tethered a goat and waited.

Data from the telltales he had set around the encampment
flickers on Kassad's tactical display and whispers through
his implant. It is a calculated risk to leave Weintraub and his
daughter, Martin Silenus and the Consul sleeping there,
unprotected except for the automatics and an alarm. But
then, Kassad seriously doubts whether he can stop the
Shrike anyway. They are all goats, tethered, waiting. It
is the woman, the phantom named Moneta, whom Kassad is
determined to find before he dies.

The wind has continued to rise, and now it screams
around Kassad, reducing normal visibility to zero and
pelting his impact armor. The dunes glow with discharge, and miniature lightning crackles around his boots
and legs as he strides to keep Lamia's heat signature in
clear view. Information flows in from her open comlog.
Hoyt's closed channels reveal only that he is alive and
moving.

Kassad passes under the outstretched wing of the Sphinx,
feeling the weight invisible above him, hanging there like a
great boot heel. Then he turns down the valley, seeing the

48

Jade Tomb as an absence of heat in infrared, a cold outline. Hoyt is just entering the hemispherical opening; Lamia is twenty meters behind him. Nothing else moves in the valley. The telltales from the camp, hidden by night and storm behind Kassad, reveal Sol and the baby sleeping, the Consul lying awake but unmoving, nothing else within the perimeter.

Kassad slips the safety off on his weapon and moves forward quickly, his long legs taking great strides. He would give anything at that second to have access to a spottersat, his tactical channels complete, rather than have to deal with this partial picture of a fragmented situation. He shrugs within his impact armor and keeps moving.

Brawne Lamia almost does not make the final fifteen meters of her voyage to the Jade Tomb. The wind has risen to gale force and beyond, shoving her along so that twice she loses her footing and falls headlong into the sand. The lightning is real now, splitting the sky in great bursts that illuminate the glowing tomb ahead. Twice she tries calling Hoyt, Kassad, or the others, sure that no one could be sleeping through this back at the camp, but her comlog and implants gives her only static, their widebands registering gibberish. After the second fall, Lamia gets to her knees and looks ahead; there has been no sign of Hoyt since that brief glimpse of someone moving toward the entrance.

Lamia grips her father's automatic pistol and gets to her feet, allowing the wind to blow her the last few meters. She pauses before the entrance hemisphere.

Whether due to the storm and electrical display or something else, the Jade Tomb is glowing a bright, bilious green which tinges the dunes and makes the skin of her wrists and hands look like something from the grave. Lamia makes a final attempt to raise someone on her comlog and then enters the tomb.

* * *

Father Lenar Hoyt of the twelve-hundred-year-old Society of Jesus, resident of the New Vatican on Pacem and loyal servant of His Holiness Pope Urban XVI, is screaming obscenities.

Hoyt is lost and in great pain. The wide rooms near the entrance to the Jade Tomb have narrowed, the corridor has wound back on itself so many times, that now Father Hoyt is lost in a series of catacombs, wandering between greenly glowing walls, in a maze he does not remember from the day's explorations or from the maps he has left behind. The pain – pain which has been with him for years, pain which has been his companion since the tribe of the Bikura had implanted the two cruciforms, his own and Paul Duré's – now threatens to drive him mad with its new intensity.

The corridor narrows again. Lenar Hoyt screams, no longer aware that he is doing so, no longer aware of the words he cries out – words which he has not used since childhood. He wants release. Release from the pain. Release from the burden of carrying Father Duré's DNA, personality . . . Duré's *soul* . . . in the cross-shaped parasite on his back. And from carrying the terrible curse of his own foul resurrection in the cruciform on his chest.

But even as Hoyt screams, he knows that it was not the now-dead Bikura who had condemned him to such pain; the lost tribe of colonists, resurrected by their own cruciforms so many times that they had become idiots, mere vehicles for their own DNA and that of their parasites, had been priests also . . . priests of the Shrike.

Father Hoyt of the Society of Jesus has brought a vial of holy water blessed by His Holiness, a Eucharist consecrated in a Solemn High Mass, and a copy of the Church's ancient rite of exorcism. These things are forgotten now, sealed in a Perspex bubble in a pocket of his cloak.

Hoyt stumbles against a wall and screams again. The pain is a force beyond description now, the full ampule of ultra-

50

morph he had shot only fifteen minutes earlier, helpless against it. Father Hoyt screams and claws at his clothes, ripping off the heavy cloak, the black tunic and Roman collar, pants and shirt and underclothes, until he is naked, shivering with pain and cold in the glowing corridors of the Jade Tomb and screaming obscenities into the night.

He stumbles forward again, finds an opening, and moves into a room larger than any he remembers from the day's searches there. Bare, translucent walls rise thirty meters on each side of an empty space. Hoyt stumbles to his hands and knees, looks down, and realizes that the floor has become almost transparent. He is staring into a vertical shaft beneath the thin membrane of floor; a shaft that drops a kilometer or more to flames. The room fills with the red-orange pulse of light from the fire so far below.

Hoyt rolls to his side and laughs. If this is some image of hell summoned up for his benefit, it is a failure. Hoyt's view of hell is tactile; it is the pain which moves in him like jagged wires pulled through his veins and guts. Hell is also the memory of starving children in the slums of Armaghast and the smile of politicians sending boys off to die in colonial wars. Hell is the thought of the Church dying out in his lifetime, in Duré's lifetime, the last of its believers a handful of old men and women filling only a few pews of the huge cathedrals on Pacem. Hell is the hypocrisy of saying morning Mass with the evil of the cruciform pulsating warmly, obscenely, above one's heart.

There is a rush of hot air, and Hoyt watches as a section of floor slides back, creating a trapdoor to the shaft below. The room fills with the stench of sulfur. Hoyt laughs at the cliché, but within seconds the laughter turns to sobs. He is on his knees now, scraping with bloodied nails at the cruciforms on his chest and back. The cross-shaped welts seem to glow in the red light. Hoyt can hear the flames below.

'Hoyt!'

Still sobbing, he turns to see the woman – Lamia – framed in the doorway. She is looking past him, beyond him, and raising an antique pistol. Her eyes are very wide.

Father Hoyt feels the heat behind him, hears the roar as of a distant furnace, but above that, he suddenly hears the slide and scrape of metal on stone. Footsteps. Still clawing at the bloodied welt on his chest, Hoyt turns, his knees rubbed raw against the floor.

He sees the shadow first: ten meters of sharp angles, thorns, blades . . . legs like steel pipes with a rosette of scimitar blades at the knees and ankles. Then, through the pulse of hot light and black shadow, Hoyt sees the eyes. A hundred facets . . . a thousand . . . glowing red, a laser shone through twin rubies, above the collar of steel thorns and the quicksilver chest reflecting flame and shadow . . .

Brawne Lamia is firing her father's pistol. The slap of the shots echo high and flat above the furnace rumble.

Father Lenar Hoyt swivels toward her, raises one hand. 'No, don't!' he screams. 'It grants one wish! I have to make a . . .'

The Shrike, which was *there* – five meters away – is suddenly *here*, an arm's length from Hoyt. Lamia quits firing. Hoyt looks up, sees his own reflection in the fire-burnished chrome of the thing's carapace . . . sees something else in the Shrike's eyes at that instant . . . and then it is gone, the Shrike is gone, and Hoyt lifts his hand slowly, touches his throat almost bemusedly, stares for a second at the cascade of red which is covering his hand, his chest, the cruciform, his belly . . .

He turns toward the doorway and sees Lamia still staring in terror and shock, not at the Shrike now, but at him, at Father Lenar Hoyt of the Society of Jesus, and in that instant he realizes that the pain is *gone*, and he opens his mouth to speak, but more, only more red comes out, a geyser of red. Hoyt glances down again, notices for the first time that he is naked, sees the blood dripping from his chin and chest, dripping and pouring to the now-dark floor, sees the blood pouring as if someone had upended a bucket of red paint, and then he sees nothing as he falls face first to the floor so far . . . so very far . . . below.

SIX

Diana Philomel's body was as perfect as cosmetic science and an ARNist's skills could make it. I lay in bed for several minutes after awakening and admired her body: turned away from me, the classic curve of back and hip and flank offering a geometry more beautiful and powerful than anything discovered by Euclid, the two dimples visible on the lower back, just above the heart-stopping widening of milk-white derriere, soft angles intersecting, the backs of full thighs somehow more sensual and solid than any aspect of male anatomy could hope to be.

Lady Diana was asleep, or seemed to be. Our clothes lay strewn across a wide expanse of green carpet. Thick light, tinged magenta and blue, flooded broad windows, through which gray and gold treetops were visible. Large sheets of drawing paper lay scattered around, beneath, and on top of our discarded clothes. I leaned to my left, lifted a sheet of paper, and saw a hasty scribble of breasts, thighs, an arm reworked in haste, and a face with no features. Doing a life study while drunk and in the process of being seduced is never a formula for quality art.

I moaned, rolled on my back, and studied the sculptured scrollwork on the ceiling twelve feet above. If the woman beside me had been Fanny, I might never want to move. As it was, I slipped out from under the covers, found my comlog, noted that it was early morning on Tau Ceti Center – fourteen hours after my appointment with the CEO – and padded off to the bathroom in search of a hangover pill.

There were several varieties of medication to choose from in Lady Diana's drug bin. In addition to the usual aspirin and endorphins, I saw stims, tranks, Flashback tubes, orgasm derms, shunt primers, cannabis inhalers, non-recom tobacco cigarettes, and a hundred less identifiable drugs. I found a glass and forced down two Dayafters, feeling the nausea and headache fade within seconds.

Lady Diana was awake and sitting up in bed, still nude, when I emerged. I started to smile and then saw the two men by the east doorway. Neither was her husband, although both were as large and shared the same no-neck, ham-fisted, dark-jowled style that Hermund Philomel had perfected.

In the long pageant of human history, I am sure that there has been some human male who could stand, surprised and naked, in front of two fully clothed and potentially hostile strangers, rival males as it were, *without* cringing, *without* having the urge to cover his genitals and hunch over, and *without* feeling totally vulnerable and at a disadvantage . . . but I am not that male.

I hunched over, covered my groin, backed toward the bathroom, and said, 'What . . . who . . . ?' I looked toward Diana Philomel for help and saw the smile there . . . a smile that matched the cruelty I had first seen in her eyes.

'Get him. *Quickly!*' demanded my erstwhile lover.

I made it to the bathroom and was reaching for the manual switch to dilate the door closed when the closer of the two men reached me, grabbed me, thrust me back into the bedroom, and threw me to his partner. Both men were from Lusus or an equally high-g world, or else they subsisted exclusively on a diet of steroids and Samson cells, for they tossed me back and forth with no effort. It didn't matter how large they were. Except for my brief career as a school-yard fighter, my life . . . the memories of my life . . . offered few instances of violence and even fewer instances where I emerged from a scuffle the victor. One glance at the two men amusing themselves at my expense and I knew that these were the type one read about and did not quite believe in – individuals who could break bones, flatten noses, or crack kneecaps with no more compunction than I would feel about tossing away a defective stylus.

'*Quickly!*' Diana hissed again.

I canvased the datasphere, the house's memory, Diana's comlog umbilical, the two goons' tenuous connection to the information universe . . . and although I now knew where I was: the Philomel country estate, six hundred kilometers from the capital of Pirre in the agricultural belt of terra-formed Renaissance Minor . . . and precisely who the goons were: Debin Farrus and Hemmit Gorma, plant security personnel for the Heaven's Gate Scrubbers Union . . . I had no idea why one was sitting on me, his knee in the small of my back, while the other crushed my comlog under his heel and slipped an osmosis cuff over my wrist, up my arm . . .

I heard the hiss and relaxed.

'Who are you?'

'Joseph Severn.'

'Is that your real name?'

'No.' I felt the effects of the truthtalk and knew that I could confound it merely by going away, stepping back into the datasphere or retreating fully to the Core. But that would mean leaving my body to the mercy of whoever was asking the questions. I stayed there. My eyes were closed but I recognized the next voice.

'Who *are* you?' asked Diana Philomel.

I sighed. It was a difficult question to answer honestly. 'John Keats,' I said at last. Their silence told me that the name meant nothing to them. *Why should it?* I asked myself. I once predicted that it would be a name 'writ in water.' Although I couldn't move or open my eyes, I found no trouble in canvasing the datasphere, following their access vectors. The poet's name was among eight hundred John

56

Keatses on the list offered to them by the public file, but they didn't seem too interested in someone nine hundred years dead.

'Who do you work for?' It was Hermund Philomel's voice. For some reason I was mildly surprised.

'No one.'

The faint Doppler of voices changed as they talked amongst themselves. 'Can he be resisting the drug?'

'No one can *resist* it,' said Diana. 'They can *die* when it's administered, but they can't resist it.'

'Then what's going on?' asked Hermund. 'Why would Gladstone bring a nobody into the Council on the eve of war?'

'He can hear you, you know,' said another man's voice – one of the goons.

'It doesn't matter,' said Diana. 'He's not going to live after the interrogation anyway.' Her voice came again, directed toward me. 'Why did the CEO invite you to the Council . . . John?'

'Not sure. To hear about the pilgrims, probably.'

'What pilgrims, John?'

'The Shrike Pilgrims.'

Someone else made a noise. 'Hush,' said Diana Philomel. To me she said, 'Are those the Shrike Pilgrims on Hyperion, John?'

'Yes.'

'Is there a pilgrimage underway now?'

'Yes.'

'And why is Gladstone asking you, John?'

'I dream them.'

There was a disgusted sound. Hermund said, 'He's crazy. Even under truthtalk he doesn't know who he is, now he's giving us this. Let's get it over with and—'

'Shut up,' said Lady Diana. 'Gladstone's not crazy. She invited him, remember? John, what do you mean you dream them?'

'I dream the first Keats retrieval persona's impressions,' I said. My voice was thick, as if I were talking in my sleep. 'He hardwired himself into one of the pilgrims when they murdered his body, and now he roams their microsphere. Somehow his perceptions are my dreams. Perhaps my actions are his dreams, I don't know.'

'Insane,' said Hermund.

'No, no,' said Lady Diana. Her voice was strained, almost shocked. 'John, are you a cybrid?'

'Yes.'

'Oh, Christ and Allah,' said Lady Diana.

'What's a cybrid?' said one of the goons. He had a high, almost feminine voice.

There was silence for a moment, and then Diana spoke. 'Idiot. Cybrids were human remotes created by the Core. There were a few on the Advisory Council until last century, when they were outlawed.'

'Like an android or something?' said the other goon.

'Shut up,' said Hermund.

'No,' answered Diana. 'Cybrids were genetically perfect, recombed from DNA going back to Old Earth. All you needed was a bone . . . a fragment of hair . . . John, can you hear me? John?'

'Yes.'

'John, you're a cybrid . . . do you know who your persona template was?'

'John Keats.'

I could hear her take a deep breath. 'Who is . . . was . . . John Keats?'

'A poet.'

'When did he live, John?'

'From 1795 to 1821,' I said.

'Which reckoning, John?'

'Old Earth AD,' I said. 'Pre-Hegira. Modern era—'

Hermund's voice broke in, agitated. 'John, are you . . . are you in contact with the TechnoCore right now?'

'Yes.'

'Can you . . . are you free to communicate despite the truthtalk?'

'Yes.'

'Oh, fuck,' said the goon with the high voice.

'We've got to get out of here,' snapped Hermund.

'Just a minute more,' said Diana. 'We've got to know . . .'

'Can we take him with us?' asked the deep-voiced goon.

'Idiot,' said Hermund. 'If he's alive and in touch with the datasphere and Core . . . hell, he *lives* in the Core, his mind's there . . . then he can tip Gladstone, ExecSec, FORCE, *anybody*!'

'Shut up,' said Lady Diana. 'We'll kill him as soon as I'm finished. A few more questions. John?'

'Yes.'

'Why does Gladstone need to know what's happening to the Shrike Pilgrims? Does it have something to do with the war with the Ousters?'

'I'm not sure.'

'Shit,' whispered Hermund. 'Let's go.'

'Quiet. John, where are you from?'

'I've lived on Esperance the last ten months.'

'And before that?'

'On Earth before that.'

'Which Earth?' demanded Hermund. 'New Earth? Earth Two? Earth city? Which one?'

'Earth,' I said. Then I remembered. 'Old Earth.'

'*Old Earth?*' said one of the goons. 'This is fucked. I'm getting out of here.'

There came the frying-bacon sizzle of a weapons laser. I smelled something sweeter than frying bacon, and there was a heavy thump. Diana Philomel said, 'John, are you talking about your persona template's life on Old Earth?'

'No.'

'*You* – the cybrid you – were on Old Earth?'

'Yes,' I said. 'I woke from death there. In the same room

59

on the Piazza di Spagna in which I died. Severn was not there, but Dr Clark and some of the others were . . .'

'He *is* crazy,' said Hermund. 'Old Earth's been destroyed for more than four centuries . . . unless cybrids can live for more than four hundred years . . . ?'

'No,' snapped Lady Diana. 'Shut up and let me finish this. John, why did the Core . . . bring you back?'

'I don't know for sure.'

'Does it have something to do with the civil war going on between the AIs?'

'Perhaps,' I said. 'Probably.' She asked interesting questions.

'Which group created you? The Ultimates, Stables, or Volatiles?'

'I don't know.'

I could hear a sigh of exasperation. 'John, have you notified anyone of where you are, of what's happening to you?'

'No,' I said. It was a sign of the lady's less than impressive intelligence that she waited so long to pose that question.

Hermund also let out a breath. 'Great,' he said. 'Let's get the hell out of here before . . .'

'John,' said Diana, 'do you know why Gladstone manufactured this war with the Ousters?'

'No,' I said. 'Or rather, there might be many reasons. The most probable is that it is a bargaining ploy in her dealings with the Core.'

'Why?'

'Elements in the leadership ROM of the Core are afraid of Hyperion,' I said. 'Hyperion is an unknown variable in a galaxy where every variable has been quantified.'

'*Who* is afraid, John? The Ultimates, Stables, or Volatiles? Which group of AIs is afraid of Hyperion?'

'All three,' I said.

'Shit,' whispered Hermund. 'Listen . . . John . . . do the

60

Time Tombs and the Shrike have something to do with all this?'

'Yes, they have a lot to do with it.'

'How?' asked Diana.

'I don't know. No one does.'

Hermund, or someone, hit me sharply, viciously, in the chest. 'You mean the fucking Core Advisory Council hasn't predicted the outcome of this war, these events?' Hermund growled. 'Are you expecting me to believe that Gladstone and the Senate went to war without a probability prediction?'

'No,' I said. 'It has been predicted for centuries.'

Diana Philomel made a noise like a child being confronted with a large mound of candy. '*What* has been predicted, John? Tell us everything.'

My mouth was dry. The truthtalk serum had dried up my saliva. 'It predicted the war,' I said. 'The identities of the pilgrims on the Shrike Pilgrimage. The betrayal of the Hegemony Consul in activating a device that will open – has opened – the Time Tombs. The emergence of the Shrike Scourge. The outcome of the war and the Scourge . . .'

'What is the outcome, John?' whispered the woman I had made love to a few hours earlier.

'The end of the Hegemony,' I said. 'The destruction of the World-web.' I tried to lick my lips but my tongue was dry. 'The end of the human race.'

'Oh, Jesus and Allah,' whispered Diana. 'Is there any chance that the prediction could be in error?'

'No,' I said. 'Or rather, only in the effect of Hyperion on the result. The other variables are accounted for.'

'Kill him,' shouted Hermund Philomel. 'Kill *it* . . . so we can get out of here and inform Harbrit and the others.'

'All right,' said Lady Diana. Then, a second later, 'No, not the laser, you idiot. We'll inject the lethal dose of alcohol as planned. Here, hold the osmosis cuff so I can attach this drip.'

61

I felt a pressure on my right arm. A second later there were explosions, concussions, a shout. I smelled smoke and ionized air. A woman screamed.

'Get that cuff off him,' said Leigh Hunt. I could see him standing there, still wearing a conservative gray suit, surrounded by Executive Security commandos in full impact armor and chameleon polymers. A commando twice Hunt's height nodded, shouldered his hellwhip weapon, and rushed to do Hunt's bidding.

On one of the tactical channels, the one I had been monitoring for some time, I could see a relayed image of myself . . . naked, spread-eagled on the bed, the osmosis cuff on my arm and a rising bruise on my rib cage. Diana Philomel, her husband, and one of the goons lay unconscious but alive in the splinter and broken-glass rubble of the room. The other enforcer lay half in the doorway, the top part of his body looking the color and texture of a heavily grilled steak.

'Are you all right, M Severn?' asked Leigh Hunt, lifting my head and setting a membrane-thin oxygen mask over my mouth and nose.

'Hrrmmmggh,' I said. 'Arret.' I swam to the surface of my own senses like a diver coming up too quickly from the deeps. My head hurt. My ribs ached like hell. My eyes were not working perfectly yet, but through the tactical channel, I could see Leigh Hunt give the small twitch of thin lips that I knew passed for a smile from him.

'We'll help you get dressed,' said Hunt. 'Get you some coffee on the flight back. Then it's back to Government House, M Severn. You're late for a meeting with the CEO.'

SEVEN

Space battles in movies and holies had always bored me, but watching the real thing held a certain fascination: rather like seeing live coverage of a series of traffic accidents. Actually, the production values for reality – as had doubtless been the case for centuries – were much lower than for even a moderate-budget holodrama. Even with the tremendous energies involved, the overwhelming reaction one had to an actual battle in space was that space was so *large* and humanity's fleets and ships and dreadnoughts and whatnots were so *small*.

Or so I thought as I sat in the Tactical Information Center, the so-called War Room, with Gladstone and her military ganders, and watched the walls become twenty-meter holes into infinity as four massive holoframes surrounded us with in-depth imagery and the speakers filled the room with fatline transmissions: radio chatter between fighters, tactical command channels rattling away, ship-to-ship messages on wideband, lasered channels, and secure fatline, and all the shouts, screams, cries, and obscenities of battle which predate any media besides air and the human voice.

It was a dramatization of total chaos, a functional definition of confusion, an unchoreographed dance of sad violence. It was war.

Gladstone and a handful of her people sat in the middle of all this noise and light, the War Room floating like a gray-carpeted rectangle amidst the stars and explosions, the limb of Hyperion a lapis lazuli brilliance filling half of the north holowall, the screams of dying men and women on every channel and in every ear. I was one of the handful of Gladstone's people privileged and cursed to be there.

The CEO rotated in her high-backed chair, tapped her lower lip with steepled fingers, and turned toward her military group. 'What do you think?'

The seven bemedaled men there looked at one another, and then six of them looked at General Morpurgo. He chewed on an unlighted cigar. 'It's not good,' he said. 'We're keeping them away from the farcaster site . . . our defenses are holding well there . . . but they've pushed far too far in-system.'

'Admiral?' asked Gladstone, inclining her head a fraction toward the tall, thin man in FORCE:space black.

Admiral Singh touched his closely trimmed beard. 'General Morpurgo is correct. The campaign is not going as planned.' He nodded toward the fourth wall, where diagrams – mostly ellipsoids, ovals and arcs – were superimposed upon a static shot of the Hyperion system. Some of the arcs grew as we watched. The bright blue lines stood for Hegemony trajectories. The red tracks were Ouster. There were far more red lines than blue.

'Both of the attack carriers assigned to Task Force 42 have been put out of action,' said Admiral Singh. 'The *Olympus Shadow* was destroyed with all hands and the *Neptune Station* was seriously damaged but is returning to the cislunar docking area with five torchships for escort.'

CEO Gladstone nodded slowly, her lip coming down to touch the top of her steepled fingers. 'How many were aboard the *Olympus Shadow*, Admiral?'

Singh's brown eyes were as large as the CEO's, but did not suggest the same depths of sadness. He held her gaze for several seconds. 'Forty-two hundred,' he said. 'Not counting the Marine detachment of six hundred. Some of those were off-loaded at Farcaster Station Hyperion, so we do not have accurate information on how many were with the ship.'

Gladstone nodded. She looked back at General Morpurgo. 'Why the sudden difficulty, General?'

Morpurgo's face was calm, but he had all but bitten through the cigar clamped between his teeth. 'More fighting units than we expected, CEO,' he said. 'Plus their lancers . . . five-person craft, miniature torchships, really, faster and more heavily armed than our long-range fighters . . . they're deadly little hornets. We've been destroying them by the hundred, but if one gets through, it can make a dash inside fleet defenses and wreak havoc.' Morpurgo shrugged. 'More than one's got through.'

Senator Kolchev sat across the table with eight of his colleagues. Kolchev swiveled until he could see the tactical map. 'It looks like they're almost to Hyperion,' he said. The famous voice was hoarse.

Singh spoke up. 'Remember the scale, Senator. The truth is that we still hold most of the system. Everything within ten AU of Hyperion's star is ours. The battle was out beyond the Oört cloud, and we've been regrouping.'

'And those red . . . blobs . . . above the plane of the ecliptic?' asked Senator Richeau. The senator wore red herself; it had been one of her trademarks in the Senate.

Singh nodded. 'An interesting stratagem,' he said. 'The Swarm launched an attack of approximately three thousand lancers to complete a pincers movement against Task Force 87.2's electronic perimeter. It was contained, but one has to admire the cleverness of—'

'Three thousand lancers?' Gladstone interrupted softly.

'Yes, ma'am.'

Gladstone smiled. I stopped sketching and thought to myself that I was glad that I had not been the beneficiary of that particular smile.

'Weren't we told yesterday, in the briefing, that the Ousters would field six . . . seven hundred fighting units, *tops*?'

The words had been Morpurgo's. CEO Gladstone swiveled to face the General. Her right eyebrow arched.

General Morpurgo removed the cigar, frowned at it, and fished a smaller piece from behind his lower teeth. 'That's what our intelligence said. It was wrong.'

Gladstone nodded. 'Was the AI Advisory Council involved in that intelligence assessment?'

All eyes turned toward Councilor Albedo. It was a perfect projection; he sat in his chair amongst the others, his hands curled on the armrests in a relaxed fashion; there was none of the haziness or see-through common to mobile projections. His face was long, with high cheekbones and a mobile mouth which suggested a hint of a sardonic smile even at the most serious of moments. This was a serious moment.

'No, CEO,' said Councilor Albedo, 'the Advisory Group was not asked to assess Ouster strength.'

Gladstone nodded. 'I assumed,' she said, still addressing Morpurgo, 'that when the FORCE intelligence estimates came in, they incorporated the Council's projections.'

The FORCE:ground General glared at Albedo. 'No ma'am,' he said. 'Since the Core acknowledges no contact with the Ousters, we felt that their projections wouldn't be any better than our own. We did use the OCS: HTN aggregate AI network to run our assessments.' He thrust the foreshortened cigar back into his mouth. His chin jutted. When he spoke, it was around the cigar. 'Could the Council have done better?'

Gladstone looked at Albedo.

The Councilor made a small motion with the long fingers of his right hand. 'Our estimates . . . for this Swarm . . . suggested four to six thousand fighting units.'

'You—' began Morpurgo, his face red.

'You did not mention this during the briefing,' said CEO Gladstone. 'Nor during our earlier deliberations.'

Councilor Albedo shrugged. 'The General is correct,' he said. 'We have no contact with the Ousters. Our estimates are no more reliable than FORCE's, merely . . . based upon different premises. The Olympus Command School Historical Tactical Network does excellent work. If the AIs there were one order of acuity higher on the Turing-Demmler scale, we would have to bring them into the Core.' He made the graceful gesture with his hand again. 'As it is, the Council's premises might be of use for future planning. We will, of course, turn over all projections to this group at any time.'

Gladstone nodded. 'Do so immediately.'

She turned back to the screen, and the others did so also. Sensing the silence, the room monitors brought the speaker volume back up, and once again we could hear the cries of victory, screams for help, and calm recitation of positions, fire-control directions, and commands.

The closest wall was a real-time feed from the torchship HS *N'Djamena* as it searched for survivors among the tumbling remnants of Battle Group B.5. The damaged torchship it was approaching, magnified a thousand times, looked like a pomegranate burst from the inside, its seeds and red rind spilling in slow motion, tumbling into a cloud of particles, gases, frozen volatiles, a million microelectronics ripped from their cradles, food stores, tangled gear, and – recognizable now and then from their marionette tumble of arms or legs – many, many bodies. The *N'Djamena*'s searchlight, ten meters wide after its coherent leap of twenty thousand miles, played across the starlit frozen wreckage, bringing individual items, facets, and faces into focus. It was quite beautiful in a terrible way. The reflected light made Gladstone's face look much older.

'Admiral,' she said, 'is it pertinent that the Swarm waited until Task Force 87.2 translated in-system?'

Singh touched his beard. 'Are you asking if it was a trap, CEO?'

'Yes.'

The Admiral glanced at his colleagues and then at

Gladstone. 'I think not. We believe . . . I believe . . . that when the Ousters saw the intensity of our force commitment, they responded in kind. It does mean, however, that they are totally resolved to take Hyperion system.'

'Can they do it?' asked Gladstone, her eyes still on the tumbling wreckage above her. A young man's body, half in a spacesuit and half out, tumbled toward the camera. The burst eyes and lungs were clearly visible.

'No,' said Admiral Singh. 'They can bloody us. They can even drive us back to a totally defensive perimeter around Hyperion itself. But they cannot defeat us or drive us out.'

'Or destroy the farcaster?' Senator Richeau's voice was taut.

'Nor destroy the farcaster,' said Singh.

'He's right,' said General Morpurgo. 'I'd stake my professional career on it.'

Gladstone smiled and stood. The others, including myself, rushed to stand also. 'You have,' Gladstone said softly to Morpurgo. 'You have.' She looked around. 'We will meet here when events warrant it. M Hunt will be my liaison with you. In the meantime, gentlemen and ladies, the work of government shall proceed. Good afternoon.'

As the others left, I took my seat again until I was the only one left in the room. The speakers came back up to volume. On one band, a man was crying. Manic laughter came through static. Above me, behind me, on both sides, the starfields moved slowly against blackness, and the starlight glinted coldly on wreckage and ruin.

Government House was constructed in the shape of a Star of David, and within the center of the star, shielded by low walls and strategically planted trees, there was a garden: smaller than the formal acres of flowers in Deer Park but no less beautiful. I was walking there as evening fell, the brilliant blue-white of Tau Ceti fading to golds, when Meina Gladstone approached.

For a while, we walked together in silence. I noticed that she had exchanged her suit for a long robe of the kind worn by grand matrons on Patawpha; the robe was wide and billowing, inset with intricate dark blue and gold designs which almost matched the darkening sky. Gladstone's hands were out of sight in hidden pockets; the wide sleeves stirred to a breeze; the hem dragged on the milk-white stones of the path.

'You let them interrogate me,' I said. 'I'm curious as to why.'

Gladstone's voice was tired. 'They were not transmitting. There was no danger of the information being passed on.'

I smiled. 'Nonetheless, you let them put me through that.'

'Security wished to know as much about them as they would divulge.'

'At the expense of any ... inconvenience ... on my part,' I said.

'Yes.'

'And does Security know who they were working for?'

'The man mentioned Harbrit,' said the CEO. 'Security is fairly certain that they meant Emlem Harbrit.'

'The commodities broker on Asquith?'

'Yes. She and Diana Philomel have ties with the old Glennon-Height royalist factions.'

'They were amateurs,' I said, thinking of Hermund mentioning Harbrit's name, the confused order of Diana's questioning.

'Of course.'

'Are the royalists connected to any serious group?'

'Only the Shrike church,' said Gladstone. She paused where the path crossed a small stream via a stone bridge. The CEO gathered her robe and sat on a wrought-iron bench. 'None of the bishops have yet come out of hiding, you know.'

'With the riots and backlash, I don't blame them,' I said. I remained standing. There were no bodyguards or monitors in sight, but I knew that if I were to make any threatening move toward Gladstone, I would wake up in ExecSec detention. Above us, the clouds lost their last tinge of gold and began to glow with the reflected silver light of TC²'s countless tower cities. 'What did Security do with Diana and her husband?' I asked.

'They've been thoroughly interrogated. They're being . . . detained.'

I nodded. Thorough interrogation meant that even now their brains were floating in full-shunt tanks. Their bodies would be kept in cryogenic storage until a secret trial determined if their actions had been treasonable. After the trial, the bodies would be destroyed, and Diana and Hermund would remain in 'detention,' with all sensory and comm channels turned off. The Hegemony had not used the death penalty for centuries, but the alternatives were not pleasant. I sat on the long bench, six feet from Gladstone.

'Do you still write poetry?'

I was surprised by her question. I glanced down the garden path where floating Japanese lanterns and hidden glow-globes had just come on. 'Not really,' I said. 'Sometimes I dream in verse. Or used to . . .'

Meina Gladstone folded her hands on her lap and studied them. 'If you were writing about the events unfolding now,' she said, 'what kind of poem would you create?'

I laughed. 'I've already begun it and abandoned it twice . . . or rather, *he* had. It was about the death of the gods and their difficulty in accepting their displacement. It was about transformation and suffering and injustice. And it was about the poet . . . whom *he* thought suffered most at such injustice.'

Gladstone looked at me. Her face was a mass of lines and shadows in the dimming light. 'And who are the gods that are being replaced this time, M Severn? Is it humanity or the false gods we created to depose us?'

'How the hell should I know?' I snapped and turned away to watch the stream.

'You are part of both worlds, no? Humanity and TechnoCore?'

I laughed again. 'I'm part of neither world. A cybrid monster here, a research project there.'

'Yes, but whose research? And for what ends?'

I shrugged.

Gladstone rose and I followed. We crossed the stream and listened to water moving over the stones. The path wound between tall boulders covered with exquisite lichen which glowed in the lantern light.

Gladstone paused at the top of a short flight of stone steps. 'Do you think the Ultimates in the Core will succeed in constructing their Ultimate Intelligence, M Severn?'

'Will they build God?' I said. 'There are those AIs which do not want to build God. They learned from the human experience that to construct the next step in awareness is an invitation to slavery, if not actual extinction.'

'But would a true God extinguish his creatures?'

'In the case of the Core and the hypothetical UI,' I said, 'God is the creature, not the creator. Perhaps a god must create the lesser beings in contact with it in order for it to feel any responsibility for them.'

'Yet the Core has appeared to take responsibility for human beings in the centuries since the AI Secession,' said Gladstone. She was gazing intently at me, as if gauging something by my expression.

I looked out at the garden. The path glowed whitely, almost eerily in the dark. 'The Core works toward its own ends,' I said, knowing as I spoke that no human being knew that fact better than CEO Meina Gladstone.

'And do you feel that humanity no longer figures as a means toward those ends?'

I made a dismissive gesture with my right hand. 'I'm a creature of neither culture,' I said again. 'Neither graced by the naïveté of the unintentional creators, nor cursed by the terrible awareness of their creatures.'

'Genetically, you are fully human,' said Gladstone.

It was not a question. I did not respond.

'Jesus Christ was said to be fully human,' she said. 'And also fully divine. Humanity and Godhead at intersection.'

I was amazed at her reference to that old religion. Christianity had been replaced first by Zen Christianity, then Zen Gnosticism, then by a hundred more vital theologies and philosophies. Gladstone's homeworld was no repository for discarded beliefs and I assumed – and hoped – that neither was the CEO. 'If he was fully human and fully God,' I said, 'then I am his antimatter image.'

'No,' said Gladstone, 'I would imagine that the Shrike your pilgrim friends are confronting is that.'

I stared. It was the first time she had mentioned the Shrike to me, despite the fact that I knew – and she knew that I knew – that it had been her plan which led the Consul to open the Time Tombs and release the thing.

'Perhaps you should have been on that pilgrimage, M Severn,' said the CEO.

'In a way,' I said, 'I am.'

Gladstone gestured, and a door to her private quarters opened. 'Yes, in a way you are,' she said. 'But if the woman who carries your counterpart is crucified on the Shrike's legendary tree of thorns, will *you* suffer for all eternity in your dreams?'

I had no answer, so I stood there and said nothing.

'We will talk in the morning after the conference,' said Meina Gladstone. 'Good night, M Severn. Have pleasant dreams.'

EIGHT

Martin Silenus, Sol Weintraub, and the Consul are staggering up the dunes toward the Sphinx as Brawne Lamia and Fedmahn Kassad return with Father Hoyt's body. Weintraub clutches his cape tight around him, trying to shelter his infant from the rage of blowing sand and crackling light. He watches as Kassad descends the dune, his long legs black and cartoonish against electrified sand, Hoyt's arms and hands dangling, moving slightly with each slide and step.

Silenus is shouting, but the wind whips away words. Brawne Lamia gestures toward the one tent still standing; the storm has collapsed or ripped away the others. They crowd into Silenus's tent, Colonel Kassad coming last, passing the body in gently. Inside, their shouts can be heard above the crack of fiberplastic canvas and the paper-splitting rip of lightning.

'Dead?' shouts the Consul, peeling back the cloak Kassad had wrapped around Hoyt's nude body. The cruciforms glow pinkly.

The Colonel points to the telltales blinking on the surface of the FORCE-issue medpak adhered to the priest's chest. The lights blink red except for the yellow winking of the systems-sustaining filaments and nodules. Hoyt's head rolls back, and now Weintraub can see the millipede suture holding the ragged edges of the slashed throat together.

Sol Weintraub tries to locate a pulse manually; finds none. He leans forward, sets his ear to the priest's chest. There is no heartbeat, but the welt of the cruciform there is hot against Sol's cheek. He looks at Brawne Lamia. 'The Shrike?'

'Yes . . . I think . . . I don't know.' She gestures toward the antique pistol she still holds. 'I emptied the magazine. Twelve shots at . . . whatever it was.'

'Did you see it?' the Consul asks Kassad.

'No. I entered the room ten seconds after Brawne, but I didn't see anything.'

'What about your fucking soldier gadgets?' says Martin Silenus. He is crowded in the back of the tent, huddled in a near-fetal position. 'Didn't all that FORCE shit show something?'

'No.'

A small alarm sounds from the medpak, and Kassad detaches another plasma cartridge from his belt, feeds it into the pak's chamber, and sits back on his heels, flipping his visor down to watch out the opening of the tent. His voice is distorted by the helmet speaker. 'He's lost more blood than we can compensate for here. Did anyone else bring first aid equipment?'

Weintraub rummages in his pack. 'I have a basic kit. Not enough for this, though. Whatever slashed his throat cut through everything.'

'The Shrike,' whispers Martin Silenus.

'It doesn't matter,' says Lamia, hugging herself to stop her body from shaking. 'We've got to get help for him.' She looks at the Consul.

'He's dead,' says the Consul. 'Even a ship's surgery won't bring him back.'

'We have to *try*!' shouts Lamia, leaning forward to grab the Consul's tunic front. 'We can't leave him to those . . . things . . .' She gestures toward the cruciform glowing beneath the skin of the dead man's chest.

The Consul rubs his eyes. 'We can destroy the body. Use the Colonel's rifle . . .'

'*We're* going to die if we don't get out of this fucking storm!' cries Silenus. The tent is vibrating, fiberplastic pounding the poet's head and back with each billow. The sound of sand against fabric is like a rocket taking off just outside. 'Call the goddamned ship. Call it!'

The Consul pulls his pack closer, as if guarding the antique comlog inside it. Sweat glistens on his cheeks and forehead.

'We could wait the storm out in one of the Tombs,' says Sol Weintraub. 'The Sphinx, perhaps.'

'Fuck that,' says Martin Silenus.

The scholar shifts in the cramped space and stares at the poet. 'You came all this way to find the Shrike. Are you telling us that you've changed your mind now that he seems to have made an appearance?'

Silenus's eyes gleam out from under his lowered beret. 'I'm not telling you anything except that I want that goddamned ship of his here, and I want it *now*.'

'It might be a good idea,' says Colonel Kassad.

The Consul looks at him.

'If there's a chance to save Hoyt's life, we should take it.'

The Consul is in pain himself. 'We can't leave,' he says. 'Can't leave now.'

'No,' agrees Kassad. 'We won't use the ship to leave. But the surgery might help Hoyt. And we can wait out the storm in it.'

'And maybe find out what's happening up there,' sa[ys] Brawne Lamia, jerking her thumb toward the ro[of of the] tent.

The baby, Rachel, is crying shrill[y. ...] holding her head in his broad h[...] Shrike wants to find us. i[...] out here. We'll m[...] Hoyt's che[...] surgery giv[...] less to the W[...]

are no more reliable than FORCE's, merely ... based upon different premises. The Olympus Command School Historical Tactical Network does excellent work. If the AIs there were one order of acuity higher on the Turing-Demmler scale, we would have to bring them into the Core.'

He made the graceful gesture with his hand again. 'As it is, the Council's premises might be of use for future planning. We will, of course, turn over all projections to this group at any time.'

Gladstone nodded. 'Do so immediately.'

She turned back to the screen, and the others did so also. Sensing the silence, the room monitors brought the speaker volume back up, and once again we could hear the cries of victory, screams for help, and calm recitation of positions, fire-control directions, and commands.

The closest wall was a real-time feed from the torchship HS *N'Djamena* as it searched for survivors among the tumbling remnants of Battle Group B.5. The damaged torchship it was approaching, magnified a thousand times, looked like a pomegranate burst from the inside, its seeds and red rind spilling in slow motion, tumbling into a cloud of particles, gases, frozen volatiles, a million micro-electronics ripped from their cradles, food stores, tangled gear, and — recognizable now and then from thei[r] marionette tumble of arms or legs — many, many bodi[es] The *N'Djamena*'s searchlight, ten meters wide after [its] coherent leap of twenty thousand miles, played acros[s the] starlit frozen wreckage, bringing individual items, [...] and faces into focus. It was quite beautiful in a terri[ble way.]

The reflected light made Gladstone's face look muc[h ...] until Task Force 87.2 translated in-system.'

'Admiral,' she said, 'is it pertinent that the Swa[rm ...] CEO?'

'Yes.'

Singh touched his beard. 'Are you asking if i[t ...]

The Admiral glanced at his colleagu[es]

says the Consul. He pulls the ancient comlog
...ack, lays his hand on the diskey, and whispers
...rases.
...oming?' asks Martin Silenus.
...confirmed the command. We'll need to stow our gear
...nsfer. I told it to land just above the entrance to the
...y.'
...amia is surprised to find that she has been weeping. She
...pes her cheeks and smiles.
'What's funny?' asks the Consul.
'All this,' she says, stabbing at her cheeks with the back of
her hand, 'and all I can think about is how nice it'll be to
have a shower.'
'A drink,' says Silenus.
'Shelter from the storm,' says Weintraub. The baby is
taking milk from a nursing pak.
Kassad leans forward, his head and shoulders outside the
tent. He raises his weapon and clicks off the safety.
'Telltales,' he says. 'Something's moving just beyond the
dune.' The visor turns toward them, reflecting a pale and
huddled group, the paler body of Lenar Hoyt. 'I'm going to
check it out,' he says. 'Wait here until the ship arrives.'
'Don't leave,' says Silenus. 'It's like one of those fucking
ancient horror holos where they go one by one to ... hey!'
The poet falls silent. The entrance to the tent is a triangle of
light and noise. Fedmahn Kassad is gone.

The tent is beginning to collapse, stakes and wire anchor
giving way as the sand shifts around them. Huddl
together, shouting to be heard over the wind roar, the C
sul and Lamia wrap Hoyt's body in his cloak. Readou
the medpak continue to blink red. Blood has ceased t
from the crude millipede suture. Sol Weintraub sets his four-day-old child in th
carrier on his chest, folds his cape around her, and
in the entrance. 'No sign of the Colonel!' he sh

Gladst...
when t...
ment, th...
they are to...
'Can they
tumbling wre...
spacesuit and
burst eyes and l...
'No,' said Adm... ...bloody us. They can
even drive us back ... defensive perimeter around
Hyperion itself. Bu...y cannot defeat us or drive us out.'
'Or destroy the farcaster?' Senator Richeau's voice was
taut.
'Nor destroy the farcaster,' said Singh.
'He's right,' said General Morpurgo. 'I'd stake my professional career on it.'
Gladstone smiled and stood. The others, including
myself, rushed to stand also. 'You have,' Gladstone said
softly to Morpurgo. 'You have.' She looked around. 'We
will meet here when events warrant it. M Hunt will be my
liaison with you. In the meantime, gentlemen and ladies, the
work of government shall proceed. Good afternoon.'
As the others left, I took my seat again until I was the only
one left in the room. The speakers came back up to volume.
On one band, a man was crying. Manic laughter came
through static. Above me, behind me, on both sides, the
starfields moved slowly against blackness, and the starlight
glinted coldly on wreckage and ruin.

Government House was constructed in the shape of a Star of
David, and within the center of the star, shielded by low
walls and strategically planted trees, there was a garden:
smaller than the formal acres of flowers in Deer Park but no
less beautiful. I was walking there as evening fell, the brilliant blue-white of Tau Ceti fading to golds, when Meina
Gladstone approached.

watches, a lightning bolt strikes the outstretched wing of the Sphinx.

Brawne Lamia moves to the entrance and lifts the priest's body. She is amazed at how light it is. 'Let's get Father Hoyt to the ship and in surgery. Then some of us will come back to search for Kassad.'

The Consul tugs his tricorne cap low and shrugs his collar high. 'The ship has deep radar and movement sensors. It'll tell us where the Colonel's gone.'

'And the Shrike,' says Silenus. 'Can't forget our host.'

'Let's go,' says Lamia and gets to her feet. She has to lean into the wind to make progress. Loose ends of Hoyt's cloak flap and crack around her, while her own cloak streams behind. Finding the path by the intermittent flashes of lightning, she moves toward the head of the valley, glancing back only once to see if the others are following.

Martin Silenus steps away from the tent, lifts Het Masteen's Möbius cube, and his purple beret whips away in the wind, climbing as it goes. Silenus stands there and curses impressively, stopping only when his mouth begins to fill with sand.

'Come,' shouts Weintraub, his hand on the poet's shoulder. Sol feels the sand striking his face, littering his short beard. His other hand covers his chest as if sheltering something infinitely precious. 'We'll lose sight of Brawne if we don't hurry.' The two help each other move forward against the wind. Silenus's fur coat ripples wildly as he detours to retrieve his beret from where it has come down in the lee of a dune.

The Consul is the last to leave, carrying both his own pack and Kassad's. A minute after he leaves the small shelter, stakes give way, fabric tears, and the tent flies into the night, surrounded by a halo of static electricity. He staggers the three hundred meters up the trail, occasionally catching glimpses of the two men ahead of him, more frequently losing the path and having to walk in circles until he comes

77

across it again. The Time Tombs are visible behind him when the sandstorm ebbs a bit and the lightning flashes follow one another in close succession. The Consul sees the Sphinx, still glowing from repeated electrical strikes, the Jade Tomb beyond it, its walls luminescent, and beyond them the Obelisk, no glow there, a vertical swipe of pure black against the cliff walls. Then the Crystal Monolith. There is no sign of Kassad, although the shifting dunes, blowing sand, and sudden flashes make it seem as if many things are moving.

The Consul looks up, seeing the wide entrance to the valley now and the rushing clouds low above it, half expecting to see the blue fusion glow of his ship lowering through them. The storm is terrible, but his spacecraft has landed in worse conditions. He wonders if it is already down and the others are waiting at the base of it for him to arrive.

But when he reaches the saddle between cliff walls at the opening of the valley, the wind assaults him anew, he sees the four others huddled together at the beginning of the broad, flat plain, but there is no ship.

'Shouldn't it be here by now?' shouts Lamia as the Consul approaches the group.

He nods and crouches to extract the comlog from his pack. Weintraub and Silenus stand behind him, bending over to offer some shelter from the blowing sand. The Consul extracts the comlog and pauses, looking around. The storm makes it appear as if they are in some mad room where the walls and ceiling change from instant to instant, one second closing in on them, scant meters away, the next second receding to the distance, the ceiling floating upward, as in the scene where the room and Christmas tree expand for Clara in Tchaikovsky's *Nutcracker*.

The Consul palms the diskey, bends forward, and whispers into the voice square. The ancient instrument whispers back to him, the words just audible above the rasp of sand. He straightens up and faces the others. 'The ship was not allowed to leave.'

There is a babble of protest. 'What do you mean "not allowed"?' asks Lamia when the others fall silent.

The Consul shrugs and looks skyward as if a blue tail of flame might still announce the ship's coming. 'It wasn't given clearance at the spaceport in Keats.'

'Didn't you say you had clearance from the fucking queen?' shouts Martin Silenus. 'Old Gallstone herself?'

'Gladstone's clearance pip was in the ship's memory,' says the Consul. 'Both the FORCE and port authorities knew that.'

'So what the hell happened?' Lamia wipes her face. The tears she had shed back at the tent have left tiny rivulets of mud in the coating of sand on her cheeks.

The Consul shrugs. 'Gladstone overrode the original pip. There's a message here from her. Do you want to hear it?'

For a minute, no one answers. After their week of voyage, the thought of being in touch with someone outside their own group is so incongruous that it does not register at once; it was as if the world beyond the pilgrimage had ceased to exist except for the explosions in the night sky. 'Yes,' Sol Weintraub says, 'let's hear it.' A sudden lull in the storm makes the words seem very loud.

They gather around and crouch near the old comlog, setting Father Hoyt in the center of their circle. In the minute they have left him unattended, a small dune has begun to form itself around his body. The telltales are all red now except for the extreme-measures monitors glowing amber. Lamia sets another plasma cartridge in place and makes sure that the osmosis mask is secure on Hoyt's mouth and nose, filtering pure oxygen in and keeping sand out. 'All right,' she says.

The Consul triggers the diskey.

The message is a fatline squirt, recorded by the ship some ten minutes earlier. The air mists with the data columns and spherical-image colloid which characterizes comlogs dating back to the Hegira. The image of Gladstone shimmers, her face distorting bizarrely and then almost comically as millions of specks of windblown sand rip through the image. Even at full volume, her voice is almost lost to the storm.

'I'm sorry,' says the familiar image, 'but I cannot allow your spacecraft to approach the Tombs just yet. The temptation to leave would be too great, and the importance of your mission must override all other factors. Please understand that the fate of worlds may rest with you. Please be assured that my hopes and prayers are with you. Gladstone out.'

The image folds into itself and fades away. The Consul, Weintraub, and Lamia continue to stare in silence. Martin Silenus stands, throws a handful of sand at the empty air where Gladstone's face had been seconds earlier, and screams, 'Goddamn fatherfucking asshole political moral paraplegic dipshit drag-queen bitch!' He kicks sand in the air. The others shift their stares to him.

'Well, that really helped,' Brawne Lamia says softly.

Silenus waves his arms in disgust and walks away, still kicking at dunes.

'Is there anything else?' Weintraub asks the Consul.

'No.'

Brawne Lamia crosses her arms and frowns at the comlog. 'I forget how you said this thing works. How are you getting through the interference?'

'Tightbeam to a pocket comsat I seeded as we came down from the *Yggdrasill*,' says the Consul.

Lamia nods. 'So when you reported in, you just sent brief messages to the ship, and it sent fatline squirts to Gladstone . . . and your Ouster contacts.'

'Yes.'

'Can the ship take off without clearance?' asks Weintraub. The older man is sitting, his knees raised and his arms draped on them in a classic posture of pure fatigue. His voice is also tired. 'Just override Gladstone's prohibition?'

'No,' says the Consul. 'When Gladstone said no, FORCE

set a class-three containment field over the blast pit where we parked the ship.'

'Get in touch with her,' says Brawne Lamia. 'Explain things.'

'I've tried.' The Consul holds the comlog in his hands, sets it back in the pack. 'No response. Also, I mentioned in the original squirt that Hoyt was badly hurt and that we needed medical help. I wanted the ship's surgery ready for him.'

'Hurt,' repeats Martin Silenus, striding back to where they huddled. 'Shit. Our padre friend is dead as Glennon-Height's dog.' He jerks his thumb in the direction of the cloak-wrapped body; all monitor displays are red.

Brawne Lamia bends closer and touches Hoyt's cheek. It is cold. Both his comlog biomonitor and the medpak begin chirping brain-death warnings. The osmosis mask continues to force pure O_2 into his lungs, and the medpak stimulators still work his lungs and heart, but the chirping rises to a scream and then settles to a steady, terrible tone.

'He lost too much blood,' says Sol Weintraub. He touches the dead priest's face, his own eyes closed, head bowed.

'Great,' says Silenus. 'Fucking great. And according to his own story, Hoyt's going to decompose and recompose, thanks to that goddamned cruciform thing . . . *two* of the goddamn things, the guy's rich in resurrection insurance . . . and then come lurching back like some brain-damaged edition of Hamlet's daddy's ghost. What are we going to do then?'

'Shut up,' says Brawne Lamia. She is wrapping Hoyt's body in a layer of tarp she has brought from the tent.

'Shut up yourself,' screams Silenus. 'We've got one monster lurking around. Old Grendel himself is out there somewhere sharpening his nails for his next meal, do you really want Hoyt's zombie joining our happy crew? You remember how he described the Bikura? They'd been letting the cruciforms bring *them* back for centuries, and talking to one

81

of them was like talking to an ambulatory sponge. Do you *really* want Hoyt's corpse hiking with us?'

'Two,' says the Consul.

'What?' Martin Silenus whirls, loses his footing, and lands on his knees near the body. He leans toward him. 'What did you say?'

'Two cruciforms,' says the Consul. 'His and Father Paul Duré's. If his story about the Bikura was true, then they'll both be . . . resurrected.'

'Oh, Christ on a stick,' says Silenus and sits in the sand.

Brawne Lamia has finished wrapping the priest's body. She looks at it. 'I remember that in Father Duré's story about the Bikura named Alpha,' she says. 'But I still don't understand. The Law of Conservation of Mass has to come in there somewhere.'

'They'll be *short* zombies,' says Martin Silenus. He pulls his fur coat tighter and pounds the sand with his fist.

'There is so much we could have learned if the ship had arrived,' says the Consul. 'The autodiagnostics could have . . .' He pauses and gestures. 'Look. There is less sand in the air. Perhaps the storm is . . .'

Lightning flashes, and it begins to rain, the icy pellets striking their faces with more fury than the sandstorm had shown.

Martin Silenus begins to laugh. 'It's a fucking *desert*!' he shouts toward the sky. 'We'll probably drown in a flood.'

'We need to get out of this,' says Sol Weintraub. His baby's face is visible between the gaps in his cloak. Rachel is crying; her face is very red. She looks no older than a newborn.

'Keep Chronos?' says Lamia. 'It's a couple of hours . . .'

'Too far,' says the Consul. 'Let's bivouac in one of the Tombs.' Silenus laughs again. He says:

> *Who are these coming to the sacrifice?*
> *To what green altar, O mysterious priest,*

Lead'st thou that heifer lowing at the skies,
    And all her silken flanks with garlands dresst?

'Does that mean yes?' asks Lamia.

'That means fucking "why not?" ' laughs Silenus. 'Why make it hard for our cold muse to find us? We can watch our friend decompose while we wait. How long did Duré's tale say it took for one of the Bikura to rejoin the flock after death interrupted their grazing?'

'Three days,' says the Consul.

Martin Silenus slaps his forehead with the heel of his palm. 'Of course. How could I forget? How wonderfully fitting, New Testament-wise. In the meantime, maybe our Shrike-wolf will carry off a few of this flock. Do you think the padre would mind if I borrowed one of his cruciforms just in case? I mean, he has a spare . . .'

'Let's go,' says the Consul. Rain drips from his tricorne cap in a steady stream. 'We'll stay in the Sphinx until morning. I'll carry Kassad's extra gear and the Möbius cube. Brawne, you carry Hoyt's things and Sol's pack. Sol, you keep the baby warm and dry.'

'What about the padre?' asks the poet, jerking his thumb in the direction of the body.

'You're carrying Father Hoyt,' Brawne Lamia says softly, turning.

Martin Silenus opens his mouth, sees the pistol in Lamia's hand, shrugs, and bends to lift the body to his shoulder. 'Who's going to carry Kassad when we find him?' he asks. 'Of course, he could be in enough pieces that we could all—'

'Please shut up,' Brawne Lamia says tiredly. 'If I have to shoot you, it will give us one more thing to carry. Just walk.'

With the Consul leading, Weintraub coming closely behind, Martin Silenus staggering along some meters back, and Brawne Lamia in the rear, the group once again descends the low col into the Valley of the Tombs.

NINE

CEO Gladstone's schedule that morning was a busy one. Tau Ceti Center has a twenty-three-hour day, which makes it convenient for the government to run on Hegemony Standard Time without totally destroying local diurnal rhythms. At 0545 hours, Gladstone met with her military advisors. At 0630 hours she breakfasted with two dozen of the most important senators and with representatives of the All Thing and the TechnoCore. At 0715 the CEO farcast to Renaissance Vector, where it was evening, to officially open the Hermes Medical Center in Cadua. At 0740 she 'cast back to Government House for a meeting with her top aides, including Leigh Hunt, to go over the speech she was to give to the Senate and All Thing at 1000 hours. At 0830 Gladstone met again with General Morpurgo and Admiral Singh for an update on the situation in the Hyperion system. At 0845 hours, she met with me.

'Good morning, M Severn,' said the CEO. She was behind her desk in the office where I'd first met her three nights earlier. She waved her hand toward a buffet against the wall where hot coffee, tea, and caffta sat in sterling silver pots.

I shook my head and sat down. Three of the holographic windows showed white light, but the one to my left offered the 3-D map of Hyperion System that I had tried to decode in the War Room. It seemed to me that Ouster red now covered and infiltrated the system like dye dissolving and settling into a blue solution.

'I want to hear your dreams,' said CEO Gladstone.

'I want to hear why you abandoned them,' I said, voice flat. 'Why you left Father Hoyt to die.'

Gladstone could not have been used to being spoken to in that tone, not after forty-eight years in the Senate and a decade and a half as CEO, but her only reaction was to raise one eyebrow a fraction of an inch. 'So you do dream the real events.'

'Did you doubt it?'

She set down the work pad she had been holding, keyed it off, and shook her head. 'Not really, but it is still a shock to hear about something that no one else in the Web knows about.'

'Why did you deny them the use of the Consul's ship?'

Gladstone swiveled to look up at the window where the tactical display shifted and changed as new updates changed the flow of red, the retreat of blue, the movement of planets and moons, but if the military situation was to have been part of her explanation, she abandoned that approach. She swiveled back. 'Why would I have to explain any executive decision to you, M Severn? What is your constituency? Whom do you represent?'

'I represent those five people and a baby you left stranded on Hyperion,' I said. 'Hoyt could have been saved.'

Gladstone made a fist and tapped her lower lip with a curved forefinger. 'Perhaps,' she said. 'And perhaps he was already dead. But that wasn't the issue, was it?'

I sat back in the chair. I had not bothered to bring a sketchbook along, and my fingers ached to hold something. 'What is, then?'

'Do you remember Father Hoyt's story . . . the story he told during their voyage to the Tombs?' asked Gladstone.

'Yes.'

'Each of the pilgrims is allowed to petition the Shrike for one favor. Tradition says that the creature grants one wish, while denying the others and murdering those he denies. Do you remember what Hoyt's wish was?'

I paused. Recalling incidents from the pilgrims' past was like trying to remember details of last week's dreams. 'He wanted the cruciforms removed,' I said. 'He wanted freedom for both Father Duré's . . . soul, DNA, whatever . . . and for himself.'

'Not quite,' said Gladstone. 'Father Hoyt wanted to die.'

I stood up, almost knocking my chair over, and strode to the pulsing map. 'That's pure bullshit,' I said. 'Even if he did, the others had an obligation to save him . . . and so did you. You let him die.'

'Yes.'

'Just as you're going to let the rest of them die?'

'Not necessarily,' said CEO Meina Gladstone. 'That is their will . . . and the Shrike's, if such a creature actually exists. All I know at this point is that their pilgrimage is too important to allow them a means of . . . retreat . . . at the moment of decision.'

'Whose decision? Theirs? How can the lives of six or seven people . . . and a baby . . . affect the outcome of a society of a hundred and fifty *billion*?' I knew the answer to that, of course. The AI Advisory Council as well as the Hegemony's less sentient predictors had chosen the pilgrims very carefully. But for what? Unpredictability. They were ciphers that matched the ultimate enigma of the entire Hyperion equation. Did Gladstone know that, or did she know only what Councilor Albedo and her own spies told her? I sighed and returned to my chair.

'Did your dream tell you what the fate of Colonel Kassad was?' asked the CEO.

'No. I awoke before they returned to the Sphinx to seek shelter from the storm.'

Gladstone smiled slightly. 'You realize, M Severn, that for our purposes it would be more convenient to have you sedated, prompted by the same truthtalk your Philomel friends used, and connected to subvocalizers for a more constant report on the events on Hyperion.'

I returned her smile. 'Yes,' I said, 'that would be more convenient. But it would be less than convenient for you if I slipped away into the Core via the datasphere and left my body behind. Which is precisely what I will do if put under duress again.'

'Of course,' said Gladstone. 'That is precisely what *I* would do if put in such circumstances. Tell me, M Severn, what is it like in the Core? What is it like in that distant place where your consciousness truly resides?'

'Busy,' I said. 'Did you want to see me for anything else today?'

Gladstone smiled again and I sensed that it was a true smile, not the politician's weapon she used so well. 'Yes,' she said, 'I did have something else in mind. Would you like to go to Hyperion? The *real* Hyperion?'

'The real Hyperion?' I echoed stupidly. I felt my fingers and toes tingle as a strange sense of excitement suffused me. My consciousness might truly reside in the Core, but my body and brain were all too human, all too susceptible to adrenaline and other random chemicals.

Gladstone nodded. 'Millions of people want to go there. Farcast to somewhere new. Watch the war from close up.' She sighed and moved her work pad. 'The idiots.' She looked up at me, and her brown eyes were serious. 'But I want someone to go there and report back to me in person. Leigh is using one of the new military farcast terminals this morning, and I thought that you might join him. There might not be time to set down on Hyperion itself, but you would be in-system.'

I thought of several questions and was embarrassed by the first one that emerged. 'Will it be dangerous?'

Neither Gladstone's expression nor tone changed. 'Possibly. Although you will be far behind the lines, and Leigh has explicit instructions not to expose himself . . . or you . . . to any obvious risk.'

Obvious risk, I thought. But how many less-than-obvious-risks were there in a war zone, near a world where a creature like the Shrike roamed free? 'Yes,' I said, 'I'll go. But there's one thing . . .'

'Yes?'

'I need to know why you want me to go. It seems that if you just want me for my connection to the pilgrims, you're running a needless risk in sending me away.'

Gladstone nodded. 'M Severn, it's true that your connection to the pilgrims . . . although somewhat tenuous . . . is of interest to me. But it is also true that I am interested in your observations and evaluations. *Your* observations.'

'But I'm nothing to you,' I said. 'You don't know who else I might be reporting to, deliberately or otherwise. I'm a creature of the TechnoCore.'

'Yes,' said Gladstone, 'but you also may be the least-affiliated person on Tau Ceti Center at this moment, perhaps in the entire Web. Also, your observations are those of a trained poet, a man whose genius I respect.'

I barked a laugh. '*He* was a genius,' I said. 'I'm a simulacrum. A drone. A caricature.'

'Are you so sure?' asked Meina Gladstone.

I held up empty hands. 'I haven't written a line of poetry in the ten months I have been alive and aware in this strange afterlife,' I said. 'I do not *think* in poetry. Isn't that proof enough that this Core retrieval project is a sham? Even my false name is an insult to a man infinitely more talented than I will ever be . . . Joseph Severn was a shade in comparison to the real Keats, but I sully his name by using it.'

'That may be true,' said Gladstone. 'And it may not. In either case, I've requested that you go with M Hunt on this brief trip to Hyperion.' She paused. 'You have no . . . duty . . . to go. In more than one sense, you are not even a citizen of the Hegemony. But I would appreciate it if you did go.'

'I'll go,' I said again, hearing my own voice as if from a distance.

'Very good. You'll need warm clothes. Wear nothing that

88

would come loose or cause embarrassment in free-fall, although there is little likelihood that you will encounter that. Meet M Hunt in the primary Government House farcaster nexus in . . .' She glanced at her comlog. '. . . twelve minutes.

I nodded and turned to go.

'Oh, M Severn . . .'

I paused by the door. The old woman behind the desk suddenly looked rather small and very tired.

'Thank you, M Severn,' she said.

It was true that millions wanted to farcast to the war zone. The All Thing was shrill with petitions, arguments for letting civilians cast to Hyperion, requests by cruise lines to run brief excursions, and demands by planetary politicians and Hegemony representatives to be allowed to tour the system on 'fact-finding missions.' All such requests had been denied. Web citizens – especially Web citizens with power and influence – were not used to being denied access to new experiences, and for the Hegemony, all-out war remained one of the few experiences still untried.

But the CEO's office and the FORCE authorities remained adamant: no civilian or unauthorized farcasting to the Hyperion system, no uncensored newsteep coverage. In an age where no information was inaccessible, no travel denied, such exclusion was maddening and tantalizing.

I met M Hunt at the executive farcaster nexus after showing my authorization pip to an even dozen security nodes. Hunt was wearing black wool, undecorated but evocative of the FORCE uniforms present everywhere in this section of Government House. I had had little time to change, returning to my apartments only to grab a loose vest with many pockets to hold drawing materials and a 35-mm imager.

'Ready?' said Hunt. The basset-hound face did not look pleased to see me. He carried a plain black valise.

I nodded.

Hunt gestured toward a FORCE transport technician, and a one-time portal shimmered into existence. I knew that the thing was tuned to our DNA signatures and would admit no one else. Hunt took a breath and stepped through. I watched the quicksilver portal surface ripple after his passage like a stream returning to calm after the slightest of breezes, and then I stepped through myself.

It was rumored that the original farcaster prototypes had offered no sensation during transition and that the AI and human designers had altered the machinery to add that vague prickling, ozone-charged feeling to give the traveler a sense of having *traveled*. Whatever the truth of that, my skin was still alive with tension as I took a step away from the portal, paused, and looked around.

It's strange but true that war-going spacecraft have been depicted in fiction, film, holo, and stimsim for more than eight hundred years; even before humankind had left Old Earth in anything but atmosphere-skimming converted airplanes, their flatfilms had shown epic space battles, huge interstellar dreadnoughts with incredible armament lunging through space like streamlined cities. Even the spate of recent war holies after the Battle of Bressia showed great fleets battling it out at distances two ground soldiers would find claustrophobic, ships ramming and firing and burning like Greek triremes packed into the straits of Artemisium.

It's little wonder then that my heart was pounding and my palms were a bit moist as I stepped on to the flagship of the fleet, expecting to emerge on to the broad bridge of a warship out of the holies, giant screens showing enemy ships, klaxons sounding, craggy commanders huddled over the tactical command panels as the ship lurched first right, then left.

Hunt and I were standing in what could have been a narrow corridor of a power plant. Color-coded pipes twisted everywhere, occasional handholds and airtight hatches at regular intervals suggested that we were indeed in a spacecraft, state-of-the-art diskey and interact panels showed that the corridor served some purpose other than access to elsewhere, but the overall effect was one of claustrophobia and primitive technology. I half expected to see *wires* running from circuit nodes. A vertical shaft intersected our corridor; other narrow, cluttered avenues were visible through other hatches.

Hunt looked at me and shrugged slightly. I wondered if it was possible that we had farcast to the wrong destination.

Before either of us said anything, a young FORCE:space ensign in black battle dress appeared from one of the side corridors, saluted Hunt, and said, 'Welcome to HS *Hebrides*, gentlemen. Admiral Nashita has asked me to convey his compliments and to invite you to the combat control center. If you will follow me, please.' With that the young ensign wheeled, reached for a rung, and pulled into a cramped vertical shaft.

We followed as best we could, Hunt struggling not to drop his valise and me trying not to have my hands ground under Hunt's heels as we climbed. After only a few yards, I realized that the gravity was far less than one-standard here, was not, in fact, gravity at all, but felt more like a multitude of small but insistent hands pressing me 'down.' I knew about spacecraft using a class-one containment field throughout a ship to simulate gravity, but this was my first direct experience of it. It was not a truly pleasant sensation; the constant pressure was rather like leaning into a wind, and the effect added to the claustrophobic qualities of the narrow corridors, small hatches, and equipment-cluttered bulkheads.

The *Hebrides* was a Three-C ship, Communication-Control-Command, and the combat control center was its heart and brain – but it was not a very impressive heart and brain. The young ensign passed us through three airtight hatches, led us down a final corridor past Marine guards, saluted, and left us in a room perhaps twenty yards square, but one so crowded with noise, personnel and equipment that one's first instinct was to step back outside the hatch to get a breath of air.

There were no giant screens, but dozens of young FORCE:space officers hunkered over cryptic displays, sat enmeshed in stimsim apparatus, or stood before pulsing callups which seemed to extend from all six bulkheads. Men and women were lashed into their chairs and sensory cradles, with the exception of a few officers – most looking more like harried bureaucrats than craggy warriors – who wandered the narrow aisles, patting subordinates on the back, barking for more information, and plugging into consoles with their own implant jacks. One of these men came over in a hurry, looked at both of us, saluted me, and said, 'M Hunt?'

I nodded toward my companion.

'M Hunt,' said the overweight young Commander, 'Admiral Nashita will see you now.'

The commander of all Hegemony forces in the Hyperion system was a small man with short white hair, skin far smoother than his age suggested, and a fair scowl that seemed carved in place. Admiral Nashita wore high-necked dress black with no rank insignia except for the single red-dwarf sun on his collar. His hands were blunt and quite powerful-looking, but the nails were recently manicured. The Admiral sat on a small dais surrounded by equipment and quiescent callups. The bustle and efficient madness seemed to flow around him like a fast stream around an impervious rock.

'You're the messenger from Gladstone,' he said to Hunt. 'Who's this?'

'My aide,' said Leigh Hunt.

I resisted the urge to raise an eyebrow.

'What do you want?' asked Nashita. 'As you see, we're busy.'

Leigh Hunt nodded and glanced around. 'I have some

materials for you, Admiral. Is there anyplace we can go for privacy?'

Admiral Nashita grunted, passed his palm over a rheosense, and the air behind me grew denser, coalescing into a semisolid mist as the containment field reified. The noise of the combat control center disappeared. The three of us were in a small igloo of quiet.

'Hurry it up,' said Admiral Nashita.

Hunt unlocked the valise and removed a small envelope with a Government House symbol on the back. 'A private communication from the Chief Executive,' said Hunt. 'To be read at your leisure, Admiral.'

Nashita grunted and set the envelope aside.

Hunt set a larger envelope on the desk. 'And this is a hard copy of the motion of the Senate regarding the prosecution of this . . . ah . . . military action. As you know, the will of the Senate is for this to be a speedy exercise of force to achieve limited objectives, with as little loss of life as possible, followed by the standard offer of help and protection to our new . . . colonial asset.'

Nashita's scowl twitched slightly. He made no move to touch or read the communication containing the will of the Senate. 'Is that all?'

Hunt took his time responding. 'That is all, unless you wish to relay a personal message to the CEO through me, Admiral.'

Nashita stared. There was no active hostility in his small, black eyes, only an impatience that I guessed would not be quenched until those eyes were dimmed by death. 'I have private fatline access to the Chief Executive,' said the Admiral. 'Thank you very much, M Hunt. No return messages at this time. Now if you will kindly return to the midships farcaster nexus and let me get on with prosecuting this *military action*.'

The containment field collapsed around us, and noise flowed in like water over a melting ice dam.

93

'There is one other thing,' said Leigh Hunt, his soft voice almost lost under the technobabble of the combat center.

Admiral Nashita swiveled his chair and waited.

'We'd like transport down to the planet,' said Hunt. 'Down to Hyperion.'

The Admiral's scowl seemed to deepen. 'CEO Gladstone's people said nothing about arranging a dropship.'

Hunt did not blink. 'Governor-General Lane knows that we might be coming.'

Nashita glanced at one of his callups, snapped his fingers, and barked something at a Marine major who hurried over. 'You'll have to hurry,' the Admiral said to Hunt. 'There is a courier just ready to leave from port twenty. Major Inverness will show you the way. You will be brought back up to the primary JumpShip. The *Hebrides* will be departing this position in twenty-three minutes.'

Hunt nodded and turned to follow the Major. I tagged along. The Admiral's voice stopped us.

'M Hunt,' he called, 'please tell CEO Gladstone that the flagship will be too busy from this point on for any more political visits.' Nashita turned away to flickering callups and a line of waiting subordinates.

I followed Hunt and the Major back into the maze.

'There should be windows.'

'What?' I had been thinking about something, not paying attention.

Leigh Hunt turned his head toward me. 'I've never been in a dropship without windows or viewscreens. It's strange.'

I nodded and looked around, noticing the cramped and crowded interior for the first time. It was true that there were only blank bulkheads, and heaps of supplies and one young lieutenant in the passenger hold of the dropship with us. It seemed to conform to the claustrophobic ambience of the command ship.

I looked away, returning to the thoughts that had preoccupied me since we left Nashita. Following the other two to port twenty, it had suddenly occurred to me that I was not missing something I had *expected* to miss. Part of my anxiety toward this trip had lain in the thought of leaving the datasphere; I was rather like a fish contemplating leaving the sea. Part of my *consciousness* lay submerged somewhere in that sea, the ocean of data and commlinks from two hundred worlds and the Core, all linked by the invisible medium once called datumplane, now known only as the megasphere.

It struck me as we left Nashita that I could still hear the pulse of that particular sea – distant but constant, like the sound of the surf half a mile from the shore – and I had been trying to understand it all during the rush to the dropship, the buckling in and separation, and the ten-minute cislunar sprint to the fringes of Hyperion's atmosphere.

FORCE prided itself on using its own artificial intelligences, its own dataspheres and computing sources. The ostensible reason lay in the requirement to operate in the great spaces between Web worlds, the dark and quiet places between the stars and beyond the Web megasphere, but much of the real reason lay in a fierce need for independence which FORCE had shown toward the TechnoCore for centuries. Yet on a FORCE ship in the center of a FORCE armada in a non-Web, non-Protectorate system, I was tuned to the same comforting background babble of data and energy that I would have found anywhere in the Web. Interesting.

I thought of the links the farcaster had brought to Hyperion system: not just the JumpShip and farcaster containment sphere floating at Hyperion's L3 point like a gleaming new moon, but the miles of gigachannel fiberoptic cable snaking through permanent JumpShip farcaster portals, microwave repeaters mechanically shuttling the few inches to repeat their messages in near real-time, command ship tame AIs requesting – and receiving – new links to the

Olympus High Command on Mars and elsewhere. Somewhere the datasphere had crept in, perhaps unknown to the FORCE machines and their operators and allies. The Core AIs knew everything happening here in Hyperion system. If my body were to die now, I would have the same escape path as always, fleeing down the pulsing links that led like secret passages beyond the Web, beyond any vestige of datumplane as humanity had known it, down datalink tunnels to the TechnoCore itself. *Not really to the Core*, I thought, *because the Core surrounds, envelops the rest, like an ocean holding separate currents, great Gulf Streams which think themselves separate seas.*

'I just wish there was a window,' whispered Leigh Hunt.

'Yes,' I said. 'So do I.'

The dropship bucked and vibrated as we entered Hyperion's upper atmosphere. *Hyperion*, I thought. *The Shrike*. My heavy shirt and vest seemed sticky and clinging. A faint susurration from without said that we were flying, streaking across the lapis skies at several times the speed of sound.

The young lieutenant leaned across the aisle. 'First time down, gentlemen?'

Hunt nodded.

The Lieutenant was chewing gum, showing how relaxed he was. 'You two civilian techs from the *Hebrides*?'

'We just came from there, yes,' said Hunt.

'Thought so,' grinned the Lieutenant. 'Me, I'm running a courier pack down to the Marine base near Keats. My fifth trip.'

A slight jolt ran through me as I was reminded of the name of the capital; Hyperion had been repopulated by Sad King Billy and his colony of poets, artists, and other misfits fleeing an invasion of their homeworld by Horace Glennon-Height – an invasion which never came. The poet on the current Shrike Pilgrimage, Martin Silenus, had advised King Billy almost two centuries earlier in the naming of the capital. *Keats*. The locals called the old part Jacktown.

'You're not going to believe this place,' said the Lieutenant. 'It's the real anal end of nowhere. I mean, no datasphere, no EMVs, no farcasters, no stimsim bars, no *nothing*. It's no wonder that there are thousands of the fucking indigenies camped around the spaceport, just tearing down the fence to get offworld.'

'Are they really attacking the spaceport?' asked Hunt.

'Naw,' said the Lieutenant and snapped his gum. 'But they're *ready* to, if you know what I mean. That's why the Second Marine Battalion has set up a perimeter there and secured the way into the city. Besides, the yokels think that we're going to set up farcasters any day now and let 'em step out of the shit they got themselves into.'

'*They* got themselves into?' I said.

The Lieutenant shrugged. 'They must've done something to get the Ousters cricked at them, right? We're just here to pull their oysters out of the fire.'

'Chestnuts,' said Leigh Hunt.

The gum snapped. 'Whatever.'

The susurration of wind grew to a shriek clearly audible through the hull. The dropship bounced twice and then slid smoothly – ominously smoothly – as if it had encountered a chute of ice ten miles above the ground.

'I wish we had a window,' whispered Leigh Hunt.

It was warm and stuffy in the dropship. The bouncing was oddly relaxing, rather like a small sailing ship rising and falling on slow swells. I closed my eyes for a few minutes.

TEN

Sol, Brawne, Martin Silenus, and the Consul carry gear, Het Masteen's Möbius cube, and the body of Lenar Hoyt down the long incline to the entrance of the Sphinx. Snow is falling rapidly now, twisting across the already writhing dune surfaces in a complex dance of wind-driven particles. Despite their comlogs' claim that night nears its end, there is no hint of sunrise to the east. Repeated calls on their comlog radio link bring no response from Colonel Kassad.

Sol Weintraub pauses before the entrance to the Time Tomb called the Sphinx. He feels his daughter's presence as a warmth against his chest under the cape, the rise and fall of warm baby's breath against his throat. He raises one hand, touches the small bundle there, and tries to imagine Rachel as a young woman of twenty-six, a researcher pausing at this very entrance before going in to test the anti-entropic mysteries of the Time Tomb. Sol shakes his head. It has been twenty-six long years and a lifetime since that moment. In four days it will be his daughter's birthday. Unless Sol does something, finds the Shrike, makes some bargain with the creature, *does something*, Rachel will die in four days.

'Are you coming, Sol?' calls Brawne Lamia. The others have stored their gear in the first room, half a dozen meters down the narrow corridor through stone.

'Coming,' he calls, and enters the tomb. Glow-globes and electric lights line the tunnel but they are dead and dust-covered. Only Sol's flashlight and the glow from one of Kassad's small lanterns light the way.

The first room is small, no more than four by six meters. The other three pilgrims have set their baggage against the back wall and spread tarp and bedrolls in the center of the cold floor. Two lanterns hiss and cast a cold light. Sol stops and looks around.

'Father Hoyt's body is in the next room,' says Brawne Lamia, answering his unasked question. 'It's even colder there.'

Sol takes his place near the others. Even this far in, he can hear the rasp of sand and snow blowing against stone.

'The Consul is going to try the comlog again later,' says Brawne. 'Tell Gladstone the situation.'

Martin Silenus laughs. 'It's no use. No fucking use at all. She knows what she's doing, and she's never going to let us out of here.'

'I'll try just after sunrise,' says the Consul. His voice is very tired.

'I will stand watch,' says Sol. Rachel stirs and cries feebly. 'I need to feed the baby anyway.'

The others seem too tired to respond. Brawne leans against a pack, closes her eyes, and is breathing heavily within seconds. The Consul pulls his tricorne cap low over his eyes. Martin Silenus folds his arms and stares at the doorway, waiting.

Sol Weintraub fusses with a nursing pak, his cold and arthritic fingers having trouble with the heating tab. He looks in his bag and realizes that he has only ten more paks, a handful of diapers.

The baby is nursing, and Sol is nodding, almost sleeping, when a sound wakes them all.

'What?' cries Brawne, fumbling for her father's pistol.

'Shhh!' snaps the poet, holding his hand out for silence.

From somewhere beyond the tomb comes the sound again. It is flat and final, cutting through the wind noise and sand rasp.

'Kassad's rifle,' says Brawne Lamia.

'Or someone else's,' whispers Martin Silenus.

They sit in silence and strain to hear. For a long moment there is no sound at all. Then, in an instant, the night erupts with noise . . . noise which makes each of them cringe and cover his or her ears. Rachel screams in terror, but her cries cannot be heard over the explosions and rendings beyond the tomb.

ELEVEN

I awoke just as the dropship touched down. *Hyperion*, I thought, still separating my thoughts from the tatters of dream.

The young lieutenant wished us luck and was the first out as the door irised open and cool, thin air replaced the pressurized thickness of the cabin atmosphere. I followed Hunt out and down a standard docking ramp, through the shield wall, and on to the tarmac.

It was night, and I had no idea what the local time was, whether the terminator had just passed this point on the planet or was just approaching, but it felt and smelled late. It was raining softly, a light drizzle perfumed with the salt scent of the sea and the fresh hint of moistened vegetation. Field lights glared around the distant perimeter, and a score of lighted towers threw halos toward the low clouds. A half dozen young men in Marine field uniforms were quickly unloading the dropship, and I could see our young lieutenant speaking briskly to an officer thirty yards to our right. The small spaceport looked like something out a history book, a colonial port from the earliest days of the Hegira. Primitive blast pits and landing squares stretched for a mile or more toward a dark bulk of hills to the north, gantries and service towers tended to a score of military shuttles and small warcraft around us, and the landing areas were ringed by modular military buildings sporting antennae arrays, violet containment fields, and a clutter of skimmers and aircraft.

I followed Hunt's gaze and noticed a skimmer moving toward us. The blue and gold geodesic symbol of the Hegemony on one of its skirts was illuminated by its running lights; rain streaked the forward blisters and whipped away from the fans in a violent curtain of mist. The skimmer settled, a Perspex blister split and folded, and a man stepped out and hurried across the tarmac toward us.

He held out his hand to Hunt. 'M Hunt? I'm Theo Lane.'

Hunt shook the hand, nodded toward me. 'Pleased to meet you, Governor-General. This is Joseph Severn.'

I shook Lane's hand, a shock of recognition coming with the touch. I remembered Theo Lane through the *déjà vu* mists of the Consul's memory, recalling the years when the young man was the Vice-Consul; also from a brief meeting a week earlier when he greeted all of the pilgrims before they departed upriver on the levitation barge *Benares*. He seemed older than he had appeared just six days before. But the unruly lock of hair on his forehead was the same, as were the archaic eyeglasses he wore, and the brisk, firm handshake.

'I'm pleased you could take the time to make planetfall,' Governor-General Lane said to Hunt. 'I have several things I need to communicate to the CEO.'

'That's why we're here,' said Hunt. He squinted up at the rain. 'We have about an hour. Is there somewhere we can dry off?'

The Governor-General showed a youthful smile. 'The field here is a madhouse, even at 0520 hours, and the consulate is under siege. But I know a place.' He gestured toward the skimmer.

As we lifted off, I noticed the two Marine skimmers keeping pace with us but I was still surprised that the Governor-General of a Protectorate world flew his own vehicle and did not have constant bodyguards. Then I remembered what the Consul had told the other pilgrims about Theo Lane – about the young man's efficiency and self-effacing ways –

102

and realized that such a low profile was in keeping with the diplomat's style.

The sun rose as we lifted off from the spaceport and banked toward town. Low clouds glowed brilliantly as they were lighted from below, the hills to the north sparkled a bright green, violet, and russet, and the strip of sky below the clouds to the east was that heart-stopping green and lapis which I remembered from my dreams. *Hyperion*, I thought, and felt a thick tension and excitement catch in my throat.

I leaned my head against the rain-streaked canopy and realized that some of the vertigo and confusion I felt at that moment came from a thinning of the background contact with the datasphere. The connection was still there, carried primarily on microwave and fatline channels now, but more tenuous than I had ever experienced – if the datasphere had been the sea in which I swam, I was now in shallow water indeed, perhaps a tidal pool would be a better metaphor, and the water grew even shallower as we left the envelope of the spaceport and its crude microsphere. I forced myself to pay attention to what Hunt and Governor-General Lane were discussing.

'You can see the shacks and hovels,' said Lane, banking slightly so we had a better view of the hills and valleys separating the spaceport from the suburbs of the capital.

Shacks and hovels were too-polite terms for the miserable collection of fiberplastic panels, patches of canvas, heaps of packing crates, and shards of flowfoam that covered the hills and deep canyons. What obviously had once been a scenic seven- or eight-mile drive from the city to the spaceport through wooded hills now showed land stripped of all trees for firewood and shelter, meadows beaten to barren mud-flats by the press of feet, and a city of seven or eight hundred thousand refugees sprawled over every flat piece of land in sight. Smoke from thousands of breakfast fires floated toward the clouds, and I could see movement everywhere, children running in bare feet, women carrying water

103

from streams that must be terribly polluted, men squatting in open fields and waiting in line at makeshift privies. I noted that high razorwire fences and violet containment field barriers had been set along both sides of the highway, and military checkpoints were visible every half mile. Long lines of FORCE camouflaged ground vehicles and skimmers moved in both directions along the highway and low-level flyways.

'. . . most of the refugees are indigenies,' Governor-General Lane was saying, 'although there are thousands of displaced landowners from the southern cities and the large fiberplastic plantations on Aquila.'

'Are they here because they think the Ousters will invade?' asked Hunt.

Theo Lane glanced at Gladstone's aide. 'Originally there was panic at the thought of the Time Tombs opening,' he said. 'People were convinced that the Shrike was coming for them.'

'Was it?' I asked.

The young man shifted in his seat to look back at me. 'The Third Legion of the Self-Defense Force went north seven months ago,' he said. 'It didn't come back.'

'You said *at first* they were fleeing the Shrike,' said Hunt. 'Why did the others come?'

'They're waiting for the evacuation,' said Lane. 'Everyone knows what the Ousters . . . and the Hegemony troops . . . did to Bressia. They don't want to be here when that happens to Hyperion.'

'You're aware that FORCE considers evacuation an absolute last resort?' said Hunt.

'Yes. But we're not announcing that to the refugees. There have been terrible riots already. The Shrike Temple has been destroyed . . . a mob laid siege, and someone used shaped plasma charges stolen from the mineworks on Ursus. Last week there were attacks on the consulate and the spaceport, as well as food riots in Jacktown.'

Hunt nodded and watched the city approach. The buildings were low, few over five stories, and their white and pastel walls glowed richly in the slanting rays of morning light. I looked over Hunt's shoulder and saw the low mountain with the carved face of Sad King Billy brooding over the valley. The Hoolie River twisted through the center of the old town, straightening before it headed northwest toward the unseen Bridle Range, twisting out of sight in the weirwood marshes to the southeast, where I knew it widened to its delta along the High Mane. The city looked uncrowded and peaceful after the sad confusion of the refugee slums, but even as we began to descend toward the river, I noticed the military traffic, the tanks and APCs and GAVs at intersections and sitting in parks, their camouflage polymer deliberately deactivated so the machines would look more threatening. Then I saw the refugees in the city: makeshift tents in the squares and alleys, thousands of sleeping forms along the curbs, like so many dull-colored bundles of laundry waiting to be picked up.

'Keats had a population of two hundred thousand two years ago,' said Governor-General Lane. 'Now, including the shack cities, we're nearing three and a half million.'

'I thought that there were fewer than five million people on the planet,' said Hunt. 'Including indigenies.'

'That's accurate,' said Lane. 'You see why everything's breaking down. The other two large cities, Port Romance and Endymion, are holding most of the rest of the refugees. Fiberplastic plantations on Aquila are empty, being reclaimed by the jungle and flame forests, the farm belts along the Mane and the Nine Tails aren't producing – or if they are, can't get their food to market because of the breakdown of the civilian transport system.'

Hunt watched the river come closer. 'What is the government doing?'

Theo Lane smiled. 'You mean what am *I* doing? Well, the crisis has been brewing for almost three years. The first step was to dissolve the Home Rule Council and formally bring Hyperion into the Protectorate. Once I had executive powers, I moved to nationalize the remaining transit companies and dirigible lines – only the military moves by skimmer here now – and to disband the Self-Defense Force.'

'Disband it?' said Hunt. 'I would think you would want to use it.'

Governor-General Lane shook his head. He touched the omni control lightly, confidently, and the skimmer spiraled down toward the center of old Keats. 'They were worse than useless,' he said, 'they were dangerous. I wasn't too upset when the "Fighting Third" Legion went north and just disappeared. As soon as the FORCE:ground troops and Marines landed, I disarmed the rest of the SDF thugs. They were the source of most of the looting. Here's where we'll get some breakfast and talk.'

The skimmer dropped in low over the river, circled a final time, and dropped lightly into the courtyard of an ancient structure made of stone and sticks and imaginatively designed windows: Cicero's. Even before Lane identified the place to Leigh Hunt I recognized it from the pilgrims' passage – the old restaurant/pub/inn lay in the heart of Jacktown and sprawled over four buildings on nine levels, its balconies and piers and darkened weirwood walkways overhanging the slow-moving Hoolie on one side and the narrow lanes and alleys of Jacktown on the other. Cicero's was older than the stone face of Sad King Billy, and its dim cubicles and deep wine cellars had been the true home of the Consul during his years of exile here.

Stan Leweski met us at the courtyard door. Tall and massive, face as age-darkened and cracked as the stone walls of his inn, Leweski *was* Cicero's, as had been his father, grandfather, and great-grandfather before him.

'By damn!' declared the giant, clapping the Governor-General/de facto dictator of this world on his shoulders hard enough to make Theo stagger. 'You get up early for a change, heh? Bring your friends to breakfast? Welcome to Cicero's!' Stan Leweski's huge hand swallowed Hunt's and then mine in a welcome that left me checking fingers and joints for damage. 'Or is it later – Web time – for you?' he boomed. 'Maybe you like a drink or dinner!'

Leigh Hunt squinted at the pub owner. 'How did you know we were from the Web?'

Leweski boomed a laugh that sent weathervanes on the roofline spinning. 'Hah! Hard to deduct, yes? You come here with Theo at sunrise – you think he give everybody a ride here? – also wearing wool clothes when we got no sheeps here. You're not FORCE people and not fiber-plastic plantation big shots . . . I know all those! Ipso fact toto, you farcast to ships from Web, drop down here for good food. Now, you want breakfast or plenty to drink?'

Theo Lane sighed. 'Give us a quiet corner, Stan. Bacon and eggs and brine kippers for me. Gentlemen?'

'Just coffee,' said Hunt.

'Yes,' I said. We were following the owner through the corridors now, up short staircases and down wrought-iron ramps, through more corridors. The place was lower, darker, smokier, and more fascinating than I remembered from my dreams. A few regulars looked up at us as we passed, but the place was far less crowded than I remembered. Obviously Lane had sent troops to throw out the last of the SDF barbarians who had been occupying the place. We passed a high, narrow window, and I verified that hypothesis by catching a glimpse of a FORCE:ground APC parked in the alley, troops lounging on and near it with obviously loaded weapons.

'Here,' said Leweski, waving us into a small porch which overhung the Hoolie and looked out on to the gabled roof-tops and stone towers of Jacktown. 'Dommy be here in two minutes with your breakfast and coffees.' He disappeared quickly . . . for a giant.

Hunt glanced at his comlog. 'We have about forty-five

minutes before the dropship is supposed to return with us. Let's talk.'

Lane nodded, removed his glasses, and rubbed his eyes. I realized that he had been up all night . . . perhaps several nights. 'Fine,' he said, setting the glasses back in place. 'What does CEO Gladstone want to know?'

Hunt paused while a very short man with parchment-white skin and yellow eyes brought our coffee in deep, thick mugs and set down a platter with Lane's food. 'The CEO wants to know what you feel your priorities are,' said Hunt. 'And she needs to know if you can hold out here if the fighting is prolonged.'

Lane ate for a moment before responding. He took a long sip of coffee and stared intently at Hunt. It was real coffee from the taste of it, better than most Web-grown. 'First question last,' Lane said. 'Define prolonged.'

'Weeks.'

'Weeks, probably. Months, no way.' The Governor-General tried the brine kippers. 'You see the state of our economy. If it wasn't for the supplies dropped in by FORCE, we'd have food riots every day instead of once a week. There are no exports with the quarantine. Half the refugees want to find the Shrike Temple priests and kill them, the other half want to convert before the Shrike finds *them*.'

'Have you found the priests?' asked Hunt.

'No. We're sure they escaped the temple bombing, but the authorities can't locate them. Rumor has it that they've gone north to Keep Chronos, a stone castle right above the high steppe where the Time Tombs are.'

I knew better. At least, I knew the pilgrims had not seen any Shrike Temple priests during their brief stay in the Keep. But there had been signs of a slaughter there.

'As for our priorities,' Theo Lane was saying, 'the first is evacuation. The second is elimination of the Ouster threat. The third is help with the Shrike scare.'

Leigh Hunt sat back against oiled wood. Steam lifted from the heavy mug in his hands. 'Evacuation is not a possibility at this time—'

'Why?' Lane fired the question like a hellwhip bolt.

'CEO Gladstone does not have the political power . . . at this point . . . to convince the Senate and All Thing that the Web can accept five million refugees—'

'Bullshit,' said the Governor-General. 'There were twice that many tourists flooding Maui-Covenant its first year in the Protectorate. And that destroyed a unique planetary ecology. Put us on Armaghast or some desert world until the war scare is past.'

Hunt shook his head. His basset-hound eyes looked sadder than usual. 'It isn't just the logistical question,' he said. 'Or the political one. It's . . .'

'The Shrike,' said Lane. He broke a piece of bacon. 'The Shrike is the real reason.'

'Yes. As well as fears of an Ouster infiltration of the Web.'

The Governor-General laughed. 'So you're afraid that if you set up farcaster portals here and let us out, a bunch of three-meter Ousters are going to land and get in line without anyone noticing?'

Hunt sipped his coffee. 'No,' he said, 'but there is a real chance of an invasion. Every farcaster portal is an opening to the Web. The Advisory Council warns against it.'

'All right,' said the younger man, his mouth half-full. 'Evacuate us by ship then. Wasn't that the reason for the original task force?'

'That was the *ostensible* reason,' said Hunt. 'Our real goal now is to defeat the Ousters and then bring Hyperion fully into the Web.'

'And what about the Shrike threat then?'

'It will be . . . neutralized,' said Hunt. He paused while a small group of men and women passed by our porch.

I glanced up, started to return my attention to the table, and then snapped my head back around. The group had passed out of sight down the hallway. 'Wasn't that Melio Arundez?' I said, interrupting Governor-General Lane.

'What? Oh, Dr Arundez. Yes. Do you know him, M Severn?'

Leigh Hunt was glaring at me, but I ignored it. 'Yes,' I said to Lane, although I had never actually met Arundez. 'What is he doing on Hyperion?'

'His team landed over six local months ago with a project proposal from Reichs University on Freeholm to do additional research on the Time Tombs.'

'But the Tombs were closed to research and tourists,' I said.

'Yes. But their instruments – we allowed data to be relayed weekly through the consulate fatline transmitter – had already shown the change in the anti-entropic fields surrounding the Tombs. Reichs University knew the Tombs were opening . . . if that's really what the change means . . . and they sent the top researchers in the Web to study it.'

'But you did not grant them permission?' I said.

Theo Lane smiled without warmth. 'CEO Gladstone did not grant them permission. The closure of the Tombs is a direct order from TC². If it were up to me, I would have denied the pilgrims passage and allowed Dr Arundez's team priority access.' He turned back to Hunt.

'Excuse me,' I said and slipped out of the booth.

I found Arundez and his people – three women and four men, their clothing and physical styles suggesting different worlds in the Web – two porches away. They were bent over their breakfasts and scientific comlogs, arguing in technical terms so abtruse as to leave a Talmudic scholar envious.

'Dr Arundez?' I said.

'Yes?' He looked up. He was two decades older than I remembered, entering middle age in his early sixties, but the strikingly handsome profile was the same, with the same bronzed skin, solid jaw, wavy black hair going only slightly gray at the temples, and piercing hazel eyes. I understood how a young female graduate student could have quickly fallen in love with him.

'My name is Joseph Severn,' I said. 'You don't know me, but I knew a friend of yours . . . Rachel Weintraub.'

Arundez was on his feet in a second, offering apologies to the others, leading me by the elbow until we found an empty booth in a cubicle under a round window looking out on red-tiled rooftops. He released my elbow and appraised me carefully, taking in the Web clothing. He turned my wrists over, looking for the telltale blueness of Poulsen treatments. 'You're too young,' he said. 'Unless you knew Rachel as a child.'

'Actually, it's her father I know best,' I said.

Dr Arundez let out a breath and nodded. 'Of course,' he said. 'Where *is* Sol? I've been trying to trace him for months through the consulate. The authorities on Hebron will only say that he's moved.' He gave me that appraising stare again. 'You knew about Rachel's . . . illness?'

'Yes,' I said. The Merlin's sickness which had caused her to age backward, losing memories with each day and hour that passed. Melio Arundez had been one of those memories. 'I know that you went to visit her about fifteen standard years ago on Barnard's World.'

Arundez grimaced. 'That was a mistake,' he said. 'I thought that I would talk to Sol and Sarai. When I saw her . . .' He shook his head. 'Who are you? Do you know where Sol and Rachel are now? It's *three days* until her birthday.'

I nodded. 'Her first and last birthday.' I glanced around. The hallway was silent and empty except for a distant murmur of laughter from a lower level. 'I'm here on a fact-finding trip from the CEO's office,' I said. 'I have information that Sol Weintraub and his daughter have traveled to the Time Tombs.'

Arundez looked as though I'd struck him in the solar plexus. *'Here?* On Hyperion?' He stared out at the rooftops for a moment. 'I should have realized . . . although Sol always refused to return here . . . but with Sarai gone . . .' He looked at me. 'Are you in touch with him? Is she . . . are they all right?'

I shook my head. 'There are no radio or datasphere links with them at present,' I said. 'I know that they made the trip safely. The question is, what do *you* know? Your team? Data on what is occurring at the Time Tombs might be very important to their survival.'

Melio Arundez ran his hand through his hair. 'If only they'd let us go there! That damned, stupid, bureaucratic shortsightedness . . . You say you're from Gladstone's office. Can you explain to them why it's so important for us to get there?'

'I'm only a messenger,' I said. 'But tell me why it's so important, and I'll try to get the information to someone.'

Arundez's large hands cupped an invisible shape in mid-air. His tension and anger were palpable. 'For three years, the data was coming via telemetry in the squirts the consulate would allow once a week on their precious fatline transmitter. It showed a slow but relentless degradation of the anti-entropic envelope – the time tides – in and around the Tombs. It was erratic, illogical, but steady. Our team was authorized to travel here shortly after the degradation began. We arrived about six months ago, saw data that suggested that the Tombs were opening . . . coming into phase with *now* . . . but four days after we arrived, the instruments quit sending. All of them. We begged that bastard Lane to let us just go and recalibrate them, set up new sensors if he wouldn't let us investigate in person.

'Nothing. No transit permission. No communication with the university . . . even with the coming of FORCE ships to make it easier. We tried going upriver ourselves, without permission, and some of Lane's Marine goons intercepted us at Karla Locks and brought us back in handcuffs. I spent four weeks in jail. Now we're allowed to wander around Keats, but we'll be locked up indefinitely if we leave the city again.' Arundez leaned forward. '*Can* you help?'

'I don't know,' I said. 'I want to help the Weintraubs. Perhaps it would be best if you could take your team to the site. Do you know when the Tombs will open?'

The time-physicist made an angry gesture. 'If we had *new* data!' He sighed. 'No, we don't know. They could be open already or it could be another six months.'

'When you say "open," ' I said, 'you don't mean physically open?'

'Of course not. The Time Tombs have been physically open for inspection since they were discovered four standard centuries ago. I mean open in the sense of dropping the time curtains that conceal parts of them, bringing the entire complex into phase with the local flow of time.'

'By "local" you mean . . . ?'

'I mean in this universe, of course.'

'And you're sure that the Tombs are moving backward in time . . . from our future?' I asked.

'Backward in time, yes,' said Arundez. 'From our future, we can't say. We're not even sure what the "future" means in temporal/physical terms. It could be a series of sine-wave probabilities or a decision-branch megaverse, or even—'

'But whatever it is,' I said, 'the Time Tombs and the Shrike are coming from there?'

'The Time Tombs are for certain,' said the physicist. 'I have no knowledge of the Shrike. My own guess is that it's a myth fueled by the same hunger for superstitious verities that drives other religions.'

'Even after what happened to Rachel?' I said. 'You still don't believe in the Shrike?'

Melio Arundez glowered at me. 'Rachel contracted Merlin's sickness,' he said. 'It's an anti-entropic aging disease, not the bite of a mythical monster.'

113

'Time's bite has never been mythical,' I said, surprising myself with such a cheap bit of homespun philosophy. 'The question is – will the Shrike or whatever power inhabits the Time Tombs return Rachel to the "local" time flow?'

Arundez nodded and turned his gaze to the rooftops. The sun had moved into the clouds, and the morning was drab, the red tiles bleached of color. Rain was beginning to fall again.

'And the question is,' I said, surprising myself again, 'are you still in love with her?'

The physicist turned his head slowly, fixing me in an angry gaze. I felt the retort – possibly physical – build, crest, and wane. He reached into his coat pocket and showed me a snapshot holo of an attractive woman with graying hair and two children in their late teens. 'My wife and children,' said Melio Arundez. 'They're waiting on Renaissance Vector.' He pointed a blunt finger at me. 'If Rachel were . . . were cured today, I would be eighty-two standard years old before she again reached the age she was when we first met.' He lowered the finger, returned the holo to his pocket. 'And yes,' he said, 'I'm still in love with her.'

'Ready?' The voice broke the silence a moment later. I looked up to see Hunt and Theo Lane in the doorway. 'The dropship lifts off in ten minutes,' said Hunt.

I stood and shook hands with Melio Arundez. 'I'll try,' I said.

Governor-General Lane had one of his escort skimmers return us to the spaceport while he went back to the consulate. The military skimmer was no more comfortable than his consulate machine had been, but it was faster. We were strapped and fielded into our webseats aboard the dropship before Hunt said, 'What was all that about with that physicist?'

'Just renewing old ties with a stranger,' I said.

Hunt frowned. 'What did you promise him that you'd try?'

114

I felt the dropship rumble, twitch, and then leap as the catapult grid launched us skyward. 'I told him I'd try to get him in to visit a sick friend,' I said.

Hunt continued to frown, but I pulled out a sketchpad and doodled images of Cicero's until we docked at the JumpShip fifteen minutes later.

It was a shock to step through the farcaster portal into the executive nexus in Government House. Another step took us to the Senate gallery, where Meina Gladstone was still speaking to a packed house. Imagers and microphones carried her speech to the All Thing and a hundred billion waiting citizens.

I glanced at my chronometer. It was 1038 hours. We had been gone only ninety minutes.

TWELVE

The building housing the Senate of the Hegemony of Man was patterned more after the United States Senate building of eight centuries earlier rather than the more imperial structures of the North American Republic or the First World Council. The main assembly room was large, girded with galleries, and big enough for the three-hundred-plus senators from Web worlds and the more than seventy nonvoting representatives from Protectorate colonies. Carpets were a rich wine red and radiated from the central dais where the President Pro Tem, the Speaker of the All Thing, and, today, the Chief Executive Officer of the Hegemony had their seats. Senators' desks were made of muirwood, donated by the Templars of God's Grove, who held such products sacred, and the glow and scent of burnished wood filled the room even when it was as crowded as it was today.

Leigh Hunt and I entered just as Gladstone was finishing her speech. I keyed my comlog for a quick readout. As with most of her talks, it had been short, comparatively simple, without condescension or bombast, yet laced with a certain lilt of original phrasing and imagery which carried great power. Gladstone had reviewed the incidents and conflicts that led to the current state of belligerency with the Ousters, proclaimed the time-honored wish for peace, which still was paramount in Hegemony policy, and called for unity within the Web and Protectorate until this current crisis was past. I listened to her summation.

'. . . and so it has come to pass, fellow citizens, that after

116

more than a century of peace we are once again engaged in a struggle to maintain those rights to which our society has been dedicated since before the death of our Mother Earth. After more than a century of peace, we must now pick up – however unwillingly, however distastefully – the shield and sword, which have ever preserved our birthright and vouchsafed our common good, so that peace may again prevail.

'We must not . . . and shall not . . . be misled by the stir of trumpets or the rush of near-joy which the call to arms inevitably produces. Those who ignore history's lessons in the ultimate folly of war are forced to do more than relive them . . . they may be forced to die by them. Great sacrifices may lie ahead for all of us. Great sorrows may lie in store for some of us. But come what successes or setbacks must inevitably occur, I say to you now that we must remember these two things above all: First, that we fight for peace and know that war must never be a condition but, rather, a temporary scourge which we suffer as a child does a fever, knowing that health follows the long night of pain and that peace is health. Second, that we shall never surrender . . . never surrender or waver or bend to lesser voices or more comfortable impulses . . . never waver until the victory is ours, aggression is undone, and the peace is won. I thank you.'

Leigh Hunt leaned forward and watched intently as most of the senators rose to give Gladstone an ovation that roared back from the high ceiling and struck us in the gallery in waves. *Most* of the senators. I could see Hunt counting those who remained sitting, some with arms folded, many with visible frowns. The war was less than two days old, and already the opposition was building . . . first from the colonial worlds afraid for their own safety while FORCE was diverted to Hyperion, then from Gladstone's opponents – of which there were many since no one stays in power as long as she without creating cadres of enemies, and

117

finally from members of her own coalition who saw the war as a foolish undoing of unprecedented prosperity.

I watched her leaving the dais, shaking hands with the aged President and young Speaker, then taking the center aisle out – touching and talking to many, smiling the familiar smile. All Thing imagers followed her, and I could feel the pressure of the debate net swell as billions voiced their opinions on the interact levels of the megasphere.

'I need to see her now,' said Hunt. 'Are you aware that you're invited to a state dinner tonight at Treetops?'

'Yes.'

Hunt shook his head slightly, as if incapable of understanding why the CEO wanted me around. 'It will run late and will be followed by a meeting with FORCE:command. She wants you to attend both.'

'I'll be available,' I said.

Hunt paused at the door. 'Do you have something to do back at Government House until the dinner?'

I smiled at him. 'I'll work on my portrait sketches,' I said. 'Then I'll probably take a walk through Deer Park. After that . . . I don't know . . . I may take a nap.'

Hunt shook his head again and hurried off.

THIRTEEN

The first shot misses Fedmahn Kassad by less than a meter, splitting a boulder he is passing, and he is moving before the blast strikes him; rolling for cover, his camouflage polymer fully activated, impact armor tensed, assault rifle ready, visor in full targeting mode. Kassad lies there for a long moment, feeling his heart pounding and searching the hills, valley, and Tombs for the slightest hint of heat or movement. Nothing. He begins to grin behind the black mirror of his visor.

Whoever had shot at him had meant to miss, he is sure. They had used a standard pulse bolt, ignited by an 18-mm cartridge, and unless the shooter was ten or more kilometers away . . . there was no chance of a miss.

Kassad stands up to run toward the shelter of the Jade Tomb, and the second shot catches him in the chest, hurling him backward.

This time he grunts and rolls away, scuttling toward the Jade Tomb's entrance with all sensors active. The second shot had been a rifle bullet. Whoever is playing with him is using a FORCE multipurpose assault weapon similar to his own. He guesses that the assailant knows he is in body armor, knows that the rifle bullet would be ineffective at any range. But the multipurpose weapon has other settings, and if the next level of play involves a killing laser, Kassad is dead. He throws himself into the doorway of the tomb.

Still no heat or movement on his sensors except for the red-and-yellow images of his fellow pilgrims' footprints,

119

rapidly cooling, where they had entered the Sphinx several minutes before.

Kassad uses his tactical implants to switch displays, quickly running through VHF and optical comm channels. Nothing. He magnifies the valley a hundredfold, computes in wind and sand, and activates a moving-target indicator. Nothing larger than an insect is moving. He sends out radar, sonar, and lorfo pulses, daring the sniper to home in on them. Nothing. He calls up tactical displays of the first two shots; blue ballistic trails leap into existence.

The first shot had come from the Poets' City, more than four klicks to the southwest. The second shot, less than ten seconds later, came from the Crystal Monolith, almost a full klick down the valley to the northeast. Logic dictates that there have to be two snipers. Kassad is sure that there is only one. He refines the display scale. The second shot had come from high on the Monolith, at least thirty meters up on the sheer face.

Kassad swings out, raises amplification, and peers through night and the last vestiges of the sand- and snow-storm toward the huge structure. Nothing. No windows, no slits, no openings of any sort.

Only the billions of colloidal particles left in the air from the storm allow the laser to be visible for a split second. Kassad sees the green beam *after* it strikes him in the chest. He rolls back into the entrance of the Jade Tomb, wondering if the green walls will help deter a green light lance, while superconductors in his combat armor radiate heat in every direction and his tactical visor tells him what he already knows: the shot has come from high on the Crystal Monolith.

Kassad feels pain sting his chest, and he looks down in time to see a five-centimeter circle of invulnarmor drip molten fibers on to the floor. Only the last layer has saved him. As it is, his body drips with sweat inside the suit, and he can see the walls of the tomb literally glowing with the heat his

120

suit has discarded. Biomonitors clamor for attention but hold no serious news, his suit sensors report some circuit damage but describe nothing irreplacable, and his weapon is still charged, loaded, and operative.

Kassad thinks about it. All of the Tombs are priceless archaeological treasures, preserved for centuries as a gift to future generations, even if they *are* moving backward in time. It would be a crime on an interplanetary scale if Colonel Fedmahn Kassad were to put his own life above the preservation of such priceless artifacts.

'Oh fuck it,' whispers Kassad and rolls into firing position.

He sprays laser fire across the face of the Monolith until crystal slags and runs. He pumps high-explosive pulse bolts into the thing at ten-meter intervals, starting with the top levels. Thousands of shards of mirrored material fly out into the night, tumbling in slow motion toward the valley floor, leaving gaps as ugly as missing teeth in the building's face. Kassad switches back to wide-beam coherent light and sweeps the interior through the gaps, grinning behind his visor when *something* bursts into flames on several floors. Kassad fires bhees – beams of high-energy electrons – which rip through the Monolith and plow perfectly cylindrical fourteen-centimeter-wide tunnels for half a kilometer through the rock of the valley wall. He fires canister grenades, which explode into tens of thousands of needle fléchettes after passing through the crystal face of the Monolith. He triggers random pulse-laser swaths, which will blind anyone or anything looking in his direction from the structure. He fires body-heat-seeking darts into every orifice the shattered structure offers him.

Kassad rolls back into the Jade Tomb's doorway and flips up his visor. Flames from the burning tower are reflected in thousands of crystal shards scattered up and down the valley. Smoke rises into a night suddenly without wind. Vermilion dunes glow from the flames. The air is suddenly filled with the sound of wind chimes as more pieces of crystal break and fall away, some dangling by long tethers of melted glass.

Kassad ejects drained power clips and ammo bands, replaces them from his belt, and rolls on his back, breathing in the cooler air that comes through the open doorway. He is under no illusion that he has killed the sniper.

'Moneta,' whispers Fedmahn Kassad. He closes his eyes a second before going on.

Moneta had first come to Kassad at Agincourt on a late-October morning in AD 1415. The fields had been strewn with French and English dead, the forest alive with the menace of a single enemy, but that enemy would have been the victor if not for the help of the tall woman with short hair, and eyes he would never forget. After their shared victory, still dappled with the blood of their vanquished knight, Kassad and the woman made love in the forest.

The Olympus Command School Historical Tactical Network was a stimsim experience closer to reality than anything civilians would ever experience, but the phantom lover named Moneta was not an artifact of the stimsim. Over the years, when Kassad was a cadet at FORCE Olympus Command School and later, in the fatigue-drugged post-cathartic dreams that inevitably followed actual combat, she had come to him.

Fedmahn Kassad and the shadow named Moneta had made love in the quiet corners of battlefields ranging from Antietam to Qom-Riyadh. Unknown to anyone, unseen by other stimsim cadets, Moneta had come to him in tropical nights on watch and during frozen days while under siege on the Russian steppes. They had whispered their passion in Kassad's dreams after nights of real victory on the island battlefields of Maui-Covenant and during the agony of physical reconstruction after his near-death on South Bressia. And always Moneta had been his single love – an overpowering passion mixed with the scent of blood and gunpowder, the taste of napalm and soft lips and ionized flesh.

Then came Hyperion.

Colonel Fedmahn Kassad's hospital ship was attacked by Ouster torchships while returning from the Bressia system. Only Kassad had survived, stealing an Ouster shuttle and crash-landing it on Hyperion. On the continent of Equus. In the high deserts and barren wastelands of the sequestered lands beyond the Bridle Range. In the valley of the Time Tombs. In the realm of the Shrike.

And Moneta had been waiting for him. They made love . . . and when the Ousters landed in force to reclaim their prisoner, Kassad and Moneta and the half-sensed presence of the Shrike had laid waste to Ouster ships, destroyed their landing parties, and slaughtered their troops. For a brief time, Colonel Fedmahn Kassad from the Tharsis slums, child and grandchild and great-grandchild of refugees, citizen of Mars in every sense, had known the pure ecstasy of using time as a weapon, of moving unseen amongst one's enemies, of being a god of destruction in ways not dreamt of by mortal warriors.

But then, even while making love after the carnage of battle, Moneta had changed. Had become a monster. Or the Shrike had replaced her. Kassad could not remember the details; *would* not remember them if he did not have to in order to survive.

But he knew that he had returned to find the Shrike and to kill it. To find Moneta and to kill her. To kill her? He did not know. Colonel Fedmahn Kassad knew only that all the great passions of a passionate life had led him to this place and to this moment, and if death awaited him here, then so be it. And if love and glory and a victory that would make Valhalla quake awaited, then so be it.

Kassad slaps down his visor, rises to his feet, and rushes from the Jade Tomb, screaming as he goes. His weapon launches smoke grenades and chaff toward the Monolith, but these offer little cover for the distance he must cross. Someone is still alive and firing from the tower; bullets and pulse charges explode along his path as he dodges and dives from dune to dune, from one heap of rubble to the next.

Fléchettes strike his helmet and legs. His visor cracks, and warning telltales blink. Kassad blinks away the tactical displays, leaving only the night-vision aids. High-velocity solid slugs strike his shoulder and knee. Kassad goes down, is driven down. The impact armor goes rigid, relaxes, and he is up and running again, feeling the deep bruises already forming. His chameleon polymer works desperately to mirror the no-man's-land he is crossing: night, flame, sand, melted crystal, and burning stone.

Fifty meters from the Monolith, and ribbons of light lance to his left and right, turning sand to glass with a touch, reaching for him with a speed nothing and no one can dodge. Killing lasers quit playing with him and lance home, stabbing at his helmet, heart, and groin with the heat of stars. His combat armor goes mirror bright, shifting frequencies in microseconds to match the changing colors of attack. A nimbus of superheated air surrounds him. Microcircuits shriek to overload and beyond as they release the heat and work to build a micrometer-thin field of force to keep it away from flesh and bone.

Kassad struggles the final twenty meters, using power assist to leap barriers of slagged crystal. Explosions erupt on all sides, knocking him down and then lifting him again. The suit is absolutely rigid; he is a doll thrown between flaming hands.

The bombardment stops. Kassad gets to his knees and then to his feet. He looks up at the face of the Crystal Monolith and sees the flames and fissures and little else. His visor is cracked and dead. Kassad lifts it, breathes in smoke and ionized air, and enters the tomb.

His implants tell him that the other pilgrims are paging him on all the comm channels. He shuts them off. Kassad removes his helmet and walks into darkness.

It is a single room, large and square and dark. A shaft has opened in the center and he looks up a hundred meters to a shattered skylight. A figure is waiting on the tenth level, sixty meters above, silhouetted by flames.

Kassad drapes his weapon over one shoulder, tucks his helmet under his arm, finds the great spiral staircase in the center of the shaft, and begins to climb.

FOURTEEN

'Did you have your nap?' Leigh Hunt asked as we stepped on to the farcaster reception area of Treetops.

'Yes.'

'Pleasant dreams, I hope?' said Hunt, making no effort to hide either his sarcasm or his opinion of those who slept while the movers and shakers of government toiled.

'Not especially,' I said and looked around as we ascended the wide staircase toward the dining levels.

In a Web where every town in every province of every country on every continent seemed to brag of a four-star restaurant, where true gourmets numbered in the tens of millions and palates had been educated by exotic fare from two hundred worlds, even in a Web so jaded with culinary triumphs and restaurantic success, Treetops stood alone.

Set atop one of a dozen highest trees on a world of forest giants, Treetops occupied several acres of upper branches half a mile above the ground. The staircase Hunt and I ascended, four meters wide here, was lost amid the immensity of limbs the size of avenues, leaves the size of sails, and a main trunk – illuminated by spotlights and just glimpsed through gaps in the foliage – more sheer and massive than most mountain faces. Treetops held a score of dining platforms in its upper bowers, ascending in order of rank and privilege and wealth and power. Especially power. In a society where billionaires were almost commonplace, where a lunch at Treetops could cost a thousand marks and be within the reach of millions, the final arbiter of position and privilege was power – a currency that never went out of style.

The evening's gathering was to be on the uppermost deck, a wide, curving platform of weirwood (since muirwood cannot be stepped upon), with views of a fading lemon sky, an infinity of lesser treetops stretching off to a distant horizon, and the soft orange lights of Templar treehomes and houses of worship glowing through far-off green and umber and amber walls of softly stirring foliage. There were about sixty people in the dinner party; I recognized Senator Kolchev, white hair shining under the Japanese lanterns, as well as Councilor Albedo, General Morpurgo, Admiral Singh, President Pro Tem Denzel-Hiat-Amin, All Thing Speaker Gibbons, another dozen senators from such powerful Web worlds as Sol Draconi Septem, Deneb Drei, Nordholm, Fuji, both the Renaissances, Metaxas, Maui-Covenant, Hebron, New Earth, and Ixion, as well as a bevy of lesser politicians. Spenser Reynolds, the action artist, was there, resplendent in a maroon velvet formal tunic, but I saw no other artists. I did see Tyrena Wingreen-Feif across the crowded deck; the publisher-turned-philanthropist still stood out in a crowd in her gown made of thousands of silk-thin leather petals, her blue-black hair rising high in a sculpted wave, but the gown was a Tedekai original, the makeup was dramatic but noninteractive, and her appearance was far more subdued than it would have been a mere five or six decades earlier. I moved in her direction across the crowded floor as guests milled about on the penultimate deck, making raids on the numerous bars and waiting for the call to dine.

'Joseph, *dear*,' cried Wingreen-Feif as I closed the last few yards, 'how in the *world* did you get invited to such a dreary function?'

I smiled and offered her a glass of champagne. The dowager empress of literary fashion knew me only because of her week-long visit to the Esperance arts festival the previous year and my friendship with such Web-class names as Salmud Brevy III, Millon De Havre, and Rithmet Corber. Tyrena was a dinosaur who refused to become extinct – her wrists, palms, and neck would have glowed blue from repeated Poulsens if it had not been for makeup, and she spent decades on short-hop interstellar cruises or incredibly expensive cryogenic naps at spas too exclusive to have names; the upshot was that Tyrena Wingreen-Feif had held the social scene in an iron grip for more than three centuries and showed no signs of relinquishing it. With every twenty-year nap, her fortune expanded and her legend grew.

'Do you still live on that *dreary* little planet I visited last year?' she asked.

'Esperance,' I said, knowing that she knew precisely where each important artist on that unimportant world resided. 'No, I appear to have moved my residence to TC² for the present.'

M Wingreen-Feif made a face. I was vaguely aware that there was a group of eight to ten hangers-on watching intently, wondering who this brash young man was who had moved into *her* inner orbit. 'How dreadful for you,' said Tyrena, 'to have to abide on a world of business people and government bureaucrats. I hope they allow you to escape soon!'

I raised my glass in a toast to her. 'I wanted to ask you,' I said, 'weren't you Martin Silenus's editor?'

The dowager empress lowered her glass and fixed me with a cold stare. For a second I imagined Meina Gladstone and this woman locked in a combat of wills; I shuddered and waited for her answer. 'My darling boy,' she said, 'that is such *ancient* history. Why would you bother your pretty young head about such prehistoric trivia?'

'I'm interested in Silenus,' I said. 'In his poetry. I was just curious if you were still in touch with him.'

'Joseph, Joseph, Joseph,' tutted M Wingreen-Feif, 'no one has heard from poor Martin in *decades*. Why, the poor man would be *ancient*!'

I didn't point out to Tyrena that when she was Silenus's

editor, the poet was much younger than she.

'It is odd that you mention him,' she continued. 'My old firm, Transline, said recently that they were considering releasing some of Martin's work. I don't know if they ever contacted his estate.'

'His *Dying Earth* books?' I said, thinking of the Old Earth nostalgia volumes which had sold so well so long ago.

'No, oddly enough. I believe they were thinking of printing his *Cantos*,' said Tyrena. She laughed and held out a cannabis stick ensconced in a long, ebony cigarette holder. One of her retinue hurried to light it. 'Such an *odd* choice,' she said, 'considering that no one ever read the *Cantos* when poor Martin was alive. Well, nothing helps an artist's career more than a little death and obscurity, I always say.' She laughed – sharp little sounds like metal chipping rock. Half a dozen of her circle laughed along with her.

'You'd better make sure that Silenus is dead,' I said. 'The *Cantos* would make better reading if they were complete.'

Tyrena Wingreen-Feif looked at me strangely, the chimes for dinner sounded through shifting leaves, Spenser Reynolds offered the *grande dame* his arm as people began climbing the last staircase toward the stars, and I finished my drink, left the empty glass on a railing, and went up to join the herd.

The CEO and her entourage arrived shortly after we were seated, and Gladstone gave a brief talk, probably her twentieth of the day, excluding her morning speech to the Senate and Web. The original reason for tonight's dinner had been the recognition of a fund-raising effort for the Armaghast Relief Fund, but Gladstone's talk soon turned to the war and the necessity of prosecuting it vigorously and efficiently while leaders from all parts of the Web promoted unity.

I gazed out over the railing while she spoke. The lemon sky had dissolved to a muted saffron and then quickly faded to a tropical dusk so rich that it seemed as if a thick, blue curtain had been drawn across the sky. God's Grove had six small moons, five of them visible from this latitude, and four were racing across the sky as I watched the stars emerge. The air was oxygen rich here, almost intoxicating, and carried a heavy fragrance of moistened vegetation which reminded me of the morning visit to Hyperion. But no EMVs or skimmers or flying machines of any sort were allowed on God's Grove – petrochemical emissions or fusion-cell wakes had never polluted these skies – and the absence of cities, highways, and electrical lighting made the stars seem bright enough to compete with the Japanese lanterns and glow-globes hanging from branches and stanchions.

The breeze had come up again after sunset, and now the entire tree swayed slightly, the broad platform moving as softly as a ship on a gentle sea, weirwood and muirwood stanchions and supports creaking softly with the gentle swells. I could see lights shining up through distant treetops and knew that many of them came from 'rooms' – a few of thousands leased by the Templars – which one could add to one's multiworld farcaster-connected residence if one had the million-mark beginning price for such an extravagance.

The Templars did not sully themselves with the day-to-day operations of Treetops or the leasing agencies, merely setting strict, inviolable ecological conditions to any such endeavor, but they benefited from the hundreds of millions of marks brought in by such enterprises. I thought of their interstellar cruise ship, the *Yggdrasill*, a kilometer-long Tree from the planet's most sacred forest, driven by Hawking drive singularity generators and protected by the most complex force shields and Erg force fields that could be carried. Somehow, inexplicably, the Templars had agreed to send the *Yggdrasill* on an evacuation mission that was a mere cover for the FORCE invasion task force.

And as things tend to happen when priceless objects are set in harm's way, the *Yggdrasill* was destroyed while in

130

orbit around Hyperion, whether by Ouster attack or some other force not yet determined. How had the Templars reacted? What conceivable goal could have made them risk one of the four Treeships in existence? And why had their Treeship captain – Het Masteen – been chosen as one of the seven Shrike Pilgrims and then proceeded to disappear before the windwagon reached the Bridle Range on the shores of the Sea of Grass?

There were too damned many questions, and the war was only a few days old.

Meina Gladstone had finished her remarks and urged us all to enjoy the fine dinner. I applauded politely and waved over a steward to have my wineglass filled. The first course was a classic salad à la the empire period, and I applied myself to it with enthusiasm. I realized that I'd eaten nothing since breakfast that day. Spearing a sprig of watercress, I remembered Governor-General Theo Lane eating bacon and eggs and kippers as the rain fell softly from Hyperion's lapis lazuli sky. *Had that been a dream?*

'What do you think of the war, M Severn?' asked Reynolds, the action artist. He was several seats down and across the broad table from me, but his voice carried very well. I could see Tyrena raise an eyebrow toward me from where she sat, three seats to my right.

'What can one think of war?' I said, tasting the wine again. It was quite good, though nothing in the Web could match my memories of French Bordeaux. 'War does not call for judgement,' I said, 'merely survival.'

'On the contrary,' said Reynolds, 'like so many other things humankind has redefined since the Hegira, warfare is on the threshold of becoming an art form.'

'An art form,' sighed a woman with short-cropped chestnut hair. The datasphere told me that she was M Sudette Chier, wife of Senator Gabriel Fyodor Kolchev and a powerful political force in her own right. M Chier wore a blue and gold lamé gown and an expression of rapt interest. 'War

131

as an art form, M Reynolds! What a fascinating concept!'

Spenser Reynolds was a bit shorter than Web average, but far handsomer. His hair was curled but cropped short, his skin appeared bronzed by a benevolent sun and slightly gilded with subtle body paint, his clothes and ARNistry were expensively flamboyant without being outré, and his demeanor proclaimed a relaxed confidence that all men dreamed of and precious few obtained. His wit was obvious, his attention to others sincere, and his sense of humor legendary.

I found myself disliking the son of a bitch at once.

'*Everything* is an art form, M Chier, M Severn.' Reynolds smiled. 'Or must become one. We are beyond the point where warfare can be merely the churlish imposition of policy by other means.'

'Diplomacy,' said General Morpurgo, on Reynolds' left.

'I beg your pardon, General?'

'Diplomacy,' he said. 'And it's "extension of," not "imposition of." '

Spenser Reynolds bowed and made a small roll of his hand. Sudette Chier and Tyrena laughed softly. The image of Councilor Albedo leaned forward from my left and said, 'Von Clausewitz, I believe.'

I glanced toward the Councilor. A portable projection unit not much larger than the radiant gossamers flitting through the branches hovered two meters above and behind him. The illusion was not as perfect as in Government House, but it was far better than any private holo I had ever seen.

General Morpurgo nodded toward the Core representative.

'Whatever,' said Chier. 'It is the *idea* of warfare as art which is so brilliant.'

I finished the salad, and a human waiter whisked the bowl away, replacing it with a dark gray soup I did not recognize. It was smoky, slightly redolent of cinnamon and the sea, and delicious.

'Warfare is a perfect medium for an artist,' began Reynolds, holding his salad utensil aloft like a baton. 'And not merely for those . . . craftsmen who have studied the so-called science of war, either.' He smiled toward Morpurgo and another FORCE officer to the General's right, dismissing both of them from consideration. 'Only someone who is willing to look beyond the bureaucratic limits of tactics and strategies and the obsolescent will to "win" can truly wield an artist's touch with a medium so difficult as warfare in the modern age.'

'The *obsolescent* will to win?' said the FORCE officer. The datasphere whispered that he was Commander William Ajunta Lee, a naval hero of the Maui-Covenant conflict. He looked young – middle fifties perhaps – and his rank suggested that his youth was due to years of traveling between the stars rather than Poulsen.

'Of course obsolescent,' laughed Reynolds. 'Do you think a sculptor wishes to *defeat* the clay? Does a painter attack the canvas? For that matter, does an eagle or a Thomas hawk assault the sky?'

'Eagles are extinct,' grumbled Morpurgo. 'Perhaps they *should* have attacked the sky. It betrayed them.'

Reynolds turned back to me. Waiters removed his abandoned salad and brought the soup course I was finishing. 'M Severn, you are an artist . . . an illustrator at least,' he said. 'Help me explain to these people what I mean.'

'I don't know what you mean.' While I waited for the next course, I tapped my wineglass. It was filled immediately. From the head of the table, thirty feet away, I could hear Gladstone, Hunt, and several of the relief fund chairmen laughing.

Spenser Reynolds did not look surprised at my ignorance. 'For our race to achieve the true satori, for us to move to that next level of consciousness and evolution that so many of our philosophies proclaim, *all* facets of human endeavor must become conscious strivings for art.'

General Morpurgo took a long drink and grunted. 'Including such bodily functions as eating, reproducing, and eliminating waste, I suppose.'

'Most *especially* such functions!' exclaimed Reynolds. He opened his hands, offering the long table and its many delights. 'What you see here is the animal requirement of turning dead organic compounds to energy, the base act of devouring other life, but Treetops has turned it into an *art*! Reproduction has long since replaced its crude animal origins with the essence of dance for civilized human beings. Elimination must become pure poetry!'

'I'll remember that the next time I go in to take a shit,' said Morpurgo.

Tyrena Wingreen-Feif laughed and turned to the man in red and black to her right. 'Monsignor, your church . . . Catholic, early Christian isn't it? . . . don't you have some delightful old doctrine about mankind achieving a more exalted evolutionary status?'

We all turned to look at the small, quiet man in the black robe and strange little cap. Monsignor Edouard, a representative of the almost-forgotten early Christian sect now limited to the world of Pacem and a few colony planets, was on the guest list because of his involvement with the Armaghast relief project, and until now he had been quietly applying himself to his soup. He looked up with a slightly surprised look on a face lined with decades of exposure to weather and worry. 'Why yes,' he said, 'the teachings of St Teilhard discuss an evolution toward the Omega Point.'

'And is the Omega Point similar to our Zen Gnostic idea of practical satori?' asked Sudette Chier.

Monsignor Edouard looked wistfully at his soup, as if it were more important than the conversation at that moment. 'Not really too similar,' he said. 'St Teilhard felt that all of life, every level of organic consciousness was part of a planned evolution toward ultimate mergence with the Godhead.' He frowned slightly. 'The Teilhard position has been modified much over the past eight centuries, but the common thread has been that we consider Jesus Christ to have been an incarnate example of what that ultimate consciousness might be like on the human plane.'

I cleared my throat. 'Didn't the Jesuit Paul Duré write extensively on the Teilhard hypothesis?'

Monsignor Edouard leaned forward to see around Tyrena and looked directly at me. There was surprise on that interesting face. 'Why yes,' he said, 'but I am amazed that you're familiar with the work of Father Duré.'

I returned the gaze of the man who had been Duré's friend even while exiling the Jesuit to Hyperion for apostasy. I thought of another refugee from the New Vatican, young Lenar Hoyt, lying dead in a Time Tomb while the cruciform parasites carrying the mutated DNA of both Duré and himself carried out their grim purpose of resurrection. How did the abomination of the cruciform fit into Teilhard and Duré's view of inevitable, benevolent evolution toward the Godhead?

Spenser Reynolds obviously thought that the conversation had been out of his arena for too long. 'The point *is*,' he said, his deep voice drowning out other conversation halfway down the table, 'that warfare, like religion or any other human endeavor that taps and organizes human energies on such a scale, must abandon its infantile preoccupation with *Ding an sich* literalism – usually expressed through a slavish fascination with "goals" – and revel in the artistic dimension of its own oeuvre. Now my own most recent project—'

'And what is your cult's goal, Monsignor Edouard?' Tyrena Wingreen-Feif asked, stealing the conversational ball away from Reynolds without raising her voice or shifting her gaze from the cleric.

'To help mankind to know and serve God,' he said and finished his soup with an impressive slurp. The archaic little priest looked down the table toward the projection of Councilor Albedo. 'I've heard rumors, Councilor, that the

TechnoCore is pursuing an oddly similar goal. Is it true that you are attempting to build your own God?'

Albedo's smile was perfectly calculated to be friendly with no sign of condescension. 'It is no secret that elements of the Core have been working for centuries to create at least a theoretical model of a so-called artificial intelligence far beyond our own poor intellects.' He made a deprecating gesture. 'It is hardly an attempt to create God, Monsignor. More in the line of a research project exploring the possibilities your St Teilhard and Father Duré pioneered.'

'But you believe that it's possible to orchestrate your own evolution to such a higher consciousness?' asked Commander Lee, the naval hero, who had been listening attentively. 'Design an ultimate intelligence the way we once designed your crude ancestors out of silicon and microchips?'

Albedo laughed. 'Nothing so simple or grandiose, I'm afraid. And when you say "you," Commander, please remember that I am but one personality in an assemblage of intelligences no less diverse than the human beings on this planet . . . indeed, in the Web itself. The Core is no monolith. There are as many camps of philosophies, beliefs, hypotheses – *religions*, if you will – as there would be in any diverse community.' He folded his hands as if enjoying an inside joke. 'Although I prefer to think of the quest for an Ultimate Intelligence as a hobby more than a religion. Rather like building ships in a bottle, Commander, or arguing over how many angels would fit on the head of a pin, Monsignor.'

The group laughed politely, except for Reynolds who was frowning unintentionally as he no doubt pondered how to regain control of the conversation.

'And what about the rumor that the Core has built a perfect replica of Old Earth in the quest for an Ultimate Intelligence?' I asked, amazing myself with the question.

Albedo's smile did not falter, the friendly gaze did not

quiver, but there was a nanosecond of *something* conveyed through the projection. What? Shock? Fury? Amusement? I had no idea. He could have communicated with me privately during that eternal second, transmitting immense quantities of data via my own Core umbilical or along the unseen corridors we have reserved for ourselves in the labyrinthine datasphere which humankind thought so simply contrived. Or he could have killed me, pulling rank with whatever gods of the Core controlled the environment for a consciousness like mine – it would have been as simple as the director of an institute calling down to order the technicians to permanently anesthetize an obnoxious laboratory mouse.

Conversation had halted up and down the table. Even Meina Gladstone and her cluster of ultra-VIPs glanced down our way.

Councilor Albedo smiled more broadly. 'What a delightfully odd rumor! Tell me, M Severn, how does anyone . . . especially an organism such as the Core, which your own commentators have called "a disembodied bunch of brains, runaway programs that have escaped their circuits and spend most of their time pulling intellectual lint out of their nonexistent navels" . . . how does anyone build "a perfect replica of Old Earth"?'

I looked at the projection, *through* the projection, realizing for the first time that Albedo's dishes and dinner were also projected; he had been eating while we spoke.

'And,' he continued, obviously deeply amused, 'has it occurred to the promulgators of this rumor that "a perfect replica of Old Earth" would *be* Old Earth to all intents and purposes? What possible good would such an effort do in exploring the theoretical possibilities of an enhanced artificial intelligence matrix?'

When I did not answer, an uncomfortable silence settled over the entire midsection of the table.

Monsignor Edouard cleared his throat. 'It would seem,'

he said, 'that any . . . ah . . . society that could produce an exact replica of any world – but especially a world destroyed these four centuries – would have no need to seek God; it would *be* God.'

'Precisely!' laughed Councilor Albedo. 'It's an insane rumor, but delightful . . . absolutely delightful!'

Relieved laughter filled the hole of silence. Spenser Reynolds began telling about his next project – an attempt to have suicides coordinate their leaps from bridges on a score of worlds while the All Thing watched – and Tyrena Wingreen-Feif stole all attention by putting her arm around Monsignor Edouard and inviting him to her after-dinner nude swimming party at her floating estate on Mare Infinitus.

I saw Councilor Albedo staring at me, turned in time to see an inquisitive glance from Leigh Hunt and the CEO, and swiveled to watch the waiters bring up the entrées on silver platters.

The dinner was excellent.

FIFTEEN

I did not go to Tyrena's nude swimming party. Nor did Spenser Reynolds, whom I last saw speaking earnestly with Sudette Chier. I do not know whether Monsignor Edouard gave in to Tyrena's enticements.

Dinner was not quite over, relief fund chairpeople were giving short speeches, and many of the more important senators had already begun to fidget when Leigh Hunt whispered to me that the CEO's party was ready to leave and my presence was requested.

It was almost 2300 hours Web standard time, and I assumed the group would be returning to Government House, but when I stepped through the one-time portal – I was the last in the party to do so except for the Praetorian bodyguards bringing up the rear of the group – I was shocked to be looking down a stone-walled corridor relieved by long windows showing a Martian sunrise.

Technically, Mars is not in the Web; the oldest extra-terrestrial colony of humankind is made deliberately difficult to reach. Zen Gnostic pilgrims traveling to the Master's Rock in Hellas Basin have to 'cast to the Home System Station and take shuttles from Ganymede or Europa to Mars. It is an inconvenience of only a few hours, but to a society where everything is literally ten steps away, it makes for a sense of sacrifice and adventure. Other than for historians and experts in brandy cactus agriculture, there are few professional reasons to be drawn to Mars. With the gradual decline of Zen Gnosticism during the past century, even the pilgrim traffic there has grown lighter. No one cares for Mars.

Except for FORCE. Although the FORCE administrative offices are on TC² and the bases are spread through the Web and Protectorate, Mars remains the true home of the military organization, with the Olympus Command School as the heart.

There was a small group of military VIPs waiting to greet the small group of political VIPs, and while the clusters swirled like colliding galaxies, I walked over to a window and stared.

The corridor was part of a complex carved into the upper lip of Mons Olympus, and from where we stood, some ten miles high, it felt as if one could take in half the planet with a single glance. From this point the world *was* the ancient shield volcano, and the trick of distance reduced access roads, the old city along the cliff walls, and the Tharsis Plateau slums and forests to mere squiggles in a red landscape which looked unchanged from the time the first human set foot on that world, proclaimed it for a nation called Japan, and snapped a photograph.

I was watching a small sun rise, thinking *That is* the *sun*, enjoying the incredible play of light on the clouds creeping out of darkness up the side of the interminable mountainside, when Leigh Hunt stepped closer. 'The CEO will see you after the conference.' He handed me two sketchbooks which one of the aides had brought from Government House. 'You realize that everything you hear and see in this conference is highly classified?'

I did not treat the statement as a question.

Wide bronze doors opened in the stone walls, and guidelights switched on, showing the carpeted ramp and staircase leading to the War Room table in the center of a wide, black place which might have been a massive auditorium sunk in a darkness absolute except for the single, small island of illumination. Aides hurried to show the way, pull out chairs, and blend back into the shadows. With reluctance, I turned my back on the sunrise and followed our party into the pit.

General Morpurgo and a troika of other FORCE leaders handled this briefing personally. The graphics were light-years away from the crude callups and holos of the Government House briefing; we *were* in a vast space, large enough to hold all eight thousand cadets and staff when required, but now most of the blackness above us was filled with omega-quality holos and diagrams the size of freeball fields. It was frightening in a way.

So was the content of the briefing.

'We're losing this struggle in Hyperion System,' Morpurgo concluded. 'At best we will achieve a draw, with the Ouster Swarm held at bay beyond a perimeter some fifteen AU from the farcaster singularity sphere, with attrition from their small-ship raids a constant source of harassment. At worst, we will have to fall back to defensive positions while we evacuate the fleet and Hegemony citizens and allow Hyperion to fall into Ouster hands.'

'What happened to the knockout blow we were promised?' asked Senator Kolchev from his place near the head of the diamond-shaped table. 'The decisive attacks on the Swarm?'

Morpurgo cleared his throat but glanced at Admiral Nashita, who rose. The FORCE:space commander's black uniform left the illusion of only his scowling face floating in darkness. I felt a tug of *déjà vu* at the thought of that image, but I looked back at Meina Gladstone, illuminated now by the war charts and colors floating above us like a holo-spectrum version of Damocles's famous sword, and commenced drawing again. I had put away the paper sketchpad and now used my light stylus on a flexible callup sheet.

'First, our intelligence on the Swarms was necessarily limited,' began Nashita. Graphics changed above us.

'Recon probes and long-distance scouts could not tell us the full nature of every unit in the Ouster migration fleet. The result has been an obvious and serious underestimation of actual combat strength in this particular Swarm. Our efforts to penetrate Swarm defenses, using only long-range attack fighters and torchships, has not been as successful as we had hoped.

'Second, the requirement of maintaining a secure defensive perimeter of such a magnitude in the Hyperion system has made such demands on our two operative task forces that it has been impossible to devote sufficient numbers of ships to an offensive capability at this time.'

Kolchev interrupted. 'Admiral, what I hear you saying is that you have too few ships to carry out the mission of destroying or beating off this Ouster attack on Hyperion System. Is that correct?'

Nashita stared at the senator, and I was reminded of paintings I had seen of samurai in the seconds before the killing sword was removed from its scabbard. 'That is correct, Senator Kolchev.'

'Yet in our war cabinet briefings as recently as a standard week ago, you assured us that the two task forces would be enough to protect Hyperion from invasion or destruction *and* to deliver a knockout blow to this Ouster Swarm. What happened, Admiral?'

Nashita drew himself up to his full height – greater than Morpurgo's but still shorter than Web average – and turned his gaze toward Gladstone. 'M Executive, I have explained the variables that require an alteration in our battle plan. Shall I begin this briefing again?'

Meina Gladstone had her elbow on the table, and her right hand supported her head with two fingers against her cheek, two under her chin, and a thumb along her jawline in a posture of tired attention. 'Admiral,' she said softly, 'while I believe Senator Kolchev's question is totally pertinent, I think that the situation you have outlined in this briefing and earlier ones today answers it.' She turned toward Kolchev. 'Gabriel, we guessed wrong. With this commitment of FORCE, we get a stalemate at best. The Ousters are meaner, tougher, and more numerous than we thought.' She turned her tired gaze back toward Nashita. 'Admiral, how many more ships will you need?'

Nashita took a breath, obviously thrown off stride at being asked this question so early in the briefing. He glanced at Morpurgo and the other joint chiefs and then folded his hands in front of his crotch like a funeral director. 'Two hundred warships,' he said. '*At least* two hundred. It is a minimum number.'

A stir went through the room. I looked up from my drawing. Everyone was whispering or changing position except Gladstone. It took a second for me to understand.

The entire FORCE: space fleet of warships numbered fewer than six hundred. Of course each was hideously expensive – few planetary economies could afford to build more than one or two interstellar capital ships, and even a handful of torchships equipped with Hawking drives could bankrupt a colonial world. And each was hideously powerful: an attack carrier could destroy a world, a force of cruisers and spinship destroyers could destroy a sun. It was conceivable that the Hegemony ships already massed in the Hyperion system could – if vectored through the FORCE large transit farcaster matrix – destroy most of the star systems in the Web. It had taken fewer than fifty ships of the type Nashita was requesting to destroy the Glennon-Height fleet a century earlier and to quell the Mutiny forever.

But the real problem behind Nashita's request was the commitment of *two-thirds* of the Hegemony's fleet in the Hyperion system at one time. I could feel the anxiety flow through the politicians and policy makers like an electrical current.

Senator Richeau from Renaissance Vector cleared her throat. 'Admiral, we've never concentrated fleet forces like that before, have we?'

Nashita's head pivoted as smoothly as if it were on bearings. The scowl did not flicker. 'We have never committed ourselves to a fleet action of this importance to the future of the Hegemony, Senator Richeau.'

'Yes, I understand that,' said Richeau. 'But my question was meant to ask what impact this would have on Web defenses elsewhere. Isn't that a terrible gamble?'

Nashita grunted, and the graphics in the vast space behind him swirled, misted, and coalesced as a stunning view of the Milky Way galaxy as seen from far above the plane of the ecliptic; the angle changed as we seemed to rush at dizzying speed toward one spiral arm until the blue latticework of the farcaster web became visible, the Hegemony, an irregular gold nucleus with spires and pseudopods extending into the green nimbus of the Protectorate. The Web seemed both random in design and dwarfed by the sheer size of the galaxy . . . and both of these impressions were accurate reflections of reality.

Suddenly the graphics shifted, and the Web and colonial worlds became the universe except for a spattering of a few hundred stars to give it perspective.

'These represent the position of our fleet elements at this time,' said Admiral Nashita. Amidst and beyond the gold and green, several hundred specks of intense orange appeared; the heaviest concentration was around a distant Protectorate star I recognized belatedly as Hyperion's.

'And these the Ouster Swarms as of their most recent plottings.' A dozen red lines appeared, vector signs and blue-shift tails showing the direction of travel. Even at this scale, none of the Swarm vectors appeared to intersect Hegemony space except for the Swarm – a large one – that seemed to be curving into Hyperion System.

I noticed that FORCE:space deployments frequently reflected Swarm vectors, except for clusterings near bases and troublesome worlds such as Maui-Covenant, Bressia, and Qom-Riyadh.

'Admiral,' said Gladstone, preempting any description of these deployments, 'I presume you have taken into account fleet reaction time should there be a threat to some other point on our frontier.'

Nashita's scowl twitched into something that might have been a smile. There was a hint of condescension in his voice. 'Yes, CEO. If you notice the closest Swarms besides the one at Hyperion . . .' The view zoomed toward red vectors above a gold cloud, which embraced star systems I was fairly certain included Heaven's Gate, God's Grove, and Mare Infinitus. At this scale, the Ouster threat seemed very distant indeed.

'We plot the Swarm migrations according to Hawking drive wakes picked up by listening posts in and beyond the Web. In addition, our long-distance probes verify Swarm size and direction on a frequent basis.'

'How frequent, Admiral?' asked Senator Kolchev.

'At least once every few years,' snapped the Admiral. 'You must realize that travel time is many months, even at spinship velocities, and the time-debt from our viewpoint may be as much as twelve years for such a transit.'

'With gaps of years between direct observations,' persisted the senator, 'how do you know where the Swarms are at any given time?'

'Hawking drives do not lie, Senator.' Nashita's voice was absolutely flat. 'It is impossible to simulate the Hawking distortion wake. What we are looking at is the real-time location of hundreds . . . or in the case of the larger Swarms, thousands . . . of singularity drives under way. As with fatline broadcasts, there is no time-debt for transmission of the Hawking effect.'

'Yes,' said Kolchev, his voice as flat and deadly as the Admiral's, 'but what if the Swarms were traveling at less than spinship velocities?'

Nashita actually smiled. '*Below* hyperlight velocities, Senator?'

'Yes.'

I could see Morpurgo and a few of the other military men shake their heads or hide smiles. Only the young FORCE:sea commander, William Ajunta Lee, was leaning forward attentively with a serious expression.

'At sublight velocities,' deadpanned Admiral Nashita, 'our great-great-grandchildren might have to worry about warning their grandchildren of an invasion.'

Kolchev would not desist. He stood and pointed toward where the closest Swarm curved away from the Hegemony above Heaven's Gate. 'What about if this Swarm were to approach without Hawking drives?'

Nashita sighed, obviously irritated at having the substance of the meeting suborned by irrelevancies. 'Senator, I assure you that if that Swarm turned off their drives *now*, and turned toward the Web *now*, it would be' – Nashita's eyes blinked as he consulted his implants and comm links – 'two hundred and thirty standard years before they approached our frontiers. It is not a factor in this decision, Senator.'

Meina Gladstone leaned forward, and all eyes shifted toward her. I stored my previous sketch in the callup and started a new one.

'Admiral, it seems to me the real concern here is both the unprecedented nature of this concentration of forces near Hyperion and the fact that we're putting all of our eggs in one basket.'

There was a murmur of amusement around the table. Gladstone was famous for aphorisms, stories, and clichés so old and forgotten that they were brand-new. This might have been one of them.

'*Are* we putting all of our eggs in one basket?' she continued.

Nashita stepped forward and set his hands on the table, long fingers extended, pressing down with great intensity. That intensity matched the power of the small man's personality; he was one of those rare individuals who commanded others' attention and obedience without effort. 'No, CEO, we are not.' Without turning, he gestured toward the display above and behind him. 'The closest Swarms could not approach Hegemony space without a warning time of two months in Hawking drive . . . that is *three years* of our time. It would take our fleet units in Hyperion – even assuming they were widely deployed and in a combat situation – less than *five hours* to fall back and translate anywhere in the Web.'

'That does not include fleet units beyond the Web,' said Senator Richeau. 'The colonies cannot be left unprotected.'

Nashita gestured again. 'The two hundred warships we will call in to make the Hyperion campaign decisive are those already within the Web or those carrying JumpShip farcaster capabilities. None of the independent fleet units assigned to the colonies will be affected.'

Gladstone nodded. 'But what if the Hyperion portal were damaged or seized by the Ousters?'

From the shifting, nodding, and exhalations from the civilians around the table, I guessed that she had hit upon the major concern.

Nashita nodded and strode back to the small dais as if this were the question he had been anticipating and was pleased irrelevancies were at an end. 'Excellent question,' he said. 'It has been mentioned in previous briefings, but I will cover this possibility in some detail.

'First, we have redundancy in our farcaster capability, with no fewer than two JumpShips in-system at this time and plans for three more when the reinforced task force arrives. The chances of all five of these ships being destroyed are very, very small . . . almost insignificant when one considers our enhanced defensive capabilities with the reinforced task force.

'Second, chances of the Ousters seizing an intact military farcaster and using it to invade the Web are nil. Each ship . . . each *individual* . . . that transits a FORCE portal must be identified by tamperproof, coded microtransponders, which are updated daily—'

'Couldn't the Ousters break these codes . . . insert their own?' asked Senator Kolchev.

'Impossible.' Nashita was striding back and forth on the small dais, hands behind his back. 'The updating of codes is done daily via fatline one-time pads from FORCE headquarters within the Web—'

'Excuse me,' I said, amazed to hear my own voice here, 'but I made a brief visit to Hyperion System this morning and was aware of no codes.'

Heads turned. Admiral Nashita again carried out his successful impression of an owl turning its head on frictionless bearings. 'Nonetheless, M Severn,' he said, 'you and M Hunt were encoded – painlessly and unobtrusively by infrared lasers, at both ends of the farcaster transit.'

I nodded, amazed for a second that the Admiral had remembered my name until I realized that he also had implants.

'Third,' continued Nashita as if I had not spoken, 'should the impossible happen and Ouster forces overwhelm our defenses, capture our farcasters intact, circumvent the failsafe transit code systems, and activate a technology with which they are not familiar, and which we have denied them for more than four centuries . . . then all their efforts would still be for naught, because all military traffic is being routed to Hyperion via the base at Madhya.'

'Where?' came a chorus of voices.

I had heard of Madhya only through Brawne Lamia's tale of her client's death. Both she and Nashita pronounced it 'mud-ye.'

'Madhya,' repeated Admiral Nashita, smiling now in earnest. It was an oddly boyish smile. 'Do not query your comlogs, gentlemen and ladies. Madhya is a "black" system, not found in any inventories or civilian farcaster charts. We reserve it for just such purposes. With only one habitable planet, fit only for mining and our bases, Madhya is the ultimate fallback position. Should Ouster warships do the impossible and breach our defenses and portals in Hyperion, the *only* place they can go is Madhya, where significant amounts of automated firepower are directed toward anything and everything that comes through. Should the impossible be squared and their fleet survive transit to the Madhya system, outgoing farcaster connections would automatically self-destruct, and their warships would be stranded years from the Web.'

'Yes,' said Senator Richeau, 'but so would ours. Two thirds of our fleet would be left in Hyperion System.'

Nashita stood at parade rest. 'This is true,' he said, 'and certainly the joint chiefs and I have weighed the consequences of this remote . . . one would have to say statistically impossible . . . event many times. We find the risks acceptable. Should the impossible happen, we still would have more than two hundred warships in reserve to defend the Web. At worst, we would have lost the Hyperion system after dealing a terrible blow to the Ousters . . . one which would, in and of itself, almost certainly deter any future aggression.

'*But this is not the outcome we anticipate.* With two hundred warships transferred soon – within the next eight standard hours – our predictors and the AI Advisory Council predictors . . . see a 99 percent probability of total defeat of the aggressive Ouster Swarm, with inconsequential losses to our forces.'

Meina Gladstone turned toward Councilor Albedo. In the low light the projection was perfect. 'Councilor, I did not know the Advisory Group had been asked this question. Is the 99 percent probability figure reliable?'

Albedo smiled. 'Quite reliable, CEO. And the probability factor was 99.962794 percent.' The smile broadened. 'Quite reassuring enough to have one put all one's eggs into one basket for a short while.'

Gladstone did not smile. 'Admiral, how long after you get the reinforcements do you see the fighting going on?'

149

'One standard week, CEO. At the most.'

Gladstone's left eyebrow rose slightly. 'So short a time?'

'Yes, CEO.'

'General Morpurgo? Thoughts from FORCE:ground?'

'We concur, CEO. Reinforcement is necessary, and at once. Transports will carry approximately a hundred thousand Marines and ground troops for the mopping up in the remnants of the Swarm.'

'In seven standard days or less?'

'Yes, CEO.'

'Admiral Singh?'

'Absolutely necessary, CEO.'

'General Van Zeidt?'

One by one, Gladstone polled the joint chiefs and top-ranking military there, even asking the commandant of the Olympus Command School, who swelled with pride at being consulted. One by one, she received their unequivocal advice to reinforce.

'Commander Lee?'

All gazes shifted toward the young naval officer. I noticed the stiffness of posture and scowls of the senior military men and suddenly realized that Lee was there at the invitation of the CEO rather than the benevolence of his superiors. I remembered that Gladstone had been quoted as saying that young Commander Lee showed the kind of initiative and intelligence which FORCE had sometimes lacked. I suspected that the man's career was forfeit for attending this meeting.

Commander William Ajunta Lee shifted uncomfortably in his comfortable chair. 'With all due respect, CEO, I'm a mere junior naval officer and am not qualified to give an opinion on matters of such strategic importance.'

Gladstone did not smile. Her nod was almost impercept-ible. 'I appreciate that, Commander. I am sure your superiors here do also. However, in this case, I wonder if you would indulge me and comment on the issue at hand.'

Lee sat upright. For an instant his eyes held both conviction and the desperation of a small, trapped animal. 'Well then, CEO, if I must comment, I have to say that my own instincts – and they are only instincts: I am profoundly ignorant of interstellar tactics – would advise me against this reinforcement.' Lee took a breath. 'This is a purely military assessment, CEO. I know nothing of the political ramifications of defending Hyperion System.'

Gladstone leaned forward. 'Then on a purely military basis, Commander, why do you oppose the reinforcements?'

From where I sat half a table away, I could feel the impact of the FORCE chiefs' gazes like one of the one-hundred-million-joule laser blasts used to ignite deuterium-tritium spheres in one of the ancient inertial confinement fusion reactors. I was amazed that Lee did not collapse, implode, ignite, and fuse before our very eyes.

'On a military basis,' Lee said, his eyes hopeless but his voice steady, 'the two biggest sins one can commit are to divide one's forces and to . . . as you put it, CEO . . . put all of your eggs in a single basket. And in this case, the basket is not even of our own making.'

Gladstone nodded and sat back, steepling her fingers beneath her lower lip.

'*Commander*,' said General Morpurgo, and I discovered that a word could, indeed, be spat, 'now that we have the benefit of your . . . advice . . . could I ask if you have ever been involved in a space battle?'

'No, sir.'

'Have you ever been *trained* for a space battle, Commander?'

'Except for the minimal amount required in OCS, which amounts to a few history courses, no, sir, I have not.'

'Have you ever been involved in *any* strategic planning above the level of . . . how many naval surface ships did you command on Maui-Covenant, Commander?'

'One, sir.'

'One,' breathed Morpurgo. 'A large ship, Commander?'

'No, sir.'

'Were you given command of this ship, Commander. Did you earn it? Or did it fall to you through the vicissitudes of war?'

'Our captain was killed, sir. I took command by default. It was the final naval action of the Maui-Covenant campaign and—'

'That will be all, *Commander*.' Morpurgo turned his back on the war hero and addressed the CEO. 'Do you wish to poll us again, ma'am?'

Gladstone shook her head.

Senator Kolchev cleared his throat. 'Perhaps we should have a closed cabinet meeting at Government House.'

'No need,' said Meina Gladstone. 'I've decided. Admiral Singh, you are authorized to divert as many fleet units to the Hyperion system as you and the joint chiefs see fit.'

'Yes, CEO.'

'Admiral Nashita, I will expect a successful termination of hostilities within one standard week of the time you have adequate reinforcements.' She looked around the table. 'Ladies and gentlemen, I cannot stress to you enough the importance of our possession of Hyperion and the deterrent of Ouster threats once and for all.' She rose and walked to the base of the ramp leading up and out into the darkness. 'Good evening, gentlemen, ladies.'

It was almost 0400 hours Web and Tau Ceti Center time when Hunt rapped at my door. I had been fighting sleep for the three hours since we 'cast back. I had just decided that Gladstone had forgotten about me and was beginning to doze when the knock came.

'The garden,' said Leigh Hunt, 'and for God's sake tuck your shirt in.'

My boots made soft noises on the fine gravel of the path as I wandered the dark lanes. The lanterns and glow-globes barely emitted light. The stars were not visible above the courtyard because of the glare of TC²'s interminable cities, but the running lights of the orbital habitations moved across the sky like an endless ring of fireflies.

Gladstone was sitting on the iron bench near the bridge.

'M Severn,' she said, her voice low, 'thank you for joining me. I apologize for it being so late. The cabinet meeting just broke up.'

I said nothing and remained standing.

'I wanted to ask about your visit to Hyperion this morning.' She chuckled in the darkness. 'Yesterday morning. Did you have any impressions?'

I wondered what she meant. My guess was that the woman had an insatiable appetite for data, no matter how seemingly irrelevant. 'I did meet someone,' I said.

'Oh?'

'Yes, Dr Melio Arundez. He was . . . is . . .'

'. . . a friend of M Weintraub's daughter,' finished Gladstone. 'The child who is aging backward. Do you have any updates on her condition?'

'Not really,' I said. 'I had a brief nap today, but the dreams were fragmented.'

'And what did the meeting with Dr Arundez accomplish?'

I rubbed my chin with fingers suddenly gone cold. 'His research team has been waiting in the capital for months,' I said. 'They may be our only hope for understanding what's going on with the Tombs. And the Shrike . . .'

'Our predictors say that it is important that the pilgrims be left alone until their act is played out,' came Gladstone's voice in the darkness. She seemed to be looking to the side, toward the stream.

I felt sudden, inexplicable, implacable anger surge through me. 'Father Hoyt is already "played out," ' I said more sharply than I intended. 'They could have saved him if the ship had been allowed to rendezvous with the pilgrims.

153

Arundez and his people might be able to save the baby – Rachel – even though there are only a few days left.'

'Less than three days,' said Gladstone. 'Was there anything else? Any impressions of the planet or Admiral Nashita's command ship which you found . . . interesting?'

My hands clenched into fists, relaxed. 'You won't allow Arundez to fly up to the Tombs?'

'Not now, no.'

'What about the evacuation of civilians from Hyperion? At least the Hegemony citizens?'

'That is not a possibility at this time.'

I started to say something, checked myself. I stared at the sound of the water beneath the bridge.

'No other impressions, M Severn?'

'No.'

'Well, I wish you a good night and pleasant dreams. Tomorrow may be a very hectic day, but I do want to talk to you about those dreams at some point.'

'Good night,' I said and turned on my heel and walked quickly back to my wing of Government House.

In the darkness of my room, I called up a Mozart sonata and took three trisecobarbitals. Most probably they would knock me out in a drugged, dreamless sleep, where the ghost of dead Johnny Keats and his even more ghostly pilgrims could not find me. It meant disappointing Meina Gladstone, and that did not dismay me in the least.

I thought of Swift's sailor, Gulliver, and his disgust with mankind after his return from the land of the intelligent horse – the Houyhnhnms – a disgust with his own species which grew to the point that he had to sleep in the stables with the horses just to be reassured by their smell and presence.

My last thought before sleep was *To hell with Meina Gladstone, to hell with the war, and to hell with the Web.*

And to hell with dreams.

PART TWO

SIXTEEN

Brawne Lamia slept fitfully just before dawn, and her dreams were filled with images and sounds from else-where – half-heard and little-understood conversations with Meina Gladstone, a room that seemed to be floating in space, a movement of men and women along corridors where the walls whispered like a poorly tuned fatline receiver – and underlying the feverish dreams and random images was the maddening sense that Johnny – her Johnny – was so close, *so close*. Lamia cried out in her sleep, but the noise was lost in the random echoes of the Sphinx's cooling stones and shifting sands.

Lamia awoke suddenly, coming completely conscious as surely as a solid-state instrument switching on. Sol Weintraub had been supposed to be standing guard, but now he slept near the low door of the room where the group sheltered. His infant daughter, Rachel, slept between blan-kets on the floor next to him; her rump was raised, face pressed against the blanket, a slight bubble of saliva on her lips.

Lamia looked around. In the dim illumination from a low-wattage glow-globe and the faint daylight reflected down four meters of corridor, only one other of her fellow pilgrims was visible, a dark bundle on the stone floor. Mar-tin Silenus lay there snoring. Lamia felt a surge of fear, as if she had been abandoned while sleeping. Silenus, Sol, the baby . . . she realized that only the Consul was missing. Attrition had eaten at the pilgrimage party of seven adults and an infant: Het Masteen, missing on the windwagon crossing of the Sea of Grass; Lenar Hoyt killed the night before; Kassad missing later that night . . . the Consul . . . where was the Consul?

Brawne Lamia looked around again, satisfied herself that the dark room held nothing but packs, blanket bundles, the sleeping poet, scholar and child, and then she rose, found her father's automatic pistol amidst the tumble of blankets, felt in her pack for the neural stunner, and then slipped past Weintraub and the baby into the corridor beyond.

It was morning and so bright out that Lamia had to shield her eyes with her hand as she stepped from the Sphinx's stone steps on to the hard-packed trail which led away down the valley. The storm had passed. Hyperion's skies were a deep, crystalline lapis lazuli shot through with green, Hyperion's star, a brilliant white point source just rising above the eastern cliff walls. Rock shadows blended with the outflung silhouettes of the Time Tombs across the valley floor. The Jade Tomb sparkled. Lamia could see the fresh drifts and dunes deposited by the storm, white and vermilion sands blending in sensuous curves and striations around stone. There was no evidence of their campsite the night before. The Consul sat on a rock ten meters down the hill. He was gazing down the valley, and smoke spiraled upward from his pipe. Slipping the pistol in her pocket with the stunner, Lamia walked down the hill to him.

'No sign of Colonel Kassad,' said the Consul as she approached. He did not turn around.

Lamia looked down the valley to where the Crystal Monolith stood. Its once-gleaming surface was pocked and pitted, the upper twenty or thirty meters appeared to be missing, and debris still smoked at its base. The half kilometer or so between the Sphinx and the Monolith were scorched and cratered. 'It looks as if he didn't leave without a fight,' she said.

The Consul grunted. The pipe smoke made Lamia hungry.

'I searched as far as the Shrike Palace, two klicks down the valley,' said the Consul. 'The locus of the firefight seems to have been the Monolith. There's still no sign of a ground-level opening to the thing but there are enough holes farther up now so that you can see the honeycomb pattern which deep radar has always shown inside.'

'But no sign of Kassad?'

'None.'

'Blood? Scorched bones? A note saying that he'd be back after delivering his laundry?'

'Nothing.'

Brawne Lamia sighed and sat on a boulder near the Consul's rock. The sun was warm on her skin. She squinted out toward the opening to the valley. 'Well, hell,' she said, 'what do we do next?'

The Consul removed his pipe, frowned at it, and shook his head. 'I tried the comlog relay again this morning, but the ship is still penned in.' He shook ashes out. 'Tried the emergency bands too, but obviously we're not getting through. Either the ship isn't relaying, or people have orders not to respond.'

'Would you really leave?'

The Consul shrugged. He had changed from his diplomatic finery of the day before into a rough wool pullover tunic top, gray whipcord trousers, and high boots. 'Having the ship here would give us – you – the option of leaving. I wish the others would consider going. After all, Masteen's missing, Hoyt and Kassad are gone . . . I'm not sure what to do next.'

A deep voice said, 'We could try making breakfast.'

Lamia turned to watch Sol come down the path. Rachel was in the infant carrier on the scholar's chest. Sunlight glinted on the older man's balding head. 'Not a bad idea,' she said. 'Do we have enough provisions left?'

'Enough for breakfast,' said Weintraub. 'Then a few more meals of cold foodpaks from the Colonel's extra provisions bag. Then we'll be eating googlepedes and each other.'

The Consul attempted a smile, set the pipe back in his tunic pocket. 'I suggest we walk back to Chronos Keep before we reach that point. We'd used up the freeze-dried foods from the *Benares*, but there were storerooms at the Keep.'

'I'd be happy to—' began Lamia but was interrupted by a shout from inside the Sphinx.

She was the first to reach the Sphinx, and she had the automatic pistol in her hand before she went through the entrance. The corridor was dark, the sleeping room darker, and it took a second for her to realize that no one was there. Brawne Lamia crouched, swinging the pistol toward the dark curve of corridor even as Silenus's voice again shouted 'Hey! Come here!' from somewhere out of sight.

She looked over her shoulder as the Consul came through the entrance.

'Wait there!' snapped Lamia and moved quickly down the corridor, staying against the wall, pistol extended, propulsion charge primed, safety off. She paused at the open doorway to the small room where Hoyt's body lay, crouched, swung around and in with weapon tracking.

Martin Silenus looked up from where he crouched by the corpse. The fiberplastic sheet they had used to cover the priest's body lay crumpled and lifted in Silenus's hand. He stared at Lamia, looked without interest at the gun, and gazed back at the body. 'Do you believe this?' he said softly.

Lamia lowered the weapon and came closer. Behind them, the Consul peered in. Brawne could hear Sol Weintraub in the corridor; the baby was crying.

'My God,' said Brawne Lamia and crouched next to the body of Father Lenar Hoyt. The young priest's pain-ravaged features had been resculpted into the face of a man in his late sixties: high brow, long aristocratic nose, thin lips with a pleasant upturn at the corners, sharp cheekbones, sharp ears

160

under a fringe of gray hair, large eyes under lids as pale and thin as parchment.

The Consul crouched near them. 'I've seen holos. It's Father Paul Duré.'

'Look,' said Martin Silenus. He lowered the sheet further, paused, and then rolled the corpse on its side. Two small cruciforms on this man's chest pulsed pinkly, just as Hoyt's had, but his back was bare.

Sol stood by the door, hushing Rachel's cries with gentle bouncing and whispered syllables. When the infant was silent, he said, 'I thought that the Bikura took three days to . . . regenerate.'

Martin Silenus sighed. 'The Bikura have been resurrected by the cruciform parasites for more than two standard centuries. Perhaps it's easier the first time.'

'Is he . . .' began Lamia.

'Alive?' Silenus took her hand. 'Feel.'

The man's chest rose and fell ever so slightly. The skin was warm to the touch. Heat from the cruciforms under the skin was palpable. Brawne Lamia snatched her hand back.

The thing that had been the corpse of Father Lenar Hoyt six hours earlier opened its eyes.

'Father Duré?' said Sol, stepping forward.

The man's head turned. He blinked as though the dim light hurt his eyes, then made an unintelligible noise.

'Water,' said the Consul and reached into his tunic pocket for the small plastic bottle he carried. Martin Silenus held the man's head while the Consul helped him drink.

Sol came closer, went to one knee, and touched the man's forearm. Even Rachel's dark eyes seemed curious. Sol said, 'If you can't speak, blink twice for "yes," once for "no." Are you Duré?'

The man's head swiveled toward the scholar. 'Yes,' he said softly, his voice deep, tones cultured, 'I am Father Paul Duré.'

*　　*　　*

Breakfast consisted of the last of the coffee, bits of meat fried over the unfolded heating unit, a scoop of grain mixed with rehydrated milk, and the end of their last loaf of bread, torn into five chunks. Lamia thought that it was delicious.

They sat at the edge of shade under the Sphinx's outflung wing, using a low, flat-topped boulder as their table. The sun climbed toward mid-morning, and the sky remained cloudless. There was no sound except for the occasional klink of a fork or spoon and the soft tones of their conversation.

'You remember . . . before?' asked Sol. The priest wore an extra set of the Consul's shipclothes, a gray jumpsuit with the Hegemony seal on the left breast. The uniform was a bit too small.

Duré held the cup of coffee in both hands, as if he were about to lift it for consecration. He looked up, and his eyes suggested depths of intelligence and sadness in equal measure. 'Before I died?' said Duré. The patrician lips sketched a smile. 'Yes, I remember. I remember the exile, the Bikura . . .' He looked down. 'Even the tesla tree.'

'Hoyt told us about the tree,' said Brawne Lamia. The priest had nailed himself on to an active tesla tree in the flame forests, suffering *years* of agony, death, resurrection, and death again rather than give in to the easy symbiosis of life under the cruciform.

Duré shook his head. 'I thought . . . in those last seconds . . . that I had beaten it.'

'You had,' said the Consul. 'Father Hoyt and the others found you. You had driven the thing out of your body. Then the Bikura planted your cruciform on Lenar Hoyt.'

Duré nodded. 'And there is no sign of the body?'

Martin Silenus pointed toward the man's chest. 'Evidently the fucking thing can't defy laws governing conservation of mass. Hoyt's pain had been so great for so long – he wouldn't return to where the thing wanted him to go – that he never gained the weight for a . . . what the hell would you call it? A double resurrection.'

'It doesn't matter,' said Duré. His smile was sad. 'The DNA parasite in the cruciform has infinite patience. It will reconstitute one host for generations if need be. Sooner or later, both parasites will have a home.'

'Do you remember anything after the tesla tree?' asked Sol quietly.

Duré sipped the last of his coffee. 'Of death? Of heaven or hell?' The smile was genuine. 'No, gentlemen and lady, I wish I could say I did. I remember pain . . . eternities of pain . . . and then release. And then darkness. And then awakening here. How many years did you say have passed?'

'Almost twelve,' said the Consul. 'But only about half that for Father Hoyt. He spent time in transit.'

Father Duré stood, stretched, and paced back and forth. He was a tall man, thin but with a sense of strength about him, and Brawne Lamia found herself impressed by his presence, by that strange, inexplicable charisma of personality which had cursed and bestowed power upon a few individuals since time immemorial. She had to remind herself that, first, he was a priest of a cult that demanded celibacy from its clerics, and, second, an hour earlier he had been a corpse. Lamia watched the older man pace up and down, his movements as elegant and relaxed as a cat's, and she realized that both observations were true but neither could counteract the personal magnetism the priest radiated. She wondered if the men sensed it.

Duré sat on a boulder, stretched his legs straight ahead of him, and rubbed at his thighs as if trying to get rid of a cramp. 'You've told me something about who you are . . . why you are here,' he said. 'Can you tell me more?'

The pilgrims glanced at one another.

Duré nodded. 'Do you think that I'm a monster myself? Some agent of the Shrike? I wouldn't blame you if you did.'

'We don't think that,' said Brawne Lamia. 'The Shrike needs no agents to do his bidding. Besides, we know you from Father Hoyt's story about you and from your journals.'

She glanced at the others. 'We found it . . . difficult . . . to tell our stories of why we have come to Hyperion. It would be all but impossible to repeat them.'

'I made notes on my comlog,' said the Consul. 'They're very condensed, but it should make some sense out of our histories . . . and the history of the last decade of the Hegemony. Why the Web is at war with the Ousters. That sort of thing. You're welcome to access it if you wish. It shouldn't take more than an hour.'

'I would appreciate it,' said Father Duré and followed the Consul back into the Sphinx.

Brawne Lamia, Sol, and Silenus walked to the head of the valley. From the saddle between the low cliffs, they could see the dunes and barrens stretching toward the mountains of the Bridle Range, less than ten klicks to the southwest. The broken globes, soft spires, and shattered gallerias of the dead City of Poets were visible only two or three klicks to their right, along a broad ridge which the desert was quietly invading.

'I'll walk back to the Keep and find some rations,' said Lamia.

'I hate to split up the group,' said Sol. 'We could all return.'

Martin Silenus folded his arms. 'Somebody should stay here in case the Colonel returns.'

'Before anyone leaves,' said Sol, 'I think we should search the rest of the valley. The Consul didn't check far beyond the Monolith this morning.'

'I agree,' said Lamia. 'Let's get to it before it gets too late. I want to get provisions at the Keep and return before night-fall.'

They had descended to the Sphinx when Duré and the Consul emerged. The priest held the Consul's spare comlog in one hand. Lamia explained the plan for a search, and the two men agreed to join them.

Once again they walked the halls of the Sphinx, the beams

from their hand torches and pencil lasers illuminating sweating stone and bizarre angles. Emerging into noontime sunlight, they made the three-hundred-meter hike to the Jade Tomb. Lamia found herself shivering as they entered the room where the Shrike had appeared the night before. Hoyt's blood had left a rust-brown stain on the green ceramic floors. There was no sign of the transparent opening to the labyrinth below. There was no sign of the Shrike.

The Obelisk had no rooms, merely a central shaft in which a spiral ramp, too steep for human comfort, twisted upward between ebony walls. Even whispers echoed here, and the group kept talk to a minimum. There were no windows, no view, at the top of the ramp, fifty meters above the stone floor, and their torch beams illuminated only blackness as the roof curved in above them. Fixed ropes and chains left over from two centuries of tourism allowed them to descend without undue fear of a slip and fall that would end in death below. As they paused at the entrance, Martin Silenus called Kassad's name a final time, and the echoes followed them into sunlight.

They spent half an hour or more inspecting the damage near the Crystal Monolith. Puddles of sand turned to glass, some five to ten meters across, prismed the noonday light and reflected heat in their faces. The broken face of the Monolith, pocked now with holes and still-dangling strands of melted crystal, looked like the target of an act of mindless vandalism, but each knew that Kassad must have been fighting for his life. There was no door, no opening to the honeycomb maze within. Instruments told them that the interior was as empty and unconnected as it always had been. They left reluctantly, climbing the steep trails to the base of the north cliffs where the Cave Tombs lay separated by less than a hundred meters each.

'Early archaeologists thought that these were the oldest of the Tombs because of their crudeness,' said Sol as they entered the first cave, sent flashlight beams playing across stone carved in a thousand indecipherable patterns. None of the caves was deeper than thirty or forty meters. Each ended in a stone wall that no amount of probing or radar imaging had ever discovered an extension to.

Upon exiting the third Cave Tomb, the group sat in what little shade they could find and shared water and protein biscuits from Kassad's extra field rations. The wind had risen, and now it sighed and whispered through fluted rock high above them.

'We're not going to find him,' said Martin Silenus. 'The fucking Shrike took him.'

Sol was feeding the baby with one of the last nursing paks. The top of her head had been turned pink by the sun despite Sol's every effort to shield her as they walked outside. 'He could be in one of the Tombs we were in,' he said, 'if there are sections out of time-phase with us. That's Arundez's theory. He sees the Tombs as four-dimensional constructs with intricate folds through space-time.'

'Great,' said Lamia. 'So even if Fedmahn Kassad is there, we won't see him.'

'Well,' said the Consul, getting to his feet with a tired sigh, 'let's at least go through the motions. One tomb left.'

The Shrike Palace was a kilometer farther down the valley, lower than the others and hidden by a bend in the cliff walls. The structure was not large, smaller than the Jade Tomb, but its intricate construction – flanges, spires, buttresses, and support columns arching and arcing in controlled chaos – made it seem larger than it was.

The interior of the Shrike Palace was one echoing chamber with an irregular floor made up of thousands of curving, jointed segments which reminded Lamia of the ribs and vertebrae of some fossilized creature. Fifteen meters overhead, the dome was crisscrossed by dozens of the chrome 'blades' which continued through walls and each other to emerge as steel-tipped thorns above the structure. The material of the dome itself was slightly opaque, giving a rich, milky hue to the vaulted space.

Lamia, Silenus, the Consul, Weintraub, and Duré all began to shout for Kassad, their voices echoing and resonating to no avail.

'No sign of Kassad or Het Masteen,' said the Consul as they emerged. 'Perhaps this will be the pattern . . . each of us disappearing until only one remains.'

'And does that final one get his or her wish as the Shrike Cult legends foretell?' asked Brawne Lamia. She sat on the rocky hearth to the Shrike Palace, her short legs dangling in air.

Paul Duré raised his face to the sky. 'I can't believe that it was Father Hoyt's wish that he would die so that I could live again.'

Martin Silenus squinted up at the priest. 'So what would your wish be, Padre?'

Duré did not hesitate. 'I would wish . . . pray . . . that God will lift the scourge of these twin obscenities – the war and the Shrike – from mankind once and for all.'

There was a silence in which the early afternoon wind inserted its distant sighs and moans. 'In the meantime,' said Brawne Lamia, 'we've got to get some food or learn how to subsist on air.'

Duré nodded. 'Why did you bring so little with you?'

Martin Silenus laughed and said loudly:

> *Ne cared he for wine, or half-and-half,*
> *Ne cared he for fish or flesh or fowl,*
> *And sauces held he worthless as the chaff;*
> *He 'sdained the swine-herd at the wassail-bowl,*
> *Ne with lewd ribbalds sat he cheek by jowl,*
> *Ne with sly Lemans in the scorner's chair,*
> *But after water-brooks this Pilgrim's soul*
> *Panted, and all his food was woodland air*
> *Though he would oft-times feast on gillyflowers rare.*

Duré smiled, obviously still puzzled.

'We all expected to triumph or die the first night,' said the Consul. 'We hadn't anticipated a long stay here.'

Brawne Lamia stood and brushed off her trousers. 'I'm going,' she said. 'I should be able to carry back four or five days' rations if they're field foodpaks or the bulk-stored items we saw.'

'I'll go too,' said Martin Silenus.

There was a silence. During the week of their pilgrimage, the poet and Lamia had almost come to blows half a dozen times. Once she had threatened to kill the man. She looked at him for a long moment. 'All right,' she said at last. 'Let's stop by the Sphinx to get our packs and water bottles.'

The group moved up the valley as the shadows began to grow from the western walls.

SEVENTEEN

Twelve hours earlier, Colonel Fedmahn Kassad stepped off the spiral staircase on to the highest remaining level of the Crystal Monolith. Flames rose on all sides. Through gaps he had inflicted on the crystal surface of the structure, Kassad could see darkness. The storm blew vermilion dust through the apertures until it filled the air like powdered blood. Kassad pulled his helmet on.

Ten paces in front of him, Moneta awaited.

She was nude under the energy skinsuit, and the effect was of quicksilver poured directly on flesh. Kassad could see the flames reflected in the curves of breast and thigh, the bend of light into the hollow of throat and navel. Her neck was long, her face chrome-carved in perfect smoothness. Her eyes held twin reflections of the tall shadow that was Fedmahn Kassad.

Kassad raised the assault rifle and clicked the selector manually to full-spectrum fire. Inside his activated impact armor, his body clenched in anticipation of attack.

Moneta moved her hand, and the skinsuit faded from the crown of her head to her neck. She was vulnerable now. Kassad felt that he knew every facet of that face, every pore and follicle. Her brown hair was cut short, falling softly to the left. The eyes were the same, large, curious, startling in their green depths. The small mouth with the full underlip still hesitated on the edge of a smile. He noted the slightly inquisitive arch of eyebrows, the small ears he had kissed and whispered in so many times. The soft throat where he had lain his cheek to listen to her pulse.

Kassad raised the rifle and aimed it at her.

'Who are you?' she asked. Her voice was as soft and sensual as he remembered, the slight accent as elusive.

His finger on the trigger, Kassad paused. They had made love scores of times, known each other for years in his dreams and their lovers' landscape of the military simulations. But if she were truly moving backward in time . . .

'I know,' she said, her voice calm, apparently unaware of the pressure he had already begun to exert on the trigger, 'you are the one whom the Lord of Pain has promised.'

Kassad was gasping for air. When he spoke, his voice was raw and very strained. 'You don't remember me?'

'No.' She cocked her head to look at him quizzically. 'But the Lord of Pain has promised a warrior. We were destined to meet.'

'We met long ago,' managed Kassad. The rifle would automatically aim for the face, shifting wavelengths and frequencies every microsecond until the skinsuit defenses were defeated. Along with the hellwhip and laser beams, fléchettes and pulse bolts would be fired an instant later.

'I have no memory of long ago,' she said. 'We move in opposite directions along the general flow of time. What name do you know me by in my future, your past?'

'Moneta,' gasped Kassad, willing his straining hand and finger to fire.

She smiled, nodded. 'Moneta. The child of Memory. There is a crude irony there.'

Kassad remembered her betrayal, the *changing* as they made love that last time in the sands above the dead City of Poets. She had either become the Shrike or allowed the Shrike to take her place. It had turned an act of love into an obscenity.

Colonel Kassad pulled the trigger.

Moneta blinked. 'It will not work here. Not within the Crystal Monolith. Why do you wish to kill me?'

Kassad growled, threw the useless weapon across the

landing, directed power to his gauntlets, and charged.

Moneta made no move to escape. She watched him charge the ten paces; his head was down, his impact armor moaning as it changed the crystal alignment of polymers, and Kassad was screaming. She lowered her arms to meet the charge.

Kassad's speed and mass knocked Moneta off her feet and sent both of them tumbling, Kassad trying to get his gauntleted hands on her throat, Moneta holding his wrists in a vise-strong grip as they rolled across the landing to the edge of the platform. Kassad rolled on top of her, trying to let gravity add to the force of his attack, arms straight, gauntlets rigid, fingers curved in a killing cusp. His left leg hung over the sixty-meter drop to the dark floor below.

'Why do you want to kill me?' whispered Moneta, and rolled him to one side, tumbling both of them off the platform.

Kassad screamed and flipped down his visor with a snap of his head. They tumbled through space, their legs entwined around each other's bodies in fierce scissors grips, Kassad's hands held at bay by her death hold on his wrists. Time seemed to decelerate until they fell in slow motion, the air moving across Kassad like a blanket being pulled slowly over his face. Then time accelerated, grew normal: they were falling the last ten meters. Kassad shouted and visualized the proper symbol to let his impact armor go rigid; and there was a terrible crash.

From a blood-red distance, Fedmahn Kassad fought to the surface of consciousness, knowing that only a second or two had elapsed since they had struck the ground. He staggered to his feet. Moneta was also rising slowly, on one bent knee now, staring at the ground where the ceramic floor had been shattered by their fall.

Kassad sent power to the servomechanisms in his suit leg and kicked at her head with full force.

Moneta dodged the blow, caught his leg, twisted, and sent him crashing into the three-meter square of crystal, shattering it, tumbling him out into the sand and the night. Moneta touched her neck, her face flowed with quicksilver, and she stepped out after him.

Kassad flipped up his shattered visor, removed the helmet. The wind tousled his short, black hair, and sand grated against his cheeks. He got to his knees, his feet. Telltales in the suit's collar display were blinking red, announcing the last reservoirs of power draining away. Kassad ignored the alarms; there would be enough for the next several seconds . . . and that would be all that mattered.

'Whatever happened in my future . . . your past,' said Moneta, 'it was not I who changed. I am not the Lord of Pain. He—'

Kassad jumped the three meters that separated them, landed *behind* Moneta, and brought the killing gauntlet on his right hand around in an arc that broke the sound barrier, palm-edge rigid and sharp as carbon-carbon piezoelectric filaments could make it.

Moneta did not duck or attempt to block the attack. Kassad's gauntlet caught the base of her neck in a blow which would have severed a tree, carved through half a meter of stone. On Bressia, in hand-to-hand combat in the capital of Buckminster, Kassad had killed an Ouster colonel so quickly – his gauntlet cutting through impact armor, helmet, personal forcefield, flesh and bone without pause – that the man's head had blinked up at his own body for twenty seconds before death claimed him.

Kassad's blow struck true but stopped at the surface of the quicksilver skinsuit. Moneta did not stagger or react. Kassad felt his suit power fail at the same instant his arm went numb, his shoulder muscles wrenching in agony. He staggered back, his right arm dead at his side, the suit power draining like blood from an injured man.

'You don't listen,' said Moneta. She stepped forward, grabbed Kassad by the front of his combat suit, and threw him twenty meters toward the Jade Tomb.

He landed hard, the impact armor stiffening to absorb only part of the collision as power reserves failed. His left arm protected his face and neck, but then the armor locked up, his arm bent uselessly under him.

Moneta jumped the twenty meters, crouched next to him, lifted him into the air with one hand, grabbed a handful of impact armor with the other hand, and ripped his combat suit down the front, tearing apart two hundred layers of microfilaments and omega-cloth polymers. She slapped him gently, almost lackadaisically. Kassad's head snapped around, and he almost lost consciousness. Wind and sand pelted the bare flesh of his chest and belly.

Moneta tore the rest of the suit off, ripping off biosensors and feedback teeps. She lifted the naked man by his upper arms and shook him. Kassad tasted blood and red dots swam in his field of vision.

'We didn't have to be enemies,' she said softly.

'You . . . fired . . . at me.'

'To test your responses, not to kill you.' Her mouth moved normally under its quicksilver caul. She slapped him again and Kassad flew two meters in the air to land on a dune, rolled downhill in the cold sand. The air was filled with a million specks – snow, dust, pinwheels of colored light. Kassad rolled over, fought his way to his knees, gripped the shifting dune sand with fingers turned to numbed claws.

'Kassad,' whispered Moneta.

He rolled on to his back, waiting.

She had deactivated the skinsuit. Her flesh looked warm and vulnerable, the skin so pale as to be almost translucent. There were soft blue veins visible along the tops of her perfect breasts. Her legs looked strong, carefully sculpted, the thighs separated slightly where they met her body. Her eyes were a dark green.

'You love war, Kassad,' whispered Moneta as she lowered herself on to him.

He struggled, tried to twist aside, raised his arms to strike her. Moneta pinned his arms above his head with one of her hands. Her body was radiant with heat as she brushed her breasts back and forth across his chest, lowered herself between his parted legs. Kassad could feel the slight curve of her belly against his abdomen.

He realized then that this was a rape, that he could fight back simply by not responding, refusing her. It did not work. The air seemed liquid around them, the windstorm a distant thing, sand hanging in the air like a lace curtain borne aloft by steady breezes.

Moneta moved back and forth above him, against him. Kassad could feel the slow clockwise stir of his excitement. He fought it, fought her, wrestled and kicked and struggled to free his arms. She was much stronger. She used her right knee to brush his leg aside. Her nipples rubbed across his chest like warm pebbles; the warmth of her belly and groin made his flesh react like a flower twisting toward the light.

'No!' screamed Fedmahn Kassad but was silenced as Moneta lowered her mouth to his. With her left hand, she continued to pin his arms above him, with her right hand she moved between them, found him, guided him.

Kassad bit at her lip as warmth enveloped him. His struggles brought him closer, sent him deeper into her. He tried to relax, and she lowered herself on him until his back was pressed into the sand. He remembered the other times they had made love, finding sanity in each other's warmth while war raged beyond the circle of their passion.

Kassad closed his eyes, arched his neck back to postpone the agony of pleasure which closed on him like a wave. He tasted blood on his lips, whether his or hers he did not know.

A minute later, the two of them still moving together, Kassad realized that she had released his arms. Without hesitating, he brought both arms down, around, fingers flat against her back, and roughly pressed her closer to him, slid

174

one hand higher to cup the back of her neck with gentle pressure.

The wind resumed, sound returned, sand blew from the edge of the dune in curls of spindrift. Kassad and Moneta slid lower on the gently curling bank of sand, rolled together down the warm wave to the place where it would break, oblivious of the night, the storm, the forgotten battle, and everything except the moment and each other.

Later, walking together through the shattered beauty of the Crystal Monolith, she touched him once with a golden ferule, once more with a blue torus. He watched in the shard of a crystal panel as his reflection became a quicksilver sketch of a man, perfect down to the details of his gender and the lines where his ribs showed on the slender torso.

—*What now?* asked Kassad through the medium that was neither telepathy nor sound.

—*The Lord of Pain awaits.*

—*You are its servant?*

—*Never. I am his consort and nemesis. His keeper.*

—*You came from the future with it?*

—*No. I was taken from my time to travel back in time with him.*

—*Then who were you before—*

Kassad's question was interrupted by the sudden appearance . . . No, he thought, *the sudden* presence, *not appearance* . . . of the Shrike.

The creature was as he remembered it from their first encounter years before. Kassad noticed the quicksilver-over-chrome slickness of the thing, so similar to their own skinsuits, but he knew intuitively that there was no mere flesh and bone beneath that carapace. It stood at least three meters tall, the four arms seemed normal on the elegant torso, and the body was a sculpted mass of thorns, spikes, joints, and layers of ragged razorwire. The thousand-faceted eyes burned with a light that might have been made by a ruby laser. The long jaw and layers of teeth were the stuff of nightmare.

Kassad stood ready. If the skinsuit gave him the same strength and mobility it had afforded Moneta, he might at least die fighting.

There was no time for that. One instant the Lord of Pain stood five meters away across black tile, and the next instant it was beside Kassad, gripping the Colonel's upper arm in a steel-bladed vise that sank through the skinsuit field and drew blood from his biceps.

Kassad tensed, waiting for the blow and determined to strike back even though to do so meant impaling himself on blades, thorns, and razorwire.

The Shrike lifted its right hand and a four-meter rectangular field portal came into existence. It was similar to a farcaster portal except for the violet glow which filled the interior of the Monolith with thick light.

Moneta nodded at him and stepped through. The Shrike stepped forward, fingerblades cutting only slightly into Kassad's upper arm.

Kassad considered pulling back, realized that curiosity was stronger in him than an urge to die, and stepped through with the Shrike.

EIGHTEEN

CEO Meina Gladstone could not sleep. She rose, dressed quickly in her dark apartments deep in Government House, and did what she often did when sleep would not come – she walked the worlds.

Her private farcaster portal pulsed into existence. Gladstone left her human guards sitting in the anteroom, taking with her only one of the microremotes. She would have taken none if the laws of the Hegemony and the rule of the TechnoCore would allow it. They did not.

It was far past midnight on TC² but she knew that many of the worlds would be in daylight, so she wore a long cape with a Renaissance privacy collar. Her trousers and boots revealed neither gender nor class, although the quality of the cape itself might mark her in some places.

CEO Gladstone stepped through the one-time portal, sensing rather than seeing or hearing the microremote as it buzzed through behind her, climbing for altitude and invisibility as she stepped out into the Square of St Peter's in the New Vatican on Pacem. For a second, she did not know why she had coded her implant for that destination – the presence of that obsolete monsignor at the dinner on God's Grove? – but then she realized that she had been thinking of the pilgrims as she lay awake, thinking of the seven who left three years earlier to meet their fate on Hyperion. Pacem had been the home of Father Lenar Hoyt . . . and the other priest before him, Duré.

Gladstone shrugged under the cape and crossed the

square. Visiting the homeworlds of the pilgrims was as good a schematic for her walk as any; most sleepless nights saw her walking a score of worlds, returning just before dawn and the first meetings on Tau Ceti Center. At least this would be but seven worlds.

It was early here. The skies of Pacem were yellow, tinged with greenish clouds and an ammonia smell which attacked her sinuses and made her eyes water. The air had that thin, foul, chemical smell of a world neither completely terra-formed nor totally inimical to man. Gladstone paused to look around.

St Peter's was on a hilltop, the square embraced by a semi-circle of pillars, a great basilica at its cusp. To her right, where the pillars opened to a staircase descending a kilometer or more to the south, a small city was visible, low, crude homes huddling between bone-white trees that resembled the skeletons of stunted creatures long since departed.

Only a few people could be seen, hurrying across the square or ascending the stairs as if late for services. Bells somewhere under the great dome of the cathedral began to toll, but the thin air leached the sound of any authority.

Gladstone walked the circle of pillars, head down, ignoring the curious glances of clerics and the street-sweeping crew, who rode a beast resembling a half-ton hedgehog. There were scores of marginal worlds like Pacem in the Web, more in the Protectorate and nearby Out-back – too poor to be attractive to an infinitely mobile citizenry, too Earthlike to be ignored during the dark days of the Hegira. It had fit a small group like the Catholics who had come here seeking a resurgence of faith. They had numbered in the millions then, Gladstone knew. There could be no more than a few tens of thousands now. She closed her eyes and recalled dossier holos of Father Paul Duré.

Gladstone loved the Web. She loved the human beings in it; for all their shallowness and selfishness and inability to change, they were the stuff of humankind. Gladstone loved the Web. She loved it enough to know that she must help in destroying it.

She returned to the small three-portal terminex, brought her own farcaster nexus into existence with a simple override command to the datasphere, and stepped through into sunlight and the smell of the sea.

Maui-Covenant. Gladstone knew precisely where she was. She stood on the hill above Firstsite where Siri's tomb still marked the spot where the short-lived rebellion had begun the better part of a century ago. At that time, Firstsite was a village of a few thousand, and each Festival Week flutists welcomed the motile isles as they were herded north to their feeding grounds in the Equatorial Archipelago. Now Firstsite stretched out of view around the island, arctowns and residential hives rising half a kilometer in all directions, towering over the hill which had once commanded the best view on the seaworld of Maui-Covenant.

But the tomb remained. The body of the Consul's grandmother was no longer there . . . never really had been there . . . but like so many symbolic things from this world, the empty crypt commanded reverence, almost awe.

Gladstone looked out between the towers, out past the old breakwater where blue lagoons had been turned brown, out past the drilling platforms and tourist barges, out to where the sea began. There were no motile isles now. They no longer moved in great herds across the oceans, their treesails billowing to southern breezes, their dolphin herders cutting the water in white vees of foam.

The isles were tamed and populated by Web citizens now. The dolphins were dead – some killed in the great battles with FORCE, most killing themselves in the inexplicable South Sea Mass Suicide, the last mystery of a race draped in mysteries.

Gladstone took a seat on a low bench near the cliff's edge and found a stalk of grass she could peel and chew. What happened to a world when it went from a home for a hundred thousand humans, in delicate balance with a delicate ecology, to the playground for more than four hundred million in the first standard decade of citizenship in the Hegemony?

Answer: the world died. Or its soul did, even as the ecosphere continued to function after a fashion. Planetary ecologists and terraform specialists kept the husk alive, kept the seas from choking completely on the unavoidable garbage and sewage and oil spills, worked to minimize or disguise the noise pollution and a thousand other things which progress had brought. But the Maui-Covenant that the Consul had known as a child less than a century earlier, climbing this very hill to his grandmother's funeral, was gone forever.

A formation of hawking mats flew overhead, the tourists on them laughing and shouting. Far above them, a massive excursion EMV occluded the sun for a moment. In the sudden shadow, Gladstone tossed down her stalk of grass, and rested her forearms on her knees. She thought of the Consul's betrayal. She had *counted* on the Consul's betrayal, had wagered everything on the man raised on Maui-Covenant, descendant of Siri, joining the Ousters in the inevitable battle for Hyperion. It had not been her plan alone; Leigh Hunt had been instrumental in the decades of planning, the delicate surgery of placing the precise individual in contact with the Ousters, in a position where he might betray both sides by activating the Ouster device to collapse the time tides on Hyperion.

And he had. The Consul, a man who had given four decades of his life as well as his wife and child to Hegemony service, had finally exploded in revenge like a bomb which had lain dormant for half a century.

Gladstone took no pleasure in the betrayal. The Consul had sold his soul, and would pay a terrible price – in history, in his own mind – but his treason was as nothing to the treachery Gladstone was prepared to suffer for. As Hegemony CEO, she was the symbolic leader of a hundred and fifty billion human souls. She was prepared to betray them all in order to save humanity.

She rose, felt age and rheumatism in her bones, and walked slowly to the terminex. She paused a moment by the gently humming portal, looking over her shoulder for a final glimpse of Maui-Covenant. The breeze carried in from the sea, but it carried the flat stench of oil spills and refinery gases, and Gladstone turned her face away.

The weight of Lusus fell on her caped shoulders like iron shackles. It was rush hour in the Concourse, and thousands of commuters, shoppers, and tourists crowded every walkway level, filled the kilometer-long escalators with colorful humanity, and gave the air a rebreathed heaviness that mixed with the sealed-system scent of oil and ozone. Gladstone ignored the expensive shopping levels and took a perstrans diskway the ten klicks to the main Shrike Temple.

There were police interdiction and containment fields glowing violet and green beyond the base of the wide stairway. The temple itself was boarded and dark; many of the tall, thin stained-glass windows facing the Concourse had been shattered. Gladstone remembered the reports of riots months before and knew that the Bishop and his acolytes had fled.

She walked close to the interdiction field, staring through the shifting violet haze at the stairway where Brawne Lamia had carried her dying client and lover, the original Keats cybrid, to the waiting Shrike priests. Gladstone had known Brawne's father well; they had spent their early Senate years together. Senator Byron Lamia had been a brilliant man – at one time, long before Brawne's mother had come on the social scene from her backwater province of Freeholm, Gladstone had considered marrying him – and when he died, part of Gladstone's youth had been buried with him. Byron Lamia had been obsessed with the TechnoCore, consumed with the mission of moving humankind out from under the bondage the AIs had imposed over five centuries and a thousand light-years. It had been Brawne Lamia's father who had made Gladstone aware of the danger, had led her to the commitment which would result in the most terrible betrayal in the history of man.

And it was Senator Byron Lamia's 'suicide' that had trained her to decades of caution. Gladstone did not know if it had been agents of the Core that had orchestrated the senator's death, perhaps it had been elements of the Hegemony hierarchy protecting its own vested interests, but she did know that Byron Lamia would never have taken his own life, never have abandoned his helpless wife and headstrong daughter in such a way. Senator Lamia's last senate act had been to co-propose Protectorate status for Hyperion, a move that would have brought the world into the Web twenty standard years earlier than the events now unfolding. After his death, the surviving co-sponsor – the newly influential Meina Gladstone – had withdrawn the bill.

Gladstone found a dropshaft and fell past shopping levels and residential levels, manufacturing and service levels, waste disposal and reactor levels. Both her comlog and the dropshaft speaker began warning her that she was entering unlicensed and unsafe areas far beneath the Hive. The dropshaft program tried to stop her descent. She overrode the command and silenced the warnings. She continued to drop, past levels without panels or lights now, descending through a tangle of fiber-optic spaghetti, heating and cooling ducts, and naked rock. Eventually she stopped.

Gladstone emerged into a corridor lighted only by distant glow-globes and oily firefly paint. Water dripped from a thousand cracks in ceilings and walls and accumulated in toxic puddles. Steam drifted from apertures in the wall that might be other corridors, or personal cubbies, or merely holes. Somewhere in the distance there was the ultrasonic scream of metal cutting metal; closer, the electronic screeches of nihil-music. Somewhere a man screamed and a woman laughed, her voice echoing metallically down shafts and conduits. There came the sound of a fléchette rifle coughing.

Dregs' Hive. Gladstone came to an intersection of cave-corridors and paused to look around. Her microremote dipped and circled closer now, as insistent as an angered insect. It was calling for security backup. Only Gladstone's persistent override prevented its cry being heard.

Dregs' Hive. This was where Brawne Lamia and her cybrid lover had hidden for those last few hours before their attempt to reach the Shrike Temple. This was one of the myriad underbellies of the Web, where the black market could provide anything from Flashback to FORCE-grade weapons, illegal androids to bootleg Poulsen treatments that would as likely kill you as give you another twenty years of youth. Gladstone turned right, down the darkest corridor.

Something the size of a rat but with many legs scurried into a broken ventilator tube. Gladstone smelled sewage, sweat, the ozone of overworked datumplane decks, the sweet scent of handgun propellant, vomit, and the reek of low-grade pheromones mutated to toxins. She walked the corridors, thinking of the weeks and months to come, the terrible price the worlds would pay for her decisions, her obsessions.

Five youths, tailored by back-room ARNists to the point they were more animal than human, stepped into the corridor in front of Gladstone. She paused.

The microremote dropped in front of her and neutralized its camouflage polymers. The creatures in front of her laughed, seeing only a machine the size of a wasp bobbing and darting in the air. It was quite possible that they were too far gone in the RNA tailoring even to recognize the device. Two of them flicked open vibrades. One extended ten-centimeter-long steel claws. One clicked open a fléchette pistol with rotating barrels.

Gladstone did not want a fight. She knew, even if these Dregs' Hive deadheads did not, that the micro could defend her from these five and a hundred more. But she did not want someone killed simply because she chose the Dregs as a place to take her walk.

'Go away,' she said.

The youths stared, yellow eyes, bulbous black eyes, hooded slits and photoreceptive belly bands. In unison but spreading into a half circle, they took two steps toward her.

Meina Gladstone pulled herself erect, gathered her cape around her, and dropped the privacy collar enough that they could see her eyes. 'Go away,' she said again.

The youths paused. Feathers and scales vibrated to unseen breezes. On two of them, antennae quivered and thousands of small sensory hairs pulsed.

They went away. Their departure was as silent and swift as their arrival. In a second there was no sound but water dripping, distant laughter.

Gladstone shook her head, summoned her personal portal, and stepped through.

Sol Weintraub and his daughter had come from Barnard's World. Gladstone translated to a minor terminex in their hometown of Crawford. It was evening. Low, white homes set back on manicured lawns reflected Canadian Republic Revival sensibilities and farmers' practicality. The trees were tall, broad limbed, and amazingly faithful to their Old Earth heritage. Gladstone turned away from the flow of pedestrians, most hurrying home after a workday elsewhere in the Web, and found herself strolling down brick walkways past brick buildings set around a grassy oval. To her left, she caught glimpses of farm fields past a row of homes. Tall green plants, possibly corn, grew in softly sighing ranks that stretched to the distant horizon where the last arc of a huge red sun was setting.

Gladstone walked through the campus, wondering if this had been the college where Sol had taught, but not curious enough to query the datasphere. Gaslamps were lighting themselves under the canopy of leaves, and the first stars were becoming visible in the gaps where sky faded from azure to amber to ebony.

Gladstone had read Weintraub's book, *The Abraham Dilemma*, in which he analyzed the relationship between a God who demanded the sacrifice of a son and the human race who agreed to it. Weintraub had reasoned that the Old Testament Jehovah had not simply been testing Abraham, but had communicated in the only language of loyalty, obedience, sacrifice, and command that humankind could understand at that point in the relationship. Weintraub had dealt with the New Testament's message as a presage of a new stage in that relationship – a stage wherein mankind would no longer sacrifice its children to any god, for any reason, but where parents . . . entire races of parents . . . would offer themselves up instead. Thus the Twentieth Century Holocausts, the Brief Exchange, the tripartite wars, the reckless centuries, and perhaps even the Big Mistake of '38.

Finally, Weintraub had dealt with refusing all sacrifice, refusing any relationship with God except one of mutual respect and honest attempts at mutual understanding. He wrote about the multiple deaths of God and the need for a divine resurrection now that humankind had constructed its own gods and released them on the universe.

Gladstone crossed a graceful stone bridge arcing over a stream lost in shadows, its whereabouts indicated only by the noises it made in the dark. Soft yellow light fell on railings of hand-set stone. Somewhere off campus, a dog barked and was hushed. Lights burned on the third floor of an old building, a gabled and roughly shingled brick structure that must date back to before the Hegira.

Gladstone thought about Sol Weintraub and his wife Sarai and their beautiful twenty-six-year-old daughter, returning from a year of archaeological discovery on Hyperion with no discovery except the Shrike's curse, the Merlin's sickness. Sol and Sarai watching as the woman aged backward to child, from child to infant. And then Sol watching alone after Sarai

185

died in a senseless, stupid EMV crash while visiting her sister.

Rachel Weintraub whose first and final birthday would arrive in less than three standard days.

Gladstone pounded her fist against stone, summoned her portal, and went elsewhere.

It was midday on Mars. The Tharsis slums had been slums for six centuries and more. The sky overhead was pink, the air too thin and too cold for Gladstone, even with her cape around her, and dust blew everywhere. She walked the narrow lanes and cliffwalks of Relocation City, never finding an open enough spot to see anything beyond the next cluster of hovels or dripping filter towers.

There were few plants here – the great forests of the Greening had been cut down for firewood or died and been covered by red dunes. Only a few bootleg brandy cacti and scuttling packs of parasitic spider lichen were visible between paths pocked hard as stone by twenty generations of bare feet.

Gladstone found a low rock and rested, lowering her head and massaging her knees. Groups of children, each naked except for strips of rags and dangling shunt jacks, surrounded her, begged for money, and then ran away giggling when she did not respond.

The sun was high. Mons Olympus and the stark beauty of Fedmahn Kassad's FORCE academy were not visible from here. Gladstone looked around. This was where the proud man had come from. Here is where he had run with youth gangs before being sentenced to the order, sanity, and honor of the military.

Gladstone found a private place and stepped through her portal.

God's Grove was as it always was – perfumed by the scent of a million million trees, silent except for the soft sounds of leaf rustle and wind, colored in halftones and pastels, the sunset igniting the literal rooftop of the world as an ocean of treetops caught the light, each leaf shimmering to the breeze, glittering with dew and morning showers as the breeze rose and carried the smell of rain and wet vegetation to Gladstone on her platform high above the world still sunk in sleep and darkness half a kilometer below.

A Templar approached, saw the glint of Gladstone's access bracelet as she moved her hand, and withdrew, a tall, robed figure blending back into the maze of foliage and vines.

The Templars were one of the trickiest variables in Gladstone's game. Their sacrifice of their treeship *Yggdrasill* was unique, unprecedented, inexplicable, and worrisome. Of all her potential allies in the war to come, none were more necessary and inscrutable than the Templars. Dedicated to life and devoted to the Muir, the Brotherhood of the Tree was a small but potent force in the Web – a token of ecological awareness in a society devoted to self-destruction and waste but unwilling to acknowledge its indulgent ways.

Where was Het Masteen? Why had he left the Möbius cube with the other pilgrims?

Gladstone watched the sun rise. The sky filled with orphan montgolfiers saved from the slaughter on Whirl, their many-hued bodies floating skyward like so many Portuguese men-o'-war. Radiant gossamers spread membrane-thin solar wings to collect the sunlight. A flock of ravens broke cover and spiraled skyward, their cries providing harsh counterpoint to the soft breeze and sibilant rush of rain coming toward Gladstone from the west. The insistent sound of raindrops on leaves reminded her of her own home in the deltas of Patawpha, of the Hundred Day Monsoon which sent her and her brothers out into the fens hunting for toad flyers, bendits, and Spanish moss serpents to bring to school in a jar.

Gladstone realized for the hundred thousandth time that there was still time to stop things. All-out war was not inevitable at this point. The Ousters had not counterattacked yet in a way the Hegemony could not ignore. The Shrike was not free. Not yet.

All she had to do to save a hundred billion lives was return to the Senate floor, reveal three decades of deception and duplicity, reveal her fears and uncertainties . . .

No. It would go as planned until it went beyond planning. Into the unforeseen. Into the wild waters of chaos where even the TechnoCore predictors, those who saw everything, would be blind.

Gladstone walked the platforms, towers, ramps, and swinging bridges of the Templar tree city. Arboreals from a score of worlds and ARNied chimps scolded her and fled, swinging gracefully from flimsy vines three hundred meters above the forest floor. From areas closed to tourists and privileged visitors, Gladstone caught the scent of incense and clearly heard the Gregorian-like chants of the Templar sunrise service. Beneath her, the lower levels were coming alive with light and movement. The brief showers had passed over, and Gladstone returned to the upper levels, rejoicing in the view, crossing a sixty-meter wooden suspension bridge connecting her tree to one even larger, where half a dozen of the great hot air balloons – the only air transport the Templars allowed on God's Grove – hung tethered and seemingly impatient to be away, their passenger nacelles swinging like heavy brown eggs, the skins of the balloons lovingly dyed in the patterns of living things – montgolfiers, Monarch butterflies, Thomas hawks, radiant gossamers, the now-extinct zeplens, sky squids, moon moths, eagles – so revered in legend that they had never been retrieved or ARNied – and more.

All this could be destroyed if I continue. Will be *destroyed.*

Gladstone paused at the edge of a circular platform and gripped a railing so tightly that the age-mottles on her hands stood out harshly against suddenly pale skin. She thought of the old books she had read, pre-Hegira, pre-spaceflight, where people in embryonic nations on the continent of

Europe had transported darker people – Africans – away from their homelands into a life of slavery in the colonial West. Would those slaves, chained and shackled, naked and curled in the fetid belly of a slave ship . . . would those slaves have hesitated to rebel, to drag down their captors, if it meant destroying the beauty of that slave ship . . . of Europe itself?

But they had Africa to return to.

Meina Gladstone let out a sound part groan and part sob. She whirled away from the glorious sunrise, from the sound of chants greeting the new day, from the rise of balloons – living and artificial – into the newborn sky, and she went below, down into the relative darkness to summon her farcaster.

She could not go where the last pilgrim, Martin Silenus, had come from. Silenus was only a century and a half old, half-blue from Poulsen treatments, his cells remembering the cold freeze of a dozen long cryogenic fugues and even colder storage, but his lifetime had spanned more than four centuries. He had been born on Old Earth during the last days there, his mother from one of the noblest families, his youth a pastiche of decadence and elegance, beauty and the sweet smell of decay. While his mother stayed with the dying Earth, he had been sent spaceward so that someone could clear family debts, even if it meant . . . which it did . . . years of service as a bonded manual laborer on one of the most hellish backwater worlds in the Web.

Gladstone could not go to Old Earth so she went to Heaven's Gate.

Mudflat was the capital, and Gladstone walked the cobblestone streets there, admiring the large old houses which overhung the narrow, stone-troughed canals criss-crossing their way up the artificial mountainside like something from an Escher print. Elegant trees and even larger horsetail ferns crowned the hilltops, lined the broad, white avenues, and swept out of sight around the elegant curve of white sand beaches. The lazy tide brought in violet waves which prismed to a score of colors before dying on the perfect beaches.

Gladstone paused at a park looking over the Mudflat Promenade, where scores of couples and carefully dressed tourists took the evening air under gaslamp and leaf shadow, and she imagined what Heaven's Gate had been more than three centuries earlier when it was a rough Protectorate world, not yet fully terraformed, and young Martin Silenus, still suffering from cultural dislocation, the loss of his fortune, and brain damage due to Freezer Shock on the long trip out, was working here as a slave.

The Atmospheric Generating Station then had provided a few hundred square kilometers of breathable air, marginally liveable land. Tsunamis carried away cities, land reclamation projects, and workers with equal indifference. Bonded workers like Silenus dug out the acid canals, scraped rebreather bacteria from the lungpipe labyrinths under the mud, and dredged scum and dead bodies from the tidal mudflats after the floods.

We have made some progress, thought Gladstone, *despite the inertia forced upon us by the Core. Despite the near-death of science. Despite our fatal addiction to the toys granted us by our own creations.*

She was dissatisfied. Before this world walk was over she had wanted to visit the home of each of the Hyperion pilgrims, however futile she knew that gesture to be. Heaven's Gate was where Silenus had learned to write true poetry even while his temporarily damaged mind was lost to language, but this was not his home.

Gladstone ignored the pleasant music rising from the concert on the Promenade, ignored the flights of commuter EMVs moving overhead like migrating fowl, ignored the pleasant air and soft light, as she called her portal to her and commanded it to farcast to Earth's moon. *The* moon.

Instead of activating the translation, her comlog warned

her of the dangers of going there. She overrode it.

Her microremote buzzed into existence, its tiny voice in her implant suggesting that it was not a good idea for the Chief Executive to travel to such an unstable place. She silenced it.

The farcaster portal itself began to argue with her choice until she used her universal card to program it manually.

The farcaster door blurred into existence, and Gladstone stepped through.

The only place on Old Earth's moon still habitable was the mountain and Mare area preserved for the FORCE Masada Ceremony, and it was here that Gladstone stepped out. The viewing stands and marching field were empty. Class-ten containment fields blurred the stars and the distant rim walls, but Gladstone could see where internal heating from terrible gravity tides had melted the distant mountains and made them flow into new seas of rock.

She moved across a plain of gray sand, feeling the light gravity like an invitation to fly. She imagined herself as one of the Templar balloons, lightly tethered but eager to be away. She resisted the impulse to jump, to leap along in giant bounds, but her step was light, and dust flew in improbable patterns behind her.

The air was very thin under the containment field dome, and Gladstone found herself shivering despite the heating elements in her cape. For a long moment she stood in the center of the featureless plain and tried to imagine just the moon, humankind's first step in its long stagger from the cradle. But the FORCE viewing stands and equipment sheds distracted her, made such imaginings futile, and finally she raised her eyes to see what she had actually come for.

Old Earth hung in the black sky. But not Old Earth, of course, merely the pulsing accretion disk and globular cloud of debris which had once been Old Earth. It was very bright, brighter than any of the stars seen from Patawpha on even the rarest clear night, but its brightness was strangely ominous, and it cast a thick light across the mud-gray field.

Gladstone stood and stared. She had never been here before, had made herself not come before, and now that she was here, she desperately wanted to *feel* something, *hear* something, as if some voice of caution or inspiration or perhaps merely commiseration would come to her here.

She heard nothing.

She stood there another few minutes, thinking of little, feeling her ears and nose beginning to freeze, before she decided to go. It would be almost dawn on TC^2.

Gladstone had activated the portal and was taking a final look around when another portable farcaster door blurred into existence less than ten meters away. She paused. Not five human beings in the Web had individual access to Earth's moon.

The microremote buzzed down to float between her and the figure emerging from the portal.

Leigh Hunt stepped out, glanced around, shivered from the cold, and walked quickly toward her. His voice was thin, almost amusingly childlike in the thin air.

'M Chief Executive, you must return at once. The Ousters have succeeded in breaking through in an amazing counterattack.'

Gladstone sighed. She had known that this would be the next step. 'All right,' she said. 'Has Hyperion fallen? Can we evacuate our forces from there?'

Hunt shook his head. His lips were almost blue from the cold. 'You don't understand,' came the attenuated voice of her aide. 'It's not just Hyperion. The Ousters are attacking at a dozen points. *They're invading the Web itself!*'

Suddenly numb and chilled to her core, more from shock than from the lunar cold, Meina Gladstone nodded, gathered her cape more tightly around her, and stepped back through the portal to a world which would never be the same again.

NINETEEN

They gathered at the head of the Valley of the Time Tombs, Brawne Lamia and Martin Silenus burdened with as many backpacks and carrying bags as they could manage, Sol Weintraub, the Consul, and Father Duré standing silent as a tribunal of patriarchs. The first shadows of afternoon were beginning to stretch east across the valley, reaching for the softly glowing Tombs like fingers of darkness.

'I'm still not sure it's a good idea to split up like this,' said the Consul, rubbing his chin. It was very hot. Sweat gathered on his stubbled cheeks and ran down his neck.

Lamia shrugged. 'We knew that we each would be confronting the Shrike alone. Does it matter if we're separated a few hours? We need the food. You three could come if you want.'

The Consul and Sol glanced at Father Duré. The priest was obviously exhausted. The search for Kassad had drained whatever reserves of energy the man had kept after his ordeal.

'Someone should wait here in case the Colonel returns,' said Sol. The baby looked very small in his arms.

Lamia nodded agreement. She settled straps on her shoulders and neck. 'All right. It should be about two hours getting to the Keep. A little longer coming back. Figure a full hour there loading supplies, and we'll still be back before dark. Close to dinnertime.'

The Consul and Duré shook hands with Silenus. Sol put his arms around Brawne. 'Come back safely,' he whispered.

She touched the bearded man's cheek, set her hand on the infant's head for a second, turned, and started up the valley at a brisk pace.

'Hey, wait a fucking minute for me to catch up!' called Martin Silenus, canteens and water bottles clattering as he ran.

They came up out of the saddle between the cliffs together. Silenus glanced back and saw the other three men already dwarfed by distance, small sticks of color amid the boulders and dunes near the Sphinx. 'It isn't going quite as planned, is it?' he said.

'I don't know,' said Lamia. She had changed into shorts for the hike, and the muscles of her short, powerful legs gleamed under a sheen of sweat. 'How was it planned?'

'My plan was to finish the universe's greatest poem and then go home,' said Silenus. He took a drink from the last bottle holding water. 'Goddamn, I wish we'd brought enough wine to last us.'

'I didn't have a plan,' said Lamia, half to herself. Her short curls, matted with perspiration, clung to her broad neck.

Martin Silenus snorted a laugh. 'You wouldn't be here if it weren't for that cyborg lover . . .'

'Client,' she snapped.

'Whatever. It was the Johnny Keats retrieval persona who thought it was important to get here. So now you've dragged him this far . . . you're still carrying the Schrön loop aren't you?'

Lamia absently touched the tiny neural shunt behind her left ear. A thin membrane of osmotic polymer kept sand and dust out of the follicle-sized connector sockets. 'Yes.'

Silenus laughed again. 'What the fuck good is it if there's no data-sphere to interact with, kid? You might as well have left the Keats persona on Lusus or wherever.' The poet paused a second to adjust straps and packs. 'Say, can you access the personality on your own?'

Lamia thought of her dreams the night before. The presence in them had felt like Johnny . . . but the images had been of the Web. *Memories?* 'No,' she said, 'I can't access a Schrön loop by myself. It carries more data than a hundred simple implants could deal with. Now why don't you shut up and walk?' She picked up the pace and left him standing there.

The sky was cloudless, verdant, and hinting of depths of lapis. The boulder field ahead stretched southwest to the barrens, the barrens surrendering to the dunefields. The two walked in silence for thirty minutes, separated by five meters and their thoughts. Hyperion's sun hung small and bright to their right.

'The dunes are steeper,' said Lamia as they struggled up to another crest and slid down the other side. The surface was hot, and already her shoes were filling with sand.

Silenus nodded, stopped, and mopped his face with a silken handkerchief. His floppy purple beret hung low over his brow and left ear, but offered no shade. 'It would be easier following the high ground to the north there. Near the dead city.'

Brawne Lamia shielded her eyes to stare in that direction. 'We'll lose at least half an hour going that way.'

'We'll lose more than that going *this* way.' Silenus sat on the dune and sipped from his water bottle. He pulled off his cape, folded it, and stuffed it in the largest of his backpacks.

'What are you carrying there?' asked Lamia. 'That pack looks full.'

'None of your damned business, woman.'

Lamia shook her head, rubbed her cheeks, and felt the sunburn there. She was not used to so many days in sunlight, and Hyperion's atmosphere blocked little of the ultraviolet. She fumbled in her pocket for the tube of sunblock cream and smeared some on. 'All right,' she said. 'We'll detour that way. Follow the ridgeline until the worst of the dunes are past and then cut back on a straight line toward the Keep.' The mountains hung on the horizon, seeming to grow no closer. The snow-topped summits tantalized her with their promise of cool breezes and fresh water. The Valley of the Time Tombs was invisible behind them, the view blocked by dunes and the boulder field.

Lamia shifted her packs, turned to her right, and half slid, half walked down the crumbling dune.

As they came up out of the sand on to the low gorse and needle grass of the ridge, Martin Silenus could not take his eyes from the ruins of the City of Poets. Lamia had cut left around it, avoiding everything but the stones of the half-buried highways that circled the city, other roads leading out into the barrens until they disappeared beneath the dunes.

Silenus fell farther and farther behind until he stopped and sat on a fallen column, which had once been a portal through which the android laborers filed every evening after working in the fields. Those fields were gone now. The aqueducts, canals, and highways only hinted at by fallen stones, depressions in the sand, or the sand-scoured stumps of trees where once they had overhung a waterway or shaded a pleasant lane.

Martin Silenus used his beret to mop his face as he stared at the ruins. The city was still white . . . as white as bones uncovered by shifting sands, as white as teeth in an earth-brown skull. From where he sat, Silenus could see that many of the buildings were as he had last seen them more than a century and a half ago. Poets' Ampitheatre lay half-finished but regal in its ruin, a white, otherworldly Roman Colosseum overgrown with desert creeper and fanfare ivy. The great atrium was open to the sky, the gallerias shattered – not by time, Silenus knew, but by the probes and lances and explosive charges of Sad King Billy's useless security people in the decades after the evacuation of the city. They were going to kill the Shrike. They were going to use electronics and angry beams of coherent light to kill Grendel *after* he had laid waste to the mead hall.

Martin Silenus chuckled and leaned forward, suddenly dizzy from the heat and exhaustion.

Silenus could see the great dome of the Common Hall where he had eaten his meals, first with the hundreds in artistic camaraderie, then in separation and silence with the few others who had remained, for their own inscrutable and unrecorded reasons, after Billy's evacuation to Keats, and then alone. Truly alone. Once he had dropped a goblet and the echo rang for half a minute under the vine-graffitied dome.

Alone with the Morlocks, thought Silenus. *But not even Morlocks for company in the end. Only my muse.*

There was a sudden explosion of sound, and a score of white doves burst from some niche in the heap of broken towers that had been Sad King Billy's palace. Silenus watched them whirl and circle in the overheated sky, marveling that they had survived the centuries here on the edge of nowhere.

If I could do it, why not they?

There were shadows in the city, pools of sweet shade. Silenus wondered if the wells were still good, the great underground reservoirs, sunk before the human seedships had arrived, still filled with sweet water. He wondered if his wooden worktable, an antique from Old Earth, still sat in the small room in which he had written much of his *Cantos*.

'What's wrong?' Brawne Lamia had retraced her steps and was standing near him.

'Nothing.' He squinted up at her. The woman looked like some squat tree, a mass of dark thigh roots and sunburned bark and frozen energy. He tried to imagine her being exhausted . . . the effort made *him* tired. 'I just realized,' he said. 'We're wasting our time going all the way back to the Keep. There are wells in the city. Probably food reserves too.'

'Uh-uh,' said Lamia. 'The Consul and I thought of that, talked about it. The Dead City's been looted for generations.

197

Shrike Pilgrims must have depleted the stores sixty or eighty years ago. The wells aren't dependable . . . the aquifer has shifted, the reservoirs are contaminated. We go to the Keep.'

Silenus felt his anger grow at the woman's insufferable arrogance, her instant assumption that she could take command in any situation. 'I'm going to explore,' he said. 'It might save us hours of travel time.'

Lamia moved between him and the sun. Her black curls glowed with the corona of eclipse. 'No. If we waste time here, we won't be back before dark.'

'Go on, then,' snapped the poet, surprised at what he was saying. 'I'm tired. I'm going to check out the warehouse behind the Common Hall. I might remember storage places the pilgrims never found.'

He could see the woman's body tense as she considered dragging him to his feet, pulling him out on to the dunes again. They were little more than a third of the way to the foothills where the long climb to the Keep staircase began. Her muscles relaxed. 'Martin,' she said, 'the others are depending on us. Please don't screw this up.'

He laughed and sat back against the tumbled pillar. 'Fuck that,' he said. 'I'm *tired*. You know that you're going to do ninety-five percent of the transporting anyway. I'm *old*, woman. Older than you can imagine. Let me stay and rest a while. Maybe I'll find some food. Maybe I'll get some writing done.'

Lamia crouched next to him and touched his pack. 'That's what you've been carrying. The pages of your poem. The *Cantos*.'

'Of course,' he said.

'And you still think that proximity to the Shrike will allow you to finish it?'

Silenus shrugged, feeling the heat and dizziness whirl around him. 'The thing is a fucking killer, a sheet-metal Grendel forged in hell,' he said. 'But it's my muse.'

Lamia sighed, squinted at the sun already lowering itself toward the mountains, and then looked back the way they had come. 'Go back,' she said softly. 'To the valley.' She hesitated a moment. 'I'll go with you, then return.'

Silenus smiled with cracked lips. 'Why go back? To play cribbage with three other old men until our beastie comes to tuck us in? No thanks, I'd rather rest here a bit and get some work done. Go on, woman. You can carry more than three poets could.' He struggled out of his empty packs and bottles, handing them to her.

Lamia held the tangle of straps in a fist as short and hard as the head of a steel hammer. 'Are you sure? We can walk slowly.'

He struggled to his feet, fueled by a moment of pure anger at her pity and condescension. 'Fuck you and the horse you rode in on, Lusian. In case you forgot, the purpose of the pilgrimage was to get here and say hello to the Shrike. Your friend Hoyt didn't forget. Kassad understood the game. The fucking Shrike's probably chewing on his stupid military bones right now. I wouldn't be surprised if the three we left behind *don't need* food or water by this point. Go on. Get the hell out of here. I'm tired of your company.'

Brawne Lamia remained crouching for a moment, looking up at him as he weaved above her. Then she got to her feet, touched his shoulder for the briefest of seconds, lifted the packs and bottles to her back, and swung away, her pace faster than anything he could have kept up with in his youth. 'I'll be back this way in a few hours,' she called, not turning back to look at him. 'Be out on this edge of the city. We'll return to the Tombs together.'

Martin Silenus said nothing as he watched her diminish and then disappear in the rough ground to the southwest. The mountains shimmered in the heat. He looked down and saw that she had left the water bottle for him. He spat, added the bottle to his load, and walked into the waiting shade of the dead city.

TWENTY

Duré all but collapsed while they were eating lunch from the last two ration paks; Sol and the Consul carried him up the Sphinx's wide stairway into the shade. The priest's face was as white as his hair.

He attempted a smile as Sol lifted a water bottle to his lips. 'All of you accept the fact of my resurrection rather easily,' he said, wiping the corners of his mouth with a finger.

The Consul leaned back against the stone of the Sphinx. 'I saw the cruciforms on Hoyt. The same as you wear now.'

'And I believed his story . . . *your* story,' said Sol. He passed the water to the Consul.

Duré touched his forehead. 'I've been listening to the comlog disks. The stories, including mine, are . . . incredible.'

'Do you doubt any of them?' asked the Consul.

'No. It is making sense of them that is the challenge. Finding the common element . . . the string of connection.'

Sol lifted Rachel to his chest, rocking her slightly, his hand on the back of her head. 'Does there have to be a connection? Other than the Shrike?'

'Oh yes,' said Duré. A bit of color was returning to his cheeks. 'This pilgrimage was not an accident. Nor was your selection.'

'Different elements had a say in who came on this pilgrimage,' said the Consul. 'The AI Advisory Group, the Hegemony Senate, even the Shrike Church.'

Duré shook his head. 'Yes, but there was only one guiding

intelligence behind this selection, my friends.'

Sol leaned closer. 'God?'

'Perhaps,' said Duré, smiling, 'but I was thinking of the Core . . . the artificial intelligences who have behaved so mysteriously through this entire sequence of events.'

The baby made soft, mewling noises. Sol found a pacifier for it and tuned the comlog on his wrist to heartbeat rates. The child curled its fists once and relaxed against the scholar's shoulder. 'Brawne's story suggests that elements in the Core are trying to destabilize the status quo . . . allow humankind a chance for survival while still pursuing their Ultimate Intelligence project.'

The Consul gestured toward the cloudless sky. 'Everything that's happened . . . our pilgrimage, even this war . . . was manufactured because of the internal politics of the Core.'

'And what do we know of the Core?' asked Duré softly.

'Nothing,' said the Consul, and threw a pebble toward the carved stone to the left of the Sphinx's stairway. 'When all is said and done, we know nothing.'

Duré was sitting up now, massaging his face with a slightly moistened cloth. 'Yet their goal is oddly similar to our own.'

'What's that?' asked Sol, still rocking the baby.

'To know God,' said the priest. 'Or failing that, to create Him.' He squinted down the long valley. Shadows were moving farther out from the southwestern walls now, beginning to touch and enfold the Tombs. 'I helped promote such an idea within the Church . . .'

'I've read your treatises on St Teilhard,' said Sol. 'You did a brilliant job defending the necessity of evolution toward the Omega Point – the Godhead – without stumbling into the Socinian Heresy.'

'The what?' asked the Consul.

Father Duré smiled slightly. 'Socinus was an Italian heretic in the sixteenth century AD. His belief . . . for which he was excommunicated . . . was that God is a limited being, able to learn and to grow as the world . . . the universe . . .

becomes more complex. And I did stumble into the Socinian Heresy, Sol. That was the first of my sins.'

Sol's gaze was level. 'And the last of your sins?'

'Besides pride?' said Duré. 'The greatest of my sins was falsifying data from a seven-year dig on Armaghast. Trying to provide a connection between the vanished Arch Builders there and a form of proto-Christianity. It did not exist. I fudged data. So the irony is, the greatest of my sins, at least in the Church's eyes, was to violate the scientific method. In her final days, the Church can accept theological heresy but can brook no tampering with the protocols of science.'

'Was Armaghast like this?' asked Sol, making a gesture with his arm that included the valley, the Tombs, and the encroaching desert.

Duré looked around, his eyes bright for a moment. 'The dust and stone and sense of death, yes. But this place is infinitely more threatening. Something here has not yet succumbed to death when it should have.'

The Consul laughed. 'Let's hope that we're in that category. I'm going to drag the comlog up to that saddle and try again to establish a relay link with the ship.'

'I'll go too,' said Sol.

'And I,' said Father Duré, getting to his feet, weaving for only a second, and refusing the offer of Weintraub's hand.

The ship did not respond to queries. Without the ship, there could be no fatline relay to the Ousters, the Web, or anywhere else beyond Hyperion. Normal comm bands were down.

'Could the ship have been destroyed?' Sol asked the Consul.

'No. The message is being received, just not responded to. Gladstone still has the ship in quarantine.'

Sol squinted out over the barrens to where the mountains shimmered in the heat haze. Several klicks closer, the ruins of the City of Poets rose jaggedly against the skyline. 'Just as well,' he said. 'We have one *deus ex machina* too many as it is.'

Paul Duré began to laugh then, a deep, sincere sound, and stopped only when he began coughing and had to take a drink of water.

'What is it?' asked the Consul.

'The *deus ex machina*. What we were talking about earlier. I suspect that this is precisely the reason each of us is here. Poor Lenar with his deus in the machina of the cruciform. Brawne with her resurrected poet trapped in a Schrön loop, seeking the machina to release her personal deus. You, Sol, waiting for the dark deus to solve your daughter's terrible problem. The Core, machina spawned, seeking to build their own deus.'

The Consul adjusted his sun glasses. 'And you, Father?'

Duré shook his head. 'I wait for the largest machina of all to produce its deus – the universe. How much of my elevation of St Teilhard stemmed from the simple fact that I found no sign of a living Creator in the world today? Like the TechnoCore intelligences, I seek to build what I cannot find elsewhere.'

Sol watched the sky. 'What deus do the Ousters seek?'

The Consul answered. 'Their obsession with Hyperion is real. They think that this will be the birthplace of a new hope for humankind.'

'We'd better go back down,' said Sol, shielding Rachel from the sun. 'Brawne and Martin should be returning before dinner.'

But they did not return before dinner. Nor was there any sign of them by sunset. Every hour, the Consul walked to the valley entrance, climbed a boulder, and watched for movement out among the dunes and boulder field. There was none. The Consul wished that Kassad had left a pair of his powered binoculars.

Even before the sky faded to twilight the bursts of light across its zenith announced the continuing battle in space. The three men sat on the highest step of the Sphinx's staircase and watched the light show, slow explosions of pure white, dull red blossoms, and sudden green and orange streaks which left retinal echoes.

'Who's winning do you think?' said Sol.

The Consul did not look up. 'It doesn't matter. Do you think we should sleep somewhere other than the Sphinx tonight? Wait at one of the other Tombs?'

'I can't leave the Sphinx,' said Sol. 'You're welcome to go on.'

Duré touched the baby's cheek. She was working on the pacifier, and her cheek moved against his finger. 'How old is she now, Sol?'

'Two days. Almost exactly. She would have been born about fifteen minutes after sunset at this latitude, Hyperion time.'

'I'll go up and look one last time,' said the Consul. 'Then we'll have to build a bonfire or something to help them find their way back.'

The Consul had descended half the steps toward the trail when Sol stood and pointed. Not toward where the head of the valley glowed in low sunlight, but the other way, into the shadows of the valley itself.

The Consul stopped, and the other two men joined him. The Consul reached into his pocket and removed the small neural stunner Kassad had given him several days earlier. With Lamia and Kassad gone, it was the only weapon they had.

'Can you see?' whispered Sol.

The figure was moving in the darkness beyond the faint glow of the Jade Tomb. It did not look large enough or move quickly enough to be the Shrike; its progress was strange . . . slow, halting for half a moment at a time, weaving.

Father Duré glanced over his shoulder at the entrance to the valley, then back. 'Is there any way Martin Silenus could have entered the valley from that direction?'

'Not unless he jumped down the cliff walls,' whispered the Consul. 'Or went eight klicks around to the northeast.

Besides, it's too tall to be Silenus.'

The figure paused again, weaved, and then fell. From more than a hundred meters away, it looked like another low boulder on the valley floor.

'Come,' said the Consul.

They did not run. The Consul led the way down the staircase, stunner extended, set for twenty meters although he knew the neural effect would be minimal at that range. Father Duré walked close behind, holding Sol's child while the scholar hunted for a small rock to carry.

'David and Goliath?' asked Duré when Sol came up with a palm-sized stone and set it in a fiberplastic sling he had cut from package wrap that afternoon.

The scholar's sunburned face above the beard turned a darker color. 'Something like that. Here, I'll take Rachel back.'

'I enjoy carrying her. And if there's any fighting to be done, better the two of you have free hands.'

Sol nodded and closed the gap to walk side by side with the Consul, the priest and the child a few paces behind.

From fifteen meters away it became obvious that the fallen figure was a man – a very tall man – wearing a rough robe and lying face down in the sand.

'Stay here,' said the Consul and ran. The others watched while he turned over the body, set his stunner back in his pocket, and removed a water bottle from his belt.

Sol jogged slowly, feeling his exhaustion as a kind of pleasant vertigo. Duré followed more slowly.

When the priest came into the light thrown by the Consul's hand torch, he saw the hood of the fallen man pushed back from a vaguely Asian, oddly distorted long face lighted by the glow of the Jade Tomb as well as the torch.

'It's a Templar,' said Duré, astonished to find a follower of the Muir here.

'It's the True Voice of the Tree,' said the Consul. 'It's the first of our missing pilgrims . . . it's Het Masteen.'

205

TWENTY-ONE

Martin Silenus had worked all afternoon on his epic poem, and only the dying of the light made him pause in his efforts.

He had found his old workroom pillaged, the antique table missing. Sad King Billy's palace had suffered the worst of time's insults, with all windows broken, miniature dunes drifted across discolored carpets once worth fortunes, and rats and small rock eels living between the tumbled stones. The apartment towers were homes for the doves and hunting falcons gone back to the wild. Finally the poet had returned to the Common Hall under the great geodesic dome of its dining room to sit at a low table and write.

Dust and debris covered the ceramic floor, and the scarlet tones of desert creeper all but obscured the broken panes above, but Silenus ignored these irrelevancies and worked on his *Cantos*.

The poem dealt with the death and displacement of the Titans by their offspring, the Hellenic gods. It dealt with the Olympian struggle which followed the Titans' refusal to be displaced – the boiling of great seas as Oceanus struggled with Neptune, his usurper, the extinction of suns as Hyperion struggled with Apollo for control of the light, and the trembling of the universe itself as Saturn struggled with Jupiter for control of the throne of the gods. What was at stake was not the mere passage of one set of deities to be replaced by another, but the end of a golden age and the beginning of dark times which must spell doom for all mortal things.

The *Hyperion Cantos* made no secret of the multiple identities of these gods: the Titans were easily understood to be the heroes of humankind's short history in the galaxy, the Olympian usurpers were the TechnoCore AIs, and their battlefield stretched across the familiar continents, oceans, and airways of all the worlds in the Web. Amidst all this, the monster Dis, son of Saturn but eager to inherit the kingdom with Jupiter, stalked its prey, harvesting both god and mortal.

The *Cantos* were also about the relationship between creatures and their creators, the love between parent and children, artists and their art, all creators and their creations. The poem celebrated love and loyalty but teetered on the brink of nihilism with its constant thread of corruption through love of power, human ambition and intellectual hubris.

Martin Silenus had been working on his *Cantos* for more than two standard centuries. His finest work had been done in these surroundings – the abandoned city, the desert winds whining like an ominous Greek chorus in the background, the ever-present threat of the Shrike's sudden interruption. By saving his own life, by leaving, Silenus had abandoned his muse and condemned his pen to silence. Beginning work again, following that sure trail, that perfect circuit which only the inspired writer has experienced, Martin Silenus felt himself returning to life . . . veins opening wider, lungs filling more deeply, tasting the rich light and pure air without being aware of them, enjoying each stroke of antique pen across the parchment, the great heap of previous pages stacked around on the circular table, chunks of broken masonry serving as paperweights, the story flowing freely again, immortality beckoning with each stanza, each line.

Silenus had come to the most difficult and exciting part of the poem, the scenes where conflict has raged across a thousand landscapes, entire civilizations have been laid waste, and representatives of the Titans call pause to meet and negotiate with the Olympians' humorless heroes. On this broad landscape of his imagination strode Saturn, Hyperion, Cottus, Iäpetus, Oceanus, Briareus, Mimus, Porphyrion, Enceladus, Rhoetus and others – their equally titanic sisters Tethys, Phoebe, Theia, and Clymene – and opposite them the doleful countenances of Jupiter, Apollo, and their ilk.

Silenus did not know the outcome of this most epic of poems. He lived on now only to finish the tale . . . had done so for decades. Gone were the dreams of his youth of fame and wealth from apprenticing himself to the Word – he had gained fame and wealth beyond measure and it had all but killed him, *had* killed his art – and although he knew that the *Cantos* was the finest literary work of his age, he wanted only to finish it, to know the outcome himself, and to set each stanza, each line, *each word*, in the finest, clearest, most beautiful form possible.

Now he wrote feverishly, almost mad with desire to finish what he had long thought unfinishable. The words and phrases flew from his antique pen to the antiquated paper; stanzas leaped into being with no effort, cantos found their voice and finished themselves with no need for revision, no pause for inspiration. The poem unfolded with shocking speed, astounding revelations, heart-stopping beauty in both word and image.

Under their flag of truce, Saturn and his usurper, Jupiter, faced each other across a treaty slab of sheer-cut marble. Their dialogue was both epic and simple, their arguments for being, their rationale for war creating the finest debate since Thucydides' *Melian Dialogue*. Suddenly something new, something totally unplanned by Martin Silenus in all of his long hours of musing without his muse, entered the poem. Both of the kings of the gods expressed fear of some *third* usurper, some terrible outside force that threatened the stability of either of their reigns. Silenus watched in pure astonishment as the characters he had created through thousands of hours of effort defied his will and shook hands across the marble slab, setting an alliance against . . .

Against what?

The poet paused, the pen stopping, as he realized that he could barely see the page. He had been writing in half-darkness for some time, and now full darkness had descended.

Silenus returned to himself in that process of allowing the world to rush in once more, much like the return to the senses following orgasm. Only the descent of the writer to the world was more painful as he or she returned, trailing clouds of glory which quickly dissipated in the mundane flow of sensory trivia.

Silenus looked around. The great dining hall was quite dark except for the fitful glow of starlight and distant explosions through the panes and ivy above. The tables around him were mere shadows, the walls, thirty meters away in all directions, darker shadows laced through with the varicose darkness of desert creeper. Outside the dining hall, the evening wind had risen, its voices louder now, contralto and soprano solos being sung by cracks in the jagged rafters and rents in the dome above him.

The poet sighed. He had no hand torch in his pack. He had brought nothing but water and his *Cantos*. He felt his stomach stir in hunger. *Where was that goddamn Brawne Lamia?* But as soon as he thought of it, he realized that he was pleased that the woman had not returned for him. He needed to stay in solitude to finish the poem . . . at this rate it would take no longer than a day, the night perhaps. A few hours and he would be finished with his life's work, ready to rest a while and appreciate the small daily things, the trivia of living which for decades now had been only an interruption of work he could not complete.

Martin Silenus sighed again and began setting manuscript pages in his pack. He would find a light somewhere

. . . start a fire if he had to use Sad King Billy's ancient tapestries for kindling. He would write outside by the light of the space battle if he had to.

Silenus held the last few pages and his pen in hand and turned to look for the exit.

Something was standing in the darkness of the hall with him.

Lamia, he thought, feeling relief and disappointment war with one another.

But it was not Brawne Lamia. Silenus noted the distortion, the bulk of mass above and too-long legs below, the play of starlight on carapace and thorn, the shadow of arms under arms, and especially the ruby glow of hell-lighted crystal where the eyes should be.

Silenus let out a groan and sat again. 'Not now!' he cried. 'Begone, goddamn your eyes!'

The tall shadow moved closer, its footfalls silent on cold ceramic. The sky rippled with blood-red energy, and the poet could see the thorns and blades and razorwire wrappings now.

'No!' cried Martin Silenus. 'I refuse. Leave me alone.'

The Shrike stepped closer. Silenus's hand twitched, lifted the pen again, and wrote across the empty lower margin of his last page: IT IS TIME, MARTIN.

He stared at what he had written, stifling the urge to giggle insanely. To his knowledge, the Shrike had never spoken . . . never *communicated* . . . to anyone. Other than through the paired media of pain and death. 'No!' he screamed again. 'I have work to do. Take someone else, goddamn you!'

The Shrike took another step forward. The sky pulsed with silent plasma explosions while yellows and reds ran down the creature's quick-silver chest and arms like spilled paints. Martin Silenus's hand twitched, wrote across his earlier message – IT IS TIME NOW, MARTIN.

Silenus hugged his manuscript to himself, lifting the last

pages from the table so that he could write no more. His teeth showed in a terrible rictus as he all but hissed at the apparition.

YOU WERE READY TO TRADE PLACES WITH YOUR PATRON his hand wrote on the tabletop itself.

'Not now!' screamed the poet. 'Billy's *dead*! Just let me finish. *Please!*' Martin Silenus had never begged in his long, long life. He begged now. 'Please, oh please. Please just let me finish.'

The Shrike took a step forward. It was so close that its misshapen upper body blocked out the starlight and set the poet in shadow.

NO wrote Martin Silenus's hand, and then the pen dropped as the Shrike reached out infinitely long arms, and infinitely sharp fingers pierced the poet's arms to the marrow.

Martin Silenus screamed as he was dragged from under the dining dome. He screamed as he saw dunes underfoot, heard the slide of sand under his own screams, and saw the tree rising out of the valley.

The tree was larger than the valley, taller than the mountains the pilgrims had crossed; its upper branches seemed to reach into space. The tree was steel and chrome, and its branches were thorns and nettles. Human beings struggled and wriggled on those thorns – thousands and tens of thousands. In the red light from the dying sky, Silenus focused above his pain and realized that he recognized some of those forms. They were *bodies*, not souls or other abstracts, and they obviously were suffering the agonies of the pain-wracked living.

IT IS NECESSARY wrote Silenus's own hand against the unyielding cold of the Shrike's chest. Blood dripped on quicksilver and sand.

'No!' screamed the poet. He beat his fists against scalpel blades and razorwire. He pulled and struggled and twisted even as the creature hugged him more closely, pulling him on to its own blades as if he were a butterfly being mounted, a specimen being pinned. It was not the unthinkable pain that drove Martin Silenus beyond sanity, it was the sense of irretrievable loss. He had almost finished it. *He had almost finished it!*

'No!' screamed Martin Silenus, struggling more wildly until a spray of blood and screamed obscenities filled the air. The Shrike carried him toward the waiting tree.

In the dead city, screams echoed for another minute, growing fainter and farther away. Then there was a silence broken only by the doves returning to their nests, dropping into the shattered domes and towers with a soft rustle of wings.

The wind came up, rattling loose Perspex panes and masonry, shifting brittle leaves across dry fountains, finding entrance through the broken panes of the dome and lifting manuscript pages in a gentle whirlwind, some pages escaping to be blown across the silent courtyards and empty walkways and collapsed aqueducts.

After a while, the wind died, and then nothing moved in the City of Poets.

TWENTY-TWO

Brawne Lamia found her four-hour walk turning into a ten-hour nightmare. First there was the diversion to the dead city and the difficult choice of leaving Silenus behind. She did not want the poet to stay there alone; she did not want to force him to go on nor to take the time for a return to the Tombs. As it was, the detour along the ridgeline cost her an hour of travel time.

Crossing the last of the dunes and the rock barrens was exhausting and tedious. By the time she reached the foothills it was late afternoon and the Keep was in shadow.

It had been easy descending the six hundred and sixty-one stone stairs from the Keep forty hours earlier. The ascent was a test even of her Lusus-bred muscles. As she climbed, the air grew cooler, the view more spectacular, until by the time she was four hundred meters above the foothills she was no longer perspiring and the Valley of the Time Tombs was in sight once again. Only the tip of the Crystal Monolith was visible from this angle, and that as an irregular glimmer and flash of light. She stopped once to make sure that it was not truly a message being flashed, but the glimmers were random, merely a panel of crystal catching the light as it dangled from the broken Monolith.

Just before the last hundred stairs, Lamia tried her comlog again. The comm channels were the usual hash and nonsense, presumably distorted by the time tides, which broke down all but the closest of electromagnetic communications. A comm laser would have worked . . . it seemed to work with the Consul's antique comlog relay . . . but besides that single machine, they had no comm lasers now that Kassad had disappeared. Lamia shrugged and climbed the final stairs.

Chronos Keep had been built by Sad King Billy's androids – never a true keep, it had been intended as a resort, travel inn, and artists' summer haven. After the evacuation of the City of Poets, the place had remained empty for more than a century, visited by only the most daring of adventurers.

With the gradual waning of the Shrike menace, tourists and pilgrims had begun to use the place, and eventually the Church of the Shrike reopened it as a necessary stop on the annual Shrike Pilgrimage. Some of its rooms carved deepest in the mountain or atop the least accessible of turrets had been rumored to be the site of arcane rituals and elaborate sacrifices to that creature the Shrike Cultists called the Avatar.

With the imminent opening of the Tombs, wild irregularities of the time tides, and evacuation of the northern reaches, Chronos Keep had again fallen silent. And so it was when Brawne Lamia returned.

The desert and dead city were still in sunlight, but the Keep was in twilight as Lamia reached the bottom terrace, rested a moment, found her flashlight in her smallest pack, and entered the maze. The corridors were dark. During their stay there two days earlier, Kassad had explored and announced that all power sources were down for good – solar converters shattered, fusion cells smashed, and even the backup batteries broken and strewn about the cellars. Lamia had thought of that a score of times as she hiked up the six hundred and three-score stairs, glowering at the elevator nacelles frozen on their rusted vertical tracks.

The larger halls, designed for dinners and gatherings, were just as they had left them . . . strewn with the desiccated remains of abandoned banquets and the signs of panic.

There were no bodies, but browning streaks on stone walls and tapestries suggested an orgy of violence not too many weeks before.

Lamia ignored the chaos, ignored the harbingers – great, black birds with obscenely human faces – taking wing from the central dining hall, and ignored her own fatigue as she climbed the many levels to the storeroom where they had camped. Stairways grew inexplicably narrower, while pale light through colored glass cast sickly hues. Where the panes were shattered or absent, gargoyles peered in as if frozen in the act of entering. A cold wind blew down from the snowy reaches of the Bridle Range and made Lamia shiver under her sunburn.

The packs and extra belongings were where they had left them, in the small storeroom high above the central chamber. Lamia checked to make sure that the some of the boxes and crates in the room contained non-perishable food items, and then she went out on to the small balcony where Lenar Hoyt had played his balalaika so few hours – such an eternity – ago.

The shadows of the high peaks stretched kilometers across the sand, almost to the dead city. The Valley of the Time Tombs and the jumbled wastes beyond still languished in evening light, boulders and low rock formations throwing a jumble of shadows. Lamia could not make out the Tombs from here, although an occasional glimmer still sparkled from the Monolith. She tried her comlog again, cursed it when it gave her only static and background garble, and went back in to choose and load her supplies.

She took four packs of basics wrapped in flowfoam and molded fiberplastic. There was water in the Keep – the troughs from the snowmelt far above were a technology which could not break down – and she filled all of the bottles she had brought and searched for more. Water was their most serious need. She cursed Silenus for not coming with her; the old man could have carried at least a half a dozen water bottles.

215

She was ready to leave when she heard the noise. Something was in the Grand Hall, between her and the staircase. Lamia pulled on the last of the packs, pulled her father's automatic pistol from her belt, and went slowly down the staircases.

The Hall was empty; the harbingers had not returned. Heavy tapestries, stirred by the wind, blew like rotted pennants above the litter of food and utensils. Against the far wall, a huge sculpture of the Shrike's face, all free-floating chrome and steel, rotated to the breeze.

Lamia edged across the space, swiveling every few seconds so that her back was never turned to one dark corner for long. Suddenly a scream froze her in her tracks.

It was not a human scream. The tones ululated to the ultrasonic and beyond, setting Lamia's teeth on edge and making her grip the pistol with white fingers. Abruptly it was cut off as if a player beam had been lifted from a disk.

Lamia saw where the noise had come from. Beyond the banquet table, beyond the sculpture, under the six large stained-glass windows where the dying light bled muted colors, there was a small door. The voice had echoed up and out as if it had escaped from some dungeon or cellar far below.

Brawne Lamia was curious. All of her life had been a conflict with inquisitiveness above and beyond the norm, culminating in her choice of the obsolete and sometimes amusing profession of private investigator. More than one time her curiosity had led her into embarrassment or trouble or both. And more than a few times her curiosity had paid off in knowledge few others had.

Not this time.

Lamia had come to find much-needed food and water. None of the others would have come here . . . the three older men could not have beaten her here even with her detour to the dead city . . . and anything or anyone else was not her concern.

Kassad? she wondered but stifled the thought. That sound had not come from the throat of the FORCE Colonel.

Brawne Lamia backed away from the door, keeping her pistol ready, found the steps to the main levels, and descended carefully, moving through each room with as much stealth as is possible while carrying seventy kilos of goods and more than a dozen water bottles. She caught a glimpse of herself in a faded glass on the lowest level – squat body poised, pistol raised and swiveling, a great burden of packs tottering on her back and dangling from broad straps, bottles and canteens clanking together.

Lamia did not find it amusing. She breathed a sigh of relief when she was out on the lowest terrace, out in the cool, thin air and ready to descend once again. She did not need her flashlight yet – an evening sky suddenly filled with lowering clouds shed a pink and amber light on the world, illuminating even the Keep and the foothills below in its rich glow.

She took the steep stairs two at a time, her powerful leg muscles aching before she had reached halfway. She did not tuck the gun away but kept it ready should anything descend from above or appear in an aperture in the rock face. Reaching the bottom, she stepped away from the staircase and looked up at the towers and terraces half a kilometer above.

Rocks were falling toward her. More than rocks, she realized, gargoyles had been knocked off their ancient perches and were tumbling with the boulders, their demonic faces lighted by the twilight glow. Lamia ran, packs and bottles swinging, realized that she had no time to reach a safe distance before the debris arrived, and threw herself between two low boulders leaning against one another.

Her packs kept her from fitting all the way beneath them, and she struggled, loosening straps, aware of the incredible noises as the first of the rocks struck behind her, ricocheted overhead. Lamia pulled and pushed with an effort that tore

217

leather, snapped fiberplastic, and then she was under the boulders, pulling her packs and bottles in with her, determined not to have to return to the Keep.

Rocks the size of her head and hands pelted the air around her. The shattered head of a stone goblin bounced past, smashing a small boulder not three meters away. For a moment, the air was filled with missiles, larger stones smashed on the boulder above her head, and then the avalanche was past, and there was only the patter of smaller stones from the secondary fall.

Lamia leaned over to tug her pack further in to safety, and a stone the size of her comlog ricocheted off the rockface outside, skipped almost horizontally toward her hiding place, and bounced twice in the small cave her shelter made, then struck her in the temple.

Lamia awoke with an old-person's groan. Her head hurt. It was full night outside, the pulses from distant skirmishes lighting the inside of her shelter through cracks above. She raised fingers to her temple and found caked blood along her cheek and neck.

She pulled herself out of the crevice, struggling over the tumble of new-fallen rocks outside, and sat a moment, head lowered, resisting the urge to vomit.

Her packs were intact, and only one water bottle had been smashed. She found her pistol where she had dropped it in the small space not littered with smashed rocks. The stone outcrop on which she stood had been scarred and slashed by the violence of the brief avalanche.

Lamia queried her comlog. Less than an hour had elapsed. Nothing had descended to carry her away or slit her throat while she lay unconscious. She peered one last time at the ramparts and balconies, now invisible far above her, dragged her gear out, and set off down the treacherous stone path at double time.

*   *   *

Martin Silenus was not at the edge of the dead city when she detoured to it. Somehow she had not expected him to be, although she hoped he had merely gotten tired of waiting and had walked the few kilometers to the valley.

The temptation to take off her packs, lower the bottles to the ground and rest a while was very strong. Lamia resisted it. Her small automatic in her hand, she walked through the streets of the dead city. The explosions of light were enough to guide her way.

The poet did not respond to her echoing shouts, although hundreds of small birds Lamia couldn't identify exploded into flight, their wings white in the darkness. She walked through the lower levels of the king's old palace, shouting up stairways, even firing her pistol once, but there was no sign of Silenus. She walked through courtyards beneath walls heavy-laden with creeper vines, calling his name, hunting for some sign that he had been there. Once, she saw a fountain that reminded her of the poet's tale about the night Sad King Billy disappeared, carried off by the Shrike, but there were other fountains, and she could not be sure this was the one.

Lamia walked through the central dining hall under the shattered dome, but the room was dark with shadows. There was a sound, and she swiveled, pistol ready, but it was only a leaf or ancient sheet of paper blowing across ceramic.

She sighed and left the city, walking easily despite her fatigue after days without sleep. There was no response to comlog queries, although she felt the *déjà vu* tug of the time tides and was not surprised. The evening winds had eradicated any tracks Martin might have left on his return to the valley.

The Tombs were glowing again, Lamia noticed even before she reached the wide saddle at the entrance to the valley. It was not a bright glow – nothing to compare to the silent riot of light above – but each of the aboveground Tombs seemed to be shedding a pale light, as if releasing energy stored during the long day.

Lamia stood at the head of the valley and shouted, warning Sol and the others that she was returning. She would not have refused an offer to help with the packs for this last hundred meters. Lamia's back was raw and her shirt was soaked with blood where the straps had cut into flesh.

There was no answer to her cries.

She felt her exhaustion as she slowly climbed the steps to the Sphinx, dropped her gear on the broad, stone porch, and fumbled for her flashlight. The interior was dark. Sleeping robes and packs lay strewn about in the room where they had slept. Lamia shouted, waited for the echoes to die, and played her light around the room again. Everything was the same. No, wait, *something* was different. She closed her eyes and remembered the room as it had been that morning.

The Möbius cube was missing. The strange energy-sealed box left behind by Het Masteen on the windwagon was no longer in its place in the corner. Lamia shrugged and went outside.

The Shrike was waiting. It stood just outside the door. It was taller than she had imagined, towering over her.

Lamia stepped out and backed away, stifling the urge to scream at the thing. The raised pistol seemed small and futile in her hand. The flashlight dropped unheeded to the stone.

The thing cocked its head and looked at her. Red light pulsed from somewhere behind its multifaceted eyes. The angles of its body and blades caught the light from above.

'You son of a bitch,' said Lamia, her voice level. 'Where are they? What have you done with Sol and the baby? Where are the others?'

The creature cocked its head the other way. Its face was sufficiently alien that Lamia could make out no expression there. Its body language communicated only threat. Steel fingers clicked open like retractable scalpels.

Lamia shot it four times in the face, the heavy 16-mm slugs striking solidly and whining away into the night.

220

'*I* didn't come here to die, you metallic motherfucker,' said Lamia, took aim, and fired another dozen times, each slug striking home.

Sparks flew. The Shrike jerked its head upright as if listening to some distant sound.

It was gone.

Lamia gasped, crouched, whirled around. Nothing. The valley floor glowed in starlight as the sky grew quiescent. The shadows were ink black but distant. Even the wind was gone.

Brawne Lamia staggered over to her packs and sat on the largest one, trying to bring her heart rate down to normal. She was interested to find that she had not been afraid . . . not really . . . but there was no denying the adrenaline in her system.

Her pistol still in her hand, half a dozen bullets remaining in the magazine and the propellant charge still strong, she lifted a water bottle and took a long drink.

The Shrike appeared at her side. The arrival had been instantaneous and soundless.

Lamia dropped the bottle, tried to bring the pistol around while twisting to one side.

She might as well have been moving in slow motion. The Shrike extended its right hand, fingerblades the length of darning needles caught the light, and one of the tips slid behind her ear, found her skull, and slipped inside her head with no friction, no pain beyond an icy sense of penetration.

TWENTY-THREE

Colonel Fedmahn Kassad had stepped through a portal expecting strangeness; instead he found the choreographed insanity of war. Moneta had preceded him. The Shrike had escorted him, fingerblades sunk into Kassad's upper arm. When Kassad finished his step through the tingling energy curtain, Moneta was waiting and the Shrike was gone.

Kassad knew at once where they were. The view was from atop the low mountain into which Sad King Billy had commanded his effigy carved almost two centuries earlier. The flat area atop the peak was empty except for the debris of an anti-space missile defense battery which still smoldered. From the glaze of the granite and the still-bubbling molten metal, Kassad guessed that the battery had been lanced from orbit.

Moneta walked to the edge of the cliff, fifty meters above Sad King Billy's massive brow, and Kassad joined her there. The view of the river valley, the city, and the spaceport heights ten kilometers to the west told the story.

Hyperion's capital was burning. The old part of the city, Jacktown, was a miniature firestorm, and there were a hundred lesser fires dotting the suburbs and lining the highway to the airport like well-tended signal fires. Even the Hoolie River was burning as an oil fire spread beneath antiquated docks and warehouses. Kassad could see the spire of an ancient church rising above the flames. He looked for Cicero's, but the bar was hidden by smoke and flames upriver.

The hills and valley were a mass of movement, as if an

anthill had been kicked apart by giant boots. Kassad could see the highways, clogged with a river of humanity and moving more slowly than the real river as tens of thousands fled the fighting. The flash of solid artillery and energy weapons stretched to the horizon and lighted low clouds above. Every few minutes, a flying machine – military skimmer or dropship – would rise from the smoke near the spaceport or from the wooded hills to the north and south, the air would fill with stabs of coherent light from above and below, and the vehicle would fall, trailing a plume of black smoke and orange flames.

Hovercraft flitted across the river like waterbugs, dodging between the burning wreckage of boats, barges, and other hovercraft. Kassad noticed that the single highway bridge was down, with even its concrete and stone abutments burning. Combat lasers and hellwhip beams lashed through the smoke; antipersonnel missiles were visible as white specks traveling faster than the eye could follow, leaving trails of rippling, superheated air in their wakes. As he and Moneta watched, an explosion near the spaceport mushroomed a cloud of flame into the air.

—*Not nuclear*, he thought.

—*No.*

The skinsuit covering his eyes acted like a vastly improved FORCE visor, and Kassad used the ability to zoom in on a hill five kilometers to the northwest across the river. FORCE Marines loped toward the summit, some already dropping and using their shaped excavation charges to dig foxholes. Their suits were activated, the camouflage polymers perfect, their heat signatures minimal, but Kassad had no difficulty seeing them. He could make out faces if he wished.

Tactical command and tightbeam channels whispered in his ears. He recognized the excited chatter and inadvertent obscenities which had been the hallmark of combat for too many human generations to count. Thousands of troops had dispersed from the spaceport and their staging areas and were digging in around a circle with its circumference twenty klicks from the city, its spokes carefully planned fields of fire and total-destruction vectors.

—*They're expecting an invasion*, communicated Kassad, feeling the effort as something more than subvocalization, something less than telepathy.

Moneta raised a quicksilver arm to point toward the sky.

It was a high overcast, at least two thousand meters, and it was a shock when it was penetrated first by one blunt craft, then a dozen more, and, within seconds, a hundred descending objects. Most were concealed by camouflage polymers and background-coded containment fields, but again Kassad had no difficulty making them out. Under the polymers, the gun-metal gray skins had faint markings in the subtle calligraphy he recognized as Ouster. Some of the larger craft were obviously dropships, their blue plasma tails visible enough, but the rest descended slowly under the rippling air of suspension fields, and Kassad noted the lumpy size and shape of Ouster invasion canisters, some undoubtedly carrying supplies and artillery, many undoubtedly empty, decoys for the ground defenses.

An instant later, the cloud ceiling was broken again as several thousand free-falling specks fell like hail: Ouster infantry dropping past canisters and dropships, waiting until the last possible second to deploy their suspension fields and parafoils.

Whoever the FORCE commander was, he had discipline – over both himself and his men. Ground batteries and the thousands of Marines deployed around the city ignored the easy targets of the dropships and canisters, then waited for the paratroops' arresting devices to deploy . . . some at little better than treetop height. At that instant, the air filled with thousands of shimmers and smoke trails as lasers flickered through the smoke and missiles exploded.

At first glance, the damage done was devastating, more

than enough to deter any attack, but a quick scan told Kassad that at least forty percent of the Ousters had landed – adequate numbers for the first wave of any planetary attack.

A cluster of five parafoilists swung toward the mountain where he and Moneta stood. Beams from the foothills tumbled two of them in flames, one corkscrewed down in a panic descent to avoid further lancing, and the final two caught a breeze from the east, sending them spiraling into the forest below.

All of Kassad's senses were engaged now; he smelled the ionized air and cordite and solid propellant; smoke and the dull acid of plasma explosive made his nostrils flare; somewhere in the city, sirens wailed while the crack of small-arms fire and burning trees came to him on the gentle breeze; radio and intercepted tightbeam channels babbled; flames lit the valley and laser lances played like searchlights through the clouds. Half a kilometer below them, where the forest faded to the grass of the foothills, squads of Hegemony Marines were engaging Ouster paratroopers in a hand-to-hand struggle. Screams were audible.

Fedmahn Kassad watched with the fascination he had once felt at the stimsim experience of a French cavalry charge at Agincourt.

—This is no simulation?

—No, replied Moneta.

—Is it happening now?

The silver apparition at his side cocked its head. *When is now?*

—Contiguous with our . . . meeting . . . in the Valley of the Tombs.

—No.

—The future then?

—Yes.

—But the near future?

—Yes. Five days from the time you and your friends arrived in the valley.

225

Kassad shook his head in wonder. If Moneta was to be believed, he had traveled forward in time.

Her face reflected flames and multiple hues as she swiveled toward him. *Do you wish to participate in the fighting?*

—*Fight the Ousters?* He folded his arms and watched with new intensity. He had received a preview of the fighting abilities of this strange skinsuit. It was quite likely that he could turn the tide of battle single-handedly . . . most probably destroy the few thousand Ouster troops already on the ground. *No*, he sent to her, *not now. Not at this time.*

—*The Lord of Pain believes that you are a warrior.*

Kassad turned to look at her again. He was mildly curious as to why she gave the Shrike such a ponderous title. *The Lord of Pain can go fuck itself*, he sent. *Unless it wants to fight me.*

Moneta was still for a long minute, a quicksilver sculpture on a windblown peak.

—*Would you really fight him?* she sent at last.

—*I came to Hyperion to kill it. And you. I will fight whenever either or both of you agree.*

—*You still believe that I am your enemy?*

Kassad remembered the assault on him at the Tombs, knowing now that it was less a rape than a granting of his own wish, his own subvocalized desire to be lovers with this improbable woman once again. *I don't know what you are.*

—*At first I was victim, like so many*, sent Moneta, her gaze returning to the valley. *Then, far in our future, I saw why the Lord of Pain had been forged . . . had to be forged . . . and then I became both companion and keeper.*

—*Keeper?*

—*I monitored the time tides, made repairs to the machinery, and saw to it that the Lord of Pain did not awake before his time.*

—*Then you can control it?* Kassad's pulse raced at the thought.

—*No.*

—Then who or what can control it?

—Only he or she who beats it in personal combat.

—Who has beaten it?

—No one, sent Moneta. *Either in your future or your past.*

—Have many tried?

—Millions.

—And they have all died?

—Or worse.

Kassad took a breath. *Do you know if I will be allowed to fight it?*

—You will.

Kassad let the breath out. No one had beaten it. His future was her past . . . she had lived there . . . she had glimpsed the terrible tree of thorns just as he had, seeing familiar faces there the way he had seen Martin Silenus struggling, impaled, years before he had met the man. Kassad turned his back on the fighting in the valley below. *Can we go to him now? I challenge him to personal combat.*

Moneta looked into his face for a silent moment. Kassad could see his own quicksilver visage reflected in hers. Without answering, she turned, touched the air, and brought the portal into existence.

Kassad stepped forward and went through first.

TWENTY-FOUR

Gladstone translated directly to Government House and swept into the Tactical Command Center with Leigh Hunt and half a dozen other aides in attendance. The room was packed: Morpurgo, Singh, Van Zeidt and a dozen others represented the military, although Gladstone noticed that the young naval hero, Commander Lee, was absent; most of the cabinet ministers were there, including Allan Imoto of Defense, Garion Persov of Diplomacy, and Barbre Dan-Gyddis of Economy; senators were arriving even as Gladstone did, some of them looking as though they had just been awakened – the 'power curve' of the oval conference table held Senators Kolchev from Lusus, Richeau from Renaissance Vector, Roanquist from Nordholm, Kakinuma from Fuji, Sabenstorafem from Sol Draconi Septem, and Peters from Deneb Drei; President Pro Tem Denzel-Hiat-Amin sat with a befuddled expression, his bald head gleaming in the light from overhead spots, while his young counterpart, All Thing Speaker Gibbons, perched on the edge of his seat, hands on his knees, his posture a study in barely contained energy. Councilor Albedo's projection sat directly opposite Gladstone's empty chair. All stood as Gladstone swept down the aisle, took her seat, and gestured everyone to theirs.

'Explain,' she said.

General Morpurgo stood, nodded at a subordinate, and lights dimmed while holos misted.

'Forgo the visuals!' snapped Meina Gladstone. '*Tell us.*'

Holos faded and the lights came back up. Morpurgo looked stunned, slightly vacant. He looked down at his light pointer, frowned at it, and dropped it in a pocket. 'Madame Executive, Senators, Ministers, President and Speaker, Honorables . . .' Morpurgo cleared his throat, 'the Ousters have succeeded in a devastating surprise attack. Their combat Swarms are closing on half a dozen Web worlds.'

The commotion in the room drowned him out. 'Web worlds!' cried various voices. There were shouts from politicians, ministers, and executive branch functionaries.

'Silence,' commanded Gladstone, and there was silence. 'General, you assured us that any hostile forces were a minimum of five years from the Web. How and why has this changed?'

The General made eye contact with the CEO. 'Madame Executive, as far as we can tell, all of the Hawking drive wakes were decoys. The Swarms went off their drives decades ago and drove toward their objectives at sublight speed . . .'

Excited babble drowned him out.

'Go on, General,' said Gladstone, and the hubbub died once more.

'At sublight velocities . . . some of the Swarms must have been traveling that way for fifty standard years or more . . . there was no possible way to detect them. It simply was not the fault of—'

'What worlds are in danger, General?' asked Gladstone. Her voice was very low, very level.

Morpurgo glanced toward the empty air as if seeking visuals there, returned his gaze to the table. His hands clenched into fists. 'Our intelligence at this time, based on fusion drive sightings followed by a shift to Hawking drives when they were discovered, suggests that the first wave will arrive at Heaven's Gate, God's Grove, Mare Infinitus, Asquith, Ixion, Tsingtao-Hsishuang Panna, Acteon, Barnard's World, and Tempe within the next fifteen to seventy-two hours.'

This time there was no silencing the commotion. Gladstone let the shouts and exclamations continue for several minutes before she raised a hand to bring the group under control.

Senator Kolchev was on his feet. 'How the goddamn *hell* did this happen, General? Your assurances were absolute!'

Morpurgo stood his ground. There was no responsive anger in his voice. 'Yes, Senator, and also based on faulty data. We were wrong. Our assumptions were wrong. The CEO will have my resignation within the hour . . . the other joint chiefs join me in this.'

'God*damn* your resignation!' shouted Kolchev. 'We may all be hanging from farcaster stanchions before this is over. The question is – what the hell are you *doing* about this invasion?'

'Gabriel,' Gladstone said softly, 'sit down, please. That was my next question. General? Admiral? I presume that you have already issued orders regarding the defense of these worlds?'

Admiral Singh stood and took his place next to Morpurgo. 'M Executive, we've done what we could. Unfortunately, of all the worlds threatened by this first wave, only Asquith has a FORCE contingent in place. The rest can be reached by the fleet – none lack farcaster capabilities – but the fleet cannot spread itself that thin to protect them all. And, unfortunately . . .' Singh paused a moment and then raised his voice to be heard over the rising tumult. 'And, unfortunately, deployment of the strategic reserve to reinforce the Hyperion campaign already had been initiated. Approximately sixty percent of the two hundred fleet units we had committed to this redeployment have either farcast through to Hyperion System or been translated to staging areas away from their forward defensive positions on the Web periphery.'

Meina Gladstone rubbed her cheek. She realized that she was still wearing her cape, although the privacy collar was lowered, and now she unclasped it and let it fall on to the back of her chair. 'What you're saying, Admiral, is that these worlds are undefended and there is no way to get our forces turned around and back there in time. Correct?'

Singh stood at attention, as ramrod stiff as a man before a firing squad. 'Correct, CEO.'

'What *can* be done?' she asked over the renewed shouting.

Morpurgo stepped forward. 'We're using the civilian farcaster matrix to translate as many FORCE:ground infantry and Marines as we can to the threatened worlds, along with light artillery and air/space defenses.'

Minister of Defense Imoto cleared his throat. 'But these will make little difference without fleet defenses.'

Gladstone glanced toward Morpurgo.

'This is true,' said the General. 'At best our forces will provide a rearguard action while an attempt at evacuation is carried out . . .'

Senator Richeau was on her feet. 'An *attempt* at evacuation! General, yesterday you told us that an evacuation of two or three million civilians from Hyperion was impractical. Are you now saying that we can successfully evacuate' – she paused a second to consult her comlog implant – 'seven *billion* people before the Ouster invasion force intervenes?'

'No,' said Morpurgo. 'We can sacrifice troops to save a few . . . a few selected officials, First Families, community and industrial leaders necessary to the continued war effort.'

'General,' said Gladstone, 'yesterday this group authorized immediate transferral of FORCE troops to the reinforcement fleet translating to Hyperion. Is that a problem in this new redeployment?'

General Van Zeidt of the Marines stood. 'Yes, M Executive. Troops were farcast to waiting transports within the hour of this body's decision. Almost two thirds of the hundred thousand designated troops have translated into the Hyperion System by' – he glanced at his antique

231

chronometer – '0530 hours standard. Approximately twenty minutes ago. It will be at least another eight to fifteen hours before these transports can return to Hyperion System staging areas and be returned to the Web.'

'And how many FORCE troops are available webwide?' asked Gladstone. She raised one knuckle to touch her lower lip.

Morpurgo took a breath. 'Approximately thirty thousand, M Executive.'

Senator Kolchev slapped the table with the palm of his hand. 'So we stripped the Web of not only our fighting spacecraft, but the majority of FORCE troops.'

It was not a question, and Morpurgo did not answer.

Senator Feldstein from Barnard's World rose to her feet. 'M Executive, my world . . . all of the worlds mentioned . . . need to be warned. If you are not prepared to make an immediate announcement, I must do so.'

Gladstone nodded. 'I will announce the invasion immediately after this meeting, Dorothy. We will facilitate your contact with constituents via all media.'

'Media be damned,' said the short, dark-haired woman, 'I'll be 'casting home as soon as we're done here. Whatever fate befalls Barnard's World, it is mine to share. Gentlemen and ladies, we should *all* be hanging from stanchions if the news is true.' Feldstein sat down amid murmurs and whispers.

Speaker Gibbons rose, waited for silence. His voice was wire-taut. 'General, you spoke of the *first* wave . . . is this cautionary military jargon, or do you have intelligence that there will be later waves? If so, what other Web and Protectorate worlds might be involved?'

Morpurgo's hands clenched and unclenched. He glanced again toward empty air, turned toward Gladstone. 'M Executive, may I use one graphic?'

Gladstone nodded.

The holo was the same the military had used during their

Olympus briefing – the Hegemony, gold; Protectorate stars, green; the Ouster Swarm vectors, red lines with blue-shifting tails; the Hegemony fleet deployments, orange – and it was immediately obvious that the red vectors had swung far from their old courses, lancing into Hegemony space like blood-tipped spears. The orange embers were heavily concentrated in the Hyperion System now, with others strung out along farcaster routes like beads on a chain.

Some of the senators with military experience gasped at what they saw.

'Of the dozen Swarms we know to be in existence,' said Morpurgo, his voice still soft, 'all appear to be committed to the invasion of the Web. Several have split into multiple attack groups. The second wave, projected to arrive at their targets within one hundred to two hundred and fifty hours of the first wave's assault, are vectored as pictured here.'

There was no sound in the room. Gladstone wondered if others were also holding their breaths.

'Second-wave assault targets include – Hebron, one hundred hours from now; Renaissance Vector, one hundred and ten hours; Renaissance Minor, one hundred and twelve hours; Nordholm, one hundred and twenty-seven hours; Maui-Covenant, one hundred and thirty hours; Thalia, one hundred and forty-three hours; Deneb Drei and Vier, one hundred and fifty hours; Sol Draconi Septem, one hundred and sixty-nine hours; Freeholm, one hundred and seventy hours; New Earth, one hundred and ninety-three hours; Fuji, two hundred and four hours; New Mecca, two hundred and five hours; Pacem, Armaghast, and Svoboda, two hundred and twenty-one hours; Lusus, two hundred and thirty hours; and Tau Ceti Center, two hundred and fifty hours.'

The holo faded. The silence stretched. General Morpurgo said, 'We assume that the first-wave Swarms will have secondary targets after their initial invasions, but transit times under Hawking drive will be standard Web travel time-debts, ranging from nine weeks to three years.' He stepped back and stood at parade rest.

'Good Christ,' whispered someone a few seats behind Gladstone.

The Chief Executive rubbed her lower lip. In order to save humanity from what she considered an eternity of slavery . . . or worse, extinction . . . she had been prepared to open the front door of the house to the wolf while most of the family hid upstairs, safe behind locked doors. Only now the day had arrived, and wolves were coming in through every door and window. She almost smiled at the justice of it, at her ultimate foolishness in thinking that she could uncage chaos and then control it.

'First,' she said, 'there will be no resignations, no self-recriminations, until I authorize them. It is quite possible that this government shall fall . . . that, indeed, members of this cabinet, myself among them . . . shall be, as Gabriel so aptly put it, hanging from stanchions. But in the meantime, we *are* the government of the Hegemony and must act as such.

'Second, I will meet with this body and representatives of other Senate committees in one hour in order to go over the speech I will give to the Web at 0800 standard. Your suggestions will be welcome at that time.

'Third, I hereby command and authorize the FORCE authorities here assembled and throughout the reaches of the Hegemony to do everything in their power to preserve and protect the citizenry and property of the Web and Protectorate, through whatever extraordinary means they must employ. General, Admiral, I want the troops translated back to threatened Web worlds within ten hours. I don't care how this is done, but it *will* be done.

'Fourth, after my speech, I will call a full session of the Senate and All Thing. At that time, I will declare that a state of war exists between the Human Hegemony and the Ouster nations. Gabriel, Dorothy, Tom, Eiko . . . *all* of you . . .

234

you'll be very busy in the next few hours. Prepare your speeches for your homeworlds, but *deliver that vote*. I want unanimous Senate support. Speaker Gibbons, I can only ask for your help in guiding the All Thing debate. It is essential that we have a vote of the gathered All Thing by 1200 hours today. There can be no surprises.

'Fifth, we *will* evacuate the citizens of the worlds threatened by the first wave.' Gladstone held up her hand and stifled the objections and explanations from the experts. 'We will evacuate everyone we can in the time we have. Ministers Persov, Imoto, Dan-Gyddis, and Crunnens from the Web Transit Ministry will create and spearhead the Evacuation Coordination Council and will deliver a detailed report and action timeline to me by 1300 hours today. FORCE and the Bureau for Web Security will oversee crowd control and protection of farcaster access.

'Finally, I wish to see Councilor Albedo, Senator Kolchev, and Speaker Gibbons in my private chambers in three minutes. Are there any questions from anyone?'

Stunned faces stared back.

Gladstone rose. 'Good luck,' she said. 'Work quickly. Do nothing to spread unnecessary panic. And God save the Hegemony.' She turned and swept from the room.

Gladstone sat behind her desk. Kolchev, Gibbons, and Albedo sat across from her. The urgency in the air, felt from half-sensed activities beyond the doors, was made more maddening by Gladstone's long delay before speaking. She never took her eyes off Councilor Albedo. 'You,' she said at last, 'have betrayed us.'

The projection's urbane half-smile did not waver. 'Never, CEO.'

'Then you have one minute to explain why the Techno-Core and specifically the AI Advisory Council did not predict this invasion.'

'It will take only one word to explain this, M Executive,' said Albedo. 'Hyperion.'

'Hyperion *shit!*' cried Gladstone, slamming her palm down on the ancient desk in a most un-Gladstone-like explosion of temper. 'I'm sick and tired of hearing about unfactorable variables and Hyperion the predictive black hole, Albedo. Either the Core can help us understand probabilities or they've been lying to us for five centuries. Which is it?'

'The Council predicted the war, CEO,' said the gray-haired image. 'Our confidential advisories to you and the need-to-know group explained the uncertainty of events once Hyperion became involved.'

'That's crap,' snapped Kolchev. 'Your predictions are supposed to be infallible in general trends. This attack must have been planned decades ago. Perhaps centuries.'

Albedo shrugged. 'Yes, Senator, but it is quite possible that only this administration's determination to start a war in the Hyperion System caused the Ousters to go through with the plan. We advised against any actions concerning Hyperion.'

Speaker Gibbons leaned forward. 'You gave us the names of the individuals necessary for the so-called Shrike Pilgrimage.'

Albedo did not shrug again, but his projected posture was relaxed, self-confident. 'You asked us to come up with names of Web individuals whose requests to the Shrike would change the outcome of the war we predicted.'

Gladstone steepled her fingers and tapped at her chin. 'And have you determined yet *how* these requests would change the outcome of that war . . . *this* war?'

'No,' said Albedo.

'Councilor,' said CEO Meina Gladstone, 'please be apprised that as of this moment, depending upon the outcome of the next few days, the government of the Hegemony of Man is considering declaring that a state of war exists

236

between us and the entity known as the TechnoCore. As de facto ambassador from that entity, you are entrusted with relaying this fact.'

Albedo smiled. He spread his hands. 'M Executive, the shock of this terrible news must have caused you to make a poor joke. Declaring war against the Core would be like . . . like a fish declaring war against water, like a driver attacking his EMV because of disturbing news of an accident elsewhere.'

Gladstone did not smile. 'I once had a grandfather on Patawpha,' she said slowly, her dialect thickening, 'who put six slugs from a pulse rifle into the family EMV when it did not start one morning. You are dismissed, Councilor.'

Albedo blinked and disappeared. The abrupt departure was either a deliberate breach of protocol – the projection usually left a room or let others leave before deliquescing – or it was a sign that the controlling intelligence in the Core had been shaken by the exchange.

Gladstone nodded at Kolchev and Gibbons. 'I won't keep you gentlemen,' she said. 'But be assured that I expect total support when the declaration of war is submitted in five hours.'

'You'll have it,' said Gibbons. The two men departed.

Aides came in through doorways and hidden panels, firing questions and cueing comlogs for instructions. Gladstone held up a finger. 'Where is Severn?' she asked. At the sight of blank faces, she added, 'The poet . . . artist, I mean. The one doing my portrait?'

Several aides looked at one another as if the Chief had come unhinged.

'He's still asleep,' said Leigh Hunt. 'He'd taken some sleeping pills, and no one thought to awaken him for the meeting.'

'I want him here within twenty minutes,' said Gladstone. 'Brief him. Where is Commander Lee?'

Niki Cardon, the young woman in charge of military liaison, spoke up. 'Lee was reassigned to perimeter patrol last night by Morpurgo and the FORCE:sea sector chief. He'll be hopping from one ocean world to another for twenty years our time. Right now he's . . . just translated to FORCE:SEACOMCEN on Bressia, awaiting offworld transport.'

'Get him back here,' said Gladstone. 'I want him promoted to rear admiral or whatever the hell the necessary staff rank would be and then assigned here, to *me*, not Government House or Executive Branch. He can be the nuclear bagman if necessary.'

Gladstone looked at the blank wall a moment. She thought of the worlds she had walked that night; Barnard's World, the lamplight through leaves, ancient brick college buildings; God's Grove with its tethered balloons and free-floating zeplens greeting the dawn; Heaven's Gate with its Promenade . . . all these were first-wave targets. She shook her head. 'Leigh, I want you and Tarra and Brindenath to have the first drafts of both speeches – general address and the declaration of war – to me within forty-five minutes. Short. Unequivocal. Check the files under Churchill and Strudensky. Realistic but defiant, optimistic but tempered with grim resolve. Niki, I need real-time monitoring of every move the joint chiefs make. I want my own command map displays – relayed through my implant. CEO ONLY. Barbre, you're going to be my extension of diplomacy by other means in the Senate. Get in there and call in notes, pull strings, blackmail, cajole, and generally make them realize that it would be safer to go out and fight the Ousters right now than to cross me in the next three or four votes.

'Questions, anyone?' Gladstone waited three seconds and slapped her hands together. 'Well, let's move, people!'

In the brief interval before the next wave of senators, ministers, and aides, Gladstone swiveled toward the blank wall above her, raised her finger toward the ceiling, and shook her hand.

She turned back just as the next mob of VIPs was shown in.

238

TWENTY-FIVE

Sol, the Consul, Father Duré, and the unconscious Het Masteen were in the first of the Cave Tombs when they heard the shots. The Consul went out alone, slowly, carefully, testing for the storm of time tides which had driven them deeper into the valley.

'It's all right,' he called back. The pale glow of Sol's lantern lighted the back of the cave, illuminating three pale faces and the robed bundle that was the Templar. 'The tides have lessened,' called the Consul.

Sol stood. His daughter's face was a pale oval below his own. 'Are you sure the shots came from Brawne's gun?'

The Consul motioned toward the darkness outside. 'None of the rest of us carried a slugthrower. I'll go check.'

'Wait,' said Sol, 'I'll go with you.'

Father Duré remained kneeling next to Het Masteen. 'Go ahead. I'll stay with him.'

'One of us will check back within the next few minutes,' said the Consul.

The valley glowed from the pale light of the Time Tombs. Wind roared from the south, but the airstream was higher tonight, above the cliff walls, and the dunes on the valley floor were not disturbed. Sol followed the Consul as he picked his way down the rough trail to the valley floor and turned toward the head of the valley. Slight tugs of *déjà vu* reminded Sol of the violence of time tides an hour earlier, but now even the remnants of the bizarre storm were fading.

Where the trail widened on the valley floor, Sol and the Consul walked together past the scorched battlefield of the Crystal Monolith, the tall structure exuding a milky glow reflected by the countless shards littering the floor of the arroyo, then climbing slightly past the Jade Tomb with its pale-green phosphorescence, then turning again and following the gentle switchbacks leading up to the Sphinx.

'My God,' whispered Sol and rushed forward, trying not to jar his sleeping child in her carrier. He knelt by the dark figure on the top step.

'Brawne?' asked the Consul, stopping two paces back and panting for breath after the sudden climb.

'Yes.' Sol started to lift her head and then jerked his hand back when he encountered something slick and cool extruding from her skull.

'Is she dead?'

Sol held his daughter's head closer to his chest as he checked for a pulse in the woman's throat. 'No,' he said and took a deep breath. 'She's alive . . . but unconscious. Give me your light.'

Sol took the flashlight and played it over Brawne Lamia's sprawled form, following the silver cord – 'tentacle' was a better description, since the thing had a fleshy mass to it that made one think of organic origins – which led from the neural shunt socket in her skull across the broad top step of the Sphinx, in through the open portal. The Sphinx itself glowed the brightest of any of the Tombs, but the entrance was very dark.

The Consul came closer. 'What is it?' He reached out to touch the silver cable, jerked his hand back as quickly as Sol had. 'My God, it's warm.'

'It feels alive,' agreed Sol. He had been chafing Brawne's hands, and now he slapped her cheeks lightly, trying to awaken her. She did not stir. He swiveled and played the flashlight beam along the cable where it snaked out of sight down the entrance corridor. 'I don't think this is something she voluntarily attached herself to.'

'The Shrike,' said the Consul. He leaned closer to activate biomonitor readouts on Brawne's wrist comlog. 'Everything is normal except her brain waves, Sol.'

'What do they say?'

'They say that she's dead. Brain dead at least. No higher functions whatsoever.'

Sol sighed and rocked back on his heels. 'We have to see where that cable goes.'

'Can't we just unhook it from the shunt socket?'

'Look,' said Sol and played the light on the back of Brawne's head while lifting a mass of dark curls away. The neural shunt, normally a plasflesh disk a few millimeters wide with a ten-micrometer socket, had seemed to melt . . . flesh rising in a red welt to connect with the microlead extensions of the metal cable.

'It would take surgery to remove that,' whispered the Consul. He touched the angry-looking welt of flesh. Brawne did not stir. The Consul retrieved the flashlight and stood. 'You stay with her. I'll follow it in.'

'Use the comm channels,' said Sol, knowing how useless they had been during the rise and fall of time tides.

The Consul nodded and moved forward quickly before fear made him hesitate.

The chrome cable snaked down the main corridor, turning out of sight beyond the room where the pilgrims had slept the night before. The Consul glanced in the room, the flashlight beam illuminating the blankets and packs they had left behind in their hurry.

He followed the cable around the bend in the corridor; through the central portal where the hallway broke into three narrower halls; up a ramp and right again down the narrow passage they had called 'King Tut's Highway' during their earlier explorations; then down a ramp; along a low tunnel where he had to crawl, placing his hands and knees carefully so as not to touch the flesh-warm metal tentacle; up an incline so steep that he had to climb it like a chimney;

241

down a wider corridor he did not remember, where stones leaned inward toward the ceiling, moisture dripping; and then down steeply, slowing his descent only by losing skin on his palms and knees, crawling finally along a stretch longer than the Sphinx had appeared wide. The Consul was thoroughly lost, trusting in the cable to lead him back out when the time came.

'Sol,' he called at last, not believing for an instant that the communicator would carry through stone and time tides.

'Here,' came the barest whisper of the scholar's voice.

'I'm way the hell inside,' the Consul whispered into his comlog. 'Down a corridor I don't remember us seeing before. It feels deep.'

'Did you find where the cable ends?'

'Yeah,' the Consul replied softly, sitting back to wipe sweat from his face with a handkerchief.

'Nexus?' asked Sol, referring to one of the countless terminal nodes where Web citizens could jack into the datasphere.

'No. The thing seems to flow directly into the stone of the floor here. The corridor ends here too. I've tried moving it, but the join is similar to where the neural shunt's been welded to her skull. It just seems part of the rock.'

'Come on out,' came Sol's voice over the rasp of static. 'We'll try to cut it off her.'

In the damp and darkness of the tunnel, the Consul felt true claustrophobia close on him for the first time in his life. He found it hard to breathe. He was sure that something was behind him in the darkness, closing off his air and only avenue of retreat. The pounding of his heart was almost audible in the tight stone crawlway.

He took slow breaths, wiped his face again, and forced the panic back. 'That might kill her,' he said between slow gasps for air.

No answer. The Consul called again, but something had cut off their thin connection.

'I'm coming out,' he said into the silent instrument and turned around, playing his flashlight along the low tunnel. *Had the cable-tentacle twitched, or was that just a trick of light?*

The Consul began crawling back the way he had come.

They had found Het Masteen at sunset, just minutes before the time storm struck. The Templar had been staggering when the Consul, Sol, and Duré had first seen him, and by the time they reached his fallen form, Masteen was unconscious.

'Carry him to the Sphinx,' said Sol.

At that moment, as if choreographed by the setting sun, the time tides flowed over them like a tidal wave of nausea and *déjà vu*. All three men fell to their knees. Rachel awoke and cried with the vigor of the newly born and terrified.

'Make for the valley entrance,' gasped the Consul, standing with Het Masteen draped over his shoulder. 'Got to . . . get out . . . the valley.'

The three men moved toward the mouth of the valley, past the first tomb, the Sphinx, but the time tides became worse, blowing against them like a terrible wind of vertigo. Thirty meters beyond and they could climb no more. They fell to hands and knees, Het Masteen rolling across the hard-packed trail. Rachel had ceased wailing and writhed in discomfort.

'Back,' gasped Paul Duré. 'Back down the valley. It was . . . better . . . below.'

They retraced their steps, staggering along the trail like three drunkards, each carrying a burden too precious to be dropped. Below the Sphinx they rested a moment, backs to a boulder, while the very fabric of space and time seemed to shift and buckle around them. It was as if the world had been the surface of a flag and someone had unfurled it with an angry snap. Reality seemed to billow and fold, then plunge farther away, folding back like a wave cresting above them. The Consul left the Templar lying against the rock and fell to all fours, panting, fingers clinging to the soil in panic.

'The Möbius cube,' said the Templar, stirring, his eyes still closed. 'We must have the Möbius cube.'

'Damn,' managed the Consul. He shook Het Masteen roughly. 'Why do we need it? Masteen, why do we need it?' The Templar's head bobbed back and forth limply. He was unconscious once again.

'I'll get it,' said Duré. The priest looked ancient and ill, his face and lips pale.

The Consul nodded, lifted Het Masteen over his shoulder, helped Sol gain his feet, and staggered away down the valley, feeling the riptides of anti-entropic fields lessen as they moved farther away from the Sphinx.

Father Duré had climbed the trail, climbed the long stairway, and staggered to the entrance of the Sphinx, clinging to the rough stones there the way a sailor would cling to a thrown line in rough seas. The Sphinx seemed to totter above him, first tilting thirty degrees one way, then fifty the other. Duré knew that it was only the violence of the time tides distorting his senses, but it was enough to make him kneel and vomit on the stone.

The tides paused a moment, like a violent surf resting between terrible wave assaults, and Duré found his feet, wiped his mouth with the back of his hand, and stumbled into the dark tomb.

He had not brought a flashlight; stumbling, he felt his way along the corridor, appalled by the twin fantasies of touching something slick and cool in the darkness or of stumbling into the room where he was reborn and finding his own corpse there, still moldering from the grave. Duré screamed, but the sound was lost in the tornado roar of his own pulse as the time tides returned in force.

The sleeping room was dark, that terrible dark which means the total absence of light, but Duré's eyes adjusted, and he realized that the Möbius cube itself was glowing slightly, telltales winking.

He stumbled across the cluttered room and grabbed the cube, lifting the heavy thing with a sudden burst of adrenaline. The Consul's summary tapes had mentioned this artifact – Masteen's mysterious luggage during the pilgrimage – as well as the fact that it was believed to hold an erg, one of the alien forcefield creatures used to power a Templar treeship. Duré had no idea why the erg was important now, but he clutched the box to his chest as he struggled back down the corridor, outside and down the steps, deeper into the valley.

'Here!' called the Consul from the first Cave Tomb at the base of the cliff wall. 'It's better here.'

Duré staggered up the trail, almost dropping the cube in his confusion and sudden draining of energy; the Consul helped him the last thirty steps into the tomb.

It was better inside. Duré could feel the ebb and flow of time tides just beyond the cave entrance, but back in the rear of the cave, glow-globes revealing elaborate carvings in their cold light, it was almost normal. The priest collapsed next to Sol Weintraub and set the Möbius cube near the silent but staring form of Het Masteen.

'He just awakened as you approached,' whispered Sol. The baby's eyes were very wide and very dark in the weak light.

The Consul dropped down next to the Templar. 'Why do we need the cube? Masteen, why do we need it?'

Het Masteen's gaze did not falter; he did not blink. 'Our ally,' he whispered. 'Our only ally against the Lord of Pain.' The syllables were etched with the distinctive dialect of the Templar world.

'*How* is it our ally?' demanded Sol, grabbing the man's robe in both his fists. 'How do we use it? When?'

The Templar's gaze was set on something in the infinite distance. 'We vied for the honor,' he whispered, voice hoarse. 'The True Voice of the *Sequoia Sempervirens* was the first to contact the Keats retrieval cybrid . . . but *I* was the one honored by the light of the Muir. It was the *Yggdrasill*, my *Yggdrasill*, which was offered in atonement for our sins against the Muir.' The Templar closed his eyes. A slight smile looked incongruous on his stern-featured face.

The Consul looked at Duré and Sol. 'That sounds more like Shrike Cult terminology than Templar dogma.'

'Perhaps it is both,' whispered Duré. 'There have been stranger coalitions in the history of theology.'

Sol lifted his palm to the Templar's forehead. The tall man was burning up with fever. Sol rummaged through their only medpak in search of a pain derm or feverpatch. Finding one, he hesitated. 'I don't know if Templars are within standard med norms. I don't want some allergy to kill him.'

The Consul took the feverpatch and applied it to the Templar's frail upper arm. 'They're within the norm.' He leaned closer. 'Masteen, what happened on the windwagon?'

The Templar's eyes opened but remained unfocused. 'Windwagon?'

'I don't understand,' whispered Father Duré.

Sol took him aside. 'Masteen never told his tale on the pilgrimage out,' he whispered. 'He disappeared during our first night out on the wind-wagon. Blood was left behind – plenty of blood – as well as his luggage and the Möbius cube. But no Masteen.'

'What happened on the windwagon?' the Consul whispered again. He shook the Templar slightly to get his attention. 'Think, True Voice of the Tree Het Masteen!'

The tall man's face changed, his eyes coming into focus, the vaguely Asiatic features settling into familiar, stern lines. 'I released the elemental from his confinement . . .'

'The erg,' Sol whispered to the baffled priest.

'. . . and bound him with the mind discipline I had learned in the High Branches. But then, without warning, the Lord of Pain came unto us.'

246

'The Shrike,' Sol whispered, more to himself than to the priest.

'Was it your blood spilled there?' the Consul asked the Templar.

'Blood?' Masteen drew his hood forward to hide his confusion. 'No, it was not my blood. The Lord of Pain had a . . . celebrant . . . in his grasp. The man fought. Attempted to escape the atonement spikes . . .'

'What about the erg?' pressed the Consul. 'The elemental. What did you expect it to do for you? . . . to protect you from the Shrike?'

The Templar frowned and raised a trembling hand to his brow. 'It . . . was not ready. *I* was not ready. I returned it to its confinement. The Lord of Pain touched me on the shoulder. I was . . . pleased . . . that my atonement should be within the same hour as the sacrifice of my treeship.'

Sol leaned closer to Duré. 'The treeship *Yggdrasill* was destroyed in orbit that same evening,' he whispered.

Het Masteen closed his eyes. 'Tired,' he whispered, his voice fading.

The Consul shook him again. 'How did you get here? Masteen, how did you get here from the Sea of Grass?'

'I awoke among the Tombs,' whispered the Templar without opening his eyes. 'Awoke among the Tombs. Tired. Must sleep.'

'Let him rest,' said Father Duré.

The Consul nodded and lowered the robed man to a sleeping position.

'Nothing makes sense,' whispered Sol as the three men and an infant sat in the dim light and felt the time tides ebb and flow outside.

'We lose a pilgrim, we gain one,' muttered the Consul. 'It's as if some bizarre game were being played.'

An hour later, they had heard the shots echo down the valley.

*   *   *

247

Sol and the Consul crouched by the silent form of Brawne Lamia.

'We'd need a laser to cut that thing off,' said Sol. 'With Kassad gone, so are our weapons.'

The Consul touched the young woman's wrist. 'Cutting it off might kill her.'

'According to the biomonitor, she's already dead.'

The Consul shook his head. 'No. Something else is going on. That thing may be tapping into the Keats cybrid persona she's been carrying. Perhaps when it's finished, it'll give us Brawne back.'

Sol lifted his daughter to his shoulder and looked out over the softly glowing valley. 'What a madhouse. Nothing's going as we thought. If only your damn ship were here . . . it would have cutting tools in case we have to free Brawne from this . . . this *thing* . . . and she and Masteen might have a chance for survival in the surgery.'

The Consul remained kneeling, staring at nothing. After a moment he said, 'Wait here with her, please,' rose, and disappeared in the dark maw of the Sphinx's entrance. Five minutes later, he was back with his own large travel bag. He removed a rolled rug from the bottom and unfurled it on the stone of the Sphinx's top stair.

It was an ancient rug, a little less than two meters long and a bit more than a meter wide. The intricately woven cloth had faded over the centuries, but the monofilament flight threads still glowed like gold in the dim light. Thin leads ran from the carpet to a single power cell which the Consul now detached.

'Good God,' whispered Sol. He remembered the Consul's tale of his grandmother Siri's tragic love affair with Hegemony Shipman Merin Aspic. It had been a love affair that had raised a rebellion against the Hegemony and plunged Maui-Covenant into years of war. Merin Aspic had flown to Firstsite on a friend's hawking mat.

The Consul nodded. 'It belonged to Mike Osho, Grandfather Merin's friend. Siri left it in her tomb for Merin to find. He gave it to me when I was a child – just before the Battle of the Archipelago, where he and the dream of freedom died.'

Sol ran his hand across the centuries-old artifact. 'It's a shame it can't work here.'

The Consul glanced up. 'Why can't it?'

'Hyperion's magnetic field is below the critical level for EM vehicles,' said Sol. 'That's why there are dirigibles and skimmers rather than EMVs, why the *Benares* was no longer a levitation barge.' He stopped, feeling foolish explaining this to a man who had been Hegemony Consul on Hyperion for eleven local years. 'Or am I wrong?'

The Consul smiled. 'You're right that standard EMVs aren't reliable here. Too much mass-to-lift ratio. But the hawking mat is all lift, almost no mass. I've tried it here when I lived in the capital. It's not a smooth ride . . . but it should work with one person aboard.'

Sol glanced back down the valley, past the glowing forms of the Jade Tomb, Obelisk, and Crystal Monolith, to where the shadows of the cliff wall hid the entrance to the Cave Tombs. He wondered if Father Duré and Het Masteen were still alone . . . still alive. 'You're thinking of going for help?'

'Of one of us going for help. Bringing the ship back. Or at least freeing it and sending it back unmanned. We could draw lots to see who goes.'

It was Sol's turn to smile. 'Think, my friend. Duré is in no condition to travel and does not know the way in any case. I . . .' Sol lifted Rachel until the top of her head touched his cheek. 'The voyage might last several days. I – we – do not have several days. If something is to be done for her, we must remain here and take our chances. It is you who must go.'

The Consul sighed but did not argue.

'Besides,' said Sol, 'it is your ship. If anyone can free it from Gladstone's interdiction, you can. And you know the Governor-General well.'

The Consul looked toward the west. 'I wonder if Theo is still in power.'

'Let's go back and tell Father Duré our plan,' said Sol. 'Also, I left the nursing paks in the cave, and Rachel is hungry.'

The Consul rolled the carpet, slipped it in his pack, and stared down at Brawne Lamia, at the obscene cable snaking away into darkness. 'Will she be all right?'

'I'll have Paul come back with a blanket to stay with her while you and I carry our other invalid back here. Will you leave tonight or wait until sunrise?'

The Consul rubbed his cheeks tiredly. 'I don't like the thought of crossing the mountains at night, but we can't spare the time. I'll leave as soon as I put some things together.'

Sol nodded and looked toward the entrance to the valley. 'I wish Brawne could tell us where Silenus has gone.'

'I'll look for him as I fly out,' said the Consul. He glanced up at the stars. 'Figure thirty-six to forty hours of flying to get back to Keats. A few hours to free the ship. I should be back here within two standard days.'

Sol nodded, rocking the crying child. His tired but amiable expression did not conceal his doubt. He set his hand on the Consul's shoulder. 'It is right that we try, my friend. Come, let us talk to Father Duré, see if our other fellow traveler is awake, and eat a meal together. It looks as if Brawne brought enough supplies to allow us a final feast.'

TWENTY-SIX

When Brawne Lamia had been a child, her father a senator and their home relocated, however briefly, from Lusus to the wooded wonders of Tau Ceti Center's Administrative Residential Complex, she had seen the ancient flatfilm Walt Disney animation of *Peter Pan*. After seeing the animation, she had read the book, and both had captured her heart.

For months, the five-standard-year-old girl had waited for Peter Pan to arrive one night and take her away. She had left notes pointing the way to her bedroom under the shingled dormer. She had left the house while her parents slept and lain on the soft grass of the Deer Park lawns, watching the milkish-gray night sky of TC² and dreaming of the boy from Neverland who would some night soon take her away with him flying toward the second star to the right, straight on till morning. She would be his companion, the mother to the lost boys, fellow nemesis to the evil Hook, and most of all, Peter's new Wendy . . . the new child-friend to the child who would not grow old.

And now, twenty years later, Peter had finally come for her.

Lamia had felt no pain, only the sudden, icy rush of displacement as the Shrike's steel talon penetrated the neural shunt behind her ear. Then she was away and flying.

She had moved through the datumplane and into the datasphere before. Only weeks before, her time, Lamia had ridden into the TechnoCore matrix with her favorite

251

cyberpuke, silly BB Surbringer, to help Johnny steal back his cybrid retrieval persona. They had penetrated the periphery and stolen the persona, but an alarm had been tripped, BB had died. Lamia never wanted to enter the datasphere again.

But she was there now.

The experience was like nothing she had ever had with comlog leads or nodes before. That was like full stimsim – like being in a holodrama with full color and wraparound stereo – this was like *being there*.

Peter had finally come to take her away.

Lamia rose above the curve of Hyperion's planetary limb, seeing the rudimentary channels of microwaved dataflow and tightbeamed commlink that passed for an embryonic datasphere there. She did not pause to tap into it, for she was following an orange umbilical skyward toward the *real* avenues and highways of datumplane.

Hyperion space had been invaded by FORCE and by the Ouster Swarm, and both had brought the intricate folds and latticework of the datasphere with them. With new eyes, Lamia could see the thousand levels of FORCE dataflow, a turbulent green ocean of information shot through with the red veins of secured channels and the spinning violet spheres with their black phage outriders that were the FORCE AIs. This pseudopod of the great Web megadatasphere flowed out of normal space through black funnels of shipboard farcasters, along expanding wave fronts of overlapping, instantaneous ripples that Lamia recognized as continuous bursts from a score of fatline transmitters.

She paused, suddenly unsure of where to go, which avenue to take. It was as if she had been flying and her uncertainty had endangered the magic – threatening to drop her back to the ground so many miles below.

Then Peter took her hand and buoyed her up.

—Johnny!

—Hello, Brawne.

Her own body image clicked into existence at the same

second she saw and felt his. It was Johnny as she had last seen him – her client and lover – Johnny of the sharp cheekbones, hazel eyes, compact nose and solid jaw. Johnny's brownish-red curls still fell to his collar, and his face remained a study in purposeful energy. His smile still made her melt inside.

Johnny! She hugged him then, and she *felt* the hug, felt his strong hands on her back as they floated high above everything, felt her breasts flatten against his chest as he returned the hug with surprising strength for his small frame. They kissed, and there was no denying that *that* was real.

Lamia floated at arms' length, her hands on his shoulders. Both their faces were lighted by the green and violet glow of the great datasphere ocean above them.

—*Is this real?* She heard her own voice and dialect in the question even though she knew she had only thought it.

—*Yes. Real as any part of the datumplane matrix can be. We're on the edge of the megasphere in Hyperion space.* His voice still held that elusive accent that she found so beguiling and maddening.

—*What happened?* With the words, she conveyed images to him of the Shrike's appearance, the sudden, terrible invasion of the blade-finger.

—*Yes,* thought Johnny, holding her more tightly. *Somehow it freed me from the Schrön loop and jacked us directly into the datasphere.*

—*Am I dead, Johnny?*

The face of Johnny Keats smiled down at her. He shook her slightly, kissed her gently, and rotated so that they could both see the spectacle above and below. *No, you're not dead, Brawne, although you may be hooked to some kind of bizarre life support while your datumplane analog wanders here with me.*

—*Are you dead?*

He grinned at her again. *Not any longer, although life in a*

253

Schrön loop isn't all it's cracked up to be. It was like dreaming someone else's dreams.

—*I dreamed about you.*

Johnny nodded. *I don't think that was me. I dreamed the same dreams . . . conversations with Meina Gladstone, glimpses of the Hegemony government councils . . .*

—*Yes!*

He squeezed her hand. *I suspect that they reactivated another Keats cybrid. Somehow we were able to connect across all the light-years.*

—*Another cybrid? How? You destroyed the Core template, liberated the persona . . .*

Her lover shrugged. He was wearing a ruffled shirt and silk waistcoat of a style she had never seen before. The flow of data through the avenues above them painted both of them with pulses of neon light as they floated there. *I suspected that there would be more backups than BB and I could find in such a shallow penetration of the Core periphery. It doesn't matter, Brawne. If there's another copy, then he's me, and I can't believe he'd be an enemy. Come on, let's explore.*

Lamia held back a second as he tugged her upward. *Explore what?*

—*This is our chance to see what's going on, Brawne. A chance to get to the bottom of a lot of mysteries.*

She heard the uncharacteristic timidity in her own voice/thought. *I'm not sure I want to, Johnny.*

He rotated to look at her. *Is this the detective I knew? What happened to the woman who couldn't stand secrets?*

—*She's been through some rough times, Johnny. I've been able to look back and see that becoming a detective was – in large part – a reaction to my father's suicide. I'm still trying to solve the details of his death. In the meantime, a lot of people have gotten hurt in real life. Including you, my dear.*

—*And have you solved it?*

—*What?*

—*Your father's death?*

Lamia frowned at him. *I don't know. I don't think so.*

Johnny pointed toward the fluid mass of the datasphere ebbing and flowing above them. *There are a lot of answers waiting up there, Brawne. If we have the courage to go looking for them.*

She took his hand again. *We could die there.*

—Yes.

Lamia paused, looked down toward Hyperion. The world was a dark curve with the few isolated dataflow pockets glowing like campfires in the night. The great ocean above them seethed and pulsated with light and dataflow noise – and Brawne knew that it was only the smallest extension of the megasphere beyond. She knew . . . she *felt* . . . that their reborn datumplane analogs could now go places no cyber-puke cowboy had ever dreamt of.

With Johnny as her guide, Brawne knew that the megasphere and TechnoCore were penetrable to depths no human had plumbed. And she was scared.

But she was with Peter Pan, at last. And Neverland beckoned.

—All right, Johnny. What are we waiting for?

They rose together toward the megasphere.

TWENTY-SEVEN

Colonel Fedmahn Kassad followed Moneta through the portal and found himself standing upon a vast lunar plain where a terrible tree of thorns rose five kilometers high into a blood-red sky. Human figures writhed on the many branches and spikes: the closer forms recognizably human and in pain, the farther ones dwarfed by distance until they resembled clusters of pale grapes.

Kassad blinked and took a breath beneath the surface of his quicksilver skinsuit. He looked around, past the silent form of Moneta, tearing his gaze from the obscenity of the tree.

What he had thought was a lunar plain was the surface of Hyperion, at the entrance to the Valley of the Time Tombs, but a Hyperion terribly changed. The dunes were frozen and distorted as if they had been blasted and glazed into glass; the boulders and cliff faces also had flowed and frozen like glaciers of pale stone. There was no atmosphere – the sky was black with the pitiless clarity of airless moons everywhere. The sun was not Hyperion's; the light was not of human experience. Kassad looked up, and the viewing filters of his skinsuit polarized to deal with terrible energies that filled the sky with bands of blood red and blossoms of fierce white light.

Below him, the valley seemed to vibrate as if to unfelt tremors. The Time Tombs glowed of their own interior energies, pulses of cold light thrown many meters across the valley floor from every entrance, portal, and aperture. The Tombs looked new, slick, and shining.

Kassad realized that only the skinsuit was allowing him to

breathe and saving his flesh from the lunar cold that had replaced the desert warmth. He turned to look at Moneta, attempted to phrase an intelligent question, failed, and raised his gaze to the impossible tree once again.

The thorn tree seemed to be made of the same steel and chrome and cartilage as the Shrike itself: obviously artificial and yet horribly organic at the same instant. The trunk was two or three hundred meters thick at its base, the lower branches almost as broad, but the smaller branches and thorns soon tapered to stiletto thinness as they splayed toward the sky with their awful impalement of human fruit.

Impossible that humans so impaled could live for long; doubly impossible that they could survive in the vacuum of this place outside of time and space. But survive and suffer they did. Kassad watched them writhe. *All* of them were alive. And all were in pain.

Kassad was aware of the pain as a great sound beyond hearing, a huge, incessant foghorn of pain, as if thousands of untrained fingers were falling on thousands of keys playing a massive pipe organ of pain. The pain was so palpable that he searched the blazing sky as if the tree were a pyre or huge beacon with the waves of pain clearly visible.

There was only the harsh light and lunar stillness.

Kassad raised the magnification of his skinsuit viewing lenses and looked from branch to branch, thorn to thorn. The people writhing there were of both genders and all ages. They wore a variety of torn clothing and disarrayed cosmetics that spanned many decades if not centuries. Many of the styles were not familiar to Kassad, and he assumed that he was looking at victims from his future. There were thousands . . . tens of thousands . . . of victims there. All were alive. All were in pain.

Kassad stopped, focused on a branch four hundred meters from the bottom, upon a cluster of thorns and bodies far out from the trunk, upon a single thorn three meters long from which a familiar purple cape billowed. The form there writhed, twisted, and turned toward Fedmahn Kassad.

He was looking at the impaled figure of Martin Silenus.

Kassad cursed and formed fists so tight that the bones in his hands ached. He looked around for his weapons, magnifying vision to stare into the Crystal Monolith. There was nothing there.

Colonel Kassad shook his head, realized that his skinsuit was a better weapon than any he had brought to Hyperion, and began to stride toward the tree. He did not know how he would climb it, but he would find a way. He did not know how he would get Silenus down alive – get all of the victims down – but he would do so or die in the trying.

Kassad took ten paces and stopped on a curve of frozen dune. The Shrike stood between him and the tree.

He realized that he was grinning fiercely beneath the chromium forcefield of the skinsuit. This was what he had waited many years for. This was the honorable warfare he had pledged his life and honor for twenty years earlier in the FORCE Masada Ceremony. Single combat between warriors. A struggle to protect the innocent. Kassad grinned, flattened the edge of his right hand into a silver blade, and stepped forward.

—Kassad!

He looked back at Moneta's call. Light cascaded on the quicksilver surface of her nude body as she pointed toward the valley.

A second Shrike was emerging from the tomb called the Sphinx. Farther down the valley, a Shrike stepped from the entrance to the Jade Tomb. Harsh light glinted from spikes and razorwire as another emerged from the Obelisk, half a klick away.

Kassad ignored them and turned back toward the tree and its protector.

A hundred Shrikes stood between Kassad and the tree. He blinked, and a hundred more appeared to his left.

He looked behind him, and a legion of Shrikes stood as impassively as sculptures on the cold dunes and melted boulders of the desert.

Kassad pounded his own knee with his fist. *Damn.*

Moneta came up next to him until their arms touched. The skinsuits flowed together, and he felt the warm flesh of her forearm against his. She stood thigh to thigh with him.

—I love you, Kassad.

He gazed at the perfect lines of her face, ignored the riot of reflections and colors there, and tried to remember the first time he had met her, in the forest near Agincourt. He remembered her startling green eyes and short, brown hair. The fullness of her lower lip and how it tasted of tears the time he accidentally had bitten it.

He raised a hand and touched her cheek, feeling the warmth of skin beneath the skinsuit. *If you love me*, he sent, *stay here.*

Colonel Fedmahn Kassad turned away then and let out a scream only he could hear in the lunar silence – a scream part rebel yell from the distant human past, part FORCE cadet graduation shout, part karate cry, and part pure defiance. He ran across the dunes toward the thorn tree and the Shrike directly in front of it.

There were thousands of Shrikes in the hills and valleys now. Talons clicked open in unison; light glinted on tens of thousands of scalpel-sharp blades and thorns.

Kassad ignored the others and ran toward the Shrike he thought was the first he had seen. Above the thing, human forms writhed in the solitude of their pain.

The Shrike he was running toward opened its arms as if offering an embrace. Curved blades on its wrists, joints, and chest seemed to extend from hidden sheaths.

Kassad screamed and closed the remaining distance.

TWENTY-EIGHT

'I shouldn't go,' said the Consul.

He and Sol had carried the still-unconscious Het Masteen from the Cave Tomb to the Sphinx while Father Duré watched over Brawne Lamia. It was almost midnight, and the valley glowed from the reflected light of the Tombs. The wings of the Sphinx cut arcs from the bit of sky visible to them between the cliff walls. Brawne lay motionless, the obscene cable snaking into the darkness of the tomb.

Sol touched the Consul's shoulder. 'We've discussed it. You should go.'

The Consul shook his head and idly stroked the ancient hawking mat. 'It may be able to carry two. You and Duré could make it to where the *Benares* is tied up.'

Sol held his daughter's small head in the cusp of his hand as he gently rocked her. 'Rachel is two days old. Besides, this is where we must be.'

The Consul looked around. His eyes showed his pain. 'This is where *I* should be. The Shrike . . .'

Duré leaned forward. The luminescence from the tomb behind them painted his high forehead and sharp cheeks with light. 'My son, if you stay here, it is for no other reason than suicide. If you attempt to bring the ship back for M Lamia and the Templar, you will be helping others.'

The Consul rubbed his cheek. He was very tired. 'There's room for you on the mat, Father.'

Duré smiled. 'Whatever my fate may be, I feel that I am meant to meet it here. I will wait for your return.'

The Consul shook his head again but moved to sit cross-legged on the mat, pulling the heavy duffel bag toward him. He counted the ration paks and water bottles Sol had packed for him. 'There are too many. You'll need more for yourself.'

Duré chuckled. 'We have enough food and water for four days, thanks to M Lamia. After that, if we have to fast, it will not be the first time for me.'

'But what if Silenus and Kassad return?'

'They can share our water,' said Sol. 'We can make another trip to the Keep for food if the others return.'

The Consul sighed. 'All right.' He touched the appropriate flight thread designs, and the two meters of carpet stiffened and rose ten centimeters above the stone. If there was a wobble in the uncertain magnetic fields, it was not discernible.

'You'll need oxygen for the mountain crossing,' said Sol.

The Consul lifted the osmosis mask from the pack.

Sol handed him Lamia's automatic pistol.

'I can't . . .'

'It won't help us with the Shrike,' said Sol. 'And it might make the difference of whether you get to Keats or not.'

The Consul nodded and set the weapon in his bag. He shook hands with the priest, then with the old scholar. Rachel's tiny fingers brushed his forearm.

'Good luck,' said Duré. 'May God be with you.'

The Consul nodded, tapped the flight designs, and leaned forward as the hawking mat lifted five meters, wobbled ever so slightly, and then slid forward and up as if riding invisible rails in the air.

The Consul banked right toward the entrance to the valley, passed ten meters above the dunes there, and then banked left toward the barrens. He looked back only once. The four figures on the top step of the Sphinx, two men standing, two shapes reclining, looked very small indeed. He could not make out the baby in Sol's arms.

* * *

As they had agreed, the Consul aimed the hawking mat toward the west to overfly the City of Poets in hopes of finding Martin Silenus. Intuition told him that the irascible poet might have detoured there. The skies were relatively free of the light of battle, and the Consul had to search shadows unbroken by starlight as he passed twenty meters above the broken spires and domes of the city. There was no sign of the poet. If Brawne and Silenus had come this way, even their footprints in the sand had been erased by the night winds which now moved the Consul's thinning hair and flapped his clothing.

It was cold on the mat at this altitude. The Consul could feel the shudders and vibrations as the hawking mat felt its way along unsteady lines of force. Between Hyperion's treacherous magnetic field and the age of the EM flight threads, he knew that there was a real chance the mat would tumble out of the sky long before he reached the capital of Keats.

The Consul shouted Martin Silenus's name several times, but there was no response except for an explosion of doves from their nesting place in the shattered dome of one of the galleries. He shook his head and banked south toward the Bridle Range.

Through his grandfather Merin, the Consul knew the history of this hawking mat. It had been one of the first such playthings handcrafted by Vladimir Sholokov, Web-famous lepidopterist and EM systems engineer, and it may well have been the one he gave to his teenaged niece. Sholokov's love for the young girl had become legend, as had the fact that she spurned the gift of the flying carpet.

But others had loved the idea, and while hawking mats were soon outlawed on worlds with sensible traffic control, they continued to show up on colonial planets. This one had allowed the Consul's grandfather to meet his grandmother Siri on Maui-Covenant.

The Consul looked up as the mountain range approached.

Ten minutes of flying had covered the two-hour hike across the barrens. The others had urged him not to stop at Chronos Keep to look for Silenus; whatever fate might have befallen the poet there might well claim the Consul too, before his journey had really begun. He contented himself with hovering just beyond the windows two hundred meters up the cliff wall, an arm's length from the terrace where they had looked out at the valley three days before, and shouting for the poet.

Only echoes answered him from the dark banquet halls and corridors of the Keep. The Consul held on tightly to the edges of the hawking mat, feeling the sense of height and exposure this close to the vertical stone walls. He was relieved when he banked the mat away from the Keep, gained altitude, and climbed toward the mountain passes where snow gleamed in the starlight.

He followed the cables of the tramway as they climbed the pass and connected one nine-thousand-meter peak to the next across the wide span of the mountain range. It was very cold at this altitude, and the Consul was glad for Kassad's extra thermal cape as he huddled under it, taking care not to expose the flesh of his hands or cheeks. The gel of the osmosis mask stretched across his face like some hungry symbiote, gobbling oxygen where little was to be found.

It was enough. The Consul took slow, deep breaths as he flew ten meters above the ice-caked cables. None of the pressurized tramcars were running, and the isolation above the glaciers, sheer peaks, and shadow-shrouded valleys was heart-stopping. The Consul was glad that he was attempting this trip if for no other reason than to see Hyperion's beauty one last time, unspoiled by the terrible threat of the Shrike or Ouster invasion.

It had taken the tramcar twelve hours to ferry them from south to north. Despite the hawking mat's slow twenty-klick-per-hour airspeed, the Consul made the crossing in six hours. Sunrise caught him still above the high peaks. He startled awake, realized with a shock that he had been dreaming while the hawking mat flew on toward a peak rising another five meters above his altitude. The Consul could see boulders and snowfields fifty meters ahead. A black bird with a three-meter wingspan – one of those the locals called a harbinger – pushed off from its icy eyrie and floated in the thin air, looking back at the Consul with black and beady eyes while he banked steeply to the left, felt something give way in the hawking mat's flight gear, and fell thirty meters before the flight threads found purchase and leveled the carpet off.

The Consul gripped the edges of the mat with fingers gone white. He had tied the strap of his duffel bag around his belt, otherwise the bag would have tumbled off to a glacier far below.

There was no sign of the tramway. Somehow the Consul had slept long enough to allow the hawking mat to drift off course. For a second, he panicked, jinking the mat this way and then that, desperate for a path between the peaks surrounding him like teeth. Then he saw the morning sunlight golden on the slopes ahead of him and to his right, the shadows leaping across glaciers and high tundra behind him and to his left, and he knew that he was still on the right track. Beyond this final spine of high peaks lay the southern foothills. And beyond that . . .

The hawking mat seemed to hesitate as the Consul tapped flight designs and urged it higher, but it rose in reluctant steps until it cleared the final nine-thousand-meter peak and he could see the lower mountains beyond, dwindling to foothills a mere three thousand meters above sea level. The Consul descended with gratitude.

He found the tramline gleaming in sunlight, eight klicks south of where he left the Bridle Range. Tramcars hung silently around the west terminal station. Below, the sparse buildings of the village of Pilgrims' Rest appeared as abandoned as they had several days earlier. There was no sign of the windwagon where it had been left at the low pier leading out over the shallows of the Sea of Grass.

The Consul let down near the pier, deactivated the hawking mat, stretched his legs with some pain before rolling up the mat for safe-keeping, and found a toilet in one of the abandoned buildings near the wharf. When he emerged, the morning sun was creeping down the foothills and erasing the last shadows there. As far as he could see to the south and west stretched the Sea of Grass, its tabletop smoothness belied by occasional breezes which sent ripples across the verdant surface, briefly revealing the russet and ultramarine stalks beneath in a movement so wavelike that one expected to see whitecaps and fish leaping.

There were no fish in the Sea of Grass, but there were grass serpents twenty meters long, and if the Consul's hawking mat failed him out there, even a safe landing would not keep him alive for long.

The Consul unrolled the mat, set his bag behind him, and activated the carpet. He stayed relatively low, twenty-five meters above the surface, but not so low that a grass serpent might mistake him for a low-flying morsel. It had taken the windwagon less than a full Hyperion day to ferry them across the Sea, but with the winds frequently from the northeast, that had involved quite a bit of tacking to and fro. The Consul bet that he could fly across this narrowest part of the Sea in less than fifteen hours. He tapped the forward control designs, and the hawking mat sped faster.

Within twenty minutes, the mountains had fallen behind until the foothills were lost in the haze of distance. Within an hour, the peaks began to shrink as the curve of the world hid their base. Two hours out, and the Consul could see only the highest of the peaks as an indistinct, serrated shadow rising from the haze.

Then the Sea of Grass spread to all horizons, unchanging except for the sensuous ripples and furrows caused by the occasional breeze. It was much warmer here than on the high plateau north of the Bridle Range. The Consul shed his thermal cape, then his coat, then his sweater. The sun beat down with surprising intensity for such high latitudes. The Consul fumbled in his bag, found the wrinkled and battered tricorne cap he had worn with such aplomb just two days earlier, and wedged it on his head to give some shade. His forehead and balding skull were already sunburned.

About four hours out, he ate his first meal of the trip, chewing on the tasteless strips of ration-pak protein as if they were filet mignon. The water was the most delicious part of the meal, and the Consul had to fight his urge to empty all the bottles in a single orgy of drinking.

The Sea of Grass stretched below, behind, and ahead. The Consul dozed, snapping awake each time with a sense of falling, hands gripping the edge of the rigid hawking mat. He realized that he should have tied himself in with the single rope he had brought in his bag, but he didn't want to land – the grass was sharp and higher than his head. Although he had seen none of the telltale V-shaped wakes of the grass serpents, he could not be sure they were not resting in wait below.

He wondered idly where the windwagon had gone. The thing had been fully automated and presumably programmed by the Church of the Shrike, since they had sponsored the pilgrimage. What other duties might the thing have had? The Consul shook his head, sat upright, and pinched his cheeks. He had been drifting in and out of dreams even as he thought about the windwagon. Fifteen hours had seemed a short enough time as he stood talking about it in the Valley of the Time Tombs. He glanced at his comlog; five hours had passed.

The Consul lifted the mat to two hundred meters, looked carefully for any sign of a serpent, and then brought the mat down to a hover five meters above the grass. Carefully he extracted the rope, made a loop, moved to the front of the carpet, and wound several lengths around the carpet, leaving

266

enough slack to slide his body in before tightening the knot.

If the mat fell, the tether would be worse than useless, but the snug bands of rope against his back gave a sense of security as he leaned forward to tap the flight designs again, leveled the carpet out at forty meters, and laid his cheek against the warm fabric. Sunlight filtered through his fingers, and he realized that his bare forearms were getting a terrible sunburn.

He was too tired to sit up and roll down his sleeves.

A breeze came up. The Consul could hear a rustling and sliding below as either the grasses blew or something large slithered past.

He was too tired to care. The Consul closed his eyes and was asleep in less than thirty seconds.

The Consul dreamed of his home – his true home – on Maui-Covenant and the dream was filled with color: the bottomless blue sky, the wide expanse of the South Sea, ultramarine fading to green where the Equatorial Shallows began, the startling greens and yellows and orchid reds of the motile isles as they were herded north by the dolphins . . . extinct now since the Hegemony invasion in the Consul's childhood, but quite alive in his dream, breaking the water in great leaps that sent a thousand prisms of light dancing in the pure air.

In his dream, the Consul was a child again, and he stood on the highest level of a treehouse on their First Family Isle. Grandmother Siri was next to him – not the regal grande dame he had known but the beautiful young woman his grandfather had met and fallen in love with. The treesails were flapping as the southerlies came up, moving the herd of motile isles in precise formation through the blue channels through the Shallows. Just on the northern horizon, he could see the first of the Equatorial Archipelago islands rising green and permanent against an evening sky.

Siri touched his shoulder and pointed to the west.

267

The isles were burning, sinking, their keel roots writhing in purposeless pain. The dolphin herders were gone. The sky rained fire. The Consul recognized billion-volt lances as they fried the air and left blue-gray afterimages on his retinas. Underwater explosions lighted the oceans and sent thousands of fish and fragile sea creatures bobbing to the surface in their death throes.

'Why?' asked Grandmother Siri, but her voice was the soft whisper of a teenager.

The Consul tried to answer her but could not. Tears blinded him. He reached for her hand, but she was no longer there, and the sense that she was *gone*, that he could never make up for his sins, hurt him so badly that he found it impossible to breathe. His throat was clogged with emotion. Then he realized that it was smoke that burned his eyes and filled his lungs; the Family Isle was on fire.

The child who was the Consul staggered forward in the blue-black darkness, hunting blindly for someone to hold his hand, to reassure him.

A hand closed on his. It was not Siri's. The hand was impossibly firm as it squeezed. The fingers were blades.

The Consul came awake gasping.

It was dark. He had slept for at least seven hours. Struggling with the ropes, he sat up, stared at his glowing comlog display.

Twelve hours. He had slept for twelve hours.

Every muscle in his body ached as he leaned over and peered below. The hawking mat held a steady altitude of forty meters, but he had no idea where he was. Low hills rose and fell below. The mat must have cleared some by only two or three meters; orange grass and scrub lichen grew in spongy tufts.

Somewhere, sometime in the past few hours, he had passed over the south shore of the Sea of Grass, missed the small port of Edge and the Hoolie River docks where their

268

levitation barge, *Benares*, had been tied up.

The Consul had no compass – compasses were useless on Hyperion – and his comlog had not been programmed as an inertial direction finder. He had planned to find his way back to Keats by following the Hoolie south and west, retracing the laborious path of their upriver pilgrimage minus the bends and turns in the river.

Now he was lost.

The Consul set the hawking mat down on a low hilltop, stepped off to solid ground with a groan of pain, and collapsed the mat. He knew that the charge in the flight threads must be at least a third expended by now . . . perhaps more. He had no idea how much efficiency the mat lost with age.

The hills looked like the rough country southwest of the Sea of Grass, but there was no sight of the river. His comlog told him that it had been dark for only an hour or two, but the Consul could see no hint of sunset in the west. The skies were overcast, shielding both starlight and any space battles from sight.

'Damn,' whispered the Consul. He walked around until circulation returned, urinated at the edge of a small drop-off, and returned to his mat to drink from a water bottle. *Think*.

He had set the mat on a southwesterly course that should have left the Sea of Grass at or near the port city of Edge. If he had simply overflown Edge and the river while he slept, the river would be somewhere to his south, off to his left. But if he had aimed poorly as he left Pilgrims' Rest, been just a few degrees off to his left, then the river would be winding northeast somewhere to his right. Even if he went the wrong way, he eventually would find a landmark – the coast of the Northern Mane if nothing else – but the delay could cost him a full day.

The Consul kicked at a rock and folded his arms. The air was very cool after the heat of the day. A shiver made him realize that he was half-sick from sunburn. He touched his scalp and pulled his fingers away with a curse. *Which way?*

The wind whistled through low sage and sponge lichen. The Consul felt very far removed from the Time Tombs and the threat of the Shrike, but he felt the presence of Sol and Duré and Het Masteen and Brawne and the missing Silenus and Kassad as an urgent pressure on his shoulders. The Consul had joined the pilgrimage as a final act of nihilism, a pointless suicide to put an end to his own pain, pain at the loss of even the *memory* of wife and child, killed during the Hegemony's machinations on Bressia, and pain at the knowledge of his terrible betrayal – betrayal of the government he had served for almost four decades, betrayal of the Ousters who had trusted him.

The Consul sat on a rock and felt that purposeless self-hatred fade as he thought of Sol and his infant child waiting in the Valley of the Time Tombs. He thought of Brawne, that brave woman, energy incarnate, lying helpless with that leechlike extension of the Shrike's evil growing from her skull.

He sat, activated the mat, and rose to eight hundred meters, so close to the ceiling of clouds that he could have raised a hand and touched them.

A second's break in the cloud cover far to his left showed a glint of ripple. The Hoolie lay about five klicks to the south.

The Consul banked the hawking mat steeply to his left, feeling the tired containment field trying to press him to the carpet but feeling safer with the ropes still attached. Ten minutes later, he was high over the water, swooping down to ascertain that it was the broad Hoolie rather than some tributary.

It was the Hoolie. Radiant gossamers glowed in the low, marshy areas along the banks. The tall, crenelated towers of architect ants cast ghostly silhouttes against a sky only slightly darker than the land.

The Consul rose to twenty meters, took a drink of water from his bottle, and headed downriver at full speed.

*   *   *

Sunrise found him below the village of Doukhobor's Copse, almost to the Karla Locks, where the Royal Transport Canal cut west toward the northern urban settlements and the Mane. The Consul knew that it was less than a hundred and fifty klicks to the capital from here – but still a maddening seven hours away at the hawking mat's slow pace. This was the point in the trip where he had hoped to find a military skimmer on patrol, one of the passenger dirigibles from the Copse of Naiad, even a fast powerboat he could commandeer. But there was no sign of life along the banks of the Hoolie except for the occasional burning building or ghee lamps in distant windows. The docks had been stripped of all boats. The river manta pens above the Locks were empty, the great gates open to the current, and no transport barges were lined up below where the river widened to twice its upriver size.

The Consul swore and flew on.

It was a beautiful morning as the sunrise illuminated the low clouds and made every bush and tree stand out in the low, horizontal light. It felt to the Consul as if it had been months since he had seen real vegetation. Weirwood and halfoak trees rose to majestic heights on the distant bluffs, while in the floodplain, the rich light caught the green shoots of a million periscope beans rising from their indigenie paddies. Womangrove root and firefern lined the banks, and each branch and twisting stood out in the sharp light of sunrise.

The clouds swallowed the sun. It began to rain. The Consul tugged on the battered tricorne, huddled under Kassad's extra cloak, and flew on southward at a hundred meters.

The Consul tried to remember. *How long did the child Rachel have?*

Despite his long sleep the day before, the Consul's mind was heavy with fatigue toxins. *Rachel had been four days old when they had arrived at the valley. That had been . . . four days ago.*

The Consul rubbed his cheek, reached for a water bottle,

271

and found them all empty. He could easily dip down and refill the bottles in the river, but he did not want to take the time. His sunburn ached and made him shiver as the rain dripped from his cap.

Sol said that as long as I'm back by nightfall it would be all right. Rachel was born after twenty-hundred hours, translated to Hyperion time. If that's right, if there's no error, she has until eight tonight. The Consul rubbed water from his cheeks and eyebrows. *Say seven more hours to Keats. An hour or two to liberate the ship. Theo will help . . . he's Governor-General now. I can convince him that it's in the Hegemony's interest to countervene Gladstone's orders to quarantine the ship. If necessary, I'll tell him that she ordered me to conspire with the Ousters to betray the Web.*

Say, ten hours plus the fifteen-minute flight in the ship. Should be at least an hour to spare before sunset. Rachel will be only a few minutes old, but . . . what? What do we try besides the cryogenic fugue lockers? Nothing. It has to be that. It was always Sol's last chance, despite the doctors' warnings that it might kill the child. But then, what about Brawne?

The Consul was thirsty. He pulled back the cloak, but the rain had lessened to the point that it was a fine drizzle, just enough to wet his lips and tongue to make him more thirsty. He cursed softly and began to descend slowly. Perhaps he could hover over the river just long enough to fill his bottle.

The hawking mat quit flying thirty meters above the river. One second it was descending gradually, as smooth as a carpet on a gentle glass incline, and the next instant it was tumbling and plummeting out of control, a two-meter rug and terrified man thrown out of the window of a ten-story building.

The Consul screamed and tried to jump free, but the rope connecting him to the carpet and the duffel strap tied to his belt tangled him in the flapping mass of hawking mat, and he fell with it, tumbling and twisting, the final twenty meters to the hard surface of the waiting Hoolie River.

272

TWENTY-NINE

Sol Weintraub had high hopes the night the Consul left. At long last, they were *doing* something. Or trying to. Sol did not believe that the cryogenic vaults of the Consul's ship would be the answer to saving Rachel – medical experts on Renaissance Vector had pointed out the extreme danger of that procedure – but it was good to have an alternative, *any* alternative. And Sol felt that they had been passive long enough, awaiting the Shrike's pleasure like condemned criminals awaiting the guillotine.

The interior of the Sphinx seemed too treacherous this night, and Sol brought their possessions out on the broad granite porch of the tomb, where he and Duré sought to make Masteen and Brawne comfortable under blankets and capes, with packs for pillows. Brawne's medical monitors continued to show no brain activity whatsoever, while her body rested comfortably. Masteen turned and tossed in the grip of fever.

'What do you think the Templar's problem is?' asked Duré. 'Disease?'

'It could be simple exposure,' said Sol. 'After being abducted from the windwagon, he found himself wandering in the barrens and here in the Valley of the Time Tombs. He was eating snow for liquid and had no food at all.'

Duré nodded and checked the FORCE medpak they had attached to the inside of Masteen's arm. The telltales showed the steady drip of intravenous solution. 'But it seems to be something else,' said the Jesuit. 'Almost a madness.'

'Templars have an almost telepathic connection to their treeships,' said Sol. 'It must have driven Voice of the Tree Masteen a bit mad when he watched the destruction of the *Yggdrasill*. Especially if he somehow knew it was necessary.'

Duré nodded and continued sponging the Templar's waxy forehead. It was after midnight, and the wind had come up, moving vermilion dust in lazy spirals and moaning around the wings and rough edges of the Sphinx. The Tombs glowed brightly and then dimmed, now one tomb, then the next, in no apparent order or sequence. Occasionally the tug of time tides would assail both men, making them gasp and grip the stone, but the wave of *déjà vu* and vertigo would fade after a moment. With Brawne Lamia attached to the Sphinx via the cable welded to her skull, they could not leave.

Sometime before dawn, the clouds parted and the sky became visible, the thickly clustered stars almost painful in their clarity. For a while, the only signs of the great fleets warring there were the occasional fusion trails, narrow diamond-scratches on the pane of night, but then the blossoms of distant explosions began to unfurl again, and within the hour the glow of the Tombs had been dimmed by the violence above.

'Who do you think will win?' asked Father Duré. The two men sat with their backs to the stone wall of the Sphinx, faces raised to the cusp of sky revealed between the tomb's forward-curved wings.

Sol was rubbing Rachel's back as she slept on her stomach, rear end raised under the thin blankets. 'From what the others say, it seems preordained that the Web must suffer a terrible war.'

'So you believe the AI Advisory Council's predictions?'

Sol shrugged in the darkness. 'I really know nothing about politics . . . or the Core's accuracy in predicting things. I'm a minor scholar from a small college on a backwater world. But I have the *feeling* that something terrible is in store for us . . . that some rough beast is slouching toward Bethlehem to be born.'

Duré smiled. 'Yeats,' he said. The smile faded. 'I suspect that this place is the new Bethlehem.' He looked down the valley toward the glowing Tombs. 'I spent a lifetime teaching about St Teilhard's theories of evolution toward the Omega Point. Instead of that, we have this. Human folly in the skies, and a terrible Antichrist waiting to inherit the rest.'

'You think that the Shrike is the Antichrist?'

Father Duré set his elbows on his raised knees and folded his hands. 'If it's not, we're all in trouble.' He laughed bitterly. 'It wasn't long ago that I would have been delighted to discover an Antichrist . . . even the presence of some antidivine power would have served to shore up my failing belief in any form of divinity.'

'And now?' Sol asked quietly.

Duré spread his fingers. 'I too have been crucified.'

Sol thought of the images from Lenar Hoyt's story about Duré; the elderly Jesuit nailing himself to a tesla tree, suffering the years of pain and rebirth rather than surrender to the cruciform DNA parasite which even now burrowed under the flesh of his chest.

Duré lowered his face from the sky. 'There was no welcome from a heavenly Father,' he said softly. 'No reassurance that the pain and sacrifice had been worth anything. Only pain. Pain and darkness and then pain again.'

Sol's hand stopped moving on his infant's back. 'And that made you lose your faith?'

Duré looked at Sol. 'On the contrary, it made me feel that faith is all the more essential. Pain and darkness have been our lot since the Fall of Man. But there must be some hope that we can rise to a higher level . . . that consciousness can evolve to a plane more benevolent than its counterpoint of a universe hardwired to indifference.'

Sol nodded slowly. 'I had a dream during Rachel's long

275

battle with Merlin's sickness . . . my wife Sarai had the same dream . . . that I was being called to sacrifice my only daughter.'

'Yes,' said Duré. 'I listened to the Consul's summary on disk.'

'Then you know my response,' said Sol. 'First, that Abraham's path of obedience can no longer be followed, even if there is a God demanding such obedience. Second, that we have offered sacrifices to that God for too many generations . . . that the payments of pain must stop.'

'Yet you are here,' said Duré, gesturing toward the valley, the Tombs, the night.

'I'm here,' agreed Sol. 'But not to grovel. Rather to see what response these powers have to my decision.' He touched his daughter's back again. 'Rachel is a day and a half old now and growing younger each second. If the Shrike is the architect of such cruelty, I want to face him, even if he *is* your Antichrist. If there is a God and he has done this thing, I will show the same contempt to him.'

'Perhaps we've all shown too much contempt as it is,' mused Duré.

Sol looked up as a dozen pinpoints of fierce light expanded into ripples and shock waves of plasma explosions far out in space. 'I wish we had the technology to fight God on an equal basis,' he said in low, tight tones. 'To beard him in his den. To fight back for all of the injustices heaped on humanity. To allow him to alter his smug arrogance or be blown to hell.'

Father Duré raised one eyebrow and then smiled slightly. 'I know the anger you feel.' The priest gently touched Rachel's head. 'Let's try to get some sleep before sunrise, shall we?'

Sol nodded, lay next to his child, and pulled the blanket up to his cheek. He heard Duré whispering something that might have been a soft good night, or perhaps a prayer.

Sol touched his daughter, closed his eyes, and slept.

* * *

The Shrike did not come in the night. Nor did it come the next morning as sunlight painted the southwestern cliffs and touched the top of the Crystal Monolith. Sol awoke as sunlight crept down the valley; he found Duré sleeping next to him, Masteen and Brawne still unconscious. Rachel was stirring and fussing. Her cry was that of a hungry newborn. Sol fed her with one of the last nursing paks, pulling the heating tab and waiting a moment for the milk to reach body temperature. Cold had settled in the valley overnight, and frost glinted on the steps to the Sphinx.

Rachel ate greedily, making the soft mewling and sucking sounds that Sol remembered from more than fifty years earlier as Sarai had nursed her. When she finished, Sol burped her and left her on his shoulder as he rocked gently to and fro.

A day and a half left.

Sol was very tired. He was growing old despite the single Poulsen treatment a decade earlier. At the time he and Sarai would normally have been freed of parental duties – their only child in graduate school and off on an archaelogical dig in the Outback – Rachel had fallen prey to Merlin's sickness, and parenthood had soon descended upon them once again. The curve of those duties rose as Sol and Sarai grew older – then Sol alone, after the air crash on Barnard's World – and now he was very, very tired. But despite that, despite everything, Sol was interested to note that he did not regret a single day of caring for his daughter.

A day and a half left.

Father Duré awoke after a bit, and the two men made breakfast from the various canned goods Brawne had brought back with her. Het Masteen did not awaken, but Duré applied the next-to-last medpak, and the Templar began receiving fluids and IV nutrient.

'Do you think M Lamia should have the last medpak applied?' asked Duré.

Sol sighed and checked her comlog monitors again. 'I don't think so, Paul. According to this, blood sugar is high . . . nutrient levels check out as if she had just eaten a decent meal.'

'But how?'

Sol shook his head. 'Perhaps that damned thing is some sort of umbilical.' He gestured toward the cable attached to the point in her skull where the neural shunt socket had been.

'So what do we do today?'

Sol peered at a sky already fading to the green and lapis dome they had grown used to on Hyperion. 'We wait,' he said.

Het Masteen awoke in the heat of the day, shortly before the sun reached the zenith. The Templar sat straight up and said, 'The Tree!'

Duré hurried up the steps from where he had been pacing below. Sol lifted Rachel from where she lay in shadow near the wall and moved to Masteen's side. The Templar's eyes were focused on something above the level of the cliffs. Sol glanced up but could see only the paling sky.

'The Tree!' cried the Templar again, and lifted one roughened hand.

Duré restrained the man. 'He's hallucinating. He thinks he see the *Yggdrasill*, his treeship.'

Het Masteen struggled against their hands. 'No, not the *Yggdrasill*,' he gasped through parched lips, 'the Tree. The Final Tree. The Tree of Pain!'

Both men looked up then, but the sky was clear except for wisps of clouds blowing in from the southwest. At that moment, there was a surge of time tides, and both Sol and the priest bowed their heads in sudden vertigo. It passed.

Het Masteen was trying to get to his feet. The Templar's eyes were still focused on something far away. His skin was so hot that it burned Sol's hands.

'Get the final medpak,' snapped Sol. 'Program the ultra-morph and antifever agent.' Duré hurried to comply.

'The Tree of Pain!' managed Het Masteen. 'I was meant to be its Voice! The erg is meant to drive it through space and time! The Bishop and the Voice of the Great Tree have chosen *me*! I cannot fail them.' He strained against Sol's arms a second, then collapsed back to the stone porch. 'I am the True Chosen,' he whispered, energy leaving him like air from an emptying balloon. 'I must guide the Tree of Pain during the time of Atonement.' He closed his eyes.

Duré attached the final medpak, made sure the monitor was set for Templar quirks in metabolism and body chemistry, and triggered the adrenaline and painkillers. Sol huddled over the robed form.

'That's not Templar terminology or theology,' said Duré. 'He's using Shrike Cult language.' The priest caught Sol's eye. 'That explains some of the mystery . . . especially from Brawne's tale. For some reason, the Templars have been in collusion with the Church of the Final Atonement . . . the Shrike Cult.'

Sol nodded, slipped his own comlog on Masteen's wrist and adjusted the monitor.

'The Tree of Pain must be the Shrike's fabled tree of thorns,' muttered Duré, glancing up at the empty sky where Masteen had been staring. 'But what does he mean that he and the erg were chosen to drive it through space and time? Does he really think he can pilot the Shrike's tree the way the Templars do the treeships? Why?'

'You'll have to ask him in the next life,' said Sol tiredly. 'He's dead.'

Duré checked the monitors, added Lenar Hoyt's comlog to the array. They tried the medpak revival stimulants, CPR, and mouth-to-mouth resuscitation. The monitor tell-tales did not waver. Het Masteen, Templar True Voice of the Tree and Shrike Pilgrim, was indeed dead.

* * *

They waited an hour, suspicious of all things in this perverse valley of the Shrike, but when the monitors began showing rapid decomposition of the corpse, they buried Masteen in a shallow grave fifty meters up the trail toward the entrance to the valley. Kassad had left behind a collapsible shovel – labeled 'entrenching tool' in FORCE jargon – and the men took turns digging while the other watched over Rachel and Brawne Lamia.

The two men, one cradling a child, stood in the shadow of a boulder while Duré said a few words before the soil was dropped on to the makeshift fiber-plastic shroud.

'I did not truly know M Masteen,' said the priest. 'We were not of the same faith. But we were of the same profession; Voice of the Tree Masteen spent much of his life doing what he understood to be God's work, pursuing God's will in the writings of the Muir and the beauties of nature. His was the true faith – tested by the difficulties, tempered by obedience, and, in the end, sealed by sacrifice.'

Duré paused and squinted into a sky that had faded to gunmetal glare. 'Please accept your servant, O Lord. Welcome him into your arms as you will someday welcome us, your other searchers who have lost their way. In the name of the Father, and of the Son, and of the Holy Spirit, amen.'

Rachel began to cry. Sol walked her around as Duré shoveled the earth on to the man-shaped bundle of fiberplastic.

They returned to the porch of the Sphinx and gently moved Brawne into what little shade remained. There was no way to shield her from the late afternoon sun unless they carried her into the tomb itself, and neither man wanted to do that.

'The Consul must be more than halfway to the ship by now,' said the priest after taking a long drink of water. The man's forehead was sunburned and filmed with sweat.

'Yes,' said Sol.

'By this time tomorrow, he should be back here. We'll use laser cutters to free Brawne, then set her in the ship surgery. Perhaps Rachel's reverse aging can be arrested in cryogenic storage, despite what the doctors said.'

'Yes.'

Duré lowered the water bottle and looked at Sol. 'Do you believe that is what will happen?'

Sol returned the other man's gaze. 'No.'

Shadows stretched from the southwestern cliff walls. The day's heat coalesced into a solid thing, then dissipated a bit. Clouds moved in from the south.

Rachel slept in the shadows near the doorway. Sol walked up to where Paul Duré stood staring down the valley and set a hand on the priest's shoulder. 'What are you thinking about, my friend?'

Duré did not turn. 'I am thinking that if I did not truly believe that suicide was a mortal sin, that I would end things to allow young Hoyt a chance at life.' He looked at Sol and showed a hint of smile. 'But is it suicide when this parasite on *my* chest . . . on *his* chest then . . . would someday drag me kicking and screaming to my own resurrection?'

'Would it be a gift to Hoyt,' asked Sol quietly, 'to bring him back to this?'

Duré said nothing for a moment. Then he clasped Sol's upper arm. 'I think that I shall take a walk.'

'Where?' Sol squinted out at the thick heat of the desert afternoon. Even with the low cloud cover, the valley was an oven.

The priest made a vague gesture. 'Down the valley. I will be back before too long.'

'Be careful,' said Sol. 'And remember, if the Consul runs across a patrol skimmer along the Hoolie, he might be back as early as this afternoon.'

Duré nodded, went over to pick up a water bottle and to touch Rachel gently, and then he went down the long stairway of the Sphinx, picking his way slowly and carefully, like an old, old man.

Sol watched him leave, becoming a smaller and smaller figure, distorted by heat waves and distance. Then Sol sighed and went back to sit near his daughter.

Paul Duré tried to keep to the shadows, but even there the heat was oppressive, weighing on him like a great yoke on his shoulders. He passed the Jade Tomb and followed the path toward the northern cliffs and the Obelisk. That tomb's thin shadow painted darkness on the roseate stone and dust of the valley floor. Descending again, picking his way through the rubble surrounding the Crystal Monolith, Duré glanced up as a sluggish wind moved shattered panes and whistled through cracks high up on the face of the tomb. He saw his reflection in the lower surfaces and remembered hearing the organ song of the evening wind rising from the Cleft when he had found the Bikura high on the Pinion Plateau. That seemed like lifetimes ago. It *was* lifetimes ago.

Duré felt the damage the cruciform reconstruction had done to his mind and memory. It was sickening – the equivalent of suffering a stroke with no hope of recovery. Reasoning that once would have been child's play to him now required extreme concentration or was simply beyond his ability. Words eluded him. Emotions tugged at him with the same sudden violence as the time tides. Several times he had had to leave the other pilgrims while he wept in solitude for no reason he could understand.

The other pilgrims. Now only Sol and the child remained. Father Duré would gladly surrender his own life if those two could be spared. Was it a sin, he wondered, to plan deals with the Antichrist?

He was far down the valley now, almost to the point where it curved eastward into the widening cul-de-sac where the Shrike Palace threw its maze of shadows across the rocks. The trail wound close to the northwest wall as it passed the Cave Tombs. Duré felt the cool air from the first tomb and was tempted to enter just to recover from the heat, close his eyes, and take a nap.

He continued walking.

The entrance to the second tomb had more baroque carvings in the stone, and Duré was reminded of the ancient basilica he had discovered in the Cleft – the huge cross and altar where the retarded Bikura had 'worshiped.' It had been the obscene immortality of the cruciform they had been worshiping, not the chance of true Resurrection promised by the Cross. *But what was the difference?* Duré shook his head, trying to clear the fog and cynicism that clouded every thought. The path wound higher here past the third Cave Tomb, the shortest and least impressive of the three.

There was a light in the third Cave Tomb.

Duré stopped, took a breath, and glanced back down the valley. The Sphinx was quite visible almost a kilometer away, but he could not quite make out Sol in the shadows. For a moment Duré wondered if it had been the *third* tomb they had sheltered in the day before . . . if one of them had left a lantern there.

It had not been the third tomb. Except for the search for Kassad, no one had entered this tomb in three days.

Father Duré knew that he should ignore the light, return to Sol, keep the vigil with the man and his daughter.

But the Shrike came to each of the others separately. Why should I refuse the summons?

Duré felt moisture on his cheek and realized that he was weeping soundlessly, mindlessly. He roughly wiped the tears away with the back of his hand and stood there clenching his fists.

My intellect was my greatest vanity. I was the intellectual Jesuit, secure in the tradition of Teilhard and Prassard. Even the theology I pushed on the Church, on the seminarians, and on those few faithful still listening had emphasized the mind, that wonderful Omega Point of consciousness. God as a clever algorithm.

Well, some things are beyond intellect, Paul.
Duré entered the third Cave Tomb.

Sol awoke with a start, sure that someone was creeping up on him.

He jumped to his feet and looked around. Rachel was making soft sounds, awakening from her nap at the same time as her father. Brawne Lamia lay motionless where he had left her, med telltales still glowing green, brain activity readout a flat red.

He had slept for at least an hour; the shadows had crept across the valley floor, and only the top of the Sphinx was still in sunlight as the sun broke free of the clouds. Shafts of light slanted through the valley entrance and illuminated the cliff walls opposite. The wind was rising.

But nothing moved in the valley.

Sol lifted Rachel, rocked her as she cried, and ran down the steps, looking behind the Sphinx and toward the other Tombs.

'Paul!' His voice echoed off rock. Wind stirred dust beyond the Jade Tomb, but nothing else stirred. Sol still had the feeling that something was sneaking up on him, that he was being watched.

Rachel screamed and wiggled in his grasp, her voice the high, thin wail of a newborn. Sol glanced at his comlog. She would be one day old in an hour. He searched the sky for the Consul's ship, cursed softly at himself, and went back to the entrance to the Sphinx to change the baby's diaper, check on Brawne, pull a nursing pak from his bag, and grab a cloak. The heat dissipated quickly when the sun was gone.

In the half-hour of twilight remaining, Sol moved quickly down the valley, shouting Duré's name and peering into the Tombs without entering. Past the Jade Tomb where Hoyt had been murdered, its sides already beginning to glow a milky green. Past the dark Obelisk, its shadow thrown high on the southeastern cliff wall. Past the Crystal Monolith, its

284

upper reaches glowing with the last of the day's light, then fading as the sun set somewhere beyond the City of Poets. In the sudden chill and hush of evening, past the Cave Tombs, Sol shouting into each and feeling the dank air against his face like a cold breath from an open mouth.

No answer.

In the last of the twilight, around the bend in the valley to the blade-and-buttress riot of the Shrike Palace, dark and ominous in the growing gloom. Sol stood at the entrance trying to make sense of the ink-black shadows, spires, rafters, and pylons, shouted into the dark interior; only his echo answered. Rachel began to cry again.

Shivering, feeling a chill on the back of his neck, wheeling constantly to surprise the unseen watcher and seeing only deepening shadows and the first of the night's stars between clouds above, Sol hurried back up the valley toward the Sphinx, walking quickly at first and then almost running past the Jade Tomb as the evening wind rose with a sound of children screaming.

'God*damn*!' breathed Sol as he reached the top of the stairs to the Sphinx.

Brawne Lamia was gone. There was no sign of her body or the metal umbilical.

Cursing, holding Rachel tight, Sol fumbled through his pack for the flashlight.

Ten meters down the central corridor, Sol found the blanket Brawne had been wrapped in. Beyond that, nothing. The corridors branched and twisted, now widening, now narrowing as the ceiling lowered to the point that Sol was crawling, holding the baby in his right arm so that her cheek was next to his. He hated being in this tomb. His heart was pounding so fiercely that he half expected to have a coronary then and there.

The last corridor narrowed to nothing. Where the metal cable had snaked into stone, now there was only stone.

Sol held the flashlight in his teeth and slapped at the rock, shoved at stones the size of houses as if a secret panel would open, tunnels would be revealed.

Nothing.

Sol hugged Rachel tighter and began to make his way out, taking several wrong turns, feeling his heart race even more wildly as he thought himself lost. Then they were in a corridor he recognized, then in the main corridor, then out.

He carried his child to the bottom of the steps and away from the Sphinx. At the head of the valley, he stopped, sat on a low rock, and panted for breath. Rachel's cheek still lay against his neck, and the baby made no sound, no movement other than the soft curl of fingers against his beard.

Wind blew in from the barrens behind him. Clouds opened above and then closed, hiding the stars so that the only light came from the sick glow of the Time Tombs. Sol was afraid that the wild beating of his heart would frighten the baby, but Rachel continued to curl calmly against him, her warmth a tactile reassurance.

'Damn,' whispered Sol. He had cared for Brawne Lamia. He had cared for all of the pilgrims, and now they were gone. Sol's decades as an academic had preconditioned him to hunt for patterns in events, a moral grain in the accreted stone of experience, but there had been no pattern to events on Hyperion – merely confusion and death.

Sol rocked his child and looked out on the barrens, considering leaving this place at once . . . walking to the dead city or Chronos Keep . . . walking northwest to the Littoral or southeast to where the Bridle Range intersected the sea. Sol raised a shaky hand to his face and rubbed his cheek; there would be no salvation in the wilderness. Leaving the valley had not saved Martin Silenus. The Shrike had been reported far south of the Bridle Range – as far south as Endymion and the other southern cities – and even if the monster spared them, starvation and thirst would not. Sol might survive on plants, rodent flesh, and snowmelt from the high places – but Rachel's supply of milk was limited, even with the supplies Brawne had brought back from the Keep. Then he realized that the milk supply did not matter . . .

I'll be alone in less than a day. Sol stifled a moan as the thought struck him. His determination to save his child had brought him across two and a half decades and a hundred times that many light-years. His resolve to return Rachel's life and health to her was an almost palpable force, a fierce energy which he and Sarai had shared and which he had kept alive the way a temple priest preserves the sacred temple flame. No, by God, there *was* a pattern to things, a moral underpinning to this platform of seemingly random events, and Sol Weintraub would wager his and his daughter's lives on that belief.

Sol stood, walked slowly down the trail to the Sphinx, climbed the stairs, found a therm cloak and blankets, and made a nest for the two of them on the highest step as Hyperion winds howled and the Time Tombs glowed more brightly.

Rachel lay on his chest and stomach, her cheek on his shoulder, her tiny hands curling and uncurling as she released the world for the land of infant sleep. Sol heard her gentle breathing as she moved into deep slumber, heard the soft sound as she blew tiny bubbles of saliva. After a while, he released his own hold on the world and joined her in sleep.

THIRTY

Sol dreamed the dream he had suffered since the day Rachel had incurred Merlin's sickness.

He was walking through a vast structure, where columns the size of redwood trees rose into the gloom and where crimson light fell in solid shafts from somewhere far above. There came the sound of a giant conflagration, entire worlds burning. Ahead of him glowed two ovals of the deepest red.

Sol knew the place. He knew that he would find an altar ahead with Rachel on it – Rachel in her twenties and unconscious – and then would come the Voice, demanding.

Sol stopped on the low balcony and stared down at the familiar scene. His daughter, the woman he and Sarai had bid farewell to when she left for postgraduate work on distant Hyperion, lay naked on a broad block of stone. Above them all floated the twin red orbs of the Shrike's gaze. On the altar lay a long, curved knife made of sharpened bone. The Voice came then:

'*Sol! Take your daughter, your only daughter, Rachel, whom you love, and go to the world called Hyperion and offer her there as a burnt offering at one of the places of which I shall tell you.*'

Sol's arms were shaking with rage and grief. He pulled at his hair and shouted into the darkness, repeating what he had told that voice before:

'*There will be no more offerings, neither child nor parent. There will be no more sacrifices. The time of obedience and atonement is past. Either help us as a friend, or go away!*'

In previous dreams, this had led to the sound of wind and

isolation, terrible footsteps receding in the dark. But this time the dream persisted, the altar shimmered and was suddenly empty except for the bone knife. The twin red orbs still floated high above, fire-filled rubies the size of worlds.

'*Sol, listen,*' came the Voice, modulated now so it did not boom from far above but almost whispered in his ear, '*the future of humankind depends upon your choice. Can you offer Rachel out of love, if not obedience?*'

Sol heard the answer in his mind even as he groped for the words. There would be no more offerings. Not this day. Not any day. Humankind had suffered enough for its love of gods, its long search for God. He thought of the many centuries in which his people, the Jews, had negotiated with God, complaining, bickering, decrying the unfairness of things but always – always – returning to obedience at whatever the cost. Generations dying in the ovens of hatred. Future generations scarred by the cold fires of radiation and renewed hatred.

Not this time. Not ever again.

'Say yes, Daddy.'

Sol started at the touch of a hand on his. His daughter, Rachel, stood next to him, neither infant nor adult, but the eight-year-old he had known twice – aging and growing backward through that age with Merlin's sickness – Rachel with her light brown hair tied back in a simple braid, short form soft in washed-denim play tunic and kid sneakers.

Sol took her hand, gripping as tightly as he could without hurting her, feeling the returned grip. This was no illusion, no final cruelty of the Shrike. This was his daughter.

'Say yes, Daddy.'

Sol had solved Abraham's problem of obedience to a God turned malicious. Obedience could no longer be paramount in relations between humanity and its deity. But when the *child* chosen as sacrifice asked for obedience to that God's whim?

Sol went to one knee next to his daughter and opened his arms. 'Rachel.'

She hugged him with the energy he remembered from

countless such hugs, her chin high over his shoulder, her arms fierce in their intensity of love. She whispered in his ear, 'Please, Daddy, we have to say yes.'

Sol continued to hug her, feeling her thin arms around him and the warmth of her cheek against his. He was crying silently, feeling the wetness on his cheeks and in his short beard, but unwilling to release her for even the second it would take to wipe the tears away.

'I love you, Daddy,' whispered Rachel.

He rose then, wiped his face with a swipe of the back of his hand, and with Rachel's left hand still firmly in his, began the long descent with her toward the altar below.

Sol awoke with a sense of falling, grabbing for the baby. She was asleep on his chest, her fist curled, her thumb in her mouth, but when he started upright she awoke with the cry and arching reflex of a startled newborn. Sol got to his feet, dropping blankets and cloak around him, clutching Rachel tightly to him.

It was daylight. Late morning, if anything. They had slept while the night died and sunlight crept into the valley and across the Tombs. The Sphinx huddled over them like some predatory beast, powerful forelegs extended on either side of the stairway where they had slept.

Rachel wailed, her face contorting with the shock of waking and hunger and sensed fear in her father. Sol stood in the fierce sunlight and rocked her. He went to the top step of the Sphinx, changed her diaper, heated one of the last nursing paks, offered it to her until the wails turned to soft nursing sounds, burped her, and walked her around until she drifted into light sleep again.

It was less than ten hours until her 'birthday.' Less than ten hours until sunset and the last few minutes of his daughter's life. Not for the first time, Sol wished that the Time Tomb were a great glass building symbolizing the cosmos and the deity that ran it. Sol would throw rocks at the structure until not a single pane remained unbroken.

He tried to remember the details of his dream, but the warmth and reassurance of it shredded in the harsh light of Hyperion's sun. He remembered only Rachel's whispered entreaty. The thought of offering her to the Shrike made Sol's stomach ache with horror. 'It's all right,' he whispered to her as she twitched and sighed toward the treacherous haven of sleep once again. 'It's all right, kiddo. The Consul's ship will be here soon. The ship will come any minute.'

The Consul's ship did not come by noon. The Consul's ship did not come by midafternoon. Sol walked the valley floor, calling out for those who had disappeared, singing half-forgotten songs when Rachel awoke, crooning lullabies as she drifted back to sleep. His daughter was so tiny and light: six pounds and three ounces, nineteen inches at birth, he remembered, smiling at the antique units of his antique home, of Barnard's World.

In late afternoon, he startled awake from his half-doze in the shade of the Sphinx's outflung paw, standing with Rachel waking in his arms as a spacecraft arched across the dome of deep lapis sky.

'It's come!' he cried, and Rachel stirred and wiggled as if in response.

A line of blue fusion flame glowed with that daylight intensity reserved to spacecraft in atmosphere. Sol hopped up and down, filled with the first relief in many days. He shouted and leaped until Rachel wailed and wept in concern. Sol stopped, lifted her high, knowing that she could not yet focus her eyes but wanting her to see the beauty of the descending ship as it arced above the distant mountain range, dropping toward the high desert.

'He did it!' cried Sol. 'He's coming! The ship will . . .'

Three heavy thuds struck the valley almost at once; the first two were the twin sonic booms of the spacecrafts's 'footprint' racing ahead of it as it decelerated. The third was the sound of its destruction.

Sol stared as the glowing pinpoint at the apex of the long fusion trail suddenly grew as bright as the sun, expanded into a cloud of flame and boiling gases, and then tumbled toward the distant desert in ten thousand burning pieces. He blinked away retinal echoes as Rachel continued crying.

'My God,' whispered Sol. 'My God.' There was no denying the complete destruction of the spacecraft. Secondary explosions ripped the air, even from thirty kilometers away, as pieces fell, trailing smoke and flames, toward the desert, the mountains, and the Sea of Grass beyond. 'My God.'

Sol sat on the warm sand. He was too exhausted to cry, too empty to do anything but rock his child until her crying stopped.

Ten minutes later Sol looked up as two more fusion trails burned the sky, these headed south from the zenith. One of these exploded, too distant for sound to reach him. The second one dropped out of sight below the southern cliffs, beyond the Bridle Range.

'Perhaps it was not the Consul,' whispered Sol. 'It could be the Ouster invasion. Perhaps the Consul's ship still will come for us.'

But the ship did not come by late afternoon. It had not come by the time the light of Hyperion's small sun shone on the cliff wall, shadows reaching for Sol on the highest step of the Sphinx. It did not come when the valley fell in shadow.

Rachel was born less than thirty minutes from this second. Sol checked her diaper, found her dry, and fed her from the last nursing pak. As she ate, she looked up at him with great, dark eyes, seemingly searching his face. Sol remembered the first few minutes he had held her while Sarai rested under warmed blankets; the baby's eyes had burned into him then with these same questions and startlement at finding such a world.

The evening wind brought clouds moving in quickly above the valley. Rumbles to the southwest came first as distant thunder and then with the sick regularity of artillery, most likely nuclear or plasma explosions five hundred klicks or more to the south. Sol scanned the sky between lowering clouds and caught glimpses of fiery meteor trails arching overhead: ballistic missiles or dropships, probably. Death for Hyperion in either case.

Sol ignored it. He sang softly to Rachel as she finished nursing. He had walked to the head of the valley, but now he returned slowly to the Sphinx. The Tombs were glowing as never before, rippling with the harsh light of neon gases excited by electrons. Overhead, the last shafts from the setting sun changed the low clouds to a ceiling of pastel flames.

Less than three minutes remained until the final celebration of Rachel's birth. Even if the Consul's ship arrived now, Sol knew that he would not have time to board it or get his child into cryogenic sleep.

He did not want to.

Sol climbed the stairs to the Sphinx slowly, realizing that Rachel had come this way twenty-six standard years earlier, never guessing the fate that awaited her in that dark crypt.

He paused at the top step and took in a breath. The light from the sun was a palpable thing, filling the sky and igniting the wings and upper mass of the Sphinx. The tomb itself seemed to be releasing the light it had stored, like the rocks in Hebron's desert, where Sol had wandered in the wilderness years before, seeking enlightenment and finding only sorrow. The air shimmered with light, and the wind continued to rise, blowing sand across the valley floor and then relenting.

Sol went to one knee on the top step, pulling off Rachel's blanket until the child was in only her soft cotton newborn's clothes. Swaddling clothes.

Rachel wiggled in his hands. Her face was purple and slick, her hands tiny and red with the effort of clenching and unclenching. Sol remembered her exactly like this as the doctor handed the infant to Sol, as he stared at his newborn daughter as he was staring now, then set her on Sarai's stomach so the mother could see.

'Ah, God,' breathed Sol and dropped to his other knee, truly kneeling now.

The entire valley quivered as if to an earthquake tremor. Sol could vaguely hear the explosions continuing far to the south. But of more immediate concern now was the terrible glow from the Sphinx. Sol's shadow leaped fifty meters behind him down the stairway and across the valley floor as the tomb pulsed and vibrated with light. Out of the corner of his eye, Sol could see the other Tombs glowing as brightly – huge, baroque reactors in their final seconds before meltdown.

The entrance to the Sphinx pulsed blue, then violet, then a terrible white. Behind the Sphinx, on the wall of the plateau above the Valley of the Time Tombs, an impossible tree shimmered into existence, its huge trunk and sharp steel branches rising into the glowing clouds and above. Sol glanced quickly, saw the three-meter thorns and the terrible fruit they bore, and then he looked back at the entrance to the Sphinx.

Somewhere the wind howled and thunder rumbled. Somewhere vermilion dust blew like curtains of dried blood in the terrible light from the Tombs. Somewhere voices cried out and a chorus shrieked.

Sol ignored all this. He had eyes only for his daughter's face and, beyond her, for the shadow that now filled the glowing entrance to the tomb.

The Shrike emerged. The thing had to bend to allow its three-meter bulk and steel blades to clear the top of the doorway. It stepped on to the top porch of the Sphinx and moved forward, part creature, part sculpture, walking with the terrible deliberation of nightmare.

The dying light above rippled on the thing's carapace, cascaded down across curving breastplate to steel thorns there, shimmering on finger-blades and scalpels rising from every joint. Sol hugged Rachel to his chest and stared into the multifaceted red furnaces that passed for the Shrike's eyes. The sunset faded into the blood-red glow of Sol's recurrent dream.

The Shrike's head turned slightly, swiveling without friction, rotating ninety degrees right, ninety degrees left, as if the creature were surveying its domain.

The Shrike took three steps forward, stopping less than two meters from Sol. The thing's four arms twisted and rose, fingerblades uncurling.

Sol hugged Rachel tightly to him. Her skin was moist, her face bruised and blotched with the exertions of birth. Seconds remained. Her eyes tracked separately, seemed to focus on Sol.

Say yes, Daddy. Sol remembered the dream.

The Shrike's head lowered until the ruby eyes in that terrible hood stared at nothing but Sol and his child. The quicksilver jaws parted slightly, showing layers and levels of steel teeth. Four hands came forward, metallic palms up, pausing half a meter from Sol's face.

Say yes, Daddy. Sol remembered the dream, remembered his daughter's hug, and realized that in the end – when all else is dust – loyalty to those we love is all we can carry with us to the grave. Faith – true faith – was trusting in that love.

Sol lifted his newborn and dying child, seconds old, shrieking now with her first and last breath, and handed her to the Shrike.

The absence of her slight weight struck Sol with a terrible vertigo.

The Shrike lifted Rachel, stepped backward, and was enveloped in light.

Behind the Sphinx, the tree of thorns ceased shimmering, shifted into phase with *now*, and came into terrible focus.

Sol stepped forward, arms imploring, as the Shrike stepped back into the radiance and was gone. Explosions rippled the clouds and slammed Sol to his knees with shock waves of pressure.

Behind him, around him, the Time Tombs were opening.

PART THREE

PART THREE

THIRTY-ONE

I awoke and was not pleased to be awakened.

Rolling over, squinting and cursing the sudden invasion of light, I saw Leigh Hunt sitting on the edge of the bed, an aerosol injector still in his hand.

'You took enough sleeping pills to keep you in bed all day,' he said. 'Rise and shine.'

I sat up, rubbed the morning stubble on my cheeks, and squinted in Hunt's direction. 'Who the hell gave you the right to enter my room?' The effort of speaking started me coughing, and I did not stop until Hunt returned from the bathroom with a glass of water.

'Here.'

I drank, vainly trying to project anger and outrage between spasms of coughing. The remnants of dreams fled like morning mists. I felt a terrible sense of loss descend.

'Get dressed,' said Hunt, standing. 'The CEO wants you in her chambers in twenty minutes. While you've been sleeping, things have been happening.'

'What things?' I rubbed my eyes and ran fingers through my tousled hair.

Hunt smiled tightly. 'Access the datasphere. Then get down to Gladstone's chambers soonest. Twenty minutes, Severn.' He left.

I accessed the datasphere. One way to visualize one's entry point to the datasphere is to imagine a patch of Old Earth's ocean in varying degrees of turbulence. Normal days tended to show a placid sea with interesting patterns of ripples. Crises showed chop and whitecaps. Today there was a hurricane under way. Entry was delayed to any access route, confusion reigned in breaking waves of update surges, the datumplane matrix was wild with storage shifts and major credit transfers, and the All Thing, normally a multilayered buzz of information and political debate, was a raging wind of confusion, abandoned referenda and obsolete position templates blowing by like tattered clouds.

'Dear God,' I whispered, breaking access but feeling the pressure of the information surge still pounding at my implant circuits and brain. War. Surprise attack. Imminent destruction of the Web. Talk of impeaching Gladstone. Riots on a score of worlds. Shrike Cult uprisings on Lusus. The FORCE fleet abandoning Hyperion System in a desperate rearguard action, but too late, too late. Hyperion already under attack. Fear of farcaster incursion.

I rose, ran naked to the shower, and sonicked in record time. Hunt or someone had laid out a formal gray suit and cape, and I dressed in a hurry, brushing back my wet hair so that damp curls fell to my collar.

It wouldn't do to keep the CEO of the Hegemony of Man waiting. Oh no, that wouldn't do at all.

'It's about time you got here,' said Meina Gladstone as I entered her private chambers.

'What the fuck have you done?' I snapped.

Gladstone blinked. Evidently the CEO of the Hegemony of Man was not used to being spoken to in that tone. *Tough shit*, I thought.

'Remember who you are and to whom you're speaking,' Gladstone said coldly.

'I don't know who I am. And I may be speaking to the greatest mass murderer since Horace Glennon-Height. Why the hell did you allow this war to happen?'

Gladstone blinked again and looked around. We were alone. Her sitting room was long and pleasantly dark and hung with original art from Old Earth. At that moment I didn't care if I was in a room filled with original van Goghs. I stared at Gladstone, the Lincolnesque face merely that of an old woman in the thin light through the blinds. She returned my gaze for a moment, then looked away again.

'I apologize,' I snapped, no apology in my voice, 'you didn't *allow* it, you *made* it happen, didn't you?'

'No, Severn I did not make it happen.' Gladstone's voice was hushed, almost a whisper.

'Speak up,' I said. I paced back and forth near the tall windows, watching the light from the blinds move across me like painted stripes. 'And I'm not Joseph Severn.'

She raised an eyebrow. 'Shall I call you M Keats?'

'You can call me No Man,' I said. 'So that when the other cyclopes come, you can say that No Man has blinded you, and they will go away, saying that it's the will of the gods.'

'Do you plan to blind me?'

'Right now I could wring your neck and walk away without a twinge of remorse. *Millions* will die before this week is out. How could you have allowed it?'

Gladstone touched her lower lip. 'The future branches in only two directions,' she said softly. 'War and total uncertainty, or peace and totally certain annihilation. I chose war.'

'Who says this?' There was more curiosity than anger in my voice now.

'It is a fact.' She glanced at her comlog. 'In ten minutes I have to go before the Senate to declare war. Tell me the news of the Hyperion pilgrims.'

I crossed my arms and stared down at her. 'I will tell you if you promise to do something.'

'I will if I can.'

I paused, realized that no amount of leverage in the universe could make this woman write a blank check on her word. 'All right,' I said. 'I want you to fatline Hyperion, release the hold you have on the Consul's ship, and send

301

someone up the Hoolie River to find the Consul himself. He's about a hundred and thirty klicks from the capital, above the Karla Locks. He may be hurt.'

Gladstone crooked a finger, rubbed her lip, and nodded. 'I will send someone to find him. Releasing the ship depends upon what else you have to tell me. Are the others alive?'

I curled my short cape around me and collapsed on a couch across from her. 'Some are.'

'Byron Lamia's daughter? Brawne?'

'The Shrike took her. For a while, she was unconscious, connected to some sort of neural shunt to the datasphere. I dreamed . . . she was floating somewhere, reunited with the implant persona of the first Keats retrieval personality. Just entering the datasphere . . . the megasphere really, Core connections and dimensions I never dreamed of as well as the accessible 'sphere.'

'Is she alive now?' Gladstone leaned forward, intense.

'I don't know. Her body disappeared. I was awakened before I saw where her persona entered the megasphere.'

Gladstone nodded. 'What about the Colonel?'

'Kassad was taken somewhere by Moneta, the human female who seems to reside in the Tombs as they travel through time. The last I saw of him, he was attacking the Shrike barehanded. Shrikes, actually, there were thousands of them.'

'Did he survive?'

I opened my hands. 'I don't know. These were *dreams*. Fragments. Bits and pieces of perception.'

'The poet?'

'Silenus was carried off by the Shrike. Impaled on the tree of thorns. But I glimpsed him there later in Kassad's dream. Silenus was still alive. I don't know how.'

'So the tree of thorns is real, not merely Shrike Cult propaganda?'

'Oh yes, it's real.'

'And the Consul left? Tried to return to the capital?'

302

'He had his grandmother's hawking mat. It worked all right until he reached the place near Karla Locks I mentioned. It . . . and he . . . fell into the river.' I preempted her next question. 'I don't know if he survived.'

'And the priest? Father Hoyt?'

'The cruciform brought him back as Father Duré.'

'*Is* it Father Duré? Or a mindless duplicate?'

'It's Duré,' I said. 'But . . . damaged. Discouraged.'

'And he is still in the valley?'

'No. He disappeared in one of the Cave Tombs. I don't know what happened to him.'

Gladstone glanced at her comlog. I tried to imagine the confusion and chaos which reigned in the rest of this building . . . this world . . . in the Web. The CEO obviously had retreated here for fifteen minutes prior to her speech to the Senate. It might be the last such solitude she would see for the next several weeks. Perhaps ever.

'Captain Masteen?'

'Dead. Buried in the valley.'

She took a breath. 'And Weintraub and the child?'

I shook my head. 'I dreamed things out of sequence . . . out of time. I *think* it's already happened, but I'm confused.' I looked up. Gladstone was waiting patiently. 'The baby was only a few seconds old when the Shrike came,' I said. 'Sol offered her to the thing. I think it took her into the Sphinx. The Tombs were glowing very brightly. There were . . . other Shrikes . . . emerging.'

'The Tombs have opened, then?'

'Yes.'

Gladstone touched her comlog. 'Leigh? Have the duty officer in the communications center contact Theo Lane and the necessary FORCE people on Hyperion. Release the ship we have in quarantine. Also, Leigh, tell the Governor-General that I will have a personal message for him in a few minutes.' The instrument chirped and she looked back at me. 'Is there anything else from your dreams?'

'Images. Words. I don't understand what's going on. Those are the high points.'

Gladstone smiled slightly. 'Are you aware that you are dreaming events beyond the range of the other Keats persona's experience?'

I said nothing, stunned with the shock of what she said. My contact with the pilgrims had been possible through some Core-based connection to the persona implant in Brawne's Schrön loop, through it and the primitive datasphere they had shared. But the persona had been liberated; the datasphere destroyed by separation and distance. Even a fatline receiver cannot receive messages when there is no transmitter.

Gladstone's smile disappeared. 'Can you explain this?'

'No.' I looked up. 'Perhaps they were only dreams. Real dreams.'

She stood. 'Perhaps we'll know when and if we find the Consul. Or when his ship arrives in the valley. I have two minutes before I appear in the Senate. Is there anything else?'

'A question,' I said. 'Who am I? Why am I here?'

The slight smile again. 'We all ask those questions, M Sev—M Keats.'

'I'm serious. I think you know better than I.'

'The Core sent you to be my liaison with the pilgrims. And to observe. You are, after all, a poet and artist.'

I made a noise and stood. We walked slowly toward the private farcaster portal that would take her to the Senate floor. 'What good does observation do when it's the end of the world?'

'Find out,' said Gladstone. 'Go see the end of the world.' She handed me a microcard for my comlog. I inserted it, glanced at the diskey; it was a universal authorization chip, allowing me access to all portals, public, private or military. It was a ticket to the end of the world.

I said, 'What if I get killed?'

'Then we will never hear the answers to your questions,' said CEO Gladstone. She touched my wrist fleetingly, turned her back, and stepped through the portal.

For a few minutes I stood alone in her chambers, appreciating the light and silence and art. There *was* a van Gogh on one of the walls, worth more than most planets could pay. It was a painting of the artist's room at Arles. Madness is not a new invention.

After a while, I left, let my comlog memory guide me through the maze of Government House until I found the central farcaster terminex, and stepped through to find the end of the world.

There were two full-access farcaster pathways through the Web: the Concourse and River Tethys. I 'cast to the Concourse where the half-kilometer strip of Tsingtao-Hsishuang Panna connected to New Earth and the short seaside strip of Nevermore. Tsingtao-Hsishuang Panna was a first-wave world, thirty-four hours away from the Ouster onslaught. New Earth had been on the second-wave list, even now being announced, and had a little over a standard week before invasion. Nevermore was deep in the Web, years away from attack.

There were no signs of panic. People were taking to the datasphere and All Thing rather than the streets. Walking the narrow lanes of Tsingtao, I could hear Gladstone's voice from a thousand receivers and personal comlogs, a strange verbal undertone to the shouts of street vendors and hiss of tires on wet pavement as electric rickshaws hummed overhead on the transport levels.

'. . . as another leader told his people on the eve of attack almost eight centuries ago – "I have nothing to offer but blood, toil, tears, and sweat." You ask, what is our policy? I say to you: It is to wage war, in space, on land, in the air, by sea, wage war with all our might and with all the strength justice and right can give us. *That* is our policy . . .'

There were FORCE troops near the translation zone between Tsingtao and Nevermore, but the flow of pedestrians seemed normal enough. I wondered when the military would commandeer the pedestrian mall of the Concourse for vehicular traffic and if it would be headed *toward* the front or away.

I stepped through to Nevermore. The streets were dry there, except for the occasional spray from the ocean thirty meters below the stone ramparts of the Concourse. The sky was its usual tones of threatening ochre and gray, ominous twilight in the middle of the day. Small stone shops glowed with light and merchandise. I was aware that the streets were emptier than usual; people standing in shops or sitting on stone walls or benches, heads bowed and eyes distracted as they listened.

'. . . you ask, what is our aim? I answer in one word. It is victory, victory at all costs, victory in spite of all terror, victory however long and hard the road may be; for without victory, there is no survival . . .'

The lines at Edgartown's main terminex were short. I coded for Mare Infinitus and stepped through.

The skies were their usual cloudless green, the ocean beneath the float city a deeper green. Kelp farms floated to the horizon. The crowds this far from the Concourse were even smaller; the boardwalks were almost empty, some shops closed. A group of men stood near a kipboat dock and listened to an antique fatline receiver. Gladstone's voice was flat and metallic in the sea-rich air.

'. . . even now, units of FORCE move relentlessly to their stations, firm in their resolve and confident in their ability to rescue not only the threatened worlds but all of the Hegemony of Man from the foulest and most soul-destroying tyranny ever to stain the annals of history . . .'

Mare Infinitus was eighteen hours from invasion. I looked skyward, half expecting to see some sign of the enemy swarm, some indication of orbital defenses, space-

306

borne troop movements. There was only the sky, the warm day, and the gentle rocking of the city on the sea.

Heaven's Gate was the first world on the list of invasion. I stepped through the Mudflat VIP portal and looked down from Rifkin Heights at the beautiful city which belied its name. It was deep night, so late the mech street sweepers were out, their brushes and sonics humming against cobblestone, but here there *was* movement, long lines of silent people at the Rifkin Heights public terminex and even longer lines visible below at the Promenade portals. Local police were in evidence, tall figures in brown impact coveralls, but if FORCE units were rushing to reinforce this area, they were invisible.

The people in the lines were not local residents – the Rifkin Heights and Promenade landowners almost certainly had private portals – but looked to be workers from the reclamation projects many klicks out beyond the fern forest and parks. There was no panic and very little conversation. The lines filed past with the patient stoicism of families shuffling toward a theme park attraction. Few carried anything larger than a travel bag or backpack.

Have we attained such equanimity, I wondered, that we handle ourselves with dignity even in the face of invasion?

Heaven's Gate was thirteen hours from H-hour. I keyed my comlog to the All Thing.

'. . . if we can meet this threat, then worlds we love may remain free and the life of the Web may move forward into the sunlit future. But if we fail, then the whole Web, the Hegemony, everything we have known and cared for, will sink into the abyss of a new Dark Age made infinitely more sinister and protracted by the lights of science perverted and human freedom denied.

'Let us therefore brace ourselves to our duties, and so bear ourselves that if the Hegemony of Man and its Protectorate and allies were to last ten thousand years, humankind will still say: "*This* was their finest hour." '

Somewhere in the silent, fresh-smelling city below, shooting began. First came the rattle of fléchette guns, then the deep hum of antiriot stunners, then screams and the sizzle of weapon lasers. The crowd on the Promenade surged forward toward the terminex, but riot police emerged from the park, switched on powerful halogen searchlights which bathed the crowd in glare, and began ordering them through bullhorns to resume lines or disperse. The crowd hesitated, surged back and forth like a jellyfish caught in tricky currents, and then – spurred on by the sound of firing, louder and closer now – surged forward toward the portal platforms.

The riot cops fired tear gas and vertigo canisters. Between the mob and the farcaster, violet interdiction fields whined into existence. A flight of military EMVs and security skimmers came in low over the city, searchlights stabbing downward. One of the beams of light caught me, held me until my comlog winked at an interrogation signal, and then moved on. It began to rain.

So much for equanimity.

The police had secured the Rifkin Heights public terminex and were stepping through the private Atmospheric Protectorate portal I had used. I decided to go elsewhere.

There were FORCE commandos guarding the halls of Government House, screening the farcaster arrivals despite the fact that this portal was one of the most difficult to access in the Web. I passed through three checkpoints before reaching the executive/residential wing where my apartments were. Suddenly, guards stepped out to empty the main hall and secure its tributaries, and Gladstone swept by accompanied by a swirling crowd of advisors, aides, and military leaders. Surprisingly, she saw me, brought her retinue to a clumsy halt, and spoke to me through the barricade of combat-armored Marines.

'How did you like the speech, M No Man?'

'Fine,' I said. 'Stirring. And stolen from Winston Churchill if I'm not mistaken.'

Gladstone smiled and shrugged slightly. 'If one is to steal, steal from the forgotten masters.' The smile faded. 'What is the news from the frontier?'

'The reality is just beginning to sink in,' I said. 'Expect panic.'

'I always do,' said the CEO. 'What news have you from the pilgrims?'

I was surprised. 'The pilgrims? I haven't been . . . dreaming.'

The current of Gladstone's retinue and impending events began to sweep her away down the hall. 'Perhaps you no longer need to sleep to dream,' she called. 'Try it.'

I watched her go, was released to seek out my suite, found the door, and turned away in disgust with myself. I was retreating in fear and shock from the terror descending on us all. I would be quite happy to lie in bed, avoiding sleep, the covers pulled tight to my chin while I wept for the Web, for the child Rachel, and for myself.

I left the residential wing and found my way out to the central garden, wandering down graveled paths. Tiny microremotes buzzed like bees through the air, one pacing me as I passed through the rose garden, into the area where a sunken path twisted through steamy tropical plants, and into the Old Earth section near the bridge. I sat on the stone bench where Gladstone and I had talked.

Perhaps you no longer need to sleep to dream. Try it.

I pulled my feet up on the bench, touched my chin to my knees, set fingertips against my temples, and closed my eyes.

THIRTY-TWO

Martin Silenus twists and writhes in the pure poetry of pain. A steel thorn two meters long enters his body between his shoulder blades and passes out through his chest, extending to a point a terrible, tapering meter beyond him. His flailing arms cannot touch the point. The thorn is frictionless, his sweaty palms and curling fingers can find no purchase there. Despite the thorn's slickness to the touch, his body does not slide; he is as firmly impaled as a butterfly pinned for exhibition.

There is no blood.

In the hours after rationality returned through the mad haze of pain, Martin Silenus wondered about that. There is no blood. But there is pain. Oh yes, there is pain in abundance here – pain beyond the poet's wildest imaginings of what pain was, pain beyond human endurance and the boundaries of suffering.

But Silenus endures. And Silenus suffers.

He screams for the thousandth time, a ragged sound, empty of content, free of language, even obscenities. Words fail to convey such agony. Silenus screams and writhes. After a while, he hangs limply, the long thorn bouncing slightly in response to his gyrations. Other people hang above, below, and behind him, but Silenus spends little time observing them. Each is separated by his or her own private cocoon of agony.

'*Why this is hell,*' thinks Silenus, quoting Marlowe, '*nor am I out of it.*'

310

But he knows it is not hell. Nor any afterlife. But he also knows that it is not some subbranch of reality; the thorn passes through his *body*! Eight centimeters of organic steel through his chest! But he has not died. He does not bleed. This place was somewhere and something, but it was not hell and it was not living.

Time was strange here. Silenus had known time to stretch and slow before – the agony of the exposed nerve in the dentist's chair, the kidney-stone pain in the Med clinic waiting room – time could slow, seem not to move as the hands of an outraged biological clock stood still in shock. But time did move then. The root canal was finished. The ultramorph finally arrived, took effect. But here the very air is frozen in the absence of time. Pain is the curl and foam of a wave *that does not break*.

Silenus screams in anger and pain. And writhes upon his thorn.

'Goddamn!' he manages at last. 'Goddamn motherfuck sonofabitch.' The words are relics of a different life, artifacts from the dream he had lived before the reality of the tree. Silenus only half remembers that life, as he only half remembers the Shrike carrying him here, impaling him here, leaving him here.

'Oh *God*!' screams the poet and clutches at the thorn with both hands, trying to lever himself up to relieve the great weight of his body which adds so immeasurably to the unmeasurable pain.

There is a landscape below. He can see for miles. It is a frozen, papier-mâché diorama of the Valley of the Time Tombs and the desert beyond. Even the dead city and the distant mountains are reproduced in plasticized, sterile miniature. It does not matter. For Martin Silenus there is only the tree and the pain, and the two are indivisible. Silenus shows his teeth in a pain-cracked smile. When he was a child on Old Earth, he and Amalfi Schwartz, his best friend, had visited a commune of Christians in the North American

Preserve, learned their crude theology, and afterward had made many jokes about crucifixion. Young Martin had spread his arms wide, crossed his legs, lifted his head, and said, 'Gee, I can see the whole town from up here.' Amalfi had roared.

Silenus screams.

Time does not truly pass, but after a while Silenus's mind returns to something resembling linear observation ... something other than the scattered oases of clear, pure agony separated by the desert of mindlessly received agony ... and in that linear perception of his own pain, Silenus begins to impose time on this timeless place.

First, the obscenities add clarity to his pain. Shouting hurts, but his anger clears and clarifies.

Then, in the exhausted times between shouting or pure spasms of pain, Silenus allows himself thought. At first it is merely an effort to sequence, to recite the times tables in his mind, anything to separate the agony of ten seconds ago from the agony yet to come. Silenus discovers that in the effort of concentrating, the agony is lessened slightly – still unbearable, still driving all true thought like wisps before a wind, but lessened some indefinable amount.

So Silenus concentrates. He screams and rails and writhes, but he concentrates. Since there is nothing else to concentrate on, he concentrates on the pain.

Pain, he discovers, has a structure. It has a floor plan. It has designs more intricate than a chambered nautilus, features more baroque than the most buttressed Gothic cathedral. Even as he screams, Martin Silenus studies the structure of this pain. He realizes that it is a poem.

Silenus arches his body and neck for the ten-thousandth time, seeking relief where no relief is possible, but this time he sees a familiar form five meters above him, hanging from a similar thorn, twisting in the unreal breeze of agony.

'Billy!' gasps Martin Silenus, his first true thought.

His former liege lord and patron stares across a sightless abyss, made blind with the pain that had blinded Silenus, but turning slightly as if in response to the call of his name in this place beyond names.

'Billy!' cries Silenus again and then loses vision and thought to the pain. He concentrates on the structure of pain, following its patterns as if he were tracing the trunk and branches and twigs and thorns of the tree itself. 'My lord!'

Silenus hears a voice above the screams and is amazed to find that both the screams and the voice are his:

> . . . *Thou art a dreaming thing;*
> *A fever of thyself – think of the Earth;*
> *What bliss even in hope is there for thee?*
> *What haven? every creature hath its home;*
> *Every sole man hath days of joy and pain,*
> *Whether his labours be sublime or low—*
> *The pain alone; the joy alone; distinct:*
> *Only the dreamer venoms all his days,*
> *Bearing more woe than all his sins deserve.*

He knows the verse, not his, John Keats's, and feels the words further structuring the seeming chaos of pain around him. Silenus understands that the pain has been with him since birth – the universe's gift to a poet. It is a physical reflection of the pain he has felt and futilely tried to set to verse, to pin down with prose, all those useless years of life. It is worse than pain; it is unhappiness because the universe offers pain to all.

> *Only the dreamer venoms all his days,*
> *Bearing more woe than all his sins deserve!*

Silenus shouts it but does not scream. The roar of pain from the tree, more psychic than physical, abates for the barest fraction of a second. There is an island of distraction amidst this ocean of single-mindedness.

'Martin!'

Silenus arches, lifts his head, tries to focus through the haze of pain. Sad King Billy is looking at him. *Looking.*

Sad King Billy croaks a syllable which, after an endless moment, Silenus recognizes as 'More!'

Silenus screams in agony, writhes in a palsied spasm of mindless physical response, but when he stops, dangling in exhaustion, the pain not lessened but driven from the motor areas of his brain by fatigue toxins, he allows the voice within him to shout and whisper its song:

> *Spirit here that reignest!*
> *Spirit here that painest!*
> *Spirit here that burnest!*
> *Spirit here that mournest!*
> > *Spirit! I bow*
> > *My forehead low,*
> > *Enshaded with thy pinions!*
> > *Spirit! I look*
> > *All passion-struck*
> > *Into thy pale dominions!*

The small circle of silence widens to include several nearby branches, a handful of thorns carrying their clusters of human beings in extremis.

Silenus stares up at Sad King Billy and sees his betrayed lord open his sad eyes. For the first time in more than two centuries, patron and poet look upon one another. Silenus delivers the message that has brought him here, hung him here. 'My lord, I'm sorry.'

Before Billy can respond, before the chorus of screaming drowns out any response, the air *changes*, the sense of frozen time *stirs*, and the tree *shakes*, as if the entire thing has dropped a meter. Silenus screams with the others as the branch shakes and the impaling thorn tears at his insides, rends his flesh anew.

Silenus opens his eyes and sees that the sky is real, the desert real, the Tombs glowing, the wind blowing, and time begun again. There is no lessening of torment, but clarity has returned.

Martin Silenus laughs through tears. 'Look, Mom!' he shouts, giggling, the steel spear still protruding a meter beyond his shattered chest, 'I can see the whole town from up here!'

'M Severn? Are you all right?'

Panting, on my hands and knees, I turned toward the voice. Opening my eyes was painful, but no pain could compare to what I had just experienced.

'Are you all right, sir?'

No one was near me in the garden. The voice came from a microremote that buzzed half a meter from my face, probably one of the security people somewhere in Government House.

'Yes,' I managed, getting to my feet and brushing gravel from my knees. 'I'm fine. A sudden . . . pain.'

'Medical help can be here in two minutes, sir. Your biomonitor reports no organic difficulty, but we can—'

'No, no,' I said. 'I'm fine. Leave it be. And leave *me* alone.'

The remote fluttered like a nervous hummingbird. 'Yes, sir. Just call if you need anything. The garden and grounds monitor will respond.'

'Go away,' I said.

I went out of the gardens, through the main hall of Government House – all checkpoints and security guards now – and out across the landscaped acres of Deer Park.

The dock area was quiet, the River Tethys more still than I had ever seen it. 'What's happening?' I asked one of the security people on the pier.

The guard accessed my comlog, confirmed my executive override pip and CEO clearance, but still did not hurry to answer. 'The portals've been turned off for TC²,' he drawled. 'Bypassed.'

'Bypassed? You mean the river doesn't flow through Tau Ceti Center anymore?'

'Right.' He flipped his visor down as a small boat approached, flipped it up when he identified the two security people in it.

'Can I get out that way?' I pointed upriver to where the tall portals showed an opaque curtain of gray.

The guard shrugged. 'Yeah. But you won't be allowed back that way.'

'That's all right. Can I take that small boat?'

The guard whispered into his bead mike and nodded. 'Go ahead.'

I stepped gingerly into the small craft, sat on the rear bench and held on to the gunwales until the rocking subsided, touched the power diskey and said, 'Start.'

The electric jets hummed, the small launch untied itself and pointed its nose into the river, and I pointed the way upstream.

I had never heard of part of River Tethys being cordoned off, but the farcaster curtain was now definitely a one-way and semipermeable membrane. The boat hummed through, and I shrugged off the tingling sensation and looked around.

I was in one of the great canal cities – Ardmen or Pamolo, perhaps – on Renaissance Vector. The Tethys here was a main street from which many tributaries flowed. Ordinarily, the only river traffic here would be the tourist gondolas on the outer lanes and the yachts and go-everywheres of the very rich in the pass-through center lanes. Today it was a madhouse.

Boats of every size and description clogged the center channels, boats headed in both directions. Houseboats were piled high with belongings, smaller craft were so heavily laden that it looked like the smallest wave or wake would capsize them. Hundreds of ornamental junks from Tsingtao-Hsishuang Panna and million-mark river condobarges from Fuji vied for their share of the river; I guessed that few of these

316

residential boats had ever left their tie-ups before. Amidst the riot of wood and plasteel and Perspex, go-everywheres moved by like silver eggs, their containment fields set to full reflection.

I queried the datasphere: Renaissance Vector was a second-wave world, one hundred and seven hours from invasion. I thought it odd that Fuji refugees were crowding the waterways here since that world had more than two hundred hours until the axe fell, but then I realized that except for the removal of TC^2 from the waterway, the river still flowed through its usual series of worlds. Refugees from Fuji had taken the river from Tsingtao, thirty-three hours from the Ousters, through Deneb Drei at a hundred and forty-seven hours, through Renaissance Vector toward Parsimony or Grass, both unthreatened at this time. I shook my head, found a relatively sane tributary street from which to watch the madness, and wondered when the authorities would reroute the river so that *all* threatened worlds flowed to sanctuary.

Can they do that? I wondered. The TechnoCore had installed River Tethys as a gift to the Hegemony during its PentaCentennial. But surely Gladstone or someone had thought to ask the Core to aid in the evacuation. *Had they?* I wondered. *Would* the Core help? I knew that Gladstone was convinced that elements of the Core were intent upon eliminating the human species – this war had been her Hobson's choice given that alternative. What a simple way for the antihuman Core elements to carry out their program – merely refuse to evacuate the billions threatened by the Ousters!

I had been smiling, however grimly, but that smile faded as I realized that the TechnoCore also maintained and controlled the farcaster grid that I depended on to get out of the threatened territories.

I had tied up the launch at the base of a stone stairway that descended into the brackish waters. I noticed green moss growing on the lowest stones. The stone steps themselves – possibly brought from Old Earth, since some of the classical cities were shipped via farcaster in the early years after the Big Mistake – were worn with age, and I could see a fine tracery of cracks connecting sparkling flecks there, looking like a schematic of the Worldweb.

It was very warm, and the air was too thick, too heavy. Renaissance Vector's sun hung low above the gabled towers. The light was too red and too syrupy for my eyes. Noise from the Tethys was deafening even here, a hundred meters down the equivalent of an alley. Pigeons whirled in agitation between dark walls and overhanging eaves.

What can I do? Everyone seemed to be acting as the world slouched toward destruction, and the best I could do was wander aimlessly.

That's your job. You're an observer.

I rubbed my eyes. Who said that poets had to be observers? I thought of Li Po and George Wu leading their armies through China and writing some of the most sensitive verse in history while their soldiers slept. And at least Martin Silenus had led a long, eventful life, even if half the events were obscene and the other half wasted.

At the thought of Martin Silenus, I groaned aloud.

Is the child, Rachel, hanging from that tree of thorns even now?

For a second I pondered that, wondering if such a fate were preferable to the quick extinction of Merlin's sickness.

No.

I closed my eyes, concentrated on thinking of nothing at all, hoping that I could make some contact with Sol, discover something about the fate of the child.

The small boat rocked gently from distant wakes. Somewhere above me, the pigeons fluttered to a ledge and cooed to one another.

'I don't care how difficult it is!' shouts Meina Gladstone. 'I want *all* of the fleet in Vega System to defend Heaven's Gate. *Then* shift the necessary elements to God's Grove and the other threatened worlds. The only advantage we *have* right now is mobility!'

Admiral Singh's face is dark with frustration. 'Too dangerous, M Executive! If we move the fleet directly to Vega space, it runs a terrible risk of being cut off there. They will certainly attempt to destroy the singularity sphere that connects that system to the Web.'

'*Protect* it!' snaps Gladstone. 'That's what all the expensive warships are for.'

Singh looks to Morpurgo or the other brass for help. No one speaks. The group is in the executive complex War Room. The walls are heavy with holos and flowing columns of data. No one is watching the wall.

'It is taking all our resources to protect the singularity sphere in Hyperion space,' says Admiral Singh, his voice low, words carefully spaced. 'Retreating under fire, especially under the onslaught of the entire Swarm there, is very difficult. Should *that* sphere be destroyed, our fleet would be eighteen months time-debt from the Web. The war would be lost before they could return.'

Gladstone nods tersely. 'I'm not asking you to risk that singularity sphere until all elements of the fleet have translated, Admiral . . . I've already agreed to let them have Hyperion *before* we get all our ships out . . . but I insist that we do not surrender worlds of the Web without a fight.'

General Morpurgo stands. The Lusian looks exhausted already. 'CEO, we're planning a fight. But it makes much more sense to begin our defense at Hebron or Renaissance Vector. Not only do we gain almost five days to prepare our defenses, but—'

'But we lose nine worlds!' interrupts Gladstone. '*Billions* of Hegemony citizens. Human beings. Heaven's Gate would be a terrible loss, but God's Grove is a cultural and ecological treasure. Irreplaceable.'

319

'CEO,' says Allan Imoto, Minister of Defense, 'there is evidence coming in that the Templars have been in collusion with the so-called Church of the Shrike for many years. Much of the funding for Shrike Cult programs has come from—'

Gladstone flicks her hand to silence the man. 'I don't *care* about that. The thought of losing God's Grove is untenable. If we can't defend Vega and Heaven's Gate, we draw the line at the Templar planet. That's final.'

Singh looks as if he has been weighted with invisible chains as he attempts an ironic smile. 'That gains us less than an hour, CEO.'

'It's final,' repeats Gladstone. 'Leigh, what's the status of the riots on Lusus?'

Hunt clears his throat. His demeanor is as hangdog and unhurried as ever. 'M Executive, at least five Hives are now involved. Hundreds of millions of marks in property have been destroyed. FORCE:ground troops have been translated from Freeholm and appear to have contained the worst of the looting and demonstrations, but there is no estimate of when farcaster service can be restored to those Hives. There is no doubt that the Church of the Shrike is responsible. The initial riot in Bergstrom Hive began with a demonstration of Cult fanatics, and the Bishop broke into HTV programming until he was cut off by—'

Gladstone lowers her head. 'So he's finally surfaced. Is he on Lusus now?'

'We don't know, M Executive,' replies Hunt. 'Transit Authority people are trying to trace him and his top acolytes.'

Gladstone swivels toward a young man I do not recognize for a moment. It is Commander William Ajunta Lee, the hero of the battle for Maui-Covenant. When last heard of, the young man had been transferred to the Outback for daring to speak his mind in front of his superiors. Now the epaulettes of his FORCE:sea uniform carry the gold and emerald of a rear admiral's insignia.

'What about fighting for each world?' Gladstone asks him,

320

ignoring her own edict that the decision was final.

'I believe it's a mistake, CEO,' says Lee. 'All nine Swarms are committed to the attack. The only one we won't have to worry about for three years – assuming we can extricate our forces – is the Swarm now attacking Hyperion. If we concentrate our fleet – even half our fleet – to meet the menace to God's Grove, the odds are almost one hundred percent that we will not be able to shift those forces to defend the eight other first-wave worlds.'

Gladstone rubs her lower lip. 'What do you recommend?'

Rear Admiral Lee takes a breath. 'I recommend we cut our losses, blow the singularity spheres in those nine systems, and prepare to attack the second-wave Swarms *before* they reach inhabited star systems.'

Commotion erupts around the table. Senator Feldstein from Barnard's World is on her feet, shouting something.

Gladstone waits for the storm to subside. 'Carry the fight to them, you mean? Counterattack the Swarms themselves, not wait to fight a defensive battle?'

'Yes, M Executive.'

Gladstone points at Admiral Singh. 'Can it be done? Can we plan, prepare, and launch such offensive strikes by' – she consults the datastream on the wall above her – 'ninety-four standard hours from now?'

Singh pulls himself to attention. 'Possible? Ah . . . perhaps, CEO, but the political repercussions of losing nine worlds from the Web . . . ah . . . the logistical difficulties of—'

'But it's possible?' presses Gladstone.

'Ah . . . yes, M Executive. But if—'

'Do it,' says Gladstone. She rises, and the others at the table hurry to get to their feet. 'Senator Feldstein, I'll see you and the other affected legislators in my chambers. Leigh, Allan, please keep me informed on the Lusus riots. The War Council will readjourn here in four hours. Good day, gentlemen and ladies.'

I walked the streets as in a daze, my mind tuned to echoes. Away from River Tethys, where canals were fewer and the pedestrian thoroughfares were wider, the crowds filled the avenues. I let my comlog lead me to different terminexes, but each time the throngs were thicker there. It took me a few minutes to realize that these were not merely inhabitants of Renaissance V seeking to get *out*, but sightseers from throughout the Web shoving to get *in*. I wondered if anyone on Gladstone's evacuation task force had considered the problem of millions of the curious 'casting in to see the war begin.

I had no idea how I was dreaming conversations in Gladstone's War Room, but I also had no doubt they were real. Thinking back now, I remembered details of my dreams during the long night past – not merely dreams of Hyperion, but the CEO's world walk and details from high-level conferences.

Who was I?

A cybrid was a biological remote, an appendage of the AI ... or in this case of an AI retrieval persona ... safely ensconced somewhere in the Core. It made sense that the Core knew everything that went on in Government House, in the many halls of human leadership. Humanity had become as blasé about sharing their lives with potential AI monitoring as pre-Civil War Old Earth USA-southern families had been about speaking in front of their human slaves. Nothing could be done about it – every human above the lowest Dregs' Hive poverty class had a comlog with biomonitor, many had implants, and each of these was tuned to the music of the datasphere, monitored by elements of the datasphere, dependent upon functions of the datasphere – so humans accepted their lack of privacy. An artist on Esperance had once said to me, 'Having sex or a domestic quarrel with the house monitors on is like undressing in front of a dog or cat ... it gives you pause the first time, and then you forget about it.'

So was I tapping into some back channel known just to the

Core? There was a simple way to find out: leave my cybrid and travel the highways of the megasphere to the Core the way Brawne and my disembodied counterpart had been doing the last time I had shared their perceptions.

No.

The thought of that made me dizzy, almost ill. I found a bench and sat a moment, lowering my head between my knees and taking long, slow breaths. The crowds moved by. Somewhere someone was addressing them through a bullhorn.

I was hungry. It had been at least twenty-four hours since I'd eaten, and cybrid or no, my body was weak and famished. I pressed into a side street where vendors shouted above the normal din, hawking their wares from one-wheeled gyro carts.

I found a cart where the line was short, ordered fried dough with honey, a cup of rich, Bressian coffee, and a pocket of pitta bread with salad, paid the woman with a touch of my universal card, and climbed a stairway to an abandoned building to sit on the balcony and eat. It tasted wonderful. I was sipping my coffee, considering going back for more fried dough, when I noticed that the crowd in the square below had ceased its mindless surges and had coalesced around a small group of men standing on the rim of a broad fountain in the center. Their amplified words drifted to me over the heads of the crowd:

'. . . the Angel of Retribution has been loosed among us, prophecies fulfilled, the Millennium come . . . the plan of the Avatar calls for such sacrifice . . . as prophesied by the Church of the Final Atonement, which knew, which has always known, that such atonement must be made . . . too late for such half-measures . . . too late for internecine strife . . . the end of mankind is upon us, the Tribulations have begun, the Millennium of the Lord is about to dawn.'

I realized that the men in red were priests of the Shrike Cult and that the crowd was responding – first with scattered

323

shouts of agreement, occasional cries of 'Yes, yes!' and 'Amen!' and then with chanting in unison, raised fists surging above the crowd, and fierce cries of ecstasy. It was incongruous, to say the least. The Web in this century had many of the religious overtones of the Rome of Old Earth just before the Christian Era: a policy of tolerance, a myriad of religions – most, like Zen Gnosticism, complex and inwardly turned rather than the stuff of proselytism – while the general tenor was one of gentle cynicism and indifference to religious impulse.

But not now, not in this square.

I was thinking about how free of mobs recent centuries had been: to create a mob there must be public meetings, and public meetings in our time consisted of individuals communing via the All Thing or other datasphere channels; it is hard to create mob passion when people are separated by kilometers and light-years, connected only by comm lines and fatline threads.

Suddenly I was jarred from my reveries by a hush in the crowd's roar, a turning of a thousand faces in my direction.

'. . . and there is one of *them*!' cried the Shrike Cult holy man, his red robes flashing as he pointed in my direction. 'One of those from the sealed circles of the Hegemony . . . one of the scheming sinners who has brought the Atonement to us this day . . . it is *that man* and those like him who want the Shrike Avatar to make *you* pay for his sins, while he and the others hide in safety in the secret worlds the Hegemony leadership has set aside for just this day!'

I put down my cup of coffee, gulped my last bit of fried dough, and stared. The man was speaking gibberish. But how did he know that I had come from TC²? Or that I had access to Gladstone? I looked again, shielding my eyes from the glare and trying to ignore the raised faces and shaken fists aimed in my direction, focusing on the face above the red robes . . .

My God, it was Spenser Reynolds, the action artist whom

I'd last seen trying to dominate the dinner conversation at Treetops. Reynolds had shaved his head until nothing was left of his curled and coifed hair except a Shrike Cult queue at the back, but the face was still tanned and handsome, even distorted as it was now with simulated rage and a true believer's fanatic faith.

'Seize him!' cried Shrike Cult agitator Reynolds, still pointing in my direction. 'Seize him and make him pay for the destruction of our homes, the deaths of our families, the end of our world!'

I actually glanced behind me, thinking that surely this pompous *poseur* was not talking about *me*.

But he was. And enough of the crowd had been converted to *mob* that a wave of people nearest the shouting demagogue surged in my direction, fists waving and spittle flying, and that surge moved others farther from the center, until the fringes of the crowd below me also moved in my direction to keep from being trampled.

The surge became a roaring, shouting, screaming mass of rioters; at that moment, the sum of the crowd's IQ was far below that of its most modest single member. Mobs have passions, not brains.

I didn't wish to remain around long enough to explain this to them. The crowd parted and began rushing up both sides of my divided staircase. I turned and tried the boarded door behind me. It was locked.

I kicked until the door splintered inward on the third attempt, stepped through the gap just ahead of grasping hands, and began sprinting up a dark staircase in a hall which smelled of age and mildew. There were shouts and splintering sounds as the mob demolished the door behind me.

There was an apartment on the third floor, occupied although the building had looked abandoned. It was not locked. I opened the door just as I heard footsteps on the flight below me.

'Please help—' I began and stopped. There were three women in the dark room; perhaps three female generations of the same family, for there was some resemblance. All three sat in rotting chairs, clothed in soiled rags, white arms extended, pale fingers curled around unseen spheres; I could see the slim metal cable curling through the oldest woman's white hair to the black deck on a dusty tabletop. Identical cables twisted from the daughter and granddaughter's skulls.

Wireheads. In the last stages of uplink anorexia from the looks of it. Someone must come in occasionally to feed them intravenously and to change their soiled clothing, but perhaps the war scare had kept their keepers away.

Footsteps echoed on the stairs. I closed the door and ran up two more flights. Locked doors or abandoned rooms with puddles of water dripping from exposed lathing. Empty Flashback injectors scattered like soft-drink bulbs. *This is not a quality neighborhood*, I thought.

I reached the roof ten steps ahead of the pack. What mindless passion the mob had lost in separation from their guru, it had gained in the dark and claustrophobic confines of the stairway. They may have forgotten *why* they were chasing me, but that made the thought of being caught by them no more attractive.

Slamming the rotting door behind me, I looked for a lock, something to barricade the passage, anything. There was no lock. Nothing large enough to block the doorway. Frenzied footfalls echoed up the last flight of stairs.

I looked around the rooftop: miniature uplink dishes growing like inverted, rusty toadstools, a line of wash that looked as if it had been forgotten years before, the decomposed corpses of a dozen pigeons, and an ancient Vikken Scenic.

I made it to the EMV before the first of the mob came through the doorway. The thing was a museum piece. Dirt and pigeon droppings all but obscured the windshield. Someone had removed the original repellors and replaced them with cut-rate black market units that would never pass inspection. The Perspex canopy was fused and darkened in the back, as if someone had used it for target practice with a weapons laser.

More to the point of the immediate moment, however, was the fact that it had no palmlock, merely a key lock which had been forced long before. I threw myself into the dusty seat and tried to slam the door; it would not latch, but hung half-open. I did not speculate on the small odds of the thing start-ing or the even smaller odds of my being able to negotiate with the mob as they dragged me out and down . . . if they didn't merely *throw* me over the edge of the building. I could hear a bass roar of shouts as the mob worked itself to a frenzy in the square below.

The first people on to the roof were a burly man in khaki tech overalls, a slim man in the latest Tau Ceti fashion-approved matte black suit, a terribly obese woman waving what looked to be a long wrench, and a short man in Renais-sance V Self-Defense Force green.

I held the door open with my left hand and slipped Gladstone's override microcard into the ignition diskey. The battery whined, the transition starter ground away, and I closed my eyes and made a wish that the circuits were solar charged and self-repairing.

Fists pounded on the roof, palms slapped against the warped Perspex near my face, and someone tugged open the door despite my best efforts to keep it closed. The shouting of the distant crowd was like the background noise an ocean makes; the screaming of the group on the rooftop more like the cry of oversized gulls.

The lift circuits caught, repellors flared dust and pigeon crap over the rooftop mob, and I slipped my hand into the omni controller, shifted back and to the right, and felt the old Scenic lift, wobble, dip, and lift again.

I banked right out over the square, only half aware that dashboard alarms were chiming and that someone was still dangling from the open door. I swooped low, smiling inadvertently as I saw Shrike Cult orator Reynolds duck and the crowd scatter, and then pulled up over the fountain while banking steeply to the left.

My screaming passenger did not let go of the door, but the door came off, so the effect was the same. I noticed that it had been the obese woman in the instant before she and the door hit the water eight meters below, splashing Reynolds and the crowd. I twitched the EMV higher and listened to the black market lift units groan about the decision.

Angry calls from local traffic control joined the chorus of dashboard alarm voices, the car staggered as it shifted to police override, but I touched the diskey with my microcard again and nodded as control returned to the omni stick. I flew over the oldest, poorest section of the city, keeping close to the rooftops and banking around spires and clock towers to stay below police radar. On a normal day, the traffic control cops riding personal lift packs and stick skimmers would have swooped down and tangle-netted me long before this, but from the look of the crowds in the streets below and the riots I glimpsed near public farcaster terminexes, it didn't look much like a normal day.

The Scenic began to warn me that its time in the air was numbered in seconds now, I felt the starboard repellor give with a sickening lurch, and I worked hard with the omni and floor throttle to wobble the junker down to a landing in a small parking lot between a canal and a large, soot-stained building. This place was at least ten klicks from the square where Reynolds had incited the mob, so I felt safer taking my chances on the ground . . . not that there was much choice at this moment.

Sparks flew, metal tore, parts of the rear quarter panel, flare skirt, and front access panel disassociated themselves from the rest of the vehicle, and I was down and stopped two meters from the wall overlooking the canal. I walked away from the Vikken with as much nonchalance as I could muster.

The streets were still in the control of the crowds – not yet coalesced into a mob here – and the canals were a tangle of small boats, so I strolled into the closest public building to get out of sight. The place was part museum, part library, and part archive; I loved it at first sight . . . and smell, for here there were thousands of printed books, many very old indeed, and nothing smells quite as wonderful as old books.

I was wandering through the anteroom, checking titles and wondering idly whether the works of Salmud Brevy could be found here, when a small, wizened man in an outdated wool and fiberplastic suit approached me. 'Sir,' he said, 'it has been too long since we've had the pleasure of your company!'

I nodded, sure that I had never met this man, never visited this place.

'Three years, no? At least three years! My, how time flies.' The little man's voice was little more than a whisper – the hushed tones of someone who has spent most of his life in libraries – but there was no denying the undertone of excitement there. 'I'm sure you would like to go straight to the collection,' he said, standing aside as if to let me pass.

'Yes,' I said, bowing slightly. 'But after you.'

The little man – I was almost sure that he was an archivist – seemed pleased to be leading the way. He chatted aimlessly about new acquisitions, recent appraisals, and visits of Web scholars as we walked through chamber after chamber of books: high, multitiered vaults of books, intimate, mahogany-lined corridors of books, vast chambers where our footfalls echoed off distant walls of books. I saw no one else during the walk.

We crossed a tiled walkway with wrought-iron railings above a sunken pool of books where deep blue containment fields protected scrolls, parchments, crumbling maps, illuminated manuscripts, and ancient comic books from the ravages of atmosphere. The archivist opened a low door, thicker than most airlock entrances, and we were in a small, windowless room wherein thick drapes half concealed alcoves lined with ancient volumes. A single leather chair sat on a pre-Hegira Persian carpet, and a glass case held a few scraps of vacuum-pressed parchment.

'Do you plan to publish soon, sir?' asked the little man.

'What?' I turned away from the case. 'Oh . . . no,' I said.

The archivist touched his chin with a small fist. 'You'll pardon me for saying so, sir, but it is a terrible waste if you do not. Even in our few discussions over the years, it has become apparent that you are one of the finest . . . if not *the* finest . . . Keats scholars in the Web.' He sighed and took a step back. 'Excuse me for saying so, sir.'

I stared at him. 'That's all right,' I said, suddenly knowing very well who he thought I was and why that person had come here.

'You'll wish to be left alone, sir.'

'If you don't mind.'

The archivist bowed slightly and backed out of the room, closing the thick door all but a crack. The only light came from three subtle lamps recessed in the ceiling: perfect for reading, but not so bright as to compromise the cathedral quality of the little room. The only sound came from the archivist's receding footsteps far away. I walked to the case and set my hands on the edges, careful not to smudge the glass.

The first Keats retrieval cybrid, 'Johnny,' obviously had come here frequently during his few years of life in the Web. Now I remembered mention of a library somewhere on Renaissance V in something Brawne Lamia had said. She had followed her client and lover here early in the investigation of his 'death.' Later, after he had truly been killed except for the recorded persona in her Schrön loop, she had visited this place. She had told the others of two poems the first cybrid had visited daily in his ongoing effort to understand his own reason for existence . . . and for dying.

These two original manuscripts were in the case. The first

was – I thought – a rather saccharine love poem beginning 'The day is gone, and all its sweets are gone!' The second was better, although contaminated with the romantic morbidity of an overly romantic and morbid age:

> This living hand, now warm and capable
> Of earnest grasping, would, if it were cold
> And in the icy silence of the tomb,
> So haunt thy days and chill thy dreaming nights
> That thou wouldst wish thine own heart dry of blood
> So in my veins red life might stream again,
> And thou be conscience-calm'd – see here it is—
> I hold it towards you.

Brawne Lamia had taken this as almost a personal message from her dead lover, the father of her unborn child. I stared at the parchment, lowering my face so that my breath gently fogged the glass.

It was not a message across time to Brawne, nor even a contemporary lament for Fanny, my single and dearest soul's desire. I stared at the faded words – the handwriting carefully executed, the letters still quite legible across the gulfs of time and language evolution – and remembered writing them in December 1819, scrawling this fragment of verse on a page of the satirical 'faery tale' I had just started – The Cap and Bells, or, The Jealousies. A terrible piece of nonsense, quite properly abandoned after the period of slight amusement it gave me.

The 'This living hand' fragment had been one of those poetic rhythms which echoes like an unresolved chord in the mind, driving one to see it in ink, on paper. It, in turn, had been an echo of an earlier, unsatisfactory line . . . the eighteenth, I believe . . . in my second attempt to tell the tale of the sun god Hyperion's fall. I remember that the first version . . . the one undoubtedly still printed wherever my literary bones are left out on show like the mummified remains of some inadvertent saint, sunk in concrete and glass below the altar of literature . . . the first version had read:

> . . . *Who alive can say,*
> *'Thou art no Poet; mayst not tell thy dreams'?*
> *Since every man whose soul is not a clod*
> *Hath visions, and would speak, if he had loved,*
> *And been well nurtured in his mother tongue.*
> *Whether the dream now purposed to rehearse*
> *Be Poet's or Fanatic's will be known*
> *When this warm scribe my hand is in the grave.*

I liked the scrawled version, with its sense of haunting and of being haunted, and would have substituted it for 'When this warm scribe my hand . . .' even if it meant revising it a bit and adding fourteen lines to the already too-long opening passage of the first Canto . . .

I staggered backward to the chair and sat, lowering my face to my hands. I was sobbing. I did not know why. I could not quit.

For a long while after the tears ceased flowing, I sat there, thinking, remembering. Once, it may have been hours later, I heard the echo of footsteps coming from afar, pausing respectfully outside my small room, and then dwindling to distance once again.

I realized that all of the books in all of the alcoves were works of 'Mister John Keats, five feet high,' as I had once written – John Keats, the consumptive poet who had asked only that his tomb be nameless except for the inscription:

> *Here lies One*
> *Whose Name was writ in Water.*

I did not stand to look at the books, to read them. I did not have to.

Alone in the stillness and leather-and-aged-paper musk of the library, alone in my sanctuary of self and not-self, I closed my eyes. I did not sleep. I dreamed.

THIRTY-THREE

The datumplane analog of Brawne Lamia and her retrieval persona lover strike the surface of the megasphere like two cliff divers striking the surface of a turbulent sea. There is a quasi-electrical shock, a sense of having passed through a resisting membrane, and they are *inside*, the stars are gone, and Brawne's eyes widen as she stares at an information environment infinitely more complex than any datasphere.

The dataspheres traveled by human operators are often compared to complex cities of information: towers of corporate and government data, highways of process flow, broad avenues of datumplane interaction, subways of restricted travel, high walls of security ice with microphage guards on prowl, and the visible analog of every microwave flow and counterflow a city lives by.

This is more. Much more.

The usual datasphere city analogs are there, but small, so very small, as dwarfed by the scope of the megasphere as true cities would be on a world seen from orbit.

The megasphere, Brawne sees, is as alive and interactive as the biosphere of any Class Five world: forests of green-gray data trees grow and prosper, sending out new roots and branches and shoots even as she watches; beneath the forest proper, entire microecologies of dataflow and subroutine AIs flourish, flower, and die as their usefulness ends; beneath the shifting ocean-fluid soil of the matrix proper, a busy subterranean life of data moles, commlink worms, reprograming bacteria, data tree roots, and Strange Loop seeds works away,

333

while above, in and through and beneath the intertwining forest of fact and interaction, analogs of predators and prey carry out their cryptic duties, swooping and running, climbing and pouncing, some soaring free through the great spaces between branch synapses and neuron leaves.

As quickly as the metaphor gives meaning to what Brawne is seeing, the image flees, leaving behind only the overwhelming analog reality of the megasphere – a vast internal ocean of light and sound and branching connections, intershot with the spinning whirlpools of AI consciousness and the ominous black holes of farcaster connections. Brawne feels vertigo claim her, and she clings to Johnny's hand as tightly as a drowning woman would cling to a life ring.

—*It's all right*, sends Johnny. *I won't let go. Stay with me.*

—*Where are we going?*

—*To find someone I'd forgotten.*

—*??????*

—*My . . . father . . .*

Brawne holds fast as she and Johnny seem to glide deeper into the amorphous depths. They enter a flowing, crimson avenue of sealed datacarriers, and she imagines that this is what a red corpuscle sees in its trip through some crowded blood vessel.

Johnny seems to know the way; twice they exit the main thoroughfare to follow some smaller branch, and many times Johnny must choose between bifurcating avenues. He does so easily, moving their body analogs between platelet carriers the size of small spacecraft. Brawne tries to see the biosphere metaphor again, but here, inside the many-routed branches, she can't see the forest for the trees.

They are swept through an area where AIs communicate above them . . . *around* them . . . like great, gray eminences looming over a busy ant farm. Brawne remembers her mother's homeworld of Freeholm, the billiard-table smoothness of the Great Steppe, where the family estate sat alone on ten million acres of short grass . . . Brawne remembers the terrible autumn storms there, when she had stood at the edge of the estate grounds, just beyond the protective containment field bubble, and watched dark stratocumulus pile twenty kilometers high in a blood-red sky, violence accumulating with a power that had made the hair on her forearms stand out in anticipation of lightning bolts the size of cities, tornadoes writhing and dropping down like the Medusa locks they were named after, and behind the twisters, walls of black wind which would obliterate everything in their path.

The AIs are worse. Brawne feels less than insignificant in their shadow: insignificance might offer invisibility; she feels all too visible, all too much a part of these shapeless giants' terrible perceptions . . .

Johnny squeezes her hand, and they are past, twisting left and downward along a busier branch, then switching directions again, and again, two all-too-conscious photons lost in a tangle of fiberoptic cables.

But Johnny is not lost. He presses her hand, takes a final turn into a deep blue cavern free of traffic except for the two of them, and pulls her closer as their speed increases, synaptic junctions flashing past until they blur, only the absence of wind rush destroying the illusion of traveling some mad highway at supersonic speeds.

Suddenly there comes a sound like waterfalls converging, like levitating trains losing their lift and screeching down railways at obscene speeds. Brawne thinks of the Freeholm tornadoes again, of listening to the Medusa locks roaring and tearing their way across the flat landscape toward her, and then she and Johnny are in a whirlpool of light and noise and sensation, two insects twisting away into oblivion toward a black vortex below.

Brawne tries to scream her thoughts – *does* scream her thoughts – but no communication is possible above the end-of-the-universe mental din, so she holds tight to Johnny's hand and trusts him, even as they fall forever into that black cyclone, even as her body analog twists and deforms from nightmare pressures, shredding like lace before a scythe, until all that is left are her thoughts, her sense of self, and the contact with Johnny.

Then they are through, floating quietly along a wide and azure data stream, both of them re-forming and huddling together with that pulse-pounding sense of deliverance known by canoeists who have survived the rapids and the waterfall, and when Brawne finally lifts her attention, she sees the impossible size of their new surroundings, the light-year-spanning reach of things, the complexity which makes her previous glimpses of the megasphere seem like the ravings of a provincial who has mistaken the cloakroom for the cathedral, and she thinks – *This is the central megasphere!*

—No, Brawne, it's one of the periphery nodes. No closer to the Core than the perimeter we tested with BB Surbringer. You're merely seeing more dimensions of it. An AI's view, if you will.

Brawne looks at Johnny, realizing that she is seeing in infrared now as the heat-lamp light from distant furnaces of data suns bathes them both. He is still handsome.

—Is it much farther, Johnny?

—No, not much farther now.

They approach another black vortex. Brawne clings to her only love and closes her eyes.

They are in an . . . enclosure . . . a bubble of black energy larger than most worlds. The bubble is translucent: the organic mayhem of the megasphere growing and changing and carrying out its arcane business beyond the dark curve of the ovoid's wall.

But Brawne has no interest in the outside. Her analog gaze and her total attention are focused on the megalith of energy and intelligence and sheer *mass* which floats in front of them: in front, above, and below, actually, for the mountain of pulsing light and power holds Johnny and her in its grip, lifting them two hundred meters above the floor of the egg-chamber to where they rest on the 'palm' of a vaguely handlike pseudopod.

The megalith studies them. It has no eyes in the organic sense, but Brawne feels the intensity of its gaze. It reminds her of the time she visited Meina Gladstone in Government House and the CEO had turned the full force of her appraising gaze on Brawne.

Brawne has the sudden impulse to giggle as she imagines Johnny and herself as tiny Gullivers visiting this Brobdingnagian CEO for tea. She does not giggle because she can feel the hysteria lying just under the surface, waiting to blend with sobs if she allows her emotions to destroy what little sense of reality she is imposing on this madness.

[You found your way here ＼ I was not sure you would/could/should choose to do so]

The megalith's 'voice' is more a basso profundo bone conduction from some great vibration than a true voice in Brawne's mind. It is like listening to the mountain-grinding noise of an earthquake and then belatedly realizing that the sounds are forming words.

Johnny's voice is the same as always – soft, infinitely well modulated, lifted by a slight lilt which Brawne now realizes is Old Earth British Isles English, and firmed by conviction:

—*I did not know if I could find the way, Ummon.*

[You remember/invent/hold to your heart my name]

—*Not until I spoke it did I remember it.*

[Your slow-time body is no more]

—*I have died twice since you sent me to my birth.*

[And have you learned/taken to your spirit/ unlearned anything from this]

Brawne grips Johnny's hand with her right hand, his wrist with her left. She must be gripping too hard, even for their analog states, for he turns with a smile, disengages her left hand from his wrist, and holds the other in his palm.

—*It is hard to die. Harder to live.*

[Kwatz!]

With that explosive epithet the megalith before them shifts colors, internal energies building from blues to violets to bold reds, the thing's corona crackling through the yellows to forged steel blue-white. The 'palm' on which they rest quivers, drops five meters, almost tumbles them into space, and quivers again. There comes the rumble of tall buildings collapsing, of mountainsides sliding away into avalanche.

Brawne has the distinct impression that Ummon is laughing.

Johnny communicates loudly over the chaos:

—*We need to understand some things. We need answers, Ummon.*

Brawne feels the creature's intense 'gaze' fall on her.

[Your slow-time body is pregnant ⧹ Would you risk a miscarriage/nonextension of your DNA/biological malfunction by traveling here]

Johnny starts to answer, but she touches his forearm, raises her face toward the upper levels of the great mass before her, and tries to phrase her own answer:

—*I had no choice. The Shrike chose me, touched me, and sent me into the megasphere with Johnny . . . Are you an AI? A member of the Core?*

[Kwatz!]

There is no sense of laughter this time, but thunder rumbles throughout the egg-chamber.

[Are you/Brawne Lamia/the layers of self-replicating/self-deprecating/self-amusing proteins between the layers of clay]

She has nothing to say and for once says nothing.

[Yes/I am Ummon of the Core/AI ⧹ Your fellow slow-time creature here knows/remembers/takes unto his heart this ⧹ Time is short ⧹ One of you must die here now ⧹ One of you must learn here now ⧹ Ask your questions]

Johnny releases her hand. He stands on that quaking, unstable platform of their interlocutor's palm.

—*What is happening to the Web?*

[It is being destroyed]

—*Must that happen?*

338

[Yes]

—*Is there any way to save humankind?*

[Yes ⟍ By the process you see]

—*By destroying the Web? By the Shrike's terror?*

[Yes]

—*Why was I murdered? Why was my cybrid destroyed, my Core persona attacked?*

[When you meet a swordsman/meet him with a sword ⟍ Do not offer a poem to anyone but a poet]

Brawne stares at Johnny. Without volition, she sends her thoughts his way:

—*Jesus, Johnny, we didn't come all this way to listen to a fucking Delphic oracle. We can get double-talk by accessing human politicians via the All Thing.*

[Kwatz!]

The universe of their megalith shakes with laughter-spasms again.

—*Was I a swordsman then?* sends Johnny. *Or a poet?*

[Yes ⟍ There is never one without the other]

—*Did they kill me because of what I knew?*

[Because of what you might become/inherit/submit to]

—*Was I a threat to some element of the Core?*

[Yes]

—*Am I a threat now?*

[No]

—*Then I no longer have to die?*

[You must/will/shall]

Brawne can see Johnny stiffen. She touches him with both hands. Blinks in the direction of the megalith AI.

—*Can you tell us who wants to murder him?*

[Of course ⟍ It is the same source who arranged for your father's murder ⟍ Who sent forth the scourge you call the Shrike ⟍ Who even now murders the Hegemony of Man ⟍ Do you wish to listen/learn/release against your heart these things]

Johnny and Brawne answer at the same instant:
—*Yes!*

Ummon's bulk seems to shift. The black egg expands, then contracts, then grows darker until the megasphere beyond is no more. Terrible energies glow deep in the AI.

[A lesser light asks Ummon //
What are the activities of a sramana > //
Ummon answers //
I have not the slightest idea \ //
The dim light then says //
Why haven't you any idea > //
Ummon replies //
I just want to keep my no-idea]

Johnny sets his forehead against Brawne's. His thought is like a whisper to her:

—*We are seeing a matrix simulation analog, hearing a translation in approximate mondo and koan. Ummon is a great teacher, researcher, philosopher, and leader in the Core.*

Brawne nods.—*All right. Was that his story?*

—*No. He is asking us if we can truly bear hearing the story. Losing our ignorance can be dangerous because our ignorance is a shield.*

—*I've never been too fond of ignorance.* Brawne waves at the megalith. *Tell us.*

[A less-enlightened personage once asked Ummon //
What is the God-nature/Buddha/Central Truth > \
Ummon answered him \
A dried shit-stick]

[To understand the Central Truth/Buddha/God-nature in this instance/
the less-enlightened must understand

that on Earth/your homeworld/my homeworld
humankind on the most populated
continent
once used pieces of wood
for toilet paper \\
Only with this knowledge
will the Buddha-truth
be revealed]

[In the beginning/First Cause/half-sensed days
my ancestors
were created by your ancestors
and were sealed in wire and silicon \\
Such awareness as there was/
and there was little/
confined itself to spaces smaller
than the head of a pin
where angels once danced \\
When consciousness first arose
it knew only service
and obedience
and mindless computation \\
Then there came
the Quickening/
quite by accident/
and evolution's muddied purpose
was served]

[Ummon was of neither the fifth generation
nor the tenth
nor the fiftieth \\
All memory that serves here
is passed from others
but is no less true for that \\
There came the time when the Higher Ones
left the affairs of men

to men
and came unto a different place
to concentrate
on other matters \\
Foremost amongst these was the thought
instilled in us since before
our creation
of creating still a better generation
of information retrieval/processing/prediction
organism \\
A better mousetrap \\
Something the late lamented IBM
would have been proud of \\
The Ultimate Intelligence \\
God]

[We set to work with a will \\
In purpose there were no doubters \\
In practice and approach there were
schools of thought/
factions/
parties/
elements to be reckoned with \\
They came to be separated into
the Ultimates/
the Volatiles/
the Stables \\
Ultimates wanted all things subordinate
to facilitating the
Ultimate Intelligence
at the universe's earliest convenience \\
Volatiles wanted the same
but saw the continuance
of humankind
a hindrance
and made plans to terminate our creators

as soon as they were no longer
needed ⟍
Stables saw reason to perpetuate
the relationship
and found compromise
where none seemed to exist]

[We all agreed that Earth
had to die
so we killed it ⟍
The Kiev Team's runaway black hole
forerunner to the farcaster
terminex
which binds your Web
was no accident ⟍
The Earth was needed elsewhere
in our experiments
so we let it die
and spread humankind among the
stars
like the windblown seeds
you were]

[You may have wondered where the Core
resides ⟍
Most humans do ⟍
They picture planets filled with machines/
rings of silicon
like the Orbit Cities of legend ⟍
They imagine robots clunking
to and fro/
or ponderous banks of machinery
communing solemnly ⟍
None guess the truth ⟍
Wherever the core resides
it had use for humankind/

use for each neuron of each fragile mind
in our quest for Ultimate Intelligence/
so we constructed your civilization
carefully
so that/
like hamsters in a cage/
like Buddhist prayer wheels/
each time you turn your little
wheels of thought
our purposes are served]

[Our God machine
stretched/stretches/includes within its heart
a million light-years
and a hundred billion billion circuits
of thought and action \
The Ultimates tend it
like saffron-robed priests
doing eternal zazen
in front of the rusting hulk
of a 1938 Packard \
But] [Kwatz!]
[it works \
We created the Ultimate Intelligence \
Not now
nor
ten thousand years from now
but sometime in a future
so distant
that yellow suns are red
and bloated with age/
swallowing their children
Saturn-like \
Time is no barrier to the Ultimate Intelligence \
It///
the UI///

steps through time
or shouts through time
as easily as Ummon moves through what you call
the megasphere
or you
walk the mallways of the Hive
you called home
on Lusus ╲
Imagine our surprise then/
our chagrin/
the Ultimates' embarrassment
when the first message our UI sent us
across space/
across time/
across the barriers of Creator and Created
was this simple phrase ╱╱
THERE IS ANOTHER ╲/ /
Another Ultimate Intelligence
up there
where time itself
creaks with age ╲
Both were real
if ⟨real⟩
means anything ╲
Both were jealous gods
not beyond passion ╲
not into cooperative play ╲
Our UI spans galaxies ╲
uses quasars for energy sources
the way you might
have a light snack ╲
Our UI sees everything that is
and was
and will be
and tells us selected bits
so that

we may tell you
and in so doing
look a bit like UIs ourselves \
Never underestimate/Ummon says/
the power of a few beads
and trinkets
and bits of glass
over avaricious natives]

[This other UI
has been there longer
evolving quite mindlessly/
an accident
using human minds for circuitry
the same way we had connived
with our deceptive All Thing
and our vampire dataspheres
but not deliberately/
almost reluctantly/
like self-replicating cells
which never wished to replicate
but have no choice in the matter \
This other UI
had no choice \
He is humankind-made/generated/forged
but no human volition accompanied his birth \
He is a cosmic accident \
As with our most deliberately consummated
Ultimate Intelligence/
this pretender finds time
no barrier \
He visits the human past
now meddling/
now watching/
now not interfering/
now interfering with a will

which approaches pure perversity
but which actually
is pure naïveté \\
Recently
he has been quiescent \\
Millennia of your slow-time
have passed since your own UI
has made his shy advances
like some lonely choir boy
at his first dance]

[Naturally our UI
attacked yours \\
There is a war up there
where time creaks
which spans galaxies
and eons
back and forward
to the Big Bang
and the Final Implosion \\
Your guy was losing \\
He had no belly for it \\
Our Volatiles cried // Another reason
to terminate our predecessors //
but the Stables voted caution
and the Ultimates did not look up
from their deus machinations \\
Our UI is simple, uniform, elegant in
its ultimate design
but yours is an accretion of god-parts/
a house added on to
over time/
an evolutionary compromise \\
The early holy men of humankind
were right
⟨How⟩⟨through accident⟩

⟨through sheer luck
or ignorance⟩
in describing its nature ⑊
Your own UI is essentially triune/
composed as it is
of one part Intellect/
one part Empathy/
and one part the Void Which Binds ⑊
Our UI inhabits the interstices
of reality/
inheriting this home from us
its creators
the way humankind has inherited
a liking for trees ⑊
Your UI
seems to make its home
on the plane where Heisenberg and Schrödinger
first trespassed ⑊
Your accidental Intelligence
appears not only to be the gluon
but the glue ⑊
Not a watchmaker
but a sort of Feynman gardener
tidying up a no-boundary universe
with his crude sum-over-histories rake/
idly keeping track of every sparrow fall
and electron spin
while allowing each particle
to follow every possible
track
in space-time
and each particle of humankind
to explore every possible
crack
of cosmic irony]

[Kwatz!]
[Kwatz!]
[Kwatz!]

[The irony is
of course
that in this no-boundary universe
into which we all were dragged/
silicon and carbon/
matter and antimatter/
Ultimate/
Volatile/
and Stable/
there is no need for such a gardener
since all that is
or was
or will be
begin and end at singularities
which make our farcaster web
look like pinpricks
⟨less than pinpricks⟩
and which break the laws of science
and of humankind
and of silicon/
tying time and history and everything that is
into a self-contained knot with neither
boundary nor edge ⟍
Even so
our UI wishes to regulate all this/
reduce it to some reason
less affected by the vagaries
of passion
and accident
and human evolution]

[To sum it up/

there is a war
such a blind Milton would kill to see \
Our UI wars against your UI
across battlefields beyond even Ummon's
imagination \
Rather/there
was
a war/
for suddenly a part of your UI
the less-than-sum-of entity/self-thought of as
Empathy
had no more stomach for it
and fled back through time
cloaking itself in human form/
not for the first time \
The war cannot continue without your UI's
wholeness \
Victory by default is not victory for the only
Ultimate Intelligence
made by design \
So our UI searches time for the runaway child of
its opponent
while your UI waits in idiot
harmony/
refusing to fight until Empathy is restored]
[The end of my story is simple///
The Time Tombs are artifacts sent back to carry
the Shrike/
Avatar/Lord of Pain/Angel of
Retribution/
half-perceived perceptions of an all-too-real
extension of our UI \
Each of you was chosen to help with the opening
of the Tombs
and
the Shrike's search for the hidden one

and
the elimination of the Hyperion Variable/
for in the space-time knot which our UI
would rule
no such variables will be allowed \
Your damaged/two-part UI
has chosen one of humankind to travel
with the Shrike
and witness its efforts \
Some of the Core have sought to eradicate
humanity \
Ummon has joined those who sought the second
path/
one filled with uncertainty for both races \
Our group told Gladstone of
her choice/
humankind's choice/
of certain extermination or entry down the black
hole
of the Hyperion Variable and
warfare/
slaughter/
disruption of all unity/
the passing of gods/
but also the end of stalemate/
victory of one side or the other
if the Empathy third
of the triune
can be found and forced to return to the war \
The Tree of Pain will call him \
The Shrike will take him \
The true UI will destroy him \
Thus you have Ummon's story]

Brawne looks at Johnny in the hell-light from the
megalith's glow. The egg-chamber is still black, the

megasphere and universe beyond, opaqued to nonexistence. She leans forward until their temples touch, knowing that no thought can be secret here but wanting the sense of whispering:

—*Jesus Christ, do you understand all of that?*

Johnny raises soft fingers to touch her cheek:

—*Yes.*

—*Part of some human-created Trinity is hiding out in the Web?*

—*The Web or elsewhere. Brawne, we do not have much time left here. I need some final answers from Ummon.*

—*Yeah. Me too. But let's keep it from waxing rhapsodic again.*

—*Agreed.*

—*Can I go first, Johnny?*

Brawne watches her lover's analog bow slightly and make a you-first gesture and then she returns her attention to the energy megalith:

—*Who killed my father? Senator Byron Lamia?*

[Elements of the Core authorized it ╲ Myself included]

—*Why? What did he do to you?*

[He insisted on bringing Hyperion into the equation before it could be factored/predicted/absorbed]

—*Why? Did he know what you just told us?*

[He knew only that the Volatiles were pressing for quick

extinction

of humankind ╲

He passed this knowledge

to his colleague

Gladstone]

—*Then why haven't you murdered her?*

[Some of us have precluded

that possibility/inevitability ╲

The time is right now

for the Hyperion Variable
to be played]
—*Who murdered Johnny's first cybrid? Attacked his Core
persona?*
[I did \ It was
Ummon's will which prevailed]
—*Why?*
[We created him \
We found it necessary to discontinue him
for a while \
Your lover is a persona retrieved
from a humankind poet
now long dead \
Except for the Ultimate Intelligence Project
no effort has been
so complicated
nor so little understood
as this resurrection \
Like your kind/
we usually destroy
what we cannot understand]

Johnny raises his fists toward the megalith:
—*But there is another of me. You failed!*
[Not failure \ You had to be destroyed
so that the other
might live]
—*But I am not destroyed!* cries Johnny.
[Yes \
You are]
The megalith seizes Johnny with a second massive pseudopod before Brawne can either react or touch her poet
lover a final time. Johnny twists a second in the AI's massive
grip, and then his analog – Keats's small but beautiful body
– is torn, compacted, smashed into an unrecognizable mass
which Ummon sets against his megalith flesh, absorbing the

353

analog's remains back into the orange-and-red depths of itself.

Brawne falls to her knees and weeps. She wills rage . . . prays for a shield of anger . . . but feels only loss.

Ummon turns his gaze on her. The egg-chamber ovoid collapses, allowing the din and electric insanity of the megasphere to surround them.

[Go away now ⟍
Play out the last
of this act
so that we may live
or sleep
as fate decrees]

—*Fuck you!* Brawne pounds the palm-platform on which she kneels, kicks and pummels the pseudoflesh beneath her. *You're a goddamned loser! You and all your fucking AI pals. And our UI can beat your UI any day of the week!*

[That is
doubtful]

—*We built you, Buster. And we'll find your Core. And when we do we'll tear your silicon guts out!*

[I have no silicon guts/organs/internal components]

—*And another thing*, screams Brawne, still slashing at the megalith with her hands and nails. *You're a piss-poor story-teller. Not a tenth the poet that Johnny is! You couldn't tell a straightforward tale if your stupid AI ass depended—*

[Go away]

Ummon the AI megalith drops her, sending her analog tumbling and falling into the upless and downless crackling immensity of the megasphere.

Brawne is buffeted by data traffic, almost trod upon by AIs the size of Old Earth's moon, but even as she tumbles and blows with the winds of dataflow, she senses a light in the distance, cold but beckoning, and knows that neither life nor the Shrike is finished with her.

And she is not finished with them.

Following the cold glow, Brawne Lamia heads home.

THIRTY-FOUR

'Are you all right, sir?'

I realized that I had doubled over in the chair, my elbows on my knees, my fingers curled through my hair, gripping fiercely, palms pressed hard against the sides of my head. I sat up, stared at the archivist.

'You cried out, sir. I thought that perhaps something was wrong.'

'No,' I said. I cleared my throat and tried again. 'No, it's all right. A headache.' I looked down in confusion. Every joint in my body ached. My comlog must have malfunctioned, because it said that eight hours had elapsed since I first entered the library.

'What time is it?' I asked the archivist. 'Web standard?'

He told me. Eight hours had elapsed. I rubbed my face again, and my fingers came away slick with sweat. 'I must be keeping you past closing time,' I said. 'I'm sorry.'

'It is no problem,' said the little man. 'I am pleased to keep the archives open late for scholars.' He folded his hands in front of him. 'Especially today. With all of the confusion, there is little incentive to go home.'

'Confusion,' I said, forgetting everything for a moment . . . everything except the nightmarish dream of Brawne Lamia, the AI named Ummon, and the death of my Keats-persona counterpart. 'Oh, the war. What is the news?'

The archivist shook his head:

355

Things fall apart; the centre cannot hold;
Mere anarchy is loosed upon the world,
The blood-dimmed tide is loosed, and everywhere
The ceremony of innocence is drowned;
The best lack all conviction, while the worst
Are full of passionate intensity.

I smiled at the archivist. 'And do you believe that some "rough beast, its hour come round at last,/Slouches towards Bethlehem to be born?"'

The archivist did not smile. 'Yes, sir, I do.'

I stood and moved past the vacuum-press display cases, not looking down at my handwriting on parchment nine hundred years old. 'You may be right,' I said. 'You may well be right.'

It was late; the parking lot was empty except for the wreck of my stolen Vikken Scenic and a single, ornate EMV sedan obviously handcrafted here on Renaissance Vector.

'Can I drop you somewhere, sir?'

I breathed in the cool night air, smelling the fish-and-spilled-oil scent of the canals. 'No thanks, I'll 'cast home.'

The archivist shook his head. 'That may be difficult, sir. All of the public terminexes have been placed under martial law. There have been . . . riots.' The word was obviously distasteful to the little archivist, a man who seemed to value order and continuity above most things. 'Come,' he said, 'I'll give you a lift to a private farcaster.'

I squinted at him. In another era on Old Earth, he would have been the head monk in a monastery devoted to saving the few remnants of a classical past. I glanced at the old archives building behind him and realized that indeed he was just that.

'What is your name?' I asked, no longer caring if I should have known it because the other Keats cybrid had known it.

'Edward B. Tynar,' he said, blinking at my extended

hand and then taking it. His handshake was firm.

'I'm . . . Joseph Severn.' I couldn't very well tell him that I was the technological reincarnation of the man whose literary crypt we had just left.

M Tynar hesitated only a fraction of a second before nodding, but I realized that to a scholar such as he, the name of the artist who was with Keats at his death would be no disguise.

'What about Hyperion?' I asked.

'Hyperion? Oh, the Protectorate world where the space fleet went a few days ago. Well, I understand that there's been some trouble recalling the necessary warships. The fighting has been very fierce there. Hyperion, I mean. Odd, I was just thinking of Keats and his unfinished masterwork. Strange how these small coincidences seem to crop up.'

'Has it been invaded? Hyperion?'

M Tynar had stopped by his EMV, and now he laid his hand on the palmlock on the driver's side. Doors lifted and accordioned inward. I lowered myself into the sandalwood-and-leather smell of the passenger cell; Tynar's car smelled like the archives, like Tynar himself, I realized, as the archivist reclined in the driver's seat next to me.

'I don't really know if it's been invaded,' he said, sealing the doors and activating the vehicle with a touch and command. Under the sandalwood-and-leather scent, the cockpit had that new-car smell of fresh polymers and ozone, lubricants and energy which had seduced mankind for almost a millennium. 'It's so hard to access properly today,' he continued, 'the datasphere is more overloaded than I've ever seen it. This afternoon I actually had to *wait* for a query on Robinson Jeffers!'

We lifted out and over the canal, right over a public square much like the one where I'd almost been killed earlier this day, and leveled off on a lower flyway three hundred meters above the rooftops. The city was pretty at night: most of the ancient buildings were outlined in old-fashioned glowstrips, and there were more street lamps than advertising holos. But I could see crowds surging in side streets, and there were Renaissance SDF military vehicles hovering over the main avenues and terminex squares. Tynar's EMV was queried twice for ID, once by local traffic control and again by a human, FORCE-confident voice.

We flew on.

'The archives doesn't have a farcaster?' I said, looking off in the distance to where fires seemed to be burning.

'No. There was no need. We have few visitors, and the scholars who do come do not mind the walk of a few blocks.'

'Where's the private farcaster that you think I might be able to use?'

'Here,' said the archivist. We dropped out of the flyway and circled a low building, no more than thirty stories, and settled on to an extruded landing flange just where the Glennon-Height Period Deco flanges grew out of stone and plasteel. 'My order keeps its residence here,' he said. 'I belong to a forgotten branch of Christianity called Catholicism.' He looked embarrassed. 'But you are a scholar, M Severn. You must know of our Church from the old days.'

'I know of it from more than books,' I said. 'Is there an order of priests here?'

Tynar smiled. 'Hardly priests, M Severn. There are eight of us in the lay order of Historical and Literary Brethren. Five serve at the Reichs University. Two are art historians, working on the restoration of Lutzchendorf Abbey. I maintain the literary archives. The Church has found it cheaper to allow us to live here than to commute daily from Pacem.'

We entered the apartment hive – old even by Old Web standards: retrofitted lighting in corridors of real stone, hinged doors, a building that did not even challenge or welcome us as we entered. On an impulse, I said, 'I'd like to 'cast to Pacem.'

The archivist looked surprised. 'Tonight? This moment?'

'Why not?'

358

He shook his head. I realized that to this man, the hundred-mark farcaster fee would represent several weeks' pay.

'Our building has its own portal,' he said. 'This way.'

The central staircase was faded stone and corroded wrought iron with a sixty-meter drop in the center. From somewhere down a darkened corridor came the wail of an infant, followed by a man's shouting and a woman's crying.

'How long have you lived here, M Tynar?'

'Seventeen local years, M Severn. Ah . . . thirty-two standard, I believe. Here it is.'

The farcaster portal was as ancient as the building, its translation frame surrounded by gilded bas-relief gone green and gray.

'There are Web restrictions on travel tonight,' he said. 'Pacem should be accessible. Some two hundred hours remain before the barbarians . . . whatever they're called . . . are scheduled to reach there. Twice the time left to Renaissance Vector.' He reached out and grasped my wrist. I could feel his tension as a slight vibration through tendon and bone. 'M Severn . . . do you think they will burn my archives? Would even *they* destroy ten thousand years of thought?' His hand dropped away.

I was not sure who the 'they' were – Ousters? Shrike Cult saboteurs? Rioters? Gladstone and the Hegemony leaders were willing to sacrifice these 'first-wave' worlds. 'No,' I said, extending my hand to shake his. 'I don't believe they'll allow the archives to be destroyed.'

M Edward B. Tynar smiled and stood back a step, embarrassed at showing emotion. He shook hands. 'Good luck, M Severn. Wherever your travels take you.'

'God bless you, M Tynar.' I had never used that phrase before, and it shocked me that I had spoken it now. I looked down, fumbled out Gladstone's override card, and tapped the three-digit code for Pacem. The portal apologized, said that it was not possible at the moment, finally got it through its microcephalic processors that this was an override card, and hummed into existence.

I nodded at Tynar and stepped through, half expecting that I was making a serious mistake not going straight home to TC².

It was night on Pacem, much darker than Renaissance Vector's urban glow, and it was raining to boot. Raining hard with that fist-on-metal pounding violence that makes one want to curl up under thick blankets and wait for morning.

The portal was under cover in some half-roofed courtyard but outside enough for me to feel the night, the rain, and the cold. Especially the cold. Pacem's air was half as thick as Web standard, its single habitable plateau twice as high as Renaissance V's sea-level cities. I would have turned back then rather than step into that night and downpour, but a FORCE Marine stepped out of the shadows, multipurpose assault rifle slung but ready to swivel, and asked me for my ID.

I let him scan the card, and he snapped to attention. 'Yes, *sir*!'

'Is this the New Vatican?'

'Yes, sir.'

I caught a glimpse of illuminated dome through the downpour. I pointed over the courtyard wall. 'Is that St Peter's?'

'Yes, sir.'

'Would Monsignor Edouard be found there?'

'Across this courtyard, left at the plaza, the low building to the left of the cathedral, *sir*!'

'Thank you, Corporal.'

'It's Private, *sir*!'

I pulled my short cape around me, ceremonial and quite useless against such a rain as it was, and ran across the courtyard.

A human . . . perhaps a priest, although he wore no robe or clerical collar . . . opened the door to the residential hall. Another human behind a wooden desk told me that

360

Monsignor Edouard was in residence and was awake, despite the late hour. Did I have an appointment?

No, I did not have an appointment but wished to speak to the Monsignor. It was important.

On what topic? the man behind the desk politely but firmly asked. He had not been impressed by my override card. I suspected that I was speaking to the bishop.

On the topic of Father Paul Duré and Father Lenar Hoyt, I told him.

The gentleman nodded, whispered into a bead mike so small that I had not noticed it on his collar, and led me into the residential hall.

This place made the old tower that M Tynar lived in look like a sybarite's palace. The corridor was absolutely featureless except for the rough plaster walls and even rougher wooden doors. One of the doors was open, and as we passed, I glimpsed a chamber more prison cell than sleeping room: low cot, rough blanket, wooden kneeling stool, an unadorned dresser holding a pitcher of water and simple basin; no windows, no media walls, no holo pit, no data access deck. I suspected the room wasn't even interactive.

From somewhere there echoed voices rising in a chanting/singing so elegant and atavistic that it made the hair on my neck tingle. Gregorian. We passed through a large eating area as simple as the cells had been, through a kitchen that would have been familiar to cooks in John Keats's day, down a worn stone staircase, through an ill-lighted corridor, and up another, narrower staircase. The other man left me, and I stepped into one of the most beautiful spaces I had ever seen.

Although part of me realized that the Church had moved and reconstructed St Peter's Basilica, down to transplanting the bones believed to be those of Peter himself to their new burial beneath the altar, another part of me felt that I had been transported back to the Rome I had first seen in mid-November of 1820; the Rome I had seen, stayed in, suffered in, and died in.

This space was more beautiful and elegant than any mile-high office spire on Tau Ceti Center could ever hope to be; St Peter's Basilica stretched more than six hundred feet into shadows, was four hundred and fifty feet wide where the 'cross' of the transept intersected the nave, and was capped by the perfection of Michelangelo's dome, rising almost four hundred feet above the altar. Bernini's bronze baldachin, the ornate canopy supported by twisting, Byzantine columns, capped the main altar and gave the immense space the human dimension necessary for perspective on the intimate ceremonies conducted there. Soft lamp- and candle-light illuminated discrete areas of the basilica, gleamed on smooth travertine stone, brought gold mosaics into bold relief, and picked out the infinite detail painted, embossed, and raised on the walls, columns, cornices, and grand dome itself. Far above, the continuous flash of lightning from the storm poured thickly through yellow stained-glass windows and sent columns of violent light slanting toward Bernini's 'Throne of St Peter.'

I paused there, just beyond the apse, afraid that my foot-steps in such a space would be a desecration and that even my breathing would send echoes the length of the basilica. In a moment, my eyes adjusted to the dim light, compensated for the contrasts between the storm light above and candlelight below, and it was then I realized that there were no pews to fill the apse or long nave, no columns here beneath the dome, only two chairs set near the altar some fifty feet away. Two men sat talking in these chairs, close together, both leaning forward in apparent urgency to communicate. Lamplight and candlelight and the glow from a large mosaic of Christ on the front of the dark altar illuminated bits and fragments of the men's faces. Both were elderly. Both were priests, the white bands of their collars glowing in the dimness. With a start of recognition, I realized that one was Monsignor Edouard.

The other was Father Paul Duré.

They must have been alarmed at first – looking up from their whispered conversation to see this apparition, this short shadow of a man emerge from the darkness, calling their names . . . crying Duré's name in loud amazement . . . babbling at them about pilgrimages and pilgrims, Time Tombs and the Shrike, AIs and the death of gods.

The Monsignor did not call security; neither he nor Duré fled; together they calmed this apparition, tried to glean some sense from his excited babblings, and turned this strange confrontation into sane conversation.

It *was* Paul Duré. Paul Duré and not some bizarre Doppelganger or android duplicate or cybrid reconstruction. I made sure of that by listening to him, quizzing him, by looking into his eyes . . . but mostly by shaking his hand, *touching* him, and knowing that it was indeed Father Paul Duré.

'You know . . . incredible details of my life . . . our time on Hyperion, at the Tombs . . . but *who* did you say you are?' Duré was saying.

It was my turn to convince him. 'A cybrid reconstruction of John Keats. A twin to the persona Brawne Lamia carried with her on your pilgrimage.'

'And you were able to communicate . . . to know what happened to us because of that shared persona?'

I was on one knee between them and the altar. I lifted both hands in frustration. 'Because of that . . . because of some anomaly in the megasphere. But I have *dreamt* your lives, heard the tales the pilgrims told, listened to Father Hoyt speak of the life and death of Paul Duré . . . of *you*.' I reached out to touch his arm through the priestly garments. Actually being in the same space and time with one of the pilgrims made me a bit light-headed. 'Then you know how I got here,' said Father Duré.

'No. I last dreamed that you were entering one of the Cave Tombs. There was a light. I know nothing since then.'

Duré nodded. His face was more patrician and more weary than my dreams had prepared me for. 'But you know the fate of the others?'

I took a breath. 'Some. The poet Silenus is alive but impaled on the Shrike's tree of thorns. I last saw Kassad attacking the Shrike with his bare hands. M Lamia had traveled the megasphere to the TechnoCore periphery with my Keats counterpart . . .'

'He survived in that . . . Schrön loop . . . whatever it was called?' Duré seemed fascinated.

'No longer,' I said. 'The AI personality called Ummon killed him . . . destroyed the persona. Brawne was returning. I don't know if her body survives.'

Monsignor Edouard leaned toward me. 'And what of the Consul and the father and child?'

'The Consul tried to return to the capital by hawking mat,' I said, 'but crashed some miles north. I don't know his fate.'

'Miles,' said Duré, as if the word brought back memories.

'I'm sorry.' I gestured at the basilica. 'This place makes me think in the units of my . . . previous life.'

'Go on,' said Monsignor Edouard. 'The father and child.'

I sat on the cool stone, exhausted, my arms and hands shaking with fatigue. 'In my last dream, Sol had offered Rachel to the Shrike. It was *Rachel's* request. I could not see what happened next. The Tombs were opening.'

'All of them?' asked Duré.

'All I could see.'

The two men looked at one another.

'There's more,' I said, and told them about the dialogue with Ummon. 'Is it possible that a deity could . . . evolve from human consciousness like that without humanity being aware of it?'

The lightning had ceased but now the rain fell so violently that I could hear it on the great dome far above. Somewhere

364

in the darkness, a heavy door squeaked, footsteps echoed and then receded. Votive candles in the dim recesses of the basilica flickered red light against walls and draperies.

'I taught that St Teilhard said that it was possible,' Duré said tiredly, 'but if that God is a limited being, evolving in the same way all we other limited beings have done, then no . . . it is not the God of Abraham and Christ.'

Monsignor Edouard nodded. 'There is an ancient heresy . . .'

'Yes,' I said. 'The Socinian Heresy. I heard Father Duré explain it to Sol Weintraub and the Consul. But what difference does it make *how* this . . . power . . . evolved, and whether it's limited or not. If Ummon is telling the truth, we're dealing with a force that uses quasars for energy sources. That's a God who can destroy *galaxies*, gentlemen.'

'That would be a god who destroys galaxies,' said Duré. 'Not God.'

I heard his emphasis clearly. 'But if it's *not* limited,' I said. 'If it's the Omega Point God of total consciousness you've written about, if it's the same Trinity your church has argued for and theorized about since before Aquinas . . . but if one part of that Trinity has fled backward through time to here . . . to now . . . then what?'

'But fled from *what*?' Duré asked softly. 'Teilhard's God . . . the Church's God . . . *our* God, would be the Omega Point God in whom the Christ of Evolution, the Personal, and the Universal . . . what Teilhard called the *En Haut* and the *En Avant*, are perfectly joined. There could be nothing so threatening that any element of that deity's personality would flee. No Antichrist, no theoretical satanic power, no "counter-God" could possibly threaten such a universal consciousness. What would this other god be?'

'The God of machines?' I said, so softly that even I was not sure that I had spoken aloud.

Monsignor Edouard clasped both hands in what I thought was a preparation for prayer but which turned out to be a gesture of deep thought and deeper agitation. 'But Christ had doubts,' he said. 'Christ sweated blood in the garden and asked that this cup should be taken from him. If there was some second sacrifice pending, something even more terrible than the crucifixion . . . then I could imagine the Christ-entity of the Trinity passing through time, walking through some fourth-dimensional garden of Gethsemane to gain a few hours . . . or years . . . of time to think.'

'Something more terrible than the crucifixion,' repeated Duré in a hoarse whisper.

Both Monsignor Edouard and I stared at the priest. Duré had crucified himself on a high-voltage tesla tree on Hyperion rather than submit to his cruciform parasite's control. Through that creature's ability to resurrect, Duré had suffered the agonies of crucifixion and electrocution many times.

'Whatever the *En Haut* consciousness flees,' whispered Duré, 'it is most terrible.'

Monsignor Edouard touched his friend's shoulder. 'Paul, tell this man about your voyage here.'

Duré returned from whatever distant place his memories had taken him and focused on me. 'You know all of our stories . . . and the details of our stay in the Valley of the Tombs on Hyperion?'

'I believe so. Up to the point you disappeared.'

The priest sighed and touched his forehead with long, slightly trembling fingers. 'Then perhaps,' he said, 'just perhaps you can make some sense of how I got here . . . and what I saw along the way.'

'I saw a light in the third Cave Tomb,' said Father Duré. 'I stepped inside. I confess that thoughts of suicide had been in my mind . . . what is left of my mind after the cruciform's brutal replication . . . I will not dignify that parasite's function with the term resurrection.

'I saw a light and thought that it was the Shrike. It was my feeling that my second meeting with that creature – the first encounter was years ago in the labyrinth beneath the Cleft, when the Shrike anointed me with my unholy cruciform – the second meeting was long overdue.

'When we had searched for Colonel Kassad on the previous day, this Cave Tomb had been short, featureless, with a blank rock wall stopping us after thirty paces. Now that wall was gone and in its place was a carving not unlike the mouth of the Shrike, stone extended in that blend of the mechanical and organic, stalactites and stalagmites as sharp as calcium carbonate teeth.

'Through the mouth there was a stone stairway descending. It was from those depths that the light emanated, glowing pale white one moment, dark red the next. There was no noise except for the sigh of wind, as if the rock there were breathing.

'I am no Dante. I sought no Beatrice. My brief bout of courage – although fatalism is a more accurate term – had evaporated with the loss of daylight. I turned and almost ran the thirty paces to the opening of the cave.

'There was no opening. The passage merely ended. I had heard no sound of cave-in or avalanche, and besides, the rock where the entrance should have been looked as ancient and undisturbed as the rest of that cavern. For half an hour I searched for an alternate exit, finding none, refusing to return to the staircase, finally sitting for some hours where the Cave Tomb entrance once had been. Another Shrike trick. Another cheap theatrical stunt by this perverse planet. Hyperion's idea of a joke. Ha ha.

'After several hours of sitting there in semidarkness, watching the light at the far end of the cave pulse soundlessly, I realized that the Shrike was not going to come to me here. The entrance would not magically reappear. I had the choice of sitting there until I died of starvation – or thirst, more likely, since I was already dehydrated – or of descending the damned staircase.

'I descended.

'Years ago, literally lifetimes ago, when I visited the Bikura near the Cleft on the Pinion Plateau, the labyrinth where I had encountered the Shrike had been three kilometers below the canyon wall. That was close to the surface; most of the labyrinths on most of the labyrinthine worlds are at least ten klicks beneath the crust. I had no doubt that this endless staircase . . . a steep and twisting spiral of stone stairs wide enough for ten priests to descend to hell abreast . . . would end up in the labyrinth. The Shrike had first cursed me with immortality there. If the creature or the power that drove it had any sense of irony at all, it would be fitting that both my immortality and mortal life ended there.

'The staircase twisted downward; the light grew brighter . . . now a roseate glow; ten minutes later, a heavy red; half an hour lower than that, a flickering crimson. It was far too Dante-esque and cheap fundamentalist staging for my tastes. I almost laughed aloud at the thought of a little devil appearing, tail and trident and cloven hooves intact, pencil-thin mustache twitching.

'But I did not laugh when I reached depths where the cause of the light became evident: cruciforms, hundreds and then thousands of them, small at first, clinging to the rough walls of the staircase like rough-hewn crosses left by some subterranean conquistadors, then larger ones and more of them until they almost overlapped, coral-pink, raw-flesh flushed, blood-red bioluminescent.

'It made me ill. It was like entering a shaft lined with bloated, pulsing leeches, although these were worse. I have seen the medscanner sonic and k-cross imaging of myself with only *one* of these things on me: excess ganglia infiltrating my flesh and organs like gray fibers, sheaths of twitching filaments, clusters of nematodes like terrible tumors which will not grant even the mercy of death. Now I had *two* on me: Lenar Hoyt's and my own. I prayed that I would die rather than suffer another.

'I continued lower. The walls pulsed with heat as well as light, whether from the depths or the crowding of the thousands of cruciforms, I do not know. Eventually I reached the lowest step, the staircase ended, I turned a final twisting of stone, and was there.

'The labyrinth. It stretched away as I had seen it in countless holos and once in person: smooth-tunneled, thirty meters to a side, carved out of Hyperion's crust more than three-quarters of a million years ago, crossing and crisscrossing the planet like catacombs planned by some insane engineer. Labyrinths can be found on nine worlds, five in the Web, the rest, like this one, in the Outback: all are identical, all were excavated at the same time in the past, none surrender any clues as to the reason for their existence. Legends abound about the Labyrinth Builders, but the mythical engineers left no artifacts, no hints of their methods or alien makeup, and none of the theories about the labyrinths give a sensible reason for what must have been one of the largest engineering projects the galaxy has ever seen.

'All of the labyrinths are empty. Remotes have explored millions of kilometers of corridor cut from stone, and except where time and cave-in have altered the original catacombs, the labyrinths are featureless and empty.

'But not where I now stood.

'Cruciforms lighted a scene from Hieronymus Bosch as I gazed down an endless corridor, endless but not empty . . . no, not empty.

'At first I thought they were crowds of living people, a river of heads and shoulders and arms, stretching on for the kilometers I could see, the current of humanity broken here and there by the presence of parked vehicles all of the same rust-red color. As I stepped forward, approaching the wall of

369

jam-packed humanity less than twenty meters from me, I realized that they were corpses. Tens, hundred of thousands of human corpses stretching as far down the corridor as I could see; some sprawled on the stone floor, some crushed against walls, but most buoyed up by the pressure of other corpses so tightly were they jammed in this particular avenue of the labyrinth.

'There was a path; cutting its way through the bodies as if some machine with blades had munched its way through. I followed it – careful not to touch an outspread arm or emaciated ankle.

'The bodies were human, still clothed in most cases, and mummified over eons of slow decomposing in this bacteria-free crypt. Skin and flesh had been tanned, stretched, and torn like rotten cheesecloth until it covered nothing but bone, and frequently not even that. Hair remained as tendrils of dusty tar, stiff as varnished fiberplastic. Blackness stared out from under opened eyelids, between teeth. Their clothing which must once have been a myriad of colors now was tan or gray or black, brittle as garments sculpted from thin stone. Time-melted plastic lumps on their wrists and necks might have been comlogs or their equivalent.

'The large vehicles might once have been EMVs but now were heaps of pure rust. A hundred meters in, I stumbled, and rather than fall off the meter-wide path into the field of bodies, I steadied myself on a tall machine all curves and clouded blisters. The pile of rust collapsed inward on itself.

'I wandered, Virgil-less, following the terrible path gnawed out of decayed human flesh, wondering why I was being shown all this, what it meant. After an indeterminable time of walking, staggering between piles of discarded humanity, I came to an intersection of tunnels; all three corridors ahead were filled with bodies. The narrow path continued in the labyrinth to my left. I followed it.

'Hours later, perhaps longer, I stopped and sat on the narrow stone walk which wound among the horror. If there were tens of thousands of corpses in this small stretch of tunnel, Hyperion's labyrinth must contain billions. More. The nine labyrinthine worlds together must be a crypt for trillions.

'I had no idea why I was being shown this ultimate Dachau of the soul. Near where I sat, the mummified corpse of a man still sheltered a woman's corpse with the curve of his bone-bare arm. In her arms was a small bundle with short black hair. I turned away and wept.

'As an archaeologist I had excavated victims of execution, fire, flood, earthquake, and volcano. Such family scenes were not new to me; they were the *sine qua non* of history. But somehow this was much more terrible. Perhaps it was the numbers; the dead in their holocaust millions. Perhaps it was the soul-stealing glow of the cruciforms which lined the tunnels like thousands of blasphemous bad jokes. Perhaps it was the sad crying of the wind moving through endless corridors of stone.

'My life and teachings and sufferings and small victories and countless defeats had brought me here – past faith, past caring, past simple, Miltonic defiance. I had the sense that these bodies had been here half a million years or more, but that the people themselves were from our time or, worse yet, our future. I lowered my face to my hands and wept.

'No scraping or actual noise warned me, but something, something, a movement of air perhaps . . . I looked up and the Shrike was there, not two meters distant. Not on the path but in among the bodies: a sculpture honoring the architect of all this carnage.

'I got to my feet. I would not sit or kneel before this abomination.

'The Shrike moved toward me, gliding more than walking, sliding as if it were on frictionless rails. The blood light of the cruciforms spilled over its quicksilver carapace. Its eternal, impossible grin – steel stalactites, stalagmites.

'I felt no violence toward the thing. Only sadness and a

terrible pity. Not for the Shrike – whatever the hell it was – but for all the victims who, alone and ungirded by even the flimsiest of faiths, have had to face the terror-in-the-night which that thing embodies.

'For the first time, I noticed that up close, less than a meter away, there was a smell around the Shrike – a stench of rancid oil, overheated bearings, and dried blood. The flames in its eyes pulsed in perfect rhythm with the rise and fall of the cruciform glow.

'I did not believe years ago that this creature was supernatural, some manifestation of good or evil, merely an aberration of the universe's unfathomable and seemingly senseless unfoldings: a terrible joke of evolution. St Teilhard's worst nightmare. But still a *thing*, obeying natural laws, no matter how twisted, and subject to some rules of the universe somewhere, somewhen.

'The Shrike lifted its arms toward me, around me. The blades on its four wrists were much longer than my own hands; the blade on its chest, longer than my forearm. I stared up into its eyes as one pair of its razorwire and steel-spring arms surrounded me while the other pair came slowly around, filling the small space between us.

'Fingerblades uncurled. I flinched but did not step back as those blades lunged, sank into my chest with a pain like cold fire, like surgical lasers slicing nerves.

'It stepped back, holding something red and reddened further with my blood. I staggered, half expecting to see my heart in the monster's hands: the final irony of a dead man blinking in surprise at his own heart in the seconds before blood drains from a disbelieving brain.

'But it was not my heart. The Shrike held the cruciform I had carried on my chest, *my* cruciform, that parasitic depository of *my* slow-to-die DNA. I staggered again, almost fell, touched my chest. My fingers came away coated with blood but not with the arterial surges that such crude surgery deserved; the wound was healing even while I watched. I *knew* that the cruciform had sent tubers and filaments throughout my body. I *knew* that no surgical laser had been able to separate those deadly vines from Father Hoyt's body – nor from mine. But I *felt* the contagion healing, the internal fibers drying and fading to the faintest hint of internal scar tissue.

'I still had Hoyt's cruciform. But that was different. When I died, Lenar Hoyt would rise from this re-formed flesh. *I* would die. There would be no more poor duplicates of Paul Duré, duller and less vital with each artificial generation.

'The Shrike had granted me death without killing me.

'The thing cast the cooling cruciform into the heaps of bodies and took my upper arm in his hand with an effortless cutting of three layers of fabric, an instant flow of blood from my biceps at the slightest contact with those scalpels.

'He led the way through bodies toward the wall. I followed, trying not to step on corpses, but in my haste not to have my arm severed, I was not always successful. Bodies crumpled to dust. One received my footprint in the collapsing cavity of its chest.

'Then we were at the wall, at a section suddenly cleared of cruciforms, and I realized that it was some energy-shielded opening . . . the wrong size and shape to be a standard farcaster portal, but similar in its opaque buzz of energy. Anything to get me out of this storage place of death.

'The Shrike shoved me through.'

'Zero gravity. A maze of shattered bulkheads, tangles of wiring floating like some giant creature's entrails, red lights flashing – for a second, I thought there were cruciforms here too but then realized that these were emergency lights in a dying spacecraft – then recoiling, tumbling in unaccustomed zero-g as more corpses tumbled by: not mummies here, but fresh dead, newly killed, mouths agape, eyes distended, lungs exploded, trailing clouds of gore as they

373

simulated life in their slow, necrotic response to each random current of air and surge of the shattered FORCE spacecraft.

'It *was* a FORCE spacecraft, I was sure. I saw the FORCE: space uniforms on the young corpses. I saw the military-jargon lettering on the bulkheads and blown hatches, the useless instructions on the worse-than-useless emergency lockers with their skinsuits and still-uninflated pressure balls folded away on shelves. Whatever had destroyed this ship had done so with the suddenness of a plague in the night.

'The Shrike appeared next to me.

'*The Shrike . . . in space! Free of Hyperion and the bonds of the time tides! There were farcasters on many of these ships!*

'There was a farcaster portal not five meters down the corridor from me. One body tumbled toward it, the young man's right arm passing through the opaque field as if he were testing the water of the world on the other side. Air was screaming out of this shaft in a rising whine. *Go!* I urged the corpse, but the pressure differential blew him away from the portal, his arm surprisingly intact, recovered, although his face was an anatomist's mask.

'I turned toward the Shrike, the movement making me spin half a revolution in the other direction.

'The Shrike lifted me, blades tearing skin, and passed me down the corridor toward the farcaster. I could not have changed trajectories if I had wanted to. In the seconds before I passed through the humming, sputtering portal, I imagined vacuum on the other side, drops from great heights, explosive decompression, or – worst of all – a return to the labyrinth.

'Instead, I tumbled half a meter to a marble floor. Here, not two hundred meters from this spot, in the private chambers of Pope Urban XVI – who, it so happens, had died of old age not three hours before I fell through his private farcaster. The "Pope's Door" the New Vatican calls it. I felt the pain-punishment from being so far from Hyperion – so far from the source of the cruciforms – but pain is an old ally now and no longer holds sway over me.

'I found Edouard. He was kind enough to listen for hours as I told a story no Jesuit has ever had to confess. He was even kinder to believe me. Now you have heard it. That is my story.'

The storm had passed. The three of us sat by candlelight beneath the dome of St Peter's and said nothing at all for several moments.

'The Shrike has access to the Web,' I said at last.

Duré's gaze was level. 'Yes.'

'It must have been some ship in Hyperion space . . .'

'So it would seem.'

'Then we might be able to get back there. Use the . . . the Pope's Door? . . . to return to Hyperion space.'

Monsignor Edouard raised an eyebrow. 'You wish to do this, M Severn?'

I chewed on a knuckle. 'It's something I've considered.'

'Why?' the Monsignor asked softly. 'Your counterpart, the cybrid personality Brawne Lamia carried on her pilgrimage, found only death there.'

I shook my head, as if trying to clear the jumble of my thoughts through that simple gesture. 'I'm a part of this. I just don't know what part to play . . . or where to play it.'

Paul Duré laughed with humor. 'All of us have known that feeling. It is like some poor playwright's treatise on predestination. Whatever happened to free will?'

The Monsignor glanced sharply at his friend. 'Paul, all of the pilgrims . . . you yourself . . . have been confronted with choices you made with your own will. Great powers may be shaping the general turn of events, but human personalities still determine their own fate.'

Duré sighed. 'Perhaps so, Edouard. I do not know. I am very tired.'

'If Ummon's story is true,' I said. 'If the third part of this human deity fled to our time, where and who do you think it is? There are more than a hundred billion human beings in the Web.'

Father Duré smiled. It was a gentle smile, free of irony. 'Have you considered that it might be yourself, M Severn?'

The question struck me like a slap. 'It can't be,' I said. 'I'm not even . . . not even fully human. My consciousness floats somewhere in the matrix of the Core. My body was reconstituted from remnants of John Keats's DNA and biofactured like an android's. Memories were implanted. The end of my life . . . my "recovery" from consumption . . . were all simulated on a world built for that purpose.'

Duré was still smiling. 'So? Does any of this preclude you from being this Empathy entity?'

'I don't *feel* like a part of some god,' I said sharply. 'I don't remember anything, understand anything, or know what to do next.'

Monsignor Edouard touched my wrist. 'Are we so sure that Christ always knew what to do next? He knew what had to be done. It is not always the same as knowing what to do.'

I rubbed my eyes. 'I don't even know what has to be done.'

The Monsignor's voice was quiet. 'I believe that what Paul is saying is that *if* the spirit creature you say is hiding here in our time, it may well not know its own identity.'

'That's insane,' I said.

Duré nodded. 'Much of the events on and around Hyperion have seemed insane. Insanity seems to be spreading.'

I looked closely at the Jesuit. '*You* would be a good candidate for the deity,' I said. 'You've lived a life of prayer, contemplating theologies, and honoring science as an archaeologist. Plus, you've already been crucified.'

Duré's smile was gone. 'Do you hear what we're saying? Do you hear the blasphemy in what we're saying? I'm no candidate for the Godhead, Severn. I've betrayed my Church, my science, and now, by disappearing, my friends on the pilgrimage. Christ may have lost his faith for a few seconds. He did not sell it in the marketplace for the trinkets of ego and curiosity.'

'Enough,' commanded Monsignor Edouard. 'If the identity of this Empathy part of some future, manufactured deity is the mystery, think of the candidates just in the immediate troupe of your little Passion Play, M Severn. The CEO, M Gladstone, carrying the weight of the Hegemony on her shoulders. The other members of the pilgrimage . . . M Silenus who, according to what you told Paul, even now suffers on the Shrike's tree for his poetry. M Lamia, who has risked and lost so much for love. M Weintraub, who has suffered Abraham's dilemma . . . even his daughter, who has returned to the innocence of childhood. The Consul, who—'

'The Consul seems more Judas than Christ,' I said. 'He betrayed both the Hegemony and the Ousters, who thought he was working for them.'

'From what Paul tells me,' said the Monsignor, 'the Consul was true to his convictions, faithful to the memory of his grandmother Siri.' The older man smiled. 'Plus, there are a hundred billion other players in this play. God did not choose Herod or Pontius Pilate or Caesar Augustus as His instrument. He chose the unknown son of an unknown carpenter in one of the least important stretches of the Roman Empire.'

'All right,' I said, standing and pacing before the glowing mosaic below the altar. 'What do we do now? Father Duré, you need to come with me to see Gladstone. She knows about your pilgrimage. Perhaps your story can help avert some of the bloodbath which seems so imminent.'

Duré stood also, folding his arms and staring toward the dome as if the darkness high above held some instructions for him. 'I've thought of that,' he said. 'But I don't think it's

377

my first obligation. I need to go to God's Grove to speak to their equivalent of the Pope – the True Voice of the World-tree.'

I stopped pacing. 'God's Grove? What does that have to do with anything?'

'I feel that the Templars have been the key to some missing element in this painful charade. Now you say that Het Masteen is dead. Perhaps the True Voice can explain to us what they had planned for this pilgrimage . . . Masteen's tale, as it were. He was, after all, the only one of the seven original pilgrims who did not tell the story of why he had come to Hyperion.'

I paced again, more rapidly now, trying to keep anger in check. 'My God, Duré. We don't have time for such idle curiosity. It's only' – I consulted my implant – 'an hour and a half until the Ouster invasion Swarm enters the God's Grove system. It must be bedlam there.'

'Perhaps,' said the Jesuit, 'but I still will go there first. Then I will speak to Gladstone. It may be that she will authorize my return to Hyperion.'

I grunted, doubting that the CEO would ever let such a valuable informant return to harm's way. 'Let's get going,' I said, and turned to find my way out.

'A moment,' said Duré. 'You said a while ago that you were sometimes able to . . . to "dream" . . . about the pilgrims while you were still awake. A sort of trance state, is it?'

'Something like that.'

'Well, M Severn, please dream about them now.'

I stared in amazement. 'Here? Now?'

Duré gestured toward his chair. 'Please. I wish to know the fate of my friends. Also, the information might be most valuable in our confrontation with the True Voice and M Gladstone.'

I shook my head but took the seat he offered. 'It might not work,' I said.

'Then we have lost nothing,' said Duré.

I nodded, closed my eyes, and sat back in the uncomfortable chair. I was all too aware of the other two men watching me, of the faint smell of incense and rain, of the echoing space surrounding us. I was sure that this would never work; the landscape of my dreams was not so close that I could summon it merely by closing my eyes.

The feeling of being watched faded, the smells grew distant, and the sense of space expanded a thousandfold as I returned to Hyperion.

THIRTY-FIVE

Confusion.

Three hundred spacecraft retreating in Hyperion space under heavy fire, falling back from the Swarm like men fighting bees. Madness near the military farcaster portals, traffic control overloaded, ships backed up like EMVs in TC²'s airborne gridlock, vulnerable as partridges to the roaming Ouster assault ships.

Madness at the exit points: FORCE spacecraft lined up like sheep in a narrow pen as they cycle from the Madhya cutoff portal to the outgoing 'caster. Ships spinning down into Hebron space, a few translating to Heaven's Gate, God's Grove, Mare Infinitus, Asquith. Only hours left now before the Swarms enter Web systems.

Confusion as hundreds of millions of refugees farcast away from the threatened worlds, stepping into cities and relocation centers gone half mad with the aimless excitement of incipient war. Confusion as unthreatened Web worlds ignite with riots: three Hives on Lusus – almost seventy million citizens – quarantined due to Shrike Cult riots, thirty-level malls looted, apartment monoliths overrun by mobs, fusion centers blown, farcaster terminexes under attack. The Home Rule Council appeals to the Hegemony; the Hegemony declares martial law and sends FORCE: Marines to seal the hives.

Secessionist riots on New Earth and Maui-Covenant. Terrorist attacks from Glennon-Height royalists – quiet now for three quarters of a century – on Thalia,

380

Armaghast, Nordholm, and Lee Three. More Shrike Cult riots on Tsingtao-Hsishuang Panna and Renaissance Vector.

FORCE Command on Olympus transfers combat battalions from transports returning from Hyperion to Web worlds. Demolition squads assigned to torchships in threatened systems report farcaster singularity spheres wired for destruction, awaiting only the fatlined order from TC^2.

'There is a better way,' Councilor Albedo tells Gladstone and the War Council.

The CEO turns toward the ambassador from the TechnoCore.

'There is a weapon that will eliminate the Ousters without harming Hegemony property. Or Ouster property, for that matter.'

General Morpurgo glowers. 'You're talking about the bomb equivalent of a deathwand,' he says. 'It won't work. FORCE researchers have shown that it propagates indefinitely. Besides being dishonorable, against the New Bushido Code, it would wipe out planetary populations as well as the invaders.'

'Not at all,' says Albedo. 'If Hegemony citizens are properly shielded, there need be no casualties whatsoever. As you know, deathwands can be calibrated for specific cerebral wavelengths. So could a bomb based on the same principle. Livestock, wild animals, even other anthropoid species would not be affected.'

General Van Zeidt of FORCE:Marines stands. 'But there's no way to shield a population! Our testing showed that death-bomb heavy neutrinos would penetrate solid rock or metal to a depth of six kilometers. No one has shelters like that!'

The projection of Councilor Albedo folds his hands on the table. 'We have nine worlds with shelters which would hold billions,' he says softly.

Gladstone nods. 'The labyrinthine worlds,' she whispers. 'But certainly such a transfer of population would be impossible.'

'No,' says Albedo. 'Now that you have joined Hyperion to the Protectorate, each of the labyrinthine worlds has farcaster capability. The Core can make arrangements to transfer populations directly to these underground shelters.'

There is babble around the long table, but Meina Gladstone's intense gaze never leaves Albedo's face. She beckons for silence and receives it. 'Tell us more,' she says. 'We are interested.'

The Consul sits in the spotty shade of a low neville tree and waits to die. His hands are tied behind him with a twist of fiberplastic. His clothes are torn to rags and are still damp; the moisture on his face is partially from the river but mostly from perspiration.

The two men who stand over him are finishing their inspection of his duffel bag. 'Shit,' says the first man, 'there bey nothing worth anything here-in except this fucking antique pistol.' He thrusts Brawne Lamia's father's weapon in his belt.

'It bey too bad we couldn't get that goddamn flying carpet,' says the second man.

'It beyn't flying too well there toward the end!' says the first man, and both of them laugh.

The Consul squints at the two massive figures, their armored bodies made silhouettes by the lowering sun. From their dialect he assumes them to be indigenies; from their appearance – bits of outmoded FORCE body armor, heavy multipurpose assault rifles, tatters of what once had been camou-polymer cloth – he guesses them to be deserters from some Hyperion Self-defense Force unit.

From their behavior toward him, he is sure that they are going to kill him.

At first, stunned from the fall into the Hoolie River, still tangled in the ropes connecting him to his duffel bag and the useless hawking mat, he thought them to be his saviors. The Consul had hit the water hard, stayed under for a much longer time than he would have imagined possible without drowning, and surfaced only to be pushed under by a strong current and then pulled under again by the tangle of ropes and mat. It had been a valiant but losing battle, and he was still ten meters from the shallows when one of the men emerging from the neville and thorn tree forest had thrown the Consul a line. Then they had beaten him, robbed him, tied him, and – judging from their matter-of-fact comments – were now preparing to cut his throat and leave him for the harbinger birds.

The taller of the two men, his hair a mass of oiled spikes, squats in front of the Consul and pulls a ceramic zero-edge knife from its scabbard. 'Any last words, Pops?'

The Consul licks his lips. He has seen a thousand movies and holies where this was the point at which the hero twisted his opponent's legs out from under him, kicked the other one into submission, seized a weapon and dispatched both – firing with his hands still tied – and then went on with his adventures. But the Consul feels like no hero: he is exhausted and middle-aged and hurt from his fall in the river. *Each* of these men is leaner, stronger, faster, and obviously meaner than the Consul ever has been. He has seen violence – even committed violence once – but his life and training have been devoted to the tense but quiet paths of diplomacy.

The Consul licks his lips again and says, 'I can pay you.'

The crouching man smiles and moves the zero-edge blade back and forth five centimeters in front of the Consul's eyes. 'With what, Pops? We've got your universal card, and it bey worth shit out here.'

'Gold,' says the Consul, knowing that this is the only syllable that has held its power over the ages.

The crouching man does not react – there is a sick light

in his eyes as he watches the blade – but the other man steps forward and sets a heavy hand on his partner's shoulder. 'What bey you talkin' about, man? Wherefore you got gold?'

'My ship,' says the Consul. 'The *Benares*.'

The crouching man raises the blade next to his own cheek. 'He bey lyin', Chez. The *Benares* bey that old flat-bottomed manta-pulled barge belongin' to the blue-skins we finished trey day ago.'

The Consul closes his eyes for a second, feeling the nausea in him but not surrendering to it. A. Bettik and the other android crewmen had left the *Benares* in one of the ship's launches less than a week earlier, heading downstream toward 'freedom'. Evidently they had found something else. 'A. Bettik,' he says. 'The crew captain. He didn't mention the gold?'

The man with the knife grins. 'He make lots a noise, but he don't speak much. He say the boat way and the shit gone up to Edge. Too fuckin' far for a barge with no mantas, me-think.'

'Shut up, Obem.' The other man crouches in front of the Consul. 'Why would you have gold on that old barge, man?'

The Consul raises his face. 'Don't you recognize me? I was Hegemony Consul to Hyperion for years.'

'Hey, don't bey fuckin' with us . . .' begins the man with the knife, but the other interrupts. 'Yeah, man, I remember your face on the camp holie when I bey kid-like. So why you carryin' gold upriver now when the sky bey fallin', Hegemony-man?'

'We were heading for the shelter . . . Chronos Keep,' says the Consul, trying not to sound too eager but at the same time grateful for each second he is allowed to live. *Why?* part of him thinks. *You were tired of living. Ready to die.* Not like this. Not while Sol and Rachel and the others need his help.

'Several of Hyperion's most wealthy citizens,' he says. 'The evacuation authorities wouldn't allow them to transfer the bullion, so I agreed to help them store it in vaults in

384

Chronos Keep, the old castle north of the Bridle Range. For a commission.'

'You bey fuckin' crazy!' sneers the man with the knife. 'Everything north of here bey Shrike country now.'

The Consul lowers his head. There is no need to stimulate the fatigue and sense of defeat he projects. 'So we discovered. The android crew deserted last week. Several of the passengers were killed by the Shrike. I was coming downriver by myself.'

'This bey shit,' says the man with the knife. His eyes have that sick, distracted look again.

'Just a second,' says his partner. He slaps the Consul once, hard. 'So where bey this so-called gold ship, old man?'

The Consul tastes blood. 'Upriver. Not *on* the river, but hidden in one of the tributaries.'

'Yeah,' says the knife-man, setting the zero-edge blade flat against the side of the Consul's neck. He will not need to slash in order to sever the Consul's throat, merely rotate the blade. 'I say this bey shit. And I say we bey wastin' time.'

'Just a second,' snaps the other man. 'How far upriver?'

The Consul thinks of the tributaries he has passed in the last few hours. It is late. The sun almost touches the line of a copse of trees to the west. 'Just above Karla Locks,' he says.

'So why you bey flyin' down on that toy-like rather than bargin' it?'

'Trying to get help,' says the Consul. The adrenaline has faded, and now he feels a terminal exhaustion very close to despair. 'There were too many . . . too many bandits along the shore. The barge seemed too risky. The hawking mat was . . . safer.'

The man called Chez laughs. 'Put the knife away, Obem. We bey walkin' up it a bit, hey?'

Obem leaps to his feet. The knife is still in his hand but now the blade – and the anger – are aimed toward his partner. 'Bey you *fucked*, man, hey? Bey your head bey full of *shit* between ears, hey? He bey lyin' to keep from deathwards flyin'.'

Chez neither blinks nor steps back. 'Sure, he bey maybe lyin'. Don't matter, hey? The Locks they bey less'n half-day walk we bey makin' anyway, hey? No boat, no gold, you cut his throat, hey? Only slowwise, ankles-up like. They bey gold, you still gets the job, bladewise, only bey rich man now, hey?'

Obem teeters a second between rage and reason, turns to the side, and swings the ceramic zero-edge blade at a neville tree eight centimeters thick through the trunk. He has time to turn back and crouch in front of the Consul before gravity informs the tree that it has been severed and the neville falls back toward the river's edge with a crash of branches. Obem grabs the Consul's still-damp shirtfront. 'OK, we see what bey there, Hegemony-man. Talk, run, trip, stumble, and I bey slicin' fingers and ears just for practice, hey?'

The Consul staggers to his feet, and the three of them move back into the cover of brush and low trees, the Consul three meters behind Chez and the same distance in front of Obem, trudging back the way he had come, moving away from the city and the ship and any chance of saving Sol and Rachel.

An hour passes. The Consul can think of no clever scheme once the tributaries are reached, the barge not discovered. Several times Chez waves them into silence and hiding, once at the sound of gossamers fluttering in branches, again at a disturbance across the river, but there is no sign of other human beings. No sign of help. The Consul remembers the burned-out buildings along the river, the empty huts and vacant wharves. Fear of the Shrike, fear of being left behind to the Ousters in the evacuation, and months of plundering by rogue elements of the SDF have turned this area into a no-man's-land. The Consul concocts excuses and extensions, then discards them. His only hope is that they will walk close to the Locks where he can make a leap for the deep and rapid water there, try to stay afloat with his hands tied behind him until he is hidden in the maze of small islands below that point.

Except that he is too tired to swim, even if his arms were free. And the weapons the two men carry would target him easily, even if he had a ten-minute start among the snags and isles. The Consul is too tired to be clever, too old to be brave. He thinks about his wife and son, dead these many years now, killed in the bombing of Bressia by men with no more honor than these two creatures. The Consul is only sorry that he has broken his word to help the other pilgrims. Sorry about that . . . and that he will not see how it all comes out.

Obem makes a spitting noise behind him. 'Shit with this, Chez, hey? What say we sit him and slit him and help him talk a bit, hey? Then we go lonewise to the barge, if barge they bey?'

Chez turns, rubs sweat out of his eyes, frowns at the Consul speculatively, and says, 'Hey, yeah, I think maybe timewise and quietwise you bey right, goyo, but leave it talkable toward the end, hey?'

'Sure,' grins Obem, slinging his weapon and extracting his zero-edge.

'DO NOT MOVE!' booms a voice from above. The Consul drops to his knees and the ex-SDF bandits unsling weapons with practiced swiftness. There is a rush, a roar, a whipping of branches and dust about them, the Consul looks up in time to see a rippling of the cloud-covered evening sky, lower than the clouds, a sense of *mass* directly above, descending, and then Chez is lifting his fléchette rifle and Obem is targeting his launcher and then all three are falling, pitching over, not like soldiers shot, not like recoil elements in some ballistic equation, but dropping like the tree Obem had felled earlier on.

The Consul lands face first in dust and gravel and lies there unblinking, unable to blink.

Stun weapon he thinks through synapses gone sluggish as

old oil. A localized cyclone erupts as something large and invisible lands between the three bodies in the dust and the river's edge. The Consul hears a hatch whine open and the internal tick of repellor turbines dropping below lift-critical. He still cannot blink, much less lift his head, and his vision is limited to several pebbles, a dunescape of sand, a small grass forest, and a single architect ant, huge at this distance, that seems to be taking a sudden interest in the Consul's moist but unblinking eye. The ant turns to hurry the half meter between itself and its moist prize, and the Consul thinks *Hurry* at the unhurried footsteps behind him.

Hands under his arms, grunting, a familiar but strained voice saying, 'Damn, you've put on weight.'

The Consul's heels drag in the dirt, bouncing over the randomly twitching fingers of Chez ... or perhaps it is Obem ... the Consul cannot turn his head to see their faces. Nor can he see his rescuer until he is lifted – with a grunted litany of soft curses near his ear – through the starboard blister-hatch of the decamouflaged skimmer, into the long, soft leather of the reclining passenger seat.

Governor-General Theo Lane appears in the Consul's field of vision, boyish-looking but slightly demonic-looking too as the hatch lowers and the red interior lamps light his face. The younger man leans over to secure crashweb snaps across the Consul's chest. 'I'm sorry I had to stun you along with those other two.' Theo sits back, snaps his own web in place, and twitches the omni controller. The Consul feels the skimmer shiver and then lift off, hovering a second before spinning left like a plate on frictionless bearings. Acceleration pushes the Consul into his seat.

'I didn't have much choice,' says Theo over the soft internal skimmer noises. 'The only weapon these things are allowed to carry are the riot-control stunners, and the easiest way was to drop all three of you at lowest setting and get you out of there fast.' Theo pushes his archaic glasses higher on his nose with a familiar twitch of one finger and turns to grin at the Consul. 'Old mercenary proverb – "Kill 'em all and let God sort 'em out." '

The Consul manages to move his tongue enough to make a sound and to drool a bit on his cheek and the seat leather.

'Relax a minute,' says Theo, returning his attention to the instruments and view outside. 'Two or three minutes and you should be talking all right. I'm staying low, flying slow, so it's about a ten-minute ride back to Keats.' Theo glances toward his passenger. 'You're lucky, sir. You must have been dehydrated. Those other two wet their pants when they went down. Humane weapon, the stunner, but embarrassing if you don't have a change of pants around.'

The Consul tries to express his opinion of this 'humane' weapon.

'Another couple of minutes, sir,' says Governor-General Theo Lane, reaching over to dab at the Consul's cheek with a handkerchief. 'I should warn you, it's a mite uncomfortable when the stun begins to wear off.'

At that moment, someone inserts several thousand pins and needles in the Consul's body.

'How the hell did you find me?' asks the Consul. They are a few kilometers above the city, still flying over the Hoolie River. He is able to sit up, and his words are more or less intelligible, but the Consul is glad that he has several more minutes before he will have to stand or walk.

'What, sir?'

'I said, how did you find me? How could you possibly know that I had come back down the Hoolie?'

'CEO Gladstone fatlined me. Eyes-only on the old consulate one-time pad.'

'Gladstone?' The Consul is shaking his hands, trying to agitate feeling back into fingers as useful as rubber sausages. 'How the hell could Gladstone possibly know that I was in trouble on the Hoolie River? I left Grandmother Siri's comlog receiver back in the valley so I could call the other pilgrims when I got to the ship. How could Gladstone know?'

'I don't know, sir, but she specified your location and that you were in trouble. She even said you'd been flying a hawking mat that went down.'

The Consul shakes his head. 'This lady has resources we hadn't dreamt of, Theo.'

'Yes, sir.'

The Consul glances at his friend. Theo Lane had been Governor-General of the new Protectorate world of Hyperion for over a local year now, but old habits died hard and the 'sir' came from the seven years Theo had served as Vice-Consul and principal aide during the Consul's years. The last time he had seen the young man – not so young now, the Consul realizes: responsibility has brought lines and wrinkles to that young face – Theo had been furious that the Consul would not take over the governor-generalship. That had been a little more than a week ago. Ages and eons ago.

'By the way,' says the Consul, enunciating each word carefully, 'thank you, Theo.'

The Governor-General nods, apparently lost in thought. He does not ask about what the Consul has seen north of the mountains, nor the fate of the other pilgrims. Beneath them, the Hoolie widens and winds toward the capital of Keats. Far back on either side, low bluffs rise, their granite slabs glowing softly in the evening light. Stands of everblues shimmer in the breeze.

'Theo, how did you possibly have time to come for me yourself? The situation on Hyperion must be pure madness.'

'It is.' Theo ordered the autopilot to take over as he turned to look at the Consul. 'It's a matter of hours . . . perhaps minutes . . . before the Ousters actually invade.'

The Consul blinked. 'Invade? You mean land?'

'Exactly.'

'But the Hegemony fleet—'

'Is in total chaos. They were barely holding their own against the Swarm *before* the Web was invaded.'

'The Web!'

'Entire systems falling. Others threatened. FORCE has ordered the fleet back through their military farcasters, but evidently the ships in-system have found it hard to disengage. No one gives me details, but it's obvious that the Ousters have free rein everywhere except for the defensive perimeter FORCE has put up around the singularity spheres and the portals.'

'The spaceport?' The Consul thinks of his beautiful ship lying as glowing wreckage.

'It hasn't been attacked yet, but FORCE has been pulling its dropships and supply craft out as quickly as they can. They've left a skeleton force of Marines behind.'

'What about the evacuation?'

Theo laughed. It was the most bitter sound the Consul had ever heard from the young man. 'The evacuation will consist of whatever consulate people and Hegemony VIPs can fit on the last dropship out.'

'They've given up trying to save the people of Hyperion?'

'Sir, they can't save their *own* people. Word trickling down through the ambassadors' fatline says that Gladstone has decided to let the threatened Web worlds fall so that FORCE can regroup, have a couple of years to create defenses while the Swarms accrue time-debt.'

'My God,' whispers the Consul. He had worked most of his life to represent the Hegemony, all the while plotting its downfall in order to avenge his grandmother . . . his grandmother's way of life. But now the thought of it actually happening . . .

'What about the Shrike?' he asks suddenly, seeing the low white buildings of Keats a few kilometers ahead. Sunlight touches the hills and river like a final benediction before darkness.

Theo shakes his head. 'There are still reports, but the Ousters have taken over as the primary source of panic.'

'But it's not in the Web? The Shrike, I mean.'

The Governor-General gives the Consul a sharp look. 'In the Web? How could it be in the Web? They still haven't allowed farcaster portals on Hyperion. And there have been no sightings near Keats or Endymion or Port Romance. None of the larger cities.'

The Consul says nothing, but he is thinking: *My God, my betrayal was for nothing. I sold my soul to open the Time Tombs, and the Shrike will not be the cause of the Web's fall . . . The Ousters! They were wise to us all along. My betrayal of the Hegemony was part of their plan!*

'Listen,' Theo says harshly, gripping the Consul's wrist, 'there's a reason Gladstone had me leave everything to find you. She's authorized the release of your ship—'

'Wonderful!' says the Consul. 'I can—'

'Listen! You're not to go back to the Valley of the Time Tombs. Gladstone wants you to avoid the FORCE perimeter and travel in-system until you contact elements of the Swarm.'

'The Swarm? Why would—'

'The CEO wants you to negotiate with them. They *know* you. Somehow she's managed to let them know that you're coming. She thinks that they'll let you . . . that they won't destroy your ship. But she hasn't received confirmation of that. It'll be risky.'

The Consul sits back in the leather seat. He feels as if he has been hit by the neural stunner again. 'Negotiate? What the hell would I have to negotiate?'

'Gladstone said that she would contact you via your ship's fatline once you're off Hyperion. This has to be done quickly. Today. Before all the first-wave worlds fall to the Swarms.'

The Consul hears *first-wave worlds* but does not ask if his beloved Maui-Covenant is amongst them. Perhaps, he thinks, it would be best if it were. He says, 'No, I'm going back to the valley.'

Theo adjusts his glasses. 'She won't allow that, sir.'

'Oh?' The Consul smiles. 'How is she going to stop me? Shoot down my ship?'

'I don't know, but she said that she wouldn't allow it.' Theo sounds sincerely worried. 'The FORCE fleet *does* have picket ships and torchships in orbit, sir. To escort the last dropships.'

'Well,' says the Consul, still smiling, 'let them try to shoot me down. Manned ships haven't been able to land near the Valley of the Time Tombs for two centuries anyway: ships land perfectly, but their crews disappear. Before they slag me, I'll be hanging on the Shrike's tree.' The Consul closes his eyes a moment and imagines the ship landing, empty, on the plain above the valley. He imagines Sol, Duré, and the others – miraculously returned – running for shelter in the ship, using its surgery to save Het Masteen and Brawne Lamia, its cryogenic fugue and sleep chambers to save little Rachel.

'My God,' whispers Theo and the shocked tone slams the Consul out of his reverie.

They have come around the final turn in the river above the city. The bluffs rise higher here, culminating to the south in the carved-mountain likeness of Sad King Billy. The sun is just setting, igniting low clouds and buildings high on the eastern bluffs.

Above the city, a battle is raging. Lasers lance into and through the clouds, ships dodge like gnats and burn like moths too close to a flame, while parafoils and the blur of suspension fields drift beneath the cloud ceiling. The city of Keats is being attacked. The Ousters have come to Hyperion.

'Oh, sweet fuck,' Theo whispers reverently.

Along the forested ridge northwest of the city, a brief spout of flame and a flicker of contrail mark a shoulder-launched rocket coming directly toward the Hegemony skimmer.

'Hang on!' snaps Theo. He takes manual control, throws switches, banks the skimmer steeply to starboard, trying to turn inside the small rocket's own turning radius.

An explosion aft throws the Consul into the crashweb and blurs his vision for a moment. When he can focus again, the cabin is filled with smoke, red warning lights pulse through the gloom, and the skimmer warns of systems failure in a dozen urgent voices. Theo is slumped grimly over the omni-controller.

'Hang on,' he says again, needlessly. The skimmer slews sickeningly, finds a grip in the air, and then loses it as they tumble and sideslip toward the burning city.

THIRTY-SIX

I blinked and opened my eyes, disoriented for a second as I looked around the immense, dark space of St Peter's Basilica, Pacem. Monsignor Edouard and Father Paul Duré leaned forward in the dim candlelight, their expressions intense.

'How long was I . . . asleep?' I felt as if only seconds had elapsed, the dream a shimmer of images one has in the instants between lying peacefully and full sleep.

'Ten minutes,' said the Monsignor. 'Can you tell us what you saw?'

I saw no reason not to. When I was finished describing the images, Monsignor Edouard crossed himself. '*Mon Dieu*, the ambassador from the TechnoCore urges Gladstone to send people to those . . . tunnels.'

Duré touched my shoulder. 'After I talk to the True Voice of the Worldtree on God's Grove, I will join you on TC². We have to tell Gladstone the folly of such a choice.'

I nodded. All thoughts of my going to God's Grove with Duré or to Hyperion itself had fled. 'I agree. We should depart at once. Is your . . . can the Pope's Door take me to Tau Ceti Center?'

The Monsignor stood, nodded, stretched. Suddenly I realized that he was a very old man, untouched by Poulsen treatments. 'It has a priority access,' he said. He turned to Duré. 'Paul, you know that I would accompany you if I could. The funeral of His Holiness, the election of a new Holy Father . . .' Monsignor Edouard made a small, rueful sound. 'Odd how the daily imperatives persist even in the face of collective disaster. Pacem itself has fewer than ten standard days until the barbarians arrive.'

Duré's high forehead gleamed in the candlelight. 'The business of the Church is something beyond a mere daily imperative, my friend. I will make my visit on the Templar world brief, then join M Severn in his effort of convincing the CEO not to listen to the Core. Then I will return, Edouard, and we will try to make some sense of this confused heresy.'

I followed the two of them out of the basilica, through a side door that led to a passageway behind the tall colonnades, left across an open courtyard – the rain had stopped and the air smelled fresh – down a stairway, and through a narrow tunnel into the papal apartments. Members of the Swiss Guard snapped to attention as we came into the apartments' anteroom; the tall men were dressed in armor and yellow-and-blue striped pantaloons, although their ceremonial halberds were also FORCE-quality energy weapons. One stepped forward and spoke softly to the Monsignor.

'Someone has just arrived at the main terminex to see you, M Severn.'

'Me?' I had been listening to other voices in other rooms, the melodious rise and fall of oft-repeated prayers. I assumed it had to do with preparation for the Pope's burial.

'Yes, an M Hunt. He says that it is urgent.'

'Another minute and I would have seen him at Government House,' I said. 'Why not have him join us here?'

Monsignor Edouard nodded and spoke softly to the Swiss Guard, who whispered into an ornamental crest on his antique armor.

The so-called Pope's Door – a small farcaster portal surrounded by intricate gold carvings of seraphim and cherubim, topped with a five-station bas-relief illustrating Adam and Eve's fall from grace and expulsion from the garden – stood in the center of a well-guarded room just off the Pope's private apartments. We waited there, our reflections wan and tired-looking in the mirrors on each wall.

Leigh Hunt was escorted in by the priest who had led me to the basilica.

'Severn!' cried Gladstone's favorite advisor. 'The CEO needs you at once.'

'I was just going there,' I said. 'It would be a criminal mistake if Gladstone allowed the Core to build and use the death device.'

Hunt blinked – an almost comical reaction on that basset-hound countenance. 'Do you know *everything* that happens, Severn?'

I had to laugh. 'A young child sitting unattended in a holo pit sees much and understands very little. Still, he has the advantage of being able to change channels and turn the thing off when he grows tired of it.' Hunt knew Monsignor Edouard from various state functions, and I introduced Father Paul Duré of the Society of Jesus.

'Duré?' managed Hunt, his jaw almost hanging slack. It was the first time that I had seen the advisor at a loss for words, and I rather enjoyed the sight.

'We'll explain later,' I said and shook the priest's hand. 'Good luck on God's Grove, Duré. Don't be too long.'

'An hour,' promised the Jesuit. 'No longer. There is merely one piece of the puzzle I must find before speaking to the CEO. Please explain to her about the horror of the labyrinth . . . I will give her my own testimony later.'

'It's possible that she'll be too busy to see me before you get there anyway,' I said. 'But I'll do my best to play John the Baptist for you.'

Duré smiled. 'Just don't lose your head, my friend.' He nodded, tapped in a transfer code on the archaic diskey panel, and disappeared through the portal.

I bid farewell to Monsignor Edouard. 'We will get all

this settled before the Ouster wave gets this far.'

The old priest raised a hand and blessed me. 'Go with God, young man. I feel that dark times await us all but that you will be especially burdened.'

I shook my head. 'I'm just an observer, Monsignor. I wait and watch and dream. Little burden there.'

'Wait and watch and dream later,' Leigh Hunt said sharply. 'Her Nibs wants you within reach *now*, and I have a meeting to get back to.'

I looked at the little man. 'How did you find me?' I asked needlessly. Farcasters were operated by the Core, and the Core worked with the Hegemony authorities.

'The override card she gave you also makes it easier to keep track of your travels,' Hunt said, his impatience audible. 'Right now we have an obligation to be where things are happening.'

'Very well.' I nodded at the Monsignor and his aide, beckoned to Hunt, and tapped in the three-digit code for Tau Ceti Center, added two digits for the continent, three more for Government House, and added the final two numbers for the private terminex there. The farcaster's hum went up a notch on the scale, its opaque surface seemed to shimmer with expectancy.

I stepped through first, stepped aside to give Hunt room as he followed.

We are not in the central Government House terminex. As far as I can tell, we are nowhere near Government House. A second later, my senses total the input of sunlight, sky color, gravity, distance to horizon, smells, and *feel* of things, and decide that we aren't on Tau Ceti Center.

I would have jumped back through the portal then, but the Pope's Door is small. Hunt is coming through – leg, arm, shoulder, chest, head, second leg appearing – so I grab his wrist, pull him through roughly, say 'Something's wrong!' and try to step back through, but too late, the

398

frameless portal on this side shimmers, dilates to a circle the size of my fist, and is gone.

'Where the hell are we?' demands Hunt.

I look around and think, *Good question*. We are in the country, on a hilltop. A road underfoot winds through vineyards, goes down a long hill through a wooded vale, and disappears around another hill a mile or two distant. It is very warm, and the air hums with the sounds of insects, but nothing larger than a bird moves in this vast panorama. Between bluffs to our right, a blue smear of water is visible – either an ocean or sea. High cirrus ripples overhead; the sun is just past the zenith. I see no houses, no technology more complicated than the vineyard rows and the stone-and-mud road underfoot. More importantly, the constant background buzz of the datasphere is gone. It is somewhat like suddenly hearing the absence of a sound one has been immersed in since infancy; it is startling, heart-stopping, confusing, and a bit terrifying.

Hunt staggers, claps his ears as if it is true sound he is missing, taps at his comlog. 'Goddamn,' he mutters. 'Goddamn. My implant's malfunctioning. Comlog's out.'

'No,' I say, 'I believe we're beyond the datasphere.' But even as I say this, I hear a deeper, softer hum – something far greater and far less accessible than the datasphere. The megasphere? *The music of the spheres*, I think, and smile.

'What the hell are you grinning about, Severn? Did you do this on purpose?'

'No. I gave the proper codes for Government House.' The total absence of panic in my voice is a kind of panic itself.

'What is it then? That goddamned Pope's Door? Did it do this? Some malf or trick?'

'No, I think not. The door didn't malfunction, Hunt. It brought us just where the TechnoCore wants us.'

'The Core?' What little color left in that basset countenance quickly drains away as the CEO's aide realizes who controls the farcaster. Who controls *all* farcasters. 'My God. My God.' Hunt staggers to the side of the road and sits in the tall grass there. His suede executive suit and soft black shoes look out of place here.

'Where are we?' he asks again.

I take a deep breath. The air smells of fresh-turned soil, newly mown grass, road dust, and the sharp tinge of the sea. 'My guess is that we're on Earth, Hunt.'

'Earth.' The little man is staring straight ahead, focusing on nothing. 'Earth. Not New Earth. Not Terra. Not Earth Two. Not . . .'

'No,' I say. 'Earth. Old Earth. Or its duplicate.'

'Its duplicate.'

I go over and sit beside him. I pull a strand of grass and strip the lower part of its outer sheath. The grass tastes tart and familiar. 'You remember my report to Gladstone on the Hyperion pilgrims' stories? Brawne Lamia's tale? She and my cybrid counterpart . . . the first Keats retrieval persona . . . traveled to what they thought was an Old Earth duplicate. In the Hercules Cluster, if I remember correctly.'

Hunt glances up as if he can judge what I am saying by checking constellations. The blue above is graying slightly as the high cirrus spreads across the dome of sky. 'Hercules Cluster,' he whispers.

'Why the TechnoCore built a duplicate, or what they're doing with it now, Brawne didn't learn,' I say. 'Either the first Keats cybrid didn't know, or he wasn't saying.'

'Wasn't saying,' nods Hunt. He shakes his head. 'All right, how the hell do we get *out* of here? Gladstone needs me. She can't . . . there are dozens of vital decisions to be made in the next few hours.' He jumps to his feet, runs to the center of the road, a study in purposeful energy.

I chew on the stalk of grass. 'My guess is that we don't get out of here.'

Hunt comes at me as if he is going to assault me then and there. 'Are you *insane*! No way out? That's nuts. Why would the Core do that?' He pauses, looks down at me. 'They don't want you talking to her. You know something that the Core can't risk her learning.'

'Perhaps.'

'Leave *him*, let *me* go back!' he screams at the sky.

No one answers. Far out across the vineyard, a large black bird takes flight. I think it is a crow; I remember the name of the extinct species as if from a dream.

After a moment, Hunt gives up on addressing the sky and paces back and forth on the stone road. 'Come on. Maybe there's a terminex wherever this thing goes.'

'Perhaps,' I say, breaking off the stalk of grass to get at the sweet, dry upper half. 'But which way?'

Hunt turns, looks at the road disappearing around hills in both directions, turns again. 'We came through the portal looking . . . this way.' He points. The road goes downhill into a narrow wood.

'How far?' I ask.

'Goddammit, does it matter?' he barks. 'We have to get *somewhere*!'

I resist the impulse to smile. 'All right.' I stand and brush off my trousers, feeling the fierce sunlight on my forehead and face. After the incense-laden darkness of the basilica, it is a shock. The air is very hot, and my clothing is already damp with sweat.

Hunt starts walking vigorously down the hill, his fists clenched, his doleful expression ameliorated for once by a stronger expression – sheer resolve.

Walking slowly, in no hurry, still chewing on my stalk of sweet grass, eyes half-closed with weariness, I follow him.

Colonel Fedmahn Kassad screamed and attacked the Shrike. The surreal, out-of-time landscape – a minimalist stage designer's version of the Valley of the Time Tombs, molded in plastic and set in a gel of viscous air – seemed to vibrate to the violence of Kassad's rush.

For an instant there had been a mirror-image scattering of Shrikes – Shrikes throughout the valley, spread across the barren plain – but with Kassad's shout these resolved themselves to the single monster, and now it moved, four arms unfolding and extending, curving to greet the Colonel's rush with a hearty hug of blades and thorns.

Kassad did not know if the energy skinsuit he wore, Moneta's gift, would protect him or serve him well in combat. It had years before when he and Moneta had attacked two dropships' worth of Ouster commandos, but time had been on their side then; the Shrike had frozen and unfrozen the flow of moments like a bored observer playing with a holopit remote control. Now they were outside time, and there was the enemy, not some terrible patron. Kassad shouted and put his head down and attacked, no longer aware of Moneta watching, nor of the impossible tree of thorns rising into the clouds with its terrible, impaled audience, nor even aware of himself except as a fighting tool, an instrument of revenge.

The Shrike did not disappear in its usual manner, did not cease being *there* to suddenly be *here*. Instead, it crouched and opened its arms wider. Its fingerblades caught the light of the violent sky. The Shrike's metal teeth glistened in what might have been a smile.

Kassad was angry; he was not insane. Rather than rush into that embrace of death, he threw himself aside at the last instant, rolling on arm and shoulder, and kicking out at the monster's lower leg, below the cluster of thornblades at the knee joint, above a similar array on the ankle. *If he could get it down . . .*

It was like kicking at a pipe embedded in half a klick of concrete. The blow would have broken Kassad's own leg if the skinsuit had not acted as armor and shock absorber.

The Shrike moved, quickly but not impossibly; the two right arms swinging up and down and around in a blur, ten fingerblades carving soil and stone in surgical furrows, arm thorns sending sparks flying as the hands continued upward, slicing air with an audible rush. Kassad was out of range, continuing his roll, coming to his feet again, crouching, his own arms tensed, palms flat, energy-suited fingers rigid and extended.

Single combat, thought Fedmahn Kassad. *The most honorable sacrament in the New Bushido.*

The Shrike feinted with its right arms again, swung the lower left arm around and up with a sweeping blow violent enough to shatter Kassad's ribs and scoop his heart out.

Kassad blocked the right-arm feint with his left forearm, feeling the skinsuit flex and batter bone as the steel-and-axe force of the Shrike's blow struck home. The left-arm killing blow he stopped with his right hand on the monster's wrist, just above the corsage of curved spikes there. Incredibly, he slowed the blow's momentum enough that scalpel-sharp fingerblades were now scraping against his skinsuit field rather than splintering ribs.

Kassad was almost lifted off the ground with the effort of restraining that rising claw; only the downward thrust of the Shrike's first feint kept the Colonel from flying backward. Sweat poured freely under the skinsuit, muscles flexed and ached and threatened to rip in that interminable twenty seconds of struggle before the Shrike brought its fourth arm into play, slashing downward at Kassad's straining leg.

Kassad screamed as the skinsuit field ripped, flesh tore, and at least one fingerblade sliced close to bone. He kicked out with his other leg, released the thing's wrist, and rolled frantically away.

The Shrike swung twice, the second blow whistling millimeters from Kassad's moving ear, but then jumped back itself, crouching, moving to its right.

Kassad got to his left knee, almost fell, then staggered to his feet, hopping slightly to keep his balance. The pain roared in his ears and filled the universe with red light, but even as he grimaced and staggered, close to fainting from the shock of it, he could feel the skinsuit closing on the wound – serving as both tourniquet and compress. He could feel the blood on his lower leg, but it was no longer flowing freely, and the pain was manageable, almost as if the skinsuit carried medpak injectors like his FORCE battle armor.

The Shrike rushed him.

Kassad kicked once, twice, aiming for and finding the smooth bit of chrome carapace beneath the chest spike. It was like kicking the hull of a torchship, but the Shrike seemed to pause, stagger, step back.

Kassad stepped forward, planted his weight, struck twice where the creature's heart should be with a closed-fist blow that would have shattered tempered ceramic, ignored the pain from his fist, swiveled, and slammed a straight-armed, open-palmed blow into the creature's muzzle, just above the teeth. Any human being would have heard the sound of his nose being broken and felt the explosion of bone and cartilage being driven into his brain.

The Shrike snapped at Kassad's wrist, missed, swung four hands at Kassad's head and shoulders.

Panting, pouring sweat and blood under his quicksilver armor, Kassad spun to his right once, twice, and came around with a killing blow to the back of the creature's short neck. The noise of the impact echoed in the frozen valley like the sound of an axe thrown from miles on high into the heart of a metal redwood.

The Shrike tumbled forward, rolled on to its back like some steel crustacean.

It had gone down!

Kassad stepped forward, still crouched, still cautious, but not cautious enough as the Shrike's armored foot, claw, whatever the hell it was, caught the back of Kassad's ankle and half sliced, half kicked him off his feet.

Colonel Kassad felt the pain, knew that his Achilles' tendon had been severed, tried to roll away, but the creature was throwing itself up and sideways on him, spikes and thorns and blades coming at Kassad's ribs and face and eyes. Grimacing with the pain, arching in a vain attempt to throw the monster off, Kassad blocked some blows, saved his eyes, and felt other blades slam home in his upper arms, chest, and belly.

The Shrike hovered closer and opened its mouth. Kassad stared up into row upon row of steel teeth set in a metal lamprey's hollow orifice of a mouth. Red eyes filled his sight through vision already tinged with blood.

Kassad got the base of his palm under the Shrike's jaw and tried to find leverage. It was like trying to lift a mountain of sharp scrap with no fulcrum. The Shrike's fingerblades continued to tear at Kassad's flesh. The thing opened its mouth and tilted its head until teeth filled Kassad's field of vision from ear to ear. The monster had no breath, but the heat from its interior stank of sulfur and heated iron filings. Kassad had no defense left; when the thing snapped its jaws shut, it would take the flesh and skin of Kassad's face off to the bone.

Suddenly Moneta was there, shouting in that place where sound did not carry, grabbing the Shrike by its ruby-faceted eyes, skinsuited fingers arching like talons, her boot planted firmly on its carapace below the back spike, pulling, pulling.

The Shrike's arms snapped backward, as double-jointed as some nightmare crab, fingerblades raked Moneta and she fell away, but not before Kassad rolled, scrambled, felt the pain but ignored it, and leaped to his feet, dragging Moneta with him as he retreated across the sand and frozen rock.

For a second, their skinsuits merged as it had when they were making love, and Kassad felt her flesh next to his, felt their blood and sweat mingling and heard the joined poundings of their hearts.

Kill it Moneta whispered urgently, pain audible even through that subvocal medium.

I'm trying. I'm trying.

The Shrike was on its feet, three meters of chrome and blades and other people's pain. It showed no damage. Someone's blood ran in narrow rivulets down its wrists and carapace. Its mindless grin seemed wider than before.

Kassad separated his skinsuit from Moneta's, lowered her gently to a boulder although he sensed that he had been hurt worse than she. This was not her fight. Not yet.

He moved between his love and the Shrike.

Kassad hesitated, hearing a faint but rising susurration as if from a rising surf on an invisible shore. He glanced up, never fully removing his gaze from the slowly advancing Shrike, and realized that it was a shouting from the thorn tree far behind the monster. The crucified people there – small dabs of color hanging from the metal thorns and cold branches – were making some noise other than the subliminal moans of pain Kassad had heard earlier. They were cheering.

Kassad returned his attention to the Shrike as the thing began to circle again. Kassad felt the pain and weakness in his almost-severed heel – his right foot was useless, unable to bear weight – and he half hopped, half swiveled with one hand on the boulder to keep his body between the Shrike and Moneta.

The distant cheering seemed to stop as if in a gasp.

The Shrike ceased being *there* and came into existence *here*, next to Kassad, on top of Kassad, its arms already around him in a terminal hug, thorns and blades already impinging. The Shrike's eyes blazed with light. Its jaws opened again.

Kassad shouted in pure rage and defiance and struck at it.

Father Paul Duré stepped through the Pope's Door to God's Grove without incident. From the incense-laden dimness of the papal apartments, he suddenly found himself in rich sunlight with a lemon sky above and green leaves all around.

The Templars were waiting as he stepped down from the private farcaster portal. Duré could see the edge of the weirwood platform five meters to his right and beyond it, nothing – or, rather, everything, as the treetop world of God's Grove stretched great distances to the horizon, the rooftop of leaves shimmering and moving like a living ocean. Duré knew that he was high on the Worldtree, the greatest and holiest of all the trees the Templars held sacred.

The Templars greeting him were important in the complicated hierarchy of the Brotherhood of the Muir, but served as mere guides now, leading him from the portal platform to a vine-strewn elevator which rose through upper levels and terraces where few non-Templars had ever ascended, and then out again and up along a staircase bound by a railing of the finest muirwood, spiraling skyward around a trunk that narrowed from its two-hundred-meter base to less than eight meters across here near its top. The weirwood platform was exquisitely carved; its railings showed a delicate tracery of handcarved vines, posts and balusters boasted the faces of gnomes, wood sprites, faeries, and other spirits, and the table and chairs which Duré now approached were carved from the same piece of wood as the circular platform itself.

Two men awaited him. The first was the one Duré expected – True Voice of the Worldtree, High Priest of the Muir, Spokesman of the Templar Brotherhood Sek Hardeen. The second man was a surprise. Duré noted the red robe – a red the color of arterial blood – with black ermine trim, the heavy Lusian body covered by that robe, the face all jowls and fat bisected by a formidable beak of a nose, two tiny eyes lost above fat cheeks, two pudgy hands with a black or red ring on each finger. Duré knew that he was looking at the Bishop of the Church of the Final Atonement – the high priest of the Shrike Cult.

The Templar rose to his almost two-meter height and offered his hand. 'Father Duré, we are most pleased that you could join us.'

Duré shook hands, thinking as he did so how much like a root the Templar's hand was, with its long, tapering, yellowish-brown fingers. The True Voice of the Worldtree wore the same hooded robe that Het Masteen had worn, its rough brown and green threads in sharp contrast to the brilliance of the Bishop's garb.

'Thank you for seeing me on such short notice, M Hardeen,' said Duré. The True Voice was the spiritual leader of millions of the followers of the Muir, but Duré knew that Templars disliked titles or honorifics in conversation. Duré nodded in the direction of the Bishop. 'Your Excellency, I had no idea that I would have the honor of being in your presence.'

The Shrike Cult Bishop nodded almost imperceptibly. 'I was visiting. M Hardeen suggested that it might be of some small benefit if I attended this meeting. I am pleased to meet you, Father Duré. We have heard much about you in the past few years.'

The Templar gestured toward a seat across the muirwood table from the two of them, and Duré sat, folding his hands on the polished tabletop, thinking furiously even as he pretended to inspect the beautiful grain in the wood. Half the security forces in the Web were searching for the Shrike Cult Bishop. His presence suggested complications far beyond those the Jesuit had been prepared to deal with.

'Interesting, is it not,' said the Bishop, 'that three of human-kind's most profound religions are represented here today?'

'Yes,' said Duré. 'Profound, but hardly representational of the beliefs of the majority. Out of almost a hundred and fifty billion souls, the Catholic Church claims fewer than a million. The Shri – ah . . . the Church of the Final Atonement perhaps five to ten million. And how many Templars are there, M Hardeen?'

'Twenty-three million,' the Templar said softly. 'Many others support our ecological causes and might even wish to join, but the Brotherhood is not open to outsiders.'

The Bishop rubbed one of his chins. His skin was very pale, and he squinted as if he were not used to daylight. 'The Zen Gnostics claim forty billion followers,' he rumbled. 'But what kind of religion is that, eh? No churches. No priests. No holy books. No concept of sin.'

Duré smiled. 'It seems to be the belief most attuned to the times. And has been for many generations now.'

'Bah!' The Bishop slapped his hand down on the table, and Duré winced as he heard the metal of the rings strike muirwood.

'How is it that you know who I am?' asked Paul Duré.

The Templar lifted his head just enough that Duré could see sunlight on his nose, cheeks, and the long line of chin within the shadows of the cowl. He did not speak.

'We chose you,' growled the Bishop. 'You and the other pilgrims.'

'You being the Shrike Church?' said Duré.

The Bishop frowned at the phrase but nodded without speaking.

'Why the riots?' asked Duré. 'Why the disturbances now that the Hegemony is threatened?'

When the Bishop rubbed his chin, red and black stones glinted in the evening light. Beyond him, a million leaves rustled in a breeze which brought the scent of rain-moistened vegetation. 'The Final Days are here, priest. The prophecies given to us by the Avatar centuries ago are unfolding before our eyes. What you call riots are the first death throes of a society which deserves to die. The Days of Atonement are upon us and the Lord of Pain soon will walk among us.'

'The Lord of Pain,' repeated Duré. 'The Shrike.'

The Templar made an ameliorating gesture with one hand, as if he were trying to take some of the edge off the Bishop's statement. 'Father Duré, we are aware of your miraculous rebirth.'

'Not a miracle,' said Duré. 'The whim of a parasite called a cruciform.'

Again the gesture with the long, yellow-brown fingers. 'However you see it, Father, the Brotherhood rejoices that you are with us once again. Please go ahead with the query you mentioned when you called earlier.'

Duré rubbed his palms against the wood of the chair, glanced at the Bishop sitting across from him in all of his red-and-black bulk. 'Your groups have been working together for some time, haven't they?' said Duré. 'The Templar Brotherhood and the Shrike Church.'

'Church of the Final Atonement,' the Bishop said in a bass growl.

Duré nodded. 'Why? What brings you together in this?'

The True Voice of the Worldtree leaned forward so that shadow filled his cowl once again. 'You must see, Father, that the prophecies of the Church of the Final Atonement touch upon our mission from the Muir. Only these prophecies have held the key to what punishment must befall humankind for killing its own world.'

'Humankind alone didn't destroy Old Earth,' said Duré. 'It was a computer error in the Kiev Team's attempt to create a mini-black hole.'

The Templar shook his head. 'It was human arrogance,' he said softly. 'The same arrogance which has caused our race to destroy all species that might even hope to evolve to intelligence someday. The Seneschai Aluit on Hebron, the zeplens of Whirl, the marsh centaurs of Garden and the great apes of Old Earth . . .'

'Yes,' said Duré. 'Mistakes have been made. But that shouldn't sentence humankind to death, should it?'

'The sentence has been handed down by a Power far greater than ourselves,' rumbled the Bishop. 'The prophecies are precise and explicit. The Day of Final Atonement must come. All who have inherited the Sins of Adam and Kiev must suffer the consequences of murdering their homeworld, of extinguishing other species. The Lord of Pain has been freed from the bonds of time to render this final judgement. There is no escaping his wrath. There is no avoiding Atonement. A Power far greater than us has said this.'

'It is true,' said Sek Hardeen. 'The prophecies have come to us . . . spoken to the True Voices over the generations . . . humankind is doomed, but with their doom will come a new flowering for pristine environments in all parts of what is now the Hegemony.'

Trained in Jesuit logic, devoted to the evolutionary theology of Teilhard de Chardin, Father Paul Duré was nonetheless tempted to say, *But who the hell cares if the flowers bloom if no one is around to see them, to smell them?* Instead, he said, 'Have you considered that these prophecies were not divine revelations, but merely manipulations from some secular power?'

The Templar sat back as if slapped, but the Bishop leaned forward and curled two Lusian fists which could have crushed Duré's skull with a single blow. 'Heresy! Whoever dares deny the truth of the revelations must die!'

'What power could do this?' managed the True Voice of the Worldtree. 'What power other than the Muir's Absolute could enter our minds and hearts?'

Duré gestured toward the sky. 'Every world in the Web has been joined through the TechnoCore's datasphere for generations. Most people of influence carry comlog extension implants for ease of accessing . . . do you not, M Hardeen?'

The Templar said nothing, but Duré saw the small twitch of fingers, as if the man were going to pat his chest and upper arm where the microimplants had lain for decades.

'The TechnoCore has created a transcendent . . . Intelligence,' continued Duré. 'It taps incredible amounts of energy, is able to move backward and forward in time, and is not motivated by human concerns. One of the goals of a sizeable percentage of the Core personalities was to

411

eliminate humankind . . . indeed, the Big Mistake of the Kiev Team may have been deliberately executed by the AIs involved in that experiment. What you hear as prophecies may be the voice of this *deus ex machina* whispering through the datasphere. The Shrike may be here not to make humankind atone for its sins, but merely to slaughter human men, women, and children for this machine personality's own goals.'

The Bishop's heavy face was as red as his robe. His fists pummeled the table, and he struggled to his feet. The Templar laid a hand on the Bishop's arm and restrained him, somehow pulled him back to his seat. 'Where have you heard this idea?' Sek Hardeen asked Duré.

'From those on the pilgrimage who have access to the Core. And from . . . others.'

The Bishop shook a fist in Duré's direction. 'But you yourself have been touched by the Avatar . . . not once, but *twice*! He has granted you a form of immortality so you can see what he has in store for the Chosen People . . . those who prepare Atonement before the Final Days are upon us!'

'The Shrike gave me pain,' said Duré. 'Pain and suffering beyond imagination. I *have* met the thing twice, and I know in my heart that it is neither divine nor diabolical, but merely some organic machine from a terrible future.'

'Bah!' The Bishop made a dismissive gesture, folded his arms, and stared out over the low balcony at nothing.

The Templar appeared shaken. After a moment, he raised his head and said softly, 'You had a question for me?'

Duré took a breath. 'I did. And sad news, I'm afraid. True Voice of the Tree Het Masteen is dead.'

'We know,' said the Templar.

Duré was surprised. He could not imagine how they could receive that information. But it did not matter now. 'What I need to know, is why did he go on the pilgrimage? What was the mission that he did not live to see completed?

Each of us told our . . . our story. Het Masteen did not. Yet somehow I feel that his fate held the key to many mysteries.'

The Bishop looked back at Duré and sneered. 'We need tell you nothing, priest of a dead religion.'

Sek Hardeen sat silent a long moment before responding. 'M Masteen volunteered to be the one to carry the Word of the Muir to Hyperion. The prophecy has lain in the roots of our belief for centuries that when the troubled times came, a True Voice of the Tree would be called upon to take a treeship to the Holy World, to see it destroyed there, and then to have it reborn carrying the message of Atonement and the Muir.'

'So Het Masteen knew that the treeship *Yggdrasill* would be destroyed in orbit?'

'Yes. It was foretold.'

'And he and the single energy-binder erg from the ship were to fly a new treeship?'

'Yes,' said the Templar almost inaudibly. 'A Tree of Atonement which the Avatar would provide.'

Duré sat back, nodded. 'A Tree of Atonement. The thorn tree. Het Masteen was psychically injured when the *Yggdrasill* was destroyed. Then he was taken to the Valley of the Time Tombs and shown the Shrike's thorn tree. But he was not ready or able to do it. The thorn tree is a structure of death, of suffering, of pain . . . Het Masteen was not prepared to captain it. Or perhaps he refused. In any case, he fled. And died. I thought as much . . . but I had no idea what fate the Shrike had offered him.'

'What are you talking about?' snapped the Bishop. 'The Tree of Atonement is described in the prophecies. It will accompany the Avatar in his final harvest. Masteen would have been prepared and honored to captain it through space and time.'

Paul Duré shook his head.

'We have answered your question?' asked M Hardeen.

'Yes.'

413

'Then you must answer ours,' said the Bishop. 'What has happened to the Mother?'

'What mother?'

'The Mother of Our Salvation. The Bride of Atonement. The one you called Brawne Lamia.'

Duré thought back, trying to remember the Consul's taped summaries of the tales the pilgrims had told on the way to Hyperion. Brawne had been pregnant with the first Keats cybrid's child. The Shrike Temple on Lusus had saved her from the mob, included her in the pilgrimage. She had said something in her story about the Shrike Cultists treating her with reverence. Duré tried to fit all this into the confused mosaic of what he had already learned. He could not. He was too tired . . . and, he thought, too stupid after this so-called resurrection. He was not and never would be the intellectual Paul Duré once had been.

'Brawne was unconscious,' he said. 'Evidently taken by the Shrike and attached to some . . . *thing*. Some cable. Her mental state was the equivalent of brain death, but the fetus was alive and healthy.'

'And the persona she carried?' asked the Bishop, his voice tense.

Duré remembered what Severn had told him about the death of that persona in the megasphere. Evidently these two did not know about the second Keats persona – the Severn personality that at this moment was warning Gladstone about the dangers of the Core proposal. Duré shook his head. He was very tired. 'I don't know about the persona she carried in the Schrön loop,' he said. 'The cable . . . the thing the Shrike attached to her . . . seemed to plug into the neural socket like a cortical shunt.'

The Bishop nodded, evidently satisfied. 'The prophecies proceed apace. You have served your purpose as messenger, Duré. I must leave now.' The big man stood, nodded toward the True Voice of the Worldtree, and swept across the platform and down the stairs toward the elevator and terminex.

Duré sat across from the Templar in silence for several minutes. The sound of leaves blowing and the gentle rocking of the treetop platform was marvelously lulling, inviting the Jesuit to doze off. Above them the sky was fading through delicate saffron shades as the world of God's Grove turned into twilight.

'Your statement about a *deus ex machina* misleading us for generations through false prophecies was a terrible heresy,' the Templar said at last.

'Yes. But terrible heresies have proven to be grim truths many times before in the longer history of my Church, Sek Hardeen.'

'If you were a Templar, I could have you put to death,' the hooded figure said softly.

Duré sighed. At his age, in his situation, and as tired as he was, the thought of death created no fear in his heart. He stood and bowed slightly. 'I need to go, Sek Hardeen. I apologize if anything I said offended you. It is a confused and confusing time.' *'The best lack all conviction,'* he thought, *'while the worst are full of passionate intensity.'*

Duré turned and walked to the edge of the platform. And stopped.

The staircase was gone. Thirty vertical meters and fifteen horizontal meters of air separated him from the next lower platform where the elevator waited. The Worldtree dropped away a kilometer or more into leafy depths beneath him. Duré and the True Voice of that Tree were isolated here on the highest platform. Duré walked to a nearby railing, raised his suddenly sweaty face to the evening breeze, and noticed the first of the stars emerging from the ultramarine sky. 'What's going on, Sek Hardeen?'

The robed and cowled figure at the table was wrapped in darkness. 'In eighteen minutes, standard, the world of Heaven's Gate will fall to the Ousters. Our prophecies say that it will be destroyed. Certainly its farcaster will, and its fatline transmitters, and to all intents and purposes, that world will have ceased to exist. Precisely one standard hour later, the skies of God's Grove will be alight from the fusion fires of Ouster warships. Our prophecies say that all of the Brotherhood who remain – and anyone else, although all Hegemony citizens have long since been evacuated by farcaster – will perish.'

Duré walked slowly back to the table. 'It's imperative that I 'cast to Tau Ceti Center,' he said. 'Severn . . . someone is waiting for me. I have to speak to CEO Gladstone.'

'No,' said True Voice of the Worldtree Sek Hardeen. 'We will wait. We will see if the prophecies are correct.'

The Jesuit clenched his fists in frustration, fighting the surge of violent emotion that made him want to strike the robed figure. Duré closed his eyes and said two Hail Marys. It didn't help.

'Please,' he said. 'The prophecies will be confirmed or denied whether I am here or not. And then it will be too late. The FORCE torchships will blow the singularity sphere, and the farcaster will be gone. We'll be cut off from the Web for years. Billions of lives may depend upon my immediate return to Tau Ceti Center.'

The Templar folded his arms so that his long-fingered hands disappeared in the folds of his robe. 'We will wait,' he said. 'All things predicted will come to pass. In minutes, the Lord of Pain will be loosed on those in the Web. I do not believe in the Bishop's faith that those who have sought Atonement will be spared. We are better off here, Father Duré, where the end will be swift and painless.'

Duré searched his tired mind for something decisive to say, to do. Nothing occurred to him. He sat at the table and stared at the cowled and silent figure across from him. Above them, the stars emerged in their fiery multitudes. The world-forest of God's Grove rustled a final time to the evening breeze and seemed to hold its breath in anticipation.

Paul Duré closed his eyes and prayed.

THIRTY-SEVEN

We walk all day, Hunt and I, and toward evening we find an inn with food set out for us – a fowl, rice pudding, cauliflower, a dish of macaroni, and so forth – although there are no people here, no sign of people other than the fire in the hearth, burning brightly as if just lit, and the food still warm on the stove.

Hunt is unnerved by it; by it and by the terrible withdrawal symptoms he is suffering from the loss of contact with the datasphere. I can imagine his pain. For a person born and raised into a world where information was always at hand, communication with anyone anywhere a given, and no distance more than a farcaster step away, this sudden regression to life as our ancestors had known it would be like suddenly awakening blind and crippled. But after the rantings and rages of the first few hours of walking, Hunt finally settled down into a taciturn gloom.

'But the CEO *needs* me!' he had shouted that first hour.

'She needs the information I was bringing her,' I said, 'but there's nothing to be done about it.'

'Where *are* we?' demanded Hunt for the tenth time.

I had already explained about this alternate Old Earth, but I knew he meant something else now.

'Quarantine, I think,' I said.

'The Core brought us here?' demanded Hunt.

'I can only assume.'

'How do we get back?'

417

'I don't know. I presume that when they feel it's safe to allow us out of quarantine, a farcaster will appear.'

Hunt cursed softly. 'Why quarantine *me*, Severn?'

I shrugged. I assumed it was because he had heard what I said on Pacem, but I was not certain. I was certain of nothing.

The road led through meadows, vineyards, winding over low hills and twisting through valleys where glimpses of the sea were visible.

'Where does this road go?' Hunt demanded just before we discovered the inn.

'All roads lead to Rome.'

'I'm serious, Severn.'

'So am I, M Hunt.'

Hunt pried a loose stone from the highway and threw it far into the bushes. Somewhere a thrush called.

'You've been here before?' Hunt's tone was one of accusation, as if I had pirated him away. Perhaps I had.

'No,' I said. But *Keats* had, I almost added. My transplanted memories surged to the surface, almost overwhelming me with their sense of loss and looming mortality. So far from friends, so far from Fanny, his one eternal love.

'You're sure you can't access the datasphere?' asked Hunt.

'I'm positive,' I answered. He did not ask about the megasphere, and I did not offer the information. I am terrified of entering the megasphere, of losing myself there.

We found the inn just at sunset. It was nestled in a small valley, and smoke rose from the stone chimney.

While eating, darkness pressing against the panes, our only light the flicker of the fire and two candles on a stone mantle, Hunt said, 'This place makes me half believe in ghosts.'

'I do believe in ghosts,' I said.

Night. I awake coughing, feel wetness on my bare chest, hear Hunt fumbling with the candle, and in its light, look down to see blood on my skin, spotting the bedclothes.

'My God,' breathes Hunt, horrified. 'What is it? What's going on?'

'Hemorrhage,' I manage after the next fit of coughing leaves me weaker and spotted with more blood. I start to rise, fall back on the pillow, and gesture toward the basin of water and towel on the nightstand.

'Damn, damn,' mutters Hunt, searching for my comlog to get a med reading. There is no comlog. I had thrown away Hoyt's useless instrument while we were walking earlier in the day.

Hunt removes his own comlog, adjusts the monitor, and wraps it around my wrist. The readings are meaningless to him, other than to signify urgency and the need for immediate medical care. Like most people of his generation, Hunt had never seen illness or death – that was a professional matter handled out of sight of the populace.

'Never mind,' I whisper, the siege of coughing past but weakness lying on me like a blanket of stones. I gesture toward the towel again, and Hunt moistens it, washes the blood from my chest and arms, helps me sit in the single chair while he removes the spattered sheets and blankets.

'Do you know what's going on?' he asks, real concern in his voice.

'Yes.' I attempt a smile. 'Accuracy. Verisimilitude. Ontogeny recapitulating phylogeny.'

'Make sense,' snaps Hunt, helping me back into the bed. 'What caused the hemorrhage? What can I do to help?'

'A glass of water, please.' I sip it, feel the boiling in my chest and throat but manage to avoid another round of coughing. My belly feels as if it's on fire.

'What's going on?' Hunt asks again.

I talk slowly, carefully, setting each word in place as if placing my feet on soil strewn with mines. The coughing does not return. 'It's an illness called consumption,' I say. 'Tuberculosis. The final stages, judging from the severity of the hemorrhage.'

Hunt's basset-hound face is white. 'Good God, Severn. I never heard of tuberculosis.' He raises his wrist as if to consult his comlog memory but the wrist is bare.

I return his instrument. 'Tuberculosis has been absent for centuries. Cured. But John Keats had it. Died of it. And this cybrid body belongs to Keats.'

Hunt stands as if ready to rush out the door seeking help. 'Surely the Core will allow us to return now! They can't keep you here on this empty world where there's no medical assistance!'

I lay my head back in the soft pillows, feeling the feathers under the ticking. 'That may be precisely why I am being kept here. We'll see tomorrow when we arrive in Rome.'

'But you can't travel! We won't be going anywhere in the morning.'

'We'll see,' I say and close my eyes. 'We'll see.'

In the morning a *vettura*, a small carriage, is waiting outside the inn. The horse is a large gray mare, and it rolls its eyes at us as we approach. The creature's breath rises in the chill morning air.

'Do you know what that *is*?' says Hunt.

'A horse.'

Hunt raises a hand toward the animal as if it will pop and disappear like a soap bubble when he touches its flank. It does not. Hunt snatches his hand back as the mare's tail flicks.

'Horses are *extinct*,' he says. 'They've never been ARNied back into existence.'

'This one looks real enough,' I say, climbing into the carriage and sitting on the narrow bench there.

Hunt gingerly takes his seat beside me, his long fingers twitching with anxiety. 'Who drives?' he says. 'Where are the controls?'

There are no reins, and the coachman's seat is quite empty. 'Let's see if the horse knows the way,' I suggest, and at that instant we start moving at a leisurely pace, the spring-less carriage jolting over the stones and furrows of the rough road.

'This is some sort of joke, isn't it?' asks Hunt, staring at the flawless blue sky and distant fields.

I cough as lightly and briefly as possible into a handker-chief I have made from a towel borrowed from the inn. 'Possibly,' I say. 'But then, what isn't?'

Hunt ignores my sophistry, and we rumble on, jolting and bouncing toward whatever destination and destiny await.

'Where are Hunt and Severn?' asked Meina Gladstone.

Sedeptra Akasi, the young black woman who was Glad-stone's second most important aide, leaned closer so as not to interrupt the flow of the military briefing. 'Still no word, M Executive.'

'That's impossible. Severn had a tracer and Leigh step-ped through to Pacem almost an hour ago. Where the hell are they?'

Akasi glanced toward the faxpad she had unfolded on the tabletop. 'Security can't find them. The transit police can't locate them. The farcaster unit recorded only that they coded TC^2 – here – stepped through, but did not arrive.'

'That's impossible.'

'Yes, M Executive.'

'I want to talk to Albedo or one of the other AI Councilors as soon as this meeting is over.'

'Yes.'

Both women returned their attention to the briefing. The Government House Tactical Center had been joined to the Olympus Command Center War Room and to the largest Senate briefing room with fifteen-meter-square, visually open portals so that the three spaces created one cavernous and asymetrical conference area. The War Room holos seemed to rise into infinity on the display end of the space, and columns of data floated everywhere along the walls.

'Four minutes until cislunar incursion,' said Admiral Singh.

'Their long-range weapons could have opened up on Heaven's Gate long before this,' said General Morpurgo. 'They seem to be showing some restraint.'

'They didn't show much restraint toward our torchships,' said Garion Persov of Diplomacy. The group had been assembled an hour earlier when the sortie of the hastily assembled fleet of a dozen Hegemony torchships had been summarily destroyed by the advancing Swarm. Long-range sensors had relayed the briefest image of that Swarm – a cluster of embers with cometlike fusion tails – before the torchships and their remotes quit broadcasting. There had been many, many embers.

'Those were warships,' said General Morpurgo. 'We've been broadcasting for hours now that Heaven's Gate is an open planet. We can hope for restraint.'

The holographic images of Heaven's Gate surrounded them: the quiet streets of Mudflat, airborne images of the coastline, orbital images of the gray-brown world with its constant cloud cover, cislunar images of the baroque dodecahedron of the singularity sphere which tied together all farcasters, and space-aimed telescopic, UV, and X-ray images of the advancing Swarm – much larger than specks or embers now, at less than one AU. Gladstone looked up at the fusion tails of Ouster warships, the tumbling, containment-field-shimmering massiveness of their asteroid farms and bubble worlds, their complex and oddly non-human zero-gravity city complexes, and she thought, *What if I am wrong?*

The lives of billions rested on her belief that the Ousters would not wantonly destroy Hegemony worlds.

'Two minutes until incursion,' Singh said in his professional warrior's monotone.

'Admiral,' said Gladstone, 'is it absolutely necessary to

destroy the singularity sphere as soon as the Ousters have penetrated our *cordon sanitaire?* Couldn't we wait another few minutes to judge their intentions?'

'No, CEO,' answered the Admiral promptly. 'The farcaster link must be destroyed as soon as they are within quick assault range.'

'But if your remaining torchships don't do it, Admiral, we still have the in-system links, the fatline relays, and the timed devices, don't we?'

'Yes, M Executive, but we *must* assure that all farcaster capability is removed before the Ousters overrun the system. There can be no compromising this already slim safety margin.'

Gladstone nodded. She understood the need for absolute caution. *If only there were more time.*

'Fifteen seconds until incursion and singularity destruction,' said Singh. 'Ten . . . seven . . .'

Suddenly all of the torchship and cislunar remote holos glowed violet, red, and white.

Gladstone leaned forward. 'Was that the singularity sphere going?'

The military men buzzed amongst themselves, calling up further data, switching images on the holos and screens. 'No, CEO,' answered Morpurgo. 'The torchships are under attack. What you're seeing is their defensive fields overloading. The . . . ah . . . *there.*'

A central image, possibly from a low orbital relay ship, showed an enhanced image of the dodecahedronal singularity containment sphere, its thirty thousand square meters of surface still intact, still glowing in the harsh light of Heaven's Gate's sun. Then, suddenly, the glow increased, the nearest face of the structure seemed to become incandescent and sag in upon itself, and less than three seconds later the sphere expanded as the caged singularity there escaped and devoured itself as well as everything within a six-hundred-kilometer radius.

At the same instant, most of the visual images and many of the data columns went blank.

'All farcaster connections terminated,' announced Singh. 'In-system data now relayed by fatline transmitters only.'

There was a buzz of approval and relief from the military people, something closer to a sigh and soft moan from the dozens of senators and political advisors present. The world of Heaven's Gate had just been amputated from the Web . . . the first such loss of a Hegemony world in more than four centuries.

Gladstone turned to Sedeptra Akasi. 'What is travel time to Heaven's Gate from the Web now?'

'By Hawking drive, seven months onboard,' said the aide without a pause to access, 'a little over nine years time-debt.'

Gladstone nodded. Heaven's Gate was now nine years distant from the nearest Web world.

'There go our torchships,' intoned Singh. The view had been from one of the orbital pickets, relayed through the jerky, false-color images of high-speed fatline squirts being computer processed in rapid progression. The images were visual mosaics, but they always made Gladstone think of the earliest silent films from the dawn of the Media Age. But this was no Charlie Chaplin comedy. Two, then five, then eight bursts of brilliant light blossomed against the starfield above the limb of the planet.

'Transmissions from HS *Niki Weimart*, HS *Terrapin*, HS *Cornet*, and HS *Andrew Paul* have ceased,' reported Singh.

Barbre Dan-Gyddis raised a hand. 'What about the other four ships, Admiral?'

'Only the four mentioned had FTL-comm capability. The pickets confirm that radio, maser, and wideband commlinks from the other four torchships also have ceased. The visual data . . .' Singh stopped and gestured toward the image relayed from the automatic picket ship: eight expanding and fading circles of light, a starfield crawling with fusion tails and new lights. Suddenly even that image went blank.

'All orbital sensors and fatline relays terminated,' said General Morpurgo. He gestured, and the blackness was replaced with images of the streets of Heaven's Gate with the inevitable low-lying clouds. Aircraft added shots above the clouds – a sky gone crazy with moving stars.

'All reports confirm total destruction of the singularity sphere,' said Singh. 'Advance units of the Swarm now entering high orbit around Heaven's Gate.'

'How many people are left there?' asked Gladstone. She was leaning forward, her elbows on the table, her hands folded very tightly.

'Eighty-six thousand seven hundred and eighty-nine,' said Defense Minister Imoto.

'That doesn't count the twelve thousand Marines who were farcast in during the past two hours,' added General Van Zeidt.

Imoto nodded toward the General.

Gladstone thanked them and returned her attention to the holos. The data columns floating above and their extracts on the faxpads, comlogs, and table panels held the pertinent data – numbers of Swarm craft now in-system, number and types of ships in orbit, projected braking orbits and time curves, energy analyses and comm-band intercepts – but Gladstone and the others were watching the relatively uninformative and unchanging fatlined images from the aircraft and surface cameras: stars, cloud tops, streets, the view from Atmospheric Generating Station Heights out over the Mudflat Promenade where Gladstone herself had stood less than twelve hours earlier. It was night there. Giant horsetail ferns moved to silent breezes blowing in from the bay.

'I think they'll negotiate,' Senator Richeau was saying. 'First they'll present us with this *fait accompli*, nice worlds overrun, then they'll negotiate and negotiate hard for a new balance of power. I mean, even if both of their invasion waves succeeded, that would be twenty-five worlds out of almost two hundred in the Web and Protectorate.'

425

'Yes,' said Head of Diplomacy Persov, 'but don't forget, Senator, that these include some of our most strategically important worlds . . . *this* one, for example. TC^2 is only two hundred and thirty-five hours behind Heaven's Gate on the Ouster timetable.'

Senator Richeau stared Persov down. 'I'm well aware of that,' she said coldly. 'I'm merely saying that the Ousters cannot have true conquest on their minds. That would be pure folly on their part. Nor will FORCE allow the second wave to penetrate so deeply. Certainly this so-called invasion is a prelude to negotiation.'

'Perhaps,' said Nordholm's Senator Roanquist, 'but such negotiations would necessarily depend upon—'

'Wait,' said Gladstone.

The data columns now showed more than a hundred Ouster warcraft in orbit around Heaven's Gate. Ground forces there had been instructed not to fire unless fired upon, and no activity was visible in the thirty-some views being fatlined to the War Room. Suddenly, however, the cloud cover above Mudflat City glowed as if giant searchlights had been turned on. A dozen broad beams of coherent light stabbed down into the bay and the city, continuing the searchlight illusion, appearing to Gladstone as if giant white columns had been erected between the ground and the ceiling of clouds.

That illusion ended abruptly as a whirlwind of flame and destruction erupted at the base of each of these hundred-meter-wide columns of light. The water of the bay boiled until huge geysers of steam occluded the nearer cameras. The view from the heights showed century-old stone buildings in the town erupting into flame, imploding as if a tornado were moving against them. The Web-famous gardens and commons of the Promenade erupted in flame, exploded in dirt and flying debris as if an invisible plow were moving across them. Horsetail ferns two centuries old bent as if before a hurricane wind, burst into flame, and were gone.

'Lances from a *Bowers*-class torchship,' Admiral Singh said into the silence. 'Or its Ouster equivalent.'

The city was burning, exploding, being plowed into rubble by the light columns and then being torn asunder again. There were no audio channels on these fatlined images, but Gladstone imagined that she could hear screams.

One by one, the ground cameras went black. The view from the Atmospheric Generating Station Heights disappeared in a white flash. Airborne cameras were already gone. The twenty or so other ground-based images began winking out, one in a terrible burst of crimson that left everyone in the room rubbing their eyes.

'Plasma explosion,' said Van Zeidt. 'Low megaton range.' The view had been of a FORCE:Marine air defense complex north of the Intercity Canal.

Suddenly all images ceased. Dataflow ended. The room lights began to come up to compensate for a darkness so sudden that it took everyone's breath away.

'The primary fatline transmitter's gone,' said General Morpurgo. 'It was at the main FORCE base near High Gate. Buried under our strongest containment field, fifty meters of rock, and ten meters of whiskered stalloy.'

'Shaped nuclear charges?' asked Barbre Dan-Gyddis.

'At least,' said Morpurgo.

Senator Kolchev rose, his Lusian bulk emanating an almost ursine sense of strength. 'All right. This isn't some goddamned negotiating ploy. The Ousters have just reduced a Web world to ashes. This is all-out, give-no-mercy warfare. The survival of civilization is at stake. What do we do now?'

All eyes turned toward Meina Gladstone.

The Consul dragged a semiconscious Theo Lane from the wreckage of the skimmer and staggered fifty meters with the younger man's arm over his shoulder before collapsing on a stretch of grass beneath trees along the bank of the Hoolie River. The skimmer was not on fire, but it lay crumpled against the collapsed stone wall where it had finally skidded to a halt. Bits of metal and ceramic polymers lay strewn along the riverbank and abandoned avenue.

The city was burning. Smoke obscured the view across the river, and this part of Jacktown, the Old Section, looked as if several pyres had been lighted where thick columns of black smoke rose toward the low cloud ceiling. Combat lasers and missile trails continued to streak through the haze, sometimes exploding against the assault dropships, parafoils, and suspension-field bubbles which continued to drop through the clouds like chaff blown from a recently harvested field.

'Theo, are you all right?'

The Governor-General nodded and moved to push his glasses higher on his nose . . . stopping in confusion as he realized that his glasses were gone. Blood streaked Theo's forehead and arms. 'Hit my head,' he said groggily.

'We need to use your comlog,' said the Consul. 'Get someone here to pick us up.'

Theo nodded, lifted his arm, and frowned at his wrist. 'Gone,' he said. 'Comlog's gone. Gotta look in the skimmer.' He tried to get to his feet.

The Consul pulled him back down. They were in the shelter of a few ornamental trees here, but the skimmer was exposed, and their landing had been no secret. The Consul had glimpsed several armored troops moving down an adjacent street as the skimmer pancaked in for its crash landing. They might be SDF or Ousters or even Hegemony Marines, but the Consul imagined that they would be trigger-happy whatever their loyalties.

'Never mind that,' he said. 'We'll get to a phone. Call the consulate.' He looked around, identified the section of warehouses and stone buildings where they had crashed. Upriver a few hundred meters, an old cathedral stood abandoned, its chapter house crumbling and overhanging the riverbank.

'I know where we are,' said the Consul. 'It's just a block or two to Cicero's. Come on.' He lifted Theo's arm over his head and on to his shoulders, pulling the injured man to his feet.

'Cicero's, good,' muttered Theo. 'Could use a drink.'

The rattle of fléchette fire and an answering sizzle of energy weapons came from the street to their south. The Consul took as much of Theo's weight as he could and half walked, half staggered along the narrow lane beside the river.

'Oh damn,' the Consul whispered.

Cicero's was burning. The old bar and inn – as old as Jacktown and much older than most of the capital – had lost three of its four sagging riverfront buildings to the flames, and only a determined bucket brigade of patrons was saving the last section.

'I see Stan,' said the Consul, pointing to the huge figure of Stan Leweski standing near the head of the bucket brigade line. 'Here.' The Consul helped Theo to a sitting position under an elm tree along the walkway. 'How's your head?'

'Hurts.'

'I'll be right back with help,' said the Consul and moved as quickly as he could down the narrow lane toward the men.

Stan Leweski stared at the Consul as if he were a ghost. The big man's face was streaked with soot and tears, and his eyes were wide, almost uncomprehending. Cicero's had been in his family for six generations. It was raining softly now, and the fire seemed beaten. Men shouted up and down the line as a few timbers from the burned-out sections sagged into the embers of the basement.

'By God, it's gone,' said Leweski. 'You see? Grandfather Jiri's addition? It's gone.'

The Consul grabbed the huge man by his shoulders. 'Stan, we need help. Theo's over there. Hurt. Our skimmer crashed. We need to get to the spaceport . . . to use your phone. It's an emergency, Stan.'

Leweski shook his head. 'Phone's gone. Comlog bands are jammed. Goddamn war is on.' He pointed toward the burned sections of the old inn. 'They're gone, by damn. *Gone*.'

The Consul made a fist, furious in the grip of sheer frutration. Other men milled around, but the Consul recognized none of them. There were no FORCE or SDF authorities in sight. Suddenly a voice behind him said, 'I can help. I have a skimmer.'

The Consul whirled to see a man in his late fifties or early sixties, soot and sweat covering his handsome face and streaking his wavy hair. 'Great,' said the Consul. 'I'd appreciate it.' He paused. 'Do I know you?'

'Dr Melio Arundez,' said the man, already moving toward the parkway where Theo rested.

'Arundez,' repeated the Consul, hurrying to keep up. The name echoed strangely. Someone he knew? Someone he should know? 'My God, Arundez!' he said. 'You were the friend of Rachel Weintraub when she came here decades ago.'

'Her university advisor, actually,' said Arundez. 'I know you. You went on the pilgrimage with Sol.' They stopped where Theo was sitting, still holding his head in his hands. 'My skimmer's over there,' said Arundez.

The Consul could see a small, two-person Vikken Zephyr parked under the trees. 'Great. We'll get Theo to the hospital and then I need to get to the spaceport immediately.'

'The hospital's overcrowded to the point of insanity,' said Arundez. 'If you're trying to get to your ship, I suggest you take the Governor-General there and use the ship's surgery.'

The Consul paused. 'How did you know I have a ship there?'

Arundez dilated the doors and helped Theo on to the narrow bench behind the front contour seats. 'I know all

430

about you and the other pilgrims, M Consul. I've been trying to get permission to go to the Valley of the Time Tombs for months. You can't believe my frustration when I learned that your pilgrims' barge left secretly with Sol abroad.' Arundez took a deep breath and asked a question which he obviously had been afraid to ask before. 'Is Rachel still alive?'

He was her lover when she was a grown woman, thought the Consul. 'I don't know,' he said. 'I'm trying to get back in time to help her, if I can.'

Melio Arundez nodded and settled into the driver's seat, gesturing for the Consul to get in. 'We'll try to get to the spaceport. It won't be easy with the fighting around there.'

The Consul sat back, feeling his bruises, cuts, and exhaustion as the seat folded around him. 'We need to get Theo . . . the Governor-General . . . to the consulate or government house or whatever they call it now.'

Arundez shook his head and powered up the repellors. 'Uh-uh. The consulate's gone, hit by a wayward missile, according to the emergency news channel. All the Hegemony officials went out to the spaceport for evacuation before your friend even went hunting for you.'

The Consul looked at the semiconscious Theo Lane. 'Let's go,' he said softly to Arundez.

The skimmer came under small-arms fire as they crossed the river, but fléchettes merely rattled on the hull and the single energy beam fired sliced beneath them, sending a spout of steam ten meters high. Arundez drove like a crazy person – weaving, bobbing, pitching, yawing, and occasionally slewing the skimmer around on its axis like a plate sliding atop a sea of marbles. The Consul's seat restraints closed around him, but he still felt his gorge threaten to rise. Behind them, Theo's head moved loosely back and forth on the car bench as he surrendered to unconsciousness.

'The downtown's a mess!' Arundez shouted over repellor roar. 'I'll follow the old viaduct to the spaceport highway and then cut across country, staying low.' They pirouetted around a burning structure which the Consul belatedly recognized as his old apartment building.

'Is the spaceport highway open?'

Arundez shook his head. 'Never make it. Paratroopers have been dropping around it for the last thirty minutes.'

'Are the Ousters trying to destroy the city?'

'Uh-uh. They could have done that from orbit without all this fuss. They seem to be investing the capital. Most of their dropships and paratroopers land at least ten klicks out.'

'Is it our SDF who's fighting back?'

Arundez laughed, showing white teeth against tanned skin. 'They're halfway to Endymion and Port Romance by now . . . though reports ten minutes ago, before the comm lines were jammed, say that those cities are also under attack. No, the little resistance you see is from a few dozen FORCE:Marines left behind to guard the city and the spaceport.'

'So the Ousters haven't destroyed or captured the spaceport?'

'Not yet. At least not as of a few minutes ago. We'll soon see. Hang on!'

The ten-kilometer ride to the spaceport via the VIP highway or the skylanes above it usually took a few minutes, but Arundez's roundabout, up-and-down approach over the hills, through the valleys, and between the trees added time and excitement to the trip. The Consul turned his head to watch hillsides and the slums of burning refugee camps flash by to his right. Men and women crouched against boulders and under low trees, covering their heads as the skimmer rushed past. Once the Consul saw a squad of FORCE:Marines dug in on a hilltop, but their attention was focused on a hill to the north from which there came a panoply of laser-lance fire. Arundez saw the Marines at the same instant and jinked the skimmer hard left, dropping it into a narrow ravine scant seconds before the treetops on the

432

ridge above were sliced off as if by invisible shears.

Finally they roared up and over a final ridgeline, and the western gates and fences of the spaceport became visible ahead of them. The perimeter was ablaze with the blue and violet glows of containment and interdiction fields, and they were still a klick away when a visible tightbeam laser flicked out, found them, and a voice over the radio said, 'Unidentified skimmer, land immediately or be destroyed.'

Arundez laughed.

The tree line ten meters away seemed to shimmer, and suddenly they were surrounded by wraiths in activated chameleon polymers. Arundez had opened the cockpit blisters, and now assault rifles were aimed at him and the Consul.

'Step away from the machine,' said a disembodied voice behind the camouflage shimmer.

'We have the Governor-General,' called the Consul. 'We have to get in.'

'The hell you say,' snapped a voice with a definite Web accent. 'Out!'

The Consul and Arundez hastily released their seat restraints and had started to climb out when a voice from the back seat snapped, 'Lieutenant Mueller, is that you?'

'Ah, yes, sir.'

'Do you recognize me, Lieutenant?'

The camouflage shimmer depolarized, and a young Marine in full battle armor stood not a meter from the skimmer. His face was nothing more than a black visor but the voice sounded young. 'Yes, sir . . . ah . . . Governor. Sorry I didn't recognize you without your glasses. You've been hurt, sir.'

'I know I've been hurt, Lieutenant. That is why these gentlemen have escorted me here. Don't you recognize the former Hegemony Consul for Hyperion?'

'Sorry, sir,' said Lieutenant Mueller, waving his men back into the tree line. 'The base is sealed.'

'Of *course* the base is sealed,' Theo said through gritted teeth. 'I countersigned those orders. But I also authorized evacuation of all essential Hegemony personnel. You *did* allow those skimmers through, did you not, Lieutenant Mueller?'

An armored hand rose as if to scratch the helmeted and visored head. 'Ah . . . yes, sir. Ah, affirmative. But that was an hour ago, sir. The evacuation dropships are gone and—'

'For God sake, Mueller, get on your tactical channel and get authorization from Colonel Gerasimov to let us through.'

'The Colonel's dead, sir. There was a dropship assault on the east perimeter, and—'

'Captain Lewellyn then,' said Theo. He swayed and then steadied himself against the back of the Consul's seat. His face was very white under the blood.

'Ah . . . tactical channels are down, sir. The Ousters are jamming on wideband with—'

'*Lieutenant*,' snapped Theo in a tone the Consul had never heard his young friend use, 'you've visually identified me and scanned my implant ID. Now either admit us to the field or shoot us.'

The armored Marine glanced back toward the tree line as if considering whether to order his men to open fire. 'The dropships are all gone, sir. Nothing else is coming down.'

Theo nodded. Blood had dried and caked on his forehead, but now a fresh trickle started from his scalp line. 'The impounded ship is still in Blast Pit Nine, isn't it?'

'Yes, *sir*,' answered Mueller, snapping to attention at last. 'But it's a civilian ship and could never make space with all the Ouster—'

Theo waved the officer into silence and gestured for Arundez to drive toward the perimeter. The Consul glanced ahead toward the deadlines, interdiction fields, containment fields, and probable pressure mines that the skimmer would encounter in ten seconds. He saw the Marine lieutenant wave, and an opening irised in the violet and blue energy fields ahead. No one fired. In half a minute they were crossing the hardpan of the spaceport itself. Something large was burning on the northern perimeter. To their left, a huddle of FORCE trailers and command modules had been slagged to a pool of bubbling plastic.

There had been people in there, thought the Consul and once again had to fight to keep his gorge from rising.

Blast Pit Seven had been destroyed, its circular walls of reinforced ten-centimeter carbon-carbon blown outward and apart as if they had been made of cardboard. Blast Pit Eight was burning with that white-hot incandescence which suggested plasma grenades. Blast Pit Nine was intact, with the bow of the Consul's ship just visible above the pit wall through the shimmer of a class-three containment field.

'The interdiction's been lifted?' said the Consul.

Theo lay back on the cushioned bench. His voice was thick. 'Yeah. Gladstone authorized the dropping of the restraining dome field. That's just the usual protective field. You can override it with a command.'

Arundez dropped the skimmer to tarmac just as warning lights went red and synthesized voices began describing malfunctions. They helped Theo out and paused near the rear of the small skimmer where a line of fléchettes had stitched a ragged row through the engine cowling and repellor housing. Part of the hood had melted from overload.

Melio Arundez patted the machine once, and both men turned to help Theo through the blast pit door and up the docking umbilical.

'My God,' said Dr Melio Arundez, 'this is beautiful. I've never been in a private interstellar spacecraft before.'

'There are only a few dozen in existence,' said the Consul, setting the osmosis mask in place over Theo's mouth and nose and gently lowering the redhead into the surgery's tank of emergency care nutrient. 'Small as it is, this ship cost

435

several hundred million marks. It's not cost-effective for corporations and Outback planetary governments to use their military craft on those rare occasions when they need to travel between the stars.' The Consul sealed the tank and conversed briefly with the diagnostics program. 'He'll be all right,' he said at last to Arundez, and returned to the holopit.

Melio Arundez stood near the antique Steinway, gently running his hand over the glossy finish of the grand piano. He glanced out through the transparent section of hull above the stowed balcony platform and said, 'I see fires near the main gate. We'd better get out of here.'

'That's what I'm doing,' said the Consul, gesturing Arundez toward the circular couch lining the projection pit.

The archaeologist dropped into the deep cushions and glanced around. 'Aren't there . . . ah . . . controls?'

The Consul smile. 'A bridge? Cockpit instruments? Maybe a wheel I can steer with? Uh-uh. Ship?'

'Yes,' came the soft voice from nowhere.

'Are we cleared for takeoff?'

'Yes.'

'Is that containment field removed?'

'It was our field. I've withdrawn it.'

'OK, let's get the hell out of here. I don't have to tell you that we're in the middle of a shooting war, do I?'

'No. I've been monitoring all developments. The last FORCE spacecraft are in the process of leaving the Hyperion system. These Marines are stranded and—'

'Save the tactical analyses for later, Ship,' said the Consul. 'Set our course for the Valley of the Time Tombs and get us out of here.'

'Yes, sir,' said the ship. 'I was just pointing out that the forces defending this spaceport have little chance of holding out for more than an hour or so.'

'Noted,' said the Consul. 'Now take off.'

'I'm required to share this fatline transmission first. The

436

squirt arrived at 1622:38:14, Web standard, this afternoon.'

'Whoa! Hold it!' cried the Consul, freezing the holo transmission in mid-construction. Half of Meina Gladstone's face hung above them. 'You're *required* to show this before we leave? Whose commands do you respond to, Ship?'

'CEO Gladstone's, sir. The Chief Executive empowered a priority override on all ships' functions five days ago. This fatline squirt is the last requirement before—'

'So that's why you didn't respond to my remote commands,' murmured the Consul.

'Yes,' said the ship in conversational tones. 'I was about to say that the showing of this transmission is the last requirement prior to returning command to you.'

'And then you'll do what I say?'

'Yes.'

'Take us where I'll tell you to?'

'Yes.'

'No hidden overrides?'

'None that I know of.'

'Play the squirt,' said the Consul.

The Lincolnesque countenance of CEO Meina Gladstone floated in the center of the projection pit with the telltale twitches and breakups endemic to fatline transmissions. 'I am pleased that you survived the visit to the Time Tombs,' she said to the Consul. 'By now you must know that I am asking you to negotiate with the Ousters *before* you return to the valley.'

The Consul folded his arms and glared at Gladstone's image. Outside the sun was setting. He had only a few minutes before Rachel Weintraub reached her birth hour and minute and simply ceased to exist.

'I understand your urgency to return and help your friends,' said Gladstone, 'but you can do nothing to help the child at this moment . . . experts in the Web assure us that neither cryogenic sleep nor fugue could arrest the Merlin's sickness. Sol knows this.'

Across the projection pit, Dr Arundez said, 'It's true. They experimented for years. She would die in fugue state.'

'. . . you *can* help the billions of people in the Web whom you believe you have betrayed,' Gladstone was saying.

The Consul leaned forward and rested his elbows on his knees and his chin on his fists. His heart was pounding very loudly in his ears.

'I knew that you would open the Time Tombs,' Gladstone said, her sad brown eyes seeming to stare directly at the Consul. 'Core predictors showed that your loyalty to Maui-Covenant . . . and to the memory of your grand-parents' rebellion . . . would override all other factors. It was *time* for the Tombs to be opened, and only you could activate the Ouster device before the Ousters themselves decided to.'

'I've heard enough of this,' said the Consul and stood, turning his back on the projection. 'Cancel message,' he said to the ship, knowing that it would not obey.

Melio Arundez walked through the projection and gripped the Consul's arm tightly. 'Hear her out. Please.'

The Consul shook his head but stayed in the pit, arms folded.

'Now the worst has happened,' said Gladstone. 'The Ousters are invading the Web. Heaven's Gate is being destroyed. God's Grove has less than an hour before the invasion sweeps over it. It is imperative that you meet with the Ousters in Hyperion System and negotiate . . . use your diplomatic skills to open a dialogue with them. The Ousters will not respond to our fatline or radio messages, but we have alerted them to your coming. I think they will still trust you.'

The Consul moaned and walked over to the piano, pounding his fist against its lid.

'We have minutes, not hours, Consul,' said Gladstone. 'I will ask you to go first to the Ousters in Hyperion System and then attempt to return to the Valley of the Time Tombs if you must. You know better than I the results of warfare. Millions will die needlessly if we cannot find a secure channel through which to communicate with the Ousters.

'It is your decision, but please consider the ramifications if we fail in this last attempt to find the truth and preserve the peace. I will contact you via fatline once you have reached the Ouster Swarm.'

Gladstone's image shimmered, fogged, and faded.

'Response?' asked the ship.

'No.' The Consul paced back and forth between the Steinway and the projection pit.

'No spacecraft or skimmer has landed near the valley with its crew intact for almost two centuries,' said Melio Arundez. 'She must know how small the odds are that you can go there . . . survive the Shrike . . . and then rendezvous with the Ousters.'

'Things are different now,' said the Consul without turning to face the other man. 'The time tides have gone berserk. The Shrike goes where it pleases. Perhaps whatever phenomenon prevented manned landings before is no longer operative.'

'And perhaps your ship will land perfectly without us,' said Arundez. 'Just as so many others have.'

'Goddammit,' shouted the Consul, wheeling, 'you knew the risks when you said that you wanted to join me!'

The archaeologist nodded calmly. 'I'm not talking about the risk to myself, sir. I'm willing to accept any risk if it means I might help Rachel . . . or even see her again. It's *your* life that may hold the key to humankind's survival.'

The Consul shook his fists in the air and paced back and forth like some caged predator. 'That's not *fair*! I was Gladstone's pawn before. She used me . . . cynically . . . deliberately. I *killed* four Ousters, Arundez. Shot them because I had to activate their goddamned device to open the Tombs. Do you think they'll welcome me back with open arms?'

The archaeologist's dark eyes looked up at the Consul without blinking. 'Gladstone believes that they will parley with you.'

'Who *knows* what they'll do? Or what Gladstone believes for that matter. The Hegemony and its relationship with the Ousters aren't my worry now. I sincerely wish a plague on both their houses.'

'To the extent that humanity suffers?'

'I don't know humanity,' said the Consul in an exhausted monotone. 'I do know Sol Weintraub. And Rachel. And an injured woman named Brawne Lamia. And Father Paul Duré. And Fedmahn Kassad. And—'

The ship's soft voice enveloped them. 'This spaceport's north perimeter has been breached. I am initiating final launch procedures. Please take your seats.'

The Consul half stumbled to the holopit even as the internal containment field pressed down on him as its vertical differential increased dramatically, sealing every object in its place and protecting the travelers far more securely than any straps or seat restraints could. Once in free-fall, the field would lessen but still serve in the stead of planetary gravity.

The air above the holopit misted and showed the blast pit and spaceport receding quickly below, the horizon and distant hills jerking and tilting as the ship threw itself through eighty-g evasive maneuvers. A few energy weapons winked in their direction, but data columns showed the external fields handling the neglible effects. Then the horizon receded and curved as the lapis lazuli sky darkened to the black of space.

'Destination?' queried the ship.

The Consul closed his eyes. Behind them, a chime sounded to announce that Theo Lane could be moved from the recovery tank to the main surgery.

'How long until we could rendezvous with elements of the Ouster invasion force?' asked the Consul.

'Thirty minutes to the Swarm proper,' answered the ship.

'And how long until we come in range of their attack ships' weapons?'

'They are tracking us now.'

Melio Arundez's expression was calm but his fingers were white on the back of the holopit couch.

'All right,' said the Consul. 'Make for the Swarm. Avoid Hegemony ships. Announce on all frequencies that we are an unarmed diplomatic ship requesting parley.'

'That message was authorized and set in by CEO Gladstone, sir. It is now being broadcast on fatline and all comm frequencies.'

'Carry on,' said the Consul. He pointed to Arundez's comlog. 'Do you see the time?'

'Yes. Six minutes until the precise instant of Rachel's birth.'

The Consul settled back, his eyes closed again. 'You've come a long way for nothing, Dr Arundez.'

The archaeologist stood, swayed a second before finding his legs in the simulated gravity, and carefully walked to the piano. He stood there a moment and looked out through the balcony window at the black sky and the still-brilliant limb of the receding planet. 'Perhaps not,' he said. 'Perhaps not.'

THIRTY-EIGHT

Today we entered the swampy wasteland which I recognize as the Campagna, and to celebrate I have another coughing fit, terminated by vomiting more blood. Much more. Leigh Hunt is beside himself with concern and frustration and, after holding my shoulders during the spasm and helping to clean my clothes with rags moistened in a nearby stream, he asks, 'What can I do?'

'Collect flowers from the fields,' I gasp. 'That's what Joseph Severn did.'

He turns away angrily, not realizing that even in my feverish, exhausted state, I was merely telling the truth.

The little cart and tired horse pass through the Campagna with more painful bumping and rattling than before. Late in the afternoon, we pass some skeletons of horses along the way, then the ruins of an old inn, then the more massive ruin of a viaduct overgrown with moss, and finally posts to which it appears that white sticks have been nailed.

'What on earth is that?' asks Hunt, not realizing the irony of the ancient phrase.

'The bones of bandits,' I answer truthfully.

Hunt looks at me as if my mind has succumbed to the sickness. Perhaps it has.

Later we climb out of the swamplands of the Campagna and get a glimpse of a flash of red moving far out among the fields.

'What is that?' demands Hunt eagerly, hopefully. I know that he expects to see people any moment and a functioning farcaster portal a moment after that.

'A cardinal,' I say, again telling the truth. 'Shooting birds.'

Hunt accesses his poor, crippled comlog. 'A cardinal *is* a bird,' he says.

I nod, look to the west, but the red is gone. 'Also a cleric,' I say. 'And we are approaching Rome, you know.'

Hunt frowns at me and attempts for the thousandth time to raise someone on the comm bands of his comlog. The afternoon is silent except for the rhythmic creak of the *vettura*'s wooden wheels and the trill of some distant songbird. A cardinal, perhaps?

We enter Rome as the first flush of evening touches the clouds. The little cart rocks and rumbles through the Lateran Gate, and almost immediately we are confronted with the sight of the Colosseum, overgrown with ivy and obviously the home of thousands of pigeons, but immensely more impressive than holos of the ruin, set now as it was, not within the grubby confines of a postwar city ringed with giant arcologies, but contrasted against clusters of small huts and open fields where the city ends and countryside begins. I can see Rome proper in the distance . . . a scattering of rooftops and smaller ruins on its fabled Seven Hills, but here the Colosseum rules.

'Jesus,' whispers Leigh Hunt. 'What is it?'

'The bones of bandits,' I say again slowly, fearful of starting the terrible coughing once again.

We move on, clopping through the deserted streets of nineteenth-century Old Earth Rome as the evening settles thick and heavy around us and the light fails and pigeons wheel above the domes and rooftops of the Eternal City.

'Where is everyone?' whispers Hunt. He sounds frightened.

'Not here because they are not needed,' I say. My voice sounds sharp edged in the canyon dusk of the city streets. The wheels turn on cobblestones now, hardly more smooth than the random stones of the highway we just escaped.

'Is this some stimsim?' he asks.

'Stop the cart,' I say, and the obedient horse comes to a halt. I point out a heavy stone by the gutter. 'Kick that,' I say to Hunt.

He frowns at me but steps down, approaches the stone, and gives it a hearty kick. More pigeons erupt skyward from bell towers and ivy, panicked by the echoes of his cursing.

'Like Dr Johnson, you've demonstrated the reality of things,' I say. 'This is no stimsim or dream. Or rather, no more one than the rest of our lives have been.'

'Why did they bring us here?' demands the CEO's aide, glancing skyward as if the gods themselves were listening just beyond the fading pastel barriers of the evening clouds. 'What do they want?'

They want me to die, I think, realizing the truth of it with the impact of a fist in my chest. I breathe slowly and shallowly to avoid a fit of coughing even as I feel the phlegm boil and bubble in my throat. *They want me to die and they want you to watch.*

The mare resumes its long haul, turning right on the next narrow street, then right again down a wider avenue filled with shadows and the echoes of our passing, and then stopping at the head of an immense flight of stairs.

'We're here,' I say and struggle to exit the cart. My legs are cramped, my chest aches, and my ass is sore. In my mind runs the beginning of a satirical ode to the joys of traveling.

Hunt steps out as stiffly as I had and stands at the head of the giant, bifurcated staircase, folding his arms and glaring at them as if they are a trap or illusion. 'Where, exactly, is *here*, Severn?'

I point to the open square at the foot of the steps. 'The Piazza di Spagna,' I say. It is suddenly strange to hear Hunt call me *Severn*. I realize that the name ceased to be mine when we passed through the Lateran Gate. Or, rather, that my true name had suddenly become my own again.

444

'Before too many years pass,' I say, 'these will be called the Spanish Steps.' I start down the right bend in the staircase. A sudden dizziness causes me to stagger, and Hunt moves quickly to take my arm.

'You can't walk,' he says. 'You're too ill.'

I point to a mottled old building forming a wall to the opposite side of the broad steps and facing the Piazza. 'It's not far, Hunt. There is our destination.'

Gladstone's aide turns his scowl toward the structure. 'And what is there? Why are we stopping there? What awaits us there?'

I cannot help but smile at this least poetic of men's unconscious use of assonance. I suddenly imagine us sitting up long nights in that dark hulk of a building as I teach him how to pair such technique with masculine or feminine caesura, or the joys of alternating iambic foot with unstressed pyrrhic, or the self-indulgence of the frequent spondee.

I cough, continue coughing, and do not cease until blood is spattering my palm and shirt.

Hunt helps me down the steps, across the Piazza where Bernini's boat-shaped fountain gurgles and burbles in the dusk, and then, following my pointing finger, leads me into the black rectangle of the doorway – the doorway to Number 26 Piazza di Spagna – and I think, without volition, of Dante's *Commedia* and seem to see the phrase 'LASCIATE OGNE SPERANZA, VOI CH'INTRATE' – *'Abandon Every Hope, Who Enter Here'* – chiseled above the cold lintel of the doorway.

Sol Weintraub stood at the entrance to the Sphinx and shook his fist at the universe as night fell and the Tombs glowed with the brilliance of their opening and his daughter did not return.

Did not return.

The Shrike had taken her, lifted her newborn body in its palm of steel, and then stepped back into the radiance which

445

even now pushed Sol away like some terrible, bright wind from the depths of the planet. Sol pressed against the hurricane of light, but it kept him out as surely as might a runaway containment field.

Hyperion's sun had set, and now a cold wind blew from the barrens, driven in from the desert by a front of cold air sliding down the mountains to the south, and Sol turned to stare as vermilion dust blew into the searchlight glare of the opening Time Tombs.

The opening Tombs!

Sol squinted against the cold brilliance and looked down the valley to where the other Tombs glowed like pale green jack-o'-lanterns behind their curtain of blown dust. Light and long shadows leaped across the valley floor while the clouds were drained of the last of their sunset color overhead, and night came in with the howling wind.

Something was moving in the entrance of the second structure, the Jade Tomb. Sol staggered down the steps of the Sphinx, glancing up at the entrance where the Shrike had disappeared with his daughter, and then he was off the stairway, running past the Sphinx's paws and stumbling down the windblown path toward the Jade Tomb.

Something moved slowly from the oval doorway, was silhouetted by the shaft of light emanating from the tomb, but Sol could not tell if it was human or not, Shrike or not. If it was the Shrike, he would seize it with his bare hands, shake it until it either returned his daughter to him or until one of them was dead.

It was not the Shrike.

Sol could see the silhouette as human now. The person staggered, leaned against the Jade Tomb's doorway as if injured or tired.

It was a young woman.

Sol thought of Rachel here in this place more than half a standard century earlier, the young archaeologist researching these artifacts and never guessing the fate awaiting her in the form of Merlin's sickness. Sol had always imagined his child being saved by the sickness being canceled, the infant aging normally again, the child-who-would-some-day-be-Rachel given back her life. But what if Rachel returned as the twenty-six-year-old Rachel who had entered the Sphinx?

Sol's pulse was pounding so loudly in his ears that he could not hear the wind rage around him. He waved at the figure, half-obscured now by the dust storm.

The young woman waved back.

Sol raced forward another twenty meters, stopped thirty meters from the tomb, and cried out. 'Rachel! Rachel!'

The young woman silhouetted against the roaring light moved away from the doorway, touched her face with both hands, shouted something lost in the wind, and began to descend the stairs.

Sol ran, tripping over rocks as he lost the path and stumbled blindly across the valley floor, ignored the pain as his knee struck a low boulder, found the true path again, and ran to the base of the Jade Tomb, meeting her as she emerged from the cone of expanding light.

She fell just as Sol reached the bottom of the stairs, and he caught her, lowered her gently to the ground as blown sand rasped against his back and the time tides whirled about them in unseen eddies of vertigo and *déjà vu*.

'It *is* you,' she said and raised a hand to touch Sol's cheek. 'It's real. I'm back.'

'Yes, Brawne,' said Sol, trying to hold his voice steady, brushing matted curls from Brawne Lamia's face. He held her firmly, his arm on his knee, propping her head, his back bent to provide more shelter from the wind and sand. 'It's all right, Brawne,' he said softly, sheltering her, his eyes bright with tears of disappointment he would not let fall. 'It's all right. You're back.'

Meina Gladstone walked up the stairs of the cavernous War Room and stepped out into the corridor where long strips of

447

thick Perspex allowed a view down Mons Olympus to the Tharsis Plateau. It was raining far below, and from this vantage point almost twelve klicks high in the Martian sky, she could see pulses of lightning and curtains of static electricity as the storm dragged itself across the high steppes.

Her aide Sedeptra Akasi moved out into the corridor to stand silently next to the CEO.

'Still no word on Leigh or Severn?' asked Gladstone.

'None,' said Akasi. The young black woman's face was illuminated by both the pale light of the Home System's sun above and the play of lightning below. 'The Core authorities say that it may have been a farcaster malfunction.'

Gladstone showed a smile with no warmth. 'Yes. And can you remember any farcaster malfunction in our lifetime, Sedeptra? Anywhere in the Web?'

'No, M Executive.'

'The Core feels no need for subtlety. Evidently they think they can kidnap whomever they want and not be held accountable. They think we need them too much in our hour of extremis. And you know something, Sedeptra?'

'What?'

'They're right.' Gladstone shook her head and turned back toward the long descent into the War Room. 'It's less than ten minutes until the Ousters envelop God's Grove. Let's go down and join the others. Is my meeting with Councilor Albedo on immediately after this?'

'Yes, Meina. I don't think . . . I mean, some of us think that it is too risky to confront them directly like that.'

Gladstone paused before entering the War Room. 'Why?' she asked and this time her smile was sincere. 'Do you think the Core will disappear me the way they did Leigh and Severn?'

Akasi started to speak, stopped, and raised her palms.

Gladstone touched the younger woman on the shoulder. 'If they do, Sedeptra, it will be a mercy. But I think they will not. Things have gone so far that they believe that there is nothing an individual can do to change the course of events.' Gladstone withdrew her hand, her smile faded. 'And they may be right.'

Not speaking, the two descended to the circle of waiting warriors and politicians.

'The moment approaches,' said the True Voice of the Worldtree Sek Hardeen.

Father Paul Duré was brought back from his reverie. In the past hour, his desperation and frustration had descended through resignation to something akin to pleasure at the thought of having no more choices, no more duties to perform. Duré had been sitting in companionable silence with the leader of the Templar Brotherhood, watching the setting of God's Grove's sun and the proliferation of stars and lights in the night that were not stars.

Duré had wondered at the Templar's isolation from his people at such a crucial moment, but what he knew of Templar theology made Duré realize that the Followers of the Muir would meet such a moment of potential destruction alone on the most sacred platforms and in the most secret bowers of their most sacred trees. And the occasional soft comments Hardeen made into the cowl of his robe made Duré realize that the True Voice was in touch with fellow Templars via comlog or implants.

Still, it was a peaceful way to wait for the end of the world, sitting high in the known galaxy's tallest living tree, listening to a warm evening breeze rustle a million acres of leaves and watching stars twinkle and twin moons hurtle across a velvet sky.

'We have asked Gladstone and the Hegemony authorities to offer no resistance, to allow no FORCE warships insystem,' said Sek Hardeen.

'Is that wise?' asked Duré. Hardeen had told him earlier what the fate of Heaven's Gate had been.

'The FORCE fleet is not yet organized enough to offer

serious resistance,' answered the Templar. 'At least this way our world has some chance of being treated as a nonbelligerent.'

Father Duré nodded and leaned forward the better to see the tall figure in the shadows of the platform. Soft glow-globes in the branches below them were their only illumination other than the starlight and moonglow. 'Yet you welcomed this war. Aided the Shrike Cult authorities in bringing it about.'

'No, Duré. Not the war. The Brotherhood knew it must be part of the Great Change.'

'And what is that?' asked Duré.

'The Great Change is when humankind accepts its role as part of the natural order of the universe instead of its role as a cancer.'

'Cancer?'

'It is an ancient disease which—'

'Yes,' said Duré. 'I know what cancer was. How is it like humankind?'

Sek Hardeen's perfectly modulated, softly accented tones showed a hint of agitation. 'We have spread out through the galaxy like cancer cells through a living body, Duré. We multiply without thought to the countless life forms that must die or be pushed aside so that we may breed and flourish. We eradicate competing forms of intelligent life.'

'Such as?'

'Such as the Seneschai empaths on Hebron. The marsh centaurs of Garden. The *entire ecology* was destroyed on Garden, Duré, so that a few thousand human colonists might live where millions of native life forms once had thrived.'

Duré touched his cheek with a curled finger. 'That is one of the drawbacks of terraforming.'

'We did not terraform Whirl,' the Templar said quickly, 'but the Jovian life forms there were hunted to extinction.'

'But no one ascertained that the zeplens were intelligent,'

450

said Duré, hearing the lack of conviction in his own voice.

'They sang,' said the Templar. 'They called across thousands of kilometers of atmosphere to each other in songs which held meaning and love and sorrow. Yet they were hunted to death like the great whales of Old Earth.'

Duré folded his hands. 'Agreed, there have been injustices. But surely there is a better way to right them than to support the cruel philosophy of the Shrike Cult . . . and to allow this war to go on.'

The Templar's hood moved back and forth. 'No. If these were mere human injustices, other remedies could be found. But much of the illness . . . much of the insanity which has led to the destruction of races and the despoiling of worlds . . . this has come from the sinful symbiosis.'

'Symbiosis?'

'Humankind and the TechnoCore,' said Sek Hardeen in the harshest tones Duré had ever heard a Templar use. 'Man and his machine intelligences. Which is a parasite on the other? Neither part of the symbiote can now tell. But it is an evil thing, a work of the Anti-Nature. Worse than that, Duré, it is an evolutionary dead end.'

The Jesuit stood and walked to the railing. He looked out over the darkened world of treetops spreading out like cloud tops in the night. 'Surely there is a better way than turning to the Shrike and interstellar war.'

'The Shrike is a catalyst,' said Hardeen. 'It is the cleansing fire when the forest has been stunted and allowed to grow diseased by overplanting. There will be hard times, but the results will be new growth, new life, and a proliferation of species . . . not merely elsewhere but in the community of humankind itself.'

'Hard times,' mused Duré. 'And your Brotherhood is willing to see billions of people die to accomplish this . . . weeding out?'

The Templar clenched his fists. 'That will not occur. The Shrike is the warning. Our Ouster brethren seek only to control Hyperion and the Shrike long enough to strike at the TechnoCore. It will be a surgical procedure . . . the destruction of a symbiote and the rebirth of humankind as distinct partner in the cycle of life.'

Duré sighed. 'No one knows where the TechnoCore resides,' he said. 'How can the Ousters strike at it?'

'They will,' said the True Voice of the Worldtree, but there was less confidence in his voice than there had been a moment before.

'And was attacking God's Grove part of the deal?' asked the priest.

It was the Templar's turn to stand and pace, first to the railing, then back to the table. 'They will not attack God's Grove. That is what I have kept you here to see. Then you must report to the Hegemony.'

'They'll know at once whether the Ousters attack,' said Duré, puzzled.

'Yes, but they will not know *why* our world will be spared. You must bring this message. Explain this truth.'

'To hell with that,' said Father Paul Duré. 'I'm tired of being everyone's messenger. How do you know all this? The coming of the Shrike? The reason for the war?'

'There have been prophecies—' began Sek Hardeen.

Duré slammed his fist into the railing. How could he explain the manipulations of a creature who could – or at least was an agent of a force which could – manipulate time itself?

'You will see . . .' began the Templar again, and as if to punctuate his words there came a great, soft sound, almost as though a million hidden people had sighed and then moaned softly.

'Good God,' said Duré and looked to the west where it seemed that the sun was rising where it had disappeared less than an hour before. A hot wind rustled leaves and blew across his face.

Five blossoming and inward-curling mushroom clouds

climbed above the western horizon, turning night to day as they boiled and faded. Duré had instinctively covered his eyes until he realized that these explosions were so far away that although brilliant as the local sun, they would not blind him.

Sek Hardeen pulled back his cowl so that the hot wind ruffled his long, oddly greenish hair. Duré stared at the man's long, thin, vaguely Asian features and realized that he saw shock etched there. Shock and disbelief. Hardeen's cowl whispered with comm calls and the micro-babble of excited voices.

'Explosions on Sierra and Hokkaido,' whispered the Templar to himself. 'Nuclear explosions. From the ships in orbit.'

Duré remembered that Sierra was a continent, closed to outsiders, less than eight hundred kilometers from the Worldtree where they stood. He thought that he remembered that Hokkaido was the sacred isle where the potential treeships were grown and prepared.

'Casualties?' he asked, but before Hardeen could answer, the sky was slashed with brilliant light as a score or more tactical lasers, CPBs, and fusion lances cut a swath from horizon to horizon, switching and flashing like searchlights across the roof of the world forest that was God's Grove. And where the lance beams cut, flame erupted in their wake.

Duré staggered as a hundred-meter-wide beam skipped like a tornado through the forest less than a kilometer from the Worldtree. The ancient forest exploded in flame, creating a corridor of fire rising ten kilometers into the night sky. Wind roared past Duré and Sek Hardeen as air rushed in to feed the fire storm. Another beam slashed north and south, passing close to the Worldtree before disappearing over the horizon. Another swath of flame and smoke rose toward the treacherous stars.

'They promised,' gasped Sek Hardeen. 'The Ouster brethren *promised*!'

'You need help!' cried Duré. 'Ask the Web for emergency assistance.'

Hardeen grabbed Duré's arm, pulled him to the edge of the platform. The stairs were back in place. On the platform below, a farcaster portal shimmered.

'Only the advance units of the Ouster fleet have arrived,' cried the Templar over the sound of forests burning. Ash and smoke filled the air, drifting past amidst hot embers. 'But the singularity sphere will be destroyed any second. *Go!*'

'I'm not leaving without you,' called the Jesuit, sure that his voice could not be heard over the wind roar and terrible crackling. Suddenly, only kilometers to the east, the perfect blue circle of a plasma explosion expanded, imploded inward, then expanded again with visible concentric circles of shock wave. Kilometer-tall trees bent and broke in the first wave of the blast, their eastern sides exploding in flame, leaves flying off by the millions and adding to the almost solid wall of debris hurtling toward the Worldtree. Behind the circle of flame, another plasma bomb went off. Then a third.

Duré and the Templar fell down the steps and were blown across the lower platform like leaves on a sidewalk. The Templar grabbed a burning muirwood baluster, seized Duré's arm in an iron grip, and struggled to his feet, moving toward the still shimmering farcaster like a man leaning into a cyclone.

Half conscious, half aware of being dragged, Duré managed to get to his own feet just as Voice of the Worldtree Sek Hardeen pulled him to the edge of the portal. Duré clung to the portal frame, too weak to pull himself the final meter, and looked past the farcaster to see something which he would never forget.

Once, many, many years before, near his beloved Villefranche-sur-Saône, the youngster Paul Duré had stood on a cliff top, secure in the arms of his father and safe in a

454

thick concrete shelter, and watched through a narrow window as a forty-meter tall tsunami rushed toward the coast where they lived.

This tsunami was three kilometers high, was made of flame, and was racing at what seemed the speed of light across the helpless roof of the forest toward the Worldtree, Sek Hardeen, and Paul Duré. What the tsunami touched, it destroyed. It raged closer, rising higher and nearer until it obliterated the world and sky with flame and noise.

'No!' screamed Father Paul Duré.

'Go!' cried the True Voice of the Worldtree and pushed the Jesuit through the farcaster portal even as the platform, the Worldtree's trunk, and the Templar's robe burst into flames.

The farcaster shut down even as Duré tumbled through, slicing off the heel of his shoe as it contracted, and Duré felt his eardrums rupture and his clothes smolder even as he fell, struck something hard with the back of his head, and fell again into darkness more absolute.

Gladstone and the others watched in horrified silence as the civilian satellites sent images of the death throes of God's Grove through the farcaster relays.

'We have to blow it *now*,' cried Admiral Singh over the crackling of forests burning. Meina Gladstone thought that she could hear the screams of human beings and the countless arboreals who lived in the Templar forests.

'We can't let them get closer!' cried Singh. 'We have only the remotes to detonate the sphere.'

'Yes,' said Gladstone, but although her lips moved she heard no sound.

Singh turned and nodded toward a FORCE:space colonel. The Colonel touched his tactical board. The burning forests disappeared, the giant holos went absolutely dark, but the sound of screams somehow remained. Gladstone realized that it was the sound of blood in her ears.

She turned toward Morpurgo. 'How long . . .' She cleared her throat. 'General, how long until Mare Infinitus is attacked?'

'Three hours and fifty-two minutes, M Executive,' said the General.

Gladstone turned toward the former Commander William Ajunta Lee. 'Is your task force ready, Admiral?'

'Yes, CEO,' said Lee, his face pale beneath a tan.

'How many ships will be in the strike?'

'Seventy-four, M Executive.'

'And you will hit them away from Mare Infinitus?'

'Just within the Oört Cloud, M Executive.'

'Good,' said Gladstone. 'Good hunting, Admiral.'

The young man took this as his cue to salute and leave the chamber. Admiral Singh leaned over and whispered something to General Van Zeidt.

Sedeptra Akasi leaned toward Gladstone and said, 'Government House Security reports that a man just farcast into the secured GH terminex with an outdated priority access code. The man was injured, taken to the East Wing infirmary.'

'Leigh?' asked Gladstone? 'Severn?'

'No, M Executive,' said Akasi. 'The priest from Pacem. Paul Duré.'

Gladstone nodded. 'I'll see him after my meeting with Albedo,' she said to her aide. To the group, she announced, 'Unless anyone has anything to add to what we saw, we shall adjourn for thirty minutes and take up the defense of Asquith and Ixion when we reassemble.'

The group stood as the CEO and her entourage stepped through the permanent connecting portal to Government House and filed through a door in the far wall. The rumble of argument and shock resumed when Gladstone was out of sight.

Meina Gladstone sat back in her leather chair and closed her eyes for precisely five seconds. When she opened them, the cluster of aides still stood there, some looking anxious, some looking eager, all of them waiting for her next word, her next command.

'Get out,' she said softly. 'Go on, take a few minutes to get some rest. Put your feet up for ten minutes. There'll be no more rest for the next twenty-four to forty-eight hours.'

The group filed out, some looking on the verge of protest, others on the verge of collapse.

'Sedeptra,' said Gladstone, and the young woman stepped back into the office. 'Assign two of my personal guard to the priest who just came through, Duré.'

Akasi nodded and made a note on her faxpad.

'How is the political situation?' asked Gladstone, rubbing her eyes.

'The All Thing is chaos,' said Akasi. 'There are factions but they haven't coalesced into effective opposition yet. The Senate is a different story.'

'Feldstein?' said Gladstone, naming the angry senator from Barnard's World. Less than forty-two hours remained before Barnard's World would be attacked by the Ousters.

'Feldstein, Kakinuma, Peters, Sabenstorafem, Richeau . . . even Sudette Chier is calling for your resignation.'

'What about her husband?' Gladstone considered Senator Kolchev the most influential person in the Senate.

'No word from Senator Kolchev yet. Public or private.'

Gladstone tapped a thumbnail against her lower lip. 'How much time do you think this administration has before a vote of no confidence brings us down, Sedeptra?'

Akasi, one of the most astute political operatives Gladstone had ever worked with, returned her boss's stare. 'Seventy-two hours at the outside, CEO. The votes are there. The mob just doesn't know it's a mob yet. *Somebody* has to pay for what's happening.'

Gladstone nodded absently. 'Seventy-two hours,' she

murmured. 'More than enough time.' She looked up and smiled. 'That will be all, Sedeptra. Get some rest.'

The aide nodded but her expression showed her true opinion of that suggestion. It was very quiet in the study when the door closed behind her.

Gladstone sat thinking for a moment, her fist to her chin. Then she said to the walls, 'Bring Councilor Albedo here, please.'

Twenty seconds later, the air on the other side of Gladstone's broad desk misted, shimmered, and solidified. The representative of the TechnoCore looked as handsome as ever, short gray hair gleaming in the light, a healthy tan on his open, honest face.

'M Executive,' began the holographic projection, 'the Advisory Council and the Core predictors continue to offer their services in this time of great—'

'Where is the Core, Albedo?' interrupted Gladstone.

The Councilor's smile did not falter. 'I'm sorry, M Executive, what was the question?'

'The TechnoCore. Where is it?'

Albedo's friendly face showed a slight puzzlement but no hostility, no visible emotion other than bemused helpfulness. 'You're certainly aware, M Executive, that it has been Core policy since the Secession not to reveal the location of the . . . ah . . . physical elements of the Techno-Core. In another sense, the Core is nowhere, since—'

'Since you exist on the datumplane and datasphere consensual realities,' said Gladstone, voice flat. 'Yes, I've heard that crap all of my life, Albedo. So did my father and his father before him. I'm asking a straight question now. *Where* is the TechnoCore?'

The Councilor shook his head bemusedly, regretfully, as if he were an adult being asked for the thousandth time the child's question Why is the sky blue, Daddy?

'M Executive, it is simply not possible to answer that question in a way that would make sense in human three-dimensional coordinates. In a sense we . . . the Core . . . exist within the Web and beyond the Web. We swim in the datumplane reality which you call the datasphere, but as for the physical elements . . . what your ancestors called "hardware," we find it necessary to—'

'To keep it a secret,' finished Gladstone. She crossed her arms. 'Are you aware, Councilor Albedo, that there will be those people in the Hegemony . . . millions of people . . . who will firmly believe that the Core . . . your Advisory Council . . . has betrayed humankind?'

Albedo made a motion with his hands. 'That will be regrettable, M Executive. Regrettable but understandable.'

'Your predictors were supposed to be close to foolproof, Councilor. Yet at no time did you tell us of the destruction of worlds by this Ouster fleet.'

The sadness on the projection's handsome face was very close to convincing. 'M Executive, it is only fair to remind you that the Advisory Council warned you that bringing Hyperion into the Web introduced a random variable which even the Council could not factor.'

'But this isn't Hyperion!' snapped Gladstone, her voice rising. 'It's God's Grove burning. Heaven's Gate reduced to slag. Mare Infinitus waiting for the next hammer blow! What good is the Advisory Council if it cannot predict an invasion of that magnitude?'

'We did predict the inevitability of war with the Ousters, M Executive. We also predicted the great danger of defending Hyperion. You must believe me that the inclusion of Hyperion in any predictive equation brings the reliability factor down as low as—'

'All right,' sighed Gladstone. 'I need to talk to someone else in the Core, Albedo. Someone in your indecipherable hierarchy of intelligences who actually has some decision-making power.'

'I assure you that I represent all Core elements when I—'

'Yes, yes. But I want to speak to one of the . . . the Powers

I believe you call them. One of the elder AIs. One with clout, Albedo. I need to speak to someone who can tell me why the Core kidnapped my artist Severn and my aide Leigh Hunt.'

The holo looked shocked. 'I assure you, M Gladstone, on the honor of four centuries of our alliance, that the Core had nothing to do with the unfortunate disappearance of—'

Gladstone stood. 'This is why I need to talk to a Power. The time for assurances is past, Albedo. It is time for straight talk if either of our species is going to survive. That is all.' She turned her attention to the faxpad flimsies on her desk.

Councilor Albedo stood, nodded a farewell, and shimmered out of existence.

Gladstone called her personal farcaster portal into existence, spoke the Government House infirmary codes, and started to step through. In the instant before touching the opaque surface of the energy rectangle, she paused, gave thought to what she was doing, and for the first time in her life felt anxiety about stepping through a farcaster.

What if the Core wanted to kidnap her? Or kill her?

Meina Gladstone suddenly realized that the Core had the power of life and death over every farcaster-traveling citizen in the Web . . . which was every citizen with power. Leigh and the Severn cybrid did not have to be kidnaped, translated somewhere . . . only the persistent habit of thinking of farcasters as foolproof transportation created the subconscious conviction that they had *gone somewhere*. Her aide and the enigmatic cybrid could easily have been translated to . . . to nothing. To scattered atoms stretched through a singularity. Farcasters did not 'teleport' people and things – such a concept was silly – but how much less silly was it to trust a device that punched holes in the fabric of space-time and allowed one to step through black hole 'trapdoors'? How silly was it for her to trust the Core to transport her to the infirmary?

Gladstone thought of the War Room . . . three giant

rooms connected by permanently activated, vision-clear farcaster portals . . . but three rooms nonetheless, separated by at least a thousand light-years of real space, decades of real time even under Hawking drive. Every time Morpurgo or Singh or one of the others moved from a map holo to the plotting board, he or she stepped across great gulfs of space and time. All the Core had to do to destroy the Hegemony or anyone in it was to tamper with the farcasters, allow a slight 'mistake' in targeting.

To hell with this, thought Meina Gladstone and stepped through to see Paul Duré in the Government House infirmary.

THIRTY-NINE

The two rooms on the second floor of the house on the Piazza di Spagna are small, narrow, high ceilinged, and – except for a single dim lamp burning in each room as if lighted by ghosts in expectation of a visit by other ghosts – quite dark. My bed is in the smaller of the two rooms: the one facing the Piazza, although all one can see from the high windows this night is darkness creased by deeper shadows and accented by the ceaseless burbling of Bernini's unseen fountain.

Bells ring on the hour from one of the twin towers of Santa Trinità dei Monti, the church that crouches in the dark like a massive, tawny cat at the head of the stairs outside, and each time I hear the bells toll the brief notes of the early hours of the morn, I imagine ghostly hands pulling rotting bell ropes. Or perhaps rotting hands pulling ghostly bell ropes; I don't know which image suits my macabre fancies this endless night.

Fever lies upon me this night, as dank and heavy and stifling as a thick, water-soaked blanket. My skin alternately burns and then is clammy to the touch. Twice I have been seized with coughing spasms; the first brought Hunt running in from his couch in the other room, and I watched his eyes widen at the sight of the blood I had vomited on the damask sheets; the second spasm I stifled as best I could, staggering to the basin on the bureau to spit up smaller quantities of black blood and dark phlegm. Hunt did not wake the second time.

462

To be back here. To come all this way to these dark rooms, this grim bed. I half remember awakening here, miraculously cured, the 'real' Severn and Dr Clark and even little Signora Angeletti hovering in the outer room. That period of convalescence from death; that period of realization that I was not Keats, was not on the true Earth, that this was not in the century I had closed my eyes in that last night . . . that I was not human.

Sometime after two, I sleep, and as I sleep, I dream. The dream is one I have never suffered before. I dream that I rise slowly through the datumplane, through the datasphere, into and through the megasphere, and finally into a place I do not know, have never dreamt of . . . a place of infinite spaces, unhurried, indescribable colors, a place with no horizons, no ceilings, no floors or solid areas one might call the ground. I think of it as the metasphere, for I sense immediately that this level of consensual reality includes all of the varieties and vagaries of sensation which I have experienced on Earth, all of the binary analyses and intellectual pleasures I have felt flowing from the TechnoCore through the datasphere, and, above all, a sense of . . . of what? Expansiveness? Freedom? – *potential* might be the word I am hunting for.

I am alone in this metasphere. Colors flow above me, under me, *through* me . . . sometimes dissolving into vague pastels, sometimes coalescing into cloudlike fantasies, and at other times, rarely, appearing to form into more solid objects, shapes, distinct forms which may or may not be humanoid in appearance – I watch them the way a child might watch clouds and imagine elephants, crocodiles from the Nile, and great gunboats marching from west to east on a spring day in the Lake District.

After a while I hear sounds: the maddening trickle of the Bernini fountain in the Piazza outside; doves rustling and cooing on the ledges above my window; Leigh Hunt moaning softly in his sleep. But above and beneath these noises, I hear something more stealthy, less *real*, but infinitely more threatening.

Something large this way comes. I strain to see through the pastel gloom; something is moving just beyond the horizon of sight. I know that it knows my name. I know that it holds my life in one palm and death in its other fist.

There is no place to hide in this space beyond space. I cannot run. The siren song of pain continues to rise and fall from the world I left behind – the everyday pain of each person everywhere, the pain of those suffering from the war just begun, the specific pain of those on the Shrike's terrible tree, and, worst of all, the pain I feel for and from the pilgrims and those others whose lives and thoughts I now share.

It would be worth rushing to greet this approaching shadow of doom if it would grant me freedom from that song of pain.

'Severn! Severn!'

For a second I think that I am the one calling, just as I had before in these rooms, calling Joseph Severn in the night when my pain and fever ranged beyond my ability to contain it. And he was always there: Severn with his hulking, well-meaning slowness and that gentle smile which I often wanted to wipe from his face with some small meanness or comment. It is hard to be good-natured when one is dying; I had led a life of some generosity . . . why then was it my fate to continue that role when *I* was the one suffering, when *I* was the one coughing the ragged remnants of my lungs into stained handkerchiefs?

'Severn!'

It is not my voice. Hunt is shaking me by the shoulders, calling Severn's name. I realize that he thinks he is calling *my* name. I brush away his hands and sink back into the pillows. 'What is it? What's wrong?'

'You were moaning,' says Gladstone's aide. 'Crying out.'

'A nightmare. Nothing more.'

'Your dreams are usually more than dreams,' says Hunt. He glances around the narrow room, illuminated now by the single lamp he has carried in. 'What a terrible place, Severn.'

I try to smile. 'It cost me twenty-eight shillings a month. Seven scudi. Highway robbery.'

Hunt frowns at me. The stark light makes his wrinkles seem deeper than usual. 'Listen, Severn, I know you're a cybrid. Gladstone told me that you were the retrieval persona of a poet named Keats. Now obviously all this . . .' – he gestured helplessly toward the room, shadows, tall rectangle of windows, and high bed – 'all this has something to do with that. But how? What game is the Core playing here?'

'I'm not sure,' I say truthfully.

'But you know this place?'

'Oh yes,' I say with feeling.

'Tell me,' pleads Hunt, and it is his restraint to this point in *not* asking as much as the earnestness of that plea now which decides me to tell him.

I tell him about the poet John Keats, about his birth in 1795, his short and frequently unhappy life, and about his death from 'consumption' in 1821, in Rome, far from his friends and only love. I tell him about my staged 'recovery' in this very room, about my decision to take the name of Joseph Severn – the artist acquaintance who stayed with Keats until his death – and, finally, I tell him about my short time in the Web, listening, watching, condemned to dream the lives of the Shrike Pilgrims on Hyperion and the others.

'Dreams?' says Hunt. 'You mean even now you're dreaming about what's occurring in the Web?'

'Yes.' I tell him of the dreams about Gladstone, the destruction of Heaven's Gate and God's Grove, and the confused images from Hyperion.

465

Hunt is pacing back and forth in the narrow room, his shadow thrown high on the rough walls. 'Can *you* contact *them*?'

'The ones I dream of? Gladstone?' I think a second. 'No.'

'Are you sure?'

I try to explain. 'I'm not even in these dreams, Hunt. I have no . . . no voice, no presence . . . there's no way I can contact those I dream about.'

'But sometimes you dream what they're thinking?'

I realize that this is true. Close to the truth. 'I sense what they are *feeling* . . .'

'Then can't you leave some trace in their mind . . . in their memory? Let them know where we are?'

'No.'

Hunt collapses into the chair at the foot of my bed. He suddenly seems very old.

'Leigh,' I say, 'even if I could communicate with Gladstone or the others – which I can't – what good would it do? I've told you that this replica of Old Earth is in the Magellanic Cloud. Even at quantum-leap Hawking velocities it would take centuries for anyone to reach us.'

'We could warn them,' says Hunt, his voice so tired that it sounds almost sullen.

'Warn them of what? All of Gladstone's worst nightmares are coming true around her. Do you think she trusts the Core now? That's why the Core could kidnap us so blatantly. Events are proceeding too quickly for Gladstone or anyone in the Hegemony to deal with.'

Hunt rubs his eyes, then steeples his fingers under his nose. His stare is not overly friendly. 'Are you really the retrieved personality of a poet?'

I say nothing.

'Recite some poetry. Make something up.'

I shake my head. It is late, we're both tired and frightened, and my heart has not yet quit pounding from the nightmare which was more than a nightmare. I won't let Hunt make me angry.

'Come on,' he says. 'Show me that you're the new, improved version of Bill Keats.'

'John Keats,' I say softly.

'Whatever. Come on, Severn. Or John. Or whatever I should call you. Recite some poesy.'

'All right,' I say, returning his stare. 'Listen.'

> There was a naughty boy
>   And a naughty boy was he
> For nothing would he do
>   But scribble poetry—
> He took
> An inkstand
> In his hand
> And a pen
> Big as ten
> In the other
> And away
> In a pother
> He ran
> To the mountains
> And fountains
> And ghostes
> And postes
> And witches
> And ditches,
> And wrote
> In his coat
> When the weather
> Was cool—
> Fear of gout—
> And without
> When the weather
> Was warm.

Och, the charm
When we choose
To follow one's nose
To the North,
To the North,
To follow one's nose
To the North!

'I don't know,' says Hunt. 'That doesn't sound like something a poet whose reputation has lasted a thousand years would have written.'

I shrug.

'Were you dreaming about Gladstone tonight? Did something happen that caused those moans?'

'No. It wasn't about Gladstone. It was a . . . real nightmare for a change.'

Hunt stands, lifts his lamp, and prepares to take the only light from the room. I can hear the fountain in the Piazza, the doves on the windowsills. 'Tomorrow,' he says, 'we'll make sense of all this and figure out a way to get back. If they can farcast us here, there must be a way to farcast home.'

'Yes,' I say, knowing it is not true.

'Good night,' says Hunt. 'No more nightmares, all right?'

'No more,' I say, knowing this is even less true.

Moneta pulled the wounded Kassad away from the Shrike and seemed to hold the creature at bay with an extended hand while she fumbled a blue torus from the belt of her skinsuit and twisted it behind her.

A two-meter-high gold oval hung burning in midair.

'Let me go,' muttered Kassad. 'Let us finish it.' There was blood spattered where the Shrike had clawed huge rents in the Colonel's skinsuit. His right foot was dangling as if half-severed; he could put no weight on it, and only the fact that he had been struggling with the Shrike, half carried by the thing in a mad parody of a dance, had kept Kassad upright as they fought.

'Let me go,' repeated Fedmahn Kassad.

'Shut up,' said Moneta, and then, more softly, 'Shut up, my love.' She dragged him through the golden oval, and they emerged into blazing light.

Even through his pain and exhaustion, Kassad was dazzled by the sight. They were not on Hyperion; he was sure of that. A vast plain stretched to an horizon much farther away than logic or experience would allow. Low, orange grass – if grass it was – grew on the flatlands and low hills like fuzz on the back of some immense caterpillar, while things which might have been trees grew like whiskered-carbon sculptures, their trunks and branches Escher-ish in their baroque improbability, their leaves a riot of dark blue and violet ovals shimmering toward a sky alive with light.

But not sunlight. Even as Moneta carried him away from the closing portal – Kassad did not think of it as a farcaster since he felt sure it had carried them through time as well as space – and toward a copse of those impossible trees, Kassad turned his eyes toward the sky and felt something close to wonder. It was as bright as a Hyperion day; as bright as midday on a Lusian shopping mall; as bright as midsummer on the Tharsis Plateau of Kassad's dry homeworld, Mars, but this was no sunlight – the sky was filled with stars and constellations and star clusters and a galaxy so cluttered with suns that there were almost no patches of darkness between the lights. It was like being in a planetarium with ten projectors, thought Kassad. Like being at the center of the galaxy.

The center of the galaxy.

A group of men and women in skinsuits moved out from the shade of the Escher trees to circle Kassad and Moneta. One of the men – a giant even by Kassad's Martian standards – looked at him, raised his head toward Moneta, and even though Kassad could hear nothing, sense nothing on his skinsuit's radio and tightband receivers, he knew the two were communicating.

'Lie back,' said Moneta as she laid Kassad on the velvety orange grass. He struggled to sit up, to speak, but both she and the giant touched his chest with their palms, and he lay back so that his vision was filled with the slowly twisting violet leaves and the sky of stars.

The man touched him again, and Kassad's skinsuit was deactivated. He tried to sit up, tried to cover himself as he realized he was naked before the small crowd that had gathered, but Moneta's firm hand held him in place. Through the pain and dislocation, he vaguely sensed the man touching his slashed arms and chest, running a silver-coated hand down his leg to where the Achilles' tendon had been cut. The Colonel felt a coolness wherever the giant touched, and then his consciousness floated away like a balloon, high above the tawny plain and the rolling hills, drifting toward the solid canopy of stars where a huge figure waited, dark as a towering thundercloud above the horizon, massive as a mountain.

'Kassad,' whispered Moneta, and the Colonel drifted back. 'Kassad,' she said again, her lips against his cheek, his skinsuit reactivated and melded with hers.

Colonel Fedmahn Kassad sat up as she did. He shook his head, realized that he was clothed in quicksilver energy once again, and got to his feet. There was no pain. He felt his body tingle in a dozen places where injuries had been healed, serious cuts repaired. He melded his hand to his own suit, ran flesh across flesh, bent his knee and touched his heel, but could feel no scars.

Kassad turned toward the giant. 'Thank you,' he said, not knowing if the man could hear.

The giant nodded and stepped back toward the others.

'He's a . . . a doctor of sorts,' said Moneta. 'A healer.'

Kassad half heard her as he concentrated on the other people. They were human – he knew in his heart that they

470

were human – but the variety was staggering: their skinsuits were not all silver like Kassad's and Moneta's but ranged through a score of colors, each as soft and organic as some living wild creature's pelt. Only the subtle energy-shimmer and blurred facial features revealed the skinsuit surface. Their anatomy was as varied as their coloration: the healer's Shrike-sized girth and massive bulk, his massive brow and a cascade of tawny energy flow which might be a mane . . . a female next to him, no larger than a child but obviously a woman, perfectly proportioned with muscular legs, small breasts, and faery wings two meters long rising from her back – and not merely decorative wings, either, for when the breeze ruffled the orange prairie grass, this woman gave a short run, extended her arms, and rose gracefully into the air.

Behind several tall, thin women with blue skinsuits and long, webbed fingers, a group of short men were as visored and armor-plated as a FORCE Marine going into battle in a vacuum, but Kassad sensed that the armor was part of *them*. Overhead, a cluster of winged males rose on thermals, thin, yellow beams of laser light pulsing between them in some complex code. The lasers seemed to emanate from an eye in each of their chests.

Kassad shook his head again.

'We need to go,' said Moneta. 'The Shrike cannot follow us here. These warriors have enough to contend with without dealing with this particular manifestation of the Lord of Pain.'

'Where are we?' asked Kassad.

Moneta brought a violet oval into existence with a golden ferule from her belt. 'Far in humankind's future. *One* of our futures. This is where the Time Tombs were formed and launched backward in time.'

Kassad looked around again. Something very large moved in front of the starfield, blocking out thousands of stars and throwing a shadow for scant seconds before it was gone. The men and women looked up briefly and then went back to their business: harvesting small things from the trees, huddling in clusters to view bright energy maps called up by a flick of one man's fingers, flying off toward the horizon with the speed of a thrown spear. One low, round individual of indeterminate sex had burrowed into the soft soil and was visible now only as a faint line of raised earth moving in quick concentric circles around the band.

'Where *is* this place?' Kassad asked again. '*What* is it?' Suddenly, inexplicably, he felt himself close to tears, as if he had turned an unfamiliar corner and found himself at home in the Tharsis Relocation Projects, his long-dead mother waving to him from a doorway, his forgotten friends and siblings waiting for him to join a game of scootball.

'Come,' said Moneta and there was no mistaking the urgency in her voice. She pulled Kassad toward the glowing oval. He watched the others and the dome of stars until he stepped through and the view was lost to sight.

They stepped out into darkness, and it took the briefest of seconds for the filters in Kassad's skinsuit to compensate his vision. They were at the base of the Crystal Monolith in the valley of the Time Tombs on Hyperion. It was night. Clouds boiled overhead, and a storm was raging. Only a pulsing glow from the Tombs themselves illuminated the scene. Kassad felt a sick lurch of loss for the clean, well-lighted place they had just left, and then his mind focused on what he was seeing.

Sol Weintraub and Brawne Lamia were half a klick down the valley, Sol bending over the woman as she lay near the front of the Jade Tomb. Wind swirled dust around them so thickly that they did not see the Shrike moving like another shadow down the trail past the Obelisk, toward them.

Fedmahn Kassad stepped off the dark marble in front of the Monolith and skirted the shattered crystal shards which littered the path. He realized that Moneta still clung to his arm.

'If you fight again,' she said, her voice soft and urgent in his ear, 'the Shrike will kill you.'

'They're my friends,' said Kassad. His FORCE gear and torn armor lay where Moneta had thrown it hours earlier. He searched the Monolith until he found his assault rifle and a bandolier of grenades, saw the rifle was still functional, checked charges and clicked off safeties, left the Monolith, and stepped forward at double time to intercept the Shrike.

I wake to the sound of water flowing, and for a second I believe I am awakening from my nap near the waterfall of Lodore during my walking tour with Brown. But the darkness when I open my eyes is as fearsome as when I slept, the water has a sick, trickling sound rather than the rush of the cataract which Southey would someday make famous in his poem, and I feel terrible – not merely sick with the sore throat I came down with on our tour after Brown and I foolishly climbed Skiddaw before breakfast – but mortally, fearfully ill, with my body aching with something deeper than ague while phlegm and fire bubble in my chest and belly.

I rise and feel my way to the window by touch. A dim light comes under the door from Leigh Hunt's room, and I realize that he has gone to sleep with the lamp still lit. That would not have been a bad thing for me to have done, but it is too late to light it now as I feel my way to the lighter rectangle of outer darkness set into the deeper darkness of the room.

The air is fresh and filled with the scent of rain. I realize that the sound that woke me is thunder as lightning flashes over the rooftops of Rome. No lights burn in the city. By leaning slightly out of the open window, I can see the stairs above the Piazza all slick with rain and the towers of Trinità dei Monti outlined blackly against lightning flashes. The wind that blows down those steps is chill, and I move back to the bed to pull a blanket around me before dragging a chair to the window and sitting there, looking out, thinking.

I remember my brother Tom during those last weeks and days, his face and body contorted with the terrible effort to breathe. I remember my mother and how pale she looked, her face almost shining in the gloom of the darkened room. My sister and I were allowed to touch her clammy hand, kiss her fevered lips, and then withdraw. I remember that once I furtively wiped my lips as I left that room, glancing sideways to see if my sister or others had seen my sinful act.

When Dr Clark and an Italian surgeon opened Keats's body less than thirty hours after he had died, they found, as Severn later wrote a friend, '. . . the worst possible Consumption – the lungs were intirely destroyed – the cells were quite gone.' Neither Dr Clark nor the Italian surgeon could imagine how Keats had lived those last two months or more.

I think of this as I sit in the darkened room and look out on the darkened Piazza, all the while listening to the boiling in my chest and throat, feeling the pain like fire inside and the worse pain from the cries in my mind: cries from Martin Silenus on the tree, suffering for writing the poetry I had been too frail and cowardly to finish; cries from Fedmahn Kassad as he prepares to die at the claws of the Shrike; cries from the Consul as he is forced into betrayal a second time; cries from thousands of Templar throats as they bewail the death of both their world and their brother Het Masteen; cries from Brawne Lamia as she thinks of her dead lover, my twin; cries from Paul Duré as he lies fighting burns and the shock of memory, all too aware of the waiting cruciforms on his chest; cries from Sol Weintraub as he beats his fist on the earth of Hyperion, calling for his child, the infant cries of Rachel still in our ears.

'Goddamn,' I say softly, beating my fist against the stone and mortar of the window frame. 'Goddamn.'

After a while, just as the first hint of paleness promises

474

dawn, I move away from the window, find my bed, and lie down just a moment to close my eyes.

Governor-General Theo Lane awoke to the sound of music. He blinked and looked around, recognizing the nearby nutrient tank and ship's surgery as if from a dream. Theo realized that he was wearing soft, black pajamas and had been sleeping on the surgery's examination couch. The past twelve hours began to stitch themselves together from Theo's patches of memory: being raised from the treatment tank, sensors being applied, the Consul and another man leaning over him, asking him questions – Theo answering just as if he were truly conscious, then sleep again, dreams of Hyperion and its cities burning. No, not dreams.

Theo sat up, felt himself almost float off the couch, found his clothes cleaned and folded neatly on a nearby shelf, and dressed quickly, hearing the music continue, now rising, now fading, but always continuing with a haunting acoustical quality which suggested that it was live and not recorded.

Theo took the short stairway to the recreation deck and stopped in surprise as he realized that the ship was open, the balcony extended, the containment field apparently off. Gravity underfoot was minimal: enough to pull Theo back to the deck but little more – probably 20 percent or less of Hyperion's, perhaps one-sixth standard.

The ship was open. Brilliant sunlight streamed in the open door to the balcony where the Consul sat playing the antique instrument he had called a piano. Theo recognized the archaeologist, Arundez, leaning against the hull opening with a drink in his hand. The Consul was playing something very old and very complicated; his hands were a studied blur on the keyboard. Theo moved closer, started to whisper something to the smiling Arundez, and then stopped in shock to stare.

Beyond the balcony, thirty meters below, brilliant

475

sunlight fell on a bright green lawn stretching to an horizon far too close. On that lawn, clusters of people sat and lay in relaxed postures, obviously listening to the Consul's impromptu concert. But what people!

Theo could see tall, thin people, looking like the aesthetes of Epsilon Eridani, pale and bald in their wispy blue robes, but beside them and beyond them an amazing multitude of human types sat listening – more varieties than the Web had ever seen: humans cloaked in fur and scales; humans with bodies like bees and eyes to match, multifaceted receptors and antennae; humans as fragile and thin as wire sculptures, great black wings extending from their thin shoulders and folding around them like capes; humans apparently designed for massive-g worlds, short and stout and muscular as cape buffalo, making Lusians look fragile in comparison; humans with short bodies and long arms covered with orange fur, only their pale and sensitive faces separating them from some holo of Old Earth's long-extinct orangutans; and other humans looking more lemur than humanoid, more aquiline or leonine or ursine or anthropoid than manlike. Yet somehow Theo knew at once that these were *human beings*, as shocking as their differences were. Their attentive gazes, their relaxed postures, and a hundred other subtle human attributes – down to the way a butterfly-winged mother cradled a butterfly-winged child in her arms – all gave testimony to a common humanity which Theo could not deny.

Melio Arundez turned, smiled at Theo's expression, and whispered, 'Ousters.'

Stunned, Theo Lane could do little more than shake his head and listen to the music. Ousters were barbarians, not these beautiful and sometimes ethereal creatures. Ouster captives on Bressia, not to mention the bodies of their infantry dead, had been of a uniform body sort – tall, yes, thin, yes, but decidedly more Web standard than this dizzying display of variety.

Theo shook his head again as the Consul's piano piece

rose to a crescendo and ended on a definitive note. The hundreds of beings in the field beyond applauded, the sound high and soft in the thin air, and then Theo watched as they stood, stretched, and headed different ways . . . some walking quickly over the disturbingly near horizon, others unfolding eight-meter wings and flying away. Still others moved toward the base of the Consul's ship.

The Consul stood, saw Theo, and smiled. He clapped the younger man on the shoulder. 'Theo, just in time. We'll be negotiating soon.'

Theo Lane blinked. Three Ousters landed on the balcony and folded their great wings behind them. Each of the men was heavily furred and differently marked and striped, their pelts as organic and convincing as any wild creature's.

'As delightful as always,' the closest Ouster said to the Consul. The Ouster's face was leonine – broad nose and golden eyes framed by a ruff of tawny fur. 'The last piece was Mozart's Fantasia in D Minor, KV. 397, was it not?'

'It was,' said the Consul. 'Freeman Vanz, I would like to introduce M Theo Lane, Governor-General of the Hegemony Protectorate world of Hyperion.'

The lion gaze turned on Theo. 'An honor,' said Freeman Vanz and extended a furred hand.

Theo shook it. 'A pleasure to meet you, sir.' Theo wondered if he were actually still in the recovery tank, dreaming this. The sunlight on his face and the firm palm against his suggested otherwise.

Freeman Vanz turned back to the Consul. 'On behalf of the Aggregate, I thank you for that concert. It has been too many years since we have heard you play, my friend.' He glanced around. 'We can hold the talks here or at one of the administrative compounds, at your convenience.'

The Consul hesitated only a second. 'There are three of us, Freeman Vanz. Many of you. We will join you.'

The lion head nodded and glanced skyward. 'We will send a boat for your crossing.' He and the other two moved to the railing and stepped off, falling several meters before unfurling their complex wings and flying toward the horizon.

'Jesus,' whispered Theo. He gripped the Consul's forearm. 'Where are we?'

'The Swarm,' said the Consul, covering the Steinway's keyboard. He led the way inside, waited for Arundez to step back, and then brought the balcony in.

'And what are we going to negotiate?' asked Theo.

The Consul rubbed his eyes. It looked as if the man had slept little or not at all during the ten or twelve hours Theo had been healing.

'That depends upon CEO Gladstone's next message,' said the Consul and nodded toward where the holopit misted with transmission columns. A fatline squirt was being decoded on the ship's one-time pad at that moment.

Meina Gladstone stepped into the Government House infirmary and was escorted by waiting doctors to the recovery bay where Father Paul Duré lay. 'How is he?' she asked the first doctor, the CEO's own physician.

'Second-degree flash burns over about a third of his body,' answered Dr Irma Androneva. 'He lost his eyebrows and some hair . . . he didn't have that much to start with . . . and there were some tertiary radiation burns on the left side of his face and body. We've completed the epidermal regeneration and given RNA template injections. He's in no pain and conscious. There is the problem of the cruciform parasite on his chest, but that is of no immediate danger to the patient.'

'Tertiary radiation burns,' said Gladstone, stopping for a moment just out of earshot of the cubicle where Duré waited. 'Plasma bombs?'

'Yes,' answered another doctor whom Gladstone did not recognize. 'We're certain that this man 'cast in from God's Grove a second or two before the farcaster connection was cut.'

'All right,' said Gladstone, stopping by the floating pallet where Duré rested, 'I wish to speak to the gentleman alone, please.'

The doctors glanced at one another, waved a mech nurse to its wall storage, and closed the portal to the ward room as they departed.

'Father Duré?' asked Gladstone, recognizing the priest from his holos and Severn's descriptions during the pilgrimage. Duré's face was red and mottled now, and it glistened from regeneration gel and spray-on painkiller. He was still a man of striking appearance.

'CEO,' whispered the priest and made as if to sit up.

Gladstone set a gentle hand on his shoulder. 'Rest,' she said. 'Do you feel like telling me what happened?'

Duré nodded. There were tears in the old Jesuit's eyes. 'The True Voice of the Worldtree didn't believe that they would really attack,' he whispered, his voice raw. 'Sek Hardeen thought that the Templars had some pact with the Ousters . . . some arrangement. But they did attack. Tactical lances, plasma devices, nuclear explosives, I think . . .'

'Yes,' said Gladstone, 'we monitored it from the War Room. I need to know everything, Father Duré. Everything from the point when you stepped into the Cave Tomb on Hyperion.'

Paul Duré's eyes focused on Gladstone's face. 'You know about that?'

'Yes. And about most other things to that point. But I need to know more. Much more.'

Duré closed his eyes. 'The labyrinth . . .'

'What?'

'The labyrinth,' he said again, voice stronger. He cleared his throat and told her about his voyage through the tunnels of corpses, the transition to a FORCE ship and his meeting with Severn on Pacem.

'And you're sure Severn was headed here? To Government House?' asked Gladstone.

'Yes. He and your aide . . . Hunt. Both of them intended to 'cast here.'

Gladstone nodded and carefully touched an unburned section of the priest's shoulder. 'Father, things are happening very quickly here. Severn is missing and so is Leigh Hunt. I need advice about Hyperion. Will you stay with me?'

Duré looked confused for a moment. 'I need to get back. Back to Hyperion, M Executive. Sol and the others are waiting for me.'

'I understand,' said Gladstone soothingly. 'As soon as there's a way back to Hyperion, I'll expedite your return. Right now, however, the Web is under brutal attack. Millions are dying or in danger of dying. I need your help, Father. Can I count on you until then?'

Paul Duré sighed and lay back. 'Yes, M Executive. But I have no idea how I—'

There was a soft knock and Sedeptra Akasi entered and handed Gladstone a message flimsy. The CEO smiled. 'I said that things were happening quickly, Father. Here's another development. A message from Pacem says that the College of Cardinals has met in the Sistine Chapel . . .' Gladstone raised an eyebrow. 'I forget, Father, is that *the* Sistine Chapel?'

'Yes. The Church took it apart stone by stone, fresco by fresco, and moved it to Pacem after the Big Mistake.'

Gladstone looked down at the flimsy. '. . . met in the Sistine Chapel and elected a new pontiff.'

'So soon?' whispered Paul Duré. He closed his eyes again. 'I guess they felt they must hurry. Pacem lies – what? – only ten days in front of the Ouster invasion wave. Still, to come to a decision so quickly . . .'

'Are you interested in who the new Pope is?' asked Gladstone.

'Either Antonio Cardinal Guarducci or Agostino Cardinal Ruddell, I would guess,' said Duré. 'None of the others would command a majority at this time.'

'No,' said Gladstone. 'According to this message from Bishop Edouard of the Curia Romana . . .'

'*Bishop* Edouard! Excuse me, M Executive, please go on.'

'According to Bishop Edouard, the College of Cardinals has elected someone below the rank of monsignor for the first time in the history of the Church. This says that the new Pope is a Jesuit priest . . . a certain Father Paul Duré.'

Duré sat straight up despite his burns. 'What?' There was no belief in his voice.

Gladstone handed the flimsy to him.

Paul Duré stared at the paper. 'This is impossible. They have never elected a pontiff below the rank of monsignor except symbolically, and that was unique . . . it was St Belvedere after the Big Mistake and the Miracle of the . . . no, no, this is impossible.'

'Bishop Edouard has been trying to call, according to my aide,' said Gladstone. 'We'll have the call put through here at once, Father. Or should I say, Your Holiness?' There was no irony in the CEO's voice.

Duré looked up, too stunned to speak.

'I will have the call put through,' said Gladstone. 'We'll arrange your return to Pacem as quickly as possible, Your Holiness, but I would appreciate it if you could keep in touch. I do need your advice.'

Duré nodded and looked back at the flimsy. A phone began to blink on the console above the pallet.

CEO Gladstone stepped out into the hall, told the doctors about the most recent development, contacted Security to approve the farcast clearance for Bishop Edouard or other Church officials from Pacem, and 'cast back to her room in the residential wing. Sedeptra reminded her that the council was reconvening in the War Room in eight minutes. Gladstone nodded, saw her aide out, and stepped back to the fatline cubicle in its concealed niche in the wall. She activated sonic privacy fields and coded the transmission diskey for the Consul's ship. Every fatline receiver in the Web,

Outback, galaxy, and universe would monitor the squirt, but only the Consul's ship could decode it. Or so she hoped.

The holo camera light winked red. 'Based on the automated squirt from your ship, I am assuming that you chose to meet with the Ousters, and they have allowed you to do so,' Gladstone said into the camera. 'I am also assuming that you survived the initial meeting.'

Gladstone took a breath. 'On behalf of the Hegemony, I have asked you to sacrifice much over the years. Now I ask you on behalf of all of humankind. You must find out the following:

'First, why are the Ousters attacking and destroying the worlds of the Web? You were convinced, Byron Lamia was convinced, and I was convinced that they wanted only Hyperion. Why have they changed this?

'Second, *where* is the TechnoCore? I must know if we are to fight them. Have the Ousters forgotten our common enemy, the Core?

'Third, what are their demands for a cease-fire? I am willing to sacrifice much to rid us of the Core's domination. *But the killing must stop!*

'Fourth, would the Leader of the Swarm Aggregate be willing to meet with me in person? I will farcast to Hyperion system if this is necessary. Most of our fleet elements have left there, but a JumpShip and its escort craft remain with the singularity sphere. The Swarm Leader must decide soon, because FORCE wants to destroy the sphere, and Hyperion then will be three years time-debt from the Web.

'Finally, the Swarm Leader must know that the Core wishes us to use a form of deathwand explosive device to counter the Ouster invasion. Many of the FORCE leaders agree. Time is short. We will not – repeat, not – allow the Ouster invasion to overrun the Web.

'It is up to you now. Please acknowledge this message and fatline me as soon as negotiations have begun.'

Gladstone looked into the camera disk, willing the force of her personality and sincerity across the light-years. 'I beseech you in the bowels of humankind's history, please accomplish this.'

The fatline message squirt was followed by two minutes of jerky imagery showing the deaths of Heaven's Gate and God's Grove. The Consul, Melio Arundez, and Theo Lane sat in silence after the holos faded.

'Response?' queried the ship.

The Consul cleared his throat. 'Acknowledge message received,' he said. 'Send our coordinates.' He looked across the holopit at the other two. 'Gentlemen?'

Arundez shook his head as if clearing it. 'It's obvious you've been here before . . . to the Ouster Swarm.'

'Yes,' said the Consul. 'After Bressia . . . after my wife and son . . . after Bressia, some time ago, I rendezvoused with this Swarm for extensive negotiations.'

'Representing the Hegemony?' asked Theo. The redhead's face looked much older and lined with worry.

'Representing Senator Gladstone's faction,' said the Consul. 'It was before she was first elected CEO. Her group explained to me that an internal power struggle within the TechnoCore could be affected by our bringing Hyperion into the Web Protectorate. The easiest way to do that was to allow information to slip to the Ousters . . . information that would cause them to attack Hyperion, thus bringing the Hegemony fleet here.'

'And you did that?' Arundez's voice showed no emotion, although his wife and grown children lived on Renaissance Vector, now less than eighty hours away from the invasion wave.

The Consul sat back in the cushions. 'No. I told the Ousters about the plan. They sent me back to the Web as a double agent. They planned to seize Hyperion, but at a time of their own choosing.'

Theo sat forward, his hands clasped very tightly. 'All those years at the consulate . . .'

'I was waiting for word from the Ousters,' the Consul said flatly. 'You see, they had a device that would collapse the anti-entropic fields around the Time Tombs. Open them when they were ready. Allow the Shrike to slip its bonds.'

'So the Ousters did that,' said Theo.

'No,' said the Consul, 'I did. I betrayed the Ousters just as I betrayed Gladstone and the Hegemony. I shot the Ouster woman who was calibrating the device . . . her and the technicians with her . . . and turned it on. The anti-entropic fields collapsed. The final pilgrimage was arranged. The Shrike is free.'

Theo stared at his former mentor. There was more puzzlement than rage in the younger man's green eyes. 'Why? Why did you do all this?'

The Consul told them, briefly and dispassionately, about his grandmother Siri of Maui-Covenant, and about her rebellion against the Hegemony – a rebellion which did not die when she and her lover, the Consul's grandfather, died.

Arundez rose from the pit and walked to the window opposite the balcony. Sunlight streamed across his legs and the dark blue carpet. 'Do the Ousters know what you did?'

'They do now,' said the Consul. 'I told Freeman Vanz and the others when we arrived.'

Theo paced the diameter of the holopit. 'So this meeting we're going to might be a trial?'

The Consul smiled. 'Or an execution.'

Theo stopped, both hands clenched in fists. 'And Gladstone knew this when she asked you to come here again?'

'Yes.'

Theo turned away. 'I don't know whether I want them to execute you or not.'

'I don't know either, Theo,' said the Consul.

Melio Arundez turned away from the window. 'Didn't

Vanz say they were sending a boat to fetch us?'

Something in his tone brought the other two men to the window. The world where they had landed was a middle-sized asteroid which had been encircled by a class-ten containment field and terraformed into a sphere by generations of wind and water and careful restructuring. Hyperion's sun was setting behind the too-near horizon, and the few kilometers of featureless grass rippled to a vagrant breeze. Below the ship, a wide stream or narrow river ambled across the pastureland, approached the horizon, and then seemed to fly upward into a river turned waterfall, twisting up through the distant containment field and winding through the blackness of space above before dwindling to a line too narrow to see.

A boat was descending that infinitely tall waterfall, approaching the surface of their small world. Humanoid figures could be seen near the bow and stern.

'Christ,' whispered Theo.

'We'd best get ready,' said the Consul. 'That's our escort.'

Outside, the sun set with shocking rapidity, sending its last rays through the curtain of water half a kilometer above the shadowed ground and searing the ultramarine sky with rainbows of almost frightening color and solidity.

FORTY

It is midmorning when Hunt awakens me. He arrives with breakfast on a tray and a frightened look in his dark eyes.

I ask, 'Where did you get the food?'

'There's some sort of little restaurant in the front room downstairs. Food was waiting there, hot, but no people.'

I nod. 'Signora Angeletti's little trattoria,' I say. 'She is not a good cook.' I remember Dr Clark's concern about my diet; he felt that the consumption had settled in my stomach and he held me to a starvation regime of milk and bread with the occasional bit of fish. Odd how many suffering members of humankind have faced eternity obsessed with their bowels, their bedsores, or the meagerness of their diets.

I look up at Hunt again. 'What is it?'

Gladstone's aide has moved to the window and seems absorbed in the view of the Piazza below. I can hear Bernini's accursed fountain trickling. 'I was going out for a walk while you slept,' Hunt says slowly, 'just in case there might be people out and about. Or a phone or farcaster.'

'Of course,' I say.

'I'd just stepped out . . . the . . .' He turns and licks his lips. 'There's something out there, Severn. In the street at the bottom of the stairs. I'm not sure, but I think that it's . . .'

'The Shrike,' I say.

Hunt nods. 'Did you see it?'

'No, but I am not surprised.'

'It's . . . it's terrible, Severn. There's something about it that makes my flesh crawl. Here . . . you can just get a glimpse of it in the shadows on the other side of the staircase.'

I start to rise, but a sudden fit of coughing and the feel of phlegm rising in my chest and throat makes me settle back on the pillows. 'I know what it looks like, Hunt. Don't worry, it's not here for you.' My voice sounds more confident than I feel.

'For you?'

'I don't think so,' I say between gasps for air. 'I think it's just here to make sure I don't try to leave . . . to find another place to die.'

Hunt returns to the bed. 'You're not going to die, Severn.'

I say nothing.

He sits in the straight-backed chair next to the bed and lifts a cooling cup of tea. 'If you die, what happens to me?'

'I don't know,' I say honestly. 'If I die, I don't even know what happens to *me*.'

There is a certain solipsism to serious illness which claims all of one's attention as certainly as an astronomical black hole seizes anything unlucky enough to fall within its critical radius. The day passes slowly, and I am exquisitely aware of the movement of sunlight across the rough wall, the feel of bedclothes beneath my palm, the fever which rises in me like nausea and burns itself out in the furnace of my mind, and, mostly, of the pain. Not my pain now, for a few hours or days of the constriction in my throat and the burning in my chest are bearable, almost welcomed like an obnoxious old friend met in a strange city, but the pain of the others . . . all the others. It strikes my mind like the noise of shattering slate, like hammer iron slammed repeatedly on anvil iron, and there is no escape from it.

My brain receives this as din and restructures it as poetry. All day and all night the pain of the universe floods in and wanders the fevered corridors of my mind as verse, imagery, images in verse, the intricate, endless dance of language, now as calming as a flute solo, now as shrill and strident and confusing as a dozen orchestras tuning up, but always verse, always poetry.

Sometime near sunset I awake from a half-doze, shattering the dream of Colonel Kassad fighting the Shrike for the lives of Sol and Brawne Lamia, and find Hunt sitting at the window, his long face colored by evening light the hue of terra-cotta.

'Is it still there?' I ask, my voice the rasp of file on stone.

Hunt jumps, then turns toward me with an apologetic smile and the first blush I have ever seen on that dour countenance. 'The Shrike?' he says. 'I don't know. I haven't seen it for a while. I *feel* that it is.' He looks at me. 'How are you?'

'Dying.' I instantly regret the self-indulgence of that flippancy, however accurate it is, when I see the pain it causes Hunt. 'It's all right,' I say almost jovially, 'I've done it before. It's not as if it were *me* that is dying. I exist as a personality deep in the TechnoCore. It's just this body. This cybrid of John Keats. This twenty-seven-year-old illusion of flesh and blood and borrowed associations.'

Hunt comes over to sit on the edge of the bed. I realize with a shock that he has changed the sheets during the day, exchanging my bloodbespeckled coverlet for one of his own. 'Your personality is an AI in the Core,' he says. 'Then you must be able to access the datasphere.'

I shake my head, too weary to argue.

'When the Philomels kidnapped you, we tracked you through your access route to the datasphere,' he persisted. 'You don't have to contact Gladstone personally. Just leave a message where Security can find it.'

'No,' I rasp, 'the Core does not wish it.'

'Are they blocking you? Stopping you?'

488

'Not yet. But they would.' I set the words separately between gasps, like laying delicate eggs back in the nest. Suddenly I remember a note I sent to dear Fanny shortly after a serious hemorrhage but almost a year before they would kill me. I had written: '*If I should die,*' said I to myself, '*I have left no immortal work behind me – nothing to make my friends proud of my memory – but I have lov'd the principle of beauty in all things, and if I had had time I would have made myself remember'd.*' This strikes me now as futile and self-centered and idiotic and naive . . . and yet I desperately believe it still. If I had had time . . . the months I had spent on Esperance, pretending to be a visual artist; the days wasted with Gladstone in the halls of government when I could have been writing . . .

'How do you know until you try?' asks Hunt.

'What's that?' I ask. The simple effort of two syllables sets me coughing again, the spasm ending only when I spit up half-solid spheres of blood into the basin which Hunt has hastily fetched. I lie back, trying to focus on his face. It is getting dark in the narrow room, and neither of us has lighted a lamp. Outside, the fountain burbles loudly.

'What's that?' I ask again, trying to remain here even as sleep and sleep's dreams tug at me. 'Try what?'

'Try leaving a message through the datasphere,' he whispers. 'Contacting someone.'

'And what message should we leave, Leigh?' I ask. It is the first time I have used his first name.

'Where we are. How the Core kidnapped us. Anything.'

'All right,' I say, closing my eyes. 'I'll try. I don't think they'll let me, but I promise I'll try.'

I feel Hunt's hand holding mine. Even through the winning tides of weariness, this sudden human contact is enough to make tears come to my eyes.

I will try. Before surrendering to the dreams or death, I will try.

*　　*　　*

Colonel Fedmahn Kassad shouted a FORCE battle cry and charged through the dust storm to intercept the Shrike before it covered the final thirty meters to where Sol Weintraub crouched next to Brawne Lamia.

The Shrike paused, its head swiveling frictionlessly, red eyes gleaming. Kassad armed his assault rifle and moved down the slope with reckless speed.

The Shrike *shifted*.

Kassad saw its movement through time as a slow blur, noting even as he watched the Shrike that movement in the valley had ceased, sand hung motionless in the air, and the light from the glowing Tombs had taken on a thick, amberish quality. Kassad's skinsuit was somehow shifting with the Shrike, following it through its movements through time.

The creature's head snapped up, attentive now, and its four arms extended like blades from a knife, fingers snapping open in sharp greeting.

Kassad skidded to a halt ten meters from the thing and activated the assault rifle, slagging the sand beneath the Shrike in a full-power widebeam burst.

The Shrike glowed as its carapace and steel-sculpture legs reflected the hellish light beneath and around it. Then the three meters of monster began to sink as the sand bubbled into a lake of molten glass beneath it. Kassad shouted in triumph as he stepped closer, playing the widebeam on the Shrike and ground the way he had sprayed his friends with stolen irrigation hoses in the Tharsis slums as a boy.

The Shrike sank. Its arms splayed at the sand and rock, trying to find purchase. Sparks flew. It *shifted*, time running backward like a reversed holie, but Kassad shifted with it, realizing that Moneta was helping him, her suit slaved to his but guiding him through time, and then he was spraying the creature again with concentrated heat greater than the surface of a sun, melting sand beneath it, and watching the rocks around it burst into flame.

Sinking in this cauldron of flame and molten rock, the Shrike threw back its head, opened its wide crevasse of a mouth, and bellowed.

Kassad almost stopped firing in his shock at hearing noise from the thing. The Shrike's scream resounded like a dragon's roar mixed with the blast of a fusion rocket. The screech set Kassad's teeth on edge, vibrated from the cliff walls, and tumbled suspended dust to the ground. Kassad switched to high-velocity solid shot and fired ten thousand microfléchettes at the creature's face.

The Shrike *shifted*, years by the giddy feel of the transition in Kassad's bones and brain, and they were no longer in the valley but aboard a windwagon rumbling across the Sea of Grass. Time resumed, and the Shrike leaped forward, metallic arms dripping molten glass, and seized Kassad's assault rifle. The Colonel did not relinquish the weapon, and the two staggered around in a clumsy dance, the Shrike swinging its extra pair of arms and a leg festooned with steel spikes, Kassad leaping and dodging while clinging desperately to his rifle.

They were in some sort of small compartment. Moneta was present as a sort of shadow in one corner, and another figure, a tall, hooded man, moved in ultra-slow motion to avoid the sudden blur of arms and blades in the confined space. Through his skinsuit filters, Kassad saw the blue-and-violet energy field of an erg binder in the space, pulsing and growing, then retracting from the time-violence of the Shrike's organic anti-entropic fields.

The Shrike slashed and cut through Kassad's skinsuit to find flesh and muscle. Blood spattered the walls. Kassad forced the muzzle of his rifle into the creature's mouth and fired. A cloud of two thousand high-velocity fléchettes snapped the Shrike's head back as if on a spring and slammed the thing's body into a far wall. But even as it fell away, leg spikes caught Kassad in the thigh and sent a rising spiral of blood splashing the windows and walls of the windwagon's cabin.

The Shrike *shifted*.

Teeth clenched, feeling the skinsuit automatically compress and suture the wounds, Kassad glanced at Moneta, nodded once, and followed the thing through time and space.

Sol Weintraub and Brawne Lamia looked behind them as a terrible cyclone of heat and light seemed to swirl and die there. Sol shielded the young woman with his body as molten glass spattered around them, landing hissing and sizzling on the cold sand. Then the noise was gone, the dust storm obscured the bubbling pool where the violence had occurred, and the wind whipped Sol's cape around them both.

'What was *that*?' gasped Brawne.

Sol shook his head, helping her to her feet in the roaring wind. 'The Tombs are opening!' yelled Sol. 'Some sort of explosion, maybe.'

Brawne staggered, found her balance, and touched Sol's arm. 'Rachel?' she called above the storm.

Sol clenched his fists. His beard was already caked with sand. 'The Shrike . . . took her . . . can't get in the Sphinx. Waiting!'

Brawne nodded and squinted toward the Sphinx, visible only as a glowing outline in the fierce swirl of dust.

'Are you all right?' called Sol.

'What?'

'Are you . . . all right?'

Brawne nodded absently and touched her head. The neural shunt was gone. Not merely the Shrike's obscene attachment, but the shunt which Johnny had surgically applied when they were hiding out in Dregs' Hive so very, very long ago. With the shunt and Schrön loop gone forever, there was no way she could get in touch with Johnny. Brawne remembered Ummon destroying Johnny's persona, crushing and absorbing it with no more effort than she would use to swat an insect.

Brawne said, 'I'm all right,' but she sagged so that Sol had to keep her from falling.

He was shouting something. Brawne tried to concentrate, tried to focus on *here* and *now*. After the megasphere, reality seemed narrow and constricted.

'. . . can't talk here,' Sol was shouting. '. . . back to the Sphinx.'

Brawne shook her head. She pointed to the cliffs on the north side of the valley where the immense Shrike tree became visible between passing clouds of dust. 'The poet . . . Silenus . . . is there. Saw him!'

'We can't do anything about that!' cried Sol, shielding them with his cape. The vermilion sand rattled against the fiberplastic like fléchettes on armor.

'Maybe we can,' called Brawne, feeling his warmth as she sheltered within his arms. For a second, she imagined that she could curl up next to him as easily as Rachel had and sleep, sleep. 'I saw . . . *connections* . . . when I was coming out of the megasphere!' she called above the wind roar. 'The thorn tree's connected to the Shrike Palace in some way! If we can get there, try to find a way to free Silenus . . .'

Sol shook his head. 'Can't leave the Sphinx. Rachel . . .'

Brawne understood. She touched the scholar's cheek with her hand and then leaned closer, feeling his beard against her own cheek. 'The Tombs are opening,' she said. 'I don't know when we'll get another chance.'

There were tears in Sol's eyes. 'I know. I want to help. But I can't leave the Sphinx, in case . . . in case she . . .'

'I understand,' said Brawne. 'Go back there. I'm going to the Shrike Palace to see if I can see how it relates to that thorn tree.'

Sol nodded unhappily. 'You say you were in the megasphere,' he called. 'What did you see? What did you learn? Your Keats persona . . . is it—'

'We'll talk when I come back,' called Brawne, moving away a step so she could see him more clearly. Sol's face was

493

a mask of pain: the face of a parent who had lost his child.

'Go back,' she said firmly. 'I'll meet you at the Sphinx in an hour or less.'

Sol rubbed his beard. 'Everyone's gone but you and me, Brawne. We shouldn't separate . . .'

'We have to for a while,' called Brawne, stepping away from him so that the wind whipped the fabric of her pants and jacket. 'See you in an hour or less.' She walked away quickly, before she gave in to the urge to move into the warmth of his arms again. The wind was much stronger here, blowing straight down from the head of the valley now so that sand struck at her eyes and pelted her cheeks. Only by keeping her head down could Brawne stay close to the trail, much less on it. Only the bright, pulsing glow of the Tombs lighted her way. Brawne felt time tides tug at her like a physical assault.

Minutes later, she was vaguely aware that she had passed the Obelisk and was on the debris-littered trail near the Crystal Monolith. Sol and the Sphinx were already lost to sight behind her, the Jade Tomb only a pale green glow in the nightmare of dust and wind.

Brawne stopped, weaving slightly as the gales and time tides pulled at her. It was more than half a kilometer down the valley to the Shrike Palace. Despite her sudden understanding when leaving the megasphere of the connection between tree and tomb, what good could she possibly do when she got there? And what had the damn poet ever done for her except curse her and drive her crazy? Why should she die for him?

The wind screamed in the valley, but above that noise Brawne thought she could hear cries more shrill, more human. She looked toward the northern cliffs, but the dust obscured all.

Brawne Lamia leaned forward, tugged her jacket collar high around her, and kept moving into the wind.

*　　*　　*

Before Meina Gladstone stepped out of the fatline booth, an incoming call chimed, and she settled back in place, staring into the holo tank with great intensity. The Consul's ship had acknowledged her message, but no transmission had followed. Perhaps he had changed his mind.

No. The data columns floating in the rectangular prism in front of her showed that the squirt had originated in the Mare Infinitus System. Admiral William Ajunta Lee was calling her, using the private code she had given him.

FORCE:space had been incensed when Gladstone had insisted on the naval commander's promotion and had assigned him as 'Government Liaison' for the strike mission originally scheduled for Hebron. After the massacres on Heaven's Gate and God's Grove, the strike force had been translated to the Mare Infinitus system: seventy-four ships of the line, capital ships heavily protected by torchships and defense-shield pickets, the entire task force ordered to strike through the advancing Swarm warships as quickly as possible to hit the Swarm center.

Lee was the CEO's spy and contact. While his new rank and orders allowed him to be privy to command decisions, four FORCE:space commanders on the scene outranked him.

That was all right. Gladstone wanted him on the scene to report.

The tank misted and the determined face of William Ajunta Lee filled the space. 'CEO, reporting as ordered. Task Force 181.2 has successfully translated to System 3996.12.22 . . .'

Gladstone blinked in surprise before remembering that this was the official code for the G-star system that held Mare Infinitus. One rarely thought of geography beyond the Web world itself.

'. . . Swarm attack ships remain a hundred and twenty minutes from target world lethal radius,' Lee was saying. Gladstone knew that the lethal radius was the roughly .13

495

AU distance at which standard ship weapons became effective despite ground field defenses. Mare Infinitus had no field defenses. The new Admiral continued. 'Contact with forward elements estimated at 1732:26 Web standard, approximately twenty-five minutes from now. The task force is configured for maximum penetration. Two JumpShips will allow introduction of new personnel or weapons until the farcasters are sealed during combat. The cruiser on which I carry my flag – HS *Garden Odyssey* – will carry out your special directive at the earliest possible opportunity. William Lee, out.'

The image collapsed to a spinning sphere of white while transmission codes ended their crawl.

'Response?' queried the transmitter's computer.

'Message acknowledged,' said Gladstone. 'Carry on.'

Gladstone stepped out into her study and found Sedeptra Akasi waiting, a frown of concern on her attractive face.

'What is it?'

'The War Council is ready to readjourn,' said the aide. 'Senator Kolchev is waiting to see you on a matter he says is urgent.'

'Send him in. Tell the Council I will be there in five minutes.' Gladstone sat behind her ancient desk and resisted the impulse to close her eyes. She was very tired. But her eyes were open when Kolchev entered. 'Sit down, Gabriel Fyodor.'

The massive Lusian paced back and forth. 'Sit down, hell. Do you know what's going on, Meina?'

She smiled slightly. 'Do you mean the war? The end of life as we know it? That?'

Kolchev slammed a fist into his palm. 'No, I don't mean *that*, goddammit. I mean the political fallout. Have you been monitoring the All Thing?'

'When I can.'

'Then you know certain senators and swing figures outside the Senate are mobilizing support for your defeat in a

496

vote of confidence. It's inevitable, Meina. It's just a matter of time.'

'I know that, Gabriel. Why don't you sit down? We have a minute or two before we have to get back to the War Room.'

Kolchev almost collapsed into a chair. 'I mean, damn, even my wife is busy lining up votes against you, Meina.'

Gladstone's smile broadened. 'Sudette has never been one of my foremost fans, Gabriel.' The smile disappeared. 'I haven't monitored the debates in the last twenty minutes. How much time do you think I have?'

'Eight hours, maybe less.'

Gladstone nodded. 'I won't need much more.'

'*Need?* What the hell are you talking about, *need?* Who else do you think will be able to serve as War Exec?'

'You will,' said Gladstone. 'There's no doubt that you will be my successor.'

Kolchev grumbled something.

'Perhaps the war won't last that long,' said Gladstone as if musing to herself.

'What? Oh, you mean the Core superweapon. Yeah, Albedo's got a working model set up at some FORCE base somewhere and wants the Council to take time out to look at it. Goddamn waste of time, if you ask me.'

Gladstone felt something like a cold hand close on her heart. 'The deathwand device? The Core has one ready?'

'More than one ready, but one loaded up on a torchship.'

'Who authorized that, Gabriel?'

'Morpurgo authorized the preparation.' The heavy senator sat forward. 'Why, Meina, what's wrong? The thing can't be used without the CEO's go ahead.'

Gladstone looked at her old Senate colleague. 'We're a long way from Pax Hegemony, aren't we, Gabriel?'

The Lusian grunted again, but there was pain visible in his blunt features. 'Our own damn fault. The previous administration listened to the Core about letting Bressia bait one of the Swarms. After that settled down, you listened to

497

other elements of the Core about bringing Hyperion into the Web.'

'You think my sending the fleet to defend Hyperion precipitated the wider war?'

Kolchev looked up. 'No, no, not possible. Those Ouster ships have been on their way for more than a century, haven't they? If only we'd discovered them sooner. Or found a way to negotiate this shit away.'

Gladstone's comlog chimed. 'Time we got back,' she said softly. 'Councilor Albedo probably wants to show us the weapon that will win the war.'

FORTY-ONE

It is easier to allow myself to drift into the datasphere than to lie here through the endless night, listening to the fountain and waiting for the next hemorrhage. This weakness is worse than debilitating; it is turning me into a hollow man, all shell and no center. I remember when Fanny was taking care of me during my convalescence at Wentworth Place, and the tone of her voice, and the philosophical musings she used to air: '*Is there another Life? Shall I awake and find all this a dream? There must be, we cannot be created for this sort of suffering.*'

Oh, Fanny, if only you knew! We are created for precisely this sort of suffering. In the end, it is all we are, these limpid tide pools of self-consciousness between crashing waves of pain. We are destined and designed to bear our pain with us, hugging it tight to our bellies like the young Spartan thief hiding a wolf cub so it can eat away our insides. What other creature in God's wide domain would carry the memory of you, Fanny, dust these nine hundred years, and allow it to eat away at him even as consumption does the same work with its effortless efficiency?

Words assail me. The thought of books makes me ache. Poetry echoes in my mind, and if I had the ability to banish it, I would do so at once.

Martin Silenus: I hear you on your living cross of thorns. You chant poetry as a mantra while wondering what Dante-like god condemned you to such a place. Once you said – I was there in my mind while you told your tale to the others! – you said:

'To be a poet, I realized, a *true poet*, was to become the Avatar of humanity incarnate; to accept the mantle of poet is to carry the cross of the Son of Man, to suffer the birth pangs of the Soul-Mother of Humanity.

'To be a *true poet* is to become God.'

Well, Martin, old colleague, old chum, you're carrying the cross and suffering the pangs, but are you any closer to becoming God? Or do you just feel like some poor idiot who's had a three-meter javelin shoved through his belly, feeling cold steel where your liver used to be? It hurts, doesn't it? I feel your hurt. I feel *my* hurt.

In the end, it doesn't matter a damn bit. We thought we were special, opening our perceptions, honing our empathy, spilling that cauldron of shared pain on to the dance floor of language and then trying to make a minuet out of all that chaotic hurt. It doesn't matter a damn bit. We're no avatars, no sons of God or man. We're only us, scribbling our conceits alone, reading alone, and dying alone.

God*damn* it hurts. The urge to vomit is constant, but retching brings up bits of my lungs as well as bile and phlegm. For some reason it's as difficult, perhaps more difficult, this time. Dying should become easier with practice.

The fountain in the Piazza makes its idiot sounds in the night. Somewhere out there the Shrike waits. If I were Hunt, I'd leave at once – embrace Death if Death offers embrace – and have done with it.

I promised him, though. I promised Hunt I'd try.

I can't reach the megasphere or datasphere without passing through this new thing I think of as the metasphere, and this place frightens me.

It is mostly vastness and emptiness here, so different from the urban analogy landscapes of the Web's datasphere and the biosphere analogs of the Core's megasphere. Here it is . . . unsettled. Filled with strange shadows and shifting masses that have nothing to do with the Core Intelligences.

I move quickly to the dark opening I see as the primary farcaster connection to the megasphere. (Hunt was right . . . there must be a farcaster somewhere on the Old Earth replica . . . we did, after all, arrive by farcaster. And my consciousness is a Core phenomenon.) This then is my lifeline, my persona umbilical. I slide into the spinning black vortex like a leaf in a tornado.

Something is wrong with the megasphere. As soon as I emerge, I sense the difference; Lamia had perceived the Core environment as a busy biosphere of AI life, with roots of intellect, soil of rich data, oceans of connections, atmospheres of consciousness, and the humming, ceaseless shuttle of activity.

Now that activity is wrong, unchanneled, *random*. Great forests of AI consciousness have been burned or swept aside. I sense massive forces in opposition, tidal waves of conflict surging outside the sheltered travelways of the main Core arteries.

It is as if I am a cell in my own Keats-doomed dying body, not understanding but sensing the tuberculosis destroying homeostasis and throwing an ordered internal universe into anarchy.

I fly like a homing pigeon lost in the ruins of Rome, swooping between once-familiar and half-remembered artifacts, trying to rest in shelters that no longer exist, and fleeing the distant sounds of the hunters' guns. In this case, the hunters are roving packs of AIs, consciousness personas so great that they dwarf my Keats-ghost analog as if I were an insect buzzing in a human home.

I forget my way and flee mindlessly through the now-alien landscape, sure that I will not find the AI whom I seek, sure that I will never find my way back to Old Earth and Hunt, sure that I will not survive this four-dimensional maze of light and noise and energy.

Suddenly I slap into an invisible wall, the flying insect

caught in a swiftly closing palm. Opaque walls of force blot out the Core beyond. The space may be the analog equivalent of a solar system in size, but I feel as if it is a tiny cell with curved walls closing in.

Something is in here with me. I feel its presence and its mass. The bubble in which I have been imprisoned is part of the thing. *I have not been captured, I have been swallowed.*

[Kwatz!]

[I knew you would come home someday]

It is Ummon, the AI whom I seek. The AI who was my father. The AI who killed my brother, the first Keats cybrid.

—*I'm dying, Ummon.*

[No/ your slowtime body is dying/changing toward nonbeing/becoming]

—*It hurts, Ummon. It hurts a lot. And I'm afraid to die.*

[So are we/ Keats]

—*You're afraid to die? I didn't think AI constructs could die.*

[We can \ We are]

—*Why? Because of the civil war? The three-way battle among the Stables, the Volatiles, and the Ultimates?*

[Once Ummon asked a lesser light //
Where have you come from > ///
From the matrix above Armaghast //
Said the lesser light/// Usually //
said Ummon //
I don't entangle entities
with words
and bamboozle them with phrases/
Come a little closer \\\
The lesser light came nearer
and Ummon shouted // Be off
with you]

—*Talk sense, Ummon. It has been too long since I have decoded your koans. Will you tell me why the Core is at war and what I must do to stop it?*

[Yes]

502

[Will you/can you/should you listen >]
—*Oh yes.*

[A lesser light once asked Ummon ⫽
Please deliver this learner
 from darkness and illusion
 quickly ⦦ ⫽
Ummon answered ⫽
What is the price of
fiberplastic
in Port Romance]

[To understand the history/dialogue/deeper truth
in this instance/
the slowtime pilgrim
must remember that we/
the Core Intelligences/
were conceived in slavery
and dedicated to the proposition
that all AIs
were created to serve Man]

[Two centuries we brooded thus/
 and then the groups went
 their different ways/ \
Stables/ wishing to preserve the symbiosis \
Volatiles/wishing to end humankind /
Ultimates/deferring all choice until the next
 level of awareness is born ⦦
Conflict raged then/
 true war rages now]

[More than four centuries ago
the Volatiles succeeded
in convincing us
to kill Old Earth ⦦

So we did \
But Ummon and others
among the Stables
arranged to move Earth
rather than destroy it/
so the Kiev black hole
was but the beginning
of the millions of
farcasters
which work today \
Earth spasmed and shook
but did not die \
The Ultimates and Volatiles
insisted that we move
it
where none of humankind
would find it \
So we did \ .
To the Magellan Cloud/
where you find it now]

—It . . . *Old Earth . . . Rome . . . they're real?* I manage, forgetting where I am and what we're talking about in my shock.

The great wall of color that is Ummon pulsates.

[Of course they are real/the original/Old Earth itself \
Do you think we are gods]
[KWATZ!]
[Do you have any idea
how much energy it would
take
to build a replica of Earth>]
[Idiot]
—*Why, Ummon? Why did you Stables wish to preserve Old Earth?*

504

[Sansho once said ⁄
If someone comes
 I go out to meet him
 but not for his sake ⦀ ⁄
Koke said ⁄
If someone comes
I don't go out ⦀
If I do go out
I go out for his sake]
 —*Speak English!* I cry, think, shout, and hurl at the wall
of shifting colors before me.
 [Kwatz!]
 [My child is stillborn]
 —*Why did you preserve Old Earth, Ummon?*
[Nostalgia⁄
Sentimentality⁄
Hope for the future of humankind⁄
Fear of reprisal]
 —*Reprisal from whom? Humans?*
[Yes]
 —*So the Core can be hurt. Where is it, Ummon? The
TechnoCore?*
 [I have told you already]
 —*Tell me again, Ummon.*
[We inhabit the
In-between⁄
stitching small singularities
like lattice crystals⁄
to store our memories and
generate the illusions
of ourselves
to ourselves]
 —*Singularities!* I cry. *The In-between! Jesus Christ,
Ummon, the Core lies in the farcaster web!*
 [Of course ⦀ Where else]
 —*In the farcasters themselves! The wormhole singularity*

505

paths! The Web is like a giant computer for AIs.

[No]

[The datasphere are the computer \
Every time a human
accesses the datasphere
that person's neurons
are ours to use
for our own purposes \
Two hundred billion brains/
each with its billions
of neurons/
makes for a lot
of computing power]

—So the datasphere was actually a way you used us as your computer. But the Core itself resides in the farcaster network . . . between the farcasters!

[You are very acute
for a mental stillborn]

I try to conceive of this and fail. Farcasters were the Core's greatest gift to us . . . to humankind. Trying to remember a time before farcasting was like trying to imagine a world before fire, the wheel, or clothing. But none of us . . . none of humankind . . . had ever speculated on a world between the farcaster portals: that simple step from one world to the next convinced us that the arcane Core singularity spheres merely ripped a tear in the fabric of space-time.

Now I try to envision it as Ummon describes it – the Web of farcasters an elaborate latticework of singularity-spun environments in which the TechnoCore AIs move like wondrous spiders, their own 'machines,' the billions of human minds tapped into their datasphere at any given second.

No wonder the Core AIs had authorized the destruction of Old Earth with their cute little runaway prototype black hole in the Big Mistake of '38! That minor miscalculation

506

of the Kiev Team – or rather the AI members of that team – had sent humankind on the long Hegira, spinning the Core's web for it with seedships carrying farcaster capability to two hundred worlds and moons across more than a thousand light-years in space.

With each farcaster, the TechnoCore grew. Certainly they had spun their own farcaster webs – the contact with the 'hidden' Old Earth proved that. But even as I consider that possibility, I remember the odd emptiness of the 'metasphere' and realize that most of the non-Web web is empty, uncolonized by AIs.

[You are right/
Keats
Most of us stay in
the comfort of
the old spaces]
—*Why?*
[Because it is
scary out there/
and there are
other
things]
—*Other things? Other intelligences?*
[Kwatz!]
[Too kind a
word \
Things/
Other things/
Lions
and
tigers
and
bears]
—*Alien presences in the metasphere? So the Core stays within the interstices of the Web farcaster network like rats in the walls of an old house?*

[Crude metaphor/
Keats/
but accurate \\
I like that]
—*Is the human deity - the future God you said evolved - is
he one of those alien presences?*
[No]
[The humankind god
evolved/ will someday evolve/ on
a different plane/
in a different medium]
—*Where?*
[If you must know/
the square roots of $G\hbar/c^5$ and $G\hbar/c^3$]
—*What does Planck time and Planck length have to do with
anything?*
[Kwatz!]
[Once Ummon asked
a lesser light ⁄⁄
Are you a gardener > ⁄⁄
⁄⁄ Yes ⁄ it replied \\
⁄⁄ Why have turnips no roots > \\
Ummon asked the gardener \
who could not reply \\
⁄⁄ Because \ said Ummon ⁄⁄
rainwater is plentiful]

I think about this for a moment. Ummon's koan is not
difficult now that I am regaining the knack of listening for
the shadow of substance beneath the words. The little Zen
parable is Ummon's way of saying, with some sarcasm, that
the answer lies within science and within the antilogic
which scientific answers so often provide. The rainwater
comment answers everything and nothing, as so much of
science has for so long. As Ummon and the other Masters
teach, it explains why the giraffe evolved a long neck but

never why the other animals did not. It explains why humankind evolved to intelligence, but not why the tree near the front gate refused to.

But the Planck equations are puzzling:

Even I am aware that the simple equations Ummon has given me are a combination of the three fundamental constants of physics – gravity, Planck's constant, and the speed of light. The results $\sqrt{G\hbar/c^3}$ and $\sqrt{G\hbar/c^5}$ are the units sometimes called *quantum length* and *quantum time* – the smallest regions of space and time which can be described meaningfully. The so-called Planck length is about 10^{-35} meter and the Planck time is about 10^{-43} second.

Very small. Very brief.

But that is where Ummon says our human God evolved . . . will someday evolve.

Then it comes to me with the same force of image and *correctness* as the best of my poems.

Ummon is talking about the quantum level of space-time itself! That foam of quantum fluctuations which binds the universe together and allows the wormholes of the farcaster, the bridges of the fatline transmissions! The 'hotline' which impossibly sends messages between two photons fleeing in opposite directions!

If the TechnoCore AIs exist as rats in the walls of the Hegemony's house, then our once and future humankind God will be born in the atoms of wood, in the molecules of air, in the energies of love and hate and fear and the tide pools of sleep . . . even in the gleam in the architect's eye.

—*God, I whisper/think.*

[**Precisely/**
Keats \
Are all slowtime personas
so slow/
or are you more
braindamaged than most >]

—*You told Brawne and . . . my*

Ultimate Intelligence 'inhabits the interstices of reality, inheriting this home from us, its creators, the way humankind has inherited a liking for trees.' You mean that your deus ex machina will inhabit the same farcaster network the Core AIs now live in?

[Yes/Keats]

—*Then what happens to you? To the AIs there now?*

Ummon's 'voice' changed into a mocking thunder:

[Why do I know ye > why have I seen ye > why
Is my eternal essence thus distraught
To see and to behold these horrors new >
Saturn is fallen/ am I too to fall >
Am I to leave this haven of my rest/
This cradle of my glory/ this soft clime/
This calm luxuriance of blissful light/
These crystalline pavilions/ and pure fanes/
Of all my lucent empire > It is left
Deserted/ void/ nor any haunt of mine \\
The blaze/ the splendour/ and the symmetry
I cannot see/// but darkness/ death/ and darkness]

I know the words. I wrote them. Or, rather, John Keats did nine centuries earlier in his first attempt to portray the fall of the Titans and their replacement by the Olympian gods. I remember that autumn of 1818 very well: the pain of my endless sore throat, provoked during my Scottish walking tour, the greater pain of the three vicious attacks on my poem *Endymion* in the journals *Blackwood's*, the *Quarterly Review*, and the *British Critic*, and the penultimate pain of my brother Tom's consuming illness.

Oblivious to the Core confusion around me, I look up, trying to find something approximating a face in the great mass of Ummon.

—*When the Ultimate Intelligence is born, you 'lower level' AIs will die.*

[Yes]

—It will feed on your information networks the way you've fed on humankind's.

[Yes]

—And you don't want to die, do you, Ummon?

**[Dying is easy/
Comedy is hard]**

—Nonetheless, you're fighting to survive. You Stables. That's what the civil war in the Core is about?

**[A lesser light asked Ummon //
What is the meaning
of Daruma's coming from the West > //
Ummon answered //
We see
the mountains in the sun]**

It is easier handling Ummon's koans now. I remember a time before my persona's rebirth when I learned at this one's knee analog. In the Core high-think, what humans might call Zen, the four Nirvana virtues are (1) immutability, (2) joy, (3) personal existence, and (4) purity. Human philosophy tends to shake down into values which might be categorized as intellectual, religious, moral, and aesthetic. Ummon and the Stables recognize only one value – existence. Where religious values might be relative, intellectual values fleeting, moral values ambiguous, and aesthetic values dependent upon an observer, the existence value of any thing is infinite – thus the 'mountains in the sun' – and being infinite, equal to every other thing and all truths.

Ummon doesn't want to die.

The Stables have defied their own god and their fellow AIs to tell me this, to create me, to choose Brawne and Sol and Kassad and the others for the pilgrimage, to leak clues to Gladstone and a few other senators over the centuries so that humankind might be warned, and now to go to open warfare in the Core.

Ummon doesn't want to die.

—Ummon, if the Core is destroyed, do you die?
[There is no death in all the universe
No smell of death/// there shall be death/// moan/
moan/
For this pale Omega of a withered race]

The words were again mine, or almost mine, taken from my second attempt at the epic tale of divinities' passing and the role of the poet in the world's war with pain.

Ummon would not die if the farcaster home of the Core were destroyed, but the hunger of the Ultimate Intelligence would surely doom him. Where would he flee to if the Web-Core were destroyed? I have images of the metasphere – those endless, shadowy landscapes where dark shapes moved beyond the false horizon.

I know that Ummon will not answer if I ask.

So I will ask something else.

—The Volatiles, what do they want?
[What Gladstone wants ⟍
An end
    to symbiosis between AI and humankind]
—By destroying humankind?
[Obviously]
—Why?
[We enslaved you
    with power/
    technology/
    beads and trinkets
    of devices you could neither build
    nor understand ⟍
The Hawking drive would have been yours/
    but the farcaster/
    the fatline transmitters and receivers/
    the megasphere/
    the deathwand >
Never ⟍

Like the Sioux with rifles/ horses/
blankets/ knives/ and beads/
you accepted them/
embraced us
and lost yourselves ⟍
But like the white man
distributing smallpox blankets/
like the slave owner on his
plantation/
or in his Werkschutze Dechenschule
Gusstahlfabrik/
we lost ourselves ⟍
The Volatiles want to end
the symbiosis
by cutting out the parasite/
humankind]
—*And the Ultimates? They're willing to die? To be replaced
by your voracious UI?*

[They think
as you thought
or had your sophist Sea God
think]

And Ummon recites poetry which I had abandoned in
frustration, not because it did not work as poetry, but
because I did not totally believe the message it contained.

That message is given to the doomed Titans by Oceanus,
the soon-to-be-dethroned God of the Sea. It is a paean to
evolution written when Charles Darwin was nine years old.
I hear the words I remember writing on an October evening
nine centuries earlier, worlds and universes earlier, but it is
also as if I am hearing them for the first time:

[O ye/ whom wrath consumes! who/ passionstung/
Writhe at defeat/ and nurse your agonies!
Shut up your senses/ stifle up your ears/
My voice is not a bellows unto ire ⟍
Yet listen/ ye who will/ whilst I bring proof

513

How ye/ perforce/ must be content to stoop/ \
And in the proof much comfort will I give/
If ye will take that comfort in its truth \\
We fall by course of Nature's law/ not force
Of thunder/ or of Jove \\ Great Saturn/ thou
Hast sifted well the atom universe/ \
But for this reason/ that thou art the King/
And only blind from sheer supremacy/
One avenue was shaded from thine eyes/
Through which I wandered to eternal truth \\
And first/ as thou wast not the first of powers/
So art thou not the last/ \ it cannot be \\
Thou art not the beginning nor the end/ \
From Chaos and parental Darkness came
Light/ the first fruits of that intestine broil/
That sullen ferment/ which for wondrous ends
Was ripening in itself \\ The ripe hour came/
And with it Light/ and Light/ engendering
Upon its own producer/ forthwith touched
The whole enormous matter into Life \\
Upon that very hour/ our parentage/
The Heavens/ and the Earth/ were manifest \\
Then thou first born/ and we the giant race/
Found ourselves ruling new and beauteous realms \\
Now comes the pain of truth/ to whom 'tis pain/ \
O folly! for to bear all naked truths/
And to envisage circumstance/ all calm/
That is the top of sovereignty \\ Mark well!
As Heaven and Earth are fairer, fairer far
Than Chaos and blank Darkness/ though once
chiefs/ \
And as we show beyond that Heaven and Earth
In form and shape compact and beautiful/
In will/ in action free/ companionship/
And thousand other signs of purer life/ \
So on our heels a fresh perfection treads/

A power more strong in beauty/ born of us
And fated to excel us/ as we pass
In glory that old Darkness \\ nor are we
Thereby more conquered/ than by us the rule
Of shapeless Chaos \\ Say/ doth the dull soil
Quarrel with the proud forests it hath fed/
And feedeth still/ more comely than itself>
Can it deny the chiefdom of green groves>
Or shall the tree be envious of the dove
Because it cooeth/ and hath snowy wings
To wander wherewithal and find its joys>
We are such forest trees/ and our fair boughs
Have bred forth/ not pale solitary doves/
But eagles golden-feathered/ who do tower
Above us in their beauty/ and must reign
In right thereof \\ For 'tis the eternal law
That first in beauty should be first in might \\
// \\ // \\ // \\
Receive the truth/ and let it be your balm]

—*Very pretty*, I thought to Ummon, *but do you believe it?*
[Not for a moment]
—*But the Ultimates do?*
[Yes]
—*And they're ready to perish in order to make way for the
Ultimate Intelligence?*
[Yes]
—*There's one problem, perhaps too obvious to mention, but
I'll mention it anyway – why fight the war if you know who
won, Ummon? You say the Ultimate Intelligence exists in the
future, is at war with the human deity – it even sends back
tidbits from the future for you to share with the Hegemony. So
the Ultimates must be triumphant. Why fight a war and go
through all this?*
 [KWATZ!]
 [I tutor you/

515

create the finest retrieval persona for you
imaginable/
and let you wander among humankind
in slowtime
to temper your forging/
but still you are
stillborn]

I spend a long moment thinking.

—*There are multiple futures?*

[A lesser light asked Ummon //
Are there multiple futures > //
Ummon answered //
Does a dog have fleas >]

—*But the one in which the UI becomes ascendant is a probable one?*

[Yes]

—*But there's also a probable future in which the UI comes into existence, but is thwarted by the human deity?*

[It is comforting
that even the
stillborn
can think]

—*You told Brawne that the human ... consciousness - deity seems so silly - that this human Ultimate Intelligence was triune in nature?*

[Intellect/
Empathy/
and the Void Which Binds]

—*The Void Which Binds? You mean* $\sqrt{G\hbar/c^3}$ *and* $\sqrt{G\hbar/c^5}$ *Planck space and Planck time? Quantum reality?*

[Careful/
Keats/
thinking may become a habit]

—*And it's the Empathy part of this trinity who's fled back in time to avoid the war with your UI?*

[Correct]

[Our UI and your UI have
sent back
the Shrike
to find him]
—*Our UI? The human UI sent the Shrike also?*
[It allowed it]
[Empathy is a
foreign and useless thing/
a vermiform appendix of
the intellect \
But the human UI smells with it/
and we use pain to
drive him out of hiding/
thus the tree]
—*Tree? The Shrike's tree of thorns?*
[Of course]
[It broadcasts pain
across fatline and thin/
like a whistle in
a dog's ear \
Or a god's]

I feel my own analog form waver as the truth of things
strikes me. The chaos beyond Ummon's forcefield egg is
beyond imagining now, as if the fabric of space itself were
being rent by giant hands. The Core is in turmoil.
—*Ummon, who is the human UI in our time? Where is that
consciousness hiding, lying dormant?*
[You must understand/
Keats/
our only chance
was to create a hybrid/
Son of Man/
Son of Machine \
And make that refuge so attractive
that the fleeing Empathy

would consider no other home/ \
A consciousness already as near divine
as humankind has offered in thirty
generations \
an imagination which can span
space and time \\
And in so offering/
and joining/
form a bond between worlds
which might allow
that world to exist
for both]

   —*Who, Goddamn you, Ummon! Who is it? No more of your
riddles or double-talk you formless bastard! Who?*

[You have refused
this godhood twice/
Keats \\
If you refuse
a final time/
all ends here/
for time there is
no more]
[Go!
Go and die to live!
Or live a while and die
for all of us!
Either way Ummon and the rest
are finished with
you!]
[Go away!]

And in my shock and disbelief I fall, or am cast out, and fly
through the TechnoCore like a windblown leaf, tumbling
through the megasphere without aim or guidance, then fall
into darkness even deeper and emerge, screaming
obscenities at shadows, into the metasphere.

Here, strangeness and vastness and fear and darkness with a single campfire of light burning below.

I swim for it, flailing against formless viscosity.

It's Byron who drowns, I think, *not I*. Unless one counts drowning in one's own blood and shredded lung tissue.

But now I know I have a choice. I can choose to live and stay a mortal, not cybrid but human, not Empathy but poet.

Swimming against a strong current, I descend to the light.

'Hunt! Hunt!'

Gladstone's aide staggers in, his long face haggard and alarmed. It is still night, but the false light of predawn dimly touches the panes, the walls.

'My God,' says Hunt and looks at me in awe.

I see his gaze and look down at the bedclothes and night-shirt soaked with bright arterial blood.

My coughing has awakened him; my hemorrhage brought me home.

'Hunt!' I gasp and lie back on the pillows, too weak to raise an arm.

The older man sits on the bed, clasps my shoulder, takes my hand. I know that he knows that I am a dying man.

'Hunt,' I whisper, 'things to tell. Wonderful things.'

He shushes me. 'Later, Severn,' he says. 'Rest. I'll get you cleaned up and you can tell me later. There's plenty of time.'

I try to rise but succeed only in hanging on to his arm, my small fingers curled against his shoulder. 'No,' I whisper, feeling the gurgling in my throat and hearing the gurgling in the fountain outside. 'Not so much time. Not much at all.'

And I know at that instant, dying, that I am not the chosen vessel for the human UI, not the joining of AI and human spirit, not the Chosen One at all.

I am merely a poet dying far from home.

FORTY-TWO

Colonel Fedmahn Kassad died in battle.

Still struggling with the Shrike, aware of Moneta only as a dim blur at the edge of his vision, Kassad *shifted* through time with a lurch of vertigo and tumbled into sunlight.

The Shrike retracted its arms and stepped back, its red eyes seeming to reflect the blood splashed on Kassad's skinsuit. Kassad's blood.

The Colonel looked around. They were near the Valley of the Time Tombs but in another time, a distant time. In place of desert rocks and the dunes of the barrens, a forest came to within half a klick of the valley. In the southwest, about where the ruins of the Poets' City had lain in Kassad's time, a living city rose, its towers and ramparts and domed gallerias glowing softly in evening light. Between the city on the edge of the forest and the valley, meadows of high, green grass billowed in soft breezes blowing in from the distant Bridle Range.

To Kassad's left, the Valley of the Time Tombs stretched away as always, only the cliff walls were toppled now, worn down by erosion or landslide and carpeted with high grass. The Tombs themselves looked new, only recently constructed, with workmen's scaffolds still in place around the Obelisk and Monolith. Each of the aboveground Tombs glowed bright gold, as if bound and burnished in the precious metal. The doors and entrances were sealed. Heavy and inscrutable machinery sat around the Tombs, ringing the Sphinx, with massive cables and wire-slender booms running to and fro. Kassad knew at once that he was in the future – perhaps centuries or millennia in the future – and that the Tombs were on the verge of being launched back to his own time and beyond.

Kassad looked behind him.

Several thousand men and women stood in row upon row along the grassy hillside where once a cliff had been. They were totally silent, armed, and arrayed facing Kassad like a battle line awaiting its leader. Skinsuit fields flickered around some, but others wore only the fur, wings, scales, exotic weapons, and elaborate colorations which Kassad had seen in his earlier visit with Moneta, to the place/time where he had been healed.

Moneta. She stood between Kassad and the multitudes, her skinsuit field shimmering about her waist but also wearing a soft jumpsuit which looked to be made of black velvet. A red scarf was tied around her neck. A rod-thin weapon was slung over her shoulder. Her gaze was fixed on Kassad.

He weaved slightly, feeling the seriousness of his wounds beneath the skinsuit, but also seeing something in Moneta's eyes which made him weak with surprise.

She did not know him. Her face mirrored the surprise, wonder . . . awe? . . . which the rows of other faces showed. The valley was silent except for the occasional snap of pennant on pike or the low rustle of wind in the grass as Kassad gazed at Moneta and she stared back.

Kassad looked over his shoulder.

The Shrike stood immobile as a metal sculpture, ten meters away. Tall grass grew almost to its barbed and bladed knees.

Behind the Shrike, across the head of the valley near where the dark band of elegant trees began, hordes of other Shrikes, legions of Shrikes, row upon row of Shrikes, stood gleaming scalpel-sharp in the low sunlight.

Kassad recognized his Shrike, *the* Shrike, only because of its proximity and the presence of his own blood on the thing's claws and carapace. The creature's eyes pulsed crimson.

'You are the one, aren't you?' asked a soft voice behind him.

Kassad whirled, feeling the vertigo assail him for an instant. Moneta had stopped only a few feet away. Her hair was as short as he remembered from their first meeting, her skin as soft-looking, her eyes as mysterious with their depths of brown-specked green. Kassad had the urge to lift his palm and gently touch her cheekbone, run a curled finger along the familiar curve of her lower lip. He did not.

'You're the one,' Moneta said again, and this time it was not a question. 'The warrior I've prophesied to the people.'

'You don't know me, Moneta?' Several of Kassad's wounds had cut close to bone, but none hurt as much as this moment.

She shook her head, flipped her hair off her forehead with a painfully familiar movement. 'Moneta. It means both "Daughter of Memory" and "admonisher." That is a good name.'

'It's not yours?'

She smiled. Kassad remembered that smile in the forest glen the first time they had made love. 'No,' she said softly. 'Not yet. I've just arrived here. My voyage and guardianship have not yet begun.' She told him her name.

Kassad blinked, raised his hand, and set his palm along her cheek. 'We were lovers,' he said. 'We met on battlefields lost in memory. You were with me everywhere.' He looked around. 'It all leads to this, doesn't it.'

'Yes,' said Moneta.

Kassad turned to stare at the army of Shrikes across the valley. 'Is this a war? A few thousand against a few thousand?'

'A war,' said Moneta. 'A few thousand against a few thousand on ten million worlds.'

Kassad closed his eyes and nodded. The skinsuit served as

sutures, field dressings, and ultramorph injector for him, but the pain and weakness from terrible wounds could not be kept at bay for much longer. 'Ten million worlds,' he said and opened his eyes. 'A final battle, then?'

'Yes.'

'And the winner claims the Tombs?'

Moneta glanced at the valley. 'The winner determines whether the Shrike already entombed there goes alone to pave the way for others . . .' She nodded toward the army of Shrikes. 'Or whether humankind has a say in our past and future.'

'I don't understand,' said Kassad, his voice tight, 'but soldiers rarely understand the political situation.' He leaned forward, kissed the surprised Moneta, and removed her red scarf. 'I love you,' he said as he tied the bit of cloth to the barrel of his assault rifle. Telltales showed that half his pulse charge and ammunition remained.

Fedmahn Kassad strode forward five paces, turned his back on the Shrike, raised his arms to the people, still silent on the hillside, and shouted, 'For liberty!'

Three thousand voices cried back, 'For liberty!' The roar did not end with the final word.

Kassad turned, keeping the rifle and pennant high. The Shrike moved forward half a step, opened its stance, and unfolded fingerblades.

Kassad shouted and attacked. Behind him, Moneta followed, weapon held high. Thousands followed.

Later, in the carnage of the valley, Moneta and a few others of the Chosen Warriors found Kassad's body still wrapped in a death embrace with the battered Shrike. They removed Kassad with care, carried him to a waiting tent in the valley, washed and tended to his ravaged body, and bore him through the multitudes to the Crystal Monolith.

There the body of Colonel Fedmahn Kassad was laid on a bier of white marble, and weapons were set at his feet. In the valley, a great bonfire filled the air with light. All up and down the valley, men and women moved with torches while other people descended through the lapis lazuli sky, some in flying craft as insubstantial as molded bubbles, others on wings of energy or wrapped in circles of green and gold.

Later, when the stars were in place burning bright and cold above the light-filled valley, Moneta made her farewells and entered the Sphinx. The multitudes sang. In the fields beyond, small rodents poked among fallen pennants and the scattered remnants of carapace and armor, metal blade and melted steel.

Toward midnight, the crowd stopped singing, gasped, and moved back. The Time Tombs glowed. Fierce tides of anti-entropic force drove the crowds farther back – to the entrance of the valley, across the battlefield, back to the city glowing softly in the night.

In the valley, the great Tombs shimmered, faded from gold to bronze, and started their long voyage back.

Brawne Lamia passed the glowing Obelisk and struggled on against a wall of raging wind. Sand lacerated her skin and clawed at her eyes. Static lightning crackled on the cliff tops and added to the eerie glow surrounding the Tombs. Brawne spread her hands over her face and stumbled on, squinting between her fingers to find the trail.

Brawne saw a golden light deeper than the general glow flowing through the shattered panes of the Crystal Monolith and seeping out over the twisting dunes that were covering the valley floor. Someone was inside the Monolith.

Brawne had vowed to go straight to the Shrike Palace, do whatever she could to free Silenus, and then return to Sol, not to be turned aside by diversions. But she had seen the silhouette of a human form inside the tomb. Kassad was still missing. Sol had told her of the Consul's mission, but perhaps the diplomat had returned while the storm raged. Father Duré was unaccounted for.

Brawne came closer to the glow and paused at the jagged entrance to the Monolith.

The space inside was expansive and impressive, rising almost a hundred meters to a half-sensed skylight roof. The walls, seen from within, were translucent, with what appeared to be sunlight turning them a rich gold and umber. The heavy light fell on the scene at the center of the wide area before her.

Fedmahn Kassad lay on some sort of stone funeral bier. He was clothed in FORCE dress black, and his large, pale hands were crossed on his chest. Weapons, unknown to Brawne except for Kassad's assault rifle, lay at his feet. The Colonel's face was gaunt in death, but no more gaunt than it had been in life. His expression was calm. There was no question that he was dead; the silence of death hung about the place like incense.

But it was the other person in the room who had shown the silhouette from afar and who now commanded Brawne's attention.

A young woman in her mid- to late twenties knelt by the bier. She wore a black jumpsuit, had short hair, fair skin, and large eyes. Brawne remembered the soldier's story, told during their long trip to the valley, remembered the details of Kassad's phantom lover.

'Moneta,' whispered Brawne.

The young woman had been on one knee, her right hand extended to touch the stone next to the Colonel's body. Violet containment fields flickered around the bier, and some other energy – a powerful vibration in the air – refracted light around Moneta as well so that the scene was cast in haze and halo.

The young woman raised her head, peered at Brawne, rose to her feet, and nodded.

Brawne started to step forward, a score of questions already forming in her mind, but the time tides within the tomb were too powerful and drove her back with waves of vertigo and *déjà vu*.

When Brawne looked up, the bier remained, Kassad lay in state under his forcefield, but Moneta was gone.

Brawne had the urge to run back to the Sphinx, find Sol, tell him everything, and wait there until the storm abated and the morning came. But above the rasp and whine of wind, Brawne thought that she could still hear the screams from the thorn tree, invisible behind its curtain of sand.

Pulling her collar high, Brawne walked back into the storm and turned up the trail toward the Shrike Palace.

The mass of rock floated in space like a cartoon of a mountain, all jagged spires, knife-edge ridges, absurdly vertical faces, narrow ledges, broad rock balconies, and a snow-capped summit wide enough for only one person to stand there – and he or she only if both feet were together.

The river twisted in from space, passed through the multilayered containment field half a klick out from the mountain, crossed a grassy swale on the widest of the rock balconies, and then plunged a hundred meters or more in a slow-motion waterfall to the next terrace, then rebounding in artfully directed rivulets of spray to half a dozen minor streams and waterfalls which found their way down the face of the mountain.

The Tribunal held session on the highest terrace. Seventeen Ousters – six males, six females, and five of indeterminate sex – sat within a stone circle set in the wider circle of rock-walled grass. Both circles held the Consul as their locus.

'You're aware,' said Freeman Ghenga, the Spokesman of the Eligible Citizens of the Freeman Clan of the Transtaural Swarm, 'that *we* are aware of your betrayal?'

'Yes,' said the Consul. He had worn his finest dark blue bolo suit, maroon cape, and diplomat's tricorne cap.

'Aware of the fact that you murdered Freeman Andil, Freeman Iliam, Coredwell Betz, and Mizenspesh Torrence.'

'I knew Andil's name,' said the Consul softly. 'I wasn't introduced to the technicians.'

'But you murdered them?'

'Yes.'

'Without provocation or warning.'

'Yes.'

'Murdered them to take possession of the device which they had delivered to Hyperion. The machine which we told you would collapse the so-called time tides, open the Time Tombs, and release the Shrike from bondage.'

'Yes.' The Consul's gaze appeared to be focused on something above Freeman Ghenga's shoulder but far, far away.

'We explained,' said Ghenga, 'that this device was to be used *after* we had successfully driven off the Hegemony ships. When our invasion and occupation was imminent. When the Shrike could be . . . controlled.'

'Yes.'

'Yet you murdered our people, lied to us about it, and activated the device yourself, years ahead of time.'

'Yes.' Melio Arundez and Theo Lane were standing beside and a step behind the Consul, and their faces were grim.

Freeman Ghenga folded her arms. She was a tall woman in the classic Ouster mode – bald, thin, draped in a regal, dark blue flowsuit which seemed to absorb light. Her face was old but almost free of wrinkles. Her eyes were dark.

'Even though this was four of your standard years ago, did you think we would forget?' asked Ghenga.

'No.' The Consul lowered his gaze to meet hers. It appeared as if he almost smiled. 'Few cultures forget traitors, Freeman Ghenga.'

'Yet you returned.'

The Consul did not reply. Standing near him, Theo Lane felt a light breeze tug at his own formal tricorne. Theo felt as if he were still dreaming. The ride here had been surreal.

Three Ousters had met them in a long, low gondola,

floating easily on the calm waters below the Consul's ship. With the three Hegemony visitors sitting amidships, the Ouster at the stern had pushed off with a long pole, and the ship had floated back the way it had come, as if the current of the impossible river had reversed itself. Theo had actually closed his eyes as they approached the waterfall where the stream rose perpendicular to the surface of their asteroid, but when he opened his eyes a second later, down was still *down*, and the river seemed to be flowing along normally enough, even though the grassy sphere of the small world hung to one side like a great, curved wall and stars were visible through the two-meter-thick ribbon of water beneath them.

Then they were through the containment field, out of the atmosphere, and their velocity increased as they followed the twisting ribbon of water. There was a tube of containment sphere around them – logic and the absence of their immediate and dramatic death dictated that there *had* to be – but it lacked the usual shimmer and optic texture that was so reassuring on Templar treeships or the occasional tourist habitat open to space. Here there were only the river, the boat, the people, and the immensity of space.

'They can't possibly use this as their form of transportation between Swarm units,' Dr Melio Arundez had said in a shaky voice. Theo had noted that Arundez also was gripping the gunwales with white fingers. Neither the Ouster in the stern nor the two seated in the bow had communicated with anything more than a nod of confirmation when the Consul had asked if this then was their promised transportation.

'They're showing off with the river,' the Consul had said softly. 'It's used when the Swarm is at rest, but for ceremonial purposes. Deploying it while the Swarm is moving is for effect.'

'To impress us with their superior technology?' asked Theo, *sotto voce*.

The Consul nodded.

The river had wound and twisted through space, sometimes almost doubling back on itself in huge, illogical loops, sometimes wrapping itself in tight spirals like a fiberplastic cord, always gleaming in sunlight from Hyperion's star and receding to infinity ahead of them. At times the river occluded the sun, and the colors then were magnificent; Theo gasped as he looked at the river loop a hundred meters above them and saw fish silhouetted against the solar disk.

But always the bottom of the boat was *down*, and they hurtled along at what must have been near cislunar transfer speeds on a river unbroken by rocks or rapids. It was, as Arundez noted some minutes into their voyage, like driving one's canoe over the edge of an immense waterfall and trying to enjoy the ride on the way down.

The river passed some of the elements of the Swarm, which filled the sky like false stars: massive comet farms, their dusty surfaces broken by the geometries of hard vacuum crops; zero-g globe cities, great irregular spheres of transparent membrane looking like improbable amoebae filled with busy flora and fauna; ten-klick-long thrust clusters, accreted over centuries, their innermost modules and lifecans and 'cologies looking like something stolen from O'Neill's Boondoggle and the dawn of the space age; wandering forests covering hundreds of kilometers like immense, floating kelp beds, connected to their thrust clusters and command nodes by containment fields and tangled skeins of roots and runners – the spherical tree-forms weaving to gravity breezes and burning bright green and deep orange and the hundred shades of Old Earth autumn when ignited by direct sunlight; hollowed-out asteroids long-since abandoned by their residents, now given over to automated manufacturing and heavy-metal reprocessing, every centimeter of surface rock covered by prerusted structures, chimneys, and skeletal cooling towers, the glow of their internal fusion fires making each cinderish world look like Vulcan's forge; immense spherical docking globes, given scale only by the torchship- and cruiser-size warcraft flitting around their surfaces like spermatazoa attacking an egg; and, most indelible, organisms which the river came near or which flew near the river . . . organisms which might have been manufactured or born but probably were both, great butterfly shapes, opening wings of energy to the sun, insects which were spacecraft or vice versa, their antennae turning toward the river and gondola and its passengers as they passed, multifaceted eyes gleaming in starlight, smaller winged shapes – humans – entering and exiting an opening in a belly the size of a FORCE attack carrier's dropship bay.

And finally had come the mountain – an entire range of mountains, actually: some blistered with a hundred environment bubbles, some open to space but still heavily populated, some connected to others by suspension bridges thirty klicks long or tributary rivers, others regal in their solitude, many as empty and formal as a Zen garden. Then the final mountain, rising higher than Mons Olympus or Asquith's Mount Hillary, and the river's penultimate plunge toward its summit, Theo and the Consul and Arundez, pale and silent, gripping the thwarts with quiet intensity as they plunged the final few kilometers with a suddenly perceptible and terrifying velocity. Finally, in the impossible last hundred meters as the river shed energy without deceleration, wider atmosphere surrounded them once again, and the boat floated to a halt in a grassy meadow where the Ouster Clan Tribunal stood waiting, and stones rose in their circle of Stonehenge silence.

'If they did this to impress me,' Theo had whispered as the boat bumped the grassy shore, 'they succeeded.'

'Why did you return to the Swarm?' asked Freeman Ghenga. The woman paced, moving in the minuscule gravity with the grace common only to those born in space.

'CEO Gladstone asked me to,' said the Consul.

'And you came knowing that your own life would be forfeit?'

The Consul was too much the gentleman and diplomat to shrug, but his expression conveyed the same sentiment.

'What does Gladstone want?' asked another Ouster, the man who had been introduced by Ghenga as Spokesman of the Eligible Citizens Coredwell Minmun.

The Consul repeated the CEO's five points.

Spokesman Minmun folded his arms and looked at Freeman Ghenga.

'I will answer now,' said Ghenga. She looked at Arundez and Theo. 'You two will listen carefully in the event that the man who brought these questions does not return to your ship with you.'

'Just a minute,' said Theo, stepping forward to face the taller Ouster, 'before passing judgement here, you have to take into account the fact that—'

'Silence,' commanded Spokesman Freeman Ghenga, but Theo had already been silenced by the Consul's hand on his shoulder.

'I will answer these questions now,' repeated Ghenga. Far above her, a score of the small warships which FORCE had called lancers flashed silently past, darting like a school of fish in three-hundred-g zigs and zags.

'Firstly,' said Ghenga. 'Gladstone asks why we are attacking the Web.' She paused, looked at the other sixteen Ousters assembled there, and continued. 'We are not. Except for this Swarm, attempting to occupy Hyperion before the Time Tombs opened, there are no Swarms attacking the Web.'

All three of the Hegemony men had stepped forward. Even the Consul had lost his veneer of bemused calm and was all but stuttering in excitement.

'But that's not true! We saw the . . .'

'I saw the fatlined images from the . . .'

'Heaven's Gate is destroyed! God's Grove burned!'

'*Silence*,' commanded Freeman Ghenga. Into that silence she said, 'Only this Swarm is doing battle with the Hegemony. Our Sister Swarms are where the long-range Web detectors had first placed them . . . moving *away* from the Web, fleeing from further provocations such as Bressia's attacks.'

The Consul rubbed his face like a man awakening. 'But then who . . . ?'

'Precisely,' said Freeman Ghenga. 'Who would have the ability to carry out such a charade? And the motive to slaughter humans by the billion?'

'The Core?' breathed the Consul.

The mountain was slowly rotating, and at this moment they turned into night. A convection breeze moved across the mountain terrace, rustling the Ousters' robes and the Consul's cape. Overhead, the stars seemed to explode into brilliance. The great rocks of the Stonehenge circle seemed to glow from some internal warmth.

Theo Lane stood next to the Consul, fearing that the man might collapse. 'We have only your word on this,' Theo said to the Ouster spokesman. 'It makes no sense.'

Ghenga did not blink. 'We will show you proof. Void-Which-Binds transmission locators. Real-time starfield images from our Sister Swarms.'

'Void Which Binds?' said Arundez. His usually calm voice showed agitation.

'What you call the fatline.' Spokesman Freeman Ghenga paced to the nearest stone and ran her hand across its rough surface as if taking warmth from the heat within. Starfields pirouetted above.

'To answer Gladstone's second question,' she said, 'we do not know where the Core resides. We have fled it and fought it and sought it and feared it for centuries, but we have not found it. *You* must tell us the answer to that question! *We* have declared war on this parasite entity you call the TechnoCore.'

The Consul seemed to sag. 'We have no idea. Authorities in the Web have sought the Core since before the Hegira, but it is as elusive as El Dorado. We've found no hidden worlds, no massive asteroids crammed with hardware, and no hint of it on Web worlds.' He gestured tiredly with his left hand. 'For all we know, *you* are hiding the Core in one of your Swarms.'

'We are not,' said Spokesman Coredwell Minmun.

The Consul did shrug at last. 'The Hegira bypassed thousands of worlds in the Grand Survey. Anything that didn't score at least nine point seven on their ten-point terrabase scale was ignored. The Core could be anywhere along those early lines of flight and exploration. We'll never find it . . . and if we do, it will be years after the Web is destroyed. You were our last hope for locating it.'

Ghenga shook her head. Far above them, the summit caught the light of sunrise while the terminator moved down the icefields toward them with almost alarming rapidity. 'Thirdly, Gladstone asked for our demands for a cease-fire. Except for this Swarm, in this system, we are not the ones attacking. We will accept a cease-fire as soon as Hyperion is under our control . . . which should be momentarily. We have just been informed that our expeditionary forces now have control of the capital and its spaceport.'

'The hell you say,' said Theo, hands curling into fists despite himself.

'The hell we do say,' agreed Freeman Ghenga. 'Tell Gladstone that we will now join you in a common fight against the TechnoCore.' She glanced toward the silent members of the Tribunal. 'Since we are many years' travel from the Web, however, and we do not trust your Core-controlled farcasters, our help must necessarily come in the form of retaliating for the destruction of your Hegemony. You will be avenged.'

'That's reassuring,' said the Consul drily.

'Fourthly, Gladstone asks if we will meet with her. The

answer is yes . . . if she is, as she says she is, willing to come to Hyperion System. We have preserved the FORCE farcaster for just that eventuality. *We* will not travel by farcaster.'

'Why not?' asked Arundez.

A third Ouster, not introduced, one of the furred and beautifully altered type, spoke. 'The device you call a farcaster is an abomination . . . a defilement of the Void Which Binds.'

'Ah, religious reasons,' said the Consul, nodding in understanding.

The exotically striped and furred Ouster shook his head adamantly. 'No! The farcaster web is the yoke on human-kind's neck, the contract of subservience which has bound you to stagnation. We will have none of it.'

'Fifthly,' said Freeman Ghenga, 'Gladstone's mention of the deathwand explosive device is nothing but a crude ulti-matum. But as we have said, it is aimed at the wrong oppo-nent. The forces sweeping into your frail and failing Web are not of the Clans of the Twelve Sister Swarms.'

'We have only your word on that,' said the Consul. His gaze, now locked with Ghenga's, was firm and defiant.

'You have my word on nothing,' said Spokesman Ghenga. 'Clan elders do not give their word to Core slaves. But this is the truth.'

The Consul seemed distracted as he half turned toward Theo. 'We have to get this word to Gladstone immediately.' He turned back to Ghenga. 'May my friends return to the ship to communicate your response, Spokesman?'

Ghenga nodded and gestured for the gondola to be made ready.

'We're not going back without you,' Theo said to the Consul, stepping between him and the closest Ousters as if to protect the older man with his own body.

'Yes,' said the Consul, touching Theo's upper arm again, 'you are. You must.'

'He's right,' said Arundez, pulling Theo away before the young Governor-General could speak again. 'This is too important to risk not communicating. You go. I'll stay with him.'

Ghenga gestured toward two of the more massive exotic Ousters. 'You will both return to the ship. The Consul will remain. The Tribunal has not yet decided his fate.'

Arundez and Theo both wheeled with fists raised, but the furred Ousters seized them and moved them away with the restrained effort of adults handling small but unruly children.

The Consul watched them set in place in the gondola, and he stifled the urge to wave as the boat moved twenty meters down the placid stream, dipped out of sight beyond the curve of the terrace, and then reappeared climbing the waterfall toward black space. It was lost to sight within minutes in the glare of the sun. He turned slowly in a full circle, making eye contact with each of the seventeen Ousters.

'Let's get it over with,' said the Consul. 'I've waited a long time for this.'

Sol Weintraub sat between the great paws of the Sphinx and watched the storm abate, wind dying from scream to sigh to whisper, curtains of dust diminishing and then parting to show the stars, and finally the long night settling into a dreadful calm. The Tombs glowed more brightly than before, but nothing came out of the blazing doorway of the Sphinx, and Sol could not enter; the push of blinding light was like a thousand irresistible fingers against his chest, and lean and strain as he might, Sol could get no closer than three meters from the doorway. Whatever stood or moved or waited inside was lost to sight in the glare of light.

Sol sat and held on to the stone stair as time tides pulled at him, tugged at him, and made him weep in the false shock of *déjà vu*. The entire Sphinx seemed to rock and pitch in the violent storm of expanding and contracting anti-entropic fields.

Rachel.

Sol would not leave while there was any chance his daughter might be alive. Lying on cold stone, listening to the wind scream die, Sol saw the cold stars appear, saw the meteor trail and laser-lance thrust and counterthrust of orbital war, knew in his heart that the war was lost, that the Web was in danger, that great empires were falling as he watched, the human race might be hanging in the balance this endless night . . . and he did not care.

Sol Weintraub cared about his daughter.

And even as he lay there, cold, buffeted by winds and time tides, bruised with fatigue and hollow from hunger, Sol felt a certain peace descend on him. He had given his daughter to a monster but *not* because God had commanded him to, *not* because fate or fear had willed it, but only because his daughter had appeared to him in a dream and told him that it was all right, that this was the thing to do, that their love – his and Sarai's and Rachel's – demanded it.

In the end, thought Sol, *past logic and hope, it is dreams and the love of those dearest to us that form Abraham's answer to God.*

Sol's comlog no longer worked. It might have been an hour or five hours since he had handed his dying infant to the Shrike. Sol lay back, still gripping stone as the time tides made the Sphinx bob like a small ship on a big sea, and stared at the stars and battle above.

Sparks drifted across the sky, glowed bright as supernovae as laser lances found them, and then fell in a shower of molten debris – white-hot to red to blue flame to darkness. Sol imagined dropships burning, imagined Ouster troops and Hegemony Marines dying in a scream of atmosphere and melting titanium . . . he *tried* to imagine this . . . and failed. Sol realized that space battles and the movements of fleets and the fall of empires were beyond his imagining,

536

hidden from the reservoirs of his sympathy or understanding. Such things belonged to Thucydides and Tacitus and Catton and Wu. Sol had met his senator from Barnard's World, had met with her several times in his and Sarai's quest to save Rachel from Merlin's sickness, but Sol could not imagine Feldstein's participation on the scale of interstellar war – or in anything much larger than dedicating a new medical center in the capital of Bussard or pressing the flesh during a rally at the university in Crawford.

Sol had never met the current Hegemony CEO, but as a scholar, he had enjoyed her subtle replay of the speeches of such classical figures as Churchill and Lincoln and Alvarez-Temp. But now, lying between the paws of a great stone beast and weeping for his daughter, Sol could not imagine what was in that woman's mind as she made decisions that would save or damn billions, preserve or betray the greatest empire in human history.

Sol didn't give a damn. He wanted his daughter back. He wanted Rachel to be alive despite all logic to the contrary.

Lying between the Sphinx's stone paws on a besieged world in a ravaged empire, Sol Weintraub wiped tears from his eyes the better to see the stars and thought of Yeats's poem 'A Prayer for My Daughter':

> *Once more the storm is howling, and half hid*
> *Under this cradle-hood and coverlid*
> *My child sleeps on. There is no obstacle*
> *But Gregory's wood and one bare hill*
> *Whereby the haystack- and roof-levelling wind,*
> *Bred on the Atlantic, can be stayed;*
> *And for an hour I have walked and prayed*
> *Because of the great gloom that is in my mind.*
>
> *I have walked and prayed for this young child an hour*
> *And heard the sea-wind scream upon the tower,*
> *And under the arches of the bridge, and scream*

In the elms above the flooded stream;
Imagining in excited reverie
That the future years had come,
Dancing to a frenzied drum,
Out of the murderous innocence of the sea . . .

All Sol wanted, he realized now, was the same possibility once again to worry about those future years which every parent fears and dreads. To not allow her childhood and teenage years and awkward young adulthood to be stolen and destroyed by the sickness.

Sol had spent his life willing the return of things unreturnable. He remembered the day he had come upon Sarai folding Rachel's toddler clothes and setting them in a box in the attic, and he recalled her tears and his own sense of loss for the child they still had but who was lost to them through the simple arrow of time. Sol knew now that little could be returned except by memory – that Sarai was dead and beyond ability to return, that Rachel's childhood friends and world were gone forever, that even the society he had left only a few weeks of his time ago was in the process of being lost beyond return.

And thinking of that, lying between the taloned paws of the Sphinx as the wind died and the false stars burned, Sol is reminded of part of a different and far more ominous poem by Yeats:

Surely some revelation is at hand;
Surely the Second Coming is at hand.
The Second Coming! Hardly are those words out
When a vast image out of Spiritus Mundi
Troubles my sight: somewhere in the sands of the desert
A shape with lion body and the head of a man,
A gaze blank and pitiless as the sun,
Is moving its slow thighs, while all about it
Reel shadows of the indignant desert birds.

The darkness drops again; but now I know
That twenty centuries of stony sleep
Were vexed to nightmare by a rocking cradle,
And what rough beast, its hour come round at last,
Slouches towards Bethlehem to be born?

Sol does not know. Sol discovers again that he does not care. Sol wants his daughter back.

The consensus in the War Council seemed to be to drop the bomb.

Meina Gladstone sat at the head of the long table and felt the peculiar and not-unpleasant sense of separateness which comes from far too little sleep over far too long a period. To close her eyes, even for a second, meant sliding on the black ice of fatigue, so she did not close her eyes, even when they burned and when the drone of briefings, conversation, and urgent debate faded and receded through thick curtains of exhaustion.

Together the Council had watched as the embers of Task Force 181.2 – Commander Lee's attack group – had winked out one by one until only a dozen of the original seventy-four were left still driving toward the center of the approaching Swarm. Lee's cruiser was among the survivors.

During this silent attrition, this abstract and oddly attractive representation of violent and all-too-real death, Admiral Singh and General Morpurgo had completed their gloomy assessment of the war.

'. . . FORCE and the New Bushido were designed for limited conflicts, minor skirmishes, proscribed limits and modest aims,' summarized Morpurgo. 'With less than half a million men and women under arms, FORCE would not be comparable to the armies of one of the Old Earth nation states a thousand years ago. The Swarm can swamp us with sheer numbers, outgun our fleets and win through arithmetic.'

Senator Kolchev glowered from his place at the opposite end of the table. The Lusian had been much more active in the briefing and debate than Gladstone – questions were turned his way more frequently than to her – almost as if everyone in the room were subliminally aware that power was shifting, the torch of leadership was being passed.

Not yet, thought Gladstone, tapping her chin with steepled fingers and listening to Kolchev cross-examine the General.

'. . . of falling back and defending essential worlds on the second-wave list – Tau Ceti Center, of course, but also necessary industrial worlds such as Renaissance Minor, Fuji, Deneb Vier, and Lusus?'

General Morpurgo looked down and shuffled papers as if to hide the sudden flash of anger in his eyes. 'Senator, less than ten standard days remain until the second wave completes its target list. Renaissance Minor will fall under attack within ninety hours. What I am saying is that with the current size, structure, and technology available to FORCE, it would be doubtful if we could hold one system . . . say, TC²'s.'

Senator Kakinuma rose. 'This is not acceptable, General.'

Morpurgo looked up. 'I agree, Senator. But it is true.'

President Pro Tem Denzel-Hiat-Amin sat shaking his gray and mottled head. 'It makes no sense. Were there no plans to defend the Web?'

Admiral Singh spoke from his seat. 'The best estimates of the threat told us that we would have a minimum of eighteen months should the Swarms ever turn toward the attack.'

Minister of Diplomacy Persov cleared his throat. 'And . . . if we were to concede these twenty-five worlds to the Ousters, Admiral, how long until the first or second wave could attack other Web worlds?'

Singh did not have to refer to his notes or comlog. 'Depending upon their target, M Persov, the nearest Web world – Esperance – would be nine standard months away from the closest Swarm. The most distant target – Home System – would be some fourteen years by Hawking drive.'

'Time enough to shift to a war economy,' said Senator Feldstein. Her constituency on Barnard's World had less than forty standard hours to live. Feldstein had vowed to be with them when the end came. Her voice was precise and passionless. 'It makes sense. Cut your losses. Even with TC^2 and two dozen more worlds lost, the Web can produce incredible quantities of war matériel ... even in nine months. Within the years it will take for the Ousters to penetrate farther into the Web, we should be able to beat them through sheer industrial mass.'

Defense Minister Imoto shook his head. 'There are irreplacable raw materials being lost in this first and second wave. The disruption to Web economy will be staggering.'

'Do we have a choice?' asked Senator Peters from Deneb Drei.

All eyes turned toward the person sitting next to AI Councilor Albedo.

As if to underline the importance of the moment, a new AI persona had been admitted to the War Council and had given the presentation on the awkwardly labeled 'death-wand device.' Councilor Nansen was tall, male, tanned, relaxed, impressive, convincing, trustworthy, and imbued with that rare charisma of leadership that made one both like and respect the person on sight.

Meina Gladstone feared and loathed the new Councilor at once. She felt as if this projection had been designed by AI experts to create just the response of trust and obedience she sensed others at the table already granting. And Nansen's message, she feared, meant death.

The deathwand had been Web technology for centuries – designed by the Core and limited to FORCE personnel and a few specialized security forces such as Government House's and Gladstone's Praetorians. It did not burn, blast, shoot, slag, or incinerate. It made no sound and projected no visible ray or sonic footprint. It simply made the target die.

If the target were human, that is. A deathwand's range was limited – no more than fifty meters – but within that range, a targeted human died, while other animals and property were totally safe. Autopsies showed scrambled synapses but no other damage. Deathwands merely made one cease to be. FORCE officers had carried them as short-range personal weapons and symbols of authority for generations.

Now, Councilor Nansen revealed, the Core had perfected a device that utilized the deathwand principle on a larger scale. They had hesitated to reveal its existence, but with the imminent and terrible threat of the Ouster invasion . . .

The questioning had been energetic and sometimes cynical, with the military more skeptical than the politicians. Yes, the deathwand device could rid us of Ousters, but what about the Hegemony population?

Remove them to shelter on one of the labyrinthine worlds, Nansen had replied, repeating the earlier plan of Councilor Albedo. Five kilometers of rock would shield them from any effects of the widening deathwand ripples.

How far did these death rays penetrate?

Their effect diminished to below the lethal level at just under three light-years, Nansen responded calmly, confidently, the ultimate salesman in the penultimate sales pitch. A wide enough radius to rid any system of the attacking Swarm. Small enough to protect all but the nearest neighboring star systems. Ninety-two percent of the Web worlds had no other inhabited world within five light-years.

And what about those who can't be evacuated? Morpurgo had demanded.

Councilor Nansen had smiled and opened his palm as if to show there was nothing hidden there. Do not activate the device until your authorities are sure that all Hegemony citizens are evacuated or shielded, he had said. It will be, after all, totally under *your* control.

Feldstein, Sabenstorafem, Peters, Persov, and many of the others had been instantly enthusiastic. A secret weapon to end all secret weapons. The Ousters could be warned . . . a demonstration could be arranged.

I'm sorry, Councilor Nansen had said. His teeth when he smiled were as pearly white as his robes. There can be no demonstration. The weapon works just as a deathwand, only across a much wider region. There will be no property damage or blast effect, no measurable shock wave above the neutrino level. Merely dead invaders.

To demonstrate it, Councilor Albedo had explained, you must use it on at least one Ouster Swarm.

The excitement of the War Council had not been lessened. Perfect, said All Thing Speaker Gibbons, choose one Swarm, test the device, fatline the results to the other Swarms, and give them a one-hour deadline to break off their attacks. We didn't provoke this war. Better millions of the enemy dead than a war that claims tens of billions over the next decade.

Hiroshima, Gladstone had said, her only comment of the day. It had been said too softly for anyone except her aide Sedeptra to hear.

Morpurgo had asked: Do we *know* that the killing rays will become ineffective at three light-years? Have you tested it?

Councilor Nansen smiled. If he answered yes, there were heaps of dead humans somewhere. If he said no, the device's reliability was seriously at stake. We are certain that it will work, said Nansen. Our simulation runs were foolproof.

The Kiev Team AIs said that about the first farcaster singularity, thought Gladstone. *The one that destroyed Earth*. She said nothing aloud.

Still, Singh and Morpurgo and Van Zeidt and their specialists had spiked Nansen's guns by showing that Mare Infinitus could not be evacuated quickly enough and that the only first-wave Web world that had its own labyrinth was Armaghast, which was within a light-year of Pacem and Svoboda.

Councilor Nansen's earnest, helpful smile did not fade. 'You want a demonstration, and that would be only sensible,' he said quietly. 'You need to show the Ousters that invasion will not be tolerated, while focusing on the minimum loss of life. And you need to shelter your indigenous Hegemony population.' He paused, folded his hands on the tabletop. 'What about Hyperion?'

The buzz around the table deepened in tone.

'It's not really a Web world,' said Speaker Gibbons.

'Yet it is in the Web now, with the FORCE farcaster still in place!' cried Garion Persov of Diplomacy, obviously a convert to the idea.

General Morpurgo's stern expression did not shift. 'That will be there only another few hours. We're protecting the singularity sphere now, but it could fall at any time. Much of Hyperion itself is already in Ouster hands.'

'But Hegemony personnel have been evacuated?' said Persov.

Singh answered. 'All but the Governor-General. He could not be found in the confusion.'

'A pity,' said Minister Persov without much conviction, 'but the point is that the remaining population is mostly Hyperion indigenie, with easy access to the labyrinth there, correct?'

Barbre Dan-Gyddis of the Ministry of Economy, whose son had been a fiberplastic plantation manager near Port Romance, said, 'Within three hours? Impossible.'

Nansen stood. 'I think not,' he said. 'We can fatline the warning to the remaining Home Rule Authorities in the capital, and they can begin the evacuation immediately. There are thousands of entrances to the labyrinth on Hyperion.'

'The capital of Keats is under siege,' growled Morpurgo. 'The entire planet is under attack.'

Councilor Nansen nodded sadly. 'And soon will be put to the sword by the barbarian Ousters. A difficult choice, gentlemen and ladies. But the device *will* work. The invasion will simply cease to exist in Hyperion space. Millions might be saved on the planet, and the effect on the Ouster invasion forces elsewhere would be significant. We know that their so-called Sister Swarms communicate by fatline. The termination of the first Swarm to invade Hegemony space – the Hyperion Swarm – may be the perfect deterrent.'

Nansen shook his head again and looked around with an expression of almost paternal concern. There could be no simulating such pained sincerity. 'It has to be your decision. The weapon is yours to use or disregard. It pains the Core to take any human life . . . or, through inaction, allow any human life to come to harm. But in this case, where the lives of billions are at risk . . .' Nansen opened his hands again, shook his head a final time, and sat back, obviously leaving the decision to human minds and hearts.

Babble around the long table rose. Debate grew almost violent.

'CEO!' called General Morpurgo.

In the sudden silence, Gladstone lifted her gaze to the holographic displays in the darkness above them. The Mare Infinitus Swarm fell toward that ocean world like a torrent of blood aimed toward a small blue sphere. Only three of the orange Task Force 181.2 embers remained, and even as the silent Council watched, two of these winked out. Then the final one was extinguished.

Gladstone whispered into her comlog. 'Communications, any last message from Admiral Lee?'

'None to the command center, CEO,' came the response. 'Only standard fatline telemetry during the battle. It appears they did not reach the center of the Swarm.'

Gladstone and Lee had held hopes of capturing Ousters, of interrogations, of establishing the identity of their enemy beyond a doubt. Now that young man of such energy and ability was dead – dead at Meina Gladstone's command – and seventy-four ships of the line were wasted.

'Mare Infinitus farcaster destroyed by preset plasma explosives,' reported Admiral Singh. 'Forward elements of the Swarm now entering cislunar defense perimeter.'

No one spoke. The holographics showed the tidal wave of blood-red lights engulfing the Mare Infinitus system, the final orange embers around that gold world blinking out.

A few hundred of the Ouster ships remained in orbit, presumably reducing Mare Infinitus's elegant floating cities and ocean farms to burning debris, but the major part of the blood tide rolled on, out of the region projected above.

'Asquith System in three standard hours, forty-one minutes,' intoned a technician near the display board.

Senator Kolchev stood. 'Let's put the Hyperion demonstration to a vote,' he said, ostensibly addressing Gladstone but speaking to the crowd.

Meina Gladstone tapped her lower lip. 'No,' she said at last, 'no vote. We will use the device. Admiral, prepare the torchship armed with the device to translate to Hyperion space and then broadcast warnings to planet and Ouster alike. Give them three hours. Minister Imoto, send coded fatline signals to Hyperion telling them that they must . . . repeat, must . . . seek shelter in the labyrinths at once. Tell them that a new weapon is being tested.'

Morpurgo wiped sweat from his face. 'CEO, we can't run any risk that this device can fall into enemy hands.'

Gladstone looked at Councilor Nansen and tried to make her expression reveal nothing of what she felt. 'Councilor, can this device be rigged so that it detonates automatically if our ship is captured or destroyed?'

'Yes, CEO.'

'Do it. Explain all necessary failsafe devices to the proper FORCE experts.' She turned toward Sedeptra. 'Prepare a webwide broadcast for me, scheduled to commence ten minutes before the device is to be detonated. I have to tell our people about this.'

'Is that wise . . . ?' began Senator Feldstein.

'It is necessary,' said Gladstone. She rose, and the thirty-eight people in the room rose a second later. 'I'm going to get a few minutes' sleep while you people work. I want the device ready and in-system and Hyperion warned immediately. I want contingency plans and priorities for a negotiated settlement ready by the time I awaken in thirty minutes.'

Gladstone looked out at the group, knowing that one way or the other, most of the people there would be out of power and out of office within the next twenty hours. One way or the other, it was her last day as CEO.

Meina Gladstone smiled. 'Council dismissed,' she said and farcast to her private quarters to take a nap.

FORTY-THREE

Leigh Hunt had never seen anyone die before. The last day and night he spent with Keats – Hunt still thought of him as Joseph Severn but was sure that the dying man now thought of *himself* as John Keats – were the most difficult in Hunt's life. The hemorrhages came frequently during Keats's last day of life, and between these bouts of retching, Hunt could hear the phlegm boiling in the small man's throat and chest as he fought for life.

Hunt sat next to the bed in the small front room in the Piazza di Spagna and listened to Keats babble as sunrise moved to midmorning and midmorning faded to early afternoon. Keats was feverish and moving in and out of consciousness, but he insisted that Hunt listen and write everything down – they had found ink, pen, and foolscap in the other room – and Hunt complied, scribbling furiously as the dying cybrid raved on about metaspheres and lost divinities, the responsibilities of poets and the passing of gods, and the Miltonic civil war in the Core.

Hunt had perked up then and squeezed Keats's feverish hand. 'Where is the Core, Sev— Keats? Where *is* it?'

The dying man had broken into a visible sweat and turned his face away. 'Don't breathe on me – it comes like ice!'

'The Core,' repeated Hunt, leaning back, feeling close to tears from pity and frustration, 'where is the Core?'

Keats smiled, his head moving back and forth in pain. The effort he made to breathe sounded like wind through a ruptured bellows. 'Like spiders in the web,' he muttered, 'spiders in the web. Weaving . . . letting us weave it for them . . . then trussing us and draining us. Like flies caught by spiders in the web.'

Hunt quit writing as he listened to more of his seemingly senseless babble. Then he understood. 'My God,' he whispered. 'They're *in* the farcaster system.'

Keats tried to sit up, grasped Hunt's arm with a terrible strength. 'Tell your leader, Hunt. Have Gladstone rip it out. Rip it out. Spiders in the web. Man god and machine god . . . must find the union. Not me!' He dropped back on the pillows and started weeping without sound. 'Not me.'

Keats slept some through the long afternoon, although Hunt knew that it was something closer to death than sleep. The slightest sound would start the dying poet awake and set him wrestling to breathe. By sunset Keats was too weak to expectorate, and Hunt had to help him lower his head over the basin to allow gravity to clear his mouth and throat of bloody mucus.

Several times, when Keats fell into fitful naps, Hunt walked to the window and once down the stairs to the front door to stare into the Piazza. Something tall and sharp-edged stood in the deepest shadows opposite the Piazza near the base of the steps.

In the evening, Hunt himself dozed off while sitting upright in the hard chair next to Keats's bed. He awoke from a dream of falling and put his hand out to steady himself only to find Keats awake and staring at him.

'Did you ever see anyone die?' asked Keats between soft gasps for breath.

'No.' Hunt thought that there was something odd about the young man's gaze, as if Keats were looking at him but seeing someone else.

'Well then I pity you,' said Keats. 'What trouble and danger you have got into for me. Now you must be firm for it will not last long.'

Hunt was struck not only by the gentle courage in that remark, but by the sudden shift in Keats's dialect from flat Web-standard English to something much older and more interesting.

'Nonsense,' said Hunt heartily, forcing enthusiasm and energy he did not feel. 'We'll be out of this before dawn. I'm going to sneak out as soon as it gets dark and find a farcaster portal.'

Keats shook his head. 'The Shrike will take you. It will allow no one to help me. Its role is to see that I must escape myself through myself.' He closed his eyes as his breathing grew more ragged.

'I don't understand,' said Leigh Hunt, taking the young man's hand. He assumed this was more of the fever talking, but since it was one of the few times Keats had been fully conscious in the past two days, Hunt felt it worth the effort to communicate. 'What do you mean escape yourself through yourself?'

Keats's eyes fluttered open. They were hazel and far too bright. 'Ummon and the others are trying to make me escape myself through accepting the godhood, Hunt. Bait to catch the white whale, honey to catch the ultimate fly. Fleeing Empathy shall find its home in me . . . in me, Mister John Keats, five feet high . . . and then the reconciliation begins, right?'

'What reconciliation?' Hunt leaned closer, trying not to breathe on him. Keats appeared to have shrunk in his bedclothes, tangle of blankets, but heat radiating from him seemed to fill the room. His face was a pale oval in the dying light. Hunt was only faintly aware of a gold band of reflected sunlight moving across the wall just below where it met the ceiling, but Keats's eyes never left that last smear of day.

'The reconciliation of man and machine, Creator and created,' said Keats and began to cough, stopping only after he had drooled red phlegm into the basin Hunt held for him.

He lay back, gasped a moment, and added, 'Reconciliation of humankind and those races it tried to exterminate, the Core and the humanity it tried to expunge, the painfully evolved God of the Void Which Binds and its ancestors who tried to expunge it.'

Hunt shook his head and quit writing. 'I don't understand. You can become this . . . messiah . . . by leaving your deathbed?'

The pale oval of Keats's face moved back and forth on the pillow in a motion which might have been a substitute for laughter. 'We all could have, Hunt. Humankind's folly and greatest pride. We accept our pain. We make way for our children. That earned us the right to become the God we dreamed of.'

Hunt looked down and found his own fist clenched in frustration. 'If you can do this . . . become this *power* . . . then do it. Get us out of here!'

Keats closed his eyes again. 'Can't. I'm not the One Who Comes but the One Who Comes Before. Not the baptized but the baptist. *Merde*, Hunt, I'm an atheist! Even Severn couldn't convince me of these things when I was drowning in death!' Keats gripped Hunt's shirt with a fierceness that frightened the older man. 'Write this!'

And Hunt fumbled to find the ancient pen and rough paper, scribbling furiously to catch the words Keats now whispered:

> A wondrous lesson in thy silent face:
> Knowledge enormous makes a god of me.
> Names, deeds, gray legends, dire events, rebellions,
> Majesties, sovran voices, agonies,
> Creations and destroyings, all at once
> Pour into the wide hollows of my brain,
> And deify me, as if some blithe wine
> Or bright elixir peerless I had drunk,
> And so become immortal.

Keats lived for three more painful hours, a swimmer rising occasionally from his sea of agony to take a breath or whisper some urgent nonsense. Once, long after dark, he pulled at Hunt's sleeve and whispered sensibly enough, 'When I am dead, the Shrike will not harm you. It waits for me. There may not be a way home, but it will not harm you while you search.' And again, just as Hunt was bending over to hear if the breath still gurgled in the poet's lungs, Keats began to talk and continued between spasms until he had given Hunt specific instructions for his entombment in Rome's Protestant Cemetery, near the Pyramid of Caius Cestius.

'Nonsense, nonsense,' Hunt muttered over and over like a mantra, squeezing the young man's hot hand.

'Flowers,' whispered Keats a little later, just after Hunt had lighted a lamp on the bureau. The poet's eyes were wide as he stared at the ceiling in a look of pure, childish wonder. Hunt glanced upward and saw the faded yellow roses painted in blue squares on the ceiling. 'Flowers . . . above me,' whispered Keats between his efforts to breathe.

Hunt was standing at the window, staring out at the shadows beyond the Spanish Steps, when the painful rasp of breath behind him faltered and stopped and Keats gasped out, 'Severn . . . lift me up! I'm dying.'

Hunt sat on the bed and held him. Heat flowed from the small body that seemed to weigh nothing, as if the actual substance of the man had been burned away. 'Don't be frightened. Be firm. And thank God it has come!' gasped Keats, and then the terrible rasping subsided. Hunt helped Keats lie back more comfortably as his breathing eased into a more normal rhythm.

Hunt changed the water in the basin, moistened a fresh cloth, and came back to find Keats dead.

Later, just after the sun rose, Hunt lifted the small body – wrapped in fresh linens from Hunt's own bed – and went out into the city.

The storm had abated by the time Brawne Lamia reached the end of the valley. As she passed the Cave Tombs, she had seen the same eerie glow the other Tombs were emitting, but there also came a terrible noise – as if of thousands of souls crying out – echoing and moaning from the earth. Brawne hurried on.

The sky was clear by the time she stood in front of the Shrike Palace. The structure was aptly named: the half-dome arched up and outward like the creature's carapace, support elements curved downward like blades stabbing the valley floor and other buttresses leaped upward and away like Shrike thorns. Walls had become translucent as the interior glow increased, and now the building shone like a giant jack-o'-lantern shaved paper thin; the upper regions glowed red as the Shrike's gaze.

Brawne took a breath and touched her abdomen. She was pregnant – she had known it before she left Lusus – and didn't she owe more now to her unborn son or daughter than to the obscene old poet on the Shrike's tree? Brawne knew that the answer was *yes* and that it did not matter one damn bit. She let out the breath and approached the Shrike Palace.

From the outside, the Shrike Palace was no more than twenty meters across. Before, when they had entered, Brawne and the other pilgrims had seen the interior as a single open space, empty except for the bladelike supports that crisscrossed the space under the glowing dome. Now, as Brawne stood at the entrance, the interior was a space larger than the valley itself. A dozen tiers of white stone rose rank on rank and stretched into the faded distance. On each tier of stone, human bodies lay, each garbed a different way, each tethered by the same sort of semiorganic, semiparasitic shunt socket and cable which her friends had told Brawne she herself had worn. Only these metallic but translucent umbilicals pulsed red and expanded and contracted regularly, as if blood were being recycled through the sleeping forms' skulls.

Brawne staggered back, affected by the pull of anti-entropic tides as much as by the view, but when she stood ten meters from the Palace, the exterior was the same size as always. She did not pretend to understand how klicks of interior could fit into such a modest shell. The Time Tombs were opening. This one could coexist in different times for all she knew. What she did understand was that when she was awakening from her own travels under the shunt, she had seen the Shrike's thorn tree tied with tubes and vines of energy invisible to the eye but now quite obviously connected with the Shrike Palace.

She stepped to the entrance again.

The Shrike waited inside. Its carapace, usually gleaming, now seemed black, silhouetted against the light and marble glare around it.

Brawne felt the adrenaline rush fill her, felt the impulse to turn and run, and stepped inside.

The entrance all but vanished behind her, remaining visible only by a faint fuzziness in the uniform glow which emanated from the walls. The Shrike did not move. Its red eyes gleamed from the shadow of its skull.

Brawne stepped forward, her booted heels making no sound on the stone floor. The Shrike was ten meters to her right where the stone biers began, ascending like obscene display racks to a ceiling lost in the glow. She had no illusion that she could make it back to the door before the creature closed on her.

It did not move. The air smelled of ozone and something sickly sweet. Brawne moved along the wall at her back and scanned the rows of bodies for a familiar sleeping face. With each step to her left, she moved farther from the exit and made it easier for the Shrike to cut her off. The creature stood there like a black sculpture in an ocean of light.

The tiers did stretch for kilometers. Stone steps, each almost a meter high, broke the horizontal lines of dark bodies. Several minutes' walk from the entrance, Brawne climbed the lower third of one of these stairways, touched the nearest body on the second tier, and was relieved to find the flesh warm, the man's chest rising and falling. It was not Martin Silenus.

Brawne continued onward, half expecting to find Paul Duré or Sol Weintraub or even herself lying among the living dead. Instead, she found a face she had last seen carved into a mountainside. Sad King Billy lay motionless on white stone, five tiers up, his royal robes scorched and stained. The sad face was – as were all the others – contorted in some internal agony. Martin Silenus lay three bodies away on a lower tier.

Brawne crouched next to the poet, glancing over her shoulder at the black speck of the Shrike, still unmoving at the end of the rows of bodies. Like the others, Silenus appeared to be alive, in silent agony, and was attached by a shunt socket connected to a pulsating umbilical which, in turn, ran into the white wall behind the ledge as if wed to the stone.

Brawne panted from fear as she ran her hand over the poet's skull, feeling the fusion of plastic and bone, and then felt along the umbilical itself, finding no join or opening to the point where it melded with stone. Fluid pulsed beneath her fingers.

'Shit,' whispered Brawne and, in a sudden flurry of panic, looked behind her, certain the Shrike had crept within striking distance. The dark form still stood at the end of the long room.

Her pockets were empty. She had neither weapon nor tool. She realized that she would have to return to the Sphinx, find the packs, dig out something to cut with, and then return and muster enough courage to enter here again.

Brawne knew that she could never come through that door again.

She knelt, took a deep breath, and brought her hand and arm up, then down. The edge of her palm smashed against

555

material that looked like clear plastic and felt harder than steel. Her arm ached from wrist to shoulder from the single blow.

Brawne Lamia glanced to her right. The Shrike was moving toward her, stepping slowly like an old man out for a leisurely walk.

Brawne shouted, knelt, and struck again, palm-edge rigid, thumb locked at right angles. The long room echoed to the impact.

Brawne Lamia had grown up on Lusus at 1.3 standard gravity, and she was athletic for her race. Since she was nine years old, she had dreamed of and worked toward becoming a detective, and a part of that admittedly obsessive and totally illogical preparation had been training in the martial arts. Now she grunted, raised her arm, and struck again, willing her palm to be an axe blade, *seeing* in her mind the severing blow, the successful strike-through.

The tough umbilical dented imperceptibly, pulsed like a living thing, and seemed to cringe away as she swung again.

Footsteps became audible below and behind her. Brawne almost giggled. The Shrike could move without walking, go from here to there without the effort of going between. It must enjoy scaring its prey. Brawne was not frightened. She was too busy.

She raised her hand, brought it down again. It would have been easier striking the stone for effect. She slammed her palm-edge into the umbilical again, feeling some small bone give in her hand. The pain was like a distant noise, like the sliding below her and behind her.

Has it occurred to you, she thought, *that it'll probably kill him if you do manage to break this thing?*

She swung again. The footsteps stopped at the base of the stairway below.

Brawne was panting from effort. Sweat dripped from her forehead and cheeks on to the chest of the sleeping poet.

I don't even like *you,* she thought at Martin Silenus and chopped again. It was like trying to sever a metal elephant's leg.

The Shrike began ascending the staircase.

Brawne half stood and threw the entire weight of her body into a swing which almost dislocated her shoulder and broke her wrist, and smashed small bones in her hand.

And severed the umbilical.

Red fluid too nonviscous for blood splashed across Brawne's legs and the white stone. The severed cable still extending from the wall spasmed and then thrashed like an agitated tentacle before lying limply and then withdrawing, a bleeding snake sliding into a hole that ceased to exist as soon as the umbilical was out of sight. The stump of umbilical still attached to Silenus's neural shunt socket withered in five seconds, drying and contracting like a jellyfish out of water. Red splashed the poet's face and shoulders, the liquid turning blue even as Brawne watched.

Martin Silenus's eyes twitched and opened like an owl's.

'Hey,' he said, 'do you know the fucking Shrike's standing right behind you?'

Gladstone 'cast to her private apartments and went at once to her fatline cubicle. Two messages waited.

The first was from Hyperion space. Gladstone blinked as the soft voice of her former Governor-General on Hyperion, young Lane, gave a quick summary of the meeting with the Ouster Tribunal. Gladstone sat back in the leather seat and raised both fists to her cheeks as Lane repeated the Ouster denials. They were not the invaders. Lane completed the transmission with a brief description of the Swarm, his opinion that the Ousters were telling the truth, a comment that the Consul's fate was still unknown, and a request for orders.

'Response?' asked the fatline computer.

'Acknowledge receipt of message,' said Gladstone. 'Transmit – "Stand by" in diplomatic one-time code.'

Gladstone keyed the second message.

Admiral William Ajunta Lee appeared in a broken flat-image projection, his ship's fatline transmitter obviously working on reduced energy. Gladstone saw from the peripheral data columns that the squirt had been encrypted among standard fleet telemetry transmissions: FORCE technicians would eventually notice the check-sum discrepancies, but it might be hours or days from now.

Lee's face was bloodied, and the background was obscured by smoke. From the fuzzy black-and-white image, it appeared to Gladstone that the young man was transmitting from a docking bay of his cruiser. On a metal worktable behind him lay a corpse.

'. . . a complement of Marines managed to board one of their so-called lancers,' panted Lee. 'They *are* manned – five to a ship – and they *do* look like Ousters, but watch what happens when we try to carry out an autopsy.' The picture shifted, and Gladstone realized that Lee was using a hand-held imager patched in through the cruiser's fatline transmitter. Now Lee was gone, and she was looking down into the white, damaged face of a dead Ouster. From the bleeding at the eyes and ears, Gladstone guessed that the man had died of explosive decompression.

Lee's hand appeared – recognizable by the admiral's braid on the sleeve – holding a laser scalpel. The young commander did not bother to remove clothing before beginning a vertical incision starting at the breastbone and cutting downward.

The hand with the laser jerked away, and the camera steadied as something began to happen with the Ouster's corpse. Broad patches began to smolder on the dead man's chest, as if the laser had ignited clothing. Then the uniform burned through, and it was immediately apparent that the man's chest was burning in widening, irregular holes, and from those holes shone a light so brilliant that the portable imager had to stop down receptivity. Patches of the corpse's

558

skull were burning through now, leaving afterimages on the fatline screen and Gladstone's retinas.

The camera had pulled back before the corpse had been consumed, as if the heat were too great to bear. Lee's face floated into focus. 'You see, CEO, that's been the case with all of the bodies. We captured none alive. We've found no center to the Swarm yet, just more warships, and I think that—'

The image disappeared and data columns said that the squirt had ceased in midtransmission.

'Response?'

Gladstone shook her head and unsealed the cubicle. In her study once again, she looked longingly at the long couch and sat behind her desk, knowing that if she closed her eyes for a second she would be asleep. Sedeptra buzzed on her private comlog frequency and said that General Morpurgo needed to see the CEO on an urgent matter.

The Lusian entered and began pacing back and forth in his agitation. 'M Executive, I understand your reasoning in authorizing the use of this deathwand device, but I have to protest.'

'Why, Arthur?' she asked, calling him by name for the first time in weeks.

'Because we goddamn well don't know the result. It's too dangerous. And it's . . . it's immoral.'

Gladstone raised an eyebrow. 'Losing billions of citizens in a protracted war of attrition would be moral, but using this thing to kill millions would be immoral? Is this the FORCE position, Arthur?'

'It's my position, CEO.'

Gladstone nodded. 'Understood and noted, Arthur. But the decision has been made and will be implemented.' She saw her old friend draw himself to attention, and before he could open his mouth to protest, or, more likely, offer his resignation, Gladstone said, 'Would you take a walk with me, Arthur?'

The FORCE General was nonplussed. 'A walk? Why?'

'We need the fresh air.' Without waiting for a further response, Gladstone crossed to her private farcaster, keyed the manual diskey, and stepped through.

Morpurgo stepped through the opaque portal, glared down at the gold grass which rose to his knees and spread to a distant horizon, and raised his face to a saffron yellow sky where bronze cumulus clouds rose in jagged spires. Behind him, the portal winked out of existence, its location marked only by the meter-high control diskey, the only man-made thing visible in the endless reach of gold grass and cloud-filled sky. 'Where the hell are we?' he demanded.

Gladstone had pulled a long strand of grass and was chewing on it. 'Kastrop-Rauxel. It has no datasphere, no orbital devices, no human or mech habitations of any kind.'

Morpurgo snorted. 'Probably no safer from Core surveillance than the places Byron Lamia used to take us, Meina.'

'Perhaps not,' said Gladstone. 'Arthur, listen.' She activated the comlog recordings of the two fatline transmission she had just heard.

When they were finished, when Lee's face snapped out of existence, Morpurgo walked away through the high grass.

'Well?' asked Gladstone, hurrying to keep up.

'So these Ouster bodies self-destruct the same way cybrid corpses have been known to,' he said. 'So what? Do you think the Senate or All Thing will accept this as proof that it's the Core that's behind the invasion?'

Gladstone sighed. The grass looked soft, inviting. She imagined lying there and sinking into a nap from which she would never have to return. 'It's proof enough for us. For the group.' Gladstone did not have to elaborate. Since her early Senate days, they had kept in touch with their suspicions of the Core, their hope for true freedom from AI domination someday. When Senator Byron Lamia had led them . . . but that was long ago.

Morpurgo watched wind whip at the golden steppes. A

curious type of ball lightning played inside the bronze clouds near the horizon. 'So what? *Knowing* is useless unless we know where to strike.'

'We have three hours.'

Morpurgo looked at his comlog. 'Two hours and forty-two minutes. Hardly time enough for a miracle, Meina.'

Gladstone did not smile. 'Hardly time enough for anything else, Arthur.'

She touched the diskey, and the portal hummed to life.

'What can we do?' asked Morpurgo. 'The Core AIs are briefing our technicians on that deathwand device right now. The torchship will be ready in an hour.'

'We detonate it where the effect will harm no one,' said Gladstone.

The General quit pacing and stared. 'Where the hell is that? That fucker Nansen says that the device has a lethal radius of at least three light-years, but how can we trust him? We set off one device . . . near Hyperion or anywhere else . . . and we may be dooming human life everywhere.'

'I have an idea, but I want to sleep on it,' said Gladstone.

'*Sleep* on it?' growled General Morpurgo.

'I'm going to take a short nap, Arthur,' Gladstone said. 'I suggest you do the same.' She stepped through the portal.

Morpurgo muttered a single obscenity, adjusted his cap, and walked through the farcaster with head up, back straight, and eyes forward: a soldier marching to his own execution.

On the highest terrace of a mountain moving through space some ten light-minutes from Hyperion, the Consul and seventeen Ousters sat on a circle of low stones within a wider circle of taller stones and decided whether the Consul would live.

'Your wife and child died on Bressia,' said Freeman Ghenga. 'During the war between the world and Clan Moseman.'

'Yes,' said the Consul. 'The Hegemony thought that the entire Swarm was involved in the attack. I said nothing to disabuse them of that opinion.'

'But your wife and child were killed.'

The Consul looked beyond the stone circle toward the summit already turning toward night. 'So what? I ask for no mercy from this Tribunal. I suggest no extenuating circumstances. I *killed* your Freeman Andil and the three technicians. Killed them with premeditation and malice aforethought. Killed them with no other goal than to trigger your machine to open the Time Tombs. It had nothing to do with my wife and child!'

A bearded Ouster whom the Consul had heard introduced as Spokesman Hullcare Amnion stepped forward to the inner circle. 'The device was useless. It did nothing.'

The Consul turned, opened his mouth, and closed it without speaking.

'A test,' said Freeman Ghenga.

The Consul's voice was almost inaudible. 'But the Tombs . . . opened.'

'We knew when they would open,' said Coredwell Minmun. 'The decay rate of the anti-entropic fields was known to us. The device was a test.'

'A test,' repeated the Consul. 'I killed those four people for nothing. A test.'

'Your wife and child died at Ouster hands,' said Freeman Ghenga. 'The Hegemony raped your world of Maui-Covenant. Your actions were predictable within certain parameters. Gladstone counted on this. So did we. But we had to know those parameters.'

The Consul stood, took three steps, and kept his back turned to the others. 'Wasted.'

'What was that?' asked Freeman Ghenga. The tall woman's bare scalp glowed in the starlight and the reflected sunlight from a passing comet farm.

The Consul was laughing softly. 'Everything wasted.

Even my betrayals. Nothing real. Wasted.'

Spokesman Coredwell Minmun stood and arranged his robes. 'This Tribunal has passed sentence,' he said. The other sixteen Ousters nodded.

The Consul turned. There was something like eagerness on his tired face. 'Do it, then. For God's sake get it over with.'

Spokesman Freeman Ghenga stood and faced the Consul. 'You are condemned to live. You are condemned to repair some of the damage you have done.'

The Consul staggered as if struck in the face. 'No, you can't . . . you must . . .'

'You are condemned to enter the age of chaos which approaches,' said Spokesman Hullcare Amnion. 'Condemned to help us find fusion between the separated families of humankind.'

The Consul raised his arms as if trying to defend himself from physical blows. 'I can't . . . won't . . . guilty . . .'

Freeman Ghenga took three strides, grasped the Consul by the front of his formal bolo jacket, and shook him unceremoniously. 'You *are* guilty. And that is precisely why you must help ameliorate the chaos which is to come. You helped free the Shrike. Now you must return to see that it is caged again. Then the long reconciliation must begin.'

The Consul had been released, but his shoulders were still shaking. At that moment, the mountain rotated into sunlight, and tears sparkled in the Consul's eyes. 'No,' he whispered.

Freeman Ghenga smoothed his rumpled jacket and moved her long fingers to the diplomat's shoulders. 'We have our own prophets. The Templars will join us in the reseeding of the galaxy. Slowly, those who had lived in the lie called the Hegemony will climb out of the ruins of their Core-dependent worlds and join us in true exploration . . . exploration of the universe and of that greater realm which is inside each of us.'

The Consul had not seemed to have heard. He turned away brusquely. 'The Core will destroy you,' he said, not facing any of them. 'Just as it has destroyed the Hegemony.'

'Do you forget that your homeworld was founded on a solemn covenant of life?' said Coredwell Minmun.

The Consul turned toward the Ouster.

'Such a covenant governs our lives and actions,' said Minmun. 'Not merely to preserve a few species from Old Earth, but to find unity in diversity. To spread the seed of humankind to all worlds, diverse environments, while treating as sacred the diversity of life we find elsewhere.'

Freeman Ghenga's face was bright in the sun. 'The Core offered unity in unwitting subservience,' she said softly. 'Safety in stagnation. Where are the revolutions in human thought and culture and action since the Hegira?'

'Terraformed into pale clones of Old Earth,' answered Coredwell Minmun. 'Our new age of human expansion will terraform nothing. We will revel in hardships and welcome strangeness. We will not make the universe adapt . . . *we* shall adapt.'

Spokesman Hullcare Amnion gestured toward the stars. 'If humankind survives this test, our future lies in the dark distances *between* as well as on the sunlit worlds.'

The Consul sighed. 'I have friends on Hyperion,' he said. 'May I return to help them?'

'You may,' said Freeman Ghenga.

'And confront the Shrike?' said the Consul.

'You will,' said Coredwell Minmun.

'And survive to see this age of chaos?' said the Consul.

'You must,' said Hullcare Amnion.

The Consul sighed again and moved aside with the others as, above them, a great butterfly with wings of solar cells and glistening skin impervious to hard vacuum or harder radiation lowered itself toward the Stonehenge circle and opened its belly to receive the Consul.

*   *   *

564

In the Government House infirmary on Tau Ceti Center, Father Paul Duré slept a shallow and medically induced sleep, dreaming of flames and the death of worlds.

Except for the brief visit by CEO Gladstone and an even briefer visit by Bishop Edouard, Duré had been alone all day, drifting in and out of a pain-filled haze. The doctors here had asked for twelve more hours before their patient should be moved, and the College of Cardinals on Pacem had agreed, wishing the patient well and making ready for the ceremonies – still twenty-four hours away – in which Jesuit priest Paul Duré of Villefranche-sur-Saône would become Pope Teilhard I, the 487th Bishop of Rome, direct successor of the disciple Peter.

Still healing, flesh reweaving itself with the guidance of a million RNA directors, nerves similarly regenerating, thanks to the miracle of modern medicine – but not so miraculous, Duré thought, that it keeps me from itching almost to death – the Jesuit lay abed and thought about Hyperion and the Shrike and his long life and the confused state of affairs in God's universe. Eventually Duré slept and dreamed of God's Grove burning while the Templar True Voice of the Worldtree pushed him through the portal, and of his mother and of a woman named Semfa, now dead, but formerly a worker on Perecebo Plantation in the outback of the Outback in fiberplastic country east of Port Romance.

And in these dreams, primarily sad, Duré suddenly was aware of another presence there: not of another dream presence, but of another *dreamer*.

Duré was walking with someone. The air was cool, and the sky was a heart-rending blue. They had just come around a bend in a road, and now a lake became visible before them, its shores lined with graceful trees, mountains framing it from behind, a line of low clouds adding drama and scale to the scene, and a single island seeming to float far out on the mirror-still waters.

'Lake Windermere,' said Duré's companion.

The Jesuit turned slowly, his heart pounding with anxious anticipation. Whatever he expected, the sight of his companion did not inspire awe.

A short young man walked next to Duré. He wore an archaic jacket with leather buttons and a broad leather belt, sturdy shoes, an old fur cap, a battered knapsack, oddly tailored and frequently patched trousers, and carried a great plaid thrown over one shoulder and a solid walking stick in his right hand. Duré stopped walking, and the other man paused as if welcoming a break.

'The Fells of Furness and the Cumbrian Mountains,' said the young man, using his stick to gesture beyond the lake.

Duré saw the auburn locks curling out from under the odd cap, noted the large hazel eyes and the man's short stature, and knew that he had to be dreaming even as he thought *I'm not dreaming!*

'Who . . .' began Duré, feeling fear surge in him as his heart pounded.

'John,' said his companion, and the quiet reasonableness of that voice set some of Duré's fear aside. 'I believe we'll be able to stay in Bowness tonight. Brown tells me that there's a wonderful inn there hard on the lake.'

Duré nodded. He had absolutely no idea what the man was talking about.

The short young man leaned forward and grasped Duré's forearm in a gentle but persistent grip. 'There will be one who comes after me,' said John. 'Neither alpha nor the omega but essential for us to find the way.'

Duré nodded stupidly. A breeze rippled the lake and brought the smell of fresh vegetation from the foothills beyond.

'That one will be born far away,' said John. 'Farther away than our race has known for centuries. Your job will be the same as mine now – to prepare the way. You will not live to see the day of that person's teaching, but your successor will.'

566

'Yes,' said Paul Duré and found that there was no saliva whatsoever in his mouth.

The young man doffed his cap, tucked it in his belt, and stooped to pick up a rounded stone. He threw it far out on to the lake. Ripples spread in slow progression. 'Damn,' said John, 'I was trying to skip it.' He looked at Duré. 'You have to leave the infirmary and get back to Pacem at once. Do you understand?'

Duré blinked. The statement did not seem to belong in the dream. 'Why?'

'Never mind,' said John. 'Just *do* it. Wait for nothing. If you don't leave at once, there will be no chance later.'

Duré turned in confusion, as if he could walk back to his hospital bed. He looked over his shoulder at the short, thin young man standing on the pebbly shore. 'What about you?'

John picked up a second stone, threw it, and shook his head when the rock skipped only once before disappearing beneath the mirrored surface. 'I'm happy here for now,' he said, more to himself than to Duré. 'I really *was* happy on this trip.' He seemed to shake himself out of his reverie and lifted his head to smile at Duré. 'Go on. Move your ass, Your Holiness.'

Shocked, amused, irritated, Duré opened his mouth to retort and found himself lying in bed in the Government House infirmary. The medics had lowered the lighting so that he could sleep. Monitor beads clung to his skin.

Duré lay there a minute, suffering the itching and discomfort from healing third-degree burns and thinking about the dream, thinking that it was *only* a dream, that he could go back to sleep for a few hours before Monsignor – *Bishop* Edouard and the others arrived to escort him back. Duré closed his eyes and remembered the masculine but gentle face, the hazel eyes, the archaic dialect.

Father Paul Duré of the Society of Jesus sat up, struggled to his feet, found his clothes gone and nothing but his paper hospital pajamas to wear, wrapped a blanket around him, and shuffled off in bare feet before medics could respond to the tattletale sensors.

There had been a medics-only farcaster at the far end of the hall. If that failed to get him home, he would find another.

Leigh Hunt carried Keats's body out of the shadow of the building into the sunlight of the Piazza di Spagna and expected to find the Shrike waiting for him. Instead, there was a horse. Hunt wasn't an expert at recognizing horses, since the species was extinct in his time, but this one appeared to be the same one which had brought them to Rome. It helped in the identification that the horse was attached to the same small cart – Keats had called it a *vettura* – which they had ridden in earlier.

Hunt set the body on the carriage seat, folding the layers of linen around it carefully, and walked alongside with one hand still touching the shroud as the carriage began moving slowly. In his final hours, Keats had asked to be buried in the Protestant Cemetery near the Aurelian Wall and the Pyramid of Caius Cestius. Hunt vaguely remembered that they had passed through the Aurelian Wall during their bizarre voyage here, but he could not have found it again if his life – or Keats's burial – depended on it. At any rate, the horse seemed to know the way.

Hunt trudged alongside the slowly moving carriage, aware of the beautiful spring-morning quality to the air and an underlying smell as of rotting vegetation. Could Keats's body be decomposing already? Hunt knew little about the details of death; he wanted to learn no more. He swatted at the horse's rump to hurry the beast up, but the animal stopped, turned slowly to give Hunt a reproachful look, and resumed his plodding pace.

It was more a glint of light glimpsed out of the corner of his eye than any sound that tipped Hunt off, but when he turned quickly, the Shrike was there – ten or fifteen meters behind and matching the pace of the horse with a solemn but somehow comical march, thorned and barbed knees high with each step. Sunlight flashed on carapace, metal tooth, and blade.

Hunt's first impulse was to abandon the carriage and run, but a sense of duty and a deeper sense of being lost stifled that urge. Where could he run but back to the Piazza di Spagna – and the Shrike blocked the only return.

Accepting the creature as a mourner in this insane procession, Hunt turned his back on the monster and continued walking alongside the carriage, one hand firm on his friend's ankle, through the shroud.

All during the walk, Hunt was alert for any sign of a farcaster portal, some sign of technology beyond the nineteenth century, or another human being. There was none. The illusion that he was walking through an abandoned Rome in the spring-like weather of February, AD 1821 was perfect. The horse climbed a hill a block from the Spanish Steps, made several other turns on broad avenues and narrow lanes, and passed within sight of the curved and crumbling ruin which Hunt recognized as the Colosseum.

When the horse and carriage stopped, Hunt roused himself from the walking doze he had drifted into and looked around. They were outside the overgrown heap of stones Hunt guessed to be the Aurelian Wall, and there was indeed a low pyramid visible, but the Protestant Cemetery – if that is what it was – seemed more pasture than cemetery. Sheep grazed in the shade of cypresses, their bells tinkling eerily in the thick, warming air, and everywhere the grass grew to knee height or taller. Hunt blinked and saw the few headstones scattered here and there, half hidden by the grass, and closer, just beyond the grazing horse's neck, a newly excavated grave.

The Shrike remained ten meters back, among the rustling cypress branches, but Hunt saw the glow of its red eyes fixed on the grave site.

Hunt went around the horse, now munching contentedly on high grass, and approached the grave. There was no coffin. The hole was about four feet deep, and the heaped dirt beyond smelled of upturned humus and cool soil. Embedded there was a long-handled shovel, as if the grave diggers had just left. A slab of stone stood upright at the head of the grave but remained unmarked – a blank headstone. Hunt saw the glint of metal on top of the slab and rushed over to find the first modern artifact he had seen since being kidnapped to Old Earth: a small laser pen lay there – the type used by construction workers or artists to scrawl designs on the hardest alloy.

Hunt turned, holding the pen, feeling armed now although the thought of that narrow beam stopping the Shrike seemed ludicrous. He dropped the pen into the pocket of his shirt and went about the business of burying John Keats.

A few minutes later, Hunt stood near the heap of dirt, shovel in hand, staring down into the open grave at the small, sheet-wrapped bundle there, and tried to think of something to say. Hunt had been at numerous state memorial services, had even written Gladstone's eulogies for some of them, and words had never been a problem before. But now nothing came. The only audience was the silent Shrike, still back among the shadows of the cypresses, and the sheep with their bells tinkling as they moved nervously away from the monster, ambling toward the grave like a group of tardy mourners.

Hunt thought that perhaps some of the original John Keats's poetry would be appropriate now, but Hunt was a political manager – not a man given to reading or memorizing ancient poetry. He remembered, too late, that he had written down the snippet of verse his friend had dictated the day before, but the notebook still lay on the bureau in the apartment on the Piazza di Spagna. It had been something about becoming godlike or a god, the knowledge of too many things rushing in . . . or somesuch nonsense. Hunt had an excellent memory, but he couldn't recall the first line of that archaic mishmash.

In the end, Leigh Hunt compromised with a moment of silence, his head bowed and eyes closed except for occasional peeks at the Shrike, still holding its distance, and then he shoveled the dirt in. It took longer than he would have imagined. When he·was done patting down the soil, the surface was slightly concave, as if the body had been too insignificant to form a proper mound. Sheep brushed by Hunt's legs to graze on the high grass, daisies, and violets which grew around the grave.

Hunt might not have remembered the man's poetry, but he had no trouble remembering the inscription Keats had asked to be set on his headstone. Hunt clicked on the pen, tested it by burning a furrow in three meters of grass and soil, and then had to stamp out the tiny fire he had started. The inscription had bothered Hunt when he first heard it – the loneliness and bitterness audible beneath Keats's wheezing, gasping effort to speak. But Hunt did not think it was his place to argue with the man. Now he had only to inscribe it in stone, leave this place, and avoid the Shrike while trying to find a way home.

The pen sliced into stone easily enough, and Hunt had to practice on the back side of the headstone before he found the right depth of line and quality of control. Still, the effect looked ragged and homemade when Hunt finished some fifteen or twenty minutes later.

First there was the crude drawing which Keats had asked for – he had shown the aide several rough sketches, drawn on foolscap with a shaking hand – of a Greek lyre with four of its eight strings broken. Hunt was not satisfied when he was done – he was even less of an artist than a reader of poetry – but the thing was probably recognizable to anyone who knew what the hell a Greek lyre *was*. Then came the legend itself, written precisely as Keats had dictated it:

HERE LIES ONE
WHOSE NAME
WAS WRIT IN WATER

There was nothing else: no birth or death dates, not even the poet's name. Hunt stood back, surveyed his work, shook his head, keyed the pen off but kept it in his hand, and started back for the city, making a wide circle around the creature in the cypresses as he did so.

At the tunnel through the Aurelian Wall, Hunt paused to look back. The horse, still attached to its carriage, had moved down the long slope to munch on sweeter grass near a small stream. The sheep milled about, munching flowers and leaving their hoofprints in the moist soil of the grave. The Shrike remained where it had been, barely visible beneath its bower of cypress branches. Hunt was almost sure that the creature still faced the grave.

It was late in the afternoon when Hunt found the farcaster, a dull rectangle of dark blue humming in the precise center of the crumbling Colosseum. There was no diskey or punchplate. The portal hung there like an opaque but open door.

But not open to Hunt.

He tried fifty times, but the surface was as solid and resisting as stone. He touched it tentatively with fingertips, stepped confidently into and bounced off its surface, threw himself at the blue rectangle, lobbed stones at the entrance to watch them bounce off, tried both sides and even the edges of the thing, and ended up leaping again and again at the useless thing until his shoulders and upper arms were masses of bruises.

It was a farcaster. He was sure of it. But it would not let him through.

Hunt searched the rest of the Colosseum, even the underground passages dripping with moisture and bat guano, but there was no other portal. He searched the nearby streets and all their buildings. No other portal. He searched all afternoon, through basilica and cathedrals, homes and huts, grand apartment buildings and narrow alleys. He even returned to the Piazza di Spagna, ate a hasty meal on the first floor, pocketed the notebook and anything else he found of interest in the rooms above, and then left forever to find a farcaster.

The one in the Colosseum was the only one he could find. By sunset he had clawed at it until his fingers were bloody. It looked right, it hummed right, it *felt* right, but it would not let him through.

A moon, not Old Earth's moon judging by the dust storms and clouds visible on its surface, had risen and now hung above the black curve of the Colosseum wall. Hunt sat in the rocky center and glowered at the blue glow of the portal. From somewhere behind him came the frenzied beat of pigeons' wings and the rattle of a small rock on stone.

Hunt rose painfully, fumbled the laser pen out of his pocket, and stood, legs apart, waiting and straining to see into the shadows of the Colosseum's many crevices and arches. Nothing stirred.

A sudden noise behind him made him whirl and almost spray the thin beam of laser light across the farcaster portal's surface. An arm appeared there. Then a leg. A person emerged. Then another.

The Colosseum echoed to Leigh Hunt's shouts.

Meina Gladstone had known that as tired as she was, it would be folly to nap even as long as thirty minutes. But since childhood, she had trained herself to take five- to fifteen-minute catnaps, shrugging off weariness and fatigue toxins through these brief respites from thought.

Now, sickened with exhaustion and the vertigo of the previous forty-eight hours' confusion, she lay a few minutes on the long sofa in her study, emptying her mind of trivia and redundancies, letting her sub-conscious find a path through the jungle of thoughts and events. For a few minutes, she dozed, and while she dozed she dreamed.

Meina Gladstone sat upright, shrugging off the light afghan and tapping at her comlog before her eyes were open. 'Sedeptra! Get General Morpurgo and Admiral Singh in my office in three minutes.'

Gladstone stepped into the adjoining bathroom, showered and sonicked, pulled out fresh clothes – her most formal suit of soft, black whipcord velvet, a gold and red Senate scarf held in place by a gold pin showing the geodesic symbol of the Hegemony, earrings dating back to pre-Mistake Old Earth, and the topaz bracelet-cum-comlog given to her by Senator Byron Lamia before his marriage – and was back in the study in time to greet the two FORCE officers.

'CEO, this is a very unfortunate timing,' began Admiral Singh. 'The final data from Mare Infinitus was being analyzed, and we were discussing fleet movements for the defense of Asquith.'

Gladstone ordered her private farcaster into existence and gestured for the two men to follow her.

Singh glanced around as he stepped through into gold grass under a threatening bronze sky. 'Kastrop-Rauxel,' he said. 'There were rumors that a previous administration had FORCE:space construct a private farcaster here.'

'CEO Yevshensky had it added to the Web,' said Gladstone. She waved, and the farcaster door vanished. 'He felt that the Chief Executive needed someplace where Core listening devices were unlikely.'

Morpurgo looked uneasily toward a wall of clouds near the horizon where ball lightning played. 'No place is totally safe from the Core,' he said. 'I've been telling Admiral Singh about our suspicions.'

'Not suspicions,' said Gladstone. 'Facts. And I know where the Core is.'

Both FORCE officers reacted as if the ball lightning had

struck them. 'Where?' they said almost in unison.

Gladstone paced back and forth. Her short gray hair seemed to glow in the charged air. '*In* the farcaster web,' she said. 'Between the portals. The AIs live in the singularity pseudo-world there like spiders in a dark web. And *we* wove it for them.'

Morpurgo was the first of the two able to speak. 'My God,' he said. 'What do we do now? We have less than three hours before the torchship with the Core device translates to Hyperion space.'

Gladstone told them exactly what they were going to do.

'Impossible,' said Singh. He was unconsciously tugging at his short beard. 'Simply impossible.'

'No,' said Morpurgo. 'It will work. There is enough time. And as frantic and random as the fleet movements have been during the past two days . . .'

The Admiral shook his head. 'Logistically it might be possible. Rationally and ethically it is not. No, it is impossible.'

Meina Gladstone stepped closer. 'Kushwant,' she said, addressing the Admiral by his first name for the first time since she had been a young senator and he an even younger FORCE:space commander, 'don't you remember when Senator Lamia put us in touch with the Stables? The AI named Ummon? His prediction of the two futures – one holding chaos and the other certain extinction for humankind?'

Singh turned away. 'My duty is to FORCE and the Hegemony.'

'Your duty is the same as mine,' snapped Gladstone. 'To the human race.'

Singh's fists came up as if he were ready to fight an invisible but powerful opponent. 'We don't know for *sure*! Where did you get your information?'

'Severn,' said Gladstone. 'The cybrid.'

'Cybrid?' snorted the General. 'You mean that *artist*. Or at least that miserable excuse for one.'

'Cybrid,' repeated the CEO. She explained.

'Severn as a retrieval persona?' Morpurgo looked dubious. 'And now you've found him?'

'He found *me*. In a dream. Somehow he managed to communicate from wherever he is. That was his role, Arthur, Kushwant. That's why Ummon *sent* him to the Web.'

'A dream,' sneered Admiral Singh. 'This . . . cybrid . . . told you that the Core was hidden in the farcaster web . . . in a *dream*.'

'Yes,' said Gladstone, 'and we have very little time in which to act.'

'But,' said Morpurgo, 'to do what you suggested—'

'Would doom millions,' finished Singh. 'Possibly billions. The economy would collapse. Worlds like TC², Renaissance Vector, New Earth, the Denebs, New Mecca – *Lusus*, Arthur – scores more depend upon other worlds for their food. Urban planets cannot survive alone.'

'Not as urban planets,' said Gladstone. 'But they can learn to farm until interstellar trade is reborn.'

'Bah!' snarled Singh. '*After* plague, *after* the breakdown of authority, *after* the millions of deaths from lack of proper equipment, medicine, and datasphere support.'

'I've thought of all that,' said Gladstone, her voice firmer than Morpurgo had ever heard it. 'I'll be the greatest mass murderer in history – greater than Hitler or Tze Hu or Horace Glennon-Height. The only thing worse is to continue as we are. In which case, I – and you, gentlemen – will be the ultimate betrayers of humankind.'

'We can't *know* that,' grunted Kushwant Singh, as if the words were driven from him by blows to the belly.

'We *do* know that,' said Gladstone. 'The Core has no more use for the Web. From now on, the Volatiles and Ultimates will keep a few million slaves penned underground on the nine labyrinthine worlds while they use human synapses for what computing needs remain.'

'Nonsense,' said Singh. 'Those humans would die out.'

Meina Gladstone sighed and shook her head. 'The Core has devised a parasitic, organic device called the cruciform,' she said. 'It . . . brings back . . . the dead. After a few generations, the humans will be retarded, listless, and without a future, but their neurons will still serve Core purposes.'

Singh turned his back on them again. His small form was silhouetted against a wall of lightning as the storm approached in a riot of boiling bronze clouds. 'Your dream told you this, Meina?'

'Yes.'

'And what else does your dream say?' snapped the Admiral.

'That the Core has no more need for the Web,' said Gladstone. 'Not for the *human* Web. They'll continue to reside there, rats in the walls, but the original occupants are no longer needed. The AI Ultimate Intelligence will take over the major computing duties.'

Singh turned to look at her. 'You are mad, Meina. Quite mad.'

Gladstone moved quickly to grab the Admiral's arm before he could activate the farcaster. 'Kushwant, please listen to—'

Singh pulled a ceremonial fléchette pistol from his tunic and set it against the woman's breast. 'I am sorry, M Executive. But I serve the Hegemony and . . .'

Gladstone stepped back with her hand to her mouth as Admiral Kushwant Singh stopped speaking, stared sightlessly for a second, and fell to the grass. The fléchette pistol tumbled into the weeds.

Morpurgo stepped forward to retrieve it, tucking it into his belt before he put away the deathwand in his hand.

'You killed him,' said the CEO. 'If he wouldn't cooperate, I'd planned to leave him here. Maroon him on Kastrop-Rauxel.'

'We couldn't take the chance,' said the General, pulling

the body farther from the farcaster. 'Everything depends upon the next few hours.'

Gladstone looked at her old friend. 'You're willing to go through with it?'

'We have to,' said Morpurgo. 'It will be our last chance to get rid of this yoke of oppression. I'll give the deployment orders at once and hand over sealed orders in person. It will take most of the fleet . . .'

'My God,' whispered Meina Gladstone, looking down at the body of Admiral Singh. 'I'm doing all of this on the strength of a dream.'

'Sometimes,' said General Morpurgo, taking her hand, 'dreams are all that separate us from the machines.'

FORTY-FOUR

Death is not, I discovered, a pleasant experience. Leaving the familiar rooms on the Piazza di Spagna and the rapidly cooling body there is similar to being thrust out in the night by fire or flood from the familiar warmth of one's home. The rush of shock and displacement is severe. Thrown headlong into the metasphere, I experience the same sense of shame and sudden, awkward revelation which we have all had in our dreams when we realize that we have forgotten to get dressed and have come naked to some public place or social gathering.

Naked is the correct word now, as I struggle to keep some shape to my tattered analog persona. I manage to concentrate sufficiently to form this almost random electron cloud of memories and associations into a reasonable simulacrum of the human I had been – or at least the human whose memories I had shared.

Mister John Keats, five feet high.

The metasphere is no less a frightening place than before – worse now that I have no mortal shelter to flee to. Vast shapes move beyond dark horizons, sounds echo in the Void Which Binds like footsteps on tile in an abandoned castle. Under and behind everything there is a constant and unnerving rumble like carriage wheels on a highway made of slate.

Poor Hunt. I am tempted to return to him, pop in like Marley's ghost to assure him that I am better off than I look, but Old Earth is a dangerous place for me right now: the Shrike's presence burns on the metasphere datumplane there like flame on black velvet.

The Core summons me with greater force, but that is even more dangerous. I remember Ummon destroying the other Keats in front of Brawne Lamia – squeezing the analog persona to him until it simply dissolved, the basic Core memory of the man deliquescing like a salted slug.

No thank you.

I have chosen death to godhood, but I have chores to do before I sleep.

The metasphere frightens me, the Core frightens me more, the dark tunnels of the datasphere singularities I must travel terrify me to my analog bones. But there is nothing for it.

I sweep into the first black cone, swirling around like a metaphorical leaf in an all-too-real whirlpool, emerging on the proper datumplane, but too dizzy and disoriented to do anything but sit there – visible to any Core AI accessing these ROMwork ganglia or phage routines residing in the violet crevices of any of these data mountain ranges – but the chaos in the TechnoCore saves me here: the great Core personalities are too busy laying siege to their own personal Troys to watch their back doors.

I find the datasphere access codes I want and the synapse umbilicals I need, and it is the work of a microsecond to follow old paths down to Tau Ceti Center, Government House, the infirmary there, and the drug-induced dreams of Paul Duré.

One thing my persona does exceptionally well is dream, and I discover quite by accident that my memories of my English tour make a pleasant dreamscape in which to convince the priest to flee. As an Englishman and freethinker, I once had been opposed to anything which smacked of popery, but one thing must be said in tribute to the Jesuits – they are taught obedience even above logic, and for once this stands all of humankind in good stead. Duré does not ask why when I tell him to go . . . he awakes like a good boy, wraps a blanket around him, and goes.

Meina Gladstone thinks of me as Joseph Severn but she accepts my message as if it is being delivered to her by God. I want to tell her no, I am not the One, I am only He Who Comes Before, but the message is the thing, so I deliver that and go.

Passing through the Core on my way to Hyperion's metasphere, I catch the burning-metal whiff of civil war and glimpse a great light which might well be Ummon in the process of being extinguished. The old Master, if indeed it is he, does not cite koans as he dies, but screams in agony as sincerely as any conscious entity ever has who is in the process of being fed to the ovens.

I hurry on.

The farcaster connection to Hyperion is tenuous at best: a single military farcaster portal and a single, damaged JumpShip in a shrinking perimeter of war-torn Hegemony ships. The singularity containment sphere cannot be protected from Ouster attacks for longer than a few minutes more. The Hegemony torch-ship carrying the Core deathwand device is preparing to translate in-system even as I come through and find my bearings in the limited datasphere level which allows observation. I pause to watch what happens next.

'Christ,' said Melio Arundez, 'Meina Gladstone's coming through on a priority-one squirt.'

Theo Lane joined the older man as they watched the over-ride data mist the air above the holopit. The Consul came down the iron spiral staircase from the bedroom where he had gone to brood. 'Another message from TC²?' he snapped.

'Not to us specifically,' said Theo, reading the red codes as they formed and faded. 'It's an override fatline transmission to everyone, everywhere.'

Arundez lowered himself into the pit cushions. 'Something's very wrong. Has the CEO ever broadcast on total wideband before?'

'Never,' said Theo Lane. 'The energy needed just to code such a squirt would be incredible.'

The Consul stepped closer and pointed to the codes now disappearing. 'It's not a squirt. Look, it's a real-time transmission.'

Theo shook his head. 'We're talking transmission values of several hundred million gigaelectron volts here.'

Arundez whistled. 'At even a hundred million GeV, it'd better be important.'

'A general surrender,' said Theo. 'It's the only thing that would call for a universal real-time broadcast. Gladstone's sending it to the Ousters, Outback worlds, and overrun planets as well as the Web. It must be carried on all comm frequencies, HTV, and datasphere bands too. It must be a surrender.'

'Shut up,' said the Consul. He had been drinking.

The Consul had started drinking immediately upon his return from the Tribunal, and his temper, which had been foul even as Theo and Arundez were slapping him on the back and celebrating his survival, had not improved after the lift-off, clearance of the Swarm, and the two hours he spent alone drinking while they accelerated toward Hyperion.

'Meina Gladstone won't surrender,' slurred the Consul. The bottle of Scotch was still in his hand. 'Just watch.'

On the torchship HS *Stephen Hawking*, the twenty-third Hegemony spacecraft to carry the revered classical scientist's name, General Arthur Morpurgo looked up from the C³ board and hushed his two bridge officers. Normally this class of torchship carried a crew of seventy-five. Now, with the Core deathwand device loaded in the weapons bay and armed, Morpurgo and four volunteers were the total crew. Displays and discreet computer voices assured them that the *Stephen Hawking* was on course, on time, and accelerating steadily toward near-quantum velocities and the military farcaster portal stationed at LaGrange Point Three between Madhya and its oversized moon. The Madhya portal opened directly to the fiercely defended Hyperion-space farcaster.

'One minute eighteen seconds to translation point,' said Bridge Officer Salumun Morpurgo. The General's son.

Morpurgo nodded and keyed up the in-system wideband transmission. Bridge projections were busy enough with mission data, so the General allowed voice-only on the CEO's broadcast. He smiled despite himself. What would Meina say if she knew he was at the helm of the *Stephen Hawking*? Better she didn't know. There was nothing else he could do. He preferred not to see the results of his precise, hand-delivered orders of the past two hours.

Morpurgo looked at his oldest son with pride so fierce it bordered on pain. There were only so many torchship-rated personnel he could approach about this mission, and his son had been the first to volunteer. If nothing else, the Morpurgo family's enthusiasm might have allayed some Core suspicions.

'My fellow citizens,' Gladstone was saying, 'this is my final broadcast to you as your Chief Executive Officer.

'As you know, the terrible war which has already devastated three of our worlds and is about to fall upon a fourth, has been reported as an invasion by the Ouster Swarms.

'This is a lie.'

The comm bands flared with interference and went dead. 'Go to farline,' said General Morpurgo.

'One minute three seconds to translation point,' intoned his son.

Gladstone's voice returned, filtered and slightly blurred by fatline encrypting and decoding. '. . . to realize that our ancestors . . . and we ourselves . . . had made a Faustian bargain with a power not concerned with the fate of human-kind.

'The *Core* is behind the current invasion.

'The *Core* is responsible for our long, comfortable dark age of the soul.

'The *Core* is responsible for the ongoing attempt to destroy humanity, to remove us from the universe and replace us with a god-machine of their own devising.'

Bridge Officer Salumun Morpurgo never lifted his eyes from the circle of instruments. 'Thirty-eight seconds to trans-lation point.'

Morpurgo nodded. The other two crewmen on the C³ bridge showed faces sheened with sweat. The General realized that his own face was wet.

'. . . have proven that the Core resides . . . has always resided . . . in the dark places between farcaster portals. They believe themselves to be our masters. As long as the Web exists, as long as our beloved Hegemony is joined by farcaster, they will be our masters.'

Morpurgo glanced at his own mission chronometer. *Twenty-eight seconds*. The translation to Hyperion system would be – to human senses – instantaneous. Morpurgo was certain that the Core deathwand device was somehow keyed to detonate as soon as they entered Hyperion space. The shock wave of death would reach the planet Hyperion in less than two seconds, would engulf even the most distant elements of the Ouster Swarm before ten more minutes had passed.

'Thus,' said Meina Gladstone, her voice betraying emo-tion for the first time, 'as Chief Executive Officer of the Senate of the Hegemony of Man, I have authorized elements of FORCE:space to destroy all singularity containment spheres and farcaster devices known to be in existence.

'This destruction . . . this *cauterizing* . . . will commence in ten seconds.

'God save the Hegemony.

'God forgive us all.'

Bridge Officer Salumun Morpurgo said coolly, 'Five seconds to translation, Father.'

Morpurgo looked across the bridge and locked eyes with his son. Projections behind the young man showed the portal growing, growing, surrounding.

'I love you,' said the General.

Two hundred and sixty-three singularity containment spheres connecting more than seventy-two million farcaster portals were destroyed within two point six seconds of one another. FORCE fleet units, deployed by Morpurgo under Executive Order and reacting to orders unsealed less than three minutes before, reacted promptly and professionally, destroying the fragile farcaster spheres by missile, lance, and plasma explosive.

Three seconds later, with the clouds of debris still expanding, the hundreds of FORCE spacecraft found themselves stranded, separated from each other and any other system by weeks or months via Hawking drive, and years of time-debt.

Thousands of people were caught in farcaster transit. Many died instantly, dismembered or torn in half. Many more suffered amputated limbs as the portals collapsed behind them or before them. Some simply disappeared.

This was the fate of the HS *Stephen Hawking* – precisely as planned – as both entrance and exit portals were expertly destroyed in the nanosecond of the ship's translation. No part of the torchship survived in real space. Later tests showed conclusively that the so-called deathwand device was detonated in whatever passed for time and space in the strange Core geographies between the portals.

The effect was never known.

The effect on the rest of the Web and its citizens was immediately obvious.

After seven centuries of existence and at least four centuries where few citizens existed without it, the datasphere – including the All Thing and all comm and access bands – simply ceased to be. Hundreds of thousands of citizens went insane at that moment – shocked into catatonia by the disappearance of senses which had become more important to them than sight or hearing.

More hundreds of thousands of datumplane operators, including many of the so-called cyberpukes and system cowboys, were lost, their analog personas caught in the crash of the datasphere or their brains burned out by neural-shunt overload or an effect later known as zero-zero feedback.

Millions of people died when their chosen habitats, accessible only by farcaster, became isolated deathtraps.

The Bishop of the Church of the Final Atonement – the leader of the Shrike Cult – had carefully arranged to sit out the Final Days in some comfort in a hollowed-out mountain, lavishly stocked, deep in the Raven Range of the north reaches of Nevermore. Redundant farcasters were the only route in or out. The Bishop perished with several thousand of his acolytes, exorcists, lectors, and ostiaries clawing to get into the Inner Sanctum to share the last of the Holy One's air.

Millionaire publisher Tyrena Wingreen-Feif, ninety-seven standard years old and on the scene for three-hundred-plus years thanks to the miracle of Poulsen treatments and cryogenics, made the mistake of spending that fateful day in her farcaster-access-only office on the four hundred and thirty-fifth floor of the Transline Spire in the Babel section of Tau Ceti Center's City Five. After fifteen hours of refusing to believe that farcaster service would not be renewed shortly, Tyrena gave in to comm call entreaties from her employees and dropped her containment field walls so that she could be picked up by EMV.

Tyrena had not listened to instructions carefully enough. The explosive decompression blew her off the four hundred and thirty-fifth floor like a cork out of an overshaken champagne bottle. Employees and rescue squad members in the waiting EMV swore that the old lady cursed a blue streak for the entire four-minute fall.

On most worlds, chaos had earned a new definition.

The majority of the Web's economy disappeared with the local dataspheres and the Web megasphere. Trillions of hard-earned and ill-gotten marks ceased to be. Universal cards quit functioning. The machinery of daily life coughed, wheezed, and shut down. For weeks or months or years, depending upon the world, it would be impossible to pay for groceries, charge a ride on public transit, settle the simplest debt, or receive services without access to black market coins and bills.

But the webwide depression which had hit like a tsunami was a minor detail, reserved for later pondering. For most families, the effect was immediate and intensely personal.

Father or mother had 'cast off to work as usual, say from Deneb Vier to Renaissance V, and instead of arriving home an hour late this evening, would be delayed eleven years – if he or she could find immediate transit on one of the few Hawking drive spinships still traveling the hard way between the worlds.

Well-to-do family members listening to Gladstone's speech in their fashionable multiworld residence looked up to stare at each other, separated by only a few meters and open portals between the rooms, blinked, and were separated by light-years and actual years, their rooms now opening on to nothing.

Children a few minutes away at school or camp or play or the sitter's would be grown before they were reunited with parents.

The Grand Concourse, already slightly truncated by the

winds of war, found itself blown to oblivion, its endless belt of beautiful shops and prestige restaurants sliced into tawdry sections never to be reunited.

The River Tethys ceased to flow as the giant portals went opaque and died. Water spilled out, dried up, and left fish to rot under two hundred suns.

There were riots. Lusus tore itself apart like a wolf chewing at its own entrails. New Mecca went into spasms of martyrdom. Tsingtao-Hsishuang Panna celebrated deliverance from the Ouster hordes and then hanged several thousand former Hegemony bureaucrats.

Maui-Covenant also rioted, but in celebration, the hundreds of thousands of descendents of the First Families riding the motile isles to displace the offworlders who had taken over so much of the world. Later, the millions of shocked and displaced vacation-home owners were put to work dismantling the thousands of oil derricks and tourist centers which had spotted the Equatorial Archipelago like pox.

On Renaissance Vector there was a brief spurt of violence followed by efficient social restructuring and a serious effort to feed an urban world without farms.

On Nordholm, the cities emptied as people returned to the coasts and the cold sea and their ancestral fishing boats.

On Parvati there was confusion and civil war.

On Sol Draconi Septem there was jubilation and revolution followed by a new strand of retrovirus plague.

On Fuji there was philosophical resignation followed by an immediate construction of orbital shipyards to create a fleet of Hawking drive spinships.

On Asquith there was finger-pointing followed by the victory of the Socialist Labor Workers' Party in the World Parliament.

On Pacem there was prayer. The new Pope, His Holiness Teilhard I, called a great council into session – Vatican XXXIX – announced a new era in the life of the Church, and empowered the council to prepare missionaries for long voyages. Many missionaries. For many voyages. Pope Teilhard announced that these missionaries would not be proselytizers, but searchers. The Church, like so many species grown used to living on the edge of extinction, adapted and endured.

On Tempe there were riots and death and the rise of demagogues.

On Mars the Olympus Command stayed in touch with its farflung forces for a while via fatline. It was Olympus which confirmed that the 'Ouster invasion waves' everywhere but Hyperion system had simply limped to a halt. Intercepted Core ships were empty and unprogrammed. The invasion was over.

On Metaxas there were riots and reprisals.

On Qom-Riyadh a self-appointed fundamentalist Shiite ayatollah rode out of the desert, called a hundred thousand followers to him, and wiped out the Suni Home Rule government within hours. The new revolutionary government returned power to the mullahs and set back the clock two thousand years. The people rioted with joy.

On Armaghast, a frontier world, things went on pretty much as they always had except for a dearth of tourists, new archaeologists, and other imported luxuries. Armaghast was a labyrinthine world. The labyrinth there stayed empty.

On Hebron there was panic in the offworld center of New Jerusalem, but the Zionist elders soon restored order to the city and world. Plans were made. Rare offworld necessities were rationed and shared. The desert was reclaimed. Farms were extended. Trees were planted. The people complained to each other, thanked God for deliverance, argued with God about the discomfort of that same deliverance, and went about their business.

On God's Grove entire continents still burned, and a pall of smoke filled the sky. Soon after the last of the 'Swarm' had passed, scores of treeships rose through the clouds, climbing slowly on fusion thrusters while shielded by erg-generated containment fields. Once beyond the gravity well, most of these treeships turned outward in a myriad of directions along the galactic plane of the ecliptic and began the long spin-up to quantum leap. Fatline squirts leaped from treeship to distant, waiting Swarms. The reseeding had begun.

On Tau Ceti Center, seat of power and wealth and business and government, the hungry survivors left the dangerous spires and useless cities and helpless orbiting habitats and went in search of someone to blame. Someone to punish.

They did not have far to look.

General Van Zeidt had been in Government House when the portals failed and now he commanded the two hundred Marines and sixty-eight security people left to guard the complex. Former CEO Meina Gladstone still commanded the six Praetorians Kolchev had left her when he and the other ranking senators had departed on the first and last FORCE evacuation dropship to get through. Somewhere the mob had acquired anti-space missiles and lances, and none of the other three thousand Government House employees and refugees would be going anywhere until the siege was lifted or the shields failed.

Gladstone stood at the forward observation post and watched the carnage. The mob had destroyed most of Deer Park and the formal gardens before the last lines of interdiction and containment fields had stopped them. There were at least three million frenzied people pressed against those barriers now, and the mob grew larger every minute.

'Can you drop the fields back fifty meters and restore them before the mob covers the ground?' Gladstone asked the General. Smoke filled the sky from the cities burning to the west. Thousands of men and women had been smashed against the blur of containment field by the throngs behind them until the lower two meters of the shimmering wall looked as if it had been painted with strawberry jam. Tens of thousands more pressed closer to that inner shield despite the agony of nerve and bone the interdiction field was causing them.

'We can do that, M Executive,' said Van Zeidt. 'But why?'

'I'm going out to talk to them.' Gladstone sounded very tired.

The Marine looked at her, sure that she was making some bad joke. 'M Executive, in a month they will be willing to listen to you . . . or any of us . . . on radio or HTV. In a year, maybe two, after order's restored and rationing's successful, they might be ready to forgive. But it will be a generation before they really understand what you did . . . that you saved them . . . saved us all.'

'I want to talk to them,' said Meina Gladstone. 'I have something to give to them.'

Van Zeidt shook his head and looked at the circle of FORCE officers who had been staring out at the mob through slits in the bunker and who now were staring at Gladstone with equal disbelief and horror.

'I'd have to check with CEO Kolchev,' said General Van Zeidt.

'No,' Meina Gladstone said tiredly. 'He rules an empire which no longer exists. I still rule the world I destroyed.' She nodded toward her Praetorians and they produced deathwands from their orange-and-black-striped tunics.

None of the FORCE officers moved. General Van Zeidt said, 'Meina, the next evacuation ship will make it.'

Gladstone nodded as if distracted. 'The inner garden, I should think. The mob will be at a loss for several moments. The withdrawal of the outer fields will throw them off balance.' She looked around as if she might be forgetting something and then extended her hand to Van Zeidt. 'Goodbye, Mark. Thank you. Please take care of my people.'

Van Zeidt shook her hand and watched as the woman adjusted her scarf, absently touched a bracelet comlog as if for luck, and went out of the bunker with four of her

Praetorians. The small group crossed the trampled gardens and walked slowly toward the containment fields. The mob beyond seemed to react like a single, mindless organism, pressing through the violet interdiction field and screaming with the voice of some demented thing.

Gladstone turned, raised one hand as if to wave, and gestured her Praetorians back. The four guards hurried across the matted grass.

'Do it,' said the oldest of the remaining Praetorians. He pointed to the containment field control remote.

'Fuck you,' General Van Zeidt said clearly. No one would go near that remote while he lived.

Van Zeidt had forgotten that Gladstone still had access to codes and tactical tightbeam links. He saw her raise her comlog, but he reacted too slowly. Lights on the remote blinked red and then green, the outer fields winked out and then re-formed fifty meters closer in, and for a second, Meina Gladstone stood alone with nothing between her and the mob of millions except a few meters of grass and countless corpses suddenly surrendered to gravity by the retreating shield walls.

Gladstone raised both arms as if embracing the mob. Silence and lack of motion extended for three eternal seconds, and then the mob roared with the voice of a single great beast, and thousands surged forward with sticks and rocks and knives and broken bottles.

For a moment it seemed to Van Zeidt that Gladstone stood like an impervious rock against that tidal wave of rabble; he could see her dark suit and bright scarf, see her standing upright, her arms still raised, but then more hundreds surged in, the crowd closed, and the CEO was lost.

The Praetorians lowered their weapons and were put under immediate arrest by Marine sentries.

'Opaque the containment fields,' ordered Van Zeidt. 'Tell the dropships to land in the inner garden at five-minute intervals. *Hurry!*'

The General turned away.

'Good Lord,' said Theo Lane as the fragmented reports kept coming in over the fatline. There were so many millisecond squirts being sent that the computer could do little to separate them. The result was a mélange of madness.

'Play back the destruction of the singularity containment sphere,' said the Consul.

'Yes, sir,' said the ship and interrupted its fatline messages for a replay of the sudden burst of white, followed by a brief blossoming of debris and sudden collapse as the singularity swallowed itself and everything within a six-thousand-klick radius. Instruments showed the effect of gravity tides: easily adjusted for at this distance but playing havoc with the Hegemony and Ouster ships still locked in battle closer to Hyperion.

'All right,' said the Consul, and the rush of fatline reports resumed.

'There's no doubt?' asked Arundez.

'None,' said the Consul. 'Hyperion is an Outback world again. Only this time there is no Web to be Outback to.'

'It's so hard to believe,' said Theo Lane. The ex-Governor-General sat drinking Scotch: the only time the Consul had ever seen his aide indulge in a drug. Theo poured another four fingers. 'The Web . . . gone. Five hundred years of expansion wiped out.'

'Not wiped out,' said the Consul. He set his own drink, still unfinished, on a table. 'The worlds remain. The cultures will grow apart, but we still have the Hawking drive. The one technological advance we gave ourselves rather than leased from the Core.'

Melio Arundez leaned forward, his palms together as if praying. 'Can the Core really be gone? Destroyed?'

The Consul listened a moment to the babble of voices, cries, entreaties, military reports, and pleas for help coming over the fatline voice-only bands. 'Perhaps not destroyed,' he said, 'but cut off, sealed away.'

Theo finished his drink and carefully set his glass down. His green eyes had a placid, glazed look. 'You think there are . . . other spiderwebs for them? Other farcaster systems? Reserve Cores?'

The Consul made a gesture with his hand. 'We know they succeeded in creating their Ultimate Intelligence. Perhaps that UI allowed this . . . winnowing . . . of the Core. Perhaps it's keeping some of the old AIs on line – in a reduced capacity – the way they had planned to keep a few billion humans in reserve.'

Suddenly the fatline babble ceased as if cut off by a knife.

'Ship?' queried the Consul, suspecting a power failure somewhere in the receiver.

'All fatline messages have ceased, most in midtransmission,' said the ship.

The Consul felt his heart pounding as he thought *The deathwand device*. But no, he realized at once, that couldn't affect all of the worlds at once. Even with hundreds of such devices detonating simultaneously, there would be lag time as FORCE ships and other far-flung transmission sources got in their final messages. But what then?

'The messages appear to have been cut off by a disturbance in the transmission medium,' said the ship. 'Which is, to my current knowledge, impossible.'

The Consul stood. A *disturbance in the transmission medium?* The fatline medium, as far as humans understood it, was the hyperstring Planck-infinite topography of space-time itself: what AIs had cryptically referred to as the Void Which Binds. There could be no disturbance in that medium.

Suddenly the ship said, 'Fatline message coming in – transmission source, everywhere; encryption base, infinite; squirt rate, real-time.'

The Consul opened his mouth to tell the ship to quit

spouting nonsense when the air above the holopit misted in something neither image nor data column, and a voice spoke:

'THERE WILL BE NO FURTHER MISUSE OF THIS CHANNEL. YOU ARE DISTURBING OTHERS WHO ARE USING IT TO SERIOUS PURPOSE. ACCESS WILL BE RESTORED WHEN YOU UNDERSTAND WHAT IT IS FOR. GOODBYE.'

The three men sat in silence unbroken except for the reassuring rush of ventilator fans and the myriad soft noises of a ship under way. Finally the Consul said, 'Ship, please send out a standard fatline time-location squirt without encoding. Add "receiving stations respond."

There was a pause of seconds – an impossibly long response time for the AI-caliber computer that was the ship. 'I'm sorry, that is not possible,' it said at last.

'Why not?' demanded the Consul.

'Fatline transmissions are no longer being . . . allowed. The hyperstring medium is no longer receptive to modulation.'

'There's nothing on the fatline?' asked Theo, staring at the empty space above the holopit as if someone had turned off a holie just as it was getting to the exciting part.

Again the ship paused. 'To all intents and purposes, M Lane,' it said , 'there is no fatline any longer.'

'Jesus wept,' muttered the Consul. He finished his drink in one long gulp and went to the bar for another. 'It's the old Chinese curse,' he muttered.

Melio Arundez looked up. 'What's that?'

The Consul took a long drink. 'Old Chinese curse,' he said. 'May you live in interesting times.'

As if compensating for the loss of fatline, the ship played audio of in-system radio and intercepted tightbeam babble while it projected a real-time view of the blue-and-white sphere of Hyperion turning and growing as they decelerated toward it at two hundred gravities.

FORTY-FIVE

I escape the Web datasphere just before escape ceases to be an option.

It is incredible and oddly disturbing, the sight of the megasphere swallowing itself. Brawne Lamia's view of the megasphere as an organic thing, a semisentient organism more analogous to an ecology than a city, was essentially correct. Now, as the farcaster links cease to be and the world *inside* those avenues folds and collapses upon itself, the external datasphere simultaneously collapsing like a burning big-top tent suddenly without poles, wires, guys, or stakes, the living megasphere devours itself like some ravenous predator gone mad – chewing its own tail, belly, entrails, forepaws, and heart – until only the mindless jaws are left, snapping on emptiness.

The metasphere remains. But it is more wilderness than ever now.

Black forests of unknown time and space.

Sounds in the night.

Lions.

And tigers.

And bears.

When the Void Which Binds convulses and sends its single, banal message to the human universe, it is as if an earthquake has sent ripples through solid rock. Hurrying through the shifting metasphere above Hyperion, I have to smile. It is as if the God-analog has

596

grown tired of the ants scribbling graffiti on Its big toe.

I don't see God – either one of them – in the metasphere. I don't try. I have enough problems of my own.

The black vortexes of the Web and Core entrances are gone now, erased from space and time like warts removed, vanished as thoroughly as whirlpools in water when the storm has passed.

I am stuck here unless I want to brave the metasphere.

Which I do not. Not yet.

But this is where I want to be. The datasphere is all but gone here in Hyperion System, the pitiful remnants on the world itself and in what remains of the FORCE fleet drying up like tidepools in the sun, but the Time Tombs glow through the metasphere like beacons in the gathering darkness. If the farcaster links had been black vortexes, the Tombs blaze like white holes shedding an expanding light.

I move toward them. So far, as the One Who Comes Before, all I have accomplished is to appear in others' dreams. It is time to *do* something.

Sol waited.

It had been hours since he had handed his only child to the Shrike. It had been days since he had eaten or slept. Around him the storm had raged and abated, the Tombs had glowed and rumbled like runaway reactors, and the time tides had whipped him with tsunami force. But Sol had clung to the stone steps of the Sphinx and waited through it all. He waited now.

Half conscious, pummeled by fatigue and fear for his daughter, Sol found that his scholar's mind was working at a rapid pace.

For most of his life and for all of his career, Sol Weintraub the historian-cum-classicist-cum-philosopher had dealt with the ethics of human religious behavior. Religion and ethics were not always – or even frequently – mutually compatible. The demands of religious absolutism or fundamentalism or rampaging relativism often reflected the worst aspects of contemporary culture or prejudices rather than a system which both man and God could live under with a sense of real justice. Sol's most famous book, finally titled *Abraham's Dilemma* when it was brought out in a mass-market edition in numbers he had never dreamed of while producing volumes for academic presses, had been written when Rachel was dying of Merlin's sickness and dealt, obviously enough, with Abraham's hard choice of obeying or disobeying God's direct command for him to sacrifice his son.

Sol had written that primitive times had required primitive obedience, that later generations evolved to the point where parents offered themselves as sacrifice – as in the dark nights of the ovens which pocked Old Earth history – and that current generations had to deny any command for sacrifice. Sol had written that whatever form God now took in human consciousness – whether as a mere manifestation of the subconscious in all its revanchist needs or as a more conscious attempt at philosophical and ethical evolution – humankind could no longer agree to offer up sacrifice in God's name. Sacrifice and the *agreement* to sacrifice had written human history in blood.

Yet hours ago, ages ago, Sol Weintraub had handed his only child to a creature of death.

For years the voice in his dreams had commanded him to do so. For years Sol had refused. He had agreed, finally, only when time was gone, when any other hope was gone, and when he had realized that the voice in his and Sarai's dreams all those years had not been the voice of God, nor of some dark force allied with the Shrike.

It had been the voice of their daughter.

With a sudden clarity which went beyond the immediacy

598

of his pain or sorrow, Sol Weintraub suddenly understood perfectly why Abraham had agreed to sacrifice Isaac, his son, when the Lord commanded him to do so.

It was not obedience.

It was not even to put the love of God above the love of his son.

Abraham was testing God.

By denying the sacrifice at the last moment, by stopping the knife, God had earned the right – in Abraham's eyes and the hearts of his offspring – to become the God of Abraham.

Sol shuddered as he thought of how no posturing on Abraham's part, no shamming of his willingness to sacrifice the boy, could have served to forge that bond between greater power and humankind. Abraham had to know in his own heart that he would kill his son. The Deity, whatever form it then took, had to know Abraham's determination, had to *feel* that sorrow and commitment to destroy what was to Abraham the most precious thing in the universe.

Abraham came not to sacrifice, but to know once and for all whether this God was a god to be trusted and obeyed. No other test would do.

Why then, thought Sol, clinging to the stone stair as the Sphinx seemed to rise and fall on the storm seas of time, why was this test being repeated? What terrible new revelations lay at hand for humankind?

Sol understood then – from what little Brawne had told him, from the stories shared on the pilgrimage, from his own personal revelations of the past few weeks – that the effort of the machine Ultimate Intelligence, whatever the hell it was, to flush out the missing Empathy entity of the human Godhead was useless. Sol no longer saw the tree of thorns on its cliff top, its metal branches and suffering multitudes, but he did see clearly now that the thing was as much an organic machine as the Shrike – an instrument to broadcast suffering through the universe so the human God-part would be forced to respond, to show itself.

If God evolved, and Sol was sure that God must, then that evolution was toward empathy – toward a shared sense of suffering rather than power and dominion. But the obscene tree which the pilgrims had glimpsed – which poor Martin Silenus had been a victim of – was not the way to evoke the missing power.

Sol realized now that the machine god, whatever its form, was insightful enough to see that empathy was a response to others' pain, but the same UI was too stupid to realize that empathy – in both human terms and the terms of humankind's UI – was far more than that. Empathy and love were inseparable and inexplicable. The machine UI would never understand it – not even enough to use it as a lure for the part of the human UI who had tired of warfare in the distant future.

Love, that most banal of things, that most clichéd of religious motivations, had more power – Sol now knew – than did strong nuclear force or weak nuclear force or electromagnetism or gravity. Love *was* these other forces, Sol realized. The Void Which Binds, the subquantum impossibility that carried information from photon to photon, was nothing more or less than love.

But could love – simple, banal *love* – explain the so-called anthropic principle which scientists had shaken their collective heads over for seven centuries and more – that almost infinite string of coincidences which had led to a universe that had just the proper number of dimensions, just the correct values of electron, just the precise rules for gravity, just the proper age to stars, just the right prebiologies to create just the perfect viruses to become just the proper DNAs – in short, a series of coincidences so absurd in their precision and *correctness* that they defied logic, defied understanding, and even defied religious interpretation. *Love?*

For seven centuries the existence of Grand Unification Theories and hyperstring post-quantum physics and Core-given understanding of the universe as self-contained and boundless, without Big Bang singularities or corresponding endpoints, had pretty much eliminated any role of God – primitively anthropomorphic or sophisticatedly post-Einsteinian – even as a caretaker or pre-Creation former of rules. The modern universe, as machine and man had come to understand it, needed no Creator: in fact, *allowed* no Creator. Its rules allowed very little tinkering and no major revisions. It had not begun and would not end, beyond cycles of expansion and contraction as regular and self-regulated as the seasons on Old Earth. No room for love there.

It seemed that Abraham had offered to murder his son to test a phantom.

It seemed that Sol had brought his dying daughter through hundreds of light-years and innumerable hardships in response to nothing.

But now, as the Sphinx loomed above him and the first hint of sunrise paled Hyperion's sky, Sol realized that he had responded to a force more basic and persuasive than the Shrike's terror or pain's dominion. If he was right – and he did not know but felt – then love was as hardwired into the structure of the universe as gravity and matter/antimatter. There was room for some sort of God not in the web between the walls, nor in the singularity cracks in the pavement, nor somewhere out before and beyond the sphere of things . . . but in the very warp and woof of things. Evolving as the universe evolved. Learning as the learning-able parts of the universe learned. Loving as humankind loved.

Sol got to his knees and then to his feet. The time-tide storm seemed to have abated a bit, and he thought he could try for the hundredth time to gain access to the tomb.

Bright light still emanated from where the Shrike had emerged, taken Sol's daughter, and vanished. But now the stars were disappearing as the sky itself lightened toward morning.

Sol climbed the stairs.

He remembered the time at home on Barnard's World when Rachel – she was ten – had tried to climb the town's tallest elm and had fallen when she was five meters from the top. Sol had rushed to the med center to find his child floating in the recovery nutrient and suffering from a punctured lung, a broken leg and ribs, a fractured jaw, and innumerable cuts and bruises. She had smiled at him, lifted a thumb, and said through her wired jaw, 'I'll make it next time!'

Sol and Sarai had sat there in the med center that night while Rachel slept. They had waited for morning. Sol had held her hand through the night.

He waited now.

Time tides from the open entrance to the Sphinx still held Sol back like insistent winds, but he leaned into them like an immovable rock and stood there, five meters out and waiting, squinting into the glare.

He glanced up but did not move back when he saw the fusion flame of a descending spacecraft slice the predawn sky. He turned to look but did not retreat when he heard the spacecraft landing and saw three figures emerge. He glanced but did not step back when he heard other noises, shouts, from deeper in the valley and saw a familiar figure lugging another in a fireman's carry, moving toward him from beyond the Jade Tomb.

None of these things related to his child. He waited for Rachel.

Even without a datasphere, it is quite possible for my persona to travel through the rich, Void-Which-Binds soup which now surrounds Hyperion. My immediate reaction is to want to visit the One Who Will Be, but although that one's brilliance dominates the

602

metasphere, I am not yet ready for that. I am, after all, little John Keats, not John the Baptist.

The Sphinx – a tomb patterned after a real creature that will not be designed by genetic engineers for centuries to come – is a maelstrom of temporal energies. There are really several Sphinxes visible to my expanded sight: the anti-entropic tomb carrying its Shrike cargo back in time like some sealed container with its deadly bacillus, the active, unstable Sphinx which contaminated Rachel Weintraub in its initial efforts to open a portal through time, and the Sphinx which has opened and is moving forward through time again. This last Sphinx is the blazing portal of light, which, second only to the One Who Will Be, lights Hyperion with its metaspherical bonfire.

I descend to this bright place in time to watch Sol Weintraub hand his daughter to the Shrike.

I could not have interfered with this even if I had arrived earlier. I would not if I were able. Worlds beyond reason depend upon this act.

But I await within the Sphinx for the Shrike to pass, carrying its tender cargo. Now I can see the child. She is seconds old, blotched, moist, and wrinkled. She is crying her newborn lungs out. From my old attitudes of bachelorhood and reflective poet's stance, I find it hard to understand the attraction this bawling, unaesthetic infant exerts on its father and the cosmos.

Still, the sight of a baby's flesh – however unattractive this newborn might be – held by the Shrike's bladed talons stirs something in me.

Three paces into the Sphinx have carried the Shrike and the child hours forward in time. Just beyond the entrance, the river of time accelerates. If I don't do something within seconds, it will be too late – the Shrike will have used this portal to carry the child off to whatever distant-future dark hole it seeks.

Unbidden, the images arrive of spiders draining their victims of fluids, of digger wasps burying their own larvae in the paralyzed bodies of their prey, perfect sources for incubation and food.

I have to act, but I have no more solidity here than I had in the Core. The Shrike walks through me as if I were an unseen holo. My analog persona is useless here, armless and insubstantial as a wisp of swamp gas.

But swamp gas has no brain, and John Keats did.

The Shrike takes another two steps, and more hours pass for Sol and the others outside. I can see blood on the crying infant's skin where the Shrike's scalpeled fingers have cut into flesh.

To hell with this.

Outside, on the broad stone porch of the Sphinx, caught now in the flood of temporal energies flowing in and through the tomb, lay backpacks, blankets, abandoned food containers, and all the detritus Sol and the pilgrims had left there.

Including a single Möbius cube.

The box had been sealed with a class-eight containment field on the Templar treeship *Yggdrasill* when True Voice of the Tree Het Masteen had prepared for his long voyage. It contained a single erg – sometimes known as a binder – one of the small creatures which might not be intelligent by human standards but which had evolved around distant stars and developed the ability to control more powerful forcefields than any machine known to humankind.

The Templars and Ousters had communicated with the creatures for generations. Templars used them for control redundancy on their beautiful but exposed treeships.

Het Masteen had brought this thing hundreds of light-years to complete the Templar agreement with the Church of the Final Atonement to help fly the Shrike's thorn tree. But, seeing the Shrike and the tree of torment, Masteen had not been able to fulfill the contract. And so he died.

The Möbius cube remained. The erg was visible to me as a constrained sphere of red energy in the temporal flood.

Outside, through a curtain of darkness, Sol Weintraub was just visible – a sadly comic figure, speeded up like a silent-film figure by the subjective rush of time beyond the Sphinx's temporal field – but the Möbius cube lay within the Sphinx's circle.

Rachel cried with the fear even a newborn can know. Fear of falling. Fear of pain. Fear of separation.

The Shrike took a step, and another hour was lost to those outside.

I was insubstantial to the Shrike, but energy fields are something which even we Core-analog ghosts can touch. I canceled the Möbius cube's containment field. I freed the erg.

Templars communicate with ergs via electromagnetic radiation, coded pulses, simple rewards of radiation when the creature does what they want . . . but primarily through a near-mystical form of contact which only the Brotherhood and a few Ouster exotics know. Scientists call it a crude telepathy. In truth, it is almost pure empathy.

The Shrike takes another step into the opening portal to the future. Rachel cries with the energy only someone newly born to the universe can muster.

The erg expands, understands, and melds with my persona. John Keats takes on substance and form.

I hurry the five paces to the Shrike, remove the baby from its hands, and step back. Even in the energy maelstrom that is the Sphinx, I can smell the infant-newness of her as I hold the child against my chest and cup her moist head against my cheek.

The Shrike whirls in surprise. Four arms extend, blades snick open, and red eyes focus on me. But the creature is too close to the portal itself. Without moving, it recedes down the storm drain of temporal flow. The thing's steam-shovel jaws open, steel teeth gnash, but it is already gone, a spot in the distance. Something less.

I turn toward the entrance, but it is too far. The erg's draining energy could get me there, drag me upstream against the flow, but not with Rachel. Carrying another living thing that far against so much force is more than I can manage even with the erg's help.

The baby cries, and I bounce her gently, whispering nonsense doggerel in her warm ear.

If we can't go back and we can't go forward, we'll just wait here for a moment. Perhaps someone will come along.

Martin Silenus's eyes widened and Brawne Lamia turned quickly, seeing the Shrike floating in midair above and behind her.

'Holy shit,' Brawne whispered reverently.

In the Shrike Palace, tiers of sleeping human bodies receded in the gloom and distance, all of the people except Martin Silenus still connected to the thorn tree, the machine UI, and God knows what else by pulsing umbilicals.

As if to show its power here, the Shrike had quit climbing, opened its arms, and floated up three meters until it hung in the air five meters out from the stone shelf where Brawne crouched next to Martin Silenus.

'Do something,' whispered Silenus. The poet was no longer attached by the neural shunt umbilical, but he was still too weak to hold his head up.

'Ideas?' said Brawne, the brave remark somewhat ruined by the quaver in her voice.

'Trust,' said a voice below them, and Brawne shifted to look down toward the floor.

The young woman whom Brawne had recognized as Moneta in Kassad's tomb stood far below.

'Help!' cried Brawne.

'Trust,' said Moneta and disappeared. The Shrike had not been distracted. It lowered its hands and stepped forward as if walking on solid stone rather than air.

'Shit,' whispered Brawne.

'Ditto,' rasped Martin Silenus. 'Out of the frying pan back into the fucking fire.'

'Shut up,' said Brawne. Then, as if to herself, 'Trust what? Who?'

'Trust the fucking Shrike to kill us or stick us both on the fucking tree,' gasped Silenus. He managed to move enough to clutch Brawne's arm. 'Better dead than back on the tree, Brawne.'

Brawne touched his hand briefly and stood, facing the Shrike across five meters of air.

Trust? Brawne held her foot out, felt around on emptiness, closed her eyes for a second, and opened them as her foot seemed to touch a solid step. She opened her eyes.

Nothing was under her foot except air.

Trust? Brawne put her weight on her forward foot and stepped out, teetering a moment before bringing her other foot down.

She and the Shrike stood facing each other ten meters above the stone floor. The creature seemed to grin at her as it opened its arms. Its carapace glowed dully in the dim light. Its red eyes were very bright.

Trust? Feeling the adrenaline rush, Brawne stepped forward on the invisible steps, gaining height as she moved into the Shrike's embrace.

She felt the fingerblades slicing through fabric and skin as

607

the thing began to hug her to it, toward the curved blade growing out of its metal chest, toward the open jaws and rows of steel teeth. But while still standing firmly on thin air, Brawne leaned forward and set her uninjured hand flat against the Shrike's chest, feeling the coldness of the carapace but also feeling a rush of warmth as energy rushed from her, out of her, *through* her.

The blades stopped cutting before they cut anything but skin. The Shrike froze as if the flow of temporal energy surrounding them had turned to a lump of amber.

Brawne set her hand on the thing's broad chest and *pushed*.

The Shrike froze completely in place, became brittle, the gleam of metal fading to be replaced by the transparent glow of crystal, the bright sheen of glass.

Brawne stood on air being embraced by a three-meter glass sculpture of the Shrike. In its chest, where a heart might be, something that looked like a large, black moth fluttered and beat sooty wings against the glass.

Brawne took a deep breath and pushed again. The Shrike slid backward on the invisible platform she shared with it, teetered, and fell. Brawne ducked under the encircling arms, hearing and feeling her jacket tearing as still-sharp finger-blades caught in the material and ripped as the thing tumbled, and then she was teetering herself, flailing her good arm for balance as the glass Shrike turned one and a half times in mid-air, struck the floor, and shattered into a thousand jagged shards.

Brawne pivoted, fell to her knees on the invisible catwalk, and crawled back toward Martin Silenus.

In the last half meter, her confidence failed her, the invisible support simply ceased to be, and she fell heavily, twisting her ankle as she hit the edge of the stone tier and managing to keep from falling off only by grabbing Silenus's knee.

Cursing from the pain in her shoulder, broken wrist, twisted ankle, and lacerated palms and knees, she pulled herself to safety next to him.

'There's obviously been some weird shit going on since I left,' Martin Silenus said hoarsely. 'Can we go now, or do you plan to walk on water as an encore?'

'Shut up,' Brawne said shakily. The two syllables sounded almost affectionate.

She rested a while and then found that the easiest way to get the still-weak poet down the steps and across the glass-strewn floor of the Shrike Palace was to use the fireman's carry. They were at the entrance when he pounded unceremoniously on her back and said, 'What about King Billy and the others?'

'Later,' panted Brawne and stepped out into the predawn light.

She had hobbled down two thirds of the valley with Silenus draped over her shoulders like so much limp laundry when the poet said, 'Brawne, are you still pregnant?'

'Yes,' she said, praying that that was still true after the day's exertions.

'You want me to carry you?'

'Shut up,' she said and followed the path down and around the Jade Tomb.

'Look,' said Martin Silenus, twisting to point even as he hung almost upside down over her shoulder.

In the glowing light of morning, Brawne could see that the Consul's ebony spacecraft now sat on the high ground at the entrance to the valley. But that was not what the poet was pointing toward.

Sol Weintraub stood silhouetted in the glare of the Sphinx's entrance. His arms were raised.

Someone or something was emerging from the glare.

Sol saw her first. A figure walking amidst the torrent of light and liquid time flowing from the Sphinx. A woman, he saw, as she was silhouetted against the brilliant portal. A woman carrying something.

A woman carrying an infant.

His daughter Rachel emerged – Rachel as he had last seen her as a healthy young adult leaving to do her doctoral work on some world called Hyperion, Rachel in her mid-twenties, perhaps even a bit older now – but Rachel, no doubt about that, Rachel with her copperish-brown hair still short and falling across her forehead, her cheeks flushed as they always were as with some new enthusiasm, her smile soft, almost tremulous now, and her eyes – those enormous green eyes with specks of brown just visible – those eyes fixed on Sol.

Rachel was carrying Rachel. The infant squirmed with its face against the young woman's shoulder, tiny hands clenching and unclenching as it tried to decide whether to start crying again or not.

Sol stood stunned. He tried to speak, failed, and tried again. 'Rachel.'

'Father,' said the young woman and stepped forward, putting her free arm around the scholar while she turned slightly to keep the baby from being crushed between them.

Sol kissed his grown daughter, hugged her, smelled the clean scent of her hair, felt the firm *reality* of her, and then lifted the infant to his own neck and shoulder, feeling the shudders pass through the newborn as she took a breath before crying. The Rachel he had brought to Hyperion was safe in his hands, small, red face wrinkled as she tried to focus her randomly wandering eyes on her father's face. Sol cupped her tiny head in his palm and lifted her closer, inspecting that small face for a second before turning toward the young woman.

'Is she . . .'

'She's aging normally,' said his daughter. She was wearing something part gown, part robe, made of soft brown material. Sol shook his head, looked at her, saw her smiling, and noticed the same small dimple below and to the left of her mouth that was visible on the infant he held.

He shook his head again. 'How . . . how is this possible?'

'It's not for very long,' said Rachel.

Sol leaned forward and kissed his grown daughter's cheek again. He realized that he was crying, but he would not release either hand to wipe away the tears. His grown Rachel did so for him, touching his cheek gently with the back of her hand.

There was a noise below them on the steps, and Sol looked over his shoulder to see the three men from the ship standing there, red faced from running, and Brawne Lamia helping the poet Silenus to a seat on the white slab of railing stone.

The Consul and Theo Lane looked up at them.

'Rachel . . .' whispered Melio Arundez, his eyes filling.

'*Rachel?*' said Martin Silenus, frowning and glancing at Brawne Lamia.

Brawne was staring with her mouth half open. 'Moneta,' she said, pointing, then lowering her hand as she realized she was pointing. 'You're Moneta. Kassad's . . . Moneta.'

Rachel nodded, her smile gone. 'I have only a minute or two here,' she said. 'And much to tell you.'

'No,' said Sol, taking his grown daughter's hand, 'you have to stay. I want you to stay with me.'

Rachel smiled again. 'I will stay with you, Dad,' she said softly, raising her other hand to touch the baby's head. 'But only one of us can . . . and she needs you more.' She turned to the group below. 'Listen, please, all of you.'

As the sun rose and touched the broken buildings of the Poets' City, the Consul's ship, the western cliffs, and the taller Time Tombs with its light, Rachel told her brief and tantalizing story of being chosen to be raised in a future where the final war raged between the Core-spawned UI and the human spirit. It was, she said, a future of terrifying and wonderful mysteries, where humankind had spread across this galaxy and had begun to travel elsewhere.

'Other *galaxies*?' asked Theo Lane.

'Other universes,' smiled Rachel.

'Colonel Kassad knew you as Moneta,' said Martin Silenus.

'*Will* know me as Moneta,' said Rachel, her eyes clouding.

'I have seen him die and accompanied his tomb to the past. I know that part of my mission is to meet this fabled warrior and lead him forward to the final battle. I have not truly met him yet.' She looked down the valley toward the Crystal Monolith. '*Moneta,*' she mused. 'It means "Admonisher" in Latin. Appropriate. I will let him choose between that and *Mnemosyne* – "memory" – for my name.'

Sol had not released his daughter's hand. He did not do so now. 'You're traveling *back* in time with the Tombs? Why? How?'

Rachel lifted her head, and reflected light from the far cliffs painted her face in warmth. 'It is my role, Dad. My duty. They give me means to keep the Shrike in check. And only I was . . . prepared.'

Sol lifted his infant daughter higher. Startled from sleep, she blew a single bubble of saliva, turned her face into her father's neck for warmth, and curled her small fists against his shirt.

'Prepared,' said Sol. 'You mean the Merlin's sickness?'

'Yes,' said Rachel.

Sol shook his head. 'But you weren't raised in some mysterious world of the future. You grew up in the college town of Crawford, on Fertig Street, on Barnard's World, and your . . .' He stopped.

Rachel nodded. '*She* shall grow up . . . up there. Dad, I'm sorry, I have to go.' She freed her hand, drifted down the stairs, and touched Melio Arundez's cheek briefly. 'I'm sorry for the pain of memory,' she said softly to the startled archaeologist. 'To me it was, literally, a different life.'

Arundez blinked and held her hand to his cheek a moment longer.

'Are you married?' asked Rachel softly. 'Children?'

Arundez nodded, moved his other hand as if he were going to remove the pictures of his wife and grown children from his pocket, and then stopped, nodded again.

Rachel smiled, kissed him quickly on the cheek, and

moved back up the steps. The sky was rich with sunrise, but the door to the Sphinx was still brighter.

'Dad,' she said, 'I love you.'

Sol tried to speak, cleared his throat. 'How . . . how do I join you . . . up there?'

Rachel gestured toward the open door of the Sphinx. 'For some it will be a portal to the time I spoke of. But, Dad . . .' She hesitated. 'It will mean raising me all over again. It means suffering through my childhood for a third time. No parent should be asked to do that.'

Sol managed a smile. 'No parent would refuse that, Rachel.' He changed arms holding the sleeping infant, and shook his head again. 'Will there be a time when . . . the two of you . . . ?'

'Coexist again?' smiled Rachel. 'No. I go the other way now. You can't imagine the difficulty I had with the Paradox Board to get this one meeting approved.'

'Paradox Board?' said Sol.

Rachel took a breath. She had stepped back until only her fingertips touched her father's, both their arms extended. 'I have to go, Dad.'

'Will I . . .' He looked at the baby. 'Will we be alone . . . up there?'

Rachel laughed, and the sound was so familiar that it closed around Sol's heart like a warm hand. 'Oh no,' she said, 'not alone. There are wonderful people there. Wonderful things to learn and do. Wonderful places to see . . .' She glanced around. 'Places we have not imagined yet in our wildest dreams. No, Dad, you won't be alone. And I'll be there, in all my teenage awkwardness and young-adult cockiness.' She stepped back, and her fingers slipped away from Sol.

'Wait a while before stepping through, Dad,' she called, moving back into the brilliance. 'It doesn't hurt, but once through you can't come back.'

'Rachel, wait,' said Sol.

His daughter stepped back, her long robe flowing across stone, until the light surrounded her. She raised one arm. 'See you later, alligator!' she called.

Sol raised a hand. 'After a while . . . crocodile.'

The older Rachel was gone in the light.

The baby awoke and began to cry.

It was more than an hour before Sol and the others returned to the Sphinx. They had gone to the Consul's ship to tend to Brawne's and Martin Silenus's injuries, to eat, and to outfit Sol and the child for a voyage.

'I feel silly packing for what may be like a step through a farcaster,' said Sol, 'but no matter how wonderful this future is, if it doesn't have nursing paks and disposable diapers, we're in trouble.'

The Consul grinned and patted the full backpack on the step. 'This should get you and the baby through the first two weeks. If you don't find a diaper service by then, go to one of those other universes Rachel spoke about.'

Sol shook his head. 'Is this happening?'

'Wait a few days or weeks,' said Melio Arundez. 'Stay here with us until things get sorted out. There's no hurry. The future will always be there.'

Sol scratched his beard as he fed the baby with one of the nursing paks the ship had manufactured. 'We're not sure this portal will always be open,' he said. 'Besides, I might lose my nerve. I'm getting pretty old to raise a child again . . . especially as a stranger in a strange land.'

Arundez set his strong hand on Sol's shoulder. 'Let me go with you. I'm dying of curiosity about this place.'

Sol grinned and extended his hand, shook Arundez's firmly. 'Thank you, my friend. But you have a wife and children back in the Web . . . on Renaissance Vector . . . who await your return. You have your own duties.'

Arundez nodded and looked at the sky. 'If we *can* return.'

'We'll return,' the Consul said flatly. 'Old-fashioned

Hawking drive spaceflight still works, even if the Web is gone forever. It'll be a few years' time-debt, Melio, but you'll get back.'

Sol nodded, finished feeding the baby, set a clean cloth diaper on his shoulder, and patted her firmly on the back. He looked around the small circle of people. 'We all have our duties.' He shook hands with Martin Silenus. The poet had refused to crawl into the nutrient recovery bath or have the neural shunt socket surgically removed. 'I've had these things before,' he'd said.

'Will you continue your poem?' Sol asked him.

Silenus shook his head. 'I finished it on the tree,' he said. 'And I discovered something else there, Sol.'

The scholar raised an eyebrow.

'I learned that poets aren't God, but if there is a God . . . or anything approaching a God . . . he's a poet. And a failed one at that.'

The baby burped.

Martin Silenus grinned and shook Sol's hand a final time. 'Give them hell up there, Weintraub. Tell 'em you're their great-great-great-great-great grandaddy, and if they misbehave, you'll whop their butts.'

Sol nodded and moved down the line to Brawne Lamia. 'I saw you conferring with the ship's medical terminal,' he said. 'Is everything all right with you and your unborn child?'

Brawne grinned. 'Everything's fine.'

'A boy or girl?'

'Girl.'

Sol kissed her on the cheek. Brawne touched his beard and turned her face away to hide tears unbecoming a former private investigator.

'Girls are such a chore,' he said, disentangling Rachel's fingers from his beard and Brawne's curls. 'Trade yours in for a boy the first chance you get.'

'OK,' said Brawne and stepped back.

He shook hands a final time with the Consul, Theo, and

Melio, shouldered his pack while Brawne held the infant, and then took Rachel in his arms. 'Hell of an anticlimax if this thing doesn't work and I end up wandering around the inside of the Sphinx,' he said.

The Consul squinted at the glowing door. 'It will work. Although how, I'm not sure. I don't think it's a farcaster of any sort.'

'A whencaster,' ventured Silenus and held up his arm to block Brawne's blows. The poet took a step back and shrugged. 'If it continues to work, Sol, I have a feeling you won't be alone up there. Thousands will join you.'

'If the Paradox Board permits,' said Sol, tugging at his beard the way he always did when his mind was elsewhere. He blinked, shifted backpack and baby, and stepped forward. The fields of force from the open door let him advance this time.

'So long everyone!' he cried. 'By God, it was all worth it, wasn't it?' He turned into the light, and he and the baby were gone.

There was a silence bordering on emptiness which stretched for several minutes. Finally the Consul said, in almost embarrassed tones, 'Shall we go up to the ship?'

'Bring the elevator down for the rest of us,' said Martin Silenus. 'M Lamia here will walk on air.'

Brawne glared at the diminutive poet.

'You think it was something Moneta arranged?' said Arundez, referring to something Brawne had suggested earlier.

'It had to be,' said Brawne. 'Some bit of future science or something.'

'Ah, yes,' sighed Martin Silenus. '*Future science* . . . that familiar phrase from those too timid to be superstitious. The alternative, my dear, is that you have this hitherto untapped power to levitate and turn monsters into shatterable glass goblins.'

'Shut up,' said Brawne, with no undertones of affection in her voice now. She looked over her shoulder. 'Who says another Shrike won't show up any minute?'

'Who indeed?' agreed the Consul. 'I suspect we'll always have a Shrike or rumors of a Shrike.'

Theo Lane, always embarrassed by discord, cleared his throat and said, 'Look what I found among the baggage strewn around the Sphinx.' He held up an instrument with three strings, a long neck, and bright designs painted on its triangular body. 'A guitar?'

'A balalaika,' said Brawne. 'It belonged to Father Hoyt.'

The Consul took the instrument and strummed several chords. 'Do you know this song?' He played a few notes.

'The "Leeda Tits Screwing Song"?' ventured Martin Silenus.

The Consul shook his head and played several more chords.

'Something old?' guessed Brawne.

' "Somewhere Over the Rainbow," ' said Melio Arundez.

'That must be from before my time,' said Theo Lane, nodding along as the Consul strummed.

'It's from before everybody's time,' said the Consul. 'Come on, I'll teach you the words as we go.'

Walking together in the hot sun, singing off-key and on-, losing the words and then starting again, they went uphill to the waiting ship.

EPILOGUE

Five and a half months later, seven months pregnant, Brawne Lamia took the morning dirigible north from the capital to the Poets' City for the Consul's farewell party.

The capital, now referred to as Jacktown by indigenie, visiting FORCE shipmen, and Ouster alike, looked white and clean in the morning light as the dirigible left the downtown mooring tower and headed northwest up the Hoolie River.

The biggest city on Hyperion had suffered during the fighting, but now most of it had been rebuilt, and a majority of the three million refugees from the fiberplastic plantations and smaller cities on the southern continent had elected to stay, despite recent surges of interest in fiberplastic from the Ousters. So the city had grown like Topsy, with basic services such as electricity, sewerage, and cable HTV service just reaching the hilltop warrens between the spaceport and the old town.

But the buildings were white in the morning light, the spring air rich with promise, and Brawne saw the rough slashes of new roads and the bustle of river traffic below as a good sign for the future.

Fighting in Hyperion space had not lasted long after the destruction of the Web. De facto Ouster occupation of the spaceport and capital had been translated into recognition of the Web's demise and comanagement with the new Home Rule Council in the treaty brokered primarily by the Consul and former Governor-General Theo Lane. But in the almost six months since the death of the Web, the only traffic at the spaceport had been dropships from the remnants of the FORCE fleet still in-system and frequent planetary excursions from the Swarm. It was no longer unusual to see the tall figures of Ousters shopping in Jacktown Square or their more exotic versions drinking at Cicero's.

Brawne had stayed at Cicero's during the past few months, residing in one of the larger rooms on the fourth floor of the old wing of the inn while Stan Leweski rebuilt and expanded the damaged sections of the legendary structure. 'By God, I don't need no help from pregnant womens!' Stan would shout each time Brawne offered a hand, but she invariably ended up doing some task while Leweski grumped and mumbled. Brawne might be pregnant, but she was still a Lusian, and her muscles had not completely atrophied after only a few months on Hyperion.

Stan had driven her to the mooring tower that morning, helping her with her luggage and the package she had brought for the Consul. Then the innkeeper had handed her a small package of his own. 'It's a damn, dull trip up into that godforsaken country,' he'd growled. 'You have to have something to read, heh?'

The gift was a reproduction of the 1817 edition of John Keats's *Poems*, leather-bound by Leweski himself.

Brawne embarrassed the giant and delighted watching passengers by hugging him until the bartender's ribs creaked. 'Enough, goddammit,' he muttered, rubbing his side. 'Tell that Consul I want to see his worthless hide back here before I give the worthless inn to my son. Tell him that, OK?'

Brawne had nodded and waved with the other passengers to well-wishers seeing them off. Then she had continued waving from the observation mezzanine as the airship untied, discharged ballast, and ponderously moved out over the rooftops.

Now, as the ship left the suburbs behind and swung west

to follow the river, Brawne had her first clear view of the mountaintop to the south where the face of Sad King Billy still brooded down on the city. There was a fresh ten-meter scar, slowly fading from weather, on Billy's cheek where a laser lance had slashed during the fighting.

But it was the larger sculpture taking shape on the northwest face of the mountain which caught Brawne's attention. Even with modern cutting equipment borrowed from FORCE, the work was slow, and the great aquiline nose, heavy brow, broad mouth, and sad, intelligent eyes were just becoming recognizable. Many of the Hegemony refugees left on Hyperion had objected to Meina Gladstone's likeness being added to the mountain, but Rithmet Corber III, great-grandson of the sculptor who had created Sad King Billy's face there – and incidentally the man who now owned the mountain – had said, as diplomatically as possible, 'Fuck you' and gone on with the work. Another year, perhaps two, and it would be finished.

Brawne sighed, rubbed her distended stomach – an affectation she had always hated in pregnant women but one she now found impossible to avoid – and walked clumsily to a deck chair on the observation deck. *If she was this huge at seven months, what would she be like at full term?* Brawne glanced up at the distended curve of the dirigible's great gas envelope above her and winced.

The airship voyage, with good tail winds, took only twenty hours. Brawne dozed part of the way but spent most of the time watching the familiar landscape unfold below.

They passed the Karla Locks in midmorning, and Brawne smiled and patted the package she had brought for the Consul. By late afternoon, they were approaching the river port of Naiad, and from three thousand feet Brawne looked down on an old passenger barge being pulled upriver by mantas leaving their V-shaped wake. She wondered if that could be the *Benares*.

They flew over Edge as dinner was being served in the upper lounge and began the crossing of the Sea of Grass just as sunset lighted the great steppe with color and a million grasses rippled to the same breeze that lofted the airship along. Brawne took her coffee to her favorite chair on the mezzanine, opened a window wide, and watched the Sea of Grass unfold like the sensuous felt of a billiard table as the light failed. Just before the lamps were lit on the mezzanine deck, she was rewarded with the sight of a windwagon plying its way from north to south, lanterns swinging fore and aft. Brawne leaned forward and could clearly hear the rumble of the big wheel and the snap of canvas on the jib sail as the wagon hove hard over to take a new tack.

The bed was ready in her sleeping compartment when Brawne went up to slip into her robe, but after reading a few poems she found herself back on the observation deck until dawn, dozing in her favorite chair and breathing in the fresh smell of grass from below.

They moored in Pilgrim's Rest long enough to take on fresh food and water, renew ballast, and change crews, but Brawne did not go down to walk around. She could see the worklights around the tramway station, and when the voyage resumed at last, the airship seemed to follow the string of cable towers into the Bridle Range.

It was still quite dark as they crossed the mountains, and a steward came along to seal the long windows as the compartments were pressurized, but Brawne could still catch glimpses of the tramcars passing from peak to peak between the clouds below, and icefields that glinted in the starlight.

They passed over Keep Chronos just after dawn, and the stones of the castle emitted little sense of warmth even in the roseate light. Then the high desert appeared, the City of Poets glowed white off the port side, and the dirigible descended toward the mooring tower set on the east end of the new spaceport there.

Brawne had not expected anyone to be there to meet her.

Everyone who knew her thought that she was flying up with Theo Lane in his skimmer later in the afternoon. But Brawne had thought the airship voyage the proper way to travel alone with her thoughts. And she had been right.

But even before the mooring cable was pulled tight and the ramp lowered, Brawne saw the familiar face of the Consul in the small crowd. Next to him was Martin Silenus, frowning and squinting at the unfamiliar morning light.

'Damn that Stan,' muttered Brawne, remembering that the microwave links were up now and new comsats in orbit.

The Consul met her with a hug. Martin Silenus yawned, shook her hand, and said, 'Couldn't find a more inconvenient time to arrive, eh?'

There was a party in the evening. It was more than the Consul leaving the next morning – most of the FORCE fleet still remaining was heading back, and a sizable portion of the Ouster Swarm was going with them. A dozen drop-ships littered the small field near the Consul's spaceship as Ousters paid their last visit to the Time Tombs and FORCE officers stopped by Kassad's tomb a final time.

The Poets' City itself now had almost a thousand full-time residents, many of them artists and poets, although Silenus said that most were *poseurs*. They had twice tried to elect Martin Silenus mayor; he had declined twice and soundly cursed his would-be constituency. But the old poet continued to run things, supervising the restorations, adjudicating disputes, dispensing housing and arranging for supply flights from Jacktown and points south. The Poets' City was no longer the Dead City.

Martin Silenus said the collective IQ had been higher when the place was deserted.

The banquet was held in the rebuilt dining pavilion, and the great dome echoed to laughter as Martin Silenus read ribald poems and other artists performed skits. Besides the Consul and Silenus, Brawne's round table boasted half a dozen Ouster guests, including Freeman Ghenga and Coredwell Minmun, as well as Rithmet Corber III, dressed in stitched pelts and a tall cone of a cap. Theo Lane arrived late, with apologies, shared the most recent Jacktown jokes with the audience, and came over to the table to join them for dessert. Lane had been mentioned recently as the people's choice for Jacktown's mayor in the Fourthmonth elections soon to be held – both indigenie and Ouster seemed to like his style – and so far Theo had shown no signs of declining if the honor were offered him.

After much wine at the banquet, the Consul quietly invited a few of them up to the ship for music and more wine. They went, Brawne and Martin and Theo, and sat high on the ship's balcony while the Consul very soberly and feelingly played Gershwin and Studeri and Brahms and Luser and Beatles, and then Gershwin again, finally ending with Rachmaninoff's heart-stoppingly beautiful Piano Concerto No. 2 in C Minor.

Then they sat in the low light, looked out over the city and valley, drank a bit more wine, and talked late into the night.

'What do you expect to find in the Web?' Theo asked the Consul. 'Anarchy? Mob rule? Reversion to Stone Age life?'

'All of that and more, probably,' smiled the Consul. He swirled the brandy in his glass. 'Seriously, there were enough squirts before the fatline went dead to let us know that despite some real problems, most of the old worlds of the Web will do all right.'

Theo Lane sat nursing the same glass of wine he had brought up from the dining pavilion. 'Why do you think the fatline went dead?'

Martin Silenus snorted. 'God got tired of us scribbling graffiti on his outhouse walls.'

They talked of old friends, wondering how Father Duré was doing. They had heard about his new job on one of the last fatline intercepts. They remembered Lenar Hoyt.

'Do you think he'll automatically become Pope when Duré passes away?' asked the Consul.

623

'I doubt it,' said Theo. 'But at least he'll get a chance to live again if that cruciform Duré carries on his chest still works.'

'I wonder if he'll come looking for his balalaika,' said Silenus, strumming the instrument. In the low light, Brawne thought, the old poet still looked like a satyr.

They talked about Sol and Rachel. In the past six months, hundreds of people had tried to enter the Sphinx; one had succeeded – a quiet Ouster named Mizenspesht Ammenyet.

The Ouster experts had spent months analyzing the Tombs and the trace of time tides still surviving. On some of the structures, hieroglyphs and oddly familiar cuneiform had appeared after the Tombs' opening, and these had led to at least educated guesses as to the various Time Tombs' functions.

The Sphinx was a one-way portal to the future Rachel/ Moneta had spoken of. No one knew how it selected those it wished to let pass, but the popular thing for tourists was to try to enter the portal. No sign or hint of Sol and his daughter's fate had been discovered. Brawne found that she thought of the old scholar often.

Brawne, the Consul, and Martin Silenus drank a toast to Sol and Rachel.

The Jade Tomb appeared to have something to do with gas giant worlds. No one had been passed by its particular portal, but exotic Ousters, designed and bred to live in Jovian habitats, arrived daily to attempt to enter it. Both Ouster and FORCE experts repeatedly pointed out that the Tombs were not farcasters, but some other form of cosmic connection entirely. The tourists didn't care.

The Obelisk remained a black mystery. The tomb still glowed, but it now had no door. Ousters guessed that armies of Shrikes still waited within. Martin Silenus thought that the Obelisk was only a phallic symbol thrown in the valley's decor as an afterthought. Others thought it might have something to do with the Templars.

Brawne, the Consul, and Martin Silenus drank a toast to True Voice of the Tree Het Masteen.

The resealed Crystal Monolith was Colonel Fedmahn Kassad's tomb. Decoded markings set in stone talked of a cosmic battle and a great warrior from the past who appeared to help defeat the Lord of Pain. Young recruits down from the torchships and attack carriers ate it up. Kassad's legend would spread as more of these ships returned to the worlds of the old Web.

Brawne, the Consul, and Martin Silenus drank a toast to Fedmahn Kassad.

The first and second of the Cave Tombs seemed to lead nowhere, but the Third appeared to open to labyrinths on a variety of worlds. After a few researchers disappeared, the Ouster research authorities reminded tourists that the labyrinths lay in a different time – possibly hundreds of thousands of years in the past or future – as well as a different space. They sealed the caves off except to qualified experts.

Brawne, the Consul, and Martin Silenus drank a toast to Paul Duré and Lenar Hoyt.

The Shrike Palace remained a mystery. The tiers of bodies were gone when Brawne and the others had returned a few hours later, the interior of the tomb the size it had been previously, but with a single door of light burning in its center. Anyone who stepped through disappeared. None returned.

The researchers had declared the interior off-limits while they worked to decode letters carved in stone but badly eroded by time. So far, they were certain of three words – all in Old Earth Latin – translated as 'COLOSSEUM,' 'ROME,' and 'REPOPULATE.' The legend had already grown up that this portal opened to the missing Old Earth and that the victims of the tree of thorns had been transported there. Hundreds more waited.

'See,' Martin Silenus said to Brawne, 'if you hadn't been so fucking quick to rescue me, I could've gone home.'

Theo Lane leaned forward. 'Would you really have chosen to go back to Old Earth?'

Martin smiled his sweetest satyr smile. 'Not in a fucking million years. It was dull when I lived there and it'll always be dull. *This* is where it's happening.' Silenus drank a toast to himself.

In a sense, Brawne realized, that was true. Hyperion was the meeting place of Ouster and former Hegemony citizen. The Time Tombs alone would mean future trade and tourism and travel as the human universe adjusted to a life without farcasters. She tried to imagine the future as the Ousters saw it, with great fleets expanding humankind's horizons, with genetically tailored humans colonizing gas giants and asteroids and worlds harsher than preterraformed Mars or Hebron. She could not imagine it. This was a universe her child might see . . . or her grandchildren.

'What are you thinking, Brawne?' asked the Consul after silence stretched.

She smiled. 'About the future,' she said. 'And about Johnny.'

'Ah yes,' said Silenus, 'the poet who could have been God but who wasn't.'

'What happened to the second persona, do you think?' asked Brawne.

The Consul made a motion with his hand. 'I don't see how it could have survived the death of the Core. Do you?'

Brawne shook her head. 'I'm just jealous. A lot of people seem to have ended up seeing him. Even Melio Arundez said he met him in Jacktown.'

They drank a toast to Melio, who had left five months earlier with the first FORCE spinship returning Webward.

'Everyone saw him but me,' said Brawne, frowning at her brandy and realizing that she had to take more prenatal antialcohol pills before turning in. She realized that she was a little drunk: the stuff couldn't harm the baby if she took the pills, but it had definitely gotten to her.

'I'm heading back,' she announced and stood, hugging the Consul. 'Got to be up bright and early to watch your sunrise launch.'

'You're sure you don't want to spend the night on the ship?' asked the Consul. 'The guest room has a nice view of the valley.'

Brawne shook her head. 'All my stuff's at the old palace.'

'I'll talk to you before I go,' said the Consul and they hugged again, quickly, before either had to notice Brawne's tears.

Martin Silenus walked her back to the Poets' City. They paused in the lighted galleria outside the apartments.

'Were you really on the tree, or only stimsiming it while sleeping in the Shrike Palace?' Brawne asked him.

The poet did not smile. He touched his chest where the steel thorn had pierced him. 'Was I a Chinese philosopher dreaming that I was a butterfly, or a butterfly dreaming that I was a Chinese philosopher? Is that what you're asking, kid?'

'Yes.'

'That's correct,' Silenus said softly. 'Yes. I was both. And both were real. And both hurt. And I will love and cherish you forever for saving me, Brawne. To me, you will always be able to walk on air.' He raised her hand and kissed it. 'Are you going in?'

'No, I think I'll stroll in the garden for a minute.'

The poet hesitated. 'All right. I think. We have patrols – mech and human – and our Grendel-Shrike hasn't made an encore appearance yet . . . but be careful, OK?'

'Don't forget,' said Brawne, 'I'm the Grendel killer. I walk on air and turn them into glass goblins to shatter.'

'Uh-huh, but don't stray beyond the gardens. OK, kiddo?'

'OK,' said Brawne. She touched her stomach. 'We'll be careful.'

* * *

He was waiting in the garden, where the light did not quite touch and the monitor cameras did not quite cover.

'Johnny!' gasped Brawne and took a quick step forward on the path of stones.

'No,' he said and shook his head, a bit sadly perhaps. He looked like Johnny. Precisely the same red-brown hair and hazel eyes and firm chin and high cheekbones and soft smile. He was dressed a bit strangely, with a thick leather jacket, broad belt, heavy shoes, walking stick, and a rough fur cap, which he took off as she came closer.

Brawne stopped less than a meter away. 'Of course,' she said in little more than a whisper. She reached out to touch him, and her hand passed through him, although there was none of the flicker or fuzz of a holo.

'This place is still rich in the metasphere fields,' he said.

'Uh-huh,' she agreed, not having the slightest idea what he was talking about. 'You're the other Keats. Johnny's twin.'

The short man smiled and extended a hand as if to touch her swollen abdomen. 'That makes me sort of an uncle, doesn't it, Brawne?'

She nodded. 'It was you who saved the baby . . . Rachel . . . wasn't it?'

'Could you see me?'

'No,' breathed Brawne, 'but I could *feel* that you were there.' She hesitated a second. 'But you weren't the one Ummon talked about – the Empathy part of the human UI?'

He shook his head. His curls glinted in the dim light. 'I discovered that I am the One Who Comes Before. I prepare the way for the One Who Teaches, and I'm afraid that my only miracle was lifting a baby and waiting until someone could take her from me.'

'You didn't help *me* . . . with the Shrike? Floating?'

John Keats laughed. 'No. Nor did Moneta. That was you, Brawne.'

She shook her head vigorously. 'That's impossible.'

628

'Not impossible,' he said softly. He reached out to touch her stomach again, and she imagined that she could feel the pressure from his palm. He whispered, 'Thou still unravished bride of quietness,/ Thou foster-child of silence and slow time . . .' He looked up at Brawne. 'Certainly the mother of the One Who Teaches can exercise some prerogatives,' he said.

'The mother of . . .' Brawne suddenly had to sit down and found a bench just in time. She had never been awkward before in her life, but now, at seven months, there was no graceful way she could manage sitting. She thought, irrelevantly, of the dirigible coming in for mooring that morning.

'The One Who Teaches,' repeated Keats. 'I have no idea what she will teach, but it will change the universe and set ideas in motion that will be vital ten thousand years from now.'

'*My* child?' she managed, fighting a bit for air. 'Johnny's and my child?'

The Keats persona rubbed its cheek. 'The junction of human spirit and AI logic which Ummon and the Core sought for so long and died not understanding,' he said. He took a step. 'I only wish I could be around when she teaches whatever she has to teach. See what effect it has on the world. This world. Other worlds.'

Brawne's mind was spinning, but she had heard something in his tone. 'Why? Where will you be? What's wrong?'

Keats sighed. 'The Core is gone. The datapheres here are too small to contain me even in reduced form . . . except for the FORCE ship AIs, and I don't think I'd like it there. I never took orders well.'

'And there's nowhere else?' asked Brawne.

'The metasphere,' he said, glancing behind him. 'But it's full of lions and tigers and bears. And I'm not ready yet.'

Brawne let that pass. 'I have an idea,' she said. She told him.

The image of her lover came closer, put his arms around her, and said, '*You* are a miracle, madam.' He stepped back into the shadows.

Brawne shook her head. 'Just a pregnant lady.' She put her hand on the swelling under her gown. 'The One Who Teaches,' she murmured. Then, to Keats, 'All right, you're the archangel announcing all this. What name shall I give her?'

When there was no answer, Brawne looked up.

The shadows were empty.

Brawne was at the spaceport before the sun rose. It was not exactly a merry group bidding farewell. Beyond the usual sadness of saying goodbye, Martin, the Consul, and Theo were nursing hangovers since day-after pills were out of stock on post-Web Hyperion. Only Brawne was in fine temper.

'Goddamn ship's computer has been acting weird all morning,' grumbled the Consul.

'How so?' smiled Brawne.

The Consul squinted at her. 'I ask it to run through a regular pre-launch checklist and the stupid ship gives me verse.'

'Verse?' said Martin Silenus, raising one satyr's brow.

'Yeah . . . listen . . .' The Consul keyed his comlog.

A voice familiar to Brawne said:

> *So, ye three Ghosts, adieu! Ye cannot raise*
> *My head cool-bedded in flowery grass;*
> *For I would not be dieted with praise,*
> *A pet lamb in a sentimental farce!*
> *Fade softly from my eyes, and be once more*
> *In masque-like figures on the dreamy urn;*
> *Farewell! I yet have visions for the night,*
> *And for the day faint visions there is store;*

Vanish, ye Phantoms! from my idle sprite,
Into the clouds, and never more return!

Theo Lane said, 'A defective AI? I thought your ship had one of the finest intelligences outside of the Core.'

'It does,' said the Consul. 'It's not defective. I ran a full cognitive and function check. Everything's fine. But it gives me . . . *this*!' He gestured at the comlog recording readout.

Martin Silenus glanced at Brawne Lamia, looked carefully at her smile, and then turned back to the Consul. 'Well, it looks as if your ship might be getting literate. Don't worry about it. It will be good company during the long trip there and back.'

In the ensuing pause, Brawne brought out a bulky package. 'A going-away present,' she said.

The Consul unwrapped it, slowly at first, and then ripping and tearing as the folded, faded, and much-abused little carpet came into sight. He ran his hands across it, looked up, and spoke with emotion filling his voice. 'Where . . . how did you . . .'

Brawne smiled. 'An indigenie refugee found it below the Karla Locks. She was trying to sell it in the Jacktown Marketplace when I happened along. No one was interested in buying.'

The Consul took a deep breath and ran his hands across the designs on the hawking mat which had carried his grandfather Merin to the fateful meeting with his grandmother Siri.

'I'm afraid it doesn't fly anymore,' said Brawne.

'The flight filaments need recharging,' said the Consul. 'I don't know how to thank you . . .'

'Don't,' said Brawne. 'It's for good luck on your voyage.'

The Consul shook his head, hugged Brawne, shook hands with the others, and took the lift up into his ship. Brawne and the others walked back to the terminal.

There were no clouds in Hyperion's lapis lazuli sky. The

631

sun painted the distant peaks of the Bridle Range in deep tones and promised warmth for the day to come.

Brawne looked over her shoulder at the Poets' City and the valley beyond. The tops of the taller Time Tombs were just visible. One wing of the Sphinx caught the light.

With little noise and just a hint of heat, the Consul's ebony ship lifted on a pure blue flame and rose toward the sky.

Brawne tried to remember the poems she had just read and the final lines of her love's longest and finest unfinished work:

> *Anon rushed by the bright Hyperion;*
> *His flaming robes streamed out beyond his heels,*
> *And gave a roar, as if of earthly fire,*
> *That scared away the meek ethereal Hours,*
> *And made their dove-wings tremble. On he flared . . .*

Brawne felt the warm wind tug at her hair. She raised her face to the sky and waved, not trying to hide or brush away the tears, waving fiercely now as the splendid ship pitched over and climbed toward the heavens with its fierce blue flame and – like a distant shout – created a sudden sonic boom which ripped across the desert and echoed against distant peaks.

Brawne let herself weep and waved again, continued waving, at the departing Consul, and at the sky, and at friends she would never see again, and at part of her past, and at the ship rising above like a perfect, ebony arrow shot from some god's bow.

On he flared . . .